This Cursed Valley

A Novel
by Larry K. Meredith

Larry K. Meredith

Raspberry Creek Books, Ltd.

RASPBERRY
CREEK

BOOKS

This Cursed Valley

ISBN 978-0-9851352-0-1
Library of Congress Control Number: 2012910430

Printed in the United States of America

Special 10th Anniversary Edition
First edition published by Pearl Street Publishing, Denver, CO

www.raspberrycreekbooks.com

Raspberry Creek Books, Ltd.
Gunnison, Colorado   Tulsa, Oklahoma

Thanks to my dad, Lawrence Meredith,
the Crystal River Valley, which is the "cursed" valley of this novel,
has become a very special place to several generations of his family.
I wish he could see it again. And, who knows? Maybe he does.
This book is for him.

๛๛

History is who we are and why we are the way we are.
~David McCullough

CONTENTS

Introduction

By Anne Hillerman

It's unusual for a novel to have an introduction--- but Larry K. Meredith's *This Cursed Valley* isn't your average novel. As you've probably guessed from the heft of this volume, there's a lot going on inside these covers. Meredith has created an epic adventure, an imaginative 19th-century hero's journey constructed around the facts and flesh-and-blood people who helped shape Colorado's beautiful Crystal River Valley. He celebrates the "story" in history.

When I was in school, teaching history meant battering students with dates and names to memorize. A book like Meredith's would have given me a new and happier outlook on the subject. Unlike the barrage of dry facts that tortured my spirit in the name of education, Meredith's juicy novel has black-hearted scoundrels, likable good guys, illicit romance, revenge, gunfights, lucky coincidences, ill-timed accidents and evergreen insights into what makes people tick.

The story grows from the sagas surrounding Colorado's early white settlement in the mountain towns Redstone, Carbondale, Aspen, Glenwood Springs, Schofield and Marble. This stunningly beautiful part of the Rocky Mountains frames Meredith's chronicle. Readers travel through time and geography, meeting real historical characters and those from Meredith's enlightened imagination, all representatives of the forces that shaped modern Colorado. I wish all history were told in a way as compelling as this.

As a life-long Westerner and a visitor to Colorado for decades, I appreciate Meredith's obvious affection for his adopted state and his skill in describing its peaks and valleys, rivers and winters. Readers in the unfortunate position of living elsewhere might accuse him of using a novelist's license in his poetic descriptions. Trust me, he's telling the truth.

 The curse that opens the book and gives the book its title comes from a Ute Holy Man, concerned about the displacement of his people from the land they held sacred. The Crystal Valley is as much a character as the people who live here, die here, or pass through to make their fortunes.

Although the title calls the valley "cursed," this majestic place also reflects many of nature's blessings. In the Crystal River Valley of the novel, the hope called America shines like a beacon long after it had cooled to a flicker in the East. Beginning around 1880, the story spans 50 years of booms and busts, decades packed with openings and closings of mines and the dance halls, saloons, hotels, boarding houses, schools and churches that followed.

With the open-minded character of Will Martin as our guide, author Meredith lets us know what it might have been like to have lived in this formative era, when the American dream pulsated with the energy of immigrants from the Midwest and East Coast as well as from Europe. Husband, father, rancher, explorer and risk-taker, Martin takes us through *This Cursed Valley* on foot, horseback and by railroad and finally, automobile. Readers join Will and a taciturn Bat Masterson for a meal of jerky and wild pheasant under the stars. We meet Doc Holliday and President Teddy Roosevelt who come to the valley to hunt. Martin reads the newspapers, sharing the developments that tie his isolated mountain ranch to the world outside. The readers learn about President Coolidge's resistance to the installation of electric lights in the White House, the publication of Hitler's *Mein Kampf*, the Scopes Monkey Trial, the rise of Josef Stalin and even the invention of television. Characters marvel at the telephone and question the sanitation of indoor plumbing.

Among its many compelling episodes, *This Cursed Valley* captures the hope that once blazed brightly in the high mountain town of Marble. In 1905, Col. Channing Meek, with some help from the Rockefellers, raised millions of dollars to develop the Yule Marble Quarry. The reader watches huge blocks of beautiful white stone come down from the 9500 foot mine to be shipped elsewhere. The town's marble fabricating mill becomes the largest in the world. Then avalanches, fires and an accident in which Meek dies dampen the endeavors. The town's optimism soars again when word arrives that every ton of the pure white marble needed to create the new Lincoln Memorial in far away Washington D.C. will come from its high country mine. But World War I calls most of the miners--- men of Italian and Austrian descent---back to Europe to fight for their homelands. All true, and told with a novelist's skill.

In addition to the Indian curse, these exciting times held real dangers from mining accidents, disease, unpredictable weather and unreliable people. They also held amazing opportunity for a person to make a fortune, or at least live a reasonably comfortable life, with the combination of hard work and a dash of good luck. The novel's characters ride the currents of blessed and damned as they intermingle with real events and people from the history of the times. Will, for example, knows the good luck of winning a silver mine in a poker game and the bad luck of seeing his ranch house burned to the ground by vengeful thugs. He has the good luck of fathering children and endures the bad luck of rotten apples on the family tree. Luckily for us, Will is attracted to interesting women, among them another man's wife who becomes his first love and an eccentric Swedish princess. Will's spunky daughter adds a Ute husband to the family while both his sons bring challenges and aggravation.

As with any good historical novel, the book raises the questions of how things have changed and how they have stayed the same despite time's passage. Near the end, as the Great Depression envelopes the country, we read: "There were plenty of good people in the world, Will thought to himself, and damn the stock market anyway. The country would survive."

This special re-issue coincides with the novel's 10th anniversary. In an age when books come and go quicker than a spring snowstorm in the Rockies, *This Cursed Valley's* steady popularity speaks to Meredith's skill as a storyteller and to the innate interest of the historical material that lies as bedrock to his fine tale.

Anne Hillerman, Santa Fe, N.M., 2012

Anne Hillerman is the author of the award-winning "Tony Hillerman's Landscape: On the Road with Chee and Leaphorn" and seven other books. She and husband/photographer Don Strel, in cooperation with the University of New Mexico Press, have completed an introduction and new photographs for a re-issue of mystery giant Tony Hillerman's book of non-fiction essays, "The Great Taos Bank Robbery." Her newest book, a collaboration with photographer Don Strel, "Gardens of Santa Fe," won the 2011 New Mexico Book Award and was a finalist for the prestigious Eric Hoffer Award. Anne is also the author of "Santa Fe Flavors: Best Restaurants and Recipes" (winner of the 2009 New Mexico Book Award!); "The Insiders Guide to Santa Fe," "Children's Guide to Santa Fe," "Done in the Sun," and "Ride the Wind: USA to Africa." She and photographer Strel have done scores of presentations on their books.

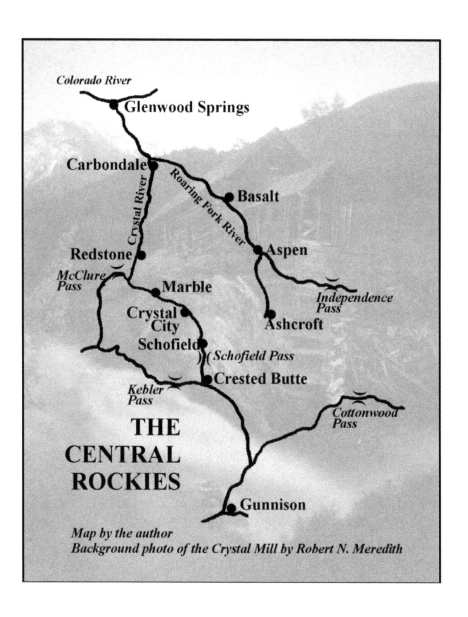

Colorado River

Glenwood Springs

Carbondale

Crystal River

Roaring Fork River

Basalt

Redstone

Aspen

McClure
Pass

Marble

Independence
Pass

Crystal
City

Ashcroft

Schofield

Schofield Pass

Crested Butte

Kebler
Pass

Cottonwood
Pass

**THE
CENTRAL
ROCKIES**

Gunnison

*Map by the author
Background photo of the Crystal Mill by Robert N. Meredith*

PROLOGUE

Fall, 1879

The thought occurred to him once again that they had killed too many.

This time he agreed with himself and groaned involuntarily, letting his usual Ute stoicism slip as he struggled to rise from the cross-legged sitting position he had assumed throughout the long night. *Too many winters*, he muttered to himself as he brushed at the dust on his store-bought Levi's. He trudged the few steps to a weathered pine tree and scratched his back against the bark, not worrying about snagging the plaid shirt he had worn since he and the others had fled the White River Agency five days ago.

It saddened him to think of what he had decided he must do as a result of what the whites were calling a "massacre." The Utes called it necessary. Nevertheless, it was done, and now he was about to use his powers as a holy man in a manner that had once been unthinkable.

Owl Man shrugged as if to say it didn't matter. In his heart, however, in the deepest secret places of his soul, it did matter.

He discussed it with himself some more.

They had killed only twenty-three, he told himself again, and thirteen of those were soldiers. One of the others, though, had been the agent Meeker. That was it, then. It had been the deaths of the agent and the women that had sent the white soldiers into such a rage they had pursued the small band of Utes down Colorado's rugged backbone to this deep, isolated valley.

He laid the thought aside and turned slightly, looking past the brush toward an army of ramrod-straight aspen trees, trying to see the woman. He had heard nothing from her for several hours and it was nearly light, the false dawn of early morning beginning to give shape to the bulk of mountain across the valley. He wanted to join the others this morning and cross the pass that would lead them to safety in the southwestern San Juan Mountains. *It would not be a good idea to stay here much longer*, he thought. The soldiers would be along much sooner than the *Nunt'z*, the People, expected them. Most of the Utes respected the soldiers for the power of their guns and because there were so many. Few, however, gave them credit for being fast or smart.

There was a moan from the aspen grove to his left. Good. Perhaps the half-Ute, half-white child would come soon and they could leave this sacred mountain.

He walked to the edge of the high outcropping and sat once more on the rock where he had waited throughout the night. His knees creaked as he bent to the boulder and he shook his head sadly at the thought of the rigors of old age. Straight gray hair with hints of the deep black of the past fell to his shoulders and framed a broad face, a flat nose that spread wide beneath still-

2

sharp and deeply set eyes and a narrow line of a mouth. The face was smooth except for the etched lines at the corners of his eyes and in his forehead, made even darker by the consternation he felt as he pondered the events of the past few months.

Few of the *Nunt'z* had listened when he told them it was inevitable. The speed at which it happened had been a surprise, though, even to him, a holy man with powers that had once made him rich and honored by his people. But when the whites laughed at him the People slowly began to doubt his power. It was Meeker, though, who turned them finally against him and many of the *Nunt'z* deserted *Inu'sakats* and turned to Meeker's Jesus.

He waved his hand at a blowfly and then stared at the palm. It was old and scarred. His life was written on that hand, the thick wrist, the short, strong fingers. That scar there between the thumb and forefinger. A Comanche knife blade might have severed the thumb entirely but he had been too quick. Something like a smile cracked his broad, dark face. That hand had killed a man, had held many babies, had caressed many women. His smile broadened slightly. Was it for the killing, the babies or the women? No, it was for his youth. Only yesterday he had been young and strong. One day young, the next old. He did not remember the transition.

Now he was old and running like a frightened rabbit from vengeful white soldiers who were angry over the deaths of twenty-three of their number, even though it was clearly their fault. It was good to grieve for those killed but they had died in battle and honorably. It had to be the women. The conclusion comforted him slightly. The whites were people, too, and they could rightly be angry and vengeful because of the women. He hoped it was the women and not simply the twenty-three deaths.

The old Indian sniffed the air and wished for the scent of a campfire and breakfast. Instead, the sharp bite of spruce, familiar to those who lived in the high country, filled his nostrils. It was a comforting smell, one he quickly associated with this place, this valley. The *Nunt'z*, the People, his band of Utes, had spent many good summers here. Game had been plentiful in those days and the People were happy. Then the miners had come and said there was value in the rocks of the mountains. "Pha!" He spat on the ground, thinking of the gleaming eyes in faces streaked with greed. He thought about it all, then, and fought the despair that threatened to overwhelm the anger. *Keep the anger*, he said to himself, *and never accept the loss of country, of pride, of identity.*

There was a sharp cry of new life behind him and soon the woman called his name. The child was already at her breast when he turned to her. "It is a man child," she said.

He saw a scraggle of black hair, a nose that was bent to the side.

3

Potentially blue eyes hinted at part of the child's parentage. Sooner than he had expected, the woman claimed she was ready to leave. He directed her to the ponies at the base of the ledge and lingered behind, waiting until she was out of the range of his voice. Then he stood and stretched his arms to the north and south. The sun cast his shadow far over the broad valley below.

He called on the *powa'a* and the *ini'pute* who had served him well for so many years. When he felt their calming presence, in a voice he hoped was angry but which betrayed the sadness that engulfed him, Owl Man placed a curse on the valley that he knew would lead to lives of pain and sorrow for all white men who walked in the shadow of the Mountain of Sanctuary.

PART I

1879 and Before

The campfire was in a buffalo wallow on the south side of an eastbound creek. Two cottonwoods and some plum bushes provided pitiful protection from the wind and glowed orange from the fire. Will Martin was just north of Indian Territory, barely in Kansas, and he was bone-tired after several days of solitary riding.

He had left the Palo Duro and twelve years of his life behind in Texas along with Charles Goodnight and the best friend a man ever had, Sagebrush Tom Cordell. Now, as the weariness truly set in and the south wind worked futilely to dry the sweat on the back of his neck, he tried to convince himself once more that all of this wasn't a big mistake.

You don't get to California by heading northeast from Texas, he told himself. But that was his plan and this time he'd do it, too.

In the deepening dusk Will had been about to give up finding water to camp by when he saw the faint glow of the fire from a mile away. Whoever was there sure wasn't trying to hide anything, but he eased up quietly anyway.

After he took a long look and saw no sign of life, he rode closer, making his tired horse prance a bit as she clattered through some loose shale. He didn't want to surprise anyone. Closer, he hollered out a "Hello!" but got no response.

At the edge of the buffalo wallow Will ground-tied the horse and walked into the shallow depression, keeping his eyes busy. "If anyone's here I'm not looking for trouble," he said loudly, "just for a place to sleep." The fire had been tended recently and was built Indian-fashion with only the ends of the cottonwood logs in the fire and fanned out like the spokes of a wheel. Will shoved a couple of them farther into the fire and it blazed up. He squatted down on his haunches and wondered.

"Like for you to just stay in that squat for a bit, mister." The voice seemed to come from the direction of the creek. Will did as he was told. "Saw you coming a good mile away," the voice said. "Where are you headed and why?"

Will didn't try to look for the man behind the voice, figuring any sudden movement and he might never see California, or anywhere else. "Dodge City," he said. "Just out of curiosity, mostly." He heard the man moving behind him. He hadn't been on the creek side after all. "If you've got a gun on me it isn't necessary."

"I don't suppose it is, but you can't be too careful." The man was beside him. "Stretch if you want. Name's Masterson."

Will pushed himself to his feet, turned and saw a medium-sized man wearing a tall sugar-loaf sombrero with a wide brim. The crown of the hat

6

might have reached Will's height of over six feet. Still, the shorter man appeared formidable. Masterson's body was compact. Looked strong like a prize fighter's. He had a bright red silk bandanna around his neck and a Mexican sash thrown over his shoulders. He was holstering a silver-plated .45 in one of two embossed holsters hanging from a wide belt slung low on his hips.

"Evenin'," Will said. "Martin. Will Martin. Mind some company?"

"Might not. Depends. Got anything to eat? I'm out."

"Got some jerky and what's left of a pheasant I killed this morning."

"Let's eat, then."

They finished the pheasant, down to picking at the bones, and then chewed the jerky a while. Will laid out his bedroll and stretched out, looking at a million stars and wondering how many there were, just like he and Sagebrush Tom had done a hundred times these past years in the canyon or out on the Llano Estacado where it was even flatter and maybe even hotter than Kansas.

Masterson was stirring, squirming around on his bedroll and tilting the brim of his enormous sombrero until it covered him to his chest bone.

"Ever been to Dodge?" Will asked.

"Yes. I have." No more of an answer than that.

"What's it like?"

A long silence. Finally: "Probably pretty much like you've heard. Noisy. Dirty." Another long pause. And then: "Cow town. Beer and whiskey, women, gambling, whatever you want. Be there tomorrow night and you'll see for yourself."

Within minutes Will could tell from the regular breathing that Masterson was asleep. For a while he thought some more about things like cattle drives up the Goodnight-Loving Trail and Sagebrush Tom Cordell. Tom had taken him under his wing back in '65 when Will was a tall-for-his-age fifteen-year-old with a rooster-tail cowlick who'd been headed for California but got hired by Mr. Goodnight instead and turned into a pretty damn good cowpuncher. Now, twelve years later, he'd set out for California again, just as he had when his dad didn't come home to their rocky Mississippi farm after the war. But he told Tom he wanted to see Dodge City first, so he took off to the north and now was about to turn east. California would still be there when he got around to it. He went to sleep, finally, and dreamed about the first pair of spurs he bought with his first money from Mr. Goodnight on his first trip to Waco way back in 1866 or so. Tom and most of the others had hustled off to the second floor of a building when some women hollered at them but Will hadn't gone, that time.

With daylight he got a better look at Masterson. Will guessed the man

7

was what women would call handsome. A square face framed slate-blue eyes that seemed to store up everything they saw for future reference. The man used them to size up Will, who figured he would probably have a good smile behind the mustache. His hair was as thick and black as Will's. He was something of a "dandy," Will decided when he saw Masterson buckle on a pair of gold-mounted spurs.

They rode all day in silence through country that was at first skillet flat and rock hard. Soon small hills swelled and the grass became thicker and bent to a south wind. They stopped twice to water the horses in shallow creeks that ran slowly with silt-filled water that Will's silent companion didn't hesitate to drink.

At dusk they topped a rise and looked down on Dodge City. A train sat silently on the siding parallel to the main street which Will would soon learn was called Front Street.

The train was the only silent thing about the town. Above the bawling of cattle penned up and grazing near the railroad siding on the edge of town, other sounds grew louder as the two touched the west end of the street lined with false fronts and board sidewalks. As they rode into town they were assaulted with a smell that Will recognized from his days as a cowboy -- the raunchy odor of hundreds of cows and the fresh and rotting cow patties that dotted the area south of the tracks and that wafted over front street on the wind that blew up from Oklahoma.

From a saloon called the Long Branch came the tinkle of a piano, almost overridden by a cacophony of women's voices that Will guessed was supposed to be singing. Other music drifted over the swinging doors of at least half a dozen other saloons — what might have been a brass band, violins, maybe a banjo. Groups of cowboys yelled good-natured obscenities at each other as they clomped over the boards, spurs clanking. A woman screamed, then laughed just as loudly.

Masterson reined his horse in front of the Long Branch. "Got to see some people here," he muttered. "Buy you a drink?"

Will felt like he wanted a bath first. "Maybe later. They got a hotel here?"

"Just passed it." Masterson gestured back toward a large, three-story frame building with "Great Western Hotel" lettered on the front. He didn't look at Will again but dismounted, casually looped the reins over a hitch rail and pushed through the doors of the saloon.

Will found a livery and took a while talking to his horse, Sally, as he rubbed her down. Groomed and fed, she nipped at him as he sidled past her on his way out of the stall. *Maybe I'll feel as frisky after a bath and a shave*, he thought to himself. First, though, he'd have a smoke. He leaned against the board-and-batten siding of the rear of the stable and looked north at the

8

silhouette of rolling hills as the twilight deepened. The sounds of the town were muffled behind him as he lit up and wondered what Sagebrush Tom was doing about now. Wondered if he'd ever see his friend again. Doubted it and thought it would be a shame, but figured that's just the way things were, and they were of his own making anyway. Wondered again if he was doing the right thing. A man just never knew.

It was suddenly dark as a bank of low-lying clouds off in the west took the last of the light and sucked it up like a gulp of water. With the darkness came voices in the livery. Will took another draw and leaned some more, listening.

"Thought you were supposed to get here yesterday." The voice was not that of a cowhand. There was something cultured in it. There was also something cruel.

"Horse went lame. Is he here?" This voice was raspy as a dull saw blade, trail-tired and not especially concerned about the first speaker's evident anger.

"He just got here." The first voice again. "Listen, when I make a contract I expect it to be filled as promised. You two horses' asses are getting good money for this. I thought you'd run out on me." So there were three people in the livery. A horse whinnied and Will could hear saddles being thrown over a rail.

"We never run out on nobody yet." The third voice, higher-pitched with a trace of whine in it, a bit muffled, maybe by a chaw in a cheek.

Then the raspy, tired voice again. "How you want it done?"

"That's up to you. But I want it done tonight. And I don't want him back-shot, you understand? Do it clean."

"Where's the money? We got expenses."

"You'll get it when the job's done."

A bridle rattled onto a nail and feet shuffled. "Been wonderin' why." Raspy-Voice coughed and spat. "What you got in your craw against him, anyhow?"

"That doesn't concern you. It goes back a long time. But there are others who feel just as I do. Make your plans. I'll see you inside."

A pair of feet marched out of the livery and Will listened to the remaining two grumble as they took care of their animals.

"Think we can pull it off?" the whiner asked.

"All you got to do is back my play, just like we said." Another cough turned into a long session of hacking and spitting. "C'mon. Let's get a drink first."

As they left, Will ground out his smoke with the heel of his boot. Shook his head as he walked around the building and headed for the hotel. *Something dirty going on*, he thought. *Town's probably full of that kind.*

9

Later, feeling refreshed after a bath and the first shave in days, Will strolled the Front Street boardwalk, peering in one saloon after another.

"Come on in, cowboy," a man said to him as he squinted through the smoke behind the swinging doors of a saloon called Varieties. "Make you forget all about that cattle drive. Best whiskey in Dodge and the fairest prices. Prettiest girls, too."

"Thanks anyway," Will said as he turned back toward the Long Branch, thinking he might see Masterson again.

He wormed his way through the crowd to get to the bar, ordered a drink and watched two women on a stage at the rear of the room. They seemed to be singing to the music of what appeared to be a five-piece orchestra. He could barely hear them over the noise. They shook their bosoms and pranced. Other "fallen doves," as he was to learn they were called, sashayed around the room, sat on laps, now and then wandered out the door with a cowboy.

Masterson was standing across the room talking to two men, one with a star on his chest. The conversation ended and the lawman and his friend left the saloon. Masterson sat down at a table and joined a card game. Will casually surveyed the room again. Above the bar was a painting of a naked lady reclining on some sort of horse-drawn wagon. It wasn't very realistic but the woman, who looked to be asleep, was a lot more appealing than the one who sidled up to Will, brazenly stroked his inner thigh, and asked him to buy her a drink. "Not tonight, honey," he started to say, but she was already rubbing her breasts against the arm of the cowboy standing next to him.

Two ragged-looking men caught Will's eye. They were deep in conversation and occasionally turned a wary glance toward Masterson who was conspicuous in his tall sombrero and red sash. As Will watched, his suspicions growing, one of the two, a short man with a patch over one eye, worked his way to a point behind and to the left of Masterson. The other, a man with a protruding belly and yellow teeth, seemed to be waiting for his friend to get in position. Then he walked past Masterson and intentionally bumped the chair hard enough to make Will's new friend spill some of his drink. Masterson was instantly on his feet, looking the man in the eye.

"Wish you hadn't done that," he said. His hands dangled at his side.

"Do you, now?" the man said — with a raspy voice. Will tensed. The hubbub in the room let up little by little as everyone turned to watch.

"Why don't you buy me another and we'll forget it," Masterson said.

The other replied with a sneer and a cough.

Will watched as Patch-Eye crept closer to Masterson.

"I don't think you want any trouble," Masterson said. "I know I don't."

Will began to move toward Patch-Eye, certain these were the two he had heard talking in the livery.

Big-Belly backed off a couple of paces. "I bet you don't want no trouble. You are a woman-stealing son-of-a-bitch and I been hopin' I'd run into you someday." He coughed.

"You have something against me?" Masterson said quietly, moving closer to Big-Belly, not letting him put too much space between them. Big-Belly spat on the floor.

"The name King mean anything to you?"

"That army sergeant from Sweetwater, Texas?"

Patch-Eye was trying to get closer to Masterson but Will pushed in front of the man. He was two long steps from Masterson by now. Patch-Eye shoved a man aside and stood next to Will.

"Melvin King was my friend and you killed him," Big-Belly said. "Before he died I told him I'd get you for him."

Masterson was a cool one, Will thought. He never took his eyes from Big-Belly's. He kept his hands loose and by his sides, near his guns.

"King shot me first. Killed a girl, too."

"King and Molly Brennan was gonna get married." Big-Belly spat again, hitting Masterson's boot.

Masterson smiled. "Molly Brennan wasn't going to marry anyone, least of all Melvin King."

"You say so," Big-Belly said. "But I say you're a bald-faced liar. What you gonna do about that?"

Patch-Eye slipped his .45 from his holster but Will caught his hand in a vice grip and, without looking at him, keeping his eyes on Masterson and Big-Belly, said softly, "Don't think you ought to get involved, friend." The man struggled to free his gun hand but Will shoved his thumb into the man's wrist and he cried out in pain.

Big-Belly heard the cry and flicked his eyes that direction for an instant. In a flash, Masterson had one of his peacemakers out and clubbed the man on the side of his head. Big-Belly fell like a dropped sandbag and lay still.

Patch-Eye dropped his pistol, twisted away from Will's grip, and ran for the door, leaving his friend crumpled on the dirty floor.

The room was suddenly alive with noise again. The piano started up playing "Pop Goes the Weasel." Men went back to their card games; women went back to the men. Masterson shot Will a nod of thanks, sat down at the table with his back to him, and resumed his game as though nothing had happened.

"Made yourself a friend there," someone said to Will. He turned to a grinning man in a twenty-dollar gray suit with a silk tie. The grin filled up his face, all but the eyes. He was as tall as Will with thin, sandy-colored hair neatly parted on the left. He held out his hand and Will took it. It was soft but

11

the man had a strong grip.

"Name's Peabody," he said. "Nathan Peabody. Let me buy you a drink since it seems the man whose life you just saved isn't going to." *A cultured voice*, Will thought. *The third man from the livery?* They found a table just being vacated and sat down.

"New in town?" Peabody asked. Will nodded. "Little old for a cowboy. Trail boss?"

"Nope," Will said, taking a lesson from Masterson about not volunteering too much information.

"Yes, well. Just what might be your business in Dodge?" The man was awfully interested, Will thought. At least Peabody looked him in the eye when he talked.

"Just passing through."

"Me, too," Peabody said. "I'll be here a while and then move on when I get tired of taking money from these folks."

A gambler, Will thought. *Might have known.*

"I liked what I saw," Peabody continued. "You played it just right. Pull a gun and you start a real ruckus. Yes, you did it right. Know whose life you saved?"

"Man's name is Masterson. Rode in with him today. Quiet man. Didn't want to tell me much about himself."

Peabody laughed a loud guffaw, slapping himself on the thigh. He shook his head. "That's Bat Masterson," he said. "He's earned quite a reputation the past few years as a man you don't mess with. His brother Ed is assistant marshal. He has another brother here, Jim, who's co-owner of a saloon down the street called Varieties."

"That so?" Will said cautiously. They must have been the two men Masterson had been visiting with earlier.

Within half an hour Will knew a great deal about this Bat Masterson. It seemed he had been trying to farm with his two brothers and parents near Wichita a few years ago when the three boys decided to try their hands at buffalo hunting in southwestern Kansas.

Ed and Jim had returned to the farm but Bat had followed the herds down through Indian Territory and into the Texas panhandle. Will answered with a simple "I been there" when Peabody asked if he knew the area.

Masterson had been part of a group of thirty-five buffalo hunters who had held off an attack of more than five hundred Kiowa, Comanche, Cheyenne and Southern Apache warriors at a small town called Adobe Walls, Peabody told Will. Later he was a scout for the Army during a full-scale campaign against the Indians. Word had spread quickly back to Dodge about Masterson's killing Melvin King in Sweetwater barely a year ago.

"He took a bullet near his privates," the gambler said. "Seems the girl tried to protect him and got killed herself. Masterson got a shot off while King was re-cocking his piece. Took King a whole day to die, I hear."

"Interesting," Will said. "You seem to know quite a bit about him." He glanced over at Masterson who was engrossed in his game, seemingly without a care in the world.

"I know him," Peabody said. "Everybody around here knows Bat Masterson. Or at least knows of him."

"Seems like a decent sort of fellow. Must of been more to that little incident than met the eye. You suppose?"

Peabody ignored the question as he and Will pulled in their legs to let Ed Masterson and another man drag Big-Belly past them on the way to somewhere—jail, perhaps. Patch-Eye was long-gone and Will knew neither man would get any money from Peabody. Will was certain Peabody was responsible for provoking Masterson into a fight.

"Are you looking for work, Martin?" Peabody touched him on the arm and Will pulled away as the gambler talked on. "We could use somebody like you who has a cool head to help us keep the peace in here. I own a bit of this place, you see. What do you say?"

"Not interested," Will said quickly. There was something about the man he didn't particularly like, something beyond his suspicion about his involvement in the fracas. "I'm not looking for work. Not yet, anyway."

"Think about it," Peabody said. "Job's yours if you want it." He stood and shook hands again, then left to join a game at the next table. He didn't look at Will again, even when he left to turn in for the night. Will wondered if he'd be able to sleep with all the noise in the town. Turned out the only problem was trying to get used to the soft bed. Finally exchanged the fluffy pillow for his saddlebags and dreamed he and Sagebrush Tom were breaking horses in the Palo Duro.

OWL MAN did not want to sleep even though his body demanded rest. When he slept, he dreamed, and the dreams were of disaster for the *Nunt'z*. So he forced himself to remain conscious until he could sleep like the dead, dreamless and unaware.

A hazy moon crept slowly over the ridge behind the towering red cliffs to the east and for a brief moment illuminated the high point on which Owl Man had years ago learned of his supernatural powers. It was 400 miles west of Dodge City and a century removed from cattle drives and railroads and saloons and all the modern trappings of a country headed hellbent for the twentieth century.

Owl Man dipped his finger in the vinegar solution he had prepared and touched it to his lips. It seemed appropriately foul, so he placed the potato in the liquid and covered the pot with a piece of ancient deerskin he had used for such purposes for many years. Soon, when the potato was thoroughly saturated, he would take it to Blue Flower, the wife of his friend Two Hawks. By morning, if Blue Flower followed Owl Man's instructions and ate the potato slowly, her terrible headache would be gone.

It was good to perform the craft that he had practiced for so long, even though few of the *Nunt'z* came to him these days. Most now went to the white physician at the agency. Owl Man sighed and fanned at the odor escaping the medicinal pot. He looked toward the moon again and saw Owl Point, the rocky outcropping that had always been his destination when he needed solitude, standing out in bold relief against the late-night sky. Owl Point, the Utes now knew, was *ihupi'arat tubut*, a haunted spot where ghosts lurked, and therefore called a power point by Owl Man, a holy man and the only one of his band allowed to visit the point.

Tomorrow he would go again. It would be a difficult climb for someone of his age but it must be done. By fall, the *Nunt'z* would be forced to live at the agency and Owl Man might never again visit the valley.

It was Ouray's fault, he thought to himself. Ouray, whom the whites called "chief of all the Utes," had agreed to the first treaty more than twenty years earlier. Other treaties had followed, all engineered by Ouray and his friend Kit Carson, the Rope Thrower. The treaties had granted ever-smaller portions of Colorado to the Utes "for as long as grasses might grow and rivers might run." Today there was almost nothing left.

Owl Man would never accept Ouray as chief. Ouray was too much Spanish, too much Apache, and only one-quarter Ute. The whites had named him chief because he could speak their language as well as Ute and Apache.

Owl Man shook his head to drive the memories from his mind. With the dawn, perhaps after a brief sleep with his wife, Sings Quietly, he would work some more to help his people. He would feed cornmeal browned with grease and water to a patient with diarrhea. He knew it would be successful, as the tobacco he had packed into a woman's aching tooth only two days ago had been successful in killing the pain.

Often he sent those with the aches and pains of arthritis and rheumatism (although he knew nothing of those names) to the hot springs to bathe in the soothing healing water. A favorite of many was the Yampa Springs, from which he had departed on his first pony raid to the east. "Yampa" meant "big medicine" and the sulfur-laden water seemed to be endowed with a mysterious healing power. Owl Man's personal favorite, though, was near a

14

narrow cut in "his" valley not far downstream from Owl Point.

Illness meant the sick person's body was out of tune with nature, Owl Man believed. He told his patients that an evil spirit had entered their body. Frequently, he called upon relatives and friends of the patient to join him in chanting and help speed the cure by driving the spirits away.

Now and then, when all else failed, Owl Man would press his forehead against the spot on the patient's body that was determined to be afflicted. Then, with great pomp and ceremony, he would spit the evil spirit from his mouth and banish it forever. Often, the patient, believing he had been cured, would immediately begin to feel better.

Those had been the good years, when the *Nunt'z* believed in him, before Meeker had come. This new agent at the White River Indian Agency in the northwest wanted the Utes to become farmers. "Pha!" Owl Man spat on the ground. He had warned his band and the other six as well. Few had listened and had, in fact, often laughed at his predictions that the whites would soon attempt to drive them all from their sacred grounds.

Most had stopped their laughter, however, when the newspapers took up the chant, "The Utes Must Go!"

Who were they, Owl Man wondered, these white men who so loudly demanded the land the Utes had claimed as their own for centuries?

The Utes had once been the sole human inhabitants of the Colorado Rockies. They had been a part of this uplifted wilderness since the *Manitou*, the great He-She spirit, had placed them there to exist kindly with the animals he created with his breath and his cane.

Early every spring they eagerly migrated to the high mountain valleys where they played, hunted and rested until the first biting chill of late autumn. Then they made their way down to the lower ranges out of the high winds and bitter cold of winter.

Seven bands of Utes claimed an area of more than a hundred thousand square miles, each band having staked out its own territory centuries ago. The Weminuche lived in the San Juan drainage of southwest Colorado, not far from the Uncompahgres. The Colorado River drained the territory of Owl Man's Grand River band, then flowed into the northwest region of the Yampah Utes. The Colorado-Utah border area was the Uintahs' while the Muaches ranged south along the Sangre de Cristo Mountains as far as Taos. The Capotes had settled in the San Luis Valley and the upper Rio Grande.

Now and then the Utes left their mountain ranges, but only when they felt the urge to experience the sheer joy of fighting with the Indians of the plains to the east. Their trips to the Front Range and beyond were usually masked with the excuse that they needed to replenish their herds of ponies. More often, it was the anticipation of the fight that prompted them to make the

15

arduous journey over high passes to a land of trackless prairie that seemed to them utterly worthless.

It was on one of those raids that Owl Man almost lost his thumb, and his life, while earning his first war name, Badger-Fast-on-his-Belly.

The morning the raiding party left the camp near Yampa Springs, the hot sulfur springs on the Grand River, his name was Walking Horse. He was barely a man that summer, having observed his sixteenth year only a month earlier. Because he was young, he and his friend Wolf had been left to guard the ponies while the other warriors, led by Black Wing, stole into the Comanche encampment just before dawn.

It seemed they waited hours for the sounds of battle that would signal them to bring the horses closer and drive the Comanche ponies away from the camp. Maybe it had been only minutes. Walking Horse signaled to Wolf to watch the ponies and walked toward the edge of their hiding place in a growth of small pines. His stride was slow and smooth. Sudden movements would catch the eye of a wary Comanche.

Above the sound of the rushing river to his left, Walking Horse thought he heard the screech of an owl but ignored it when he caught the brief flash of something on the edge of his night vision. Did he actually see, or only sense, movement? Seen or not, someone was there. He raised his hand to Wolf, still only a few feet away, and put his finger to his lips, signaling the need for quiet. Slowly, he dropped to his stomach, strained his eyes into the night and unsheathed a knife from his belt.

A figure was faintly silhouetted against the night sky. The man raised his breechclout and began to relieve himself into the river.

Walking Horse began to crawl, slowly at first, hurting his knees and stomach on the rocky ground. The man was nearly finished. Walking Horse moved quickly but as silently as a snake, his knife gripped tightly in his right hand. His heart was pumping but he felt strangely calm and sure of himself.

The man turned, saw the movement on the ground not the length of a war lance from him, pulled his own knife from somewhere and, in the same motion, leapt toward Walking Horse. The Ute rolled suddenly to his right, flashed his knife outwards and up, felt it bite into flesh and scrape on bone. The Comanche grunted, swept his knife hand downward toward Walking Horse's chest. He reacted quickly, raised his left hand in defense and again jabbed forward with his right. He felt the jarring impact of the Comanche's blow on his hand, felt his own knife enter the man's chest, felt wetness and weight and an out-thrusting of breath as the man died.

He shoved the body from his own, jumped to his feet and rolled the Comanche over with his foot. It was a boy, perhaps no older than himself. Then he heard the sound of hoofbeats and Black Wing was beside him, Wolf coming with the Ute ponies.

"The horses," Black Wing said. "It is time. Come." Later, maybe moments, hours, it was dawn. He felt pain in his left hand, which he used to wiped his sweating face. The hand was slimy, like moss on a wet boulder. Blood still seeped from a deep gash between the thumb and forefinger. Despite the pain, he pressed the thumb tightly, made a fist, and rode on. Black Wing was beside him once again.

"You did well," his leader said, kicking his horse and forging on ahead of the boy. The pain forgotten, pride swelled within. Now, years later, Owl Man still felt the pride. It was good that he had been able to enjoy that one moment of battle glory, because his life was about to undergo a change that would make him unique among his band.

It was after his return to the valley that Badger began to realize he was, indeed, different. His new name had come from Black Wing after Wolf had described Walking Horse's attack of the young Comanche.

"He was like a badger," Wolf said, "so fast on his belly that had he made a shadow it could not have kept up."

Sometime later, weeks, months, Badger-Fast-on-his-Belly admitted to himself that he was more than a sixteen-year-old youth who had killed a man in battle, more than a Ute warrior who would live his life as countless others. He was different. He was *po'rat*, a holy man with powers far exceeding those of many who claimed the name.

For long periods of time he paced the riverbank in the valley or sat quietly on a favorite rocky outcropping high on the red cliffs, thinking, going carefully over every detail of the event that gave him his name.

Had he actually seen the man in darkness? He could remember only that he *thought* he saw something move. But hadn't there been many of the small pine trees between him and the Comanche? The moon was behind the mountains and dawn was yet to come. Had he heard something? Yes, but not the man. It was an animal. A bird. An owl. It was *otus asio*, the screech owl whose sound means someone is to die.

The owl had warned him. Or had he imagined that, too? Had he actually heard the owl above the river sounds?

No, he could not have heard it. How did he know, then, that someone was near? Gradually, he convinced himself that some inner sense had given him the knowledge. The knowledge had come in an instant, a fleeting insight, a sudden awareness of a man unseen but real. Could it be that *Inu'sakats* had granted him some special ability to know of things that were yet to be?

He began to spend full days on his overlook staring up and down the valley, seeing little of reality. Instead, he saw those few moments of the dark early morning when he had found something within himself that was not of

17

himself but of *Inu'sakats*, that benevolent being who watched over all Utes but gave special favor to few.

One day when the sun was far to the west, blinding him without his being aware of it, he realized that this spot, this vantage point, was where all of his recent discoveries about himself had been made. When he was near the river or in the meadow near its headwaters, he could not think as clearly, and couldn't reach the decisions that came to him here with such impact.

This spot was *ihupi'arat tubut*, a haunted spot. *Inu'sakats* had led him there. To ponder. To consider himself. To discover.

Finally one day, alone in his usual spot high above the valley, he knew. He was, indeed, *po'rat*, a holy man. He had sat for hours, unmoving, eyes closed, perhaps in a deep trance. Finally, opening his eyes and staring directly into the flushed face of the setting sun, he saw *otus asio*, the screech owl, flying slowly toward him. It came as though at half speed, wings outstretched, floating. It came silently in the last light of day, its enormous eyes fixed on his own. Nearly upon him, *otus asio* spoke as a man. "You may know," the owl said, gracefully pointed its left wing downward and, banking to the north, swept grandly down toward the river where it disappeared into the twilight.

A sparrow followed, then another and then a dozen, more than a dozen. "You may lead," they said and they, too, turned in unison and flew toward the valley floor.

Finally came the eagle, its wingspan wider than a man was tall. It came like the owl, slowly, grandly, proudly. "You may see," it said. And it disappeared into the darkness below as the sun ended its daily journey and left, as a day-ending gift, a sky red as blood.

Almost immediately, it seemed, it was dawn. Badger was surprised when the sky began to lighten. He had sat unmoving throughout the night, attempting to understand the meaning of it all. As the light began little by little to walk the valley floor, it became suddenly clear to him. He bounded to his feet, ignoring the aches in his legs. He was wide awake in an instant, heart pounding with the knowledge, eyes bright and alert, every sense searching for a greater awareness of what was, of what was yet to be. He had the wisdom of *otus asio*, the owl. The sparrows, the small birds with little power, had represented the *Nunt'z* who sought his leadership.

And the eagle, the grandest of all, the one who flew highest and saw all, had told him of his ability to see that which was to come.

Badger felt the heat of the sun on his back, raised his arms to the sky, to *Inu'sakats* himself, and shouted a greeting to the god who had blessed him above all others. His voice echoed across the valley, resounded to the north toward the Mountain of Sanctuary, to the south and the headwaters of the river he loved, to the very sky itself.

Near the river far below, women looked up from their cooking fires. Children, still wiping night from their eyes, gazed in wonder toward the cliff where they knew Badger sat. Men smiled and nodded knowingly at one another. All knew that Badger had found what he sought. It was good.

The shadow of the young medicine man, arms outstretched, legs spread, head thrown back, covered the entire face of the mountain and ran down to the very river itself, up the bank and across the whole of the camp.

For two days Badger kept his secret but, knowing he needed advice, finally turned to Long Hand. His leader listened to Badger's story with closed eyes and when it was finished placed his hand on the boy's shoulder.

"You have a power that has been spoken of in stories told to us by the old ones," he said. "It is rare and it is dangerous, I think, for one so young. You must think long and hard about how you will use your power. You can use it for your own gain, or for the benefit of those with whom you live. You must decide now. The decisions you make will affect us all and our lives can be enriched by what you know. Or you can lead us to disaster. I cannot help you. I can only hope that *Inu'sakats* has endowed you with wisdom as well as the power to see."

Then Long Hand told Badger of the *powa'a* and the boy listened, at first with a growing fear and then, as the story unfolded, with relief and comfort.

Inside Badger, Long Hand said, lived a tiny being — the *powa'a* — who directed the use of his power. This supernatural entity, perhaps itself a part of the great god *Inu'sakats*, had been known always in the past as a benevolent creature who dictated that the power of the *po'rat*, the holy man, be used in positive ways for the good of all. Always, though, there had been the fear that someday an evil *ini'pute*, one of the ghosts who inhabited the *ihupi'arat tubut* where Badger had discovered his power, would overcome the kind *powa'a* and infect the medicine man with evil intent.

"That is why I say it is up to you," Long Hand said. "You must be always aware that the power within you is of such magnitude that it can destroy us all. May you never have to fight an evil *powa'a* and may all your decisions be made for the good of the People." He then told Badger that from this day he would be known as Owl Man, and that no other name could ever replace this one.

Two days later, standing on the outermost point of the red cliff that he had named Owl Point, the newly named holy man gave himself up to *Inu'sakats* and let the *powa'a* within him lift his thoughts to a plane beyond which he had not gone before.

In his trancelike state he saw a broad meadow where Indian ponies raced ahead of the wind, Ute riders urging them on as the *Nunt'z* cheered. Then he saw, on the edge of the meadow but behind the Ute teepees, a structure of

19

wood with holes in the side and front. He had heard of such things. White men lived in them and the holes were called windows. A white man stood in front of the building watching the horses race. He was tall and gaunt. His face was not clear, yet Owl Man could see that it was an unhappy face.

The white man turned and walked inside as the race ended. Seething clouds covered the sky and it became dark. Then the clouds disappeared and it was again light. The horses were gone. All the Utes were in the meadow striking the ground with strange implements.

They worked silently, slowly. He himself was there. He held a long stick with a piece of metal on the end. As he swung it hard against the ground it broke the earth. In unison the *Nunt'z* lifted their sticks. Together they brought them arcing across the sky and into the earth, breaking it apart, turning it over, exposing dark clods of dirt and burying the grasses beneath. Again, and again. They worked without looking up, and behind them, the white man watched and smiled.

The vision was over. Owl Man's stomach ached. He felt dizzy and, to keep from falling headlong from the cliff, sat down abruptly.

After that first revelation had come others. Sometimes they were infrequent, seasons apart. At other times they came in groups: two, three a night, a dozen a week. Often they made no sense, seemed unworthy of the time it took to unravel their mystery. But some of the dreams, if dreams they were, startled him with their clarity.

He anticipated the movement of elk to the higher valleys in the spring. He told Ute hunters where to find game. He foretold storms and drought.

When he predicted the coming of the white man and warned the People of the dangers of his coming, many of them scoffed at him. It was the first of his visions they chose to ignore.

Now, perhaps it was too late. The white man's government had decreed something called Manifest Destiny. The land of the Utes had become a "state." Originally they called it the territory of Jefferson and now Colorado, meaning, in Spanish, "colored red." They could not even choose a Ute word, Owl Man thought, and became more depressed.

The sky brightened suddenly and the northern tip of the Mountain of Sanctuary began to gleam as the rising sun brushed its snow-laden rocks. The whites were calling it Mount Sopris after one of their own.

To the south more sunlight dazzled him with its glare as it bounced from the glacier-like build-up of snow in the bowl of what the whites called Chair Mountain.

Owl Man sighed wearily. He had not slept that night after all. *There will be much time for sleep*, he thought. *Soon, I will sleep forever*. But before that time he knew he was to see the end of the Utes as they now existed.

20

He knew it as surely as he knew the fall would come followed by the winter. He knew it because he had recognized the man in his vision of years ago. The man was Meeker and Meeker was in charge of the agency where the *Nunt'z* would soon be forced to live.

BAT MASTERSON barely glanced at the snow-white piles of buffalo bones as he and Will Martin rode past. The bones, the results of the carnage that had left the plains almost barren of the animals in a killing spree of barely five years, were piled fifteen feet high in places.

Masterson saw Will's stare. "Use 'em for fertilizer," he said.

Will looked toward the top of a pile of bleaching bones and shook his head. "Took a heap of animals to make a pile that high."

"Used to kill 'em by the hundreds. 'Bout all gone now." Masterson wasn't much interested.

He wasn't much interested in practicing shooting with Will, either, but he was doing it out of a sense of duty. Bat and his brother Ed, the assistant marshal of Dodge City, had cornered Will on his first morning in the cow town. There was an opening for a deputy, they said. Besides that, they owed him.

"I wasn't planning on staying," Will said. "'Sides that, I've never done anything but cowboy. Don't know anything about being a peace officer."

Half an hour later, over breakfast, they had talked Will into taking the job. It was better money than herding cows and he didn't have anything more specific in mind. He'd try it a while. "But I still aim to get to California."

Bat grudgingly agreed to help Will with some of the finer points of gunfighting. "Not that you're likely to need to shoot anybody," he said, "but it won't hurt you to know something about the art."

"Would you have shot that man in the saloon last night?" Will asked.

Masterson snapped a quick look at him, then slowly lifted his .45 and weighed it in his hand. "If I'd had to."

Will decided to lay it out. "I think Peabody was behind it."

"Do you, now?" Masterson checked his chambers, reholstered the weapon, and looked at Will.

Quickly, Will told him about the conversation he'd overheard. "I didn't know who they were talking about or I'd have warned you," he concluded.

"'Preciate it," Masterson said. "Peabody's been after me for a long time. Caught him cheating last winter and would have gunned him down then but he wasn't armed. So I just clubbed him around a bit. He's been riled ever since."

"He'd kill you for that?"

"Peabody riles easy. Holds grudges. Besides, I shamed him in front of too many people. It's a lesson you learn pretty quick around here," Masterson said softly. "Some of these sons-a-bitches'll shoot you for less than that. You want to learn to shoot or what?"

Will practiced but never did feel comfortable drawing, cocking, aiming and firing the single-action revolver all in the same motion. He desperately hoped he'd never get in a situation where he had to use the pistol in any manner other than as a club.

In the Long Branch, Peabody fawned over Will, offered him free drinks and free women, patted him on the back and greeted him with fake smiles that reeked of insincerity. Finally, Will shoved the man into a corner and told him in no uncertain terms to "back off and give me some breathing space."

Peabody, visibly shaken by the encounter, backed off. Now Will received a nod or a hello but little more.

After that he didn't mind going into the Long Branch. Enjoyed it, even, and liked to see himself in the big mirror, standing up there at the bar looking official and admiring the naked lady.

In the fall of 1877, Bat Masterson was elected sheriff of Ford County and Ed got himself appointed marshal of Dodge. The lawmen, including Will, sat around and played cards most of that winter, missing the fallen doves who had moved on to places of more activity during the cold weather when the trail herds weren't bringing in cowboys every day. Will kind of missed a woman named Cross-Eyed Jennie whom he'd gotten to know quite well. "Never had a regular friend that was a woman," he told Bat. "Guess I liked her 'cause she didn't have much to say. Kind of like you."

Will read old newspapers when he could find one that hadn't been torn up and used for toilet paper or seat padding. He at least read the headlines and maybe the first paragraph.

The Atchison, Topeka and Santa Fe Railroad reduced wages five percent and slashed conductors' salaries from a top of $120 per month to $75.

Eleven members of a group called The Molly Maguires were hanged in Pennsylvania after a decade of activity in mining towns. Will learned they were "an Irish-American terrorist society" and wondered which they were — Irish or American.

The cystoscope for examining the inside of the urinary bladder had been invented. "Good Lord," Will muttered.

He stared at a line drawing of a ballet dancer standing on a toe with her knickers showing. She was part of a Russian group performing a new ballet called *Swan Lake* that the reviewers didn't seem to like.

Queen Victoria had been proclaimed empress of India. "Does England own India?" Will hollered at Bat. "Stupid question," Bat replied, meaning he didn't know.

Apaches in Arizona Territory were ordered out of the Chiricahua reservation and moved to San Carlos. Any man, woman, or child found off the reservation was to be shot without being given a chance to surrender.

Osmosis was discovered, a famine killed four million in Bengal, Russia and Turkey were at war, barbed wire prices dropped from eighteen to eight cents per pound, and Secretary of the Interior Carl Schurz said timber barons were "not merely stealing trees but whole forests."

Will turned back to the ballet story with the picture.

In July of the next year, it was hotter than the Llano Estacado and the wind never stopped blowing. One night that month when it was as hot at dusk as it had been at noon, Will fired his pistol at a human for the first time.

A man named Charlie Bassett was town marshal by then and had an assistant named Wyatt Earp. Ed Masterson had wandered off to someplace else and Jim, the younger Masterson, was a policeman on the city force. Bat was still county sheriff.

Inside the saloons it was steaming. Smoke clogged the air, which was rich with the aroma of too many unwashed bodies. Even the girls were so sweaty they weren't working as hard as usual. Will broke up a couple of fights and wished the night would get over quickly.

About 3 a.m. two cowboys drifted out of the Lady Gay saloon, broke but feeling good. They retrieved their revolvers, which they weren't allowed to wear in town, and mounted up. One of them decided he hadn't had enough fun and began firing wildly in the air, riding as fast as he could up and down Front Street. Some of his bullets strayed into the Lady Gay itself. Bat Masterson was just dealing out a hand of Spanish Monte to a friend of his named Doc Holliday when the first bullet crashed into the wall behind him. Both he and Holliday hit the floor, along with everybody else in the place.

By then Jim Masterson and Wyatt Earp had raced to the scene. Not knowing it was simply a cowboy letting off steam, they started to exchange fire with the galloping rider. Will came out of the Long Branch, ducked behind a wagon and, seeing Wyatt and Jim seemingly in a deadly gunbattle, started firing himself. Finally, the cowboy and his friend, who hadn't fired a shot, took off out of town to the west. Somebody, either Masterson or Earp — nobody ever knew which — winged one of the cowboys with a lucky shot at forty yards.

That was the only damage, except that a bystander had been hit and died a few weeks later. But he was a Texan and only his friends mourned his passing. The Lady Gay had some new bullet holes in its walls and ceiling and the incident provided interesting conversation for a few days.

23

Except for that scrape and dragging a cowboy off to jail now and then for having too much fun too loudly, Will's job was getting routine. Around Christmas he told Bat he would be moving on in the spring. "I don't want to be a lawman all my life and I sure don't want to get a reputation as a gun-fighter."

"Don't think you need to worry much about that," Bat said with a laugh. "Where'll you be heading?"

"California," Will said.

So he headed east. *Well, shoot*, he mused. Somebody had told him about Wichita and Abilene and Independence and the fact that the Santa Fe Trail would get him partway to California. He could earn good money on the way, too. He'd get to California one of these days and he had nothing but time.

Sleet was blowing in his left ear when he struck out for Wichita early on a March morning. He had already said good-bye to Bat, Jim and Wyatt. Shook hands with Doc Holliday, too, although he was just getting to know the man. He was quieter even than Bat Masterson, and kept coughing into a handkerchief all the time.

There wasn't anybody on Front Street when he pointed Sally along the tracks and out of town. He followed the snow-covered banks of the Arkansas River until it wandered off to the north toward its great bend, then he struck across the prairie to Rattlesnake Creek, straight on east to the south fork of the Ninnescah. When it faded off to the south he kept pointing east until he reached the north fork. Thought to himself that there sure were a lot of rivers and creeks for such a dry country.

Wichita was as quiet as Dodge, so he spent only a couple of nights there and then headed off to the northeast, through Towanda and into the Flint Hills toward Emporia. Folks told him this bluestem grass country was the best in the world for raising cattle. Sometimes the grass got so tall a man on a horse couldn't find every head at roundup.

More rivers, the Cottonwood, Neosho, Marias des Cygnes, Wakarusa and the Kansas. Then he was riding into Independence across the Missouri.

Will spent a few weeks there, getting to know a couple of the women and then, in the spring, hired on to drive a team of jacks back across Kansas on the Santa Fe Trail. At least he would be heading in the direction of California.

"Might be the last wagon train to cross this old trail," the wagon boss told him. "They got railroad tracks laid to Colorado already and they'll get to Santa Fe itself maybe by next year this time. It's the end of a fine and wonderful thing."

The train of fifteen wagons left Westport at dawn in late May. Will had sold Sally and his rig, figuring he'd re-equip himself in Santa Fe.. Now all he owned were what clothes he had, his pistol and rifle and the original spurs he'd bought in Waco years before.

Wagons creaking, jacks braying, drivers cursing, they followed deep wagon wheel ruts to the Shawnee Indian Mission barely in Kansas, then down to Gardner and the junction of the old Oregon Trail. Some wagons still rolled for Oregon but mainly carried those people who couldn't afford to take the new train that went clear to Sacramento.

Past Burlingame on the Wakarusa they lined out for Council Grove where they joined up with another train of twelve wagons.

They headed west of Council Grove to Diamond Springs, still in the lushness of the Flint Hills, then on toward Lyons and the plains that stretched out ahead going nowhere and everywhere. Sleeping under bright stars or under the wagon while thunderstorms beat down like they were out to smash a man, Will traveled his fifteen or twenty miles a day, now and then seeing deer, maybe an antelope, lots of rabbits, a few buffalo. They passed from tallgrass to shortgrass prairie so gradually Will didn't realize it until it hit him one morning. He saw a few ragged Indians who begged for food or trinkets.

At Fort Zarah they hit the Arkansas and followed it a ways to Great Bend and Pawnee Rock. Then there was mostly dry travel, except for an occasional small creek, to Fort Dodge. They took a break there and Will went into town to say hello to Bat. He was off somewhere on sheriff business and even Cross-Eyed Jennie hadn't come back to Dodge that summer.

Will sat down at a table with Wyatt Earp and Doc Holliday after Wyatt nodded an invitation to him from across the room. Neither was much interested in what Will had been up to since he'd left.

"Where's Peabody?" Will asked. Holliday had a coughing fit and Earp didn't say anything for a long time. "He still own part of the place?"

"Nope." Wyatt sipped at his drink and surveyed the crowd. "Left town."

Will didn't really care that much but it was some kind of conversation so he pushed. "Do I get the feeling that he might not have wanted to leave?"

Holliday's coughing fit was over. "Wyatt thought he needed to go somewhere else," he said. "Got to winning too much."

"Cheating, huh?"

"Looked like it to me," Earp said. "Got to meet a man." He hauled himself to his feet and left the room. Holliday spread a deck on the table.

"Game?" he asked.

Will stood. "Not tonight." Walked out as silently as Earp and didn't care. Went back to his wagon and figured he was doing the best thing, going to California and away from Dodge. *Damn Kansans*, Will thought. *Have to pry information from 'em with a crowbar.*

West of Dodge they took the southwest cutoff rather than heading on west to Bent's Fort and La Junta. No real Indian worries anymore, just broken wagon wheels and no wood to fix them, thirst so bad your tongue got black before you hit the Middle Spring, and long days looking at the tail ends of a bunch of jacks.

Finally, Santa Fe. Buyers for the goods they carried. Rich Mexican food, liquor from Taos, and wine and brandy from El Paso. Here was gambling and women who walked proudly and looked you in the eye. Let's get this stuff unloaded and meet some of 'em.

Will collected his pay and met some of 'em. One, anyway. After a few days and nights with Maria he bought himself a horse he named Jeremiah and started for California again. This time he headed northwest since somebody told him he really ought to take a look at the Colorado Rockies.

He rode up through Alamosa, gaped at the great sand dunes and bought another horse which he called Obediah. He stocked up on food and warmer clothes. Just as the aspen leaves were changing from green to golden, the sky was the bluest and highest he'd ever seen, and the hot summer temperatures dropped down to just about perfect, he rode into Gunnison and thought he might as well settle in and wait out the winter.

NOT FAR to the north, over a narrow, treacherous pass that climbed the gnarled burl of mountains called the Elk Range, Owl Man was also admiring the vast sweep of a gold and red autumn forest. Will Martin was seeing the sight for the first time and Owl Man possibly for the last.

The Indian was not-so-patiently awaiting the birth of a half-breed child whose coming would signal the end of a way of life for Owl Man and, for that matter, all Utes. Here, where the child who would forever remind him of the most painful years of his life was to be born, was also the place he had spent his happiest days. Here, on this red point of rock that seemed to hang in the sky, was where he had come of age, where he had been often visited by the *powa'a* and the *ini'pute*. He knew they would not follow him to exile in the southwestern reservation.

The narrow valley he loved sliced south to north through a range of rugged mountains in the central Rockies just west of the Continental Divide. The whites called it the Elk Range and had given the silver stream that drained the valley the unimaginative name of Rock Creek.

White man's names! Owl Man shook his head. The enormous mass of the Mountain of Sanctuary that bulked high to its trio of pointed peaks at the valley's northern portal had been given a man's name, Sopris. The mountain deserved better. Its slide area on the north face with the shape of a fish should have conjured up a more fitting name.

26

The whites who had crossed the divide illegally on what they called Independence Day barely three months ago had known what to name the tent city they set up at the base of Aspen Mountain, though. They called it Ute City in deference to their trespass.

Owl Man stared again at the gleaming whiteness of the snow in "Chair" Mountain's bowl. Because two sharp ridges climbed to a sheer back wall on the mountain's east and west sides, it had seemed to resemble a chair to the whites. South and east of the mountain there was already the beginnings of a town. The collection of shacks and tents called Schofield was full of dirty white miners pulling ore from the ground. Soon there would be more towns, more roads, more white men. . . and no more of the *Nunt'z*.

The valley was familiar to all the Utes, few of whom would ever see it again. After the battle — what the whites were calling a "massacre" — Owl Man had convinced a group of about thirty to escape with him through the valley so they could ride at least once more through the scene of their most pleasant memories.

The most pleasant of those memories were of his time with Sings Quietly, his wife of many years. He had met her at the Bear Dance when he was eighteen years old. She was a small girl of perhaps fifteen summers with eyes the color of pine cones. When her family left with the rest of the Weminuche Utes to return to the Gunnison country she had stayed behind with Owl Man.

Always their life together had been good, although in the later years there was the problem of the white man.

For a while there had been peace. The whites were concerned with a mounting tension among themselves far to the east that some said would result in war — white against white. Owl Man was pleased with the news. *Let them fight themselves*, he thought. *Better that than an all-out war against the Utes.*

Most of the *Nunt'z* disagreed. Many Utes, among them Owl Man's friend Wolf, began to call for outright war on the white man. Not only were the Indians feeling the intense pressure of increasing white settlement on the edges of their territory, but the game upon which they depended for survival was also beginning to disappear. Commercial hunters were wiping out the once extensive herds of buffalo. Deer and elk were also less plentiful.

A few years after the 1855 treaty some of the braves of Owl Man's band returned from a hunting expedition on the eastern plains with disturbing news. White men had discovered something called placer gold in the foothills of the mountains on Cherry Creek. As many white men were there, the warriors said, as there are stars in the sky. And more were coming every day — as many as the huge herds of buffalo that once roamed the plains.

Within a year Ouray was dispatched by the Ute tribal council to seek the help of Kit Carson in negotiating another treaty, "to protect Ute lands." The treaty was signed in 1859.

By the following summer more than fifty thousand people had packed up and headed for Pikes Peak, as the entire region was called. A city called Denver was growing near Cherry Creek. Hordes of miners were rapidly encroaching on one of the last exclusively Indian domains in the country. More than five thousand of them struggled over the mountains to another gold strike at California Gulch in 1860. They were soon laboring at hundreds of claims in the thin air of ten thousand feet around another new town called Leadville.

Headlines in newspapers throughout the eastern territory screamed, "The Utes Must Go!" Ute land was evidently rich in minerals and it also included the best agricultural and grazing lands in the territory. Everywhere there were new strikes. Hundreds of acres took on the look of overgrown prairie-dog towns. The dumps of hopeful miners, most of whom knew little or nothing about mining, covered the land.

Ouray, the Arrow, negotiated another treaty. The whites and many of his own people told the chief of all the Utes that it was the greatest treaty ever made with the whites. In effect, it barred all whites from the Western Slope of the Rockies and even forced many miners already there to leave. Few mentioned that of the seven Ute bands, only the Tabeguaches had shown up at the council to negotiate, once more with Kit Carson. The treaty also promised yearly gifts to the tribe including cattle, sheep and even $10,000 in cash and another $10,000 in provisions. Ouray and other Tabeguache leaders received silver medals.

None of the Utes ever received even the first payment called for in the new treaty.

With the end of America's Civil War, thousands of homeless veterans headed west to the gold fields. By 1868 the eastern mountains were heavy with white men carrying shovels, breaking up rocks, lifting pebbles from the streams, digging more holes in the earth. Ouray granted immunity to parties of surveyors led by a geologist named Hayden. Owl Man felt the anger build again at the thought. If the mountains were to belong to the Utes "forever," what were the use of surveys? Ouray, friend to the white man, had given in to them once again, probably so he could continue to receive his thousand dollars of white man's money each year.

Nevertheless, white men were soon exploring the valley of Rock Creek. They carefully drew maps and began to refer to Hawk Peak and Hawk Creek, Elk Mountain, Rapid, Milton and Raspberry creeks, Avalanche Pass and, yes, even Hayden Peak.

Another party that same year actually gouged out a road over what they called Schofield Pass and a man named Richardson found evidence of pure white marble up a remote creek northwest of the pass.

Anthracite. Galena. Marble. Where would it end? Would there be an end at all? Owl Man had told the Utes how it would end. He had told them all, including Ouray, "Chief of all the Utes." His warnings, as usual, were fruitless. By then, agencies had been established here and there throughout the mountains. Survey parties of whites moved freely, charting the territory. Photographers made images of beautiful scenery and stern, ugly Indians. There was more wealth in Ute territory that was not getting to those who needed it, the intruders said. Those "savages" controlled a full one-third of Colorado Territory.

An entourage of Utes went to Washington to meet General Grant. They saw a circus and the newspapers reported the Indians were greatly amused by the animals with "tails at both ends." They signed the Brunot Treaty, giving up another four million acres in the rich San Juan Mountains.

An uneasy truce prevailed. Miners and soldiers were everywhere in the territory. In 1876, Colorado became a state.

In the fall of 1878 Leadville boasted a population of six thousand. By the next spring the number had doubled and men with dreams of glory and riches were coming at the rate of three hundred to five hundred a day. The Union Pacific, the Kansas Pacific, the Atchison, Topeka and Santa Fe railroads trailed scores of overloaded cars into the state. Between one and five thousand people came to Colorado every day.

"The Utes Must Go!" — the feeling expressed in that slogan was gaining strength. The reservation was a veritable storehouse of treasure, everyone said. Gold was literally exposed on top of the ground. The Elk Mountains were full of silver. Every river was lined with ore. How much came out of California Gulch up around the headwaters of the Arkansas? Millions, they said. Add in Stray Gulch and Iowa Gulch and it was $13 million in just four years. And that was just the beginning.

Life became more difficult for Owl Man and all the Utes. The Utes were blamed when several forest fires broke out. White men illegally killed deer at random, they dynamited mountain streams to kill trout, they cut forests of timber on public lands, which was also prohibited by law. Reluctantly, the Indians were forced to live near the recently established agencies to receive their meager subsidies.

In 1878, Nathan Cook Meeker, a newspaper man from New York, was appointed agent for the White River Indian Agency in northwestern Colorado. Some said Meeker had used his influence with Horace Greeley of the *New York Tribune* to get the appointment, and he appeared at a volatile moment. Meeker, who once editorialized about the "mental inferiority of the American

29

Indian," was a utopian dreamer who hoped to turn the Utes into instant farmers full of Christian zeal.

Owl Man never met Meeker. The holy man and Sings Quietly set up their own camp some distance from the agency where they and a few others would receive some sustenance from the whites but could avoid them as much as possible. He did see the agent from afar one day, however, and instantly recognized him as the white figure in his vision of 1855 — the tall, gaunt man who was supervising the breaking of ground. A shock of despair ran through Owl Man's body when he realized that his prophecy was becoming all too accurate. He quickly rode away and vowed never to see the man again.

One morning soon after the beginning of the white man's year of 1879, Owl Man rode cold and alone. The high peaks surrounding the valley were covered with snow but the valley showed only patches here and there, indications of a mild winter. Owl Man let his pony pick his way along the small stream he followed, not caring where he went.

He was lost in thought, mourning the recent death of his wife, Sings Quietly. For two days he had ridden aimlessly, grieving in silence but wanting to cry to *Inu'sakats* for a return to the days of peace.

The pony had stopped. Owl Man had no idea how long the horse might have stood there. Something jarred him out of his trance. Had it been a rifle shot? More white men hunting illegally on Ute land? He heard a scream. It was a woman. Another scream. Then silence.

The sound had come from the other side of a cottonwood grove that bordered a bend in the stream. He dismounted, felt the pain in his legs, then walked the pony to the edge of the trees and hobbled him there. He had no weapon and he was old and tired but he felt he must find out what was happening. Quietly, he slipped through the grove until he reached its far limits. He crouched down and scanned the small meadow that fell to the stream.

He sensed movement to his left. Two white men appeared from the trees. One had a grip on the arm of an Indian woman who had ceased crying out but who fought to free herself. The other dragged the body of a brave. The dead Indian lay on his back, his feet in the crooks of the white man's arms, one on either side of his body. The whites were laughing.

Owl Man was helpless. He watched in horror as the small party reached the bank of the stream.

"Here's a purty deep spot," said the one with the dead Ute. "Do somethin' with that squaw and come help me." The second man looked at the woman for an instant.

Fear was in her eyes. He picked up a heavy rock from the stream bank and clubbed her on the head. She fell without a sound.

"Hope you ain't kilt her."

"Naw," the second man said with a smirk. "Just coldcocked her a bit. She'll be good as new 'fore long." He looked like a gopher, Owl Man thought.

The other, the bigger of the two with a full growth of beard, pulled a large knife from his belt. They talked as they worked but Owl Man was unable to hear what they said. What they did was enough to pull bile from his stomach. He retched silently, as quietly as he could. He could not tear his eyes from the scene.

The big man cut the clothes from the Indian, threw them in a pile, stabbed his knife into the dead man's belly. "Shit," he said, stood up, wiped blood from his coat.

"It'll wash out," the other said. "Let's get it done."

The hairy man slit the Indian from throat to groin. The two worked feverishly, pulling intestines from the Indian and throwing them into the water. That done, they began to gather large, heavy stones which they forced into the Ute's abdomen. They picked up the disemboweled body, one at either end and, swinging it between them, they counted. On "three" they heaved the body into the stream. It made a loud splash and sank quickly to the bottom of the deep pool.

Owl Man was burning with anger. What could he do? Even if he followed his first thought and rushed the men, they would kill him.

The hairy man stood in the shallow water washing himself. He wiped the knife on his pants and replaced it in his belt. "Let's wake up that thing," he said.

Together they dragged the woman to the stream and waded in, pushing her head under water. She began to struggle.

"That's it, little girl," Gopher said. "We want you awake for this."

Owl Man closed his eyes but could not keep them closed. See and remember, he thought. Remember so you can tell the others, so you can tell Ouray himself.

The woman was awake, soaking wet. Now there was no fear in her eyes, only sadness, hopelessness.

She did not resist as they tore her clothes from her body. She lay still as they mounted her, grunted over her, laughed and rolled on their backs, panting out their pleasure. After a while they took her again, both of them.

Later, their appetites satisfied, they stood over her. She lay still, eyes open, staring at the two. The hairy man pulled a pistol and shot her just above the right breast. She jerked once and was quiet. As they casually rolled her limp body into the stream, they laughed.

They didn't look at her after that but walked back into the trees. Soon

31

Owl Man heard the sound of horses. He waited a few minutes longer, then hurried to the stream and, as gently as he could, pulled her from the water. Blood oozed from her chest as he bent his ear to her mouth to check if she was breathing.

❧❧

SEVERAL DAYS later she was strong enough to ride. *Ute women are very strong*, Owl Man said to himself. The bullet had passed through her chest and exited high on her back. Her breast bone was ruined and she had lost much blood. But she would live. The cold water might have helped her survive.

Owl Man took her to his camp, riding short distances, then resting for long periods. During the three-day ride she told him her name was Mary, a white woman's name. Her mother had been a Christian, she said, and had named her for the Virgin. Owl Man had heard the tale of Jesus and thought it had been made up by a sick man.

Mary and a brave named Runs Fast had fled their White River camp only the night before. The two young people wanted to be husband and wife but Mary's mother had forbidden it since Runs Fast was not a Christian. Her father had died a year ago. They had camped in the woods near the stream after walking most of the night to get as far away as possible. They had barely fallen asleep when the two white men woke them. Runs Fast had been killed immediately with a rifle shot to the head, and the two whites pawed Mary for some time before deciding they needed to do something with the body. Owl Man knew the remainder of the story. Owl Man apologized once again for his inability to save her.

"It is no longer important," she said. "You should have left me there to die. I have nothing to live for now."

Owl Man prayed silently to *Inu'sakats* that there might yet be some happiness in this young woman's life.

Finally, back at his camp, Mary was taken in to live with Elk Horn and his wife, Long Haired Woman. They had no children and agreed that Mary might live with them until spring. Then they would see about finding her a husband. Mary shook her head at that but smiled her thanks.

The long ride so soon after her ordeal had taken much of her strength but she healed gradually and the beauty in her face that Owl Man had seen early began to grow even more so.

Within a few weeks, however, it became apparent that Mary was pregnant.

"It is a white man's child," she said.

32

Owl Man took a deep breath. "Runs Fast?"

"We had never lain together," she said. "We might have that night but we were too tired from the running."

Mary turned her back to Owl Man and after a while he thought about leaving. "I wish you had let me die," she said softly. They continued to stay away from the agency, living on the meager amount of small game they could trap and on the supplies other members of the band brought to them when Meeker issued rations.

The news Owl Man received about the agency came from Samson Rabbit, a young man who continued to believe in the holy man's powers. "The agent Meeker has moved the agency to our meadow," Rabbit told Owl Man one summer day after catching his breath from a wild ride along the river to the holy man's camp. "He wants to plow it. He wants to plow up the grazing land and the racetrack."

Owl Man shuddered. The Utes loved to race their ponies and a track had been beaten into the earth around the meadow, the result of hundreds of races over the years and the source of many fond memories of all the Utes.

"It is not good," Owl Man said. "It is the beginning." Rabbit looked at the ground, understanding, and soon left with a promise to keep Owl Man informed of developments at the agency.

A few days later he was back telling of a building Meeker had constructed on the racetrack. "He says it is a school and he wants all the Ute children to come. He is always angry. I think he is sick in his head."

Tension continued to increase. Meeker ordered the meadow plowed and the Indians refused. He ordered them to send their children to school. "Not now," they said. "Maybe in a month when it is cooler."

Trying desperately to make the Utes follow orders, Meeker said none of the much-needed treaty supplies would be released until the plowing was done. He also made it impossible for the Utes to leave on their annual summer hunt when he required that each family, including the men, report weekly at the agency to receive rations.

Though they seemed outwardly calm, the Utes were constantly on edge. Meeker himself was badly frightened when an Indian named Canalla knocked him to the floor of his office. The agent had told Canalla he could no longer graze his herd of horses in the meadow near the new school. "You have too many horses, anyway," Meeker said curtly. "You should sell some of them." Canalla's composure broke.

He grabbed Meeker by the lapels of his coat and hit him in the face. Meeker dropped to the floor as Canalla stormed from the office.

Within an hour there was a gunshot from the edge of the meadow and the agent quickly composed a telegram to the commissioner: "Plowing stops. Life of self, family and employees not safe; want protection immediately."

In early October, Rabbit was back at Owl Man's camp with fear in his eyes. "The soldiers came and now we must leave," he said. "I think we should join the Weminuche in the San Juans."

Owl Man motioned for Rabbit to sit by the fire. "First you must tell me of it," he said. "Tell it all so we understand." About 150 soldiers had marched from Fort Steele where the Union Pacific crossed the Platte River in Wyoming. Major T. T. Thornburgh commanded three troops of cavalry and one of infantry. The Utes, in preparation for such a move, had stationed scouts far in the north to warn of any encroachment. Rabbit said Meeker knew nothing of any of this. No one had bothered to tell the agent that soldiers were anywhere near. Rabbit and others were stationed on a trail above Red Canyon when Thornburgh's command started through. His supply wagons had fallen about half a mile behind on the rough road.

We let them get just below us," Rabbit said, "and then we shot them." He talked quickly, excited about his role in what was to be the Utes' final stand against the white man.

"Well," he continued, "we didn't kill any of them right then but they ran like frightened sheep." Few of the Indians had rifles so they found cover close enough to the road for their arrows to reach. Thornburgh was hit in the side of the head with a bullet from one of the Ute rifles and fell from his horse.

The battle raged for nearly a week. "They didn't have much water," Rabbit said. "The stink of the dead horses was bad. Their chief swelled up lying out there in the hot sun. We shot some of them now and then and we heard the wounded ones moan. We would shoot and then move quickly to another hiding place. The soldiers wasted a lot of bullets shooting at places where there was no one."

The Utes sent a messenger back to the agency to report on the battle. Meeker was still unaware that only fifteen miles away a battle was underway. In fact, he began a note to Thornburgh telling him that "things are peaceable." As he wrote, the man to whom the letter was addressed lay dead.

Meanwhile, other Indians had broken into the storeroom at the agency and took the rifles.

"I wasn't there but Antelope told me about it," Rabbit said. "Quinkent led about twenty braves into the buildings and killed two white men right away. Some of them, including the women, got into the adobe milk house while Quinkent and the others burned the rest of the buildings and killed other whites. When the smoke got too bad in the milk house everyone ran. The Utes killed them all except for the women and two children."

Meeker was killed early on, Rabbit told Owl Man. Quinkent or someone else — he didn't know for sure who it was — drove a stake through the agent's mouth, pinning him to the ground. Then they cut him up some more.

As soon as they were certain that everyone was dead except some of the women, all the buildings burned and the supplies confiscated, the Utes started for their ancestral hunting grounds on Grand Mesa, across the Grand River south of the agency.

"We would have killed all the soldiers," Rabbit said, "but more soldiers with black faces came to help. Then even more came with big guns on wagons. The big bullets tore up the mountainside. I think we could have killed them, too, but we got a message from Ouray."

Owl Man raised his eyes. "Ouray! How did he know?"

"I think the whites sent a message to him," Rabbit said. "He was on a hunt in the San Juans. He told us to stop fighting."

"So you did as you were told by the Chief of all the Utes?"

"Yes." Rabbit was no longer so excited. Now he felt humbled. Had he done wrong?

"So it is over," Owl Man said. "We must go."

The small group quickly readied itself for travel. The whites were angry over the thirteen of their number who had died at Milk Creek. It was too bad the Utes had mutilated the bodies of the whites they had killed at the agency, Owl Man thought. But what was done could not be undone.

They followed the White River upstream then south to South Fork Canyon and up to the vast plateau the whites called the Flat Tops, which spread over hundreds of square miles all the way to Yampa Springs. It was a long and exhausting trip that was far out of the way. But it would take them one last time to the valley of Rock Creek.

On rock-strewn, barren ridges they crossed Indian Camp Pass near Triangle Mountain then picked their way down to Heart Lake. They crossed White Owl and Broken Rib creeks and turned west to No Name Creek, which took them off the Flat Tops and down to what the whites called the Grand River, just east of Yampa Springs.

To the west and south they found the Roaring Fork River and followed it to its juncture with Rock Creek. The Mountain of Sanctuary, Mount Sopris to the whites, spiked into the cloudless sky to the south. All eyes were on it as the tiny band of silent Indians rode slowly through the wide, wet meadow of the valley's lower end. The snows were early, whitening the gray boulders on the mountain.

All day they rode, around the mountain's boulder-packed base where the river narrowed, past Thompson Creek and Potato Bill Creek and Nettle Creek, white man's names for small streams that had no names, and needed no names when the valley belonged to the Utes. They rode past Holgate Mesa and Assignation Ridge to Avalanche Creek and the hot springs. There they set

35

up a silent camp, each lost in his own thoughts about the life that had been. They were on the move when the sun picked up the gold on the aspen the next morning. The red cliffs were hazy when they plodded below them an hour later. Owl Man squinted his eyes into the sun to pick out Owl Point. Hayes Creek trickled into the river this time of year and they picked their way carefully past the falls. Then the valley opened up again, meandered uphill to the base of Chair Mountain, bent sharply left and began a steady climb to the pass, to the headwaters of the silver stream.

"It is time for the child, I think." Mary was beside Owl Man, one hand reining her pony, the other stroking her bulging belly.

"It seems too soon." "Nevertheless."

"I have a wish to visit Owl Point," he said. "The child would have a good beginning there."

Somehow, with his help, pushing, pulling, half carrying, sharing her pain, they were there. Evening sun ringed a fat cloud with red fringes as the woman picked her way into the aspen grove while Owl Man settled down on his rocky outcropping to await the birth.

All through the night he had waited and there had been no sound from the aspen grove. Now he was old and tired and anxious to join the others. They must leave the valley before the soldiers arrived.

He heard a moan from his left and then a sharp cry of new life. He closed his eyes on today and, for a while, sat in his teepee with Sings Quietly.

Soon, the woman called his name. She held the child to her breast. "It is a man child," she said.

Owl Man stood, gently drew the blanket from the baby's head and saw blue eyes, a scraggle of black hair, a nose that was bent to the side. He tried to smile.

"You are all right?"

"I will be ready to leave soon."

Sooner than he had expected, she was at his side. She looked strong, he thought, and perhaps happy. He took her arm and began the walk down the steep mountainside to their hobbled ponies. After a few steps he heard a voice and turned.

It was the voice of Long Hand. Suddenly Owl Man was no longer old. He was again the young boy, Badger. He was barely a man and had just told his leader of a vision he had seen as he sat on this very point above the river.

Long Hand told him:

You are po'rat. You have a power that has been spoken of in stories told to us by the old ones. Inside you lives a tiny being — the powa'a — who directs the use of your power.

. . . evil ini'pute, a ghost who inhabits the ihupi'arat where you

36

discovered the power . . .

   . . . can overcome the kind powa'a . . . a rare and dangerous power.

   . . . evil ini'pute . . . lead to disaster.

   . . . overcome the kind powa'a . . .

   . . . may all of your decisions be made for the good of the Nunt'z.

Mary nudged Owl Man from behind. The boy child made a slight cry and was quiet. "Why do you stop?" she asked. "I am strong. Let us go on."

The medicine man felt youth return to his legs. "There is a thing I must do," he said. "Walk to that pine tree and follow the ridge until you can go no farther. Wait for me there."

Back on Owl Point, the *ihupi'arat tubut* where he had first felt his power, he made himself again comfortable on the red outcropping and listened to the ghosts, the *ini'pute* who dwelled there. Soon he summoned *otus asio*, the owl. He called for the sparrow and, finally, the eagle. When all had assembled he spoke to them and they listened politely, if sadly, as he talked.

"You are my friends," he said, "and I know you understand what will happen to this valley, and why. It saddens me to do this. But you can fly above it all and be affected only slightly. Hear me, then."

Legs crossed, back straight, Owl Man-Badger lifted his arms to the creator, closed his eyes and spoke.

"*Inu'sakats*, hear me! I do not desert you, as you have not deserted me. Grant me this small indulgence. This land was promised to your People for as long as rivers might run and grasses might grow. The land is no longer ours and yet I hear the river, I feel the grass. May they continue to run and to grow and to nourish all the animal brothers who can survive here with the white man." A wind rattled the aspen leaves and the once-clear blue sky began to pale behind dark clouds.

"Forgive me, little *powa'a* who have served me well. I release all ghosts who live in this place to spread themselves throughout the valley. I order them to carry out my will or the will of the one whom I will designate upon my death. *Inu'sakats* no longer lives here. It is yours, *ini'pute*. Do with it as you will. Watch the white man and hinder his every effort. I give up my soul. I give up my right to the peaceful hereafter!"

His heart beat furiously. The eyes of *otus asio* opened wide. The sparrow tucked his head beneath a wing. Only the eagle stood proudly, understanding and approving.

"I place a curse upon this valley. That the white man's life here will be one of pain and sorrow. That his efforts will be to no avail. That every *ini'pute* will cast his shadow over all white men who walk in the shadow of the Mountain of Sanctuary."

Owl Man stood, feeling the first flakes of snow on his face. He felt the

37

first onrush of icy wind, as did his brothers to the south, as did the white men who pursued them, as did the elk, the bear, the deer and the rabbit.

"Cursed be this valley to all white men!" he shouted.

Otus asio was gone, gone with the sparrow. Only the eagle remained. His eyes were fixed on Owl Man's. Opening his beak, his shrill cry was full of anguish and anger. A wing tip brushed Owl Man's wet cheek as the eagle opened up to a width greater than a tall man's height and soared from the *ihupi'arat tubut* down toward the river and disappeared in the thickening snow and lowering cloud.

Owl Man was again old as he made his way down the ridge, found Mary and her man child huddled beneath a wind-blown cedar, and went on down to the ponies.

PART II

1880

The summer morning mountain air was so clean and sharp it hurt a man's eyes just looking through it. At this altitude Will Martin figured he could see so far he might never get his eyes focused down on something close again.

Riding one horse and leading another, Will carried with him everything he owned in the world. It was little enough for a man thirty years old, he thought to himself. A pair of spurs, batwing chaps and a Texas hat with a rattlesnake band and a star on the side. A couple of shirts, a pair of boots that fit like they were part of his feet, a Colt single-action .45 revolver, a Winchester .44-.40 rifle with an extra rear sight for greater accuracy, a well-worn saddle and a bunch of odds and ends along with some flour, beans and bacon. And that's all he had to show for fifteen years of punching cows in Texas, keeping the peace in Dodge City and driving a mule train across Kansas on the Santa Fe Trail — that and $200 he had buried in the flour.

Now, here he was on top of Colorado, all alone and heading for someplace he'd never heard of just because somebody told him he ought to go take a look. He was heading for California and, sure as the wind blows in Kansas, he'd get there. But he was in no particular hurry and this was sure enough a far sight better than the high plains.

Will was still getting used to the high country, adjusting from life as a flatlander that kept you wiping dust from your eyes with one hand while you tried to keep your hat from being blown clear to Nebraska with the other. They'd told him in Gunnison that this was mighty fine country but in all his wanderings he'd never seen anything like it. He was looking for a town called Schofield, beyond which, he had been told, men were finding silver, gold, coal, lead, copper, zinc and even marble. "Finally run the damned Indians out," they said, "and a white man's got a chance to make it big over there. Not like Leadville or Aspen where all the good claims have done been took. Yessir, I had the time and money that's where I'd go. Over the pass to Schofield and even farther north."

"Why don't you go?" Will had asked.

"Well, hell, it takes a young man with no wife nor brood of kids to worry him. That's why. 'Sides, I'm goin' to California soon's I can scrape up the money."

"So am I," Will said. But first he'd have a look at this Schofield, just for the fun of it.

A sky blue as a Texas bluebonnet disappeared behind sawtooth mountain ranges with heaps of snow lying deep in crevasses. Gray and white peaks

40

ranged down to blue spruce and green cedars at timberline. Brightly colored wildflowers striped meadows of blue and green grass. Here and there a boulder big as a house shaded unmelted snow that would soon feed the stream that gurgled like a happy child meandering through the broad meadow.

Schofield probably wasn't more than a few hours' ride away but he didn't feel like hurrying. Didn't have any idea what he'd do when he got there anyway. *Shoot, this might be the end of the ride,* Will thought. *At least for a while until I set out for California again.* Now that it was about over he wasn't sure he was ready to quit. The ride up from Taos to Alamosa and into the heart of the Rocky Mountains at Gunnison had been the best he'd ever made, and getting here seemed like the end of something rather than the beginning.

The best ride ever. It surprised Will that he'd even think it, considering the rides he'd made in the past fifteen years. Of course, on practically every other trip he'd been herding cows or hauling freight and was being pushed by one trail boss or another to get there in a hurry, make some money and get back wherever it was they started from.

Yes, he thought, *this ride could be the best.* And he had a feeling these mountains might just turn out to be the best of all the places he'd ever been. Had a gut feeling. Might be just the best place of all.

He recalled the morning a week earlier when he woke up and realized he was 30 years old and, except for some vague idea about California, didn't know what he might do next. His new friend Emily, a tall coarse-voiced dancer who read a newspaper now and then, told Will there were 100 millionaires in the country. Will Martin, who had a few hundred dollars to his name and no real prospects for getting any richer anytime soon, didn't reply.

"Look," Emily said one bright morning in the spring. "It says here Singer will sell more than half a million sewing machines this year. Wish I had a sewing machine." She looked at Will but he had turned his head, pretending to be interested in something out the window, and she didn't push it.

"There's silver over Schofield Pass above Crested Butte," somebody told him a few days later. "Damn nice country, too, and the Indians has been run out."

And, shoot, Will figured, *it was kind of on the way to California.*

WILL NEGOTIATED the steep, rocky, zigzag trail over Schofield Pass with no difficulty and followed the creek on to Schofield itself. The town, set on the north edge of a broad, park-like area and surrounded by snow-capped mountains, was a surprise. Thirty or forty houses were trying to crowd together around a business district consisting of a store, a boarding house and several saloons. Next to the creek was a concentrating mill.

Will stabled his horses, made a mental note of the boarding house, wandered over to the nearest of the saloons and became the owner of a silver mine.

First, though, he ran into Nathan Peabody. Will had just made himself comfortable at the bar when he heard his name called. Peabody sat across the room from Will at a rough-hewn pine-topped table with a cigar in his mouth and a fan of cards in his hand.

"Will Martin!" Everybody in the saloon turned to look at Will as he nodded to Peabody, unable to hide his surprise at seeing the Dodge City gambler. Peabody glanced at his cards, wagged his head and put them face down on the table. "I'm out," he said. He pocketed his winnings, a few coins, and a miner quickly took his chair as he strode across the room toward Will.

"You're just about the last person in the world I ever thought to see up here," Peabody said, offering a soft hand which Will shook briefly.

"Bit of a surprise seeing you, too," he said.

Peabody blew smoke and spat in a brass spittoon. "Have a drink. I own this place." His voice was smug but he eyed Will warily.

"Seems like the first time we met you owned a bit of a place in Dodge." The two men hoisted glasses in something like a toast and downed their drinks. "Thanks," Will said.

"Yes, well, I got tired of that cow town and decided to become a part of this glorious new country where fortunes are going to be made. There is a great future ahead for this area. I believe it will surpass Leadville and Aspen both. And I figure somebody like me can play a large part in that future." He toyed with the end of a handlebar mustache which he had grown since Will had last seen him. Peabody had put on some weight, too. As tall as Will, Peabody probably outweighed him by thirty pounds.

Most noticeable was Peabody's paleness. In a country of men darkened and weathered by the elements in which they spent their lives, the light color of his face and hands made Peabody conspicuous. Here was a man who seldom saw the outdoors and, when he did, was well covered. His face had filled out with too much easy living and it ballooned when he smiled, as he did often, though Will noticed that, as in the past, it was mainly with his mouth and seemed less than genuine.

"You look kind of out of place in that suit," Will said. "I guess you aren't doing any mining yourself."

"Mining's the hard way to make it," Peabody replied. "Oh, a few of 'em will make big money. Most of 'em will make a little. They'll all spend most of it with me. I also own the general store."

Will glanced around the room. It was a far cry from the Long Branch. The bar was made of pine logs notched together and was so new it was still leaking sap. The building itself had been framed up in a hurry. No pictures decorated the walls and no windows provided an escape for the smoke which lay heavy toward the low ceiling.

"It'll look better before long," Peabody said. "You look a bit out of place yourself. We don't see many cowboys up here."

Will realized he was the only man in the place wearing a gun. The others wore rough, heavy clothes with suspenders holding up baggy pants. The clothes, for the most part, were dark-colored and dirt-stained. Some wore narrow-brimmed hats with short crowns. Will felt suddenly awkward in his tall Texas hat. He still had his chaps on, too. "Heading for California," he said. Of course, Will knew Peabody had been run out of Dodge, but he doubted Peabody was aware of that. Will wondered if anybody in Schofield knew the man's background.

A woman in a green dress swished in through the front door rubbing her arms. "Colder'n a witch's tit out there," she said loudly to anyone who was listening. A layer of makeup couldn't hide her age, or the pointed nose and jutting jaw.

"Women?" Will turned back to Peabody. "Up here?" Peabody shrugged.

"Why not? There are lots of men, lots of money. I brought Hogjaw Hannah in from Aspen. She was the only one who would come this spring but I'll get more later on."

An older man in a wrinkled dark suit and a black hat perched atop a round wrinkled face clomped across the uneven board floor to stand before Peabody. He was a short, round man with a twitch in his right eye. It blinked almost constantly as he talked.

"Good afternoon, gentlemen," he said. There was weariness in his voice, maybe a touch of sadness. "I've just mended the arm of an unlucky miner." He sighed. "It was not a pleasant afternoon." He sat without being invited and nodded at the bottle on the table, raising his eyebrows and putting a question mark in the look. Peabody shrugged and signaled for another glass. When it arrived the newcomer poured and drank quickly.

"Back in '63, '64, we would have simply cut off the arm and thrown it on the floor," he said. "Nowadays, thanks to the miracles of modern medicine, I can save it but I don't know why. About the most it will be good for is to fill up a sleeve." He poured another, drank, and turned to Will. "Hello," he said.

Peabody spoke up. "Pardon my bad manners. This is Doctor Millard Phillips, the finest sawbones this side of Aspen, if the only one."

"Thank you for that generous vote of confidence," the doctor said. He reached across the table to shake with Will. "You a Texan?"

43

"Will Martin. Used to be."

"A new acquaintance of our Mr. Peabody or an old friend come to say hello?"

Will started to answer but Peabody beat him to it. "Will was a lawman in Dodge City during my brief but splendid time there. He is now on his way to California."

Doc Phillips poured again, drank. The eye-twitching seemed to be lessening. "If it hadn't been for the war I'd be in California myself right now," he said. "Or maybe Florida or St. Louis. The damned war ruined what was shaping up as a promising career for me. I was living in Charleston, just beginning to make a name for myself when I followed the call to arms and took up the flag of the Confederate States of America. 'Won't be but a few months,' they said, 'and we'll run the Yankees clear up to Canada.' A few months later I was cutting off parts of men and throwing arms and legs on the floors of fly-ridden shacks."

"Well, Doc," Peabody cut in. "There is nothing we can do about our past, is there now?" He talked to Phillips but looked at Will. "Do you agree, Martin?"

Will looked Peabody in the eye and saw a warning there. It was no business of his and he'd be moving on soon anyway. "There's a lot of truth in that," he said.

Doc Phillips stood, took off the tall black hat and scratched at the top of a round head that was only slightly covered with stringy gray hair. "It puzzles me, though, that I should end up here, of all the great and good places of the earth, to while away the few remaining years of my life in the squalor of a mining town where cleanliness is considered the worst of sins and where culture is yet to be invented. Gentlemen, I bid you good night. I trust we shall meet again, Mr. Martin."

"'Spect so," Will said.

"Until the next time, then. I must be off to partake of what passes for dinner in this Babylon of the West."

He walked toward the door but halfway there turned back toward the pair at the table.

"Should you decide you, also, must eat," he said loudly, "there is but one almost decent establishment in this town. You will find it at the boarding house where I reside but be warned that the steak is always as tough as boot heels, the potatoes soggy, the coffee weak and the service intolerable. And, by the way, those who dare partake of sustenance there of a morning often complain that the pancakes are so thin they have but one side. Consider yourself warned and, again, good night."

A few miners laughed with Doc as he walked, slowly and majestically, out the door.

Will turned to Peabody and raised his eyebrows. Peabody shrugged again. "It isn't really that bad. His daughter does the cooking."

"His daughter?"

Peabody put his elbows on the table. "She's why he's out here. Tracey followed her husband here after he found a bit of silver up the East Fork. He was a major in the Southern army and after the war wasn't content to be a farmer. He came out here a couple of years ago on his own and sent for her when he thought he'd struck it rich."

"Are there many women up here?" Will asked. "I mean, other than Hogjaw? Doesn't seem like a very good place to bring up a family."

Peabody scratched a wooden match on the tabletop and applied the business end of it to a new cigar. Enveloped in a cloud of smoke, he laid his head back and looked down his nose at Will. "Looking for a woman, are you?"

Will tipped back his hat and smiled faintly. "Just curious."

Peabody snorted what might have passed for a friendly laugh and said, "There are a few what you might call women here. Wives, mostly. Fat women. Old. Beaten and ugly from work and worry." He paused to draw on the cigar. "All, that is, except for Tracey Collins."

"The cook? Doc's daughter?"

"She's a cook only out of necessity," Peabody said. "Randall Collins, her husband, got banged up bad last spring when he tried to drive a wagon of supplies over the pass a little too early."

"Too bad," Will said. *Life is full of surprises*, he thought to himself. *You think you know exactly what you're going to do tomorrow and you end up a cripple or dead and everything's changed.*

"Yeah," Peabody mumbled. "Too bad." He was looking around the room, surveying the activity, maybe counting the day's profits. Two men threw in their hands at a nearby table and left. Peabody played with his mustache and spoke through his fingers. "Feel like some poker? Think I'll join the boys. They'll want a fourth."

"Getting kind of hungry," Will said. "What time's supper at the boarding house?"

Peabody pulled a silver watch from a vest pocket and glanced at it. "You've got an hour," he said.

"I may have an hour but I haven't got much money."

"Stakes aren't too high in here this time of day." Peabody stood. "Coming?"

He'd be careful with Peabody. Will remembered why the gambler had left Dodge. "For a while."

45

Thirty minutes later he had parlayed $25 into $200. Most of it came from Peabody and Will found it hard to believe he was winning so easily. He had quit early on a few hands, losing only a few dollars here and there, while another man named Parkinson was losing heavily to Peabody.

Three deals and another hundred dollars later, Will realized the room was stone quiet. Most of the men were grouped around the table watching the game with a silent intensity. Only he and Parkinson were left, Peabody and the others having thrown in their hands. Will had the makings of a full house. All he needed was a jack. He threw fifty dollars to the center of the table, bringing the pot to something over three hundred dollars. Parkinson stared at the money and swallowed hard.

"Can't match that with cash," he said.

"You're out, then." Will felt sorry for the man.

Peabody sat back in his chair with hands clasped behind his head, cigar smoke wafting upwards. "That's it, boys," he said. "It's yours, Martin."

"Just a minute." Parkinson stared at the cards in his hand. He was a middle-aged miner who had a long, sad face. It looked particularly sad at this moment but Will thought he saw something in the man's eyes that indicated he just might have a winner.

"Tell you what," the man said. "I got me this little mine up toward Galena Lake. Pulls enough silver to keep me fed and goin' through the winter. But I'm tired. If I win this hand the money will get me back to Illinois where I belong. If I lose it don't matter 'cause I'll still figure how to get there. What you say to a silver mine? It's worth more'n that there pot."

Will considered. "You married?" he asked.

The long face widened in a smile and several of the surrounding men humphed a laugh. He shook his head no.

"Well, then. If that's what you want to do."

Peabody, the dealer, picked up the deck. "How many?"

"One." Both Will and Parkinson answered at the same time.

A card slid to Will, face down. He lifted a corner and saw a jack of diamonds.

Parkinson turned his card over quickly, saw a four of spades and paled. He recovered fast, though, and held out his hand to be shook by Will.

"Never have been lucky," he said. "But I reckon it don't matter much this time. Gives me the excuse I been lookin' for to head back east."

"Sorry," Will said.

"Take you out and show you the mine tomorrow." Parkinson shook his head and grinned. "Always said if I'se to buy a punkin' farm they'd call off Halloween." He was still grinning and shaking his head as he left.

Will turned to Peabody. "How'd you know I needed that jack?"

"Didn't," the gambler said and kept his eyes locked on Will's. "It's supper time." He gathered up the cards. He did not look up as Will left and walked to the boarding house.

Doc had lied but Peabody hadn't — about the girl, at least.

The steak was good, rare and tender. And Will decided the girl, Tracey Collins, just might be stunningly attractive. She was sweating from the kitchen heat, hair falling in her eyes and clothes wrinkled. She served Will without a word, barely nodding a brief acknowledgment of his presence. He was eating when Doc Phillips joined him at the long table in the center of the room.

"I see you ignored my well-intentioned advice and are risking your life by eating my daughter's cooking," he said with a friendly smile. The eye was twitching again but not as frequently as before.

Will talked around a mouthful. "Yes, and I'm wondering if I should ignore any other advice you might have, too." Doc laughed and, as Tracey passed on her way to the kitchen, took her arm.

"My dear, may I introduce our newest guest, Mr. Will Martin, out of Kansas I believe. This is my favorite, and my only, daughter, Mrs. Tracey Collins."

Will quickly wiped his mouth and stood, holding out his hand to meet hers. Behind the tired expression and beneath the hair that needed tending, she was attractive. A little long-faced, maybe, but slender where she should be and showing promise of a fuller body in other places. "Pleased, ma'am," he said.

"How do you do, Mr. Martin. Do you always eat with your hat on?" She spoke with a pronounced Southern accent, slowly, as though she was thinking through each word.

Will flushed, grabbed the hat from his head. He held it in front of him and looked down at her. The top of her head might just about touch his chin. "I'm awful sorry, ma'am."

She smiled at him like she'd caught a child stealing cookies, then self-consciously touched her hair, brushed it back from her eyes at least. "Call me Mrs. Collins, or Tracey, or 'hey you,' but don't call me ma'am."

Something about this Tracey made Will think of his mother whom he hadn't seen since he'd left home fifteen years ago. Maybe it was the smell of food cooking or the fact that she carried a pot of coffee in her hands. There was another feeling about her, too, but she was a married woman.

"Go on," she said, "sit down and finish your dinner." She held out her hand and Will stared at it. "Give me your hat and I'll hang it where it belongs." Like a child, he handed it over and she took it without comment. Will looked at her father and found him chuckling.

"Just like her mother, that one," he said. "The both of them always took such delight in making me feel like a fool. Of course that wasn't always so difficult."

Will looked up from his steak. "You're no fool."

Doc straightened his cuffs and smiled. "No."

"Why act like one, then?"

"You mean with Peabody." It wasn't a question. "A mere charade that amuses me at times. As it amuses others as well."

"They know better, though. Don't they?"

Doc laughed. "Most of them do. Those who don't will find out soon enough. Now and then, however, I do like to play a role. Just as you are playing a role."

Will stopped in the middle of a bite, put down his fork.

"Don't be upset. I meant nothing by that. But you are an oddity here — a cowboy, a peace officer, and you've come into town looking quite different from the rest of us."

"That's just me."

"Perhaps so," Doc said. "So, until we know each other better I'll play my part and you play yours. Frankly, I'd rather have your role."

Will smiled and went back to his dinner while the old man talked. Doc had come to Schofield upon hearing of Tracey's husband's accident. He told Will he had become tired of treating old people, which had become the mainstay of his Charleston practice, and he decided to explore "the wilds of the West." Collins' bad luck had given him the excuse he needed. His wife had been dead for three years and Tracey was his only child.

Will wiped his plate clean with the remains of a biscuit and popped it in his mouth. Finished, he sat back and patted his stomach. "Good," he said. "Real good."

"Surprising, isn't it, that a former Southern belle who was brought up in the genteel society of a gracious city could learn to cook so well so quickly?"

"Too bad she has to hire out as a cook to make it," Will mused.

Doc laughed again and his eye got to twitching rapidly but there was a lively twinkle in it this time. "Yes, well, actually, you see, she owns this establishment."

Will leaned forward on his elbows as he sipped his coffee. "I just thought . . . well, her husband's accident and all."

Doc patiently told him the story. Collins was making a go of it at his mine, one of the few in the area that was proving to be profitable, when his wagon went into Rock Creek from forty feet up. With him banged up, there was only Tracey to boss the crew and, after trying for a few weeks, she realized it wasn't working. By then Doc had showed up and a new

48

opportunity presented itself.

"The gentleman who built this boarding house decided he'd rather run a whorehouse in Aspen, so Tracey used the mine's profits to buy the building."

"Seems like she could be taking it easy," Will said.

Doc shook his head. "Oh, she could. But that isn't her way. She must constantly be doing something. Besides that, there are so few women out here she couldn't find one who wanted to cook, and no man would take the job."

"What's her husband think of that?"

Doc looked at the floor. "Sadly, my son-in-law doesn't seem to care about much at all these days. Or, if he does, it's impossible to tell. He's up in his room most of the time. Tracey waits on him hand and foot. I seldom see him and when I do it is late at night." Doc's voice lowered to a whisper and he seemed to be talking more to himself than to Will. "Poor girl. He's changed, you know. Randall was once quite a dashing young fellow, handsome, articulate. Now he can hardly talk and feels he must wear that mask."

Will had been politely paying attention without much interest but the word "mask" caused him to raise his eyebrows. Doc was warming to his subject.

"The accident left Randall badly injured. In addition to having a number of broken bones and many cuts and bruises, he also has a badly deformed leg that makes it difficult, if not impossible, for him to get around. Worst of all, however, is his face. The left side was so badly scraped that there was almost no skin remaining. Since everyone thought he was going to die, there was no effort made at any kind of repair work. Not that there was a doctor available, in any case."

"And he didn't die after all," Will said.

"Correct. Those who found him carried him to the shack where he and Tracey were living and told her he didn't have a chance. But they didn't know my daughter."

Will could guess the rest of the story. "She nursed him back to health and they lived happily ever after."

Doc wiped his eyes with a handkerchief, blew his nose loudly as Will waited. "You are only partly right, Mr. Martin. She did nurse him back to health. He survived, I believe, because of her but also because he was a tremendously strong man. But there has been no 'happily ever after,' I'm afraid. Randall, you see, is badly deformed, not only in his leg, but in his face as well. Particularly so in the face. One side, the right side, is still perfectly sculptured. A handsome face with the exception that there is no nose. The left side remains badly healing scars and tissue and some protruding bone. Even though he is able to get around, Randall refuses to leave his room in daylight and goes out only infrequently at night. Even then he wears a mask that

49

covers his entire face with only two holes cut for his eyes. It is a sad story, I'm afraid."

"Too bad," Will said quietly. "Bad luck."

"Yes, bad luck, indeed. Well, enough of that. So, you're on your way to California." Doc straightened, tried to smile and barely succeeded.

"I guess so. Been on my way for a long time but I don't seem to be getting any closer. Every time I stop somewhere I end up staying longer than I expected."

Doc clapped him on the shoulder. "There is no better place on Earth than here to stay longer than you expected," he said. "I firmly believe that this area, this long narrow valley, has a great deal to offer a young man like yourself."

"I'll take that as a compliment," Will said. "But I'm not so young anymore. Thirty years old and nothing to show for it but . . ." Then he remembered. "Well, I guess I own a silver mine, though."

"You own a mine? Where?"

"Well, here. I just won it from a man named Parkinson in a poker game."

Doc listened without speaking as Will told his story and, at its conclusion, leaned forward. "Parkinson is one of those strange men who should have been born a woman," he said. "Homosexuals are rare in this part of the country and he has never hit it off with the other men. I believe he would have been leaving soon at any rate."

Now Will remembered the laughter when he had asked the man if he was married.

"Parkinson's mine, the Gilded Cage I believe he calls it, is rumored to be potentially one of the finest around."

"Well, I'll be damned," Will ventured.

"Parkinson was not enough of a man to work it right, though, and most said it would take ten years at the rate he was going to get to the true vein. You might do it yourself in a year or less."

"I hadn't planned on working it," Will said. "I don't know anything about mining. I'm going to California."

"So you said." Doc smiled. "You might want to reconsider. I believe you are a lucky man, Mr. Martin."

"You're certainly right there." Will wrapped his hands around the cooling coffee cup. "I've been luckier than most during the past fifteen years." Will quickly told Doc about his time in Texas and Kansas, including his acquaintanceship with Bat Masterson.

Doc stopped him. "*The* Bat Masterson? I've heard of him."

Will nodded. "Thanks to him I ended up a lawman. After that I was one of the last to drive the Santa Fe Trail and now, just like that, I own a silver

50

mine and you tell me it might be worth something."

"That's a fascinating story. I suppose I should be the one to tell you, though. Someone else will soon enough."

"Tell me what?"

Doc leaned back in his chair and took a deep breath, letting it out in a whoosh. "This valley has all the makings of a paradise," he said. "Gold, silver, lead, copper, zinc. Even coal and marble. But strange things seem to happen to men who want to develop the area. What happened to Randall, Tracey's husband, is an example."

"Bad luck," Will said again.

"Perhaps more than that. There is a story that, as the Ute Indians left the valley, which was their summer hunting grounds, they placed a curse on it. They didn't want any white man to ever succeed here." He tried to laugh. "A silly notion, isn't it? Unfortunately, there are many who believe it."

Will sat back, relaxed. "Never was very superstitious myself."

"No, I don't suppose you are. But strange things do happen. Heart attacks when there has been no history of heart disease. Men being mauled by bears, mud slides, cave-ins, fires, anything that could cause a setback to a man who was about to become wealthy."

"Well," Will said. "This is tough country and mining appears to be risky."

"Just forget I said anything about it," Doc said. "These Indian medicine men are only so much mumbo-jumbo. Does make for interesting dinner conversation, though."

Tracey came back into the room and Will realized he and Doc Phillips were the only two remaining diners.

"More coffee?" she asked.

"Of course, my dear, of course. Why don't you join us for a moment?" Doc pulled out a chair for her and turned to Will. "It has fallen to my lot in life that I must lower myself each and every evening and descend into that pit of hell this woman calls a kitchen and help her with the dish washing and the disgusting task of cleaning up. Let us put off that degrading moment for just a while longer."

"Good idea," Tracey said as she wearily dropped into the chair across from Will.

"Sorry about your husband." It came out suddenly, not well thought-out. Will said it just for something to say and wished he hadn't.

"No need," she said and looked him in the eye. Looked for a long time as though seeking a message there, something that would answer all her questions in an instant.

"You're a friend of Peabody's," she stated. She said his name like it smelled bad.

51

"Who told you that?"

"He did." She nodded toward her father.

"I don't believe I ever said the word friend," Will said with a hint of impatience. "More like an acquaintance."

"Mr. Peabody is not one of my daughter's favorite people," Doc said.

"Humph!" Tracey snorted and fire flashed in her eyes. "That's a kind way of putting it. He hadn't been here more than a week before he was propositioning me. There's a great deal about the man I don't like. In fact, he sickens me. It's more than the fact that he's a gambler, a saloon-keeper and a whoremonger."

Will laughed with Doc. "That sounds like plenty to me." The father and daughter were both looking at Will with questions in their faces. It was Doc who spoke.

"What can you tell us about the man? He came in here claiming to have been a businessman in Kansas. He put up that saloon and brought in a woman. Now he's talking about building a road over the pass to Crested Butte."

No need to say anything about Peabody's questionable dealings in Dodge, Will thought. Not until he knew more about this town and just who was entitled to know anything. "A road doesn't seem to be such a bad idea," he said, remembering his trip into town.

"It's a good idea," Doc said. "We must have a road to get our ore out. Someday a railroad. But what about Peabody? What can you tell us?"

"Not much," Will replied. "He owned part of a saloon in Dodge when I was there. When I came back through last fall he was gone."

Tracey didn't believe him. It was obvious from the look in her eyes. Nobody spoke for a moment.

"I'm afraid I must get to my chores," Doc said. He stood and Tracey started to rise as well. "You sit a while longer, my dear. I can manage to get things started, at least."

She patted him on the arm and sat back, staring at the cup in her hands. When Doc was gone Will stole a long look at her and decided again she probably was a beautiful woman, maybe twenty-five or so, lean and tough, work-hardened but smooth yet around the face. "I heard you and my father talking," she said quietly, slowly, without looking at him. "Congratulations on the mine." The word "mine" came out more like "mahn," her strong Southern accent soft on Will's ears.

"Not sure congratulations are in order," Will said. "I don't really want to mine."

She smiled. "Nobody wants to mine. They just want to get rich."

"Not sure I want to get rich, either."

"Oh, come now, Mr. Martin." She turned her head slowly to look him in the eyes again. It was disturbing to Will but he held them just the same, wanting to hear her speak again with that accent that was gentler and more flowing than the Texas drawl he'd developed over the years. She turned the corners of her mouth up. "Just what do you want?"

If Cross-Eyed Jennie or Maria or Emily or even Hogjaw Hannah had asked him that, he'd have played along and given the rough answer. But this was a lady who was doing the asking. He thought about it for a moment.

"I guess I'm just not too sure right now," he said lamely. Did she look disappointed? "I'll be going on to California before long." He decided that, too, was pretty weak.

"I better get to work," she said.

Without thinking, Will reached across the table and put his hand on her wrist. "Don't go yet."

"Why not?"

"Well, I haven't talked to a real lady in a long time and . . ."

"I'll be around," she said. "I'm not going anywhere."

She stood. "Dinner's always at six-thirty." She was almost to the kitchen door, stopped and turned to look at Will once again. "It's nice to meet you, Mr. Will Martin. We'll talk again. Good night." And she was gone and Will sat there alone and listened to the murmur of voices from behind the closed kitchen door and to the clank of dishes and the splash of wash water.

He thought about her for a long time that night before he finally drifted off into a fitful sleep.

THE NEXT MORNING Will stood just below timberline peering into a hole in the side of the mountain. It was surrounded by debris, mine tailings and several sawed tree trunks.

"It's all yours and I can't say I'm sorry," Parkinson told him. "The Gilded Cage Mine. I just ain't cut out for this, I don't suppose."

Will turned from the mineshaft and looked out toward the northeast where, against the sun, a range of rugged blue mountains cut holes in a deeper blue sky. Will had learned Aspen lay just beyond the peaks that made up what was called the Elk Range. Some of the mountains topped out at more than fourteen thousand feet. The towering jumble of ice and snow-covered precipices looked to Will like rocks tossed into a pile and left to settle by themselves.

Parkinson was talking and Will turned back to him. "I tried Leadville," the little man said. "Aspen, too. I'se settin' in a saloon in Leadville when a bunch of footsore miners come bustin' in yellin' 'bout silver just over the pass and sayin' they's run out 'cause of an Indian uprising. They'd been illegally prospectin' across the Divide in Indian territory, don't cha know. When the Utes massacred them folks up at the White River Agency, ever'body in the territory got the hell out of there. Turned out there wasn't no more trouble. Guess you heard about the curse."

Will put his eyes back on the whitecapped peaks. "Heard some half-baked story about it."

"Seems more'n half-baked sometimes," Parkinson said, his eyes focused on some far-off place, maybe Illinois. "I swear, I think it's true and that it's workin'. Strange things happen purt near ever day. Somebody dies for no good reason or wanders off out of his mind and gets kilt by a bear. Bill Magruder's mine caved in on him even though he had it shored up stout. And ol' Charley Sonnette thought he'd found the mother lode, I reckon. Come runnin' into town to tell ever'body and dropped dead of a heart attack right in front of Peabody's saloon."

"Could happen to anybody," Will said.

"Mebbe so." Parkinson's eyes went narrow and his voice grew soft. "They's other things, too. Strange goin's on at night. Tools missin'. Wheelbarrows moved when mines are shut down. Rock slides." He looked out over the mountain greenness but didn't seem to see it. "Some say there's still Indians hereabouts. Killers. Just waitin' their chance. Knew a fella said he saw one, naked and painted. Twice as big as an ordinary man, he said he was."

Will raised his hat and brushed back his hair. "Pretty good imagination, I'd say."

Parkinson stared at him. "Don't happen like that over to Aspen. People get hurt but I ain't heard of nobody dyin' like they done here."

Will glanced once more at the hole in the mountainside. "Now that I know where it is we might as well go on down and you can sign the papers over. I'm not gonna start working it today. Maybe I can sell it to somebody."

Parkinson laughed. He seemed to be feeling good now that he was going back to Illinois. "Well, I don't give a hoot nor holler what you do with it. Hope you make a million if you want to, or sell it and walk away from it like I'm doin'. Let's get the hell outta here."

For several days Will lazily explored the area around Schofield, getting to know the mountains and where the mines were located. It wasn't that he expected to stay; he was just looking around and enjoying the solitude. He was up early every morning to ride off in one direction or another. After the first day Tracey packed a lunch for him. "Why didn't you tell me you were out roaming around without any food?"

"Well, I just never . . ."

"Oh, I suppose you cowboys are used to going all day without anything to eat. Probably why you're so skinny." She poked him in the ribs and he flushed. Her hand came up to her face and she brushed her hair out of her eyes. It was combed out and newly washed, Will noticed. Her clothes looked like they had just been ironed. He found himself staring at her and thought maybe she blushed.

Thoughts of Tracey kept swimming into his head all day, and all the next day, too, and during every ride he took into the mountains to breathe the crisp, fresh air laden with the scent of spruce and cedar and pine. He began to think about getting married, maybe in California. For the first time since he'd left home he felt empty inside.

He was still feeling weighed down as he sat in Peabody's saloon one afternoon nursing a beer. He hadn't seen the gambler since that first night and didn't hear him until he pulled out a chair and sat beside Will.

"Thought maybe you'd left," Peabody said.

Will figured Peabody had been hoping he *had* left. "Been out looking around."

"Working your mine?"

"Nope." Will didn't know at that moment if he would work it or not but figured he'd prod the gambler a bit.

"Oh?"

"Mining's not for me. Know anybody who might want to buy it?"

Peabody drew on his cigar and stroked his mustache. "Never know. I'll ask around."

"'Preciate it." Will took a swallow and put the mug on the table. "People here don't know about you, do they?"

Peabody's eyes narrowed and his neck stiffened. "What do you mean?"

"Dodge City. I heard you got run out of town for pulling the wrong card out of your sleeve."

The gambler bristled and puffed heavily on the cigar. "That's a damn lie," he said softly. "I got crosswise with Wyatt Earp one night. He lost a lot of money and accused me of cheating. After that he wouldn't leave me alone. Finally convinced the Mastersons to invite me to leave town. He didn't like losing."

"Just telling you what I heard," Will said.

Peabody leaned forward. "I run a clean game," he said, almost whispering. "These people don't need to know about Dodge City. I didn't do anything wrong there but I'd just as soon not be asked to leave another place. I've got big plans for this valley. Roads, railroads, churches. I can do a lot for these people. I expect to be a mayor, maybe even a senator. That way I could cause positive things to happen. What do you say?"

Will leaned back in his chair, away from Peabody's foul cigar breath. "I don't see any need to tell anybody anything," he said, "unless it looks like the right thing to do."

"It isn't," Peabody said, relief in his voice. "You figuring on staying here a while or are you still bound for California?"

"Haven't decided yet," Will replied.

"Yes, well." Peabody looked around the room which was almost empty this time of day. "Maybe I can find somebody who might be interested in buying your mine. That should finance your trip west."

"If I decide to go," Will said.

Hogjaw Hannah called to Peabody and he stood. "See you around," he said.

"Yeah. See you around."

"**EVERYBODY TALKS** about Leadville and Aspen," Will said to Doc that night over a dinner of venison, mashed potatoes and gravy, coffee and apple pie. "Think maybe I'll go have a look."

Tracey emerged from the kitchen with a coffee cup of her own and sat down with the two men. "Slow night," she said. There were three other diners in the room, all at one table. "Kind of a relief."

She looks tired, Will thought. *Tired but . . . sensuous*. He studied her some more, as he did every chance he got. Her face was narrow but she had full lips and a well-formed nose. Eyes as blue as a twilight sky were set deep above slightly darkening rings that told of long days and sleepless nights caring for her husband.

Doc stretched, patted his stomach. "A fine meal, my dear. Very good, indeed."

Tracey looked at Will, then at his plate which he had scraped with bread to soak up the last of the gravy and left looking as though it had just been washed. "It doesn't look as though you have any complaints, either," she said.

"Not a one," he replied, smiling. "Sure am glad your cooking didn't turn out like I was warned it might."

Tracey sat up straight. "What do you mean by that? Who said anything about my cooking?"

Will backed off, holding up his hands, palms out. "Oh, no you don't. I wouldn't anymore tell you who was spreading those stories than I'd jump off Mount Baldy."

"What kind of stories?" Her fists were clenched as Doc fidgeted in his chair.

"Well, now. Let's see. Somebody said you could make a boot out of two or three of your steaks. And I heard a miner was using your mashed potatoes for paste to keep the wind out of his shack."

Tracey jumped to her feet, almost spilling her coffee. Her eyes flashed and she put her hands on her hips, staring down at Will. "That's a bald-faced lie and you know it. I cook better than the mothers of most of these men. If I ever find out who's spreading those stories I'll take a skillet to him and he'll never eat another one of my dinners."

Doc coughed and glanced at Will with some pleading in his eyes. "Sit down, Tracey," he said. "Will is simply having some fun with you. Am I right, Mr. Martin?"

"Well," Will said, "I *did* get a warning or two. Have to admit, though, that the speaker was a sorry excuse for a man and I think maybe he'd had too much to drink."

"I'm sure that was it," Doc said. "Drunk as a dog, no doubt. Mr. Martin tells me he is thinking of leaving us." It was a neat change of subject.

Tracey sat down with a thud, looked at Will with something like distress in her face before she composed herself.

"Leaving?" That's all she got out but Will felt it, then. It was like the shock he'd felt when he lassoed a running calf and it hit the end of the rope. She'd been thinking about him, too. She held his eyes with her own and Will's stomach went upside-down. His heart was pounding so hard he was certain she could hear it. Doc was talking but Will and Tracey weren't listening. There was a rushing sound inside Will's head and he couldn't see anything but those deep blue eyes of hers. He saw clear inside her and discovered a need hidden so deeply within himself that he hadn't known it was there. Were her eyes expressing the same kind of need? He wouldn't let himself believe it might be possible. But her eyes had longing in them, and a kind of despair as well.

Doc's voice came up as though out of a mineshaft and Will made himself look away just as Tracey blinked and shook her head.

". . .some notion about seeing Aspen and Leadville," Doc concluded.

Tracey cleared her throat, took a sip of coffee. She wouldn't look back at Will now that she had broken off the eye contact. "You just got here," she said. "What about your mine?"

Will had to force himself to speak, to come back down to a mental state that allowed him to think. He couldn't look at her, turned his head toward Doc, instead.

"I'm just going to do some sightseeing," he said. His voice cracked. "Thought I'd see what I've been hearing so much about."

"You mean . . . ?" She glared at her father and actually blushed. "It's just a trip, then. You'll be back."

"Yes."

She stood. "I've got work to do. Can't sit around here lollygagging all evening." She whirled away to the kitchen and Will heard pots and pans being banged around. Right away she was back in the dining room, then back to the kitchen and back again with a coffee pot and heading for the other table to refill cups.

"Well, I'll be damned," Doc said.

ॐॐ

WELL AFTER midnight Will was awakened by a distant howling that wasn't coyotes. He rolled from the bed, pulled on his pants and a shirt, bent to the window and breathed the cool air. The smell of smoke from somebody's chimney spoiled the usual cleanliness of the mountain air at night.

For a while he stared into the darkness, hearing nothing but the slight breeze and, off to the west, the rushing of thawing mountain snows turned into water and filling Rock Creek. A half moon cast a pale light over the stillness of the town. He sat on the bed and listened but the strange noise did not return.

Tracey was just down the hall. Clapboard walls and a wedding ring made a few feet seem like a thousand miles. In better times, he thought, she might have been pampered and rich, depending on servants to do the work that now seemed a natural part of her life. He had a difficult time imagining that, however, even knowing as little about her as he did. She seemed too self-reliant, too determined to make a go of the boarding house to have ever been averse to hard work. He'd never known a woman like Tracey. But then, he admitted, he'd known few women at all other than his mother, and then only a succession of women he'd liked for reasons other than those that attracted him to Tracey.

He told himself it was useless to continue thinking about her. He told himself that over and over as he continued to think of her.

He stood, opened the door, stepped into the hallway and looked toward her rooms at the end of the building. He couldn't help himself, and he walked down the hall and stood outside her door. Her husband was in there, too, almost dead. *Might as well be dead*, Will thought. The door opened.

Tracey gasped. "You frightened me," she said in a whisper, regaining her composure. "What are you doing?"

Will was caught off guard and embarrassed. "I was just stretching," he lied. "Something woke me up."

"You heard the moaning," she said, stepping into the hall and quietly closing the door. She had on a robe, tied around the waist with a man's belt.

58

"I heard something, all right. It sounded like a wounded animal." Her robe was parted at the neck just a bit. Did she have anything on beneath it? As though she had seen where he was looking, she pulled it together.

"It's no animal. I'm going to make some coffee. Want some?" Will hesitated, looked at the closed door to her room. "Randall often drinks himself to sleep."

In the kitchen she struck a match to the coal-oil lamp and it flared brightly, blinding them both until she turned the wick down to a gentle glow. Will watched her as she busied herself shoving wood shavings into the stove, pouring water while the fire heated up, spooning out coffee. She worked quietly and efficiently, her back to him, her hips filling out the robe. The movement of her body was fluid, graceful. Finally, she sat beside him at the table, waiting for the water to boil.

"It's cool tonight," she said.

He couldn't help himself and he took her arm. "I was sweating, thinking of you."

"Don't." She pulled away, unconsciously brushed the hair from her eyes.

They sat silently and listened as the kettle began to whisper. "What did you mean, it's no animal?" he asked.

Tracey took a deep breath, then gave a short laugh. "You've heard about the curse, I'm sure." He nodded. "Some of the men say the ghost of a Ute Indian still lives in these mountains. He shows up now and then to devil the poor miners — or so they say. There is some trick of the wind that creates a moaning noise. The more superstitious of the men say it's the ghost."

Despite himself, he shuddered, just a little. "It sounded real enough."

"We only hear it now and then at night, maybe because there is so much other noise during the daytime."

Will let his hand stray toward her arm which rested on the table. Tracey quickly got to her feet and took the steaming kettle off the stove. The coffee poured and sitting in front of them, they made concerted efforts to avoid looking at one another.

"Good," Will said, taking a sip.

"Yes. I often come down here at night and sit alone. It's a beautiful time when everyone else is asleep."

"Your husband . . . ?"

She shook her head. "He's not much company. I'm sure my father must have told you about him."

Will nodded and sat there uncomfortably aware that there ought to be some words of support he could offer. Tracey took him off the hook by continuing to talk.

"Things were good here, for a while, until the accident. Randall was so

59

happy and the mine was looking good. I was even happy, just being with him, despite the terrible winter and the isolation. We are so far from anything, you know."

"It must be hard on you."

She nodded at the table, not meeting his eyes. "It is made more difficult knowing that I may never leave this place."

"Of course you will. No one has to stay."

"I do," she said quietly.

"You could leave. Go anywhere you want."

Tracey looked at Will for a long moment, until he lowered his eyes. "Randall is my husband," she whispered. "I promised to stay with him until death. I will honor that promise. This is the life the Lord has laid on me and I can't complain. I just do what I have to do. Feed him. Clean him. Wonder if he ever. . .ever wants. . .sometimes I wish. . ."

They were silent again, drinking their coffee. She stood and went to the stove. When she didn't return right away Will turned to look at her. She stood by a cabinet near the stove, her back to him, hands on the wooden counter, leaning forward. Her back jerked with silent sobs.

Will pushed back his chair and went to stand behind her. She didn't move, swallowed, and he thought she had stopped crying. When she still didn't move and said nothing, he moved behind her and put his arms out, placing his hands over hers. He felt her catch her breath as he touched her body with his own, pressed gently against her back. Her hands tensed for a brief second, then relaxed.

Something told him it was all right. He wrapped his arms around her waist and she leaned back into him, clutched his forearms with her hands. She seemed to be holding her breath. Will could hardly breathe, stood deathly still feeling the closeness of this married woman's body, dared not move.

Tracey turned in his arms until she faced him, placed her hands on his face and pulled it down to hers. The kiss was at first a tentative, soft, lingering touching of lips. Will held her more tightly, pulled her to him and kissed her with a fierceness that was matched by Tracey herself. His hand slid down her back to the softness of her hip and he felt her move into him.

Tears from Tracey's eyes wet their cheeks as they clung to one another. He explored her body with his hands and she hugged him around the neck so tightly he gasped for breath. Suddenly, she shuddered and cried out like a small animal lost in the brush. She pulled away.

"I can't," she said. "I want to. God, I want to, and He would forgive me, I know. But I just can't."

Tears coursed down her cheeks as she stood, fists clenched at her side, robe partly open showing the rounding of her breasts, hair in her eyes. "Do you understand, Will? Do you?"

He stood apart, taking deep breaths, knowing he was in love with a woman who could not be his. "I understand," he whispered. "I'd do anything to change things. I want you but I do understand." He looked at her a moment longer and she dropped her eyes to the floor as he turned and left the room.

He was gone by the time she served breakfast to the others soon after daybreak.

❧

IT WAS RAINING and Will shuddered with the cool dampness. Water dripped from his hat brim and ran in rivulets down his slicker, which kept him dry if not particularly warm. Jeremiah plodded gamely up the steep trail, slipping now and then in the mud or on a loose rock. Obediah followed obediently behind, blowing with the exertion and the thin air at around twelve thousand feet.

He was almost to the summit of Pearl Pass, which was another three hundred feet higher and a number of twists and turns ahead. The rider and two horses moved against a north wind that blew rain in their faces along with something like sleet. A few feet higher and they entered the cloud itself, slowly disappearing from the view of any living thing that might be watching.

He hadn't gone back to bed after the agonizing and short-lived fit of passion with Tracey. Instead, he had quietly wrapped some clothes and his money in his bedroll, waited until he heard her return to the rooms she shared with her husband and then had stolen from the building. He had looked up once at the darkened windows of her bedroom and then walked through the silent town to the stable where he got his horses. He left a roll of bills with a note for the livery owner in case he kept on going to California.

As the sun topped Mount Belleview he rode over Schofield Pass with the spring runoff of Rock Creek roaring in his ears. The pass wasn't particularly high but it was steep and treacherous, finally topping out near Emerald Lake. The water of the small pond was perfectly still that morning, with the deep blue sky and surrounding snow-covered peaks reflected on its mirrorlike surface. Will sat on the bank a while, thinking some more about Tracey and figuring he wasn't doing her any good and that he'd simply make life miserable for both of them if he stayed around. It didn't do any good, though, and he licked his lips, remembering her kiss. He could still taste it.

He'd learned a little more about her in the past few days, mostly from Doc. Tracey had attended a school for girls near Charleston for a short time during the Reconstruction period but, by the time she was sixteen, in 1871, she had met Randall, who thrilled her with his talk of the West. They married when she was eighteen, though he was ten years her senior. Five years later, he was on his way to Colorado. Will knew the rest of the story.

He shook his head at how the lives of millions of people, including his own, had changed after the war. Fatherless, he'd seen no future as a farmer. He gathered up a clean shirt and his father's old work boots, said good-bye to his mother and brother and headed west with tears in his eyes. Weeks later he wandered onto ranch land owned by Charles Goodnight, was hauled to the ranch headquarters by Sagebrush Tom Cordell and put to work. Pretty soon, he became a damn good cowboy, even if he did say so himself.

Now he felt about as confused as he had the day he left home fifteen years ago. He shook it off, climbed into the saddle and rode south.

In Gothic, a new town serving the mines north of Crested Butte, he found the general store and bought a barebones supply of bacon, jerky and salt. Coming out of the store, he almost ran into Nathan Peabody.

As Will pushed on past with barely a nod at the gambler Peabody pulled a fresh cheroot from his coat pocket, started to light up and spoke to Will's back.

"You leaving?"

Will put his purchases in a saddlebag and, with one hand on the saddlehorn, looked at Peabody. "Maybe."

"That much grub isn't going to get you very far."

"Far enough."

"California's a long ride."

Will put a foot in the stirrup and hauled himself into the saddle. Peabody leaned against a post and puffed smoke. "Have a good trip," he said with something like a sneer on his face. Only then did Will see the small sign to the left of the door.

GOTHIC GENERAL STORE -- Nathan Peabody, Proprietor.

"You own this, too, huh?"

"A man's got to make a living."

Will leaned forward, his hands cupped over the saddlehorn. "I don't much like you, Peabody," he said softly. Peabody stiffened, stood up from the lean and took the cheroot from his mouth. "I think maybe you thought you were doing me a favor in that card game but I don't need favors from the likes of you. And I don't like what you've got in mind for this valley."

Peabody threw the half-smoked cheroot to the ground. "You don't know any. . ."

"Shut up," Will said, still speaking quietly and looking the man in the eyes. "There's nobody around to hear so I'm going to speak my piece. I'm in that kind of mood and it might get worse so just let me talk."

"Talk away." Peabody seemed to relax, relieved that all Will was going to do was talk.

62

"I've got more'n a half-baked notion that you were behind those two yahoos who thought they could kill Bat Masterson that night in Dodge."
Peabody's eyes became mere slits and his pale face seemed to pale even more, but he kept his head up and put his hand in his pocket.

"I didn't have the proof or I'd have put you away," Will continued. "But for that reason, and for a whole bunch more, I've got a great big dislike for you that's been building ever since. You cross me once too many times, Peabody, and you and I'll do more than talk."

"This isn't Dodge City, Martin." Peabody was talking too loudly, brazening it out. "I've got plans for this valley. Big plans."

Will nudged Jeremiah closer to Peabody and leaned forward. "There's too much of Nathan Peabody in your plans and not enough of the Millard Phillips or the Tracey Collins or the miners of the valley. You're looking to get rich and you don't much care how you do it. I may not be back but, by damn, I just might be. If I am, don't you ever try to do anything for me again, and don't even think about trying to cheat me."

Peabody leaned against the post again. "It's the woman, isn't it?

"It isn't anything but you," Will said as he reined Jeremiah into the street, knowing Peabody had him figured. It was the woman, all right. He thought of her all day as he rode, and of the deepfelt need that continued to shake up his insides. In the course of a few weeks he had let a married woman turn him literally upside down. Now, they were both hurting, but she was taking it all in stride. Living the life the Lord laid on her, she'd said. And behind the facade of work and nursing was a sensuous young woman with all of a young woman's needs.

He shook it off and tried to forget about it. But all day as he rode he thought of Tracey, and of the deep-felt need that continued to shake up his insides. He had let a married woman turn him upside down. Now, they were both hurting. She had revealed more than a little of her true self in the kitchen that night and he knew she was suffering because of it, probably praying for forgiveness.

Now, lost in a rain cloud at nearly thirteen thousand feet above sea level if the Hayden Survey was right, Will saw her face before him, felt her soft body beneath the robe, tasted again her mouth and her tongue.

Jeremiah had stopped. They were at the pass and the narrow path was about to slant sharply downward into the fog of cloud. Will sat quietly in the saddle and let the horses blow. He sat there so long the sky began to brighten and the rain turned into nothing more than high humidity. Pretty soon the wind blew the high clouds on past and revealed the tops of several brown and red and snow-white peaks which poked out above a solid layer of cloud floating maybe a hundred feet below. He felt isolated in an ethereal world that

63

had no base, just fluffy cotton flooring and points of rock surrounding him like the tips of sharpened sticks on a fence.

He dismounted and shrugged off his slicker. He shook the rain from his hat and leaned back, letting the sun warm his face.

After a while the wind blew the rest of the clouds away and the Castle Creek valley opened up below. Well, Aspen was down there somewhere and he might as well go have a look-see. He tied his slicker to his saddle and pointed north, feeling better for the sunshine and trying hard to accept the fact that, as long as Randall Collins was alive, his wife would continue to be just that. She would never forget that she was a wife, and that was just the way things were.

༺༚༝

ASPEN TURNED OUT to be a collection of log cabins and tents scattered across the flats at the base of Aspen Mountain, a flat-faced, broad edifice dominating the town to the south. The Roaring Fork River gushed off Independence Pass into the east and hurried on past the town on the north to meet up with the Grand near the hot springs forty or so miles away to the northwest.

Slick-looking men in dark suits and ties talked loudly on street corners with miners who looked as though they had just climbed out of a mine shaft and hadn't brushed their britches. Women in colorful lace and long dresses that stirred up puffs of dust from the street as they moved along waved at other women in homespun or gingham who swept more dirt from shallow porches of clapboard homes or hung just-washed work clothes on a line.

It was hot, and dust rose in little clumps, hanging in the dry air as though gasping for breath before falling listlessly back to the ground. Dust hung over everything and mingled with chimney smoke and cooking fires and burning trash. It made a man thirsty just looking, so Will laid Jeremiah's reins over the rail in front of a saloon called Thunder River, went inside and met R. D. Metcalf.

The man was short and wiry with a long mane of gray hair hanging loosely out beneath the wide-brimmed, low-crowned hat he wore pushed back on his head. Heavy, dark eyebrows sprinkled with gray almost hid his eyes but Will could feel the man's gaze as he ordered a shot. It cost him a dollar but he paid without complaint. He smacked his lips and laid another silver dollar on the bar as the bartender poured. Two dollars and two drinks that only helped to whet his thirst.

"Beer's only two bits," said a slender man at the end of the bar. Will watched as the eyebrows lifted and saw a glint of friendliness in crisp blue eyes floating in a field of wrinkles.

"Obliged," Will said. "Buy you one?"

Bowlegs brought the speaker to Will's side. He put a booted foot on the rail and leaned forward in the time-honored stance of one who knew how to act in a place like this. "Never turned down the offer of a drink yet," the man said. "'Specially from another Texas cowboy."

"How'd you know?" Will asked.

"You got the look. 'Sides that, you got the hat." He sipped the newly arrived beer. "Name's Metcalf. R. D. Metcalf."

Will wiped the beer mug's dampness from his hand and shook Metcalf's. "Will Martin. Waco and the Palo Duro."

"Goodnight, huh? Heard of him. I cowboyed down on the Pecos and along the Pedernales."

They drank a while, remembering. "Never saw the Pedernales," Will said.

"Didn't miss nothin'. I never seen the Palo Duro. Good as they say?"

"Better." They remembered some more and they each paid for their own second round.

"Damn cows," Will muttered, and R. D. chuckled.

THE SUN WAS shining on the western peaks but hadn't made it over the Continental Divide when Will woke with a start. He knew immediately he shouldn't even try to move his head. It throbbed with an ache that increased each time he moved his eyes to one side or the other. R. D. was buried in a blanket on the other side of the smoldering fire, snoring louder than the rushing water of the Roaring Fork. Will tried to focus on a branch of a spruce hanging above him. He couldn't do it. He closed his eyes but the pain was worse so he opened them again and stared off at a single cloud poking along in sea-blue sky, thinking he might just as well die. *Never drank so much beer in my life*, he thought.

After a while he decided he wasn't going to die just yet so he slowly sat up. Very slowly. He saw his boots down at the end of his bedroll with his feet still in them. He found his hat beneath the blanket, reshaped it as best he could and felt better when he got it back on his head. But only for a moment. His shoulder hurt and he tried to rub it but instead grabbed the end of a long piece of wood.

"It's about time you were waking up." It was a woman's voice and, through the pain and confusion, Will managed to figure out that someone was poking him in the shoulder with a stick.

He braced himself with both hands and managed to turn his head. The woman was slender — he could tell that much — maybe a little frightened and definitely amused. In the corner of his eye he could see her holding the stick like a weapon, ready to club him with it if need be.

"What?" he managed, and that hurt, too. R. D. was still snoring. Will guessed it was R. D., anyway, since the body beneath the blanket was a short one.

"I would *appreciate* it if you would wake your friend and go somewhere else to sleep," the woman said. "You are an unwelcome *distraction*." The emphasis on certain words rang in his head like a pistol fired in a barrel.

"Distraction?" Will forced himself to turn some more and the sun, just topping the divide, blinded him and hurt like hell itself. The woman moved to her left and the sun was behind her head. He couldn't make out her face, saw only a silhouette, and had to look at the ground.

"We are *trying* to hold *class* here," she said and he could tell she was working up a good mad. There was a snicker behind her. Will shaded his eyes and thought he saw a group of midgets hiding behind the woman.

Class? A woman and a group of little people. Kids. They were kids and that meant a school. He worked his way to his feet. It seemed to take a long time. Thank God he was dressed, he thought. He was still looking into the morning sun.

"Could you move over here a little?" he asked, motioning with his hand. "Thank you." He licked his lips and wished he had a tub of water to drink.

Eight or ten youngsters moved with the woman, who turned out to be young and pretty. Not like that old woman he'd bought too many drinks for the night before. It was coming back to him now. "We are going to *attempt* to go on with our class," the woman said. "Do you think you could quietly wake your sleeping friend and move on? Perhaps to those trees over there?" The words banged around in his head. They might as well have been boulders shifting.

Will knew he was swaying and that he'd better sit down pretty quick. "Yes, ma'am," he whispered, then tried to touch his hat politely but missed. He gave up and let his hand drop to his side. He was trying to think of something else to say but realized the woman and the midgets were leaving, the kids glancing back at him and giggling.

Slowly, Will came back to himself. He spent most of the morning sitting by the Roaring Fork splashing water in his face and listening to Ardy talk. "Ardy" was somehow easier to say than "R. D." The little man had drunk just as much as Will, perhaps more, but he carried on this hot July morning as though he'd had nothing at all.

Will's mind was wandering. Hadn't he just thought something about a hot

July morning? It couldn't be July because that school teacher and those kids were supposed to be having class and school didn't meet in July. Maybe it wasn't July. Maybe it was May. He splashed more water in his face. It was July.

"What?" Ardy was saying something else.

"Thunder River. That's what the Utes called it up until a few years ago. The first prospectors up here followed it down from Independence Pass in the spring of the year and named it the Roaring Fork."

Ardy continued talking but Will only half listened. He had heard the entire history of Aspen from R. D. Metcalf the previous night and the lesson was continuing this morning. He'd heard all about the hardships faced by the men who took ten, twelve days to walk across the pass to stake their claims. Ardy knew all about the mines — the Little Nell, the Little Lotti, Best Friend, Kitty B., the Sarah Jane Shaft, Molly Gibson, Keno Gulch, Jenny Lind, Minnie Moore and the Grand Duke. There were more, too.

"You feelin' any better?" Ardy asked.

"Better'n what?"

The blue eyes sparkled and Ardy handed Will his hat. "Let's go get us some vittles," he said. "I'm hungry as a baby lookin' for tit."

Will almost lost his stomach thinking about food. But the steak and potatoes, washed down with pots of hot, black coffee, had him feeling almost fit. He sat back in the rough chair and watched Ardy gulp down a second helping of peach pie and wondered where the thin man put it. Ardy was an interesting man, and a likable one. After he had decided he'd had enough of punching cows in Texas he had found his way to Kansas where he'd married and worked for the Kansas Pacific. When his wife died giving birth to a still-born baby girl, he walked away from the little house where they lived in Salina and took the train to Denver. Eventually, he found his way to Leadville, came over the pass to Aspen and now was trying to set up a small ranch and raise horses several miles to the west. He'd come to Aspen to "raise a little hell," he told Will, and had just got to town when the two met.

"Let's get out in the sun," Ardy said, wiping his mouth on his sleeve. "You still look like the dogs had you under the house."

By midafternoon Will and Ardy sat on a rock near the base of Aspen Mountain picking their teeth with twigs and watching a tall, well-dressed man in a dark suit and a round-topped derby talk to a miner.

"That's Henry Gillespie," Ardy told Will without being asked. "He owns the Spar and the Galena mines up yonder." He motioned vaguely up the mountain. "Richest sumbitch around, I hear tell. I knew him when he was a gopher in the Kansas Pacific office in Kansas. Has a dee-gree from the Kansas Agricultural College in Manhattan. Smarter'n a professor and now

67

richer'n King Solomon." Ardy always told you more than you needed to know, Will had decided.

Gillespie's voice rose. His back was to Will and Ardy and to the mountain. He seemed to be angry about something and was giving the listener pure hell.

Something made Will turn away from the argument and look up the mountain. He blinked his eyes to double check what he thought he saw. Several large boulders were rolling down the mountain and were heading for Gillespie. A rumbling sound reached his ears. He glanced back at the two men but they were oblivious to the imminent danger. Will and Ardy stood between the boulders and the two other men. Will poked Ardy in the shoulder.

"Let's get out of here," he said, pointing up the mountain. Ardy moved fast, scrambling off the rock and hustling out of the way toward the horses. Will turned toward Gillespie.

"Hey!" he shouted. "Look out!"

The two didn't seem to hear and went on talking loudly.

Without thinking about it, Will started to run toward them, into the path of the boulders. "Where you goin'?" Ardy called. Will continued to run, shouting at the two men. They stopped their discussion, turned to look at the gangly man in a tall hat and cowboy boots running in a kind of crab-like waddle toward them waving his arms and shouting. They stood stock still. When Will reached them, he grabbed Gillespie and threw him behind a small Aspen tree, hoping it might offer some protection. Gillespie fell in the dirt and his hat rolled down the gentle slope toward town.

"What the hell do you think . . . ?" Gillespie fought Will and tried to get up, but the taller man held him down. The boulders stopped rolling a good thirty yards short of the tree. Will stood and saw the miner with whom Gillespie had been arguing doubled over in laughter. He slapped his thighs, laughing so hard tears rolled down his cheeks.

Gillespie got to his feet and began dusting himself off, swearing loudly all the time. "Just what the hell was that all about?"

Will was flustered and embarrassed. He pointed to the boulders. "I just...I thought you were about to get hit by those rocks and I..."

Gillespie stopped his dusting and his face cracked with a wide smile. The miner was sitting on the ground, weak with laughter. "Come here," Gillespie said to Will. He led the way to the boulders which Will quickly realized weren't rocks at all but large cowhide sacks.

"It's the way I get my ore down the mountain," Gillespie said. "We wrap it in cowhide and roll it down here. Saves sending wagons up the mountain." Gillespie appraised the slender man in cowboy garb. "You thought you were saving my life."

"Well," Will said, "I didn't really think," only then realizing that if the sacks had actually been boulders he might have been killed himself.

"The sacks always stop about here," Gillespie said. "There was no danger."

"I'm mighty sorry, then. Look, I'll pay to clean your suit."

Gillespie smiled again and laughed a little. "Nonsense. You did a brave thing. I should be grateful. In fact, I am grateful." He held out his hand to be shook.

"I feel damned foolish," Will said, gripping the hand. "No need," Gillespie said. "I just hope you're around sometime when I really do need saving."

He started toward the other man but turned and called back to Will. "What's your name?"

"Martin. Will Martin."

"Well, Mr. Martin, I'm giving a small party at my home tonight and I'd like for you to come. Around sundown?"

"I don't know," Will said. He gestured toward Ardy who stood calmly rolling a smoke near the horses.

"Bring him along," Gillespie called. "I insist." Will shrugged.

"Good. Ask anybody where I live. Until tonight, then." The miner slapped Gillespie on the shoulder, still laughing, and the two walked away. Gillespie stopped to pick up his derby hat and didn't look back.

"That shore was impressive," Ardy said, handing Will Jeremiah's reins.

"Oh, shut up."

GILLESPIE'S "HOME" turned out to be a 26-by-36-foot canvas-covered building known as "the big tent." When Will and Ardy arrived — Ardy attending only after long and arduous begging by Will so he would have company — the place was packed with well-dressed men and women. The two were inside before they realized how out of place they appeared in their Levi's and plaid shirts among suited men and lace- and pearl-clad women.

Gillespie spotted them immediately and hurried over to greet them, evidently unconcerned about their unusual dress. As he was introduced to Mrs. Gillespie, Will remembered to remove his hat and nudged Ardy, indicating he should do likewise. The introductions over, Gillespie climbed on a chair, raised his arms and called for quiet.

"I want you all to meet Mr. Will Martin, the man who saved me from the terrible fate of being killed by an avalanche," he said to the crowd, all of whom looked at Will with some amusement. Evidently the story had gotten around.

"And Mr. . . ."

"R. D. Metcalf," Will said.

"Mr. Metcalf. Now, we know it was an unnecessary exercise but, nevertheless, a brave one. I welcome Mr. Martin and his friend to my home and I hope all of you will make them feel they are among friends." He stepped down from the chair amid polite applause.

Gillespie took Will by the arm and led him around the room, making introductions. Ardy soon disappeared and Will later saw him near a food-laden table with a plate full of sandwiches in one hand and a drink in the other. In the course of the evening Will met several men whose stories Gillespie told with relish, bragging often about his own part in the development of Aspen.

"I came over Independence Pass last year just as soon as Ouray signed the treaty," he said. "I saw something here that was unusual for a mining camp. I saw, not only the silver and the money that was to be made, but I also saw a future of culture and dignity. That's what my vision is for Aspen. A cultural oasis in an unparalleled setting."

Despite the isolation in this rugged mountain valley, Gillespie and the others seemed quietly confident they would fulfill their dream of creating an Eden in the wilderness.

Gillespie guided Will to a settee near the wall away from the others. As he talked, Will studied him. He was tall, although not as tall as Will, with what appeared to be fragile features for a mining man. *More refined than most*, Will thought. *Neat and proper*.

Gillespie had been working as a passenger agent for the Santa Fe railroad when he heard of Leadville's silver strikes in 1877. He was in Leadville when the news of similar potential fortunes to be made in Ute City was brought over the pass by miners fleeing the Indians they feared were on the warpath.

Gillespie was soon the owner of two mines, the Spar and the Galena. Visions of a beautiful village in the Roaring Fork valley, complete with culture rivaling the East, immediately leapt to his mind.

"I went back East to drum up support for a post office at my own expense," he said. "And we needed money for a telegraph over the pass. Especially, we needed a road over Cottonwood and Taylor Passes to Buena Vista."

Only four months earlier Gillespie had been sitting in Leadville worrying about claim jumpers. "It was snowing outside — the biggest damn blizzard you ever saw — and people told me the divide was impassable. But I made it."

He waited for Will to speak and the cowboy finally realized he needed to respond. "How'd you do it?"

"On snowboats!" Gillespie puffed a cigar proudly. "Henry Staats and I built sixteen of them, one for each man in our party. They were four feet long, two feet wide and one foot deep with turned-up ends."

Traveling by night when the snow was packed hard so the boats would glide easily, the party made it over the pass in two nights, passing more than a hundred men in parties that had been on the way for more than two weeks.

"Each man pulled his own boat, each one carrying some two hundred pounds of food and blankets. The men wore snowshoes, or skis, and we waltzed into Aspen like we were on a holiday. Now I'm rolling my ore down the mountain in cowhide sacks and shipping it by jack train seventy miles to the smelter at Leadville. And, by damn, even paying four cents a pound to get it there, I'm making money. What do you think of that?"

Will didn't get a chance to reply because Gillespie's wife chose that moment to call for quiet. When she had everyone's attention she introduced a young woman who looked familiar to Will. "Recently," she said, "I prevailed upon my young niece to leave her beautiful home in Denver and join us here for the summer. Since she is an accomplished musician she has agreed to favor us with a performance on my organ, the only one on the Western Slope." She preened and her large red dress bounced as she clasped her hands. "May I present Miss Abigail Crenshaw."

Prolonged applause greeted the announcement. Will stood with Gillespie and immediately recognized the schoolteacher who had poked him with a stick that morning.

She played with confidence and poise and, though Will didn't know anything about how one should play the organ, he thought she splayed her elbows out quite a bit. When she finished everyone clapped and shouted things like "Bravo!" and seemed genuinely impressed, so he figured she must have been pretty good.

Later that evening she slipped up behind him and poked him in the shoulder. She was smiling when he turned to her.

"You needn't worry," she said. "I don't have a weapon *this* time." More details of the morning encounter came to mind, like the way she emphasized words, made them stand out like a Kansas sunflower, yellow in the green weeds, demanding attention.

"That's good," Will said reddening a bit. "Sorry about this morning."

"No harm done."

"I enjoyed your playing," he told her.

"You're very kind. I heard how you saved my uncle's life today. You must have recovered from your. . . *illness*. . .very quickly."

She seemed sure of herself with men, Will thought to himself. Must have

71

had a lot of experience. "I guess so," he said. He thought suddenly of Tracey and pictured her cleaning up the kitchen in Schofield. Abigail Crenshaw was maybe prettier than Tracey but a lot shorter and probably not as smart, Will decided.

"Mr. Martin?" She must have asked him something.

"I'm sorry. What did you say?"

"Never mind. You seemed to drift away for a moment." He tried to concentrate on the musician and when she smiled at him and rested her eyes on his for what seemed like a long time, thoughts of Tracey left his mind. Even the hardness of a word now and then seemed a bit more musical, less intimidating, actually, maybe even inviting.

"There will be *dancing* later," she said. "Perhaps you will seek me out."

That made him nervous and he answered, too quickly perhaps. "No ma'am. I just never learned to dance anything but a jig to a tinny-sounding piano. You'd be in mortal danger if you danced with me."

"In that case," she said, keeping the eye contact, "you must let me *teach* you one day."

Will felt something in his stomach again. Something like he'd felt with Tracey, but this was a bit more on the lustful side and not so much of the heart. "That'd be real nice." *Good Lord, look at those eyes*, he thought. "You were teaching school today?"

"Oh, my *no*! I was giving the children a lesson in *poetry*. There is so little *culture* for them, you know."

"Maybe you could teach me some poetry, too," he said.

"I'll be *glad* to and will look forward to it. I'm sure we will meet again," she said, and then she was gone, gliding across the plank floor and stopping to accept the praise of another group of locals.

He stayed a while longer but didn't speak to her again and she didn't even steal a glance at him the rest of the time. Not that he saw, anyway. Pretty soon Ardy came over and said he thought it was about time they got out of there. Will shook hands with Gillespie on the way out and the man told him to look him up if there was ever anything he could do.

They walked toward the bedrolls on the river, Ardy complaining about wasting his last night in Aspen before he had to get back to his "diggings" on Rock Creek and Will lost in dreams of Abigail Crenshaw teaching him to dance.

"Would you look at that!" Ardy had stopped in the middle of the street and was pointing up toward Aspen Mountain. The switchback trails covering the slopes were alive with lights, like a million fireflies popping on and off and moving up and down the mountain.

"It's the midnight shift change in the mines," Ardy said in wonderment. "I

72

heard of it but I never seen it. Guess I was always asleep or too drunk by midnight to notice."

Miners were coming and going to and from the mines all along the mountain, each one carrying his "gad," a tin can punched full of holes to let the light of a candle through. A small orchestra was playing dance music in the big tent back behind them and the music mingled with the breeze in the aspen trees and the gurgling of the river. The two men stood and watched and listened for a long time. Even Ardy was silent with the grandeur of the moment.

It sure has been a time, Will thought.

అఅ

THE NEXT DAY Ardy kept up a constant stream of chatter as the two followed the Roaring Fork northwest to its junction with the Frying Pan at a little settlement called Basalt. The river turned more to the west at that point and the valley widened.

"Glad you decided not to make the trip to Leadville," Ardy said. "Kind of dreaded the trip by myself. Nothin' to see over to Leadville anyhow 'cept for more miners and it's pure hell gettin' there."

Ardy had told Will about the ranch he was trying to develop, and about its potential to become something much larger, and he had decided to join the older cowboy. He could ride back to Schofield later, following Rock Creek upstream. He would have then made a giant circle on his ride and would have seen more of the country than he had planned to. Then he could say hello to Tracey, sell his mine and get on to California.

Near Satank, a town Ardy said some called Yellow Dog, Rock Creek emptied into the Roaring Fork. Fifteen miles or so farther north the river joined the Grand at Yampah Springs. That was something he ought to see, Ardy said. "Them hot springs'll cure whatever ails you."

Will nodded but he was more interested in a massive, gray mountain with three peaks that. once they passed Basalt, had occasionally appeared to the southwest through the saddles of lower mountains. Now it formed a seeming dead end south of Satank and looked as though it walled off access to anything beyond it. A gigantic slide area on the mountain's north face suggested a fishtail. Will's eyes were riveted to the dominating hulk of mountain. *My Lord*, he thought to himself. *That's the way a mountain ought to look.*

They turned south and followed Rock Creek that meandered gently ahead of them a few miles through a broad, fertile stretch of the valley until it came to the lower slopes of the mountain that loomed overhead with kind of protectiveness that Will found strangely comforting. R. D. identified it as Mount Sopris.

"Named for some early explorer, I hear," he said.

Small streams gushed from east and west into Rock Creek and the grass grew tall and green. Ardy pointed to a log cabin west of the river amid a stand of spruce and cottonwoods.

"There she is," he said proudly. "It ain't much, but it's mine."

That night Ardy tried to convince Will to forget about California and partner with him on the ranch. "People hereabouts are gonna need lots of horses. And mules. Cows, they got, and I'm sick of the damn cows anyhow. We can make a go of it, Will. But I need help. I'd go fifty-fifty."

"I'm tempted," Will replied, "but I don't have much money. Only about enough to get me to California. Then I'll have to go to work. Right now I'm just not ready to settle."

Ardy pulled off a boot and rubbed his toes. They were sitting on two handmade chairs out in front of the cabin, smoking and looking at the stars. "How old are you, anyway?" Ardy asked.

Will rocked back and blew smoke at the moon. "'Bout thirty and I know I ought to be thinking about settling. Just seems like there's things I want to do first."

"Like what?"

"Like going to California, for one." He was silent a moment, listening to Ardy sigh as he removed the other boot and massaged that foot.

"That all?"

"Well, no. But . . ."

"Hell, Will. I'll be fifty-one come February. When I was your age I'd had enough of horsin' around and was married. Would of worked out, too, 'cept…you know."

Will nodded. "It's just that, well, I've never amounted to much in my life and I'd kind of like to, well, have something, maybe even be somebody before I get fixed in one place for good."

"You been from Mississippi to Colorado, ain't you? And don't you got that silver mine up there? Hell, you're better off than most men around here."

Will let his chair fall forward and his feet thudded on the dirt. He put his elbows on his knees and flipped the stub of the smoke off into the dark. "You're probably right," he said. Then, changing the subject, he said, "Don't you worry about this curse everybody talks about?"

"Curse! I got more to worry about than some old Indian witch doctor's mumblin' over a sack of medicine."

"Lot of people think there's something to it."

Ardy had stopped his foot-scratching and sat leaning forward in his chair.

His hat was pulled down low and Will could barely see him in the deepening darkness.

"I knew me a cowboy once in south Texas would of believed it," Ardy said, talking softly, remembering. "Superstitious as hell. Black cats, ladders, number thirteen. Saw him get white as a sheet one morning when a blue jay flew into the bunkhouse. Said it meant somebody was gonna die. We all laughed at him. He got choked on a piece of meat two nights later and died at the dinner table."

Off behind the cabin a horse snorted and stomped his feet a bit, getting settled for the night. A little stream a few yards to the south bubbled its way to Rock Creek.

"Those things happen," Will said.

"I seen it before." Ardy stood and stretched. "Folks who believe in ghosts see ghosts. And when you're around the believers it's hard not to believe yourself. Pretty soon, things happen that wouldn't ordinarily. If you're afraid you'll step in a hole you'll probably find one to step in sooner or later. If there's supposed to be a curse on this valley those who fear it will figure out some way to make things happen that they'll blame on the Utes."

"Maybe you're right," Will said.

"I am right and don't you forget it. I'm tired, too, so I'm goin' to bed. You know where your bedroll is when you're ready."

For several days Will followed Ardy around his small acreage, admiring the fifteen horses he'd assembled, watching the little man work them. For a long time one day he sat alone on a ridge looking across the valley at Mount Sopris and thinking Ardy was probably right. Will agreed that this would be a good spot to settle, curse or no curse. But he was restless and that night he told his friend he'd be moving on the next day.

"Guess I'll go back to Schofield and see if I can sell my mine," he said.

Ardy looked up from his plate of beans and grinned at Will. "Ain't you gonna go back to Aspen and learn to dance?"

"I 'spect I can find somebody to teach me in California," Will said without looking up. But, he had to admit, the thought had occurred to him.

As Will was mounting Jeremiah for the ride upriver, Ardy once more told Will he'd like to have him as a partner.

"I'll remember," Will said. "Good luck."

"And the same to you, Will Martin."

Ardy handed Will the halter rope for Obediah and watched as he started south. Twenty yards down the trail Will stopped. "By the way, just what does R. D. stand for?"

"None of your damn business," Ardy said with a faint smile and waved him off.

75

Will let the horse set his own pace south. He planned to camp that night at some hot springs Ardy said were maybe a quarter of the way to Schofield. He figured a good soak might perk him up a bit. He felt he needed to think some things through. Like Tracey. And now Abigail, whom he barely knew.

Everything that had happened to him in the past few weeks was difficult to absorb all at once. Not only did he own a mine, but he felt like he was in love for the first time. All of his adult life he'd had a woman when he wanted one, paying for her if nothing else. He'd had some good times with some of them and really liked a few. Now, in the course of a few weeks, he'd met two women who made him consider settling down. One was unavailable, and the other was awfully young and probably from a class of society that wouldn't accept him anyway.

He pondered on it all as he rode up the narrow little valley cut by Rock Creek. Now and then the valley widened a bit, but mostly it was narrow with steep mountainsides falling down to the creek on either side. The pace of the river varied with the terrain. Here it was a rushing torrent, narrow and rock-filled with white water bouncing high and then falling into deep holes that could swallow a man and a horse. Later it would spread itself out and meander along smooth and shallow. It was crystal clear in those wide spots and its rocky bottom showed plainly with little glints of sunlight sparkling like bits of silver.

That night he felt refreshed and loose in the joints after sitting in the hot springs for more than an hour. Steam rose from the riverbank where the springs entered and the heat soothed his saddle-weary body while the steam seemed to clean out his head. He fell into a deep sleep almost the instant he got himself comfortable in his bedroll.

It was pitch dark when he jerked awake, sat up and felt for his rifle which, out of habit, he kept near him.

The two horses were also awake, snorting and shuffling in the dark. He listened for a long minute but heard nothing except the river. Some sixth sense told him something, or somebody, was out there. The fire had burned itself out and there was no moon. Something about these huge mountains spooked him. It wasn't like that out on the Llano Estacado or the Kansas plains where you could see a silhouette of an approaching man.

Then the sound that had awakened him crept into his consciousness. It started as a low moaning, a keening sort of primitive song, like the Texas lullaby he had sung to the cows not long ago. Then he was hearing words of a language he didn't recognize. It came from the south. No, the west. It seemed to come from the sky itself, at once to his right, then behind him. It came and went, always softly but sometimes not at all. Then he would hear it again as though it hadn't stopped but was being transported on wind he couldn't feel.

Nervously, he lifted the rifle from its case and fingered the trigger. He pulled the hammer back and it seemed to make a noise loud as a rock falling. The moaning continued, though, and Will slowly stood. He still couldn't make out where it was coming from. After a while he sat back down, cradled the rifle in his arms and sat there listening.

He caught himself as he almost toppled over and realized he'd been sleeping. *What time was it?* He pulled his pocket watch from his jacket and couldn't read it in the dark. *Strike a match? No, it would give away his position.* He was wide awake again. The moaning had stopped. The horses were quiet and he listened but could hear nothing through the rush of the river. He knew he was awake for good now, so he stood and walked toward the springs carrying his rifle, still cocked.

The sky began to lighten in the east and the morning chill made him shiver. Little by little, as the morning came on, he could make out more and more of the surroundings.

Steam from the springs was heavy in the morning humidity and he followed it upward. He could barely make out the top of the ridge across the river.

Something moved on it. Something erect and about the size of a man. The figure moved just as steam from the springs obscured Will's view. When it cleared and he could see the ridgeline again, there was nothing there. He watched until the sky lightened and the valley opened up before him.

THE NEXT NIGHT, after stabling his horses, he found Doc Phillips sitting alone in the dining room of the boarding house. "You're back," Doc said with a welcoming smile.

Will fell heavily into a chair. "Anything new?"

"As a matter of fact, there is something I'd like to talk with you about."

"Not tonight. Too damn tired. Thought I'd never get around those falls."

"You came from the north?" Will nodded. Doc mused about that a minute, then shoved his still-hot coffee cup over to Will, who took it gratefully. "We call it the Devil's Punch Bowl. It's a treacherous place where we've got to have a good road someday."

"Water must fall good seventy feet," Will said, warming his hands on the cup. "Where's Tracey?"

"Gone to bed bone-tired." Doc yawned and stretched. "We still have your room if you want it."

"I want it," he said, and struggled up the stairs to fall asleep fully clothed.

In the morning, Tracey flashed him a smile of welcome from across the room and hurried over to fill his coffee cup. "Dad and I had about decided you'd gone on to California," she said.

"Tracey, I . . ." Will stroked her arm but she pulled away.

"I know," she said softly.

Doc lowered himself into the chair next to Will, his eye twitching regularly. "Tell me about your trip."

Will did, leaving out the details of the first evening he'd spent drinking with Ardy. He told of Gillespie's party but didn't mention Abigail Crenshaw. And he also didn't mention the ethereal figure near the hot springs. Without all of that, it didn't make much of a story, he thought.

"You made yourself an influential friend in Henry Gillespie," Doc said, "even if you did, as you say, make an ass of yourself in the process."

"Lot of money coming out of those mountains," Will said.

Doc gulped his coffee and got a look of excitement on his face. "Speaking of that, I think I may have a solution for your mine situation."

Will forked into the eggs that Tracey placed before him and raised his eyebrows.

"There is a young man I want you to meet. In fact, he is in town and said he would be here for breakfast."

"Interested in buying the mine?"

"Not exactly. You'll see."

Within a few moments a man of about twenty-five or so, a few inches shorter than Will, broad shoulders and sandy hair cropped short stood beside Doc, hat in hand.

"George, welcome." Doc pulled out another chair without standing and motioned the man to sit. He turned to Will. "This is George Sanders. Meet Will Martin."

"Howdy," Sanders said to Will. "You own the Silver Star." His grip was firm and his gaze steady.

"The Silver Star?"

"That's what I call her. Your mine, that is. Tracey told me all about you. Said you were a tall Texan wearing a hat a foot tall with a star on the side. I know that mine. It's a good one, I think."

Will glanced at Tracey, who had joined them, and saw that she was actually blushing. Quickly, she rose. "I've got work to do," she said, and left.

"George is a mining engineer from Pittsburgh," Doc said. "He's worked in Central City, Telluride and Leadville. When he says a mine is a good one, I'd listen."

Sanders leaned forward on his elbows. "I helped Parkinson locate the mine," he said. "But he didn't have the heart for it. There's a big payoff in there. I'm sure of it."

Will looked the man over, noticing the calluses on his big hands, the clean-shaven but weathered face. He held himself well, erect and poised, ready to move quickly.

"You want to buy it?"

"Nope." The eyes held Will's. "I want to work it. Doc says . . ."

Will shot a look at the old man, who raised his hands in mock defense. "Just passing the time of day and we got to throwing around some ideas is all," he said.

"Just what did Doc say?" Will asked.

Sanders threw a look of apology at Doc but he wasn't shy about speaking his mind. "I don't have a lot of money — not nearly enough to buy a mine, and I figure all the possibles around here are already gobbled up. But I like this place, this valley. I've got a wife and a baby boy over in Leadville who want out of there mighty bad. If I don't find something to do here, some way to make some money, I'm going to have to take them someplace where we can settle."

"You coming to the point?" Will asked.

Sanders' eyes narrowed. "There's only one man in this place with enough money to pay you what your mine's worth. And Doc says you wouldn't sell to Nathan Peabody for any amount."

"You got that right."

"I'm offering to go partners with you on the Silver Star. I'll work her hard and we'll split sixty-forty. I'll work twenty hours a day if I have to and by next year we'll both be rich." He leaned forward again, eagerness in his eyes. "You don't have to give me your answer right now. Think about it. Ask around about me. I can get it done, Mr. Martin."

"Name's Will. Mr. Martin makes me feel older'n I am." Will sipped coffee, held Sanders' gaze and liked it when the younger man looked back steady and unblinking. Doc fidgeted. Behind Sanders, Will could see Tracey watching them.

"I'm not saying no," Will said. "But I never figured on staying around here."

"I've heard that."

Will turned to Doc. "You don't think there's anyone here who could buy it?"

Doc shook his head. "Only Peabody."

"Look me up in a day or so," Will said to Sanders. "I'll think on it. But I don't know. . ."

"That's all I ask right now," Sanders said. "Give it some good thought. It's a good offer. You won't be sorry if you team up with me. I promise you that."

When Sanders was gone, Will and Doc were silent. Doc didn't want to break into Will's thoughts so he let him sit there quietly. But he did raise his eyebrows at Tracey when she walked past and then winked at her. She tried not to smile but couldn't help herself.

Will thought about Sanders' offer all day. Purposely, he stayed away from the boarding house even though he wanted desperately to talk to Tracey. Somehow, despite her marriage, he had a feeling she felt something would bring them together. But her husband would probably live a long time. Damn, he thought. *Damn it all, anyway.*

Late that afternoon Will met Doc on the boardwalk and the two wandered into Peabody's saloon. Peabody wasn't around, Will noticed with some relief, and the two ordered drinks.

"Peabody's been after Tracey," Doc said without working up to it.

"Bastard," Will muttered.

"Comes around most every night, wanting her to take a walk with him, go for a ride in his buggy, stuff like that."

Will was silent, held his glass tightly. Doc ordered his second. When it came he gulped it and the eye-twitching slowed perceptibly.

"Last week he started talking to her about divorcing Randall and marrying him. Said he'd make her the silver queen of Colorado. He said he was going to get rich and then run for Congress. Take her back East, he said."

Will shook his head. "The son-of-a-bitch ought to be run out of the state like they ran him out of Dodge."

Doc gulped the last drops from his glass and signaled for another. "Ran him out of Dodge, you say?"

"Caught him cheating, I heard. He's a snake, Doc."

"Go careful," Doc said quickly. "Soon after you left town a couple of toughs wandered in and Peabody hired them. Supposedly to hold down the fights in here. But they're with him more than they're in here. Like bodyguards."

Doc saw Will's eyes on the door and turned to see Peabody and his two hired hands walk in. Peabody took in the room in one quick look and headed straight toward Will, a slanted smirk on his face.

"Heard you were back," he said. The two men with him stopped a few feet away. One was built like a bear and wore a full beard. The other, shorter, was almost as stout, and had a mustache with long ends that drooped to his jaw.

Will leaned back and looked at Peabody.

"What'll you take for your mine?" the gambler asked. "Let's talk turkey. I'll pay you good money and you can get on your Texas horse and head for paradise in California."

Will pulled the makings from his shirt and began to roll a smoke. "What do you think it's worth?"

Doc sighed and stood. He looked at Will with a sadness and clanked some coins on the table. "See you," he said, didn't look at Will again and left.

Peabody turned to the guards and jerked his head toward the bar. They clomped away as Peabody settled into Doc's chair. "That depends. I don't think there's any silver in it but I'm willing to take that chance. It'd be worth whatever you ask just to get you out of here for good."

Will blew smoke in the air. "Make me an offer." Peabody smiled broadly. "That's what I like to hear. Come by in the morning and I'll pay you cash on the barrelhead if you'll promise to get on your horse and head south by noon or north if you want. Hell, I don't care."

Will stood. "What time in the morning?"

"Nine o'clock. Right here." Peabody swelled, pulled out a cigar. "Have one?"

"No thanks," Will said. "See you tomorrow."

Tracey wouldn't look at Will that night at dinner. She slapped a plate in front of him and almost spilled the coffee she poured. Doc sat across the room from him. The story that Will was selling the mine to Peabody had gotten around town fast. He ate hurriedly and went to his room, paced the floor and finally slept.

The next morning, promptly at nine, Will walked into the saloon. Peabody stood at the bar with his two guards. The room, normally almost empty this time of day, was packed with miners who stopped their talking as Will pushed through the door.

He walked to Peabody and put his foot on the rail, shoving back his hat. "Morning."

"Good morning to you," Peabody said. "You bring your papers?"

"You got the money?"

Peabody pulled an envelope from his suit coat and held it out. "Count it if you wish."

Will took the envelope, opened it and spread the cash out on the bar. Several miners rushed to gather around and gasped at the money. Hogjaw Hannah pushed in close for a good look.

Will gathered it up and slowly replaced it in the envelope. He saw triumph written on Peabody's face.

"Tell you what," Will said. "Why don't you take this money and do one of two things with it." He saw the smile fade and Peabody's lips tightened. "You can take it back to Dodge and return it to those people you cheated. That's one thing."

He turned to the miners gathered around him. "Peabody was chased out of

81

Dodge City a year ago for cheating. Bat Masterson and Wyatt Earp put him on a horse one morning and sent him packing." There was some murmuring among those watching the proceedings. Peabody's face was grim. The two bodyguards edged closer.

Will turned back to Peabody and held out the envelope. "Or you can take the money and shove it up your ugly rear end," he said. Hogjaw Hannah laughed out loud and the big guard cuffed her on the side of the head. By then, Will had turned and was pushing his way through the crowd toward the door. It was quiet in the room for a long second and then everyone was talking at once. Outside, Will took a deep breath of the Colorado air he guessed he might as well learn to appreciate. Evidently he was going to be in it for a while.

Later that morning he found George Sanders and led him to Tracey's boarding house. "Doc here?" he asked her. She didn't answer but motioned toward the stairs.

"Get him," Will demanded. She frowned but went to the stairs and called. Doc came out almost immediately, saw Will and stopped halfway down the stairs.

"We need coffee for four," Will said, making them wait and wonder. Tracey headed for the kitchen with a question on her face and Doc joined Will and Sanders.

When the coffee was poured and the four seated, Will took off his hat and turned to Sanders. "I'll take you up on your offer," he said. Sanders' jaw dropped. Tracey choked on her coffee and had to wipe off her dress with a towel. Doc beamed.

"But it'll have to be on my terms," Will said. Sanders didn't speak, just stared. "I've got six hundred dollars to my name and I want to use most of it for something else. We'll have to raise whatever we need for equipment and men. There's a man in Aspen who I think will loan me the money to get started so I'll guarantee wages. Get good men and work the hell out of them. And get your wife and boy over here as fast as you can. I want you started on it just as soon as you can wrap up whatever else you're doing now. How long will that take?"

Sanders cleared his throat, his eyes wide. "Ten days."

"You've got a week. Can you do it?" Sanders nodded. "Good. There's just one other thing." All three looked at Will.

"It won't be sixty-forty." He waited, letting them stew. "It'll be fifty-fifty."

Doc slapped the table with his fist and coffee spilled from all four cups. Tracey beamed and Sanders sat stock still, staring at Will in near disbelief.

Quickly, Will outlined the rest of his short message. He didn't want to

82

know all the details, he told Sanders. He just wanted a regular report on how things were going.

"As long as things are going well you just tell me if we're making money or losing it," he said. "A man I used to work for named Charles Goodnight told me one of the most important things about running a business was keeping good, accurate records. You'll have to do that yourself or hire someone. Goodnight is one of the biggest ranchers in Texas and he taught me that you have to take men for what they are. He hired me when I was a snot-nosed kid and didn't know anything. Said he saw something good in me. I think I see something good in you. What do you say?" Will sat back and waited for Sanders to collect himself.

"What do I say? I say, hell, yes! And I'll have that mine going in a week or less."

"I'm counting on it," Will said. The two men stood and shook hands. Sanders looked like he'd like to hug Will.

"You won't be sorry," he said.

"I hope you're right," Will replied. "I sure do hope you're right."

THAT NIGHT Tracey came to his room.

He had watched her during the evening meal and had seen her flick her eyes toward him on several occasions, then look away quickly. He had also detected what appeared to be a growing question in the looks. Her brow wrinkled in what might have been a confused frown. Once, as she quickly turned away from him, she touched her hair with a free hand, then shook her head as though ridding it of a bad idea.

Later that night Will lay on his bed, staring out the window at nothing and thinking about Tracey and thinking maybe he had made a big mistake by deciding to become a miner. But he didn't have anything now and if the mine didn't produce he would have exactly the same.

A soft knocking at his door brought him to his feet. He started to reach for his revolver but thought better of it. He crossed the room quietly and opened the door. Tracey was wearing the same faded blue robe she'd worn the night he'd left. It was just light enough for Will to make out the outline of her body against the white wall across the hall. He stepped back and opened the door wider.

Suddenly she was in the room, closing the door quietly. Then she was up against him, her arms around his neck, holding on like she never meant to let go. He let his arms wrap themselves around her and realized there was nothing beneath her robe but the softness of her full body.

She was breathing fast. "When you left I thought I could handle it and I'd made up my mind to accept my life for what it was."

"Be quiet," he whispered. "Don't talk."

She swallowed, kissed his neck. "I've watched you all evening and I've thought of you all night. And I've fought it. There is every reason that I should not be here now but I want this one thing for myself. I have decided to be selfish." She choked back a sob, talked to the wall as her head lay on Will's shoulder. "Everything . . ." She swallowed as he kissed her neck. "Everything I've done since the accident has been for someone else. I'm so tired of it." She raised her head, pressed her lips against his, opened her mouth, pulled away, breathing heavily. "God knows, I've tried. But Randall will never . . . when I heard you were back I had this tremendous sense of relief. And then . . . what you did today for that boy. . . and to Peabody . . . oh, Will, I want you so."

Later, Tracey lay in the crook of his arm, huddling against him, trying to stay as close as possible. "It's been so long," she whispered. "I had decided that I probably never would again . . . you know."

"Hush."

They rested a while and then made love again, stretching the night, and then they both fell asleep.

Tracey was gone when Will awoke. At breakfast she hovered over him, leaving for only seconds at a time to serve the others. Doc was trying to tell Will a story he'd heard and finally became frustrated with her interruptions.

"For Pete's sake, child! Can't you leave us alone for even one minute so I can get to the point of this story?" She laughed out loud at that and tossed her hair, touched Will on the shoulder. Doc looked from one to the other and sighed. "Well, I'll be damned," he muttered. He thought they didn't even notice when he got up and left.

Will spent several weeks in Schofield, helping Sanders and putting off the time when he would have to go back to Aspen to talk to Gillespie about borrowing money. Sanders bought tools and equipment on credit and seemed to have things under control at the mine.

Tracey had made it a habit by then of coming to Will's room nightly, staying a few hours and then slipping back to her own bed. Her husband never seemed to notice her absences, she told Will.

One night, though, he waited for her a long time, lying on his bed, pacing the floor, staring out the window into the darkness. His pocket watch told him it was nearly two in the morning when he opened the door and stepped into the hallway. It was pitch dark and no light showed beneath the doors of any of the rooms. He felt his way to her door, stood beside it for a moment listening to the silence. Without knowing how, he sensed a presence behind him. The

84

hairs on the back of his neck shivered and he felt a coldness wash over him so fiercely it made his heart pound. He stood still, heard nothing but knew someone was there.

"You should have known I'd find out." The voice seemed to whisper without trying, like it was the speaker's normal way of talking. It was freakish, rasping, grating, but so quiet that even in the stillness of the night Will had to strain to make out the words. He started to turn around. "Just stay like you are." Something prodded him hard in the back, something like a gun barrel.

Will obliged. "Who are you?" he whispered.

"You know who I am." Will was sure he did. The man was silent as Will pulled himself together. "Is it Collins?"

The gun poked harder into Will's back. "I'm only saying it once, mister. Stay away from my wife."

The pressure of the gun barrel lessened and Will relaxed a bit, feeling certain now that the man didn't plan on killing him, right then at least.

"I may not be much of a man," Collins said, "but she's still my wife. She thinks I don't know much of what goes on but she's wrong. I know *everything* that happens. I listen to the two of you in your room and it makes me want to kill the both of you." Will started to reply. "Don't say anything! That's my *wife*. I stand outside your door and hear the sounds she makes. She used to make those sounds for me."

"She still loves you. She said . . ."

The gun barrel hurt Will's ribs. "I know what she said. I don't care. I'm telling you to stop seeing her." The man removed the gun, stepped back. "Now. Turn around."

Slowly, Will did as he was told. Collins was a black shape in the hallway. Suddenly a match flared and Will shaded his eyes from the glare.

"Look at me, man!"

He looked. Collins wore a black hood that covered his entire face. Two holes made blacker slots for his eyes. As Will stared, Collins whipped the hood from his head and tried to smile as Will grimaced. One side of the man's face was handsome, while the other was covered in unhealed wounds dripping fluid. His nose was gone. One side of his mouth tried to smile while the other side was nothing but exposed teeth and gums.

"Take a good look," Collins said. "This is what she sees and you say she still loves me." Deftly, he replaced the hood, dropped the match on the floor and stepped on it. "I'm not a real man anymore and I don't own anything but her. She's mine. You leave her alone."

Will wanted to retch, taking a moment to get his breath.

Collins stood there a second longer, then turned and limped away, reaching out to the wall for balance. He disappeared into the darkness and Will heard him going slowly down the stairs. He turned toward Tracey's door once more, heard nothing and went back to his room where he stayed awake the rest of the night.

The next morning Tracey brought him coffee and looked at him with reddened eyes. "I heard," she said. "I'm sorry."

They stared into each other's eyes, saying good-bye. Will wanted to touch her but kept his hands on the table.

"Can't we . . . ?"

"No. He's right, you know."

"I know."

"Good-bye, Will Martin." For a brief moment she let her gaze stay with his, then broke it off and was gone, across the room into the kitchen where the door closed behind her.

"FIGURED YOU'D be comin' around," Ardy said when Will found him on a small rise behind the cabin. He was sitting on a fallen tree trunk watching some magpies have a party in a grove of cottonwoods near a few grazing horses.

"What do you mean, you figured?"

"You'd be surprised how fast word travels up and down this valley." Ardy rolled a smoke while Will dismounted and sat beside him. "Fella rode past here a few days ago and told me how you made a fool out of some high roller. Said you put him in his place."

"So?"

"So, I figured if you wasn't sellin' that mine but was goin' in with some young feller — yeah, he told me 'bout that, too — you'd probably show up."

Will squirmed to find a more comfortable place on the log. "Did you also figure I'd decide to become a rancher?"

"Yep." Ardy reached to the ground, picked up a stick, and began to scratch in the ground with it. "I'se so sure I even made us up a brand. Call it the Double M."

Will looked at the markings in the ground. He felt a sudden tightening in his chest when he saw the brand.

Maybe he had found someplace he belonged after all, he thought.

"Kinda even looks like the mountains, don't it?" Ardy asked.

"Kinda does at that," Will said. "Metcalf and Martin. The Double M. Not bad." He laughed out loud in a spontaneous release of emotion. He was committed at both ends of the valley.

For several days Will and Ardy talked about what they would need to make the ranch work. Will almost forgot about the mine as he became caught up in Ardy's enthusiasm. He looked at the cabin and figured he and Ardy could make out just fine in it for a while but it would have to be enlarged sooner or later. Tracey, though, would never live there, he admitted.

He tried to put her out of his mind as he and Ardy went over their plans again and again. He had told Sanders he would try to raise some money from Gillespie for the mine operation. Now he believed he should also see about some funds for the ranch as well. Ardy didn't much want to borrow money but he reluctantly agreed.

"Guess the man does owe you for savin' his life," he said with more than a hint of amusement in his eyes.

"You're never going to let me live that down, are you?" Will laughed, too, but mostly with embarrassment.

৵৩৶

WILL HADN'T realized how heavy $15,000 in cash could be. Or maybe it was the knowledge that he had a hundred and fifty $100 bills in the saddlebags. He had almost quit wearing his revolver in recent weeks but with that much cash on his person he felt better with it strapped to his waist.

Will had found Gillespie holding court on a bar stool late in the afternoon he had ridden into Aspen. He sipped a beer while Gillespie regaled his listeners with a story about a man named H.A.W. Tabor who had turned a seventeen dollar grubstake into a mining company incorporated for twenty million dollars. The story wasn't that funny, but everybody laughed and slapped their thighs and Gillespie's back. As he accepted the group's response, Gillespie spun on the bar stool and saw Will sitting alone across the room.

"Ah," he said, "my savior has returned." The others looked at Will and those who recognized him and knew the story had another good laugh.

"I've got a business proposition," Will said when Gillespie sat beside him.

"I've been expecting it," Gillespie replied, sitting erect and letting his eyes scan the room.

Will sat up as straight as Gillespie. "This isn't a touch. I've got collateral and I need to raise some money. You're the richest man I know so I came to you."

"I'm the richest man anyone in this town knows," Gillespie said. "But not everyone asks me for money."

87

Will started to stand up. "Forget it. I'll find someone else."

"Sit down. You say it's a business deal so let's hear it. I owe you that much."

"You don't owe me anything."

"Have it your way." Gillespie brushed a fleck of dust from his immaculate suit coat. "But I'm listening."

Quickly, Will told him of his mine and the ranch, emphasizing the experience and knowledge of mining that George Sanders was bringing to the enterprise.

Gillespie listened, although his eyes continuously rode around the room, noting everything that went on. When Will finished he stroked his pencil-thin mustache and took a deep breath.

"I know about Schofield," he said. "I make it a point to know about everything related to silver. You've got some problems, my friend."

"Everybody has problems," Will answered. "You had a few yourself when you crawled in here in the middle of winter over that pass."

Gillespie frowned. "I've never *crawled* anywhere in my life."

"I'm not crawling either," Will said. "Even to you."

A smile wrinkled the crow's feet around Gillespie's eyes. "I think I like you, Martin. But you've still got some problems."

Will sat back and swallowed some lukewarm beer. "First of all, you've got a problem of geography. Schofield is more isolated than Aspen. You're a lot higher in altitude so your winters will be much worse than ours and you won't have as many days a year to work the mine. Mainly, though, you've got low-grade ore."

"My engineer says it's high enough grade to pay off."

Gillespie's mouth curled in a smile. "The valley is also cursed," he said.

"Are you superstitious?" Will asked. "I'm not."

"You never know about things like that. Maybe there's something to it."

Will leaned forward. "Forget the curse. It doesn't mean anything. There are at least four mines shipping jack trains of ore out to Crested Butte and Gunnison every day."

"Oh?" Gillespie perked up.

"The Shakespeare, Pride of the West, Oxford Belle and the North Pole. They're all in the basin behind Galena Mountain where the Silver Star is located."

"The Silver Star? I haven't heard of it."

"You will, if you back me."

"I see." Gillespie stood, quickly and smoothly. Startled, Will scrambled to his feet.

"You drop by my house around eight," Gillespie said. "I'll think about it until then." Without waiting for a reply, he turned and left the room.

Will sat down and signaled for another beer. Eight in the evening was still several hours away.

෴

ABIGAIL CRENSHAW answered his knock on the door of the timbered building with a canvas roof where he had met her not that long ago.

"Have you come for *dancing* lessons?" she asked with a warm smile.

"If your Uncle Henry has some good news for me, I'll be dancing without lessons." Will let her take his hat.

Gillespie was all business. "I think you just might make it, Martin," he said. "I've decided to loan you $15,000. That's all the cash I have available at the moment. The details are in the note and I'm trusting you to be honest in your accounting."

Will nodded. He was surprised at how easy it was to get money.

Gillespie had drawn up a contract and he handed it to Will for his signature. It was a simple note and Will signed it quickly. The man took it without a word and went into another room. He emerged with three bundles of cash. "Count it."

"I trust you," Will said, taking the money. "Just like you trust me."

Gillespie smiled, nodded. "Good. Now, if you'll excuse me, I do have some work to do." Not even a handshake.

"I'll show Mr. Martin out, Uncle Henry," Abigail said. Gillespie was already leaving the room and spoke without turning around. "Stay in touch," he said.

Will nodded again and then shook his head at the wonderment of it all.

"*Coming*, Mr. Martin?" Abigail stood by the door.

Will walked outside into the cooling night air and Abigail went with him, closing the door behind her. Will stared at the bills in his hands, three bundles of $5,000 each. Abigail didn't seem to notice the money.

"I'm going back to Denver next week," she said softly. He turned to her.

"Are you telling me good-bye?"

"Perhaps." She leaned against the door, hands behind her back, looking him in the eye. "I'm engaged to be married."

"He's a lucky man." Will weighed the money. He couldn't think of what he would do with it. Where he could hide it.

"He's a blithering *idiot*."

The saddlebags. He would put the money in the saddlebags and head for the ranch as fast as Jeremiah would get him there.

"My father arranged it."

"What?"

She stood up from her lean, placed her hands on her hips. "The marriage. My father expects me to marry a blithering idiot."

"Can't be too much of an idiot if he's going to marry you." He edged toward Jeremiah and the saddlebags.

She followed him. "That's nice of you to say." Her hands were clasped behind her back and she stayed close to Will.

He walked a little faster, glancing around to see if anyone was watching him hide $15,000 in his saddlebags. His mind was a soup of emotions. Tracey, whom he thought he loved, was gone. Abigail, a woman for whom he might be able to develop feelings, was trying him out. His hands were full of money that would keep him tied to the valley. Second thoughts pounded at him. Abigail kept pace as he hurried toward Jeremiah.

"I may *not* marry after all. I don't really *love* him."

"A lady like yourself ought to marry for love. But money helps."

"*You've* got money."

He was tying up the flap of the saddlebags and he stopped, really hearing her for the first time. He turned to her and she was looking up at him with eyes big as the moon, her head not quite reaching his chin. *Prettier than Tracey but not nearly the woman, yet*, Will thought. Give her a year or so. Impulsively, he reached for her, took her by the waist and pulled her to him. He kissed her soundly on her lips which she opened to him. She knew how to kiss and it was a good one, long and yielding.

He pulled away and had to gently push her away and pull her arms from around his neck. She was young, and ripe, and ready. Tracey was gone. Why not?

She stood close as he rose into the saddle. She touched his leg and the goose bumps up his spine surprised him. He wondered what kind of a man he was.

"If I *don't* marry I'll be back in the spring," she said then. There was offering in her face.

"Don't marry a blithering idiot," Will said. He couldn't seem to bring himself to spur Jeremiah. He kept looking at this young girl and thinking maybe his future had some interesting times in it.

"If you are in Aspen in June you might want to see if *I'm* here," Abigail said.

Will finally touched a rowel to the horse's belly and, as he stepped off, said, "You can count on it. Your uncle and me are partners."

He looked back after a few seconds and she was still standing there in the moonlight watching him ride off to become rich, or at least moderately wealthy. *Hell*, he thought. *"Rich" was the right word.*

ও৶৵

IT WASN'T YET light when Will wearily climbed off Jeremiah and tossed his saddlebags to Ardy, who stood in the doorway wearing only his long handles and scratching himself. "Five thousand of that goes to the ranch," he said. He led the tired horse to the small barn, unsaddled him and turned him in without a rubdown, reminding himself to do it later.

"There's a lot of money here," Ardy said when Will entered the cabin. "Gillespie?"

Will nodded and fell into a chair.

Ardy yawned, hiding the excitement he felt. "Helluva deal."

Will looked up at him. The two smiled at each other then both grinned as big as all getout. "*Helluva* deal."

Ardy held $5,000 in his hand and bounced on his toes. "How you want to spend it?"

"You're the rancher," Will said. "You figure it out."

"Already have."

"I figured."

"You did, huh? Well, figure on this for a while." Ardy handed Will a wrinkled, soiled envelope with his name on it. "Fella came by this mornin' with it. Guess you told somebody up in Schofield about our deal."

"Somebody." Will tore open the heavy envelope. Inside was a letter from Tracey. The room was dim so Will walked outside into the dawn. He leaned against a cottonwood, his back to the rising sun, and looked at the letter, turning it over and admiring the perfect handwriting. He tried to remember ever getting a letter before and couldn't. Tracey wrote with slanted letters in lines so straight on the page they might have been ruled. He read it, finally. Then read it again.

My dearest, darling Will,

It seems years since you left. I love you so greatly that I ache for you day and night. I fear I will always ache for you. You carried sunshine into my life and gave me moments to remember forever. I am a better person because of you, more confident in myself and in my womanhood.

I am pregnant. The child may be yours but Randall could also be the father. I must be forthright and honest so I will keep nothing from you. I heard Randall tell you to stop seeing me. After you left he forced me to bed and made love to me, "to prove he still could," as he put it. I did not fight him. He is, after all, still my husband. He took his hood off and made me look at him while he had his way. When I cried, he laughed. I pity him and I pray for him as I will always pray for you and for your happiness.

There is no need for you to worry about me and I beg you to seek no revenge on poor Randall. I am capable of caring for myself. Also, my father will see me through the pregnancy.

Always, I will love you and will cherish the memory of our brief time together. I will cherish our child. I choose to believe it will be our child, Will.

You are welcome here whenever you are in Schofield but no one will ever know of our love. No one but we two, Randall and, perhaps, my father. You will be an important man if you want to be and I will keep our secret. It is wonderful to be loved, isn't it?

I do love you.
Tracey

Will stood by the cottonwood for a while just holding the letter in his hands. Then he slowly wadded it up into a tiny handful, walked to the creek and tossed it into the current. He watched it float off toward Rock Creek, sat down and put his face in his hands.

Will sat by the creek until Ardy yelled at him that the biscuits was burnin' and he went inside and tried to eat.

Ardy never asked him about the contents of the letter.

PART III

1882-1884

The room was black as a midnight mine with no lights. Will rubbed his eyes and waited for them to adjust while he climbed out of a deep sleep. He had awakened suddenly, thinking he was hearing the eerie howling that miners and ranchers continued to report up and down the valley. This time, of course, it was the baby crying. The covers to his right were thrown back and she was gone, tending the child. He thought of the two of them, the baby at her breast noisily taking a before-dawn breakfast. Will Martin, father, still had trouble believing it. It had been a long ride from the Palo Duro, with no plans except for some half-baked scheme about going to California, to being a miner, rancher, husband and father.

In the space of two years he had made himself moderately wealthy, returned Gillespie's investment and then some, had broken even with the ranch and had sired a beautiful daughter. His eyes properly adjusted, he could see his wife coming back into the bedroom. He lay still as she slipped quietly into bed beside him. Thinking he was asleep, she started to turn her back to him.

"No, you don't," he whispered. He draped a long arm across her flat belly and tried to pull her close. She snorted a quick refusal, as was her habit lately, and hunched over on her side away from him, snuggling down into the thick mattress and burying her head beneath the covers. Soon she was breathing evenly and slowly. She had an aggravating ability to fall asleep quickly.

For a while he lay quietly, feeling the smooth softness of her body, tracing a finger along her hip. He wondered who this woman was and why she had so suddenly become such a consuming and frustrating part of his life. It had been good, for the first year at least. In some ways it still was good. But something gnawed at him and he knew pressures even more intense were working on his wife, slowly tearing them apart.

He nuzzled her neck and, though he knew she wouldn't hear him — and probably wouldn't care if she did — apologized to her.

"I'm sorry," he whispered. "I'm truly sorry, Abigail Martin."

THINGS HAD started out well enough. June of 1881 had finally arrived after a long, solitary winter during which he didn't see Tracey at all, thanks to heavy snows that made the route to Schofield impassable. Not that seeing her would have made things any easier. By spring he figured he had convinced himself there was absolutely no hope that Tracey would leave her husband. He also figured she was doing the right thing and he admired her for it. Little by little, he let thoughts of Abigail Crenshaw occupy his mind. Soon, she was pretty much all he thought of and he had a hunch she was thinking of him, too.

When he thought the timing was right Will had hurried to Aspen and gone directly to Gillespie's home, ostensibly to give his benefactor a progress report. As he had hoped, Abigail had been there, fresh from Denver, unmarried and exultant about it.

"I felt completely *stifled* around him," she said. "He was so *sure* of himself. *Everybody*, just absolutely *everybody* was so certain I was going to marry him. Especially *him*! I've never been taken so much for granted in my *life*!" Her eyes flashed and her shoulders seemed to hunch as she emphasized words. "So I simply *walked out*! One day I told Winfield and my father that I couldn't go through with it. Everyone was so *angry* with me but I don't care."

"Winfield?"

"Winfield *Porter*. The blithering idiot everyone expected me to marry without so much as a *thought* about my own feelings."

Life with Winfield, Abby told him, would have been a *bore*. It would have lacked *adventure*. She was tired of Denver society and being proper and demure and she had wished all winter for something *exciting* to happen. She smiled at Will and his heartbeat picked up considerably.

The long winter had been cold and lonely. Now, with the spring, Abby was warm and receptive to Will's not-so-subtle approaches. Or were the approaches hers? By midsummer he didn't care, knew only that this beautiful young girl seemed deeply in love with him and that he felt what he supposed was love for her. Often, they kissed and her body trembled as he explored it with his hands. Always, though, she stopped him.

"It's not *proper*, Will. When we're *married*."

Suddenly, they were. In the August heat a Methodist minister from Denver said the words and Will figured he was happy. Henry Gillespie hosted the wedding and, despite the fact that Abby's parents refused to attend, Will's young bride was never more beautiful nor evidently happier than at that moment.

Will took her home to a house he and Ardy had built. She smiled bravely and said she loved it, but Will saw her staring at the small rooms and figured she was remembering her parents' large home in Denver. "It'll grow," he said and she smiled again as she walked through the long living room that fronted the entire house. The kitchen adjoined the front room and two small bedrooms jutted out into the back. Suddenly, the house of which he had been so proud seemed tiny and inadequate.

Even before Evaline was born barely nine months later, Will knew they had made a mistake. The solitude, the bleakness of the winter months, Will's absences as he rode off for days at a time to tend to business here or there up and down the valley — all quickly took their toll. Early on, their love- making was enough. Abby couldn't seem to get enough of his body and she threw herself at him morning and night. When it became obvious that she was pregnant, however, the lovemaking stopped and she seemed no longer interested in him as a man.

She spent long hours reading poetry or staring morosely out the window at the gray winter snow that seemed never to stop. Her uncle, Gillespie, knowing of her love of literature, sent her the newest books: *The Portrait of a Lady* by Henry James, a book of essays by Robert Louis Stevenson called *Virginibus Puerisque*, even a new children's book titled *Heidi* by the German writer Johann Heusser.

The conversations they had were brief, and of no significance.

"I thought we'd spend more time in *Aspen*," she said. "Nothing *happens* here. I miss the sound of *music*."

The baby was born in June. Will had taken Abby to Aspen where a doctor could be called quickly. He had gone back to the ranch to help Ardy for a couple of days and the child came while he was gone. He brought them home to the valley on a gray, windy day just before the first of July and Abby took their daughter into the house without a word, went into the bedroom and shut the door.

Two months later they still had not made love and Will found more and more excuses to be gone from the ranch.

Early in September the best excuse yet presented itself on his doorstep in the person of J. C. Osgood, "of the White Breast Mining Company of Iowa," as he announced to Will, Abby, Ardy and the baby Evaline, "but also, in a way, the Chicago, Burlington and Quincy Railroad."

Osgood, with a barbered mustache, high boots that laced and a well- cut corduroy suit, told them he was looking for a guide. "They told me in Satank you know this valley better than anyone else," he said, looking up at Will. The man was short, about five-foot-seven maybe. His round face was made even rounder by the flat-brimmed, low-crowned hat he wore and the tie that seemed to squeeze his neck up into his head.

"I know the valley," Will said. "But what is it you're looking for? Surely you don't want to build a railroad up the valley."

Osgood smiled and his eyes told Will the man was honest. "I'll tell you if and when I find it," he said. "What about it?"

Will looked at Abby who shrugged and wiped Evey's mouth.

"You hired a guide, I reckon." He was already thinking about camping in the mountains.

✍

THE TRAIL petered out on a rocky shelf and Will called a halt. He turned to see Osgood urging his horse up the last part of the steep grade. The man's eyes were constantly in motion, scanning the surrounding countryside, looking for something. Osgood hadn't volunteered any information about just what it was he was looking for, and Will — still with enough Texan in him to know better — hadn't asked.

"Time for a breather?" he called.

Osgood nodded. "If you're tired, let's stop a while." There was a glint in his eye that Will had seen before, as though the Easterner was mocking him. Still, Will had come to like the man and to admire the enthusiasm he had displayed during the past few days. Osgood had matched Will for stamina as they explored a number of areas east and west of the valley. In fact, Will had been astonished at the man's energy. He had insisted on riding up every little stream that fed into Rock Creek.

"I like the looks of this particular area," Osgood said to Will when they were seated side by side on a boulder. They looked west, up a V-shaped cut that stretched a few miles farther on and always upward until it butted into a wall of north-south mountain.

"Mighty purty, all right," Will said.

Osgood seemed to catalog everything about the area as he looked. "That, too," he said.

It was the most interest Osgood had shown in any of the locales Will had shown him in four days of riding. In fact, they had looked up every small creek or defile along the way. South of the hot springs where the valley began to open up, Osgood had scanned the steep red cliffs to the east with what seemed to Will to be unusual attention. The cliffs began at a great height just beyond the shoulder of Mount Sopris and south of Avalanche Creek canyon. Their redness plummeted downward to end in a thick mat of aspen. Farther south, the cliffs seemed to be lower as the valley floor sloped upwards.

"Fantastic," Osgood murmured. "What a spot for a ranch. Or a town." Will had often admired the spot himself and had planned on somehow getting to the top of the cliffs for a better view of the valley — and to see what was on the other side.

"Look at that point up there," Osgood said, pointing to the southeast. A rocky crag jutted out into the blue sky with what appeared to be solidly anchored boulders supporting a few spruce trees with a small aspen grove behind them. "From that point you could have a perfect view up and down the

97

valley all the way from Mount Sopris to Chair Mountain."

"I've been thinking I'd like to go up there someday," Will said, grateful that Osgood could appreciate the beauty of his valley even as he looked for something else. Funny, he thought, that he should refer to it as "his" valley.

Osgood looked upward at the point for a while and then turned back to the west. "What's up there?" He nodded up a steep valley that started out wide and rapidly seemed to close around the small stream that drained it.

"Nothing that I know of," Will said. "But I bet you want to have a look anyway."

"You're right." Osgood led off without another word. During the ride, Will told Osgood about the Ute Indian curse that so many people seemed to feel was real.

"Balderdash!" Osgood snorted. "Backwoods hysterics. Surely you don't believe in that kind of poppycock."

"I'm trying real hard not to," Will said.

Now, sitting next to Osgood on the boulder, Will was glad they'd come. He hadn't been up this way for over a year. Osgood was talking to him.

"How did you get to know this country so well?"

"It was pretty easy," Will answered. "I've been out here two years and I've been up and down this valley more'n most men, I suppose." He told Osgood about his mine and the horse ranch and how he traveled frequently between them.

"So you have holdings at both ends of the fabulous valley," Osgood said. "Smart. Very smart, indeed."

Will shook his head. "Not so smart, actually. More lucky than smart." He told his story and when he finished, Osgood sat for a moment, puffing on a large cigar, still staring off into the distance. He muttered something that Will didn't catch.

"What's that?"

Osgood sat up straight, brushed dust from his pants. "The word is *destiny*, Mr. Martin. Destiny."

The two of them sat there a while and thought about the word. It sounded mighty big to Will.

Osgood began to unlace one of his high-topped boots. "You've got it written all over you, my friend," he said. He pulled the boot off and wriggled his toes. "I checked up on you very carefully in Satank before deciding you were my man. I know all about your background in Kansas. I also know all about your fortunate meeting with Henry Gillespie and his niece who is now your wife."

Will sat silently. This was a man who did his homework.

"You and I are of the same cut, Will." Osgood sighed as he worked the other boot off, stretching his short legs out in front of him. "I believe I, too, am a man of destiny. I have a restlessness of soul that wouldn't let me stay in any of the many jobs I have held. I always have known that there is something far more important, far more profitable, waiting for me in perhaps the most unlikely location."

He waved his arm grandly over the vista before them. "This just may be that place. Do we camp here tonight?"

In the darkness, after the fire had died to no more than glowing embers, Osgood told Will about himself. It didn't take long and Will hadn't asked. He simply started talking.

"I'm originally from Brooklyn, New York. My mother's maiden name was Cleveland so I am John Cleveland Osgood. My father died when I was but twelve."

Osgood had been shuffled among relatives during the Civil War years and he quit school when he was fourteen to go to work in a Rhode Island cotton mill. At sixteen he struck out alone for New York, found a job and enrolled in night classes at the Peter Cooper Institute.

"I went from clerk to cashier at a coal camp," he said, "and a few years ago gained control of the operation. I am here at the request of the Chicago, Burlington and Quincy Railroad." He waited. "You haven't asked me what I'm looking for. Why not?"

Will flicked his smoke into the fire. "Figured you'd tell me when the time was right. If you wanted to, that is."

Osgood laughed. "You were right," he said, and laid back on his bedroll. He was quiet for a few minutes and, when Will had decided the man was asleep, he spoke again. "There are incredible times ahead for America," he said. His voice was bright, enthusiastic, with no hint of weariness after the long days of riding. "And for this state of Colorado as well."

"I don't doubt it," Will murmured.

"All the money being made in the East is simply precursor to fortunes that will be made here," Osgood continued, sounding almost as though he were talking to himself, reciting lines that had more to do with building up his own self-confidence than with providing information to a listener.

"Take Rockefeller, for example," he continued. "You know of John D. Rockefeller, of course?"

Will harrumphed an answer, clearing his throat. Of course he didn't, but he knew his answer wasn't important. All Osgood needed was an indication that he was listening.

"Rockefeller incorporated the Standard Oil trust to circumvent state corporation laws and the man and his eight associates control 95 percent of the United States petroleum industry. Think of the money, man! Not that money is the most important thing, of course. Don't you agree, Martin?"

Will nodded that he did.

"It's power! Control! And it's brilliant. Using a trust rather than the usual corporate makeup."

Will wasn't sure what a trust was but he didn't ask. Osgood had raised himself to an elbow and his eyes glowed brightly in the reflection of the last of the fire. "I expect to be wealthy myself before too long," he said, his voice becoming softer. "I can feel it deep inside me. Somehow it is something I simply know."

He settled back down on his back and Will thought maybe that was the end of it. It wasn't.

"But I will be different than other wealthy men," Osgood said, his voice rising out of the dark like wind through the pines, like he was continuing to talk to himself. "I will be concerned with the common man. Not like that oaf William Vanderbilt in Chicago who has had the nerve to say 'The public be damned.' Vanderbilt, of course, is a railroad magnate who has eliminated an extra-fare mail train called the *Chicago Limited*. He told a reporter he was working for his stockholders and said if the public wants the train they should pay for it themselves."

He seemed to wait for Will to reply but, after a few seconds of silence, went on.

"I, in contrast, will be especially cognizant of the public, and of my workers. Oh, yes. I will have men working for me. Mark my words, Mr. Martin. Mark my words." He paused dramatically. "Destiny. I feel it so intensely . . ." His voice finally trailed off.

Will shook his head and pulled his Texas hat over his eyes. *This Osgood sure does keep up with the news*, he thought. The kind of things Will found interesting were a world apart from Osgood's. He may have seen a story about Standard Oil in the *Rocky Mountain News* but he'd been more interested in the fact that a twenty-one-year-old outlaw called Billy the Kid had been killed in New Mexico Territory after shooting twenty-one men. And that the law finally got rid of Jesse James when he was shot in the back of the head by somebody out for the reward.

But he'd been especially intrigued by a story about a shoot-out in Tombstone, Arizona, that had involved Wyatt Earp and his brothers Virgil and Morgan, and even Doc Holliday. Something about an O.K. Corral. He sometimes wondered about his fellow peace officers from Dodge City. Every now and then a name or two he recognized showed up in a newspaper article. They were becoming famous while he, Will Martin, tried to get comfortable on a rocky hillside.

Sure is a strange world, he thought. *It's all about money in the East and out here we don't even have a railroad. We just seem to kill people.* He snugged himself down into his bedroll and smelled spruce before he fell asleep.

THE NEXT MORNING the two men pushed on up the rapidly narrowing canyon until they had nearly reached the rock face of a towering mass of mountain that would call a definite halt to their exploration. Osgood had grown strangely quiet during the last part of the ride and Will figured he was mighty disappointed or getting really interested in something.

It turned out to be the latter.

The little man hopped down from his horse and scrambled up a small incline to stand atop a scrub-covered ridge. Will also dismounted but chose to make use of the shade cast by a pine tree. When he looked up toward the ridge Osgood was nowhere in sight. Unconcerned, he made certain the horses were grazing peacefully, stretched out, covered his eyes with his hat and quickly dozed off. Within minutes, it seemed, Osgood was nudging him with the toe of his boot.

"I think I've found what I sought," he said, looking serious and nodding his head.

Will sat up. "Already?"

"Let's stay here today," Osgood said. "I want to look around some more."

"Whatever you say."

Osgood chuckled and turned to face once more toward the ridge. "This is the end of our ride, by the way. I'll be heading back for the stage tomorrow."

LATE IN THE evening two days later, when Will rode into Schofield, he hurried to the boarding house. He found Tracey sitting alone at a table, her face in her hands. She wore a severe black dress that made her hands appear as pale as the whitewashed walls.

"Tracey?"

Slowly, she raised her head. "Will," she sighed. She stood and walked slowly to him, let him take her in his arms. "I haven't cried yet," she said.

He held her at arm's length. Her face was drained of color, expressionless. "Cried? What's going on?"

"Sit down," she said. "I'll tell you all about it."

She told him the story matter-of-factly, with little emotion. Will, on the other hand, felt the anger build as she talked. He stood, paced the floor, sat, and stood again. He clenched his fists, felt sorry for the girl, wanted to hug her to him, wanted to kill Peabody.

"Peabody came here three nights ago," she began. "He offered to marry me. I refused, of course, and he got angry. I even threw a stove lid at him."

"I hope you hit him," Will said.

She shook her head. "He knows."

"Knows? Knows what?" She kept her eyes on the floor, anywhere but on Will. "Come on, Tracey. Talk to me."

"He knows about us, about Jacob."

Will sat beside her. "He can't."

"He guessed, and the way I reacted gave it away."

"Well." Will leaned back. "What harm does it do?"

Tracey let her eyes stray toward him, found him and said, "Randall heard."

"Damn." It came out quickly and all sound died in the room as Will began to understand. The black dress, the vacant stare. "Where is Randall?"

She nodded to the east. "We buried him today."

Will felt his shoulders sag and he reached for her hand. "I'm sorry, Tracey. What happened?"

She told the story quietly, still holding back the tears, in a voice that sounded numb from retelling and reliving it.

Tracey had gone to her room after Peabody left, thinking Randall would be asleep. Instead, he was standing in the center of the room silhouetted against the faint light from the window. Moonlight glinted off the barrel of the pistol he held pointed at her. She was paralyzed with fear but managed to glance toward her son's bed in the corner.

"Don't worry about Jacob," Randall had said. "He'll be fine."

She was certain then that he fully intended to kill her but watched with astonishment and then horror as he swung the barrel away from her and placed it against his own forehead.

"I love you," he had muttered. "I don't blame you for anything."

The gunshot was a loud, dull pop with no echo, followed by the sound of his body falling to the floor, the pistol thudding dully on the carpet. His face was entirely gone. Blood and gore stained the wall and the floor.

Later, she remembered comforting Jacob. She remembered trying to still his crying. She knew her father had come quickly into the room and she thought perhaps there had been others there, too. She remembered that she did not feel faint and did not even feel remorse. She remembered only a sense of surprising relief, she told Will, comforting relief. That, and newfound, blessed, all-encompassing freedom.

They sat silently when her story was finished. "I don't know what to say,"

Will mumbled as he stroked her arm.

She shook her head and started to say something when Will leaned back and threw his hands in the air. "What is it?"

"My God, Tracey! Why didn't he do it sooner?"

"Will!"

"Well, I'm sorry again. But, don't you see? Now you're free and I'm not."

She lowered her head again. "Don't you think I know that? It's too ironic for words."

Will pulled her to him, stroked her hair.

"He — Peabody — was even at the funeral." She pulled away and walked to the window. "I hate that man more than I've hated anyone in my life."

Will stood beside her and, for a long time, held her hand as they stared into the darkness. Later, she wordlessly took her hand from his and left him alone. He heard her slow footsteps on the stairs as she went away from him — again.

THERE WAS more bad news yet to come. Sanders came in the next morning, tired and dirty. He had worked all night, he said, to confirm his suspicions.

"The mine's about played out," he said. "We're barely breaking even."

Will stared at the floor. "Guess that does it, then."

"Up here, anyway." Sanders had a grin on.

"Why do I have the feeling you're about to spring something on me?" Will said, wondering at the man's smile.

"Look," Sanders said. "Mining is about all I know. If you want to stay in the game I've got an idea."

"I've trusted you this far," Will said. "Talk."

"I think I've located a claim down valley around Crystal City that has more promise than the Silver Star."

Will laughed, almost surprised that he still could. "That's what I like about you miners. There's never a lack of optimism." Crystal City was a small mining town growing up along Rock Creek a few miles to the north. The optimism of its founders was reflected in the town's name.

Sanders wanted to move men and equipment to Crystal as fast as he could, get started before winter and spend the cold months getting as much ore ready as possible for shipment in the spring.

Will hesitated. Snow could pile up as high as twenty feet in the winter.

"I don't look forward to it," Sanders said, "but I figure it'll put us ahead of the game."

The man was persuasive and when he left, Will was convinced it might be worth the gamble, especially if the claim was as good as Sanders seemed to think.

That evening, when the mother of his son came down the stairs, he met her there. She stood on the bottom step, looking him nearly in the eye.

"Tracey . . . damn it. It all came too late, didn't it?"

She pushed past him and then turned. "Will, don't you love your wife? And your daughter?"

He didn't have an answer to the first question.

She started away but he caught her arm. "At least let me help you. I've got more money than George knows. I can set you up in Crystal City. Another boarding house."

She smiled at that. "I won't be a kept woman, Will."

He flushed. "I didn't mean that. But I owe you."

"Owe me what? I may move to Crystal, Will, but I'm going to let Peabody pay for it. I'll sell this place to him and get out. If not now, maybe by next spring."

He couldn't look at her. "Am I not to be a part of your life, then?"

She took his face in her hands and held it softly. She whispered, "You'll always be a part of my life, Will Martin. You and our son."

There was a thud from the floor above, then silence, then a whimpering as Jacob started to cry. Tracey pulled her long skirt above her calves and ran up the stairs. Will followed, clomping loudly in his boots. Tracey went to Jacob's room and, throwing open the door, found him sitting up in bed, apparently all right. "Father!" she cried.

Next door, Doc was lying on the floor beside his bed, gasping for breath, holding his chest. Will cradled the old man's head in his arms while Tracey talked to him. "What can we do?"

"Water," Doc gasped. "My bag."

Tracey ran downstairs for water and Will grabbed a pillow, put it under Doc's head, then found the physician's bag.

"In the . . . the side pocket. A bottle . . . of pills."

Tracey was back by the time Will found the pills. Doc choked down two of them and lay back, breathing easier. The two of them got him back into bed and, resting more comfortably, the man could talk.

"I've felt it coming on," he said softly. "Just a mild attack. I'll be fine, now. Been taking those pills but knew it'd happen sooner or later."

"Don't try to talk," Tracey said. "Get some sleep."

"I should take another pill by sunrise," Doc said.

"I'll be here." At Tracey's urging, and against Doc's wishes, Will carried a cot into the man's room and placed it next to his bed.

Tracey showed Will to a room down the hall and promised to call him if she needed anything.

"I'm glad you're here," she said.

He nodded. "I wish it was under different circumstances."

"So do I, Will." She walked to the door. "But we must think of Abby."

Then she was gone and he was alone again, just like he always seemed to be when he wanted to be with her. But it wasn't to be and he tried to accept the fact. He did think of Abby then and decided maybe it was best that he was alone.

The next morning Doc was feeling better. Will tucked $50 beneath Jacob's pillow without saying anything about it to Tracey. He and Sanders set out to stake the claim in Crystal.

At the Devil's Punch Bowl they stopped to rest the horses. Will had to shout to be heard over the falls. "I suppose you'll go back to Schofield and then to Gunnison to file the claim." Sanders nodded. Will moved closer so he wouldn't have to shout. "I want you to do something for me."

"Long as it isn't illegal," Sanders laughed.

"I'll help you stake out the claim at Crystal. Then I'd like for you to come on down the valley a ways and we'll file a couple of more claims west of those red cliffs."

Sanders looked puzzled. "You think there's silver up there? I've been all over that creek and it's not worth it."

"Not silver," Will said. "Coal."

Sanders looked at his boots. "I never saw any signs of coal, either."

"Trust me. I just may know something you don't."

"Well now, that's entirely possible."

"One other thing." Will pulled a piece of paper from his shirt pocket. "I want you to file the Crystal claim in your name and mine, fifty-fifty. And put yourself in for twenty percent of the coal claims."

"That's not nec . . ."

"Just shut up and listen. Put me in for forty percent. Another twenty will be for Evaline Martin."

"What about the last twenty percent?" Sanders asked.

"That'll belong to Mr. Jacob Collins."

THE SNOWS CAME early that year, the winter weather overlapping autumn so the color came and went quickly. But the snow was light, falling in a powdery consistency that melted before it could begin to pile up. Sanders

105

moved his miners down valley to Crystal City quickly, opening a hole in the side of the mountain and christening it the Princess Evaline, in honor of Will's daughter.

Will was up and down the valley several times, trying to help Sanders as much as possible. Each time he made the rugged trip he marveled at the number of people he saw. What had but a few years ago been a wilderness inhabited only by Indians was now teeming with men who explored every canyon and poked holes into pristine mountains. North of Crystal, the towns of Marble and Clarence were barely two years old, and barely a mile apart, competing for a post office and the right to survive.

Six miles upstream from Marble — but only over a treacherous trail that twisted and turned, rose and fell along precipitous cliffs and through narrow canyons — Crystal City was beginning to show signs of life that would have to wait for further development until the following spring.

Will was now pleased that Tracey had decided to stay in Schofield for the winter, finding that enough miners planned to board with her to see her through. The wagon road that had been completed from Schofield to Crystal helped give the town a lift. Even with the road, though, Sanders and his miners would be isolated for several months.

When Will returned from one of his trips to the new mine, Ardy met him with a curt "Welcome back" and then silence. Abby, on the other hand, was not so reticent about venting her anger.

"This is no *marriage*," she said to him within moments of his arrival. "You're married to that damn *mine*. I left Denver and Aspen because I loved *you*, Will, not the thought of spending every *day* alone here with Ardy and Evey. What *good* is it all? You could work for Uncle Henry in *Aspen*, or for my father in *Denver* and we could enjoy life. *Together*!"

"I've got one more trip to make up there," he told her. "After that we'll be together all winter."

"All *winter*!" She turned away. "*Snowbound* most of the time. Nobody to *visit*. No *music*. How *exciting*!"

Ardy was less vehement but just as pointed. "Gonna need more of your time, old man, or we ain't gonna make it," he said.

"Next summer things'll be different," Will promised.

One night later, Abby announced that she was going to Aspen. "I'm simply not going to stay here another *day*, especially if you're going back to those awful *mining* camps and won't even be here to say hello to your daughter, much less to *me*," she said.

"All right," Will said. "I'll find someone to drive you over. But I'll be back in ten days and you be here, too. We'll talk this whole thing over then."

Once more, then, ride past the shoulder of Mt. Sopris, trail along the river on narrow, worn paths spiked with rocks, boulders. Force the horse through a forest of aspen here, a rockfall there. Smell the sulfur of the hot springs but don't stop. The red cliffs are flecked with white and more is coming down. Push on and think about Abby and wonder what she's thinking, what has happened to her? Wonder, too, what has happened to you. There once was love. Spur the animal through six inches of snow on the level below Chair Mountain, ten inches at Marble. Switchback, hogback, steep rise and drop. The canyon floor a hundred feet below — two hundred. Can't tell for the snow that falls softly, makes a silent world twenty yards square. Watch for the landmarks and keep going. It's an early storm that will pass and melt. Abby should be all right down valley and on a well-traveled road. Ride with your head down buried in a coat that weighs as much as a big dog but that keeps you warm and dry. Is this the last slope? Smell pine burning? Relax.

Tracey was surprised when Will clomped into the boarding house, shedding his coat. "I didn't expect to see you again until spring," she said.

"Thought I'd come up and check on Doc — and Jacob," he said. "Just a tad bit interested in seeing you, too."

Her welcoming smile faded. "I don't know what to make of my father," she said. New wrinkles played around her eyes and dug deeper furrows in her forehead. *We're all aging too quickly up here*, Will thought.

"Is he worse?" Will asked.

"Not physically, I don't think," Tracey replied. "It's his head. Ever since the heart attack, if that's what it was, he simply hasn't been himself. Yesterday morning I don't think he recognized me and he refuses to play with Jacob at all."

The old man didn't know Will and ordered him out of his room when he went in to say hello. Will spent the evening carrying Jacob around on his shoulders, tossing him in the air and playing "horsey" on the floor. He didn't tell Tracey about his spat with Abby or about his growing concern over his marriage.

In the morning Doc was not in his room and Tracey woke Will at six, pounding on his door. "He's not in the building," she said. "I've looked everywhere."

"Have you checked the privy?"

They found him there, blue-lipped and coatless, sitting on the floor with his arms folded. He wore a tired look on his face as though he'd gotten that far and decided it wasn't worth it to try any more.

A FEW DAYS after Doc's funeral Will found Ardy up in the high pasture herding three ponies toward the corrals. "Only a few more to bring in," Ardy said, "and we'll have to start snuggin' 'em down for the winter." He fished in the pocket of his Levi's and pulled out a wrinkled letter. "Reminds me. Fella stopped by on the way up valley. Yesterday, it was."

Will tore the letter open and read it quickly. Then he read it again. Ardy didn't ask but he explained anyway. "Says she isn't coming home," Will said. "Says she's tired of the place and won't stay up here by herself bringing Evey up alone."

Ardy leaned on his saddle horn. "You ain't surprised, are you?"

Will crumpled the letter. He had only had two letters in his life and both of them had brought bad news. "Guess I am, a little. We had it going good for a while there." The two men rode back to the ranch house, drove the horses into the corral with the others and sat on the rail fence. "I'm gonna go get her," Will said.

Ardy rolled a smoke and spat a speck of tobacco. "Reckon she'll come?"

"She'll come. Think you can manage a few more days?" Slowly and deliberately lighting up, Ardy turned his eyes upon Will. "I been managing so far, ain't I? Look here, Will. You been gone more'n you're here and I been gettin' along. But jest barely." Will started to speak but Ardy stopped him with a raised hand. "I know you got business up the valley and I appreciate the money you've sunk into this place. But it takes more'n one beat-up old cowhand to make it work. Now you go get Abby and the girl and bring 'em back if you can. But then you need to help me some or hire us somebody who'll spell me a bit. Now, if you think I'm outta line, say so."

Will's spirits were about as low as they'd ever been. "You're right, old friend," he said. "You're sure right." Now he had everybody upset with him. Abby was close to leaving him, Tracey was clear in her intentions not to resume their affair and now Ardy had laid it on the line.

"I'll be back from Aspen in a few days and we'll make something of this place yet," Will said. He hopped off the fence and started for the house but Ardy spoke again.

"It ain't none of my business, but I got to ask."

"So. Ask."

"You got yourself a woman up there somewhere?"

Will dropped his eyes and turned toward the house again. "Nope," he said. "Not anymore, anyway." It was not easy admitting it to himself.

THEY SAT AROUND a large table in Henry Gillespie's "Big Tent" and Will felt like the outsider he was. Many of Aspen's first settlers ringed the table. There were wives and daughters, too, and there was Will sitting beside a subdued Abby.

After a bitter argument she had agreed to return with Will so they could "work things out." But first there was this vastly important dinner party which she "simply must attend." It would mark the end of another fantastic summer mining season in Aspen and it would be the final large social event before many of the rich moved to Denver or elsewhere for the winter.

Will was uncomfortable, wearing his working clothes among the suits and ties of the other guests, but had given in to Abby's pleading and attended, mainly for the sake of her desire to be a part of it all. Gillespie was making a speech.

"Leadville will die," he said, "just like Central City, Cripple Creek, Silverton and all the rest. But Aspen will survive and, before long we'll have a railroad. We'll have an opera house and hotels that will be among the finest in the land. We'll survive and prosper because of men and women like those assembled here tonight."

And, though they all knew one another, Gillespie proceeded to introduce them, one at a time.

There was B. Clark Wheeler who, with Charles Hallam, had bought eight mining and two ranch claims from Phil Pratt and Smith Steele for $5,000 down. All four were now rich and all smiled at one another across the table.

"As you all know," Gillespie continued, "our own Mr. Wheeler saw the same vision which I had for this lovely setting. Thanks to him we have our own newspaper, The Aspen Times. And, thanks to him, we don't live in a ramshackle mining camp called Ute City. We live in what is to become one of America's finest towns and it's called — at B. Clark's insistence — Aspen!"

After the applause Gillespie introduced D. R. C. Brown, who had traded $250 worth of lumber for a one-third interest in the Aspen Mine and who now, it was said, received more than $100,000 every month in dividends.

They were all introduced in turn: Isaac Cooper, William Hopkins, Charles Bennett, Henry Staats and all the others. Now millionaires, or nearly so, they were the men who had been among the first into Aspen — or at least the first into Aspen with enough money to assure their own futures.

Gillespie finished and sat down but suddenly stood again and raised his hands for quiet.

"I am remiss," he said. "During my lavish praise of Aspen and those who have made — and will make — her even greater, I neglected to pay tribute to another of our guests who has another type of vision for another, nearby, part of these mountains. I refer, of course, to Mr. Will Martin, the husband of my beautiful niece, whom all of you know well."

Will nodded as the group clapped politely.

Dinner was served, finally, and during the meal B. Clark Wheeler, sitting at the far end of the table from Will, said loudly to him: "Mr. Martin. Just how are things in your . . . your cursed valley?" There was laughter at that and Will tried not to flush. "There is a curse on it, is there not? But never mind that. Is there any ore over there worth bothering about?"

Will put down his fork and wiped his mouth with a linen napkin. "Lots of it, Mr. Wheeler. But we've got an even tougher problem getting it to the smelter than you do."

"Your Schofield will be like the others," Wheeler said. "Schofield and Crystal and all the rest. Boom and bust, Mr. Martin. You take heed, now."

"I suppose you've all heard the story about the Smuggler Mine," Gillespie interrupted. Will nodded his thanks as some of the men laughed. Gillespie continued. "Seems the first man to stake out his claim there sold it for $50 and a mule when he heard about the Ute uprising at White River. The mule, true to its disposition, died the next day and the Smuggler is now worth . . . what would you say, Hopkins or Bennett? You two owned most of the claims up there."

Bennett waved his fork in the air. "Hundreds of thousands. Maybe more."

All this talk of money in such enormous sums had begun to wear on Will and he was relieved when the dinner was over and the guests moved their chairs near Mrs. Gillespie's prized organ to hear a concert by Abby. As she played, Will compared his situation to that of those gathered. These men traded thousands of dollars a day on a whim while he worried about the comparatively small amount it took to keep the ranch going. They were confident men, certain of their right to "rule" Aspen. He wasn't that sure of his own future, much less that of a town. While Aspen had a future, Will lived in a valley that had a curse. The wives of these rich men preened over their husbands. Abby seemed to want to leave hers.

The next morning she made it plain. "I'm *going* back with you, Will," she said. "I don't know how long I'll *stay*, though. Even though we're only a few miles away from Aspen, it seems as though we're on another continent and centuries removed." She tucked Evey's arms into a coat for the ride, looked up into a gray sky, and frowned.

LOW, ANGRY CLOUDS scudded across a flat sky ahead of a gusty wind that was damp and cold. Will and Sanders took a breather within a mile of Schofield when they found a sheltered and barren spot beneath a large pine.

Sanders had been pale and gaunt that spring when Will finally was able to force his way through snowdrifts and get to Crystal. His black-rimmed eyes were set deep in a face Will hardly recognized. Cheekbones protruded where once there had been robust flesh. His shirt collar was too big for his neck.

The miner quickly brought Will up to date. He had managed to get some ore ready for shipment but the work had gone slowly. The snow had been heavy, falling for days at a time and often blocking a just-cleared trail.

The ore looked good, Sanders told Will as they warmed themselves by a potbellied stove in the little building that passed for a hotel in Crystal City. They would make some money on what he had managed to pile up. Now, they needed to hire more men and work hard all summer. It looked like their venture was going to pay off.

"But I've got to get over to Crested Butte and see my wife and kids," Sanders said. He had received only one letter from his wife all winter. Finally, they were on their way and Will's heart was pounding as much at the anticipation of seeing Tracey as at the unfamiliar exercise.

Sanders seemed unaffected by the exertion, even at this altitude. Both men were sweating beneath their layers of clothing. Will's nose was running and sweat had frozen in his three-day growth of beard. He kicked out of the snowshoes and lay flat on his back.

"Hardest work I've done all winter," he gasped. Sanders grinned and fidgeted. He had fashioned snowshoes — what he called "skis" — from eight-foot boards. The two men carried packs of food and clothing on their backs and pushed themselves along with long poles that were taller than a man.

Sanders, who had gotten to the mine on skis a number of times during the winter, was able to move quickly over the ground but Will felt like he never got the hang of it. Where the snow was shallow he could plant the pole and pull and push as he slid across the crust. In deeper snow he often had to bend almost double to find a plant for the pole. Negotiating the frequent inclines was even more difficult. After sliding backwards three feet for every two forward he gave up and maneuvered uphill in a sidestep plodding that was tiresome and much slower than Sanders' turkey trot.

"The worst is behind us now," Sanders said, moving on. He was right and, despite a few ups and downs, the going had become easier. That was fortunate since the sun, which had warmed them now and then throughout most of the day, was completely covered with clouds and the wind bit through their clothes.

Finally, as they topped a rise, they could see wisps of smoke from the chimneys of Schofield being blown parallel to the ground by the wind. Will began to feel better.

He was a full one hundred yards behind Sanders who leaned his skis against the wall of Tracey's boarding house and went inside. She was on the porch when Will got there. She stood with a shawl over her head and watched silently as he struggled up to the building and the two of them looked at each other for a moment.

"Get those boards off and come inside." She went to the door and turned. "You look terrible." Her eyes told him differently, though, and they both laughed out loud. It was good to see her. It was like coming home and Will didn't for a moment think of home as the house he shared with Abby.

Tracey wore a bulky dark green sweater and heavy black skirt. Beneath the clothes, though, he could tell she was thin. New lines creased her face and there might have been a harder look about her, one of fierce determination that kept her face in an almost perpetual frown.

That night Jacob played at Will's feet. The boy had not left his side since his arrival. "I've been telling him about you all winter," Tracey said. "He knew you would be here in the spring and he's been watching for weeks now."

Will watched the boy and thought he saw a resemblance to himself in the two-year-old face and dark hair. "He doesn't know about . . . ?"

"No, of course not." They whispered to one another as Sanders dozed a few feet away.

Will reached down and touched the boy on his shoulder. "Come up here," he said. Jacob's eyes brightened as he climbed into Will's lap where he stayed all evening until he fell asleep.

The last winter storm passed quickly, the winds shifted to the south, and sunshine began to melt the snow. It lay six to ten feet high around the buildings of Schofield and drifts piled twice that high.

Within two days of their arrival Sanders had set out for Crested Butte with a wild look of anticipation on his face. For a week Will stayed close to the boarding house. Jacob followed him everywhere, watching Will's every move and trying to imitate him, even to his walk.

"He'll be bowlegged before he even gets on a horse," Tracey said one day.

"Bowlegged? I'm not bowlegged!" *Ardy was bowlegged*, Will thought.

Tracey studied his long legs. "Oh, no?"

"Well, I'll be damned." And they both laughed. It was good to laugh. *God, it was good to laugh with a woman*, Will thought. *And mean it.*

Two nights later Will stood at the second floor window of his room and watched four men ride slowly into town from the south. One of them was obviously Nathan Peabody. He mused to himself that the pass to Crested Butte would be open wide enough now for horses, and maybe even a wagon, to make it through. Sanders would return soon, then. He watched the riders stop at Peabody's saloon and go inside.

112

The next evening Will felt he had been cooped up in the boarding house too long and wandered to Peabody's for a drink. Peabody wasn't in the bar when Will arrived. Several miners were, though, and they were restless, anxious to get to their still snowbound claims.

They were talking about the price of silver, which had fluctuated wildly the past two years but which was now at an all-time high. "But there ain't no guarantee it'll last," one man said. "Better get your ore out quick as you can."

Will also learned there was to be an assay office in Schofield. "Who's setting it up?" he asked. He winced when he was told Peabody was behind it. Even having an assay office close by would do him little good. He was sure he couldn't depend on an honest report from Peabody, or from anyone who worked for him. Will said so to a miner standing near him.

"Still trying to make trouble for me, Martin?" Peabody leaned against the doorjamb puffing on a cigar. He was much heavier than the previous fall. His face was an unhealthy, pasty color and long muttonchops reached to below his jaw.

"No more than usual," Will said, facing Peabody and resting his elbows back on the bar.

"The usual is plenty." Peabody waddled to Will's side, swinging his legs in long strides as his great girth swayed from side to side. He moved in close to Will and blew smoke in his face. "How's your kid?"

Will frowned. "She's fine."

Peabody exposed yellow teeth in a tight smile. "That's not the one I mean."

Will ignored the remark, turned to the bar and signaled for another drink. "Where you been all winter?"

The miners, tensed for a confrontation, visibly relaxed. "Here and there," Peabody said. "Got married."

"Congratulations to you," Will said, "and condolences to the bride."

"No need to be unfriendly, is there? You and I might as well get along, especially since we're neighbors."

Peabody smiled broadly when Will turned to him with a frown.

"I filed a claim next to the Princess Evaline. I suspect we'll be seeing a lot of each other."

Two men noisily entered the room, one obviously quite drunk and leaning on the other, a larger man who supported his companion. They made their way to the back of the room and sat at a table where the drunk lay his head on the tabletop, his tall Texas hat still on.

"You've got a right to file where you want," Will said. "Those two friends of yours?"

"They work for me. Brought them up from Taos to help me out a bit. I also brought in a competent assayer."

"Convenient," Will replied. There was something strangely familiar about the man whose head still rested on his arms. "They got names?"

"Assayer's name is Gordon Potts. Those two back there are Charley and Tom. I suppose they have last names but I don't remember."

Will stared at the tall Texas hat with the faded star on the side. Without a word to Peabody he left the bar and walked towards the pair at the table. The big man leaned back in his chair and watched him come. He had a week's growth of beard speckled with tobacco juice which also stained the front of his shirt. A Colt .45 rested in a holster tied down low on his right leg.

"This is Charley." Peabody was beside Will. "Good man with a gun, I hear."

Will matched Charley's stare. "What's the matter with your friend?" He nodded toward the sleeping man.

"Don't handle his likker too good, I reckon." His voice was coarse, not unfriendly. He didn't smile.

"Something familiar about him."

Charley kicked the sleeping man in the leg beneath the table. "Wake up!" he ordered.

The man whose name Peabody said was Tom started, jerked up and caused his hat to fall to the floor. Long, dirty hair fell past his shoulders and into his eyes. A mustache with long ends disappeared into an unshaven face. His cheeks were hollow and his eyes — what Will could see of them — were dull and yellowed. But there was no mistake. It was Sagebrush Tom from the Palo Duro, looking ten years older.

"Know him?" Peabody asked.

Tom had closed his eyes again and lowered his head. "Must have been thinking of somebody else," Will said.

He turned and went back to the bar, stood there a moment, waved off the bartender and walked out of the saloon. He wandered up and down the street in the cold of the evening for a while and then went back to the boarding house where he couldn't eat the dinner Tracey placed before him.

Instead, he remembered Sagebrush Tom speaking to him for the first time back in '65 or so. "We usually run strangers off the first thing," he had said when Will had wandered onto the rangeland north of Waco and west of the Brazos. "But I got a feeling you ain't no rustler."

Will had stared in awe at the first real cowboy he'd ever met and decided this Sagebrush person was the most impressive man he'd probably ever see.

Sagebrush Tom wore a tall high-crowned hat that almost hid the clean-shaven face that was brown from the eyes down to the red bandanna hung loosely around his neck. The sleeves on his dark blue work shirt disappeared into leather gloves. A pair of enormous leather chaps covered his legs and most of his saddle. A coiled lariat hung from a loop near the fork but most impressive of all was the pistol in a large black holster slung from a cartridge belt around his waist.

Later, Sagebrush Tom helped outfit Will with a dead cowboy's clothes after Mr. Goodnight hired him and then taught him the cowboy trade. They'd been best friends until Will decided to head for California. Now, here they were and there was Tom dead drunk working for a cheat. Will couldn't figure it out, and maybe, he thought, shouldn't even try. But it was a blow and he didn't know what to do about it all anyway.

The next morning Will was at the top of the stairs when Peabody came calling. He stepped back out of sight and listened as the gambler repeated his previous year's offer to buy out Tracey's boarding house.

"Get out," she ordered, motioning toward the door.

"Very well." Peabody turned, walked to the door and stopped. He struck a match and, without looking back, said quietly but just loudly enough that Will could hear: "I don't want you in my town, Mrs. Collins. I'm afraid you're going to be quite unhappy here." He blew a cloud of smoke into the air and it drifted out of the room behind him as he left.

Tracey slammed the door behind him and saw Will as she turned back into the room.

"Thought you said you were going to sell out to him and move down to Crystal," Will said.

"I'll simply lock the door and walk away before I sell to him," she said. "He'll turn the place into a whorehouse and I couldn't bear that."

Two nights later Will awoke to the sound of a strong wind. For a while he listened to it howling past the window and tried to get back to sleep. Then he realized something other than the wind had awakened him. Something smelled strange. He got out of bed and shivered in the cold, then stood in the middle of the room and tried to identify the odor.

Suddenly, he pulled on his pants and boots. Buttoning his shirt, he ran down the hall toward Tracey's room.

"Get up!" he shouted, banging on the door. "Fire!" He moved quickly back down the hall, shouting to the other two boarders, ran into Jacob's room and pulled the boy from bed. Tracey was in the hall. "Get out of here!"

He saw her run back to her room as he started for the stairs. The smoke was thickening and he could barely see as he tried to pick his way down the stairs. A wall of flame blocked his way. The fire had opened a hole in the north wall and the strong wind was feeding the flames.

With Jacob in his arms crying loudly now, he ran back upstairs, meeting Tracey and the two others. "Follow me!" A lean-to jutted out from the back of the building below Jacob's window. Will shoved the window open and climbed onto the sill, facing outward with Jacob on his lap. Without hesitating, he jumped and landed hard on the lean-to roof. He quickly leapt from there to the ground, then placed Jacob against a building next door and told him to stay put, hoping he would.

Tracey was about to jump from the window. Will stepped on a barrel and pulled himself onto the roof, and when Tracey jumped he helped break her fall. "Jacob's over there," he told her. He indicated the edge of the roof and then held her as she stepped toward it. He saw her jump, hit and roll. Then she was on her feet and running toward Jacob, who sat crying where Will had left him.

The other two boarders were on the roof and Will told them to get to the ground. They did so quickly. Will pulled himself up to Jacob's window and hauled himself inside. He threw some of the boy's clothes out the window, then ran to Tracey's room and gathered up an armload of clothes. Back in his own room, he grabbed his hat and jammed it on his head. He found his gun belt and his saddlebags. The smoke was thick in the hall and flames flew in his face. Ignoring them, he went back to Tracey's room, found a heavy coat, then saw the faded blue robe he remembered so well. He threw it over his shoulder and started back into the hallway. The way was blocked with smoke and flames.

The rest of the building was ablaze. The wind was howling and the fire was a roar. Outside, he thought he could hear voices. His shirt was full of blackened holes as cinders caught and burned.

Without thinking about it, he gathered the bundle of clothing in front of his face, ran toward Tracey's window and hurled himself through it and into space.

His arms stung as he floated free. Then he was buried in a snowdrift. He fought to work his way free, still holding the clothing. He got to his feet, struggled out of the drift and walked to the back of the building.

Tracey was standing away from the fire holding Jacob. She sobbed when Will reached her, then looked at his arms. "You're bleeding," she said.

Window glass had cut his forearms but nothing else. He realized he still clutched the bundle of clothes and his saddlebags. "Put them down," Tracey ordered. He dropped the bundle and watched as the fire quickly consumed the building and everything within it. A few men had tried to organize a bucket brigade but the fire spread too quickly and the wind removed any chance of saving anything. The firefighters moved to the building to the south and were dousing it with water in the hope that the fire would not spread.

Tracey was tearing the old robe into strips which she wrapped around Will's cuts. "What are you doing?" he asked. "Don't do that."

116

"It doesn't matter," she said.

"Yes, it does. I loved that robe."

She looked at it, then back at Will, and she understood.

"It's too late," she said. "It's too late for anything." And then, finally, she broke down and cried while he held her and saw the building collapse into a heap of burning timbers and smoldering ashes.

A WEEK LATER, after three straight days of sunshine, and clouds moving north ahead of a warm breeze, Will decided he could safely take Tracey and Jacob over the rugged trail to Crystal City.

One of the local miners had given Tracey the loan of his shack while Will slept on another miner's floor for a few days. It was just long enough to allow the cuts on his arms to heal.

The day was blustery and the wind still had a bite of winter's chill. An occasional spot of sunshine was encouraging, though, and both Will and Tracey were anxious to leave. She had finally agreed to let Will construct a new boarding house in Crystal. Will would be a partner in a business venture with Tracey, as he was with Sanders and Ardy.

They would have to walk to Crystal City. The snow would still be too deep for horses and there was no wagon road.

Will carried a heavy pack and four long skis. Tracey strapped a lighter pack to her back, tucked her long skirt up between her legs and gamely set out. They alternated carrying Jacob, who squirmed in eager anticipation of the adventure.

Only once before they reached the treacherous Punch Bowl area did they have to use the skis. Tracey mastered the clumsy boards easily and laughed as she slid downhill for fifty yards or more at one point.

There was little water going over the falls as the three rested at the top studying the snow-covered trail that snaked down the west edge of the steep canyon wall. The strong winds of the past few days had obscured any signs of recent travelers.

"We'll take it slowly," Will said. "I'll take Jacob and you follow exactly in my tracks." Because of their inexperience on skis, they would make the descent on foot. With the first few steps he knew it was going to be extremely difficult. He sank first to his knees and then even deeper. Finally, he used one of the skis to pack the snow ahead of him, stepping carefully into each hole, testing his weight and then tamping some more.

They were halfway down when he felt the snow move beneath him. He carried Jacob in his left arm and tamped with the ski with his right. He

117

stopped and stood stock still. "What's wrong?" Tracey called.

Gingerly, he poked at the snow ahead with the butt end of the ski. It seemed stable. "Nothing, I guess." But, as he shifted his weight, the side of the trail gave way with hardly a sound. Tracey could only watch helplessly as Will and Jacob tumbled down the steep embankment. Will dropped the ski and flailed his free arm, trying to find something to grab ahold of while he clutched Jacob. He fell forty feet and then stopped, half buried in snow. He seemed to be unhurt but Jacob was crying loudly with what Will hoped was only fright. But the boy was shouting now, crying and screaming, and there was something in the sound that told Will it was more than fear.

Jacob suddenly stopped crying. When Will realized the boy's right leg was bent unnaturally sideways at the knee, pointing inward toward his other leg, it became clear he had passed out from the pain.

Tracey shouted at Will from above. He waved at her to show that he, at least, was unhurt. "Stay where you are!" he called. But Tracey threw her pack down toward Will and began skidding on her backside down the slide area.

Once she hit a rock and rolled several yards, then righted herself and came to a stop twenty feet above them. She scrambled through the deep snow on hands and knees until she reached them.

"It's his leg," Will said. He squirmed around and flattened out the snow so he could free his arm from the boy. The bent leg was grotesque in its odd shape. Will pulled a knife from his belt and slit the child's pants leg. The snow beneath him reddened with blood and Tracey gasped as they saw bone protruding from just below the knee.

"Oh, my God! my God!" Tracey's face paled and Will thought for a moment that she, too, would faint. But she pulled herself together and was rummaging in the pack which she had dragged to her side. Will was in a state of shock and could only sit and stare at the little leg.

Tracey pulled a skirt from her pack and tried to tear it. Will shook his head and took the skirt from her, slit it with his knife and tore several long strips which he used to dab at the bleeding. Tracey was thinking more clearly than Will.

"Quickly," she said. "We've got to make some kind of tourniquet." She took the knife and used it to loop into the strip of skirt and twisted it above the knee. The bleeding seemed to slow.

Will's head was beginning to clear. "We've got to reset the bone, Tracey."

"My God, Will. Can you do that? Have you ever?"

"No, but I saw it done once in Texas."

Mercifully, Jacob was still unconscious. Will grasped the tiny leg, one hand above and one below the knee. His fingers went completely around and

118

he hesitated.

"Do it," Tracey said. "Do it."

The bone moved, re-entered the flesh, made a scraping noise and clicked more or less into place. The little body lay still and now the only sound was Tracey sobbing and Will breathing heavily.

"A splint. We've got to make a splint," she said.

Will looked about him. There was no timber near them; any driftwood was buried beneath the snow. He saw the heavy ski and grabbed it. The board was thick, tough. He would never know how he did it but he lifted the ski high over his head and brought it crashing down on his own knee. It splintered but didn't break. He did it again. And again. Finally, he had two ragged pieces of wood each a foot long. He placed one piece on each side of the small leg and wrapped them tightly together with more strips of cloth.

Will was exhausted and his own knee was hurting from the bashing it had taken as he broke the ski. He lay back in the snow, looked at clouds rushing overhead. He closed his eyes and silently cursed himself for attempting this foolhardy trip.

"Get up," Tracey demanded. She stared at him with a burning intensity, hands on hips. "Get up! We've got to get him somewhere. Out of the snow. To a doctor!"

Somehow he was on his feet, Jacob in his arms, splintered leg cradled as best he could. Two hundred yards down the hill was a windblown spot almost barren of snow. If he could get there. . . He staggered forward, realized the pack was still on his back. One step. Two. Another. The canyon stretched ahead, twisted and turned, rose and fell. "Move." Tracey prodded him from behind. Another step and hundreds more through snow and over rocks and around trees and across snowbridges. Pick up one foot and move it ahead. Don't think about the aching knee or the weary arms that carried a small life. Take one step and then another. Stumble but don't fall. Listen to the woman panting behind you and know, for her and for the child, you've got to keep moving. Uphill forever, feet sinking in wet snow, catching on downed tree limbs and stubbing on rocks. Downhill, now, over rocky ground that is muddy with melting snow. Wind in your face and tears in your eyes but it can't be much farther.

"Move," she says, and you do, slowly and painfully. Hours at a time. Never stopping. Plodding with the wind, praying the day won't end with you still in the wilderness.

"There," she says. "Ahead." And it is there. The town with buildings and smoke from chimneys. But it's still so far. Downhill through bending pine trees moaning with the wind. Stumbling and almost falling but scrambling ahead to catch your balance and your body hurting all over except in the feet

119

which you can't feel.

"Move." And you move and keep moving and then you're there and somebody is taking the child from you and men are hurrying here and there and then it's warm, so warm you can't stand it and your feet and toes begin to hurt like the rest of your body and you're all alone standing in a room with your eyes smarting from the kerosene lamps and you can't breathe and crumple to the floor and lay there until somebody helps you to a bed and you don't know anything else for a long time.

BY JUNE it was hot in the lower valley but Will had no trouble recalling the numbing coldness of only a few weeks before. The cuts on his forearms were now nothing more than continually itching scabs. He had received a touch of frostbite in his toes but the long, draining trek had done no other harm. Like Will, Tracey had suffered from slight frostbite but she had made that final, unrelenting dash to Crystal on little more than gritty determination. Will was on his feet the next day but Tracey had taken most of a week to recover.

A man who called himself a doctor had been able to do nothing for Jacob beyond providing some painkiller that kept the boy drugged and asleep. He did say that, while Will had reset the broken bone poorly, the child would keep the leg and no doubt would walk again. Tracey had stayed at Jacob's side constantly, her own bed moved next to his.

During the days of their convalescence Will had bought a building lot and made arrangements for the sawmill to provide lumber. He also hired three men who promised that as soon as the snow had melted enough they would begin construction of Tracey's new boarding house.

Together, Will and Tracey had drawn plans for the building. It would be much like the one in Schofield but somewhat larger. Tracey and Jacob would have three large rooms on the ground floor. Two would be bedrooms and the third a sitting room. Upstairs would be eight individual rooms and a larger one which would accommodate eight men in bunk beds. A large dining room would front the building and a kitchen would separate Tracey's apartment from the rest.

In mid-June Will left Tracey and his son and went back down valley to the Double M. He didn't want to go.

"COULDN'T GET her to come back, huh?"
Ardy had greeted Will at the front door of the ranch house when he

returned from his first trip to Aspen after the fire and the recuperation. Abby had stated her intention of staying in Aspen throughout the summer and Will hadn't put up much of an argument, figuring he would be spending a great deal of time in Crystal anyway.

Will had told Ardy the whole story, even confiding in him that he and Tracey had a son. Now, the two men sat on the bank of Rock Creek at the end of a long day. Ardy fingered a fishing pole and halfheartedly flicked a hand-tied fly toward a hole on the far bank where the rushing water eddied back and gentled.

"So what happens now?"

"I'll go back to Crystal in a few days and find out, I guess," Will replied without much enthusiasm.

"Damn!" Ardy flipped the fly out of the water and reeled it in. "Almost had one. What about the ranch?"

He could have said "What about *me?*" but that wouldn't have been like Ardy. It was what he meant, though, Will knew.

"Been thinking about that. We've got to hire some help."

Ardy tossed the pole to the ground and sat beside Will, pulled the makings from his vest and began the laborious task of rolling a smoke. "They got to know horses." He licked and lit, then blew smoke and passed it to Will.

"I 'spect some of 'em do." They sat a while.

"Rock Creek sure is an unnatural name for a river like this, ain't it?" Ardy had said it before. "Must be a couple hundred Rock Creeks in the country."

"I 'spect," Will said. They watched the water churn and boil a while. Pretty soon it got dark and they went back to the house.

UP IN CRYSTAL, Sanders had a fifty-jack team ready to haul some ore. He had bought a small two-room shack and had his wife and two children finally with him again. He was a happy man. He and Will sat in twilight on the stoop in front of the house. Tracey and Jacob had put up at what passed for a hotel while she directed the building of her boarding house. In another week or two it would be completed.

"Man from the Catalpa Mine told me they sent out over a hundred jacks yesterday," Sanders said. "Guess their ore looks pretty good."

"How many mines are there around here now?" Will asked.

"No telling. Maybe hundreds, counting every hole a man spades into a mountain. Maybe ten big ones, plus ours. 'Sides the Catalpa there's the Belle of Titusville, Eureka, Jack Whacker, the Inez, the Bear Mountain and the Daisy."

"That doesn't count the really big ones," Will said, making conversation while he thought about Tracey and Abby and Ardy and the new man they'd hired.

"There's three that are top producers," Sanders went on. "The Lead King, up in Lead King Basin, might be the biggest. But the Black Queen and Sheep Mountain Tunnel are close."

"Who's that coming?" Will nodded toward a solitary figure, silhouetted against the darkening sky, who was making his way slowly toward them. "Know him?"

"Don't think so."

The man stopped twenty feet away and shuffled his feet. By then Will had recognized the lean figure of Sagebrush Tom.

"That you, Will?" The voice was shy, unlike the Tom of the Brazos and the Palo Duro.

"It's me."

Tom stood where he had stopped. "Care to talk a while?"

Sanders glanced at Will. "Friend of yours?"

"From Texas."

"Well, I'll go see the missus a while," Sanders said as the two of them stood.

"See you," Will said. He walked slowly to Tom and the two men stood a few feet apart and looked at each other. *This isn't the way it ought to be*, Will thought. *Ought to be some sort of happy and glad with this meeting.*

"Guess you saw me with Peabody," Tom said.

Will didn't reply. Long greasy hair hung out of Tom's hat and covered a filthy shirt collar. Even in the last light of day Will could see a sorrow in his eyes. His clothes hung on him like they were made for a bigger man. At least he wasn't drunk, Will mused.

"I quit him," Tom said. "Just the other day, after I heard some of the locals talking about you."

"So?"

Tom took a deep breath. "Look, Will. I been mostly drunk since we got to Schofield and never heard your name 'til somebody told me about you and how you told Peabody where to put his money a year or so ago."

Will started walking toward the hotel and Tom followed along behind, talking. "I thought you were in California. How was I supposed to know you were right here all the time?"

California seemed like a dream Will had had once and then forgotten before he woke up.

"I started out for there myself," Tom said, talking faster. "Only got as far as Taos and some tinhorn took every dime I had in a poker game. Hung around there for a while trying to make some money. Thought about going back to the Palo Duro but, hell, I couldn't face the boys. So I just got drunk and stayed that way 'til Peabody told me he'd pay me good wages to be a bodyguard."

They were at the hotel. "Want a drink?" Will asked. Tom bowed his head. "Oh, hell, Will. I ain't had a drink since I found it was you we burned out," he said, trailing off sheepishly.

Will stiffened. "You set that fire?"

"Me'n Charley. Wait, Will. Hear me out." Will had turned and started into the hotel but stopped as Tom took his arm. "I was so drunk I didn't know what I was doing. Charley said to bring some kerosene and follow him, so I did. Now I'm sorry as I ever been for anything in my life."

"So Peabody was behind it," Will said. "I suspected it but there was no way to prove it."

Tom let go of Will's arm. "We had it good with Mr. Goodnight, didn't we? Maybe we should have stayed put."

Will looked at his old friend, the man who had taught him so much about horses and ranching, but also about friendship and trust. "Maybe so," he said. "But things change. And hardly nothing works out like you plan."

Tom stared back. "I came to say I'm sorry. Now I've said it. Reckon I'll head on out. Maybe I'll get to California yet." He nodded to Will and turned. "See you," he said quietly.

Will watched the slim, bent form walk out into the street, then called to him. "Tom?"

Sagebrush Tom stopped, didn't turn around. "Come back here, Tom."

Will's best friend ever, except maybe for Ardy, turned in the street and walked slowly back to him.

Will Martin, rancher, father, mine owner, friend, knew he couldn't let a good man go back to a bottle and a life with nothing good in it. So he wrapped his arms around Sagebrush Tom and hugged him like he'd wanted to do since he saw him first in Peabody's saloon. Will hugged Tom to his chest and felt the skin and bones of a sick man, felt him go slack and then got hugged back and the two grown men stood in a dark street hugging each other and trying not to cry.

TOM WENT to work with Sanders in the Princess Evaline for base wages and Tracey insisted that he become one of her boarders so she could "keep an eye on him."

Jacob's break was a bad one. It would heal and the boy would walk but everyone who saw the leg could tell it was set poorly. He would probably walk with a limp the rest of his life.

Peabody's crew started work on a claim next to Will's but the gambler didn't show up.

Abby, true to her word, stayed put in Aspen with Evey and Will saw them now and then when he could.

The summer of 1883 went that way. Will and Ardy worked the ranch with a hired man named Parker Woodward they found in Crystal. "Rather be workin' with animals than rocks," Will heard him say one night at dinner and gave him the chance. He and Ardy got along well.

At the mine the ore was good and each week they shipped out as much as possible on a train of fifty to one hundred mules. Sanders had become one of the happiest people Will had ever known. He worked hard, from first light until long after dark. They had increased their mining crew to eight men, including Tom, and Sanders worked longer and harder than any of them — except for Sagebrush Tom, who stayed with the mining engineer every minute he could.

"You don't have to put in those hours," Will told him. Tom shook his head. "Reckon I owe you," he said. "'Sides, it's good for me." He flexed a muscle and grinned.

In Aspen Will met a man named Jerome B. Wheeler, who was not the B. Clark Wheeler he already knew. This Wheeler was the founder of the R. H. Macy & Company of New York. The man who many called a "merchant prince" had come to Colorado to "take the waters at Manitou Springs."

When Henry Gillespie heard Wheeler was in the state he hurried off to meet the great man. He persuaded Wheeler to come to Aspen and spend a few days in Gillespie's new $35,000 home on Hallam Street. "I built it with my first real profits from the Spar," Gillespie told everyone.

It didn't take Gillespie long to convince Wheeler of Aspen's promise, and the New Yorker immediately bought A. D. Breed's interest in the Spar for $75,000. He also invested in other mines and began plans to build a smelter.

"He's a *wonderful* man," Abby told Will. "And he's so *rich!*"

She had actually seemed happy to see Will when he rode into town in late July, hot and sweating and feeling less than excited about seeing her. He was looking forward to seeing Evey, however. Over the summer he'd begun to realize his attachment to the dark-haired little beauty. The long, silent winter he had spent cooped up with a woman who evidently cared little for him had taken its toll on his marriage and his relationship with his daughter. Now, with Evey gone, he found a strange void in his life. Now and then, he filled that void with Jacob.

124

Abby had pecked him on the cheek and hovered around him, helping him move into her bedroom, asking how things were.

"Good," he told her. "Real good."

She hadn't asked for details, but had quickly launched into a description of her own summer. "Things are simply *wonderful* here," she said, talking excitedly. "We've had *concerts* and *parties* and *dinners* and you simply *must* see my new Denver gown."

"Who's this Wheeler?" Will asked when he could get in a word.

Abby told him all she knew about the man. "Mr. Wheeler and my Uncle Henry are going to make Aspen the most wonderful town in the state."

If he was surprised at the reception Abby gave him, Will was absolutely astonished at her eagerness to get him to bed. Soon after dinner that evening, she began talking about turning in. She claimed all the excitement had tired her.

In their bedroom, after they had both checked on Evey and had been assured by the nanny that the child was asleep, Will picked up a book from the bedside table. "Still keeping up with the latest literature, I see," he said. It was *Life on the Mississippi* by Mark Twain.

Abby took the book from Will and placed it beside another called *Treasure Island*. Will was trying to get a better look at it but Abby was working at his clothes. She pressed against him, rubbing her breasts against his chest, then backing off and unbuttoning his shirt. "It's been a long time, Will," she said. "Hurry!"

Will, who had anticipated a less than harmonious meeting and, certainly no lovemaking, hurried.

Abby clung to him, cried out, bit, clawed.

Well, I'll be damned, he thought. In the middle of the night when both were exhausted, Abby turned on her side away from him. "That's the best thing about being married," she said. She was quickly asleep and Will couldn't help shaking his head.

The next day, though, Abby was busy preparing for a tea she was to host that afternoon and she ignored Will. They made love again that night, but only briefly, and not again for the three additional nights he stayed.

When he left to head back to the Double M, Abby seemed relieved to see him go. *Guess that's all she needed*, he thought sadly.

THE VALLEY was becoming more and more populous. Little ranches were springing up wherever there was a meadow big enough for a pasture or a halfway level tree-covered area that could be cleared.

Across Rock Creek to the west and just downstream from Avalanche Creek, Will heard the sound of an ax and turned off the trail to investigate. He found a large, bald Swede from Illinois clearing land for a house he would build from the trees he cut. His name was Daniel Swensson. "The missus" and two kids were coming over from Denver soon, he said.

"You're getting up pretty high here," Will said apprehensively, looking with some concern at the steep mountain wall that backed the man's property.

"Mebbe so. Mighty purty spot, though."

Just to the south the valley narrowed quickly into what men had begun to call Dark Canyon. The valley opened out again where the meadow fell down to the hot springs. Will told Swensson about it. "That seems a likelier spot for a ranch," he said.

"You got that right for sure, for sure," Swensson said. "I wanted it, I did. But it seems a man named Peabody already owns it. You know this Peabody?"

"I know him." So Peabody was buying up land in the valley. It was the first Will had heard of it.

"He wanted to buy my land, too, he did. Had to ask him to leave when he wouldn't take no for an answer. I think he also threatened me and it made me mad. Yes, it did."

"What kind of threat?" Will asked gathering his reins.

"Some kind of frapdoodle about a curse on the valley and that somethin' bad would no doubt happen to me'n the missus. You know something about this curse?"

Will rubbed the stock of his rifle where it protruded from its case and told Swensson the story. "But I wouldn't let it bother me," he concluded.

Will climbed aboard his horse, this one named Nehemiah. He couldn't seem to get away from Biblical names. It was about as close as he got to the Book these days, he reminded himself.

Swensson stood beside him. "Strangest thing I heard two nights past. A howling. A singing sound that made the chills run up my back. What kind of beast makes that sound in these great mountains?"

So the strange keening had returned, Will thought. "Probably just the wind, friend," he said. "Nothing to worry about."

Farther up the valley, almost to the westward-running canyon where J. C. Osgood had bought the coal claims a year earlier, Will brought Nehemiah to a halt. He dismounted and studied the red cliffs to the east.

He sat on his haunches while the horse ripped at some grass, and he stared at the red outcropping of rocks that he and Osgood had remarked about. He decided suddenly that it was important for him to climb to that high point. A voice in his ears seemed to say go. Or did it say come? He felt a strong need,

126

as though there was nothing else so important in his life but that he climb to the red cliffs.

He looked at the sun. It was not yet directly overhead and he had plenty of time. No one was expecting him at Crystal and he carried the essentials for an extra camp.

Within fifteen minutes Will knew it was going to be a tougher climb than it looked. It was steep and rocky. He skirted a deadfall and, slipping in the scree, traversed back and forth through an aspen grove, then through spruce and pine and lots of scrub. Once, finding his way blocked by a ravine maybe twenty feet deep, he had to backtrack and sidestep over a slanting rock bed that was covered with boulders and a loose kind of shale.

"These boots ain't worth a hoot for climbin'," he muttered aloud. The sound startled him. He had been so intent on the climb he hadn't realized how quiet it had become. The sound of the river far below was blocked by the dense trees and there was little breeze. He stopped and listened, hearing nothing but the rush of almost total silence in his ears. It was a new sensation. Even on the Palo Duro or the Llano Estacado there had been sound — always sound. Wind, cows and cowboys. But here there was nothing and, for a moment, it unnerved him.

"Hello!" he called. The sound of his voice seemed to stop a short foot out of his mouth and there was no echo, no answering call, not even the flutter of a bird's wing. He coughed just to hear the sound, then spat on the ground and scuffed his feet. Finally, a breeze quaked the aspen and the rustle was comforting. He resumed his climb.

He found the rocky outlook was not quite flat when he finally stepped over the last of the rimrock and out onto the point that sloped upwards toward more mountain. A few scraggly pines and spruce grew determinedly out of the red rocks. A small aspen grove marked the south edge of the cliff.

He had kept his eyes on the ground, watching his step on the loose rocks. He raised them, finally, to a sight that was so unexpected, so totally unrelated to anything he had experienced before, that he shut his eyes, opened them again and sat down hard on a rock that was so comfortable it might have been put there just for him. The valley of Rock Creek spread out before him with a glory he found almost unnatural, almost as unnatural as the total silence that once again engulfed him.

For long moments he sat there unmoving, trying to absorb the absolute grandeur of what he saw.

To the north the valley greened up to Dark Canyon and butted into what appeared to be solid mountain. A gray wire of river slithered into view here and there, throwing sparkles of sunlight like reflected crystals before his eyes. Above what was being called Elephant Mountain, because some thought they

127

could see a humped back and a trunk, the long horizontal line of the flattops almost melted into the haze above Yampah Springs. Aspen, pine, spruce, cottonwood and scrub melded with the red stone on the mountainsides and silver peaks fringed with snow into a soft crazy quilt. The sun bore down out of a sky softened with puffs of white and reflected off the whiter snow that topped Mount Sopris.

He swung his eyes to the west. Almost directly across from him was the swiftly rising canyon of Osgood's coal. Farther south a sheer red cliff marked another narrowing of the valley which then climbed upward to the base of Chair Mountain. Tons of snow in its deep bowl bounced the sun into his eyes, and they began to water. Snowcapped peaks ranged east and south and he knew they sheltered Marble and Crystal City and Tracey and Jacob, too.

This valley, he decided, this veritable Eden hidden away in a rugged wilderness that dwarfed men and made their dreams seem insignificant — this valley was where he belonged. *Let other men have their Aspens and their Denvers and yes, even their Californias*, he thought. *Let them have their dreams of wealth and glory*. If he drew nothing from this place but this simple moment of awe, that was enough.

He sat there for most of the afternoon as a lowering sun pushed long shadows toward him.

Was there a sound behind him? He turned quickly but saw nothing. Until this moment he had been comfortable and content in his solitude. Now, though, a chilling feeling of unease crept over him, a disturbing sense of another presence. He felt eyes on him. He thought he heard a sound like the distant drumming of a thousand hummingbird wings. The sound rose and fell, seemed now nearby, then far away. He rose, touched the pistol at his side, and looked around him. There was no one, nothing there, and yet he was not alone. It was as clear a fact as he had ever been sure of, and he waited for the man, or the animal, to emerge.

Gradually the sound faded away and as he turned back to the west, in the corner of his eye he caught the shape of an owl as it glided silently across an opening in the trees to his left. As quickly as he thought he saw it, it was gone.

Suddenly, for no apparent reason, the sense of unease he had felt so strongly left him and he felt again comfortable in his surroundings. He shook it off and blamed it on the strange silence of the place. *Gettin' spooky in your old age*, he told himself.

At the back of the shelf he found the remains of a small fire. It saddened him somehow to think that another person had been there before him. *That's the way it is in this country, though*, he thought. *Somebody's always there first*. He wondered only for a swift moment who might have built the fire. He took a final, quick look out over the vast sweep of valley before him and then went on down to his horse and camped by the river. Just before dark he thought he heard an eagle scream somewhere up towards the point and, later, again saw the ghostly shape of an owl as it glided silently overhead in the last of the deepening twilight.

৵৵৽

IN OCTOBER Ardy discovered that many of their horses were developing hoof rot. This was the last thing Will needed, what with all of the trouble with Abby, the constant potential of a run-in with Peabody, and Tracey treating him more like a business partner and less like the father of her child. Hoof rot could cripple his entire herd, a financial catastrophe from which he might not recover.

Ardy told him about a herd belonging to Kit Carson's stage line from Leadville to Aspen with similar problems. "They took 'em to Yampah Springs," he said. "Didn't take no time for the hot springs to cure 'em."

When the springs also cured the Double M herd, Will breathed a deep sigh of relief. He heard that one freighter, a William Farnum, lost a fortune in horseflesh after he scoffed at the idea of taking his herd to the springs.

"Well," Will said when they had the herd back home. "That's one good thing that's happened, at least."

"What are you so down about?" Ardy asked, straightening up from rubbing his foot. "We been makin' money, ain't we? Ain't I doin' just fine runnin' this place while you're off gallavantin' around somewhere?"

Will started to reply but Ardy cut him off. "I know you got your troubles, what with Abby and all. But, from what I hear, you're makin' profits on your mine and we made some money here this year, too."

"Well, I. . ."

"Now, just shut up your yap and hear me out," Ardy interrupted. Will shut up. "You come in here ever so often and mope around like a baby for a day or so then you're off somewhere else, out climbin' around the mountains, goin' over to Aspen, up to the mine or to some woman." He raised his hand when Will opened his mouth. "Oh, I know it ain't none of my business. You told me that often enough. But, by damn, you do go somewhere and me'n Parker run this place. I make all the decisions, knowin' that if I foul up and we go broke it'll be all my fault. You put the money in the ranch and you keep puttin' more in so you got a right to do what you want. All I'm sayin' is that I'm feelin' like I'm left with the short handle and I'm diggin' a deep hole. 'Sides that, I kinda like to get off this place now'n again myself. You know how long it's been since I been over to Aspen? Hell, ol' Amelia ain't even

129

gonna recognize me if I ever get there again. Now it's purt near winter and we'll be socked in here again for months. Listen, you ain't got it so bad, you know. Now I said my piece and I'm glad. Also, I'm tired and I'm goin' to bed."

Will sat there a while after Ardy left, then finally got up and blew out the lamp. He sat in the darkness and agreed with everything Ardy had said. Few men had the kind of life he did. He didn't really work. Now and then he'd help with the herding and the branding or help put up hay then put it out for the animals in the winter. Most of the time, though, he was on his way up or down the valley, now and then going to Aspen.

But it wasn't all so good. He lacked the love of a good woman. He'd gone most of his life without giving a thought to love. Now, in the past two years, he'd been in love with two different women. He still had some mighty strong feelings for one of them, but he wasn't married to her. He had all winter to think about it, he told himself.

It was snowing outside and within a month they'd be snowed in solidly. He'd have to make one more trip to Crystal. He was glad Sanders' wife and children were going to winter up there. Tracey would have some company. He thought briefly about Jacob but his mind shifted quickly back to Tracey. He was still thinking about her as he climbed into bed and tried to sleep.

The next afternoon it was still snowing when Abby showed up. She carried Evey into the house, shaking snow from their heavy coats. She barely said hello before asking Will and Ardy to please help the man she'd hired to drive her get their luggage.

Will carried the trunk into their bedroom and set it down softly as Abby put her finger to her lips. Evey lay curled up asleep in the middle of their bed.

"She's so tired," Abby said. "So am I."

"You back to stay or just visiting?" Will stared at his daughter and thought how like her mother she looked in sleep. Soft and beautiful.

"We'll see," Abby whispered. "Who is that man in Evey's room?" Will told her about Parker. "You've got to get him out of there," she said. "Evey can't sleep in here with us."

"Guess he can move in with Ardy," Will said. "Have to build another room."

Abby turned from her trunk with an armload of clothes. "Maybe you should wait a while for that."

"Wait?"

"Wait until spring. We'll see how things are then."

She dropped her eyes and went back to unpacking. "So it is just a visit, then," Will said.

"We'll see," she replied. "This place is a mess. Don't you men ever clean

130

up after yourselves?"

A few days later Will told Abby he was going to Crystal.

"Why?" she asked.

"Well, to check on things."

"Don't you *trust* that man to run things for you?" She stared at him, her arms crossed in front of her.

"It's business."

"I don't believe you. You just want to get *away*."

She was right. He had to trust Sanders and Tom. "All right," he said. "I'll wait until spring."

That night he told Ardy to take some time off and go to Aspen. "Might as well take Parker with you," he suggested.

"Like hell," Ardy answered. "He can go to Aspen if he wants, but not with me. That old man would just slow me down."

Will knew Ardy had a good ten years on Parker.

The next morning Ardy's eyes were bright as he set out for his reunion with his woman friend. "See you in a week or so," he called as he rode off.

That day Will sat by the river until three men rode by on their way upstream. They agreed to deliver a letter he had written to Sanders, and Will watched them enviously as they headed toward the mining town. Spring seemed a long way off.

The snows that had come early stayed late. Gray day followed gray day with only intermittent periods of weak sunlight that did little to lift spirits. By late November, Will was joining Ardy and Woodward in shoveling paths through the deepening snow to the barn and corrals. Clouds crowded the mountaintops and the summit of Mount Sopris was rarely visible.

The three men had constructed a lean-to on the back of the house and Parker spent his nights there. Evey had her own room, and Will and Abby slept together in their room and occasionally made love.

It's purely physical, Will thought. As they were drawn closer together physically by the constraints of the house and the fact that they simply couldn't get far from one another, they managed to distance themselves in other ways. Abby did the cooking and cleaning, cared for Evey and spent what time she could reading her books of fiction and poetry.

Will often left early in the morning. On days when it wasn't snowing, he stayed out all day hunting, working with the other two men, or wandering the riverbank looking to the south and thinking of Tracey and Jacob snowed in far away in the high country. He was silent around Abby, and curt to Ardy and Woodward.

To Evey, though, he was a hero. He carried her on his shoulders, teased her, patted her, tucked her into bed and caught his breath each time she called him "Daddy." The feelings he had for this child were unlike any he had felt before. The passionate stirrings induced by Tracey's mere presence were mosquito bites compared to the mule-kicks he felt in his stomach when he was with Evey.

Abby let the child's dark, thick hair grow long and Will ran his fingers through it and stroked her cheeks as he mumbled nonsense phrases in her two-year-old ears. Evey soaked up the attention, cuddled and hugged and kissed him on the nose. Always, she wore a mischievous smile that everyone but Will read as an adult-like understanding that she, not Will, was in charge. Evey was his winter light and his warm campfire in the dark night of Abby's indifference.

But Abby was not always indifferent. Frequently, throughout the winter, she would seem restless as she served the evening meal. Her eyes would be filled with a fire that was not reflected from the burning wood in the fire-place. Will soon learned what her uneasiness meant. On those nights all turned in early and Abby quickly urged Will to join her in bed.

Her desire surprised him. Her experiments excited him. Her demands drained him. Her love eluded him. They learned how to please one another but not to love. They clung together feverishly but seldom looked in each other's eyes as true lovers. They made love and, spent, slept back to back alone in the bed.

In the mornings there was no kiss of hello, no secret glances of affection, no sign that their couplings were more than primal yearnings satisfied and forgotten. Will grew a mustache which Evey adored and about which Abby said absolutely nothing. Abby made new clothes, anticipating another summer of society and culture in Aspen.

Ardy watched the two and said nothing.

Christmas came and went with some attempt at false enjoyment. The new year came and went with little notice.

Will shook his head and wondered about the ways of women.

In late January he made his way to Carbondale, which people used to call Satank, and learned that J. C. Osgood, the man he had led into the valley two summers ago, had formed the Colorado Fuel Company with authorized capital stock of $50,000. Osgood, it was said, controlled more than seven hundred acres of coal land, some of it in the canyon west of Rock Creek. He planned on becoming a coal and steel magnate of some great stature.

In March of that year — 1884 — Abby told Will she was again pregnant as they lay in bed beneath a heavy comforter.

Will was silent for a while. Then he asked, "When?" "Next fall. Perhaps September."

Again they lay silently for long moments. "Are you happy?" Will asked.

132

Abby took a deep breath. "I don't know," she whispered. Will could feel her body shift as she tightened herself into a tucked-up position, exposing as little of herself as possible to the bed, the world, the future.

After a while Will laid his hand on her hip. Pretty soon, she scooted farther away toward her edge of the bed and his hand fell to the sheet behind her. He let it lay there and then pulled it back to his chest and gripped both hands together, hard.

❧

ON THE FIRST day of May the sun rose hot and stayed that way as water dripped from melting snow on the rooftop. The river, which had trickled through narrow paths of open water all winter, began to show signs of reawakening. Horses kicked and trotted. Parker Woodward announced that he would stay through the summer but didn't know if he could take another winter like this last one.

Abby told Will that when fall came and after the baby had been safely delivered, she would move — not back to the ranch for the winter, but to her parents' home in Denver.

"I made a mistake, Will," she said. She did not say "we" made a mistake and Will understood her meaning. He had done right and had reached beyond himself and his due by marrying her. She, on the other hand, had made a "mistake" in lowering herself to his level.

"Are you telling me you're not coming back? Ever?"

"I see no reason to," she replied. "Do you?"

"No. I guess not."

She busied herself at the stove. "So, that's it, then."

"If you say so."

Abby turned to him. She was as beautiful as the day he had met her, barely four years before. She was still youthful, though more mature. Her body was lithe and, though starting to show her pregnancy, trim and straight.

"Are you *surprised*?" She wouldn't look him in the eyes, and fiddled with a button on her dress.

He avoided the question, asked another. "What about my children?"

"We'll work *something* out. I don't want any money from you. My father will handle the divorce."

The word hit him in the pit of the stomach like a .45 bullet. He felt his body start to go slack and fought to stand upright. *Divorce.* Their marriage of less than three years was a failure.

He forced himself to speak. "Whatever you want," he said and walked out the back door. He went to the corrals and then to the creek bank and then

133

down by the river. Pretty soon he felt cold, realized he had not put on a coat, and went back inside.

"What's for dinner?" he asked.

"Venison. Will you call the others and get Evey ready?"

WILL URGED Nehemiah on through the snowdrifts, feeling the excitement increase. He was within a couple of hours of Crystal and could soon tell Tracey the news.

He had quickly gotten over his initial shock at Abby's announcement, particularly so when he realized he was free to once again approach Tracey. The mother of his son was of hardier stuff than Abby. She understood what life in this valley meant. She had once loved him. He was sure she still did. She would welcome him and they would be together.

As much as he longed to see Tracey, he went first to the mine. It was his duty as an owner, after all.

A hard-packed road of dirty snow led him uphill and around bends to within fifty yards of the mine opening. He heard a gunshot, then another from farther away. He spurred Nehemiah, and the horse broke into a weary lope. He could see Sanders, Tom and two other men huddled behind a pile of tailings with rifles pointed downhill, toward Peabody's claim.

Will lifted his own rifle from its scabbard as he reined the horse and flung himself to the ground beside Sanders.

"Where'd you come from?" Sanders said as he glanced at Will.

A rifle shot exploded from downhill and a second later Will heard the pop as the bullet passed overhead. Tom raised up quickly and snapped off a shot that thudded into a snowbank below the shack outside Peabody's mine. A puff of smoke drifted upwards from a window.

Will levered a shell into the chamber, peeked over the top of the pile of rocks and didn't see any movement. "You been at each other all winter?"

"Just today." Sanders waved at the others. "Hold your fire and let's see if we can put a hold on this foolishness."

"Will somebody tell me what this is all about?"

"Howdy, Will!" Tom called. "You sure did come at a good time."

Sanders rolled over onto his back and rested his rifle across his chest. "Things went good all winter," he said. "Then, this morning, we heard picking and blasting on the far side of the mine shaft wall. On Peabody's side. They're coming right into our mine, Will, trying to get to the main vein. Hell, they're so far off their own claim it can't be accidental."

Tom crawled up beside them. "George went over to have a talk with

134

Charley about it and got a pistol in his stomach instead of a conversation."

"I came back and got Tom and the others," Sanders said. "Thought maybe we could have it out. We got this far and they started banging away at us. Then you rode up."

"We ought to let the law handle it," Will said.

Sanders snorted and Tom shook his head. "What law?" Sanders peered over the top of the pile. It was silent below. "There's no law out here. Gunnison, maybe."

"Let's call off this gunfight," Will said. He crouched on his knees and yelled loudly. "Hello down there!"

For a moment there was no answer and then the unmistakable, coarse voice of Charley rumbled up the hillside. "What you want?"

"Let's talk. This isn't solving anything!"

"You talk to Peabody! He's due in Crystal!"

"I will!" Will stood, exposing himself to Charley's crew. "Let's stop shooting before somebody gets hurt!"

Sanders stood beside Will and put his rifle butt on the ground. As he turned, with his side toward Peabody's mine, the sound of a shot rattled up from below and echoed off the mountain wall. Sanders grunted and fell to the ground like a heavy lump of ore. Will quickly, impulsively, raised his rifle, saw a body in the window below and fired. The man disappeared and Will joined Tom at Sanders' side. The engineer lay still, blood oozing from his back.

"Looks like it went in the left side and out the right," Tom said. "Don't think he's dead."

Sanders slowly opened his eyes. "What happened? Did that bastard shoot me?"

"In the back," Will said. "How do you feel?"

"Feel?" Sanders panted. "Feel? I can't feel anything. I can't feel my legs, Will."

"Lie still."

Sanders' eyes were wide. He still lay on his stomach, his hands clawing at the rocks. "I can't feel my legs. Can't feel anything below my waist."

Will knew he shouldn't be moved but they couldn't let him lay in the cold much longer. "We better get him inside the shack." The four men, bending low, lifted Sanders and carried him inside the porous building standing precariously on the side of the mountain. Inside were two cots, a desk and a stove. They laid Sanders on one of the cots and worked to stop the bleeding.

Sanders was awake, talking in fits and starts. "Oh, damn. Can't feel anything." He waved his arms. "My legs won't move, Will. Tom. What's wrong with me?"

135

One of the men by the door opened it wide. Will strode to the door and saw three riders running their horses downhill toward town.

"Just three of 'em?"

"I think there were four," Tom answered, squatting beside Sanders, holding the man's hand and staring wide-eyed at the still body.

"I think maybe I shot one of 'em," Will said.

"Hope to hell so." Tom stood. "Let's get him to town." The four men rigged a stretcher and took turns carrying Sanders' limp form down the trail the two miles to town. At the edge of Crystal City, Tom climbed on his horse and hurried on ahead to warn Sanders' wife. Martha Ann met them at the door and ushered them into the small building, pointing toward the bedroom.

She stood over her husband with tears in her eyes and turned to Will. "I knew something was going to happen," she said harshly. "This valley has been no good for anyone who's ever come here." Will took her in his arms and hugged her to him, saying nothing. There were no right words.

"It's the curse," Martha Ann said. "It's the damned curse."

Tracey came to the house within a few minutes of hearing the news and announced she would stay as long as necessary. She hugged Will and then shooed him and Tom back to the boarding house. "Just stay there," she ordered. "We'll let you know how he's doing and if we need anything."

Will and Tom followed orders and left. Will had forgotten the news that he had been aching to tell Tracey.

Peabody met them in the street. He was heavier than ever and, even in the cold, his face ran with sweat. He swaggered up to the two men, stopped a few paces away, forked a cheroot from his mouth with two fingers and left the other hand in his coat pocket.

"You murdered Charley," he said, pointing the smoldering cigar at Will.

"Did I?"

Peabody took two fat steps closer. He had a sneer on his face beneath the drooping mustache. "You're gonna hang."

Will stiffened. "Maybe you ought to go have a look at Sanders first. Jury'll see it as self-defense."

Peabody guffawed loudly, crudely, then spat in the street. "Who said anything about a jury?"

"You the law now?" Will automatically felt for his .45 and then remembered he'd not worn it for months.

"Don't need the law," Peabody said. "By the way, I've got some more bad news for you."

Will held the man's stare. "Speak your piece."

Peabody's fat stomach swelled larger as he drew on the cheroot. He blew smoke which drifted up in the calmness of the day. Long shadows crept past their feet and the last sunlight lighted up the fat man's piggish eyes.

"You're mining on my claim," he said.

Tom took a step forward. "You're a lying, cheating . . ." Will stopped him with a grip on his elbow. "Your claim?

I think you better go have a look at my filing. It appears to me you've got your directions all wrong."

"Not me," Peabody said. "I just came from Gunnison and your claim's a full forty yards west of where you think it is."

"Peabody," Will said softly. "You and me are about to have it out. If you've threatened or bribed somebody . . ."

Two forms stepped forward from the deep shadows of the building to Will's right.

Peabody canted his head toward them. "Couple of new hands," he said. "Care to meet them?"

TWO DAYS LATER the sheriff of Gunnison County showed up at the boarding house and asked for Will. He had a legal claim with him that did show Will's mine was too far east. The claim was signed in Sanders' handwriting.

"Look, Sheriff," Will said. "You know as well as I do that deed's been doctored. It's outright falsification."

The sheriff, a short man with a face broader than it was tall, shrugged. "I can't prove it. You can't prove it. Peabody's got you by the balls, Martin. Reckon you haven't got any choice."

Tom's face was red as he stood beside Will. "Somebody's gonna have to kill that bastard."

The sheriff's eyes opened wide. "Now, I was you I'd talk careful, son. I been hearin' talk of a shootin' up there."

Will quickly and calmly explained what had happened. The sheriff shook his head. "Tell you what. I'm willin' to forget about that little fracas if you'll just pack up your mining gear and move along. What do you say?"

Will looked down at the smaller man's face. "What if I say to hell with that?"

He responded with a shrug and a calm reply. "Then I'll just have to take you in and charge you with trespassin' and you won't see outside for a long, long time."

Will straightened, hitched up his pants and looked at Tom who stood stiffly with his fists balled up. "I'll think about it," he said.

"You do that. And if I don't hear otherwise, I'll assume you reached the right decision and moved out. Hope I don't see you again."

After he was gone, Will sat down, took off his hat and stared at the floor.

"What do you think?" Tom asked.

Will shook his head. "I think the fat bastard's got us this time. My copy of the deed went up in Tracey's boarding house fire."

❧❧

THAT NIGHT Will paced the floor while Tom sat silently toying with his food. Neither had said much since the encounter with the sheriff. Concern over Sanders, Peabody's threat, and finally, the evident loss of the Princess Evaline had sent both men into a long period of silence.

Pretty soon the wind picked up and whined through a poorly caulked north window. Will got up and stoked the fire. Tom carried his plate, still laden with food, back to the kitchen. The sound of a banjo followed the wind down the street and Will walked to the front window. He looked at the lights of the saloon Peabody had built last summer and was pulling on his coat when Tom walked back into the room.

"Goin' out?"

"For a while."

Tom watched him button up and put on his hat. "Me, too."

Will had his hand on the doorknob. "You best stay here," he said. He was halfway out the door when Tom spoke.

"Maybe you ought to let it sit for a day or so more."

"It won't be any different by then," Will said. He closed the door and stepped out onto the porch. The wind beat at him like it had something to prove. He pulled his hat down tighter and jammed his hands in the pockets of his coat. Out in the street the wind seemed even stronger. He leaned into it, looked off to the left and saw lights in the window of Sanders' place. Tracey was there. As the noise from the saloon grew louder he put her out of his mind and wondered what he was going to do. He'd left the boarding house with no plan, simply with the thought that he couldn't let it rest. The longer he waited to confront Peabody the less chance there was that anything would come of it. He pushed open the doors and went inside to a rush of noise and warm air.

Most of the men in the saloon had heard the story by now and some of them nodded at Will as he walked past them toward the bar. Two men shoved away when they saw him and he claimed their spot, putting his boot heel on the rail and leaning back, elbows on the counter.

Peabody sat at a back table facing the door, hands folded over his protruding belly, flanked by two men Will didn't know. Two tables to Peabody's right the Gunnison County sheriff looked over his cards and

138

squinted. His flat face tightened up and his eyes and mouth disappeared into two thin horizontal lines.

Will and Peabody stared at one another and the gambler let his mouth curl up in a smirk.

"Want a drink?" the bartender asked from behind Will. "Maybe later." He kept his eyes on Peabody. He unbuttoned his coat, loosened the hat he had jammed on his head in the wind and pushed off from the bar. Peabody watched him walk toward his table.

"Too bad your hired help doesn't know how to file a proper claim," he said as Will stood before him.

"I think it's time you and I worked out our differences," Will said. He casually pulled back his coat to show he was unarmed.

"Do we have differences? The only problem I see is that you've been mining on my claim."

"I believe you know better than that."

Peabody smiled broadly, nodding toward the sheriff. "I think the law would tell you differently," he said loudly. Will glanced at the sheriff who had put his cards face down on the table and was leaning back in his chair, watching the two with no little interest. Most of the conversation in the room had died but the banjo player still plucked gamely away.

Will leaned forward, the palms of his hands on the table and his face only a couple of feet from Peabody's. The banjo player stopped and the room was quiet enough that everyone could hear Will's voice as he spoke.

"You're behind the burning of Tracey Collins' boarding house in Schofield and you, or somebody you paid off, doctored that filing of my claim."

Peabody stiffened and one of his hired hands made a move for the pistol he wore high on his right side.

"Keep your hands where I can see them," the sheriff said. He was small but he had a big voice and Peabody's man put his hands on the table. Peabody's own stayed in his lap. "You've been after me ever since Dodge," Peabody said. "I'm sick and tired of it."

"No sicker than I am."

"Then I suggest you get off my back. I'm just awful sorry about that fire up there but the place was a firetrap. As far as your errant filing goes . . ."

"You're a liar," Will snapped. It came out quickly but quietly. "A liar and a cheat." He stood up from his lean and faced the man, arms hanging limp at his side.

Peabody's face reddened. He turned to the man on his left and nodded to him. The man started to stand.

"You just keep on standing and walk over here beside me." Out of the corner of his eye Will saw Tom at the bar with his coat thrown open and the handle of a .45 plainly visible.

As Peabody's bodyguard began to walk slowly toward Tom and most of the eyes in the room followed him, the man to Peabody's right swiftly jerked his gun from its holster and fired. Will, who had never moved his eyes from Peabody's, caught the motion with his peripheral vision and stepped quickly to his right. The slug tore into his left arm.

He spun around with the shock and saw a series of actions unfold in the space of seconds. The sheriff was on his feet with his own pistol out. He fired and Will's assailant jerked backwards. The man who had been ordered by Tom to walk toward him stopped, drew and then fell forward as Tom clubbed him on the head with his Colt.

The pain in Will's arm almost blinded him. As he grabbed his left shoulder with his right hand he saw Peabody fumbling in his coat. Will instinctively grabbed a chair, swung it over his head and heard the wild shot from Peabody's derringer just as he felt the edge of the chair seat come down hard on the man's head. It made a sound like a hammer hitting a ripe melon, and Peabody fell sideways and lay over the body of the man the sheriff had shot.

Nobody moved for a moment until Will slumped forward onto the table and groaned with the pain in his arm. Then everyone was talking at once, crowding around the two men on the floor and then clearing a way for the sheriff.

"You gonna be all right?" he asked Will, who nodded.

The sheriff motioned to Tom, who holstered his pistol and helped Will stand up, then guided him to the door.

"That was about the dumbest thing I ever saw anybody do," Tom said as they walked down the street. "Goin' up against three of 'em unarmed."

"Yeah," Will said, grimacing with the pain. "I guess it probably was."

Tom got him into the boarding house, sat him down at a table and bathed the wound. "Guess I better go get Tracey," he said.

"I suppose so," Will managed to say before he fell forward face down on the table.

When he woke up he was in bed and Tracey was peering down at him. Tom stood in the background.

"Well, hi," Will said groggily.

"Hi, yourself." Tracey stroked his cheek. "How do you feel?"

"Terrific." He tried to rise but she pushed him back.

"Rest. No need to get up. You won't have to be on the run."

Will scowled. "What . . . ?"

Tom stepped forward. "The sheriff was just here," he said. "Told me everybody in the place agreed it was self defense. He won't press charges."

Will shook his head, trying to clear it. "I don't . . .What do you . . . ?"

"Peabody is dead," Tracey said. "You killed him with that chair or whatever you hit him with."

Will's eyes widened. "You mean . . . I killed him?"

"Deader'n a gut-shot rabbit," Tom said with a grin.

Will let his head fall back on the pillow. "I never meant to kill anybody," he whispered. "I just wanted to talk it out."

Tracey bent to him and kissed him on the cheek. "I know," she said. "Try to sleep now."

"How can I sleep? I just killed a man. I've killed two men, now."

"You killed somebody who needed killing, way I see it," Tom said.

Will lay on the bed looking at the two faces peering down at him. Just before he passed out from the pain that seemed to engulf his entire body he whispered, "Well, I'll be damned."

TWO DAYS LATER Will's arm was barely hurting, but he wore it in a sling. Sanders was still alive but paralyzed from his waist down. The bullet had hit his spinal column, Tracey told them. Fortunately, its quick exit and the loss of little blood had spared the man's life. "But he's through as a miner," she said. "And as a man, too."

That night the three of them — Tom, Will and Tracey — sat at a table in the boarding house. They stared at the walls, at the floor, shuffled now and then, barely spoke. Sanders' condition kept them from celebrating the news the sheriff had brought them that day — that he now agreed the paperwork on Will's claim had, indeed, been doctored. A clerk in Gunnison had confessed to accepting $500 from Peabody for doing the job. The sheriff had also given Will the official word that no charges would be filed in Peabody's death, saying all — even a judge — agreed that it was justified as self- defense.

"Nobody liked the bastard anyway," he said.

Tom had quickly agreed to take over Sanders' job at the mine and planned on getting a crew back to work right away.

"Martha Ann is going to take George back to Pennsylvania as soon as he can travel," Tracey told them.

Will and Tom had decided to pay any doctor and hospital bills and to keep Sanders on the payroll as long as the mine was making money.

Tracey reached across the table and covered Will's hand with hers. "I'm happy you are better," she said. "But poor George . . ."

"I know." Will cleared his throat. He had been waiting for the right time

141

to tell them about Abby and the fact that he would soon be a free man and that he and Tracey could finally be married. He figured now was as good a time as any. Everybody needed some cheering up.

"Listen," he began. "I have some news that I've been saving up and I want both of you to hear it."

Tracey glanced at Tom and Will saw him nod at her. She took a deep breath. *What the devil?* Will wondered.

"I think you ought to hear what we've got to say first," Tracey said. She put her hand on Will's again. "I hope you'll be pleased. Tom and I are to be married."

Will's stomach went suddenly empty and he felt his head start to spin.

"We just decided a week before you got here," Tom said with a broad, silly grin. "I knew from the first that she was the finest woman I'd ever met. Isn't that something, Will? I'm gonna be a married man. Can you believe it?"

Will watched with a growing sickness as Tom reached over and took Tracey's hand. The two looked at one another with complete joy in their faces.

"Mrs. Tom Cordell," Tracey said.

Will looked at Tom and kept the forced smile on his face. He gathered himself and held out his hand. "I'm glad for you," he lied, forcing out the words. "She's too good for you, Tom."

Tom grabbed Will's hand. "I know that for sure. But for some reason, she says she loves me."

Will leaned forward and kissed Tracey's cheek, letting his lips linger a little longer than necessary. "He's a good man," he said. "You two will be good for each other."

"Oh, I know we will, won't we Tom?" Tom had her in his arms now and kissed her full on the lips.

"I'm happier'n I've ever been in my life, Will. If only George hadn't been shot . . ."

They were all standing now and Tracey gave Will a brief hug, then backed off and, holding his good hand in hers, asked, "But what was the news you said you had?"

Will swallowed. "I'll tell you another time," he said. "It was nothing compared to this." He stood there trying to smile as Tracey buried her face in Tom's chest.

"I want you to stand up with me," Tom said. "Will you?"

"I'd be proud. And mad as hell if you hadn't asked."

He sat with them a while longer and listened as they talked excitedly about a trip to Aspen to find a preacher. It would be Tracey's first trip out of the valley in years and both wanted to see this new mining town. Things were so good now, Tracey and Tom agreed. If only George hadn't been shot, things would be perfect. Tracey decided she would have to make a new dress for the wedding, and Tom and Will would have to buy suits. *Now, that'll be something*, Will thought. Tom and Tracey asked Will if he could manage the mine while they were on their honeymoon. They talked on and on.

Pretty soon Will excused himself and went up to bed. His legs were so heavy they would hardly carry him up the stairs. He slept alone and figured that was the way it was going to be for who knew how long.

PART IV

1887-1890

Will Martin felt old. It was May of 1887 and the snow in the valley was gone. In the high country it was melting, and with a few wildflowers sneaking up out of the muddy ground and testing air as if they were gophers, Will should have been perking up, lifting out of the winter doldrums. Instead, he felt old and tired.

And way behind the times. With the snow so heavy during the past winter, he'd had plenty of time to read the weeks-old editions of the *Rocky Mountain News* he'd managed to get his hands on now and then. Several items astonished him. Some were mildly interesting, but most simply pointed out how little he knew about what was going on in the world.

The Atchison, Topeka and Santa Fe Railroad, for example, was supposed to have reached Los Angeles by this time, prompting a rate war with the Southern Pacific. Speculation was ripe that fares from Kansas City to Los Angeles would drop to one dollar.

An eighteen-year-old Frenchman had invented a "calculer" which made multiplication automatic. Will couldn't see much of a need for it.

The worst news was about the blizzards out on the plains that killed millions of open-range cattle as well as whole families found frozen in their tar-paper shacks and dugouts. Speculation was that the big ranching syndicates would go bankrupt, homesteaders would move in to farm, and range wars would break out. *At least that's something I don't have to worry about*, Will thought to himself.

He figured he was thirty-seven that morning. He'd had to force himself from bed. He walked to the kitchen yawning and poked kindling into the kitchen stove. "Happy birthday," he muttered to himself.

"What's that?" Ardy asked, leaning against the door to his room scratching his backside. If Will felt old, Ardy looked old. Will thought the man was fifty-eight but he looked ten years older.

"Nothin'," he said.

Ardy limped over to the cabinet and touched a match to the lamp. The room slowly brightened. Will watched him with some concern. "Arthritis again?"

Ardy nodded, yawned, hugged himself and rubbed his arms. He sat down by the stove and began rolling a smoke.

"You smoke too much, old man," Will said.

"Who are you, my mother? And don't call me 'old man'."

"Just a friendly term."

"Not to me, it ain't." He puffed and coughed. "What you want for

145

breakfast?"

"What we got?"

"Flapjacks."

"Well, flapjacks, then."

The two men had settled into a peaceful if uninspiring coexistence in the years since Abby had left, and each liked and respected the other. Will had become more helpful to Ardy over the years, although they continued to hire at least one additional hand each summer. The house had taken on the look and smell of a man's house. Now and then, when it was absolutely necessary, they cleaned it. When they felt like it, they shaved. Every so often they changed the bed covers.

Will sat at the table, forking food and looking around. *How long had it been since there were flowers on the table?* "Oughta be hearin' from George soon," Ardy said around a mouthful. "Wonder how he's doin'."

"Still feeling pretty low, I 'spect. Can't imagine he likes keepin' books for that Pittsburgh mine."

"He's tough. You'n Tom still sendin' him money?"

"Long as we're making some, he'll get part of it."

"You gonna eat that?" Ardy pointed to the two flapjacks still on Will's plate and when his friend shook his head, speared them and went back to his eating.

"Think I'll go to Glenwood," Will said, reaching for his coat. "Fella told me Doc Holliday was there."

"You knew him in Dodge City, didn't you? And Wyatt Earp, too, and some of those others. Bat Masterson."

"Yeah. Them, too."

"What's Holliday doin' in Glenwood?"

"That's what I'm going to find out."

Ardy didn't look up as Will left. He finished off his breakfast and piled the dishes in the tub on the counter.

Glenwood Springs was a new town growing up around Yampah Springs and catering to the wealthy from Aspen and elsewhere who believed in the healing powers of the springs.

Will found Doc Holliday playing cards in the Hotel Glenwood on the north edge of town, across the Grand River from the hot springs where he and Ardy had taken their horses a few years ago. He stood a few feet away and watched Holliday — a gambler, former dentist, gunfighter — cough into a handkerchief. Holliday slumped in his chair, a far cry from the straight-backed, alert man of Dodge City.

Finally, Holliday threw in his hand and stood. He was two years younger than Will but looked much older. His face was lean, thinner than before, and his eyes had a reddened, dirty look to them. The coughing racked him again and he leaned weakly against a chair. When he looked up Will was beside him.

"Hello, Doc," he said. "Been a long time."

Holliday studied him warily for a few seconds and then tried to smile. "Martin, isn't it?" He shook Will's hand. "Small world."

"What brings you to town?"

Holliday took off his black hat and ran a veined hand through silver hair. "You live here?" he asked, ignoring Will's question.

"Up the river a ways. A little horse ranch." They sat. "Doing some mining, too."

Holliday nodded. "You've come a long way. Married?"

"Not anymore."

"Sorry." Holliday looked around the room. "Me neither."

"Been back to Dodge lately?"

"Nope." There was silence for a moment. Holliday seemed to be remembering. When he spoke it was almost a whisper. "Went down to Tombstone for a while to help the Earps out of a scrape. I was in Leadville last winter and heard about these hot springs. Thought I'd see if they'd help me any."

"Do they?"

"Just got here." Will waited while another fit of coughing rocked Holliday. Finally, he was able to speak again. "Got a case of consumption. One sawbones in Tombstone called it tuberculosis." He paused to cough again. "Couldn't do anything for it."

"Well," Will said. "I'm sorry to hear it."

"Not half as sorry as I am."

Will hadn't seen him order it but the bartender placed a shot before Holliday. "Likker's probably killing me but I figure I'll be dead from consumption before the whiskey has a chance to work," he said. His hand shook as he lifted the glass.

"Seen anything of Bat Masterson?"

Holliday nodded. "Got married to a fine-looking woman named Emma. Last I heard he was in Las Vegas, Nevada. He was marshal of Trinidad for a while, down toward New Mexico. Before that he owned or operated saloons, dance halls, whatever. He had a place in Creede back in '82 or so. Said it was too quiet and left."

"I figured he'd stay in Dodge."

Holliday shook his head, coughed a bit. "Men like Bat — like me — have to keep moving. Somebody's always after you."

Will thought about it. "Bat's had quite a life."

147

"The Eastern newspapers say he's one of the best-known men on the Western frontier. Seems like wherever he goes he does something that makes him famous. Now, you and me, we just plod along and somebody must be covering our tracks since we don't leave many marks."

"I hear you're leaving some," Will said.

"Here and there, Martin. Here and there."

"Like to hear about it."

Holliday looked at Will for a moment, poured another drink with a trembling hand and threw it down. "Maybe I'll tell you about it sometime. Right now, there's a young woman waiting for me upstairs and I don't like to keep the ladies waiting. You got any money on you?"

The question surprised Will. "Some," he said. "Why?"

Holliday smiled. "I seem to have been cleaned out of what I carried by a wily poker player just now. Could you?" He nodded at the bottle on the table.

"Oh, well, sure." Will fished in his pockets and found some coins. The two men stood and shook hands. "If you're short . . ." Will held out what he had left.

Doc Holliday pushed the hand away. "Thanks, but no," he said. "I have plenty stashed away upstairs and tonight I'll win back what I just lost. But I appreciate the thought. Good to see you."

"You, too." Will stood at the table and watched Holliday walk to the stairs where he stopped for another spell of coughing. When it was over the slight man pulled himself toward the second floor one step at a time, hand on the banister, his chest heaving.

IT'S STRANGE *how things work out*, Will mused to himself as he rode up the Roaring Fork on his way home. Holliday was on the brink of death. *It could happen to me just like that*, he thought. *I could be dead tomorrow and there were few people who would care.* When Doc Holliday died it would make headlines across the country. Will Martin would be mourned by maybe a dozen people and remembered by fewer than that. Maybe if he'd gone on to California like he'd planned . . .

He let the horse pick his way upriver while he meandered around in his mind. He was still tortured by the fact that he and Tracey had not been able to marry. She and Tom were happy, though, and that was good. He heard from Abby now and then. In fact, he had about as much communication with her now as when they were married.

Evey was five years old by now. Will wondered what she looked like. Abby came to Aspen almost every summer and always wrote to tell him when she would be there. Somehow, though, he had always managed to be in Crystal or up in the mountains somewhere and missed her. The boy, Henry, was named for her uncle Gillespie and was three. Will had seen him for only a few weeks after his birth and then Abby had taken both children to Denver where the divorce was easy, thanks to her father's lawyer friends. Within a year she had married Winfield Porter, the "blithering idiot" she'd spurned for Will and who had remained single. They lived in a large house and were waited on by servants. It was a far cry from the ranch on Rock Creek.

"My God," Will thought. *"Even that's changed."* Rock Creek was now known as the Crystal River.

"Hell of a lot better name," Ardy had said when he'd heard it. "Rock Creek sounded like it didn't have no water." The name-change was being attributed by some to J. C. Osgood, who had bought coal claims up and down the valley as well as throughout the state.

To Will Martin, who sat at its confluence with the Roaring Fork, it was a fitting name. He stared south toward Mount Sopris, now topped with an orange glow from the setting sun, and thought sadly that the changes occurring in the Crystal River Valley were minor compared to what was probably to happen in the next few years.

Osgood's Colorado Fuel Company had bought coal claims in anticipation of beginning major mining operations in the near future. Now the Colorado Coal and Iron Company, another firm, was investing in Crystal Valley land. "Crystal Valley," he muttered. "It has a good ring."

Something else was also attracting attention in the valley. As early as 1874, when the valley officially still belonged to the Utes, a man named George Yule had found marble deposits west of the little settlement now called Marble. The stream that runs through the area was still called Yule Creek. More recently others had "rediscovered" the marble. One miner reported in 1884 that the roof of his mine on White House Mountain was composed of marble. A quarry was opened on Yule Creek that year and within a few months the owners were trying to get a contract to furnish stone for the state capitol building in Denver.

Now there were at least four quarries. Men were dynamiting marble from two-hundred-foot-high cliffs. Unfortunately, Will had heard of no contracts that would make them pay off. He watched the color disappear from the peak of Mount Sopris and nudged the horse forward toward home. Coal and marble and what next? Probably a railroad running by the front stoop of his house. A man would never get any sleep.

୶୬ঌ

149

"BEEN TALKIN' railroads for years now," Ardy muttered that night. "I'll believe it when I see one. Hard to figure, ain't it? This valley was settled from the south and that's goin' to hell and now it's all turned around. What with Glenwood Springs and Aspen and the railroad headin' that way, seems everything's happening in the north."

He was right. Schofield had practically closed down two years before and everybody moved downstream to Crystal City. The winters were too long and hard and the ore low-grade.

"I don't like it," Ardy snapped. He was trying to talk and light a smoke at the same time. "Things was always just fine and now we're talkin' railroad. Judas!"

Will suppressed a smile. "Easy, old man."

"I told you not to call me that." He puffed smoke. Will watched the man pace the floor, knowing Ardy had not felt well all winter. *He's probably afraid of getting old*, Will thought.

"How long's it been since you've been to Aspen? Is that woman still there? Ardelia, or whatever?"

Ardy stopped in mid-pace. "Amelia! By damn! How many times I got to tell you her name's Amelia? And, yes, she's still there far as I know and yes, I been thinkin' about goin' over there and yes, thanks, I'll take a couple of days and do just that." He pulled his coat from the rack and started for the door. "Think I'll go fork some hay."

The kitchen was a mess and Will reluctantly decided to have a go at cleaning it up. He started sluggishly but within half an hour was going about the job with enthusiasm. At least I can see some results, he thought. Another hour and he figured he'd done enough and only then realized Ardy hadn't returned from the barn. He pulled on a coat and went outside.

Ardy was lying on the hay in one of the stalls while a horse chewed peacefully beside him.

"Ardy?" The old man didn't move. "What the . . . ?" Will couldn't see any blood and he found a strong pulse in Ardy's wrist. As gently as he could, Will picked up the light body and cradled the man in his arms. In the house, he laid Ardy on his bed and bathed his face with a wet rag from the kitchen. Finally, Ardy slowly opened his eyes and took a while figuring out where he was.

"Somebody was out there," he said. "Spooked the horse and I got pinned against the wall. Fool animal kicked me. Busted my leg, I think."

"Which one?"

"That ol' bay mare. I should'a sold that . . ."

"Not which horse, dammit. Which leg?"

"Oh. The right one. I must'a fainted. Never did that before."

150

Will cut through the man's long underwear to the bare leg. The area around the knee was swollen but no bone had broken through the skin. He shuddered as he thought about the broken bone in Jacob's leg three years earlier. "You say there was someone out there?" he asked, to make conversation.

"Somebody was in the barn," Ardy said. "Gimme a shot of whiskey. Maybe that'll help the hurt."

Back in the room with a bottle, Will made a quick decision. "We're going to Carbondale," he said, "to see that new doctor."

Ardy wiped his mouth with a sleeve. "I 'spose we best."

"You lie still and I'll get the wagon ready."

"I ain't goin' nowhere."

Ardy was groggy from the whiskey when Will carried him to the wagon and laid him on the bed of hay behind the seat. "I think it was a damned injun," Ardy said.

"Oh, yeah?"

"Yeah. What you 'spose a injun was doin' in our barn?" Will snapped the reins and the wagon jerked forward and bounced roughly over the rocky ground.

"You sure there was something out there?"

"Not *some thing* — *some one*. A Indian."

"An Indian in our barn."

Ardy sighed. "Never knew a ride could be so rough. And, yeah, it was a Indian, all right." Carbondale seemed a long way off. "Why don't you just pay attention to what you're doin' and see if you can avoid runnin' over them big boulders."

"Go to sleep."

"Sleep? Sleep? Who can sleep with all this yakkin' and bouncin' around?" But pretty soon Ardy was sleeping with his mouth open. *Hopefully asleep and not passed out again*, Will thought.

WILL FOUND the doctor, a young one named Castle, in a little house just off the main street. The man and a good- looking woman who seemed too old for him ushered Will into an examining room where he laid Ardy on a hard table covered with a white cloth. "Feel damned foolish," Ardy muttered.

Will was shown to the cramped living room of the house where he found a comfortable sofa and was quickly asleep. He awoke with a start when the door to the examining room opened and the woman stepped through.

"How is he?" Will sat up and rubbed his eyes.

She filled the doorway, blocking the light, and her silhouette told him a great deal about her. She was full-bodied and she held herself straight and proud. Her voice had a hoarseness to it that played nicely on the ears and she wasn't shy about looking him in the eye.

"He'll be fine. How are you?"

"I'm okay. Can I take him home?" She shook her head and her long, blond hair quivered. "Well, look Mrs. Castle." Again she shook her head. "Not Mrs. Castle. I'm a nurse."

Will felt his ears burn. "Well, I'm sorry. I just . . ."

"I'm Judith Swensson. You knew my husband."

Will thought for a minute and realized he must be the big Swede he had met clearing land years ago. "Sure. I know him."

She kept her eyes level. "He died a year ago. Him and both my children."

"Judas. I'm sorry."

She averted her eyes then and turned. "A landslide in the spring. I was down by the river and it took all three of them."

"I didn't know."

"He talked about you a time or two. And we went by your place now and then on the way to town."

Will looked at the floor. "So now you're a nurse."

"I've been a nurse for a long time. In Minnesota where I met Dan. After the accident I moved to town and was taking in washing when Dr. Castle heard I was a nurse and hired me." She saw the question in Will's face and smiled faintly. "I have a room in the back. It's better since it seems someone is always needing medical care at night."

"Right. What about Ardy?"

"We'll keep him here a few days. A funny name, Ardy."

Will laughed. "Just an easy way to say R. D."

Judith Swensson smiled and the wrinkles around her eyes told Will she might be older than him. "Come have some coffee and a piece of pie."

THE NEXT morning Will went looking for some temporary help and found a young miner who said he'd been a cowhand in Montana. Will was glad to have him and was even gladder when he learned the man could cook. "Had to learn or starve," he said. His name was Fred Bancroft and that was about all Will learned. It didn't matter. If he knew horses and could cook, that was enough.

When they got to the ranch they found the corral gate open and the four horses that should have been there were gone. The two men found them on the mesa half a mile away.

That night the howling, singing, keening sound woke Will. He went into the kitchen and found Bancroft sitting at the table. "I heard it before," Bancroft said. "Lots of times. Them old miners say it's the ghost of an Indian who was drove out of the valley and put a curse on it. I don't believe in curses."

"I don't either," Will replied.

Pretty soon the sound faded away and then was gone.

A few days later Ardy was able to come home. He carried on some when Will told him Fred Bancroft was doing just fine. "Young whipper-snapper," Ardy snorted. "You should'a let me help you pick out a hand."

"Needed him then," Will said. "Not just now."

Gradually, Ardy cooled down and began to accept the man, especially after he'd had a few meals cooked by the wrangler. Ardy hobbled out to the corral almost every day and sat on a stump while he talked to Fred. One night he told Will he thought he'd picked a good man. "Be better'n you with horses 'fore long," he said.

Will was relieved to know the two were able to get along but was hesitant about leaving them alone.

"Go on," Ardy told him when he said he was thinking about going to Crystal. "But if I'se you I'd hightail it into Carbondale and have some more of nurse Swensson's apple pie."

Will grinned. "I've been thinking about that," he said. "I'll probably do it, too, right after I see Tom and Tracey."

"And Jacob," Ardy said.

TOM WAS FULL of talk of the mine. They were about to load a jack train of at least one hundred mules for the trip to Crested Butte. There had been no more trouble from the mine next door. Nathan Peabody's wife, who lived in Taos with her daughter, had showed up and hired a man to manage it and seldom showed her face.

"Things are going so well it scares me," Tom told Will. "You don't have a thing to worry about. Do what you want with your time and we'll keep you posted on the money we make."

Will made a mess out of trying to smile. Tom had the mine under control and didn't need his help. While Ardy recuperated, a temporary hand Will had found could help him run the ranch. His son called him "Uncle" and another man "Daddy." The mother of his son was married to his best friend and was so busy she barely had time for a visit. He wasn't needed and felt empty inside just thinking about it.

"Just think what a railroad would mean," Tom was saying. "We're making money even with the jack trains. Get me a railroad and I'll turn out enough to fill a train a month."

"You gettin' greedy?"

"You bet!" Tom slapped him on the shoulder. "I want to be one of those silver kings like they got over to Aspen. Wouldn't that be something?"

"It would," Will agreed. "It sure would."

As he tried to sleep that night, though, he didn't think about getting rich. He thought about Tracey and Jacob. The feeling was still there, deep inside him, and he ached with the memory of long nights of lovemaking and soft talking. He thought of Abby, too, and Evey and Henry. And he thought again that nobody needed him.

Throughout the summer he sat around the house. He tried to help with the horses but Ardy and Fred seemed to have a better time when he wasn't around. He went to Carbondale and ate more of Judith Swensson's apple pie. He rode into Glenwood and got depressed looking at the rapid deterioration of Doc Holliday. He heard more talk of railroads but never saw one. He went to Crystal and played "uncle" with Jacob and listened to Tom talk about how well things were going. He went onto the flattops above Glenwood and explored the vastness of that broad territory. He was bored and nervous and frustrated all summer.

Except for one trip to Crystal when he met Yolanda Peabody. He was at the bar of her High Country Hotel sipping tepid beer and not paying much attention to anything when someone tapped him on the shoulder. He turned to see a tall, dark woman coolly staring at him with a look on her face that could have been amusement — or hatred. Coal-black hair fell below her shoulders. Her eyes were almost as black as the hair. A long, red dress, showing more cleavage than he'd ever seen, trailed the floor. He could have spanned her waist with his hands.

"Will Martin?" There was no warmth in her voice.

"Yes."

"You killed my husband."

"You're . . . ?"

"Yolanda Peabody. *Mrs.* Peabody to you." Her eyes narrowed but there was a fire in them, like campfire embers kindled by a breath.

Will put his beer on the bar, keeping his eyes on hers. "He was about to shoot me. He did, in fact."

"Still, you killed him."

He nodded. "Didn't mean to, though."

"My daughter is three now. His daughter who he never got to see, thanks to you."

The room had quieted and all eyes watched the two. They had heard the story and most had embellished it. Tom had told Will people were talking about a huge shoot-out. They said Will ran out of ammunition, grabbed a chair and ran through a hail of bullets to club Peabody.

Yolanda Peabody sneered. There was a lot of Mexican in her, Will decided. "I don't know how," she said, loudly now. "But somehow, someday, you'll pay." She whirled and stalked off, climbed the stairs and disappeared into a far room.

"Where'd she come from?" Will asked the man at his side.

Two or three men started to talk at once. The story, as near as Will could make out, was that she had showed up early that spring to take up where her husband had left off. She made it clear she was in charge of the hotel, the mine and all of "her" property.

"Well, I'll be damned," Will said, and didn't think much more about it that summer, except now and then when he needed something else to worry about. *She is some woman*, he thought. *Wonder how Peabody ever convinced someone like her to marry him?*

THROUGHOUT THE summer people reported hearing the ghostly night singing. Sometimes it was in the high country and other times almost in Carbondale. Will didn't hear it again himself, but the reports became more and more numerous.

Tracey told Will that, on several occasions, Peabody's widow had met her on the street and had gone to great lengths to ignore her. Once, she said, the dark-haired woman had whispered something to a man and pointed at Tracey as she walked past. Another time she thought she heard the woman say something that sounded like "bastard kid." Tom still didn't know about Will being Jacob's father. "I'm afraid to tell him," Tracey said, "and I'm afraid not to. He's bound to find out sooner or later."

"Someday we'll have to tell him," Will said. "We'll wait."

He rode up and down the valley. Each time he passed the red cliffs he scanned the point, looking for signs of life. Frequently he saw two eagles circling above the cliffs and once one of them landed on the point itself, perhaps returning to an aerie it had built. Each time he had to fight the urge to visit the overlook. He would climb it again. Soon. When he was in a better mood. Maybe he could recapture the mystical feeling of that first time.

One particular feeling he was able to capture easily. It engulfed him each time he rode into Carbondale and it grew more intense as he reined his horse in front of Dr. Marvin Castle's small home and office. There was always a pie and there was always a look in Judith Swensson's eyes that made him feel little and shy. It was a look of confirmation, as though she knew he was coming, would come often, and that she could dominate him if she wished. She smiled, said little, placed the pie before him and visited in her quiet, hoarse voice. He never touched the woman. He stood always before her, hat in hand, and tried, usually unsuccessfully, to look her in the eye. As he ate she would ask about the ranch, about Ardy, about the mine. She would tell him of the many illnesses and broken bones and imagined ailments that people brought to the doctor.

The routine never varied. Will would sit and make small talk, until late sometimes, and then leave by the front door with frustration raging within him. He was always fearful of starting something that might, once again, lead to failure. Each night she stood in the doorway as he mounted his horse and he would wave his good night. When he saw her sensual form backlighted by the lamp in the hallway, he would hurt and sometimes start to go back, but he never did.

❧❧

IN MID-JULY Judith Swensson showed up at the ranch with two apple pies and a scolding for Ardy. "You missed your last check-up appointment," she told him.

"Aw," he muttered, trying to frown but unable to hide a small grin. "I'm doin' all right. Wasn't necessary to go."

"Let me see your knee," she demanded. Ardy backed off as Will and Bancroft shuffled around in the background smiling and smelling apple pie.

"No ma'am," Ardy said.

"I'm not asking you to drop your pants. Just roll up your pants leg." She stood solidly in front of him, looking down at the little man, arms folded across her chest.

Slowly, Ardy did as he was told and Judith gently touched the knee, ran her hand around it. "It's fine," she said. Turning to Will, she pointed to the kitchen. "Well, get some plates."

When she left that afternoon the men had cleaned up one of the pies and she left the other. "Bring the plate the next time you come to town," she said to Will.

"It'll be gone by tomorrow," Fred said. "We'll send it in with him."

Will took Judith's arm and guided her out the door.

"It was a nice day for a drive," she said, "and the doctor told me to get out of the house for awhile."

"Did he?"

She looked at him with that way of hers and smiled. "I wanted to see you."

Will helped her onto the wagon and dropped his gaze. "Thanks," he said. "I'll be by before long."

She nodded and, this time, there was no smile. "Come soon." He nodded back as she clucked at the horse and flicked the reins.

Back in the house, Ardy and Fred grinned at him.

"Shut up," he said.

A week later he went by her house, returned the pie plates, ate some more pie, talked a little just like always, waved goodbye and cussed himself all the way home.

∞∞∞

IN AUGUST, a Ute Indian named Colorow forayed out of his Utah reservation, started a war scare and gave Will a welcome respite from his "woman trouble," as he had begun to refer to his continuing frustration over Judith Swensson. Will hustled to Glenwood to join a posse of about one hundred men who were forming up to repel the "savage" hordes.

Jerome B. Wheeler's *Aspen Times* had the story. Colorow and a force consisting of an unknown number of savages had left the Uintah Reservation in Utah, ostensibly on their annual fall hunt. Many of the Indians had been seen at several locations near Meeker. Memories of the "bloody Meeker massacre" barely eight years ago sent waves of fear throughout the surrounding countryside. The mayor of Meeker had called upon Colorado Governor Alva Adams for "urgent military assistance."

In Glenwood the army of volunteers waited while Adams and a sizable force of "war correspondents" from newspapers across the state drank whiskey and laid plans for the attack.

Will found Doc Holliday sitting on the hotel porch. "How are you getting along?" he asked.

"Fair," Doc said. "Just fair. I breathe better when I'm in the vapor caves and sleep better after. But I'm weak as a cat."

"You're not going off to war, then?"

Holliday shook his head and shaded his eyes from the glare of the sun. "I've had enough of killing. Thought maybe the O. K. Corral was the end of it."

157

"I read something about that," Will said. "What was it all about, anyhow?"

"Just a little scrape," Doc said with a shrug. "You going out with the boys?"

"I guess so."

"Well, then." Doc turned and started back inside. "You better remember what Bat Masterson taught you about gun-fighting. These Indian warriors are bound to be truly savage." He touched his hat brim and went inside.

A few days later the armed forces gathered at Meeker. There was no sign of Indians, so they spent their time in town where they were welcomed by the local merchants. Will had never seen so much whiskey consumed by so many people. The governor went back to the Hotel Glenwood, rested a day or so, returned to Meeker, and made a speech. After ten days the militia began to break up as men wandered off toward home, disappointed that they had been cheated out of an Indian war.

The next week Governor Adams announced that the Indian War was over and the newspapers had to find something else to write about. Although no one realized it at the time, there would never be another headline inflaming the populace of Colorado with the words "Ute War!"

"THERE'S A LETTER from Abby on the kitchen table," Ardy said to Will when he and Fred returned from the "war."

"How do you know it's from Abby?"

Ardy headed for the door. "I didn't read your damn letter. I know her handwriting."

Will took the letter outside and sat by the creek to read it. She was coming to Aspen in late September or early October. Her Uncle Henry had secured a place for her and the two children on the "first train to ever reach Aspen. I will become a part of history." Husband Winfield would not be along as he had pressing business in Chicago at that time.

"I insist that you come to Aspen to see me and your children," she wrote. "I have not yet been able to understand your reluctance to visit us on any one of our frequent trips to the wilderness. We expect to be in Aspen for perhaps a month. You may visit us at any time that is convenient for you and I will see that you have ample time with your son and daughter."

IN SEPTEMBER, Doc Holliday went to bed and stayed there. "The man's sick," Will was told by the hotel clerk. "I ain't seen him for a few days."

Holliday barely nodded as Will entered his room. His neatly combed hair was silver and his face was drawn and pale. "I reckon this is probably it," he said.

"Never knew you to give up on anything," Will replied. Holliday coughed. "It isn't so much giving up as it is accepting the situation."

"Just what is the situation?"

"Bad, I guess. I never felt so weak. Chest hurts, legs don't want to work. Like that."

Will looked out the window while Doc coughed for a while. "How are things with you?" Doc asked, finally. "You making any money?"

"Enough."

"Make all you can and stay where you are. Been a long time since I had anything like a home — or a good woman."

"I don't have plans to go anywhere."

Holliday tried a smile. "You going to marry that nurse?"

"How'd you know about that?"

"Not much happens around here people don't know about."

They were silent for a while as Will mulled over the thought that a lot of people knew an awful lot about him. "You've had an unusual life," he said to Doc.

The man grunted. "That's one way of putting it. I've been all over. Met some good people, lots of bad ones. Made some money and lost it. Had a good woman and lost her. Had a — what did you call it? — an *unusual* life, and now I'm about to lose that, too.

"Fight it."

Doc barked out a laugh that set off another round of coughing. "I'm tired of fighting," he said when it was over.

Will looked away. "I understand."

"Maybe you do and maybe you don't. It doesn't matter." Holliday's eyes closed slowly. "Damn, I'm tired."

Will sat beside him for a few minutes until he thought the man was asleep, then stood and started for the door.

"Martin?"

Will turned. "Yeah?"

"I appreciate you coming by. Do it again."

"I will."

159

THAT SAME MONTH the Denver and Rio Grande Railroad was laying narrow-gauge tracks past Carbondale and heading for Aspen. For months the D&RG had been in a furious race with the Colorado Midland to be the first to Aspen. It had come by way of Tennessee Pass to Glenwood and then on up the Roaring Fork. The standard-gauge Colorado Midland was negotiating the Frying Pan to Basalt and then to Aspen.

Will and Judith rode out to the D&RG tracks late one evening. The color was gone from the surrounding mountains and a north wind bit through coats and scarves. The cold sun, lying low in the west, crept under gray clouds and reflected off the two parallel steel lines. Judith pulled her coat tighter about her neck and slid over closer to Will on the wagon seat. He felt her hip against his, put his arm around her and pulled her tight against him. She laid her head on his shoulder and it felt like it belonged there.

And yet, what did he know about this woman, this person for whom he was developing some intense feelings?

He knew she was a widow and that her marriage had been a good one. She was self-reliant and determined. *Lord, yes, she was determined!* he thought. *Straightforward. Uncompromising.*

She wasn't beautiful, he had decided some time ago. Not like Abby, certainly, nor even in the way that Tracey was beautiful. But Judith was made even more attractive by the confidence she exuded, by the honesty with which she approached everything, and by the wry sense of humor that was evident in her smile and in the look that said, "I think you're pretty funny but I'll play along with you just the same."

Will felt caught off-guard with her on many occasions, feeling like she knew what he was thinking, like she knew what he was going to say or do before he did.

He also knew she didn't like uncertainty. She made up her mind quickly and expected others — Will included — to do likewise.

Now here he was staring down an empty railroad track, and the future he was thinking of had little to do with railroads.

"Things will change now," she said. "Faster than ever."

"Change for the better, I think." He stroked her arm with a gloved hand, knowing they were talking about different kinds of change.

"I hope so. What about you?"

He looked down at her, understanding her meaning but reluctant to address the issue. "What about me?"

She sat up and he dropped his arm. "Your life. How will it change?"

He knew what she meant. "Why does it have to change?" The question he had feared was coming.

"I'm talking about the two of us," she said. She sat there looking at him

160

and waiting for him to face up to it.

A gust of wind almost took his hat off and he grabbed for it with both hands, giving him time to think. *Good Lord, I've had two months to think about it and now that she's brought it up I don't have an answer*, he thought. He had to say something.

"I think about you a lot," he said lamely.

"I know."

The words came, slowly at first, and then faster as he let his mouth rattle on. *To hell with it and let's get it out and see what happens*, he decided.

"I've been alone for about three years now," he said. "I come and go as I want. I've got an interest in a mine that another man runs and I've got a ranch that doesn't require much of my time. I get out in the mountains when I can and I've gotten pretty much used to being on my own."

Judith kept her eyes on him, not nodding, not talking, just listening and waiting for him to get to the point.

"I messed up one marriage because my wife didn't like the way we lived. I'm not sure I'd be a good husband to any woman." He turned to her, took her shoulders in his hands. "I think maybe I've fallen in love with you," he continued. "You're everything a man could want and I'd be proud to be married to you. I'm not sure you'd want to have me, though."

Judith shivered in the cold. "Maybe you should let me decide about that."

"Probably. But there's something else and I guess you ought to know everything."

Up to now the only person he'd told had been Ardy. If anyone else in the world ought to know, though, it was Judith, he decided.

"I've got a son in Crystal City," he said, and he couldn't look at her but felt her stiffen just a little. He took his hands from her shoulders and put them in his lap, then watched the low-flying clouds cover up the sun and was glad it was dark.

Judith listened quietly as he told her about Tracey and Jacob. When he finished they sat on the seat and felt the wagon jerk as the horses stomped their feet and blew into the wind.

"I haven't been much good with women," he said.

"No," she answered. "Is that it?"

"It?"

"Is that everything? Are you through?"

"Isn't that enough?"

She laughed, a laugh that came from deep in her throat, and sighed. "It's cold," she said. "Why don't you take me home?"

At her door, she didn't invite him in, but stood on the stoop half a head taller than him. "Nothing you've said makes a difference to me," she said.

"This valley is changing. The seasons change. People change. You, too. Since I've known you, you've changed. I think you've matured and have more of a handle on yourself than you may realize."

"Maybe so," he admitted. He hoped it was true.

"Don't come back for any more apple pie," she said, "or for anything else unless you come to propose."

Surprised, he stepped back.

"I love you, Will Martin. We could adjust to each other. But I can't take any more of these nights sitting at a table watching you eat and making small talk. I'll come to your house and to your bed and I'll make you a good wife — better than any other woman could. Because I understand you. But you've got to ask me. And when you do ask me I know it will be because you've made up your mind to be a good husband. I'll work at it, too, being a fine wife. You come back then and not before."

She went inside and closed the door and Will stood there a while in the cold and then felt foolish, got on the wagon and pointed the horses south. Pretty soon he was home and didn't remember the ride.

WILL AND ARDY were in Aspen when the D&RG's first train, *The Little Giant*, pulled into town on the evening of November 1, 1887. With two locomotives and twenty-five coaches, the train huffed into the new station as a brass band blared and people cheered and the engineer blew his whistle.

The dignitaries got off first and Will stood at the back of the crowd, not listening to the speeches, looking instead for Abby. Finally, a small woman carrying a child and leading another by the hand was helped down from the fifth coach and quickly disappeared into the crowd. Abby had written to Will earlier, explaining that her uncle had secured seats on the train for her and the children. She insisted in vehement terms that Will visit his children while they were in Aspen.

"Come on," Ardy said. "Let's go downtown. I hear all the saloons are giving drinks on the house."

Will followed, still looking for Abby but scanning Aspen and Smuggler Mountains, too, where bonfires, roman candles and flares blazed brightly. Fireworks brightened the skies and miners set off kegs of black powder. Men hollered at one another, women screamed and oohed and aahed at the fireworks. The streets were illuminated with Chinese lanterns. Over Mill Street, just north of Main, an arch strung with the first electric lights in the area spelled out "Welcome D&RG."

Two days later when Will, shaved and wearing clean clothes, called at

Henry Gillespie's home, Abby welcomed him warmly. "I thought you'd come *sooner*," she said.

"Figured I'd give you time to settle in." She was maturing and, in doing so, was becoming more beautiful than ever, more grown up, more a woman than a child seeking an adventure with a cowboy that, in retrospect, seemed doomed from the start. She wore a deep blue satin dress with a matching bow in her hair.

She looked him up and down and touched his arm. "It's been a *long* time," she said.

"Where are Evey and Henry?"

She motioned to a chair. "I'll get them in a minute. How have you been?"

"Fine." He fidgeted, more nervous about seeing the children than he'd been about seeing her. "And you?"

She shrugged. "You've changed."

"Oh?"

She stared at him. "Your face is fuller and you've put on weight. Has some *woman* been feeding you?"

Will felt his face flush. How could she be so perceptive? Judith Swensson's face flashed through his mind.

"I'll get the children."

In a minute — it seemed longer to Will, nervous as he was — she returned carrying Henry, now three years old. Evey walked beside her mother wearing a white dress with red ribbons. Her long hair was pulled back and pinned together in back with some kind of comb. Will stood and Evey walked directly to him. She looked up at his face.

"Hello," he said, his voice catching. He wanted to pick her up and hug her to him, but instead put his hands in his pockets and wished he'd thought to bring a present.

Her blue eyes were large and bright with what he thought must be intelligence. She examined every foot of him. "You're tall," she said. He knelt in front of her. "I'm five years old," she announced. "Henry is only three."

Will reached out and touched Evey's cheek. It was softer than he'd expected.

"You and my mother used to be married." He nodded and she put a finger to her chin. "Do you still live on a ranch and have lots of horses?"

He found it difficult to speak and answered with another nod. *How do you speak to a child?* he wondered.

"Mommy says someday I can visit you and ride them."

"I hope you'll do that." She stood straight and seemed unafraid of him. "I'd like for you to visit me."

"Can Henry come, too? And Mommy?"

163

"Sure. If they want to." This child was more than he had hoped. She would be as beautiful as Abby. She would be educated, rich. How could she fit into his life at all?

"You haven't said hello to Henry." She took his hand and he felt a shock. Evey led him to the sofa and patted it. "Sit here and you can hold Henry."

Abby handed Henry to Will and the boy immediately stuck his thumb in his mouth and hunkered down in Will's lap like a frightened rabbit. He's too young to know, Will thought.

Abby cleared her throat and Will thought he saw her wipe away a tear. "I have some things to do," she said, turned quickly and left the room.

Evey climbed on the sofa beside Will and moved close to him. "My other father couldn't come with us," she said. "He is very busy and makes lots of money."

"Is that so?"

"Yes. You're taller than he is."

Good, thought Will.

Evey reached up and tried to pull Henry's thumb from his mouth but he pushed her hand away. "He does that all the time," she said. "I am learning to play the piano. Would you like to hear me play?"

"I sure would." She climbed down from the sofa and marched to a new piano across the room. She pulled out the bench and stood beside it, made a little curtsy.

"I shall play 'My Old Kentucky Home.'"

On the bench, she placed her hands above the keys, studied them a moment, and began to play the tune. Her hair swept back and forth and she moved her head, following her little hands. Her feet swung freely above the floor.

She made another curtsy when she was finished and Will applauded. "That was wonderful."

"I have a dog," she said, seated again beside him. "His name is Boots and Henry is afraid of him."

Will looked at the boy, who had remained perfectly still except for his mouth, which continued to work on the thumb. "Henry will grow up and not be afraid of things," Will said.

Abby came back into the room and took a relieved Henry from Will's lap. "I heard Evey playing for you."

"She's just like you."

Abby studied him. "Is that all right?"

"Of course." He stood. "I think I'd better be going." He couldn't take his eyes from his daughter. "She's wonderful," he said and had to swallow hard.

Abby smiled and hugged Henry who had taken his thumb from his mouth and was fingering a necklace that dangled between his mother's breasts. "I try to see that they nap every afternoon. You can come after three to see them."

"All right. I will."

At the door she touched his arm. "Sometimes I miss you," she whispered. Her speech pattern hadn't changed, nor, evidently, had other things about her. He looked into her eyes and waited but didn't feel what he thought he might.

He was back the next day, and the next. Each time, Henry sat on his lap and, by the third visit, had stopped sucking his thumb when Will held him. Evey talked forthrightly to her father of Denver, her friends, her clothes. And she asked questions. What kind of house did he have? Where did he sleep? Were there other children nearby? Had he ever been to Denver? Why did he let Mommy leave?

"She wanted to live in a city," he answered. "Where there was music and parties. I live in the country."

"Isn't there music in the country?"

"Not much," he said, and suddenly wished there was.

ON THE fourth night the Gillespies were to dine with friends and Abby asked him to come to dinner with her and their children. A maid served them and then took Evey and Henry off to bed. Henry managed a quiet "good night" but Evey held up her arms and he picked her up. She kissed him on the cheek. "I like you," she said. "Do you like me?"

He hugged her back. "Very much."

"Good. You're a nice man." He waved as the two followed the maid out of the room.

In the sitting room Abby sat on the sofa at a comfortable distance from Will. She put her arm along the back of the sofa and pushed her breasts toward him.

"You've done a good job with them," he said.

For a while they talked about Denver and her life as a member of society. She had been to New York and attended a performance of *The Mikado* by Gilbert and Sullivan which had opened in London barely two years ago. She had seen an exhibition of French Impressionist painting. She had carried on a conversation with a friend via a telephone. There were, she said, more than two hundred thousand of them in use. Soon, Denver would have telephone service. Everything was fine except Winfield, her husband, was concerned about wheat prices which had fallen to sixty-seven cents per bushel. He invested in many areas, of course, she said, so the price of wheat, low as it might go, would not in itself ruin him.

165

The maid opened the door. "They're asleep," she said. "Is there anything else, Mrs. Porter? If not, I'll be going home."

"Thank you, Edna," Abby said. "You go ahead."

A moment later they heard the back door open and then close and they were alone in the big house with two sleeping children. Will watched the dying fire across the room and felt Abby's eyes on him. He turned to her.

"Will . . ."

"I better stoke the fire," he said and walked to it, picked up the poker and shoved the logs together. Sparks drifted up the chimney and the fire caught again. Abby laid her hand on his shoulder. He turned to her.

"There are nights when I *think* of you," she said softly. She took his hand and he let her. "Winfield is . . .well, he's not much *interested* in me at night."

"Then he's not much of a man," Will said. The heat from the fire burned his back and he took a step forward.

Abby leaned into him, misinterpreting his movement. Her arms went around him and she lifted her face. "Just for a *while* tonight it could be like it *was*," she said. She stroked his back, scratching at him with her fingernails.

He couldn't help himself. He let his hand slide down her back and pulled her tightly to him. She stood on tiptoe, stretched her neck and offered parted lips. They were thin lips, not so full as Judith's. Abby's arm was thin, her hair dark. Judith's strong arms were softer, her hair the color of straw.

"What *is* it? I want you, Will. *Damn it*, we were good together in *bed*." She tried to lead him away from the fire, toward a door across the room.

"Wait," he said, shaking his head. He wanted to make love to this woman who was once his wife. He wanted to badly and fought the impulse that urged him to relieve the hurting in his loins. "What about your husband?"

"I *told* you. He's not like *you*. Sometimes at night, even when he's beside me, I make believe you and I are . . ."

Will pulled his hand from hers. He had fallen in love once before with another man's wife and had taken her to his bed. He would not do it again. "I think I'd better be going," he said.

Abby sagged, swallowed, pulled herself together, tried to smile, straightened. "There *is* another woman, isn't there?"

After he nodded she turned away and stood still for a long moment, looking across the room. "I wish things had been *different*," she said in a whisper.

Will took her by the shoulders. "We just weren't right for each other in too many ways. But we did produce two fine kids, didn't we?"

Abby nodded again. "They are wonderful, aren't they? I'm so glad Evey liked you." She was in control of herself again, looking as prim and proper as the society of which she was a part demanded. "We'll be back next summer.

166

Will you visit us?"

"Try and keep me away." He smiled at her, picked up his hat from the rack and walked to the door. Abby stood in the middle of the room. "You have a good life," he said. "I'm glad for you."

He left the house, walked to the boarding house where he was staying and found the room empty. Ardy was still out on the town. He sat in a straight chair by the bed and stared out the window. He still felt the ache of wanting and figured it was for Abby. It had been a long time.

Then, in a moment of sudden logic, he realized the ache was not for Abby at all. Quickly, he packed his gear, left a note for Ardy, paid for him to stay two more nights at the boardinghouse. He walked to the livery, got his horse, paid the stable manager, and spurred the horse into a trot.

At four in the morning he knocked on the back door of Dr. Castle's house. In a moment a light shone behind the curtains of Judith's room and he heard her walk to the kitchen door. She pulled the curtain back then closed it. "It's all right," she called to the doctor.

Judith opened the door and looked at Will who had one foot on the ground, the other on the stoop. He grinned at her widely and she smiled back at him, brushed her hair back and opened the door wider. She wore an old and frayed green robe belted at the front. She was soft with sleep and her hair was tangled. She was beautiful.

"Come in," she said in her hoarse voice. "But I don't have any pie tonight."

Will walked through the door and heard it latch behind him. He took off his hat, rubbed his unshaven cheek. "I don't want any pie," he said.

The coal-oil lamp flickered and cast moving shadows around the room. They smiled at each other and Judith laughed low in her throat as she walked slowly to him and let him take her in his arms.

IN THE UNEASY season between fall and winter, when the color of the leaves had disappeared but before the first real snowfall, Will received news that Doc Holliday had died on November 8. When Will had gone by to see the gunfighter the hotel clerk told him Holliday had been out of bed only twice in the two months before he died.

"It's too darn bad, especially since he was only thirty-five years old," the man said. "Shoot, I thought he was at least fifty."

Two years younger than I am, Will thought.

An hour later Will brushed dirt and leaves off the small marker someone had placed at the head of the grave on Cemetery Hill. "John H. 'Doc'

Holliday" was all it said. He'd have to see about getting a more appropriate tombstone. The man's death weighed heavily.

BY MAY of 1888 Doc Holliday's death lingered in Will's mind but far in the back. He and Judith took the train to Denver, were married by a justice of the peace and spent a week in the Queen City of the West. They spent long hours in bed. He followed her from shop to shop looking at, and buying, clothes. They went to a play, ate expensive meals and learned that they could have fun together. Will decided against trying to see his children. "You'll meet them later in the summer," he told Judith.

Leaving Denver, they took the Colorado Midland to Aspen where they planned to spend a few more days. The Colorado Midland had arrived in Aspen two weeks after the D&RG and had become embroiled in the question of a location for its depot. The D&RG already had the best location and the Colorado Midland was finally given a square block on Durant Avenue between Hunter and Spring streets, two blocks from the Clarendon Hotel, Aspen's best at the time.

When Will and Judith stepped off the train, Will had to fight hard to suppress a broad grin. The two blocks they would have to walk to get to the hotel made up The Row. Judith was caught up in the beauty of the area, looking up at the bulk of Aspen Mountain and then trying to collect their luggage. Will picked up the two heavy suitcases and nodded to the west. "We go this way," he said and led off, following several other unsuspecting passengers.

Half a block down Durant he heard Judith's sharp intake of breath. She had been walking a pace behind him but caught up quickly and pressed against him. "Are those . . . ?" She nodded toward the large, fancy houses and smaller, crib-like structures.

"Yep," Will said. He kept walking and felt his face getting red. Judith had to almost trot to keep up. Heavily made-up women in long, colorful dresses and some in little more than what Will thought of as underwear sat on the porches of some of the houses. Painted over the transoms of some of the smaller buildings were names — "Nellie" and "Dollie" and "Frankie."

Judith grabbed Will's arm — for protection, he thought. He was wrong. "Slow down," she said. "I want to look." He slowed and Judith took her time. She strolled down the street like she owned it, staring at the pretty women, and at the not-so-pretty. Here and there a miner went into or out of one of the houses. A piano was being played in one.

"I don't think I've ever seen a . . . what do you call them?"

Will swallowed. "You know."

168

She smiled and nudged him in the ribs. "Come on."

"Fallen doves," he muttered.

She laughed, low in her throat. "I like that. But I thought you'd say 'whore' or something else."

Will tried to pick up the pace but she held him back, stopped him right there in the middle of the street and laughed again as one of the women blew a kiss his way.

"Did you ever . . . ? You know."

"Come on," he said, trying to get her started again.

"Tell me, Will. What do they charge? How long do you get?"

He looked at the ground and started walking again, despite her hand on his arm. "Let's get to the hotel." She gave that laugh again and kept looking back at the women until they got to the hotel and he pushed her inside.

The hotel had electric lights, and Judith's attention was drawn to the wonders of the modern world. Aspen had become the first town in Colorado to do everything by electricity. Even the Aspen Mine was operating its hoists, drills and lighting system by electricity. There was talk that the horse-drawn tramway would soon have electric cable cars.

On the wall of the hotel lobby the manager had framed a notice advertising Aspen to the world. It listed everything the "world's finest mining town" offered: three banks, ten churches, three schools, six volunteer fire companies, six newspapers, four liquor stores, eight grocers, five butchers, four hardware stores, four drugstores, four shoe shops, one hospital, six real estate offices, three stage lines, two railroads, thirteen express wagons, three lumberyards, one ore sampling works, one smelter, twenty-three hotels, twenty boarding houses, forty-three saloons, two variety theaters, five billiard halls, one brewery, one telegraph exchange, a streetcar system, two dentists, eight doctors, thirty-one lawyers, fifteen civil engineers, five hundred men owning mines producing millions every year, and fifteen hundred bachelors on the make.

It was a far cry from the Crystal Valley and Will couldn't wait to get home. Three days in Aspen was enough, and they finally boarded a train — this time the D&RG at the depot several blocks from The Row — and rode to Carbondale.

Will and Judith settled easily into their life together. Ardy quickly adjusted to Judith's presence and only occasionally wandered out to breakfast wearing nothing but his long johns.

Will and Ardy repainted the house and, soon after Judith's arrival, new curtains graced the windows, the hardwood floor took on a new shine, flowers again adorned the table and there were no more dirty dishes in the sink.

In June, Will took Judith to Crystal City. He was at first reluctant but

Judith badgered him until he agreed. Tracey had no idea Judith was aware that Will was Jacob's father, of course, and he hoped to keep it that way.

Judith turned out to be a fine horseback rider, but she surprised Will by wearing a pair of men's pants for the long ride. "You don't think I'm going to ride all the way up there sidesaddle, do you?" she asked.

They crept slowly up to the small town under a yellow-orange sky. Aspen leaves barely quivered in the stillness of the day. At the falls on the north edge of town, when the tops of some of the buildings were first in view, she reined her horse and called out to Will to stop. "I've got some fixing up to do," she said over the noise of the crashing water. Will waited while she dug into a bag carried by the packhorse and then disappeared into the aspen grove carrying clothes and hairbrushes and shoes and what other doodads he wouldn't even try to guess.

Within a few minutes, more quickly than he had expected, she emerged wearing a dress and looking like she was off to the opera. "Well, I'll be damned," he muttered to himself.

Tracey had fixed herself up and was a match for Judith. Tom beamed as the two women hugged and fussed over each other while Will scuffed his boot and watched two of the three women he'd ever loved acting like long-lost sisters.

The two whispered to each other over dinner, winked at their husbands, talked about their clothes and the foibles of their men. Tom and Will had little opportunity to talk during the meal but Will began to relax as the evening wore on and even had time to play with Jacob, who also seemed to like Judith.

After the meal, and after they had sat around the table talking some more and after the women had cleaned up and Judith had insisted on helping Tracey do what needed to be done in the dining room and the kitchen, all agreed it was time to turn in. Judith made one last trip to the kitchen, returning coffee cups, and Tracey shook her head at Will.

"I'm so happy for you both," she said. "Will, she's wonderful."

In their room, Judith sat on the edge of the bed. "Will," she said. "She's wonderful."

"They're good people," he agreed.

"And Jacob. I feel so badly about his leg. But he seems to be doing well and doesn't act like it hurts him."

He sat beside her and draped an arm over her shoulders. "I hate having him call me 'Uncle' all the time."

"I know. I'm sorry." She pulled herself free of his arm and squared around to face him. "I told her I knew about you and her — and Jacob."

Will jumped to his feet. "What?" He walked to the window and leaned against the sill, looking into blackness but seeing her reflection in the glass.

170

"The moment I met her I was certain she'd want to know I knew." She hugged him. "I think it will be easier for you now. Neither of us has to pretend anymore."

"There are times when I wish Tom knew."

"Someday he'll have to be told. It should be soon."

"I dread the time," Will said.

The next morning, before Tom left for the mine, he took Will aside. "If we had a railroad we could be another Aspen," he said. "I hear they're taking sixty to eighty carloads of ore out of that town every blessed day. There are more silver dollars jingling in more pockets over there than I ever thought existed. Ten million dollars a year! That's what the owners are making from their mines. There are twelve thousand people there now and more coming in every day."

"We'll get a railroad one of these days," Will said, "and you'll get fat and lazy from being so rich."

The smile filled Tom's face. "That'd be something," he enthused. "It'd sure be fine and nice."

That evening, as Will and Judith walked up the wide main street of Crystal City, they ran into Yolanda Peabody.

Will took Judith's elbow and was about to guide her past but Yolanda stepped in front of him. Her mouth curled into a sneer as she looked Judith up and down. "Aren't you going to introduce us?"

"I wasn't," Will said. "Mrs. Peabody, this is my wife."

"Well. How do you do?" Yolanda held out her hand and Judith took it but cast a sidelong questioning glance at Will.

Yolanda wouldn't let go of Judith's hand. "Your husband and my late husband were old friends."

Will took Judith's hand and pulled it from Yolanda's. "I wouldn't exactly say that."

"No. I suppose you wouldn't." The gambler's widow stepped back a pace and pointed a finger at Judith. "Ask him about Nathan Peabody. Ask him how he killed my husband." She nodded at Judith. "I'm so pleased to have met you. Feel free to stop by my place of business anytime."

That night Judith snuggled against Will and listened silently as he told her the entire story from Dodge City to Schofield to Crystal. He did leave out the part about Yolanda threatening to get even.

"Well," Judith said when he was finished. "I've never slept with a killer before." She chuckled and Will smiled to himself in the dark. "You do lead an interesting life, don't you, Mr. Martin?"

As he thought about it, Will allowed that maybe he did. "I can't wait to hear all the other things you must be keeping from me," Judith said. "Every time I learn something new, like you having Jacob and now about killing a man, I just love you that much more."

What a woman I've married, Will thought. *What a woman.*

ANOTHER YEAR passed and there was still no railroad in the Crystal Valley. With no good roads, the jack trains continued to carry ore to Crested Butte. Wagons hauled out marble but there were still no major contracts. Those in charge of building the state capitol in Denver had just about decided on Yule marble for the floors, at least.

In Crystal, Tom and other miners continued to bore deeper into the mountains and some of them — including Tom — were making some money. But not much.

Over in Aspen things were different. Jerome B. Wheeler built a $90,000 opera house which opened on April 23, 1889, the day after Oklahoma Territory had been opened to white homesteaders in a high-noon race to stake claims.

That November the Hotel Jerome officially opened with a fancy ball. Henry Gillespie was a member of the reception committee which also included B. Clark Wheeler and H. P. Cowenhoven.

Thanks to Abby, Will and Judith were invited to the opening.

Gillespie greeted them warmly in the reception line. "What a beautiful wife, Will!" he boomed. Judith beamed. Will's tie felt tight and the heels on the new shoes he wore were so much shorter than his boots he had trouble walking.

Gillespie introduced Judith to Wheeler, who sat to his right. As she visited with him, Gillespie leaned forward and whispered to Will. "I hear the Crystal mines aren't producing much."

Will stuck his finger in his collar, trying to breathe. "It's there," he said. "We've got to have a railroad."

"Is the ore any good?"

"It's assaying out at something over 100 ounces to the ton," Will replied.

"Good Lord, man!" Gillespie frowned but recovered and slapped Will on the shoulder. "When we get ore that bad, we dump it! You'll never get rich on that kind of rock. You know what this place cost?" When Will shook his head he continued. "It cost over $125,000. You won't make that much in a lifetime."

"You may be right," Will began, but Gillespie had already turned to welcome another guest and Will followed Judith through the line feeling frustrated and out of place.

Judith, on the other hand, was enjoying every moment of the event. They joined a tour and waited to enter a three-decker hydraulic elevator which was finished on the passenger level in carved red birch and heavy mirrors. The doors opened and Abigail Porter, formerly Abby Martin, stepped out with two of the finest-looking children Will had ever seen. Abby looked startled, then recovered.

"Will!" she said. "You look absolutely fantastic. I never thought I'd see you dressed so formally."

"How are you, Abby?" He glanced at Judith and took a deep breath. Evey took Will's hand and pulled him down to her level for a kiss on the cheek.

"You look beautiful," he said. The seven-year-old was, indeed, beautiful. Her dark hair was fixed like her mother's and she wore a floor-length blue gown.

Five-year-old Henry stood silently next to Evey. "Say hello," Abby said to him. He did. Will took his hand and the boy backed into his mother's skirts.

Abby turned to the man standing next to her. "Will, this is my husband, Winfield."

Will took the man's soft hand and studied him. He was round-faced and balding, and had a paunch and short legs. Winfield Porter said nothing, just gripped Will's hand briefly and then let go. Will introduced Judith, who was properly gracious to the adults and who then turned to the children.

"I love your dress," she said to Evey.

"It's from New York," Evey replied. "My mother and I, and Henry, went there this summer. New York is big and dirty but we purchased an electric sewing machine."

Judith and Abby examined each other, Judith towering over the much smaller woman. *Good Lord*, Will thought. *Now the cycle is complete. If Tracey was here they could all stare at each other*. They were saved from further conversation when the elevator opened and several people pushed out past them.

"Come to see the children tomorrow," Abby called. She disappeared into the crowd and Will and Judith entered the elevator.

"Well, that was interesting," Judith said when they reached the top floor and stood in the hallway. She smiled. "How could you marry me after having been in love with two such beautiful women?"

Will took her hand. "You're the most beautiful of all," he said. She laughed and squeezed his hand.

After the tour of the hotel, a buffet dinner and small talk with other guests, everyone went to the Wheeler Opera House for the evening's entertainment. As they entered the theater, Will and Judith both stopped and gasped. Eight hundred gilt opera chairs faced the stage which was flanked by

173

gold boxes, upholstered in red plush. A gilded proscenium jutted out to an orchestra pit beneath a cut-crystal chandelier that had been imported from New York. They stared like children at the opulence and moved only when pushed by the crowd behind them. They sat through an opera, the name of which Will couldn't pronounce and the foreign words of which he couldn't understand.

Afterwards, back at the Clarendon, where they were staying because the Jerome was full to capacity, Will hurriedly got out of the new clothes. "Thank God," he said, back in his Levi's.

Judith stayed in front of the mirror, fully dressed, turning this way and that, looking wistfully at herself.

"You look wonderful," Will told her. "I didn't see anyone there who could match you."

She turned to him and smiled her thanks, then ran to him and threw herself at him, pushing him back on the bed. "I'm so glad you married Abby," she said. "Otherwise, I might never have had a night like this."

Will laughed. "If I hadn't found you first you'd probably have married one of those Aspen silver kings and had a night like this once a week."

"Hush," she said. "Am I really pretty?"

"The prettiest."

Two days later, on the ride back toward the ranch, Judith was unusually quiet. "What's on your mind?" Will asked.

"Children," she said simply. "Yours are so wonderful I could cry."

"They are kind of nice," he said proudly. "Hope that boy gets some grit in him someday."

"How do you feel about children, Will?"

"What do you mean? Didn't I do all right with them?" Then he turned to her and saw the smile and figured it out.

"You don't mean . . . we're . . . ?"

She nodded. "I think we are," she said softly. The low laugh began deep down and climbed in her throat and then burst out of her mouth when Will let out a yell that scared the horses. They jerked at the wagon and it almost threw him backwards. He dropped the reins and hugged his wife. They clung to each other there in the wagon seat, laughing like it was the funniest thing they'd ever heard.

WILL STOOD outside his home in the evening a few days later and decided it looked drab and shabby. Judith continued to claim the house was just fine. "It's just a place to live in, after all," she'd said. To Will, it looked tiny, unsubstantial and unworthy of the lady who presided over it.

He leaned against the spruce and thought about the ornate homes in Aspen with gingerbread and cornices, rounded towers and bay windows, all painted bright colors and reaching tall to the sky. He thought of Bullion Row full of the silver kings' elegant showplaces. A hotel costing $125,000 and a $90,000 opera house, by damn! And silk hats, ostrich plumes, diamonds and satin-lined carriages, too.

He found more of the same in Glenwood Springs. Walter Devereux of Aspen was actually rechanneling the Grand River.

"He wants to expose the hot springs so rich Easterners and the hoity-toity from Aspen can come soak their fancy white butts in 'em," a dour-faced, short-legged woman told him as he stood on the south bank of the river and looked down at the work. "Some say he's gonna build a bathing pool and a hotel, too. Power to him, I say. We might as well have some of that money that ever'body but us seems to have plenty of."

In Carbondale, on his way home, Will stopped by the Black Nugget saloon and heard the first rumors of another Indian war. "It has something to do with an Indian Messiah named Wovoka," he told Judith and Ardy that night. "He says he had a vision and saw all the white people gone and nothing left but Indians and buffalo."

Judith shivered. "Are they going on the warpath again?"

"I don't think so. But there's also something about a ghost shirt that's supposed to stop white man's bullets."

Ardy grunted, blew smoke, coughed and frowned. "Don't sound good but it'll probably blow over when it gets cold."

"It's already cold," Judith said.

She was right. Within a week the ground was covered with snow and it was still falling steadily, sometimes floating down like soft feathers and other times being blown almost parallel to the ground by a relentless north wind. For days, even weeks at a time, they didn't see the sun, and went out of the house only rarely and at night huddled around the fire.

The house leaked cold. Drafts swirled at their feet and their hands were often so chilled they wore gloves inside. Will nailed strips of wood around the windows but succeeded in keeping out only some of the north wind. Each morning he chopped wood and the fireplace burned day and night. By late January Judith was showing her pregnancy proudly.

In February, though, she developed a cold that started with a slight sniffle and suddenly turned into a fever that kept her in bed most of the time.

"It's nothing," she snapped when Will wanted to take her to town to see Dr. Castle. "I've had colds before."

She lay in bed unmoving, groaning now and then when she thought Will

175

couldn't hear. Her face was a fiery red and her forehead hot to the touch.

After a few days and despite her protest, Will bundled her up and took her to town beneath a cold sun that seemed barely able to penetrate the gauze-like layer of high clouds.

"Frankly, I don't know what it is," the young doctor told Will. "Leave her here and we'll watch her a few days."

Will wouldn't leave, and stayed in the house with Judith in the room that had been hers before their marriage. Finally, the fever broke.

"I want to go home," she said.

"A few more days," Dr. Castle replied.

The fever stayed down and so did Judith. Her strength didn't return and she still found it difficult to eat. "Go check on Ardy," she told Will. "I'm sure he needs something. Take him some tobacco and whiskey."

"Whiskey?"

She tried to smile. "Take him some whiskey and some tobacco and something good to eat. No telling what he's been living on."

"I been livin' on a deer I shot a week ago and I been hoardin' my baccy, not knowin' when you might show up," Ardy said when Will returned home, following Judith's advice. "How's our girl?"

Will shook his head. "Doc says she needs more time."

"Well, get yourself back into town. I can take care of myself. Been doin' it for near sixty years now."

"Are you that old?"

Ardy's eyes flashed. "What if I am?"

"Don't get mad, now. Just foolin'."

"Damn fool thing to fool about."

For much of the next day, Will helped Ardy with chores that had gone undone and started for Carbondale late in the afternoon, riding against a north wind that rushed past his cold ears with the sound of a locomotive.

Judith wasn't in her room. He heard a cry and rushed into the examining room. She lay on the table, legs spread. Doctor Castle was putting something in a bag.

"Judith . . ."

The doctor turned, exposing his bloody hands. "What?"

"Wait outside, Will!"

"But . . . Judith, my God!"

"She's all right. Wait outside!" It was an order and, staggered by what he had seen, weak-kneed and gasping for breath, Will walked into the front room. A few minutes later Castle opened the door and Will jumped to his feet.

"She had a miscarriage," the doctor said. "She'll be fine."

"The baby?"

Castle shook his head.

Will sat down, head in his hands, and cried. He couldn't remember the last time he had cried, but thought he probably had as a child. "What was it?" he asked when he could talk.

"It was a girl." Castle touched Will's shoulder. "I did what I could. I'm sorry, Will."

"I know you did, Doc. Can I see her?"

"Go on in. She's asleep now but it would be good for you to be there when she wakes up."

THE WINTER stretched into April and then summer came with a rush. Hard-packed snow quickly turned into mud and the Crystal River's winter trickle became a torrent. The creek by the house swelled to twice its normal size and brought trees and boulders crashing down the ravine. Will and Ardy broke up dams almost daily, sweating under the already-hot sun. Snowbanks yards deep cascaded off of mountainsides, blocking the roads and trails. The mud slides buried meadows and left scars of uprooted trees down the steeper slopes. The river overran its banks and spread out across the valley.

Judith seemed not to notice. She did her work and spoke little. She cried late at night, her back to Will, who could find no words of consolation.

YOUNG WILDFLOWERS danced with the breeze and a willow branch whipped gracefully above the sun-ridden gold of Judith's flowing hair. She bent to a flower but left it to grow and straightened into the wind, looking at but not seeing the white line of peaks beyond Chair Mountain. Will leaned against an aspen and wished the grief hadn't taken hold of her so. He'd thought a ride would do her good and had insisted that they explore the old Ute trail that ran west from the valley toward Paonia and Delta. People were calling it McClure Pass now.

Will's failure to bring Judith out of her lethargy upset him. He'd done what he could, not that the baby's death didn't burden him, too. But Judith resisted every effort. He couldn't remember her laughing in the three months since it had happened.

Between Crystal and the gentle pass where Will waited on Judith, the valley was changing. There were more people now, and the trail along the river was being beaten into a well-worn thoroughfare as wagons and horses

177

worked their way up and down, back and forth, carrying out the commerce of an increasingly modern world.

The sun was directly overhead now and the shadows that gave depth to the mountains and exposed their shape were gone. Their massiveness was still evident but the details of cliff and gully, rise and fall, had disappeared.

He walked to Judith and touched her. She turned with sad eyes and nodded. They went back to the horses and rode silently along the fall of the river. It was twilight when they got home and Ardy had their dinner on the table.

✎✎

LITTLE BY LITTLE Judith came back to herself that summer. She got to where she could talk about her loss and, in talking, eased some of the grief.

"I've lost every child I've had," she said. "All I ever wanted was to raise children and be a good wife."

She talked and cried and talked some more. "I should have gone to the doctor at first, instead of thinking I would get over it."

At night she huddled with Will in their bed but refused his tentative advances. "I know Dr. Castle said I won't have any more children but I'm afraid, Will."

She began to pay attention to her appearance again. "Does this dress look all right?" she asked. "I lost so much weight." She put flowers on the table, and remarked, "We need new curtains. Maybe a nice sofa in front of the fire."

✎✎

IN JULY, Stephen Keene and a syndicate out of Denver bought the Yule Creek marble quarries. A group of architects and contractors from the Front Range said the marble quality was good. Prosperity was ahead for the area, they said. Keene convinced the D&RG to survey a route from Crested Butte to Marble but no railroad was built. Keene also failed in his attempt to get a wagon road built from the south. There was little interest outside of Marble itself, and even less capital. Keene went looking for more financial backing.

He would find it, Will thought, Keene or somebody else, and eventually there would be a railroad and more people and towns. *Maybe the fear of change comes with age*, he figured, *especially to a man who's seen about enough change to last him.* He fought the fear, but knew he couldn't defeat the passage of time. Despite owning part of a mine and the possibility of becoming somewhat rich with the railroad's arrival, he hoped it never came.

As Judith crept slowly out of the long nightmare of grief, Will pulled more and more into himself. He went to Crystal, finally, and talked with Tom,

178

took Jacob on a horseback ride and watched Tracey grow older.

He went to Glenwood Springs and watched Walter Devereux's crew work to fulfill the man's dream of turning the town into a healing spa where the wealthy of Aspen and the world would come to play and show off their riches.

He went to Carbondale in the fall and heard more about the ghost dancers. He listened to fearful stories of heathens preparing for vengeance, and of a people devoid of hope who saw, in an old Paiute Indian, the Messiah who would lead them back to their dreams of plenty.

Judith and Ardy had both heard bits of the story firsthand. Over dumpling stew, they shared their information.

Over the past centuries, as the tribal society of Indians throughout the West had remained strong, the Utes, the Sioux, Paiutes, Kiowas, Cheyennes, Shoshones and many of the others had resisted the Christianizing efforts of Spanish priests and, later, Protestant missionaries. As they were herded onto reservations in the late 1870s and early '80s, though, the old ways began to disappear and many Indians joined Christian churches. In time, they began to add their own variations to Christian rituals, mixing in a helping of Indian legends to come up with, as Ardy put it, "their own Christ story."

In 1870 a Paiute named Tavibo had gone into the Utah wilderness where, in a mystical revelation, he saw all of mankind swallowed into the earth. Three days later, however, all the Indians arose, along with the wild animals on which they depended. No white man was reborn.

"I thought this Wovoka started it," Ardy said.

"As near as I can figure," Will said, "Wovoka was Tavibo's son and was raised by a family of Mormons after Tavibo died."

Wovoka told his own version of the story. He predicted a flood that would destroy all of mankind and that the old Indian ways would re-emerge. Wovoka was suddenly cast in the role of an evangelist. The Ghost Dance, the Indians were told, was the means by which this would transpire. Throughout the West, Indians donned what white men soon called Ghost Shirts, made of loose-fitting white deerskin or muslin. The shirts were decorated with mystical Indian symbols — the sun, moon, stars, the eagle, the magpie and the buffalo. The shirts, the Indians said, were so powerful they were bulletproof.

Dance, they said, *and all will come to pass. Dance and you will see your long-dead relatives. Dance and the Indians will dominate the world once again.*

"It's going to lead to war, isn't it?" Judith asked.

"Wovoka's preaching peace," Will replied. "He says if they just dance, all of what he's predicting will happen peacefully."

Judith went to the bedroom and returned with a yellowed copy of *The*

179

Rocky Mountain News. She found the article she sought and read: "The Indian Messiah Wovoka says the Ghost Dancers are to do nothing but dance and sing. 'You must not hurt anybody or do harm to anyone,' he is quoted as preaching. 'You must not fight. Do right always.'"

Ardy snorted. "I don't think nothin' good's gonna come out of all this."

The eerie singing that had been heard up and down the valley for years continued into the deep fall, north and south of Marble, and near the hot springs. Valley residents, preparing for another bout with winter, were in bad enough spirits to begin with, and the continuance of the haunting sound set nerves on edge. Groups of men, many of them out of work for the winter and angry and discouraged with the lack of progress on getting a railroad into the valley, set out to locate and kill the person, or the thing, behind the noise. Armed bands roamed the mountains near where the sound had been reported.

In November Will set out on what he guessed would be his last trip of the year to Crystal. The sky was low and gray and the wind nipped at him from the back and swirled brown and yellow leaves around his horse's hooves. He rode with head down, now and then looking up as he met a horseman or a wagon.

"Snowin' hard up at Marble and Crystal?" he asked.

"Not hard but some. Won't be long now," he was told. He stopped at the hot springs and warmed his hands, let the horse stand in the steaming water and then forged on to the red cliffs. Just before it slid behind the wall of mountains to the west, the cold sun found a hole in the clouds and cast a falsely warm glow over the ridge to the east, lighting up the craggy point to which Will had climbed. He touched the reins and the horse stopped. He leaned forward in the saddle, stretching his legs, and studied the rocky outcropping. A figure moved on the point and then disappeared. He tried to focus in on the spot.

There it was again. The figure disappeared from view once again as Will waited, watching closely. Soon, though, clouds obscured the sun and he couldn't make out details on the cliff.

Will pushed the horse up the valley and camped in a heavy growth of pine on East Creek. That night he thought he heard the singing but it might have been the wind. He made a small fire, ate some cornbread and tried to sleep, curled up in a blanket.

By dawn he was on the move. He followed a deer trail for a while then struck off on his own, following his instincts through low undergrowth that tore at his pants legs and made him wish for his batwing chaps. He stopped in a small clearing, unsaddled his horse and set out on foot, carrying his old Winchester.

It was late morning when he topped a ridge and could look down and northwest toward the point. There was no one there and Will was disappointed. He had climbed a long way. Maybe he had imagined seeing someone.

Half an hour later he was on the outermost ledge of the point. The higher peaks across the valley were dusted with snow while Chair Mountain and the range behind it were bright with white. Barren aspen trees were gray against the green of pine and cedar.

Someone, or something, was behind him. He felt the hairs crawl on the back of his neck and glanced at the rifle lying on the ground beside him. He had heard nothing but, somehow, this time, he knew there was another presence on the cliff. Slowly, he let his hand drift toward the rifle.

"That will not be necessary."

The voice was old and hoarse. It cracked with age but seemed forceful because it took Will by surprise. Will stopped his hand and sat unmoving as the voice went on.

"I have seen you here before. Why do you come?"

Will swallowed, took a breath. "I wanted to know why someone would be here this time of year." Out of the corner of his eye he saw the rifle slide backwards away from him.

"You can stand up now, and turn around."

The Indian had long gray hair plaited into two braids that hung far down his back. He was as old as the dirt, and deep lines etched his broad, bronze face. He was short, but he held Will's rifle as though he knew how to use it.

"Were you unarmed?"

"I was," the Indian said. He glanced at the rifle and smiled. The Indian wore store-bought pants and a dark shirt beneath a heavy coat.

"You will come this way," the Indian said, motioning toward the trees against the back of the cliff where Will could see a bundle of clothes and maybe food hidden in a low spot. "Sit," the Indian said. He went to the bundle, his eyes rarely leaving Will's, and deftly opened it. He lifted out a length of rope. "If you cause trouble I will have to tie you up."

"I don't plan on causing any trouble."

"That is good. We will talk." The Indian sat down cross- legged, keeping the rifle barrel trained on Will.

"Talk?"

"I can talk your language." The Indian studied him. "You have been here before. Why?"

Will thought about it. "I wanted to see what it looked like from up here."

The Indian nodded, continued to stare at Will. "Because of your invasion of my sacred spot I have visited your home."

Will remembered Ardy's accident with the horse two years before, when

181

Ardy had insisted someone had been in the barn. "You spooked my horses," he said. "A man was hurt."

The Indian shrugged.

"Who are you?" Will asked.

The Indian let his eyes stray out over the valley but kept the rifle on Will. "I know your name is Martin," he said. "I know about your son." Will opened his mouth in surprise but the Indian silenced him with an upraised hand. "I know your first woman left you. I know you ride up and down this valley a great deal. I have watched you."

This is getting interesting, and frightening, Will thought. "Why?"

"Because you, among all the whites, saw a need to climb to this place. It is a sacred spot. You have felt it."

Will recalled his first climb and the intense feeling of unease that engulfed him. "I felt something."

"This is Owl Point," the Indian said. "It is *ihupi'arat tubut,* a haunted spot where ghosts live."

Owl Point? Ghosts? Will frowned beneath narrowed eyes.

"You need have no fear," the Indian continued. "The *ini'pute,* the ghosts who live here, will not harm you. They obey me."

Will looked quickly around him. His skin began to crawl.

"Inu'sakats brought me here long before white men knew of this valley. I am *po'rat,* what you call a holy man."

It was suddenly becoming clear to Will. "You are the one who does the singing."

"Singing?" The Indian's face cracked into a broad smile. "It is a chant," he said. "A chant to *Inu'sakats.*

"This *Inu* . . . this is a god? You are praying to him?" The Indian stood, heaved his ancient body upwards and swayed above Will.

"It is a curse," he said. "I have cursed this valley and I must always seek the help of *Inu'sakats* or I will lose my power."

"You . . . ?"

"I am Owl Man. I have spent many summers in the valley which is not for white men. It is for us. For Utes."

Will's eyes were wide. The curse was real, at least to this lone Indian.

"Why did you do this thing?"

Owl Man looked sad and let the rifle point to the ground. "You do not need to ask such a question."

"No. I don't."

Owl Man motioned Will up against a pine tree. "I will not kill you," he said. "But I will tie you to this tree. I must dance and sing. I have waited for you too long." Holding the rifle in his left hand, barrel against Will's side, he deftly tied Will's hands together and then looped the rope around the tree. "I knew you were coming long before you arrived. My friend, the eagle, told me. The small birds that flew from tree to tree told me of your location. You make too much noise."

Will tested the ropes and knew escape was impossible. "Many of my people have cursed a land," Owl Man said. "There are other curses but none so effective as here. And now Wovoka has awakened in my people, and in all Indians, the hope of a new world without the white man."

The Indian rummaged in the bundle again and lifted out a soiled white shirt. It was covered with Indian symbols and drawings of birds and animals.

"You have heard of the Ghost Dance?" Owl Man shrugged the white man's coat from his shoulders and pulled the Ghost Shirt on over his head. "I dance to bring back the spirits of the dead. Someday I will see my wife on this point. I will see Long Hand and Wolf and many others and we will again live in this valley."

Will slumped against the tree as Owl Man began to shuffle his feet. From the Indian's throat came a soft humming, perhaps words of the Ute language, perhaps nothing more than grunting. Owl Man ignored Will and soon seemed to forget he was there. The singing and chanting grew louder, and Will recognized it as the sound he had heard before. Owl Man's eyes seemed to glaze over as his head lowered and raised. His feet shuffled in the dirt as he sang and danced and sang.

Puffs of white clouds began to float overhead from the north and their shadows drifted over the point and over Owl Man, who seemed not to notice. All afternoon he danced the little shuffling of his feet, moving his arms, raising his head, lowering it, chanting out the words of a song known but to him and his God. Will's body ached. He spoke to Owl Man but got no response.

The sky darkened little by little all afternoon and still Owl Man danced. *The man's stamina is incredible*, Will thought, *for one so old*. The wind came up late in the afternoon and Will shivered as it clawed through his clothes. Owl Man's feet continued to shuffle but the chanting became little more than a deep rumble in his throat. Will shifted his weight, tried to spread his hands, bent his legs. A light rain, almost sleet, wet his cheek and neck. He shook with the cold. Owl Man moved in a circle, packing the damp earth, shuffling his feet, bobbing his head, and moving his arms. His braids were heavy with rain and his damp shirt clung to his body.

Will's shoulders hurt. His back felt like it would break. He stretched his legs, arched his back to the rope's limits, bent his head from side to side. It was night and the rain had stopped but the wind continued to hurl hurting shocks of cold at his unprotected body. He longed for his slicker which was

183

still neatly rolled up behind his saddle.

Against the sky he could barely make out the Indian who danced more slowly now. Only the sound of moving feet. Now and then a grunt. The sound of labored breathing. Shuffle, grunt, breathe. A deep aching in legs tied together at the boots. Numbness in hands and rope burns on wrists. His hat had blown off when he nodded somewhere around sleep and lay caught in a thicket. He had tried to lick his lips for water during the rain but now there was nothing. He slept.

He woke to the sound of an owl that hooted somewhere behind him. Owl Man's shuffling feet passed in front of him. The night was black and silent. The wind had died. Clouds seemed maybe higher in the sky. Shuffle, grunt, breathe.

Want to cry out with the pain of immobility but sit still and endure. Shift your buttocks again and again and stretch and rotate your head and move your toes if you can feel them. Long for water and apple pie and bed and softness beside you and sleep and wake again and feel the ache and try to move.

Shuffle, grunt, breathe, but slower now. Is the sky opening up? Is it almost morning? A figure looms in front of you and fades in the pre-dawn darkness. Shuffle. Grunt. Breathe.

Shuffle. Can't stand the pain in the shoulders. Grunt. No feeling in the toes. Breathe. Lick at cracked lips.

Did the Indian fall? Is he regaining his feet? The sky is gray, not black.

Shuffle. . . There. A break in the sky. The faint outline of a ridge across the valley.

Grunt. . . The wind, a breeze, stirs a pine bough. Lighter yet across the way. Now Will could see Owl Man. He stood bent at the waist, knees buckled. Breathe. . . He fell. Tried to rise. Lay still.

The morning broke of a sudden as did the wind, blowing cold clouds up the valley south. Owl Man lay on his back, eyes closed. Did his chest move? Will shifted to his right hip, pushed on the restraining ropes which cut his wrists, licked at his parched lips, heard the moan and knew it was his own. Let your head fall to your chest and relax your legs and don't worry about feet you can't feel and hope the sun will warm you soon, and sleep tied to a tree.

The sun had barely topped the ridge behind him when Will opened his eyes. An eagle cut circles out of the space above him. Small birds chirped in a tree. Far below, the narrow band of the Crystal River, made narrower by the season, glinted with points of reflected sun. Owl Man lay still.

The Indian stirred. Will couldn't tell if ten minutes or an hour had passed. Slowly, Owl Man's head turned as his eyes opened. There were questions in his ancient eyes, then awareness and remembrance. He pushed himself to a sitting position.

"Huh," he muttered and spat. The Ghost Shirt was filthy, still damp, and red from the ground. Owl Man coughed, hacked, and spat again. He looked at the white man.

"Good morning," Owl Man said to Will.

Good morning? Good morning? Is that what the old Indian said? Will marveled. *After eighteen or twenty hours of dancing and grunting and leaving me to hurt so badly I might never stand again, how can he say good morning?*

Owl Man gathered himself for a heave to his feet. He walked unsteadily to the tree, leaned against it for a moment, reached down and untied the rope.

Will let himself fall backward to the ground, stretched his legs and groaned. He felt the life trying to find its way back through arms and legs. He held out his hands and Owl Man freed them, then untied the knot that bound his ankles.

Owl Man bent to the bundle, pulled out a military canteen, drank and passed it to Will. He felt the life of his body again and Owl Man's cracked lips smiled.

Will looked at the eagle far overhead. Its circle was wider, higher. "I thought you were dead," he said. His voice was rough, little more than a whisper.

Owl Man's voice was strong. "I had a vision. It is the purpose of the dance." He walked to a nearby boulder, lifted the rifle and handed it to Will. "We are told to dance until we are taken by *Inu'sakats* to someplace where he can show us what is to come." He turned his back on Will, walked to the edge of the cliff and stared down into the broad scoop of valley that was now alive with light. The breeze whipped his braided hair.

Will fingered the rifle. "You trust me?"

Owl Man turned. "It doesn't matter. But I do not think you will kill me." His eyes glinted. "You were part of the vision."

Will shook his head. He craned his neck against the stiffness, stood, leaned the rifle against the tree and walked on weak legs to stand beside the Indian.

"I must die," Owl Man said. The Ghost Shirt flapped in the wind. "As all men must, I will die. But I must join *Inu'sakats* before the end time. I must die soon so that I may be among those who return after the three days of which Wovoka has spoken."

The Indian looked again over the valley. "My power told me to keep you here," he said, "not so much as a prisoner but as a friend."

Will found his hat, pulled it down over his head and felt better for it.

The Indian's eyes were mere slits in his face. "The end time will come soon," he said softly. "Perhaps following the last snow of this coming winter. But maybe later. I am old enough and wise enough in the ways of these things to know that it could be in yet another spring."

The eagle screamed and they each looked up as it banked into the wind and hung almost motionless above them.

"In my vision *Inu'sakats* told me a strange thing. He said that you will relieve me of my burden."

Will sighed. He could leave. He could kill this old Indian and go back to his horse. Something held him there.

"The *powa'a* must have a human being to sustain him," Owl Man continued. "I had thought this person must be of the *Nunt'z* but it has come to pass that it will be a white man."

Will was growing weaker and sat on a rock on the edge of the cliff with his head in his hands. "Bunk," he said.

"I do not know that word," the Indian replied.

"You dreamed what you wanted to dream." Will rubbed his hurting eyes.

"Perhaps." Owl Man turned away, speaking louder as the wind increased and tried to drown his words in its roar. "On this spot many years ago I discovered that I was *po'rat*, a holy man with powers exceeding your ability to understand. I also realized that this spot on which we stand is *ihupi'arat tubut.*" The old voice broke and scratched dryly. "Ghosts live here. Somehow, they drew you to them and you came here, as you say, to see the valley from on high. Yet there was another reason you came, one you yourself do not understand. But I understand."

Will struggled to his feet. "You must stop this . . . this ghostlike singing. Someone will kill you."

Owl Man laughed. "Heh!" He turned his face to the sun, lifted his head and closed his eyes. "You have felt the same love for this valley that my people have always felt. You know it as well as any Ute. You, above all others, were chosen."

Chosen. Powa'a. Ghosts. A haunted spot. Weak from hunger and thirst, his body aching, Will's head began to swim. He felt dizzy and stepped back from the brink of the cliff.

"Do you deny what I have said?"

Will tried to think. He did love the valley. He knew it better than any living man — any white man. He dreaded the changes that were sure to come with the railroad: more people, machinery and electricity, and telegraph lines and roads. He shook his head.

"My work is finished," Owl Man said.

Will let himself down to the ground again. *Where was the canteen? Where was food?*

He saw the Indian spread his arms north to south, encompassing the valley that both men loved deeply, loved with a fervor that few could

186

understand. He closed his eyes, felt himself spinning around and around and opened them again.

"I come, *Inu'sakats*," Owl Man said.

Will tried to reach for him but he was too slow. Arms outstretched, Owl Man, launched himself off the cliff and into the open air. There was no sound, only the wind rushing in Will's ears then a chattering of birds behind him, a screech from high in the sky. He stared at the emptiness where only seconds ago Owl Man had stood. He sat there a long time and then forced himself to his feet, took his rifle and walked slowly back to the clearing where he had left his horse.

◈

"I HADN'T thought about it in that way before," Will told Judith. "But when that Indian said I loved this valley I knew he was right." The two of them sat on the bed and he held her hand tightly. He had awakened Judith and Ardy late that night to tell them the story and it was now well after midnight. Ardy had trudged back to his bed but, despite his ordeal, Will knew he would not be able to sleep. Not for a while, anyway.

"There's something about this place that goes beyond beauty," he said. He stood and paced the floor, a heat in his body building up pressure that pushed for release. "I thought about it all the time I was burying the old man. The valley seems to have a life of its own, some kind of . . . of *essence*." He didn't know where the word came from, couldn't remember having used it before. He had to talk, to keep expressing himself. "It's like it actually *breathes*, maybe thinks and acts for or against whatever man throws at it. I felt something up on that point the first time I climbed to it and the old Indian told me what it was. There's a lifelike something up there. Owl Man called it ghosts, Indian names."

He sat beside her, looking at the floor and at her. "Whatever it is, I *felt* it. Owl Man said he transferred this . . this whatever it is to me. I don't believe in ghosts."

He was rambling and struggling to put something that was beyond understanding into human phrases. "I don't believe in ghosts," he said again. "But I do believe in a spiritual power that *could* give life — life like we know it — to a piece of earth. Isn't that possible? Am I crazy or is it possible?"

She touched his arm and let her eyes, full of love and a desire to understand, wash him with feeling, as if she were trying to transfer her empathy to his struggling mind. "It's possible," she said.

"I felt close to that old man," he went on. "I felt a kind of relationship with him. I *understood* him. Damn, I'm tired but my mind's so full of thinking it hurts." He reached down and pulled off a boot, then rubbed his foot. He lay back on the bed, closed his eyes, and felt his head swim again. He opened his eyes but they wouldn't stay open, so he gave in to the weariness and let his body relax and float there somewhere above the bed.

He heard the aged Indian telling him again, "You are now *po'rat*. The valley is yours to do with as you will. I pray that what I think I see in you is true." He saw again the Indian with arms outstretched and then the hole in the sky where he had been, and he felt himself move up the ridge and through the underbrush. He was standing by the body again, the broken and bleeding body lying unnaturally bent on the rocks far below the point. Again, he was moving rocks, digging with a tree limb and covering the body. Like before, he thought he saw an eagle, an owl, and hundreds of birds in the trees as he piled rocks high over the body and bent to bid the old man a farewell, wondering if there was anyone who would miss him.

Will awoke later with sun streaming in through the window and realized someone had undressed and covered him. He let the sleep take him again and he dreamed of ghosts and eagles and dancing and Indians and hurting wrists and cold and chanting. When he awoke again it was night, and he took the water that Judith brought. He fell again into sleep and didn't dream anymore, and he awoke before dawn on the second day, rested and strong. And hungry.

He started to see the valley with the eyes of a newborn. He greeted it in the early mornings as if it were a friend, a mother. He called Mount Sopris "the old man" and walked quietly on the banks of the hibernating Crystal River. He welcomed the snowfall that blanketed the valley and listened to the contented sigh from the mountains as they settled warmly beneath a coat of white. He worried about leaving footprints and said "thank you" to the trees he cut for firewood; he knew the deer he killed for meat were sent to this spot to wait for him because he needed food.

With the clouds that almost daily made the trip south to Crystal City he sent messages to Tracey and Tom and Jacob, messages of hope that he knew they received, somehow, and understood.

The snows were long and hard. They settled deep in the valley and deeper yet in the high country, and the wind blew and the sun was low and cold. But Ardy and Judith brightened when Will was with them, because they sensed he had reached an understanding within himself that set him free of the doubt that had plagued him. In December, he heard the story of Wounded Knee and was sad for Owl Man and his people, and for the Indians who had believed so strongly in a rebirth of a world in which only they and the animals existed.

Will had a strong sense that the changes that were to come for the white people of the Crystal River Valley were not so fearsome, after all.

PART V

1892-1899

Evaline Martin was ten years old and she had come to spend a month with her father at his Double M Ranch. She descended from the wagon wearing a long wine-colored gown and a hat bursting with feathers. She carried a purse, and in the two trunks which Will and Ardy struggled to lift from the wagon were clothes enough to outfit one of those fancy, and expensive, dress stores in Aspen.

Will hugged her and caught himself before he blurted out a comment about her being so tall. Instead, he held her at arm's length and said the expected: "Welcome. You're beautiful." He meant it. She looked like her mother but had Will's lean lines and long legs. Her blue eyes were big and they took in everything in one sweeping look. They shone like a lantern at night, and she smiled with her entire face as she hugged and kissed him.

"I'm not a bit homesick and I won't be, either," she announced. "Hello, Judith."

"It's so good to have you here," Judith said, giving Evey another welcoming hug.

Evey saw Ardy on the porch. "You must be Mr. Metcalf," she said and marched boldly to him, holding out her hand.

"That I am," he said. "You're prettier'n a stage actress."

Evey smiled, said, "Thank you" and walked into the house, leaving the others on the porch with her two trunks on the ground.

"Well," Will said. "I'll be damned."

Evey dominated the conversation at the evening meal and in most circumstances. She rode well on the horse Ardy had spent the spring readying for her. She was a whirlwind of activity. She dogged Judith in the kitchen, watching her cook, helping her clean. And talking. "I am not allowed in the kitchen at home. Our cook says young women should not bother her. My mother can cook, she told me, but she doesn't," Evey said. "But you don't need a cook or a maid. It's such a tiny little house. I'm glad you don't have a piano so I don't have to practice."

Ardy didn't quite know how to take her and was unusually quiet. "You don't talk very much," she said to him one night. Ardy lowered his eyes to his food and wouldn't look up. Evey watched him for a while, then stood and walked to him, bent down, and peered into his face. Ardy looked away while Will winked at Judith. Evey crept closer to him with big eyes and a mischievous smile. Suddenly, she kissed him on the cheek and Ardy, who couldn't help himself, grinned and actually blushed.

"I'll call you Uncle Ardy," Evey announced. "Is that suitable?"

190

Ardy leaned back in his chair and sighed. "That's just about as suitable as anything I can think of," he said.

A few days later they went to Crystal and were welcomed by Tom, Tracey, eleven-year-old Jacob, and Theresa, the newest of the family and now barely a year old. Jacob was shy around Evey and Will couldn't blame the boy. The few young girls he knew lacked the polish of this active young thing from the big city of Denver.

"What happened to your leg?" Evey asked him pointedly.

Jake looked at Will. "He broke it in a fall he and I took," Will said.

"Tell me about it."

"Later."

She turned to Jacob. "Then *you* tell me." Again Jacob looked to Will for help but his uncle-father shook his head.

"Might as well go ahead, boy," he said.

Tracey put her arms around the two young people and guided them toward the door. "Show Evey the town and you two can have a good talk," she said. Jacob's eyes pleaded with her to not put him through this ordeal, but she ushered them outside.

Inside, Will turned to Tom. "Things going all right?" Tom grinned. "Couldn't be better. And we'll keep on making money if we can keep Grover Cleveland from becoming President again."

"Please," Judith interrupted. "No politics today."

"Well, it's the truth," Tom retorted. "If Cleveland gets elected we go to the gold standard and there'll be no way we can afford to keep the mine operating."

"Tom's become quite an expert," Tracey said proudly.

"Some expert." Tom joined Will at the window to watch Evey and Jake walk side by side down the street. "George Sanders was the real expert. What little I know I learned from him and that's damned little compared to what he knew."

They were silent for a moment while all four of them thought about Sanders.

"Damn that Cleveland, anyhow!" Tom exclaimed, turning from the window. "He should be President right now instead of ol' Ben Harrison. We're just lucky the majority vote didn't mean anything back in eighty-eight."

"That's right," Judith said. "Harrison actually lost by ninety thousand votes but won through the Electoral College."

Evey and Jake had rounded a corner out of Will's sight and he turned from the window. "I don't want Cleveland in office any more than the rest of you," he said, "but it does seem like a stupid way to run an election."

191

"I'm for it in Harrison's case, though," Tom said. "Even if it does give the power to the big Eastern states."

"Maybe the Eastern states put him in, but I thought it was the miners and farmers," Judith said.

She sure is smart, Will thought. "Why would the farmers want him?" he asked.

"Farm prices were falling," she replied, "and we were in a period of industrialization. The farmers thought the prices were being controlled by monopolies, or trusts. They figured if the government issued enough silver money their problems would be solved."

"The Sherman Antitrust Act put a stop to the price-fixing," Tom said, "and the Treasury Notes or paper money can still be redeemed in either gold or silver. The Sherman Silver Purchase Act requires the government to buy how much silver every month?"

"Two million dollars," Tracey said. "But most people are redeeming their notes in gold and some fear too great a drain on the country's gold reserves."

"So what?" Tom said loudly. "There's enough silver to make up the difference. We've got to keep Cleveland out of the White House."

"I hear the White House has electric lights but that President Harrison and his wife are afraid to use them," Tracey said with a laugh. "I read where they actually have a White House *electrician* and they call him to turn the electric switches on and off because they're afraid of shocks."

Later, when Evey led a bewildered-looking Jacob into the house, she had him by the hand and her face was one big smile. "I like Jacob," she announced to them all. "He's quiet but once you get to know him he opens up a bit."

"I knew you two would get along," Tracey said.

Evey finally let go of Jake's hand and he looked relieved as he sat near Tom. "He showed me all of the town. It's so small, you know, that it doesn't take long. You don't have electricity here. We do in Denver, of course. I think I'll enjoy roughing it. That's what you call it, isn't it? And he told me how he hurt his leg. That was a very stupid thing to do, Father." She stood with hands on hips and pouted at Will, whose throat clogged up. He couldn't remember her calling him "father" before.

Evey turned to Tracey. "I didn't think there would be a school here."

"There wasn't until this young lady decided we needed one," Tom said, smiling at Tracey.

Evey looked from Jacob to Tracey with wide eyes. "I wish you were *my* teacher."

"That would be lovely," Tracey replied with a smile. "But it gets awfully cold up here in the winter."

Evey pondered that for a moment. "That just might be a drawback," she said, and everyone had a good laugh. Everyone except Jacob, who sat on his chair studying Evey with an odd, slack-mouthed expression.

Will saw the look and nodded to Tom who broke into another grin. "He's never been around a young filly like that one."

"She does kind of dominate, doesn't she?" Will said.

But don't get too caught up, boy, he added to himself.

"I HEAR things are picking up over your way," Henry Gillespie said to Will when he and Judith delivered Evey to Gillespie's home in Aspen later that month. "Maybe your 'cursed valley' is going to make something of itself yet."

Will ignored the barely disguised hint at sarcasm. "I hear things are going pretty well here."

"Pretty well? Things have never been better. You should have staked your claim in Aspen," Gillespie enthused. "You'd be a millionaire by now. Like me."

"Maybe so," Will said. He said his good-bye to Evey and drove Judith to the Hotel Jerome.

It appeared to Will that everyone in Aspen must be making money, even the miners themselves. If some of them could afford to pay the dollar and a quarter a day for a round trip on the cable bucket tram that carried them up and down the mountainside to and from their claims, they had to be making money.

There were upwards of twelve thousand people living in Aspen by then, and sixty to eighty carloads of ore and ten trains were running in and out of town every day. The story was that the annual ore production was averaging $10 million a year.

They drove down a street lined with handsome homes, each one larger and gaudier than the one before. Quiet ditches along the streets watered newly planted trees. Downtown, brick and stone buildings had replaced most of the original wooden structures.

"What's the feeling over in your valley about Grover Cleveland?" Gillespie asked Will the next day.

"Same as yours, probably."

"There's no question that Cleveland will adopt a gold standard and we'll all be out on the street," Gillespie said. "The Populists are putting up James Weaver, as you should know, and we'll expect your vote for him — yours and every other halfway intelligent being in the Crystal Valley."

At the hotel, Judith lingered before preparing for bed. "Won't silver be valuable, even with the gold standard?"

"Be worth something," Will said. "But not much."

"Will we be ruined if Cleveland is elected?"

Will turned from the window. "We've got the ranch."

Judith began to work her way out of her dinner dress. In a moment she flipped the switch that turned off the electric light and plunged the room into darkness. "Then come to bed," she whispered. Will tossed the cigarette out the window and felt his way across the room. He found the bed, felt the comforter, found a bare shoulder, and lay down beside it.

IN NOVEMBER Grover Cleveland won a second term as President by a margin of nearly four hundred thousand votes. Benjamin Harrison, the Republican, won only 145 electoral votes. Worse yet, James Weaver, the Populist candidate, received but twenty-two electoral votes and barely one million people voted for him. Cleveland became the only President to serve two terms that did not directly follow each other.

"Get as much ore out as you can," Will told Tom. "No telling what's going to happen."

They waited through the winter, watching whatever papers they could find and dreading the inevitable.

In Aspen, Jerome B. Wheeler's Molly Gibson mine ended 1892 with $1.2 million in paid dividends. Many of its large nuggets were 90 percent pure silver. Partly in its honor, Aspenites decided to build a colossal statue to send to the World's Fair in Chicago the next year.

The Silver Queen statue was eighteen feet tall and ten feet by twelve feet at the base. As a symbol of parity — equal rights for silver and gold — two winged gods drew a chariot and each carried a cornucopia. One poured forth gold and the other silver. The Queen's head and an eagle, which topped the chariot, were carved from solid silver nuggets.

The statue cost $10,000 and its message failed.

WILL AND TOM sat on the stoop of the boarding house in Crystal and watched as a dozen miners rode silently out of town to the south, heading for the gold fields. Will thought he could feel the valley heave a great sigh of relief as the weight of hundreds of bodies, horses, mules and equipment deserted the mountainsides and the riverbank.

The Congressional ax had dropped less than two weeks earlier — in July of 1893 — and already the town had dwindled to half the previous population.

Congress, as expected with the election of Grover Cleveland, had repealed the Sherman Act and silver had been demonetized. Most of the mines were closing, or had already shut down, and the miners who had lost jobs were heading quickly for Cripple Creek, Central City, California Gulch, anywhere the gold mines were operating or starting up again. The Princess Evaline had closed the day Will rode up the valley with the news.

Will packed a pipe. He'd been trying to quit cigarettes for a month. He got it packed, drew on it, tamped it down. "Having trouble learning how to do this," he said, just to hear himself.

Tom toed the dirt of the street. "I hear the Sheep Mountain Tunnel's staying open," he said. "They went ahead and built that mill."

"The Inez and Bear Mountain Tunnel are staying open, too," Will said.

"Hard to believe the Black Queen won't be shipping out those hundred-jack trains every day."

Will took off his hat and wiped sweat from his brow. "Wish you'd take me up on my offer," he said. "You'd be good help on the ranch. We could build you a house by winter."

Tom stretched out his legs and leaned back on his hands. "I can't figure Tracey. Says we've depended on you for too long and we should make do for ourselves."

"I'm not offering charity." Will stood, fanned himself with his hat. "You'd earn your pay. Ardy's getting old and I've got to find somebody."

"We may move down valley to Marble. Maybe build us a new boarding house. If the marble quarries get going like everybody says, I can probably hook on with one of them."

Will shrugged, feigning indifference.

That afternoon Tom went to the mine to collect whatever tools he could, thinking maybe he could sell them to one of the mines that were continuing to operate. Jacob was out somewhere and Will was alone with Tracey.

"You think Marble is the place?" he asked.

"Everybody says it's going to boom sooner or later," she said. Their voices echoed in the room. "Don't worry about us."

"All right."

"And, Will. You must stop leaving all that money for Jacob." Will had continued to leave money somewhere in the boy's room each time he visited Crystal.

"Does Tom know? About the money, I mean."

She shook her head. "Nor about anything else."

Will walked to the door, saw Tom coming from the north edge of town. "Gonna be tough when he has to know." For a moment they looked into

195

each other's eyes, remembering a brief time in another world that might as well have been centuries ago, so much had happened.

"I'd better start some supper," she said. "I've almost forgotten how to cook for so few people."

୧ৢ୨

TWO WEEKS later Will went to Aspen to visit Abby and the two children, who had come to stay with the Gillespies.

Aspen was beginning to look like the ghost town that Crystal was quickly becoming. Nearly two thousand miners had been thrown out of work. Banks had failed. Fortunes had become debts and silver barons had been reduced practically overnight from millionaires to paupers. Henry Gillespie had been wiped out.

Gillespie tried to put on a friendly face. "The fortunes of war," he said. "But, you know, I enjoyed being rich so much I think I'll try it again, someplace else."

Will and Gillespie stood outside the house the man would soon abandon. "Is everyone going down?" Will asked.

Gillespie looked at Aspen Mountain where barely a year ago the hillside had been alive with men and equipment. Now it was quiet. The bucket tram that had hauled men to and from the mines was not moving.

"Most of us are broke. I've heard that as many as 80 percent of the town's enterprises will take bankruptcy."

Will wished Evey and Henry would hurry up. "Maybe silver will come back."

Gillespie humphed a laugh. "Not likely."

Evey and Henry came from the house, finally, and Gillespie walked to the door, a broken man, but with his head up.

"How is Jacob?" Evey asked. "Will I get to see him?" "Probably not this summer."

"I think about him all the time," she said. As Will led them to the wagon he wondered where it was all heading.

୧ৢ୨

WILL FINALLY convinced Tom to accept some investment money. Now Tom was directing a crew in the building of a new boarding house in Marble. Judith rode beside Will that fall as they made their way upstream, and the two of them watched with interest the activity below Owl Point and a mile or so south.

196

A year ago J. C. Osgood had won a battle with the Colorado Coal and Iron Company and had consolidated it with his own enterprise, the Colorado Fuel Company. The resulting firm was now the Colorado Fuel and Iron Company and Osgood, as president, controlled the industrial giant of the West.

A crew of men were constructing some round-topped structures along the west bank of the Crystal River. Behind them a few shacks made up the beginning of a town Osgood had named Redstone.

"What are they building?" Judith asked. She continued to ride her horse like a man and several of the workers stared at her as the two rode past.

"Coke ovens, near as I can figure," Will said. "They'll bring the coal down from the mines about twelve miles up the creek to the west." He turned to look back at Owl Point and his stomach churned as he listened to the infernal noise of men working, shouting. He looked at Elk Mountain just south of the ovens on the west and felt its sadness. Chair Mountain, farther to the south, seemed humped down and frustrated by this new influx of men hellbent on scarring the valley, using it, and shipping its guts somewhere else for money.

Owl Man's voice came to him above the clatter: *In my vision Inu'sakats said you will relieve me of my burden . . . Ghosts live here . . . Somehow they drew you to them . . . You have the same love for this valley that my people have always felt. You, above all others, were chosen.*

"Will?" Judith nudged her horse closer to him. "Will?" He forced his eyes from the point and turned to her. "Are you all right? You seemed to be somewhere else."

He pointed to the red-rocked overlook. "Owl Point." She looked at the point then shifted her gaze to the working men.

"I understand," she said. "Let's get on to Marble."

JACOB AND THERESA had gone to bed and the four adults sat in the living room/dining room/kitchen of the small house Tom had rented while their boarding house was being built. Tracey read from the most recent issue of The Silver Lance, a small newspaper that still struggled to survive in Crystal.

"In Marble, J. C. Osgood may be the catalyst we need," she read. "The mammoth block of marble he exhibited at the Columbian Exhibition in Chicago this summer, along with that of S. W. Keene's, has resulted in orders for marble that may keep men at work in the quarries for the rest of the decade."

"I think I can get on with Osgood's Yule Creek Marble Company," Tom said. "He incorporated at $5 million."

"That's good news," Will replied. "Is there more?"

"Listen to this," Tracey said and continued reading:

"Osgood's new company has investment securities totaling more than $46 million and a labor force of sixteen thousand. The company controls 69,000 acres containing an estimated 400 million tons of steam, domestic, coking, gas, smithing, or anthracite coals. In addition, fourteen mines are operating throughout the state and producing some 12,000 tons daily. There are 800 ovens in different localities producing about twenty-five thousand tons of coke each month. There are another 2,311 acres of iron lands and nine hundred tons are produced daily in iron mines. The company owns and operates the only integrated Bessemer plant in the West. The three blast furnaces have a combined capacity of four hundred tons of foundry, pig, or ferromanganese iron each day. A rolling mill has a capacity of five hundred tons of blooms and three hundred tons of rails per day."

She stopped and took a breath. "He must be the wealthiest man in the world — or at least in the West."

"Destiny," Will muttered.

"What?" Judith brushed pie crumbs from the table.

"Several years ago I guided Osgood up the valley. I was there when he bought the coal claims up Coal Creek."

Judith's eyes widened. "You never told me that."

"We camped halfway up the creek and he told me he thought he was a man of destiny," Will said. He recalled Osgood saying that Will, too, was a man of destiny, but he kept that part to himself. "I'd almost forgotten but I own some Coal Basin claims myself."

"Will!" Judith shoved back her chair and stood.

"Sit down. I don't know if they're worth anything." He looked now at Tom and Tracey. "Whatever they're worth, George Sanders owns twenty percent."

Tracey put her hand on Tom's shoulder. "That was thoughtful of you, Will. Maybe Osgood will buy them."

"Maybe so. Another twenty percent is in Evey's name and I own forty percent."

"That's only eighty percent," Tom said.

"Right," Will said. "The rest belongs to somebody we know."

"Who?" all three listeners asked at once.

He let them wait and then leaned his head toward Jacob's room. "He's asleep in there."

There was silence for a moment and then Tracey put her face in her hands and began to sob.

"Don't get your hopes up," Will said. "I probably filed a claim on nothing but rock."

"But maybe you didn't," Judith said. "Oh, Will." And she, too, began to cry.

Will fidgeted. "I thought it might make you happy."

"It does," Tracey said as she wiped her nose and tried to smile. "It does."

THE IMMEDIATE potential of Will's coal claims was quickly reduced to nothing, however, when Osgood abruptly stopped work on the coke ovens at Redstone and the development of Coal Basin. With the crash of silver prices many smelters throughout the state had closed, resulting in a harsh reduction in the demand for coal and coke. Once again, many men were thrown out of work and another exodus from the valley began.

"Never saw such hangdog looks," Ardy said as they watched three men on horseback plod slowly past the ranch on their way to Carbondale. "Since the mines closed, anyhow."

The sun hung low in the sky, casting an orange, dusty glow over Mount Sopris. Ardy coughed almost continually and his hands had begun to shake. He still rolled his own even though it took longer than it used to.

The same sun was throwing long shadows over the almost-deserted Schofield, where those few who remained moved listlessly about their late afternoon chores. It hung on the rim above Coal Basin and blazed belligerently over the stillness of coal-mining equipment and the beginnings of a road that wound downward toward Redstone. It warmed the backs of half-built coking ovens that only a few weeks before had been tangible symbols of the valley's reawakening. The sun lighted up Owl Point, which seemed to glow with an otherworldly brightness as though from deep within the rocks a fire burned with intense heat.

"I think it knows," Will said, nodding toward Mount Sopris. Ardy looked up, hacking a cough, and flipped his spent cigarette into the yard. He shook his head and chuckled quietly.

"I believe it does," Will continued. "Sometimes I think I can feel the whole valley relaxing, like it's survived another war. Like it can sort of exhale and get ready to breathe deep in the quiet without hundreds of men tickling its bones like ants on its back."

Judith stood behind them. "You're turning into a poet. Are you pleased?"

He thought about it. "In a way. It's more like it was in the old days, when I came here for the first time."

Ardy stood and scratched his back. "Gets too much more like the old days we'll be flat broke."

"We'll make it through this," Will said. "We've got enough horses sold to last us a while."

Ardy looked away and coughed. "A while." He fished the makings from a vest pocket. "Almost glad I'm so damned old and probably won't live to see everything fall to pieces."

"You won't if you don't take Dr. Castle's advice and stop smoking so much," Judith said.

Ardy ignored her, licked the paper and lit up. The smoke hung in the air where he blew it and he sighed. He looked old in the shadows, his body and face seeming older than his sixty-three years. He walked into the yard and the sun sent his shadow straining toward the east, toward Aspen barely twenty miles away as the crow flies but almost forty on the road.

The sun was setting over Aspen, too, making sparkles dance in the dust-laden air like the glint of demonetized silver. It shone on the boarded-up houses and on the few in which men and women still lived. It strung deep shadows across Aspen Mountain and the openings of mines, some still operating but most closed down and cold in the hollowness of empty shafts. As it dipped behind the mountains it left a lingering touch on the silent Wheeler Opera House and on the nearly empty Hotel Jerome. And when it was finally dark, the town was quiet except for the barking of some lonely and hungry dog who lifted its leg against the side of a once-elegant house that now sat empty and lonely.

STARS WERE poking holes in the sky above Marble. An exception among all the mining towns west of Aspen, its townspeople were smiling. Marble, it seemed, was "on the verge." It was on the verge of getting contracts that would mean the employment of hundreds of workers. It was on the verge of getting a railroad. It was on the verge of booming so big it would put Aspen in its heyday to shame.

That's what a lot of people thought. If they could just get the contract for the new state capitol in Denver. If they could just get their bid accepted economic prosperity would be assured. If they could just convince the capitol managers that Marble could supply the 140,000 square feet on time. If they could remind the Denver capitalists that Yule marble had won first prize at the Columbian Exposition. If they could get them to commit to Colorado marble rather than that from New England and the South.

Marble submitted its bid in February of 1894 and sat back to wait. "If we get that contract," residents said. "If we just had us a railroad. Hell," they said, "if we just had a decent road." They readied the quarries that were sold and resold to firms formed just in case the contract came through. "Maybe," they said, "if we'd advertise."

❧

"YOU DID what?" Will's eyes widened as he looked at a smiling Tom that summer. He and Judith had just arrived in Marble with fourteen-year-old Evey in tow. She had immediately gone looking for Jacob while the adults settled themselves beneath a towering pine tree behind the boarding house.

Tom laughed. "Sounds crazy, doesn't it? But we'd been needing some advertising. So we issued this invitation to 'Gentleman' Jim Corbett to have his heavyweight championship fight with Charley Mitchell here in Marble."

Will looked up at blue through the green pine. "You didn't think he'd take you up on it, surely."

"Not really," Tom said. "But we did offer $75,000 cash to each fighter and a ten-ton marble monument to the one who got killed."

They were laughing at that when Evey and Jacob rounded the corner of the building. Jacob quickly jerked his hand free of Evey's and stuck both hands in his pockets. With mixed emotions, Will watched his two children walk toward him. He loved them both and dreaded having to break the news. It's got to be soon, he thought.

Evey looked at Jacob and then at Will. "You know, Father," she said, "I think he looks a lot like you."

Tracey and Will automatically shot glances at one another but, luckily, Tom didn't notice. Judith recognized the awkwardness of the moment.

"I think he's a lucky young man, in that case," she said. "Jacob, have you decided on a career?"

His face brightened. "Maybe so. Uncle Will sort of talked me out of being a cowboy so I think I should be a lawyer."

Tom beamed. "That's good thinking, boy! Maybe you could get into politics."

Evey and Jacob spent every possible moment together during the three days she was in Marble. "We're going to have to be careful," Tracey said to Will and Judith.

"I keep thinking she'll fall in love with someone in Denver," Judith mused. "The news wouldn't be so hard on her then."

Will packed his pipe. "It's going to be hard anytime."

❧

201

BECAUSE THE Gillespies were no longer in Aspen, Will and Judith took Evey to Glenwood Springs for a night in the Hotel Colorado before putting her on the train to Denver.

"A few years ago I never would have guessed that any hotel could outdo the Jerome in Aspen," Judith said as the three sat in plush chairs alongside the four-poster bed in Will and Judith's room. Will parted lace curtains framed with heavy felt drapes and shook his head at the fountain on the front lawn which spouted water maybe two hundred feet in the air. Across the street he could see the hot springs pool complex. The hotel had opened a year earlier, about the time silver prices hit bottom.

In the lobby women in finery more elaborate than any Will had seen in Aspen hung onto husbands who wore gold chains across vested potbellies. Evey picked up a printed piece.

"It says here," she read, "that the hotel is an Italian-styled edifice built from Roman brick and peachblow sandstone." She stopped walking, mouth open.

"What?" Will asked.

"The hotel cost $850,000 to build!"

"Good Lord," Will muttered. "Jerome Wheeler would have a stroke."

They walked outside near a special railroad siding. Private cars of millionaires from Denver and across the country sat silently while their owners played inside.

"Listen to this," Evey said, reading again from the pamphlet. "Walter Devereux imported architect Theodore von Rosenberg from Vienna to design and build the bathhouse for the hot springs pool complex. The walls, made of red sandstone from a quarry alongside the Frying Pan River, are two feet thick. Inside are imported mosaic floors and Roman baths with porcelain tubs."

Will peered over her shoulder at the brochure. "Pretty fancy place just to take a bath."

"Don't people come here to cure their ailments in the water?" Evey asked. "Like you did with those horses?"

"I didn't have to pay to let my horses stand in it."

Will was quiet as they strolled, watching the wealthy parade around the grounds, play in the enormous swimming pool, and drink cocktails while lounging in elegant lawn chairs. He thought about Aspen sitting quietly, her buildings rotting, only a few miles to the southeast.

Will mused that even if Glenwood Springs was booming and though Marble seemed "on the verge," many places around the country were looking more like Aspen.

Much of the country was suffering from an economic depression. The papers were predicting that some 750,000 U.S. workers would strike during the year for higher wages and shorter hours. Pullman Palace Car Company workers had gone on strike as early as May and a general strike of Western railroads began in June. Wheat prices had dropped to forty-nine cents a bushel and covered wagons were headed back East painted with the words, "In God we trusted, in Kansas we busted."

On top of everything else, the Wilson-Gorman Act included an income tax of two percent on incomes above $4,000 a year. The act was headed for an appeal but Will feared it would stand up and a general rebellion would result across the country.

Such thoughts left his mind when Will, Judith and Evey entered the Hotel Colorado's dining room. Will's eyes immediately found J. C. Osgood and his wife, Irene.

"Martin!" Osgood said loudly when he saw Will. "It's fate that you're here. I want to talk business with you."

After introductions, Osgood insisted that the three join them. He made a great fuss over Evey. "I met you when you were but a baby," he said. "I remember how beautiful you were then and you've grown into a most attractive lady."

"Thank you," Evey said, pleased with the attention. Osgood turned to Judith. "You remember. I took your husband away for a few days to guide me in the wilderness." "I'm afraid not, Mr. Osgood. That was another lady. I am the second and, I assume, the last Mrs. Martin."

Osgood flushed. "How stupid of me. I'm terribly embarrassed. Please accept my apology."

"No apology is necessary," Judith said with a smile. "Evey's mother is very beautiful and if you mistook me for her I should be flattered."

Irene Osgood leaned forward close to Judith. Her breath smelled of alcohol. "My husband frequently speaks too quickly without thinking," she said. She leaned back, took another swallow of her drink, closed her eyes and drummed her fingers on the tabletop in time with music from a piano across the room.

"Isn't that wonderful?" she asked, looking at Evey. "It's a brand new song called 'The Sidewalks of New York.' My husband, Mr. Osgood, and I heard it earlier this summer when we were actually in New York." She lifted her eyebrows. "Have you been there?"

Judith smiled bravely. "I'm afraid we haven't had the pleasure yet," she said.

"That's a shame." Irene Osgood closed her eyes and sang along: "East Side, West Side, all around the town . . ."

203

Osgood moved his chair closer to Will, ignoring his wife and the other women. "You know about my plans for Redstone and Coal Basin, of course."

Will noticed Irene's hands shake as she finished a drink and signaled for another. "I do," he said. "I also hear they're kind of on hold."

Osgood waved his hand in the air, batting away a bad idea. "Only for a time, my friend. Before long the demand for coal will rise again and I will be ready for it."

"What's that got to do with me?"

"You've bonded a claim in Coal Basin and I may be interested in purchasing it from you."

Irene downed her drink in one long swallow and Will caught Judith's concerned look. "What if I won't sell?"

Osgood leaned back and laughed. "Oh, I think you will. There's no way you could mine the coal profitably alone. You need men and equipment and roads and, by God, you've got to have a railroad."

His voice suddenly lowered and he almost whispered to Will. "There's more coal in Coal Basin than anyone has ever imagined. And I'm the one who's going to make it pay off."

He turned to Irene just as she took another glass from the tray of a waiter. He frowned and leaned toward her, whispered something in her ear. Irene tossed her head and turned back to Judith, ignoring him.

"This is another new piece," she said, nodding toward the piano. "It's called 'The Levee Song.'" Again, she sang along, this time loudly enough that people at nearby tables turned to stare at her: "I've been workin' on the railroad, all the livelong day."

Osgood talked to Will but continued to glance at Irene. "I'm sure I'll want your claim," he said. "And I'll make it worth your while. You helped me find it, after all."

Irene spilled some of her drink on her dress but didn't seem to notice. During dinner she continued to drink, even when Osgood asked her if she didn't think she had had enough. Her eyes seemed half open and her movements became slower. The waiter brought another glass and, as she reached for it, Irene hit the tray and spilled the contents in her lap.

"You clumsy fool!" she shouted at the waiter, whose eyes widened. "Can't you serve a drink properly?"

Osgood wiped at her dress with a napkin. "I'm sure he didn't mean . . . "

"He spilled that drink on me deliberately!" She stood, looking as though she might cry, took the napkin from Osgood and threw it in the waiter's face.

"I'm terribly sorry," he said. "I'll bring another."

"Just leave us," Irene demanded. "Get away from me! You've ruined my dress!"

204

Osgood put his hand on her arm. "My dear, it's all over now. There was no harm done."

"No harm?" Irene looked frantically about the room as though in a daze. "This man has ruined my Paris gown and you say there was no harm? How can you be so stupid?"

The head waiter appeared at the table. "I'm so sorry, Mrs. Osgood." He bent to her with a concerned expression. "I'm sure it was an accident."

Suddenly, Irene slapped him. "It was no accident! He did it on purpose to humiliate me!"

The waiter straightened. "I'm afraid I shall have to ask you to leave, madam," he said in as calm a voice as possible. "You are disturbing our other diners."

Osgood was quickly on his feet and stretched to his full height, which didn't come close to six feet. "How dare you insult my wife in that manner! Do you know who I am?"

"Yes sir," the man said. "I most assuredly do and it is very difficult for me to do this. But our diners have the right to expect propriety in this hotel. Now, if you will please leave quietly there will be no charge for your meal — or the lady's drinks."

Osgood threw his napkin on the table and took Irene's arm. "Come, my dear," he said. "We are checking out of this abominable excuse for a hotel this moment."

He led Irene toward the door but turned after a few steps. "I'll be in touch, Martin. And I'm sorry about this." To the room in general, he said, "To all of you, I apologize. Please enjoy your dinner. And, mark my words. Someday soon — sooner than any of you might expect — I shall construct a home that will make this stuffy hotel look like a pauper's shack. If you believe this place is the height of elegance, I advise you to watch closely." He stormed out.

Will glanced at Evey, who sat open-mouthed. "It's all right," he said. "I'm sorry you had to see that."

"I'm not," she said. "He was wonderful!" She broke into a wide smile. "He was quite mortified by everything but he certainly stood up for his wife."

Will sat back. *This little girl is very, very aware*, he thought. She missed little and Will hadn't even considered that Osgood was defending Irene. He'd taken the man's anger for concern over his own status.

"He did, didn't he?" Judith said. "Would you have done that for me, Will?"

"I'd like to think so," he replied. "But I probably wouldn't have made such a wild promise in front of so many people."

"I think he'll keep it," Judith said. "I have a feeling about that man. What did you say he called it — destiny?"

205

"I just decided something," Evey said to the two of them. "I am never, never going to drink."

"Well now," Will said. "Then the evening was certainly worthwhile."

ல௷

ASPEN CONTINUED to slumber. The beginnings of Redstone lay quietly below Owl Point. But, in 1895, Marble received the contract it had sought for so long.

A wonderful new era was underway and few took much notice when Yolanda Peabody and her eleven-year-old daughter, Inez, moved into a small house south of Marble above Beaver Lake. With her was a man she introduced as her husband, Leon Harrison. Those few who inquired were told he was an "investor."

"Why do you think she's here?" Tracey asked Will. "Who knows? Just keep out of her way and don't worry about her."

But Tracey couldn't help worrying, as she told Will during one of his trips to Marble in the spring of 1896. "She knows. I'm afraid for Jacob."

"I think she's planning on starting another saloon," Will said. "It's nothing to worry about."

Over the next two years Tracey almost forgot about the woman. Leon Harrison continued to be conspicuous by his absence most of the time and Yolanda took no part in community activities. Of far more interest to Marble residents was that, by the end of 1897, more than $100,000 worth of marble had been shipped to Denver for the interior of the capitol building. In addition, two new smelters were constructed near the town, meaning that low-grade ore could now be sold to the smelters and the mine owners didn't have to bear the cost of transporting it at great expense. Even some of the smaller mines could remain open by selling a few tons of ore at a time for cash.

"Why do you keep riding that old horse of yours up here?" Tracey asked Will. "We do have a stage line, you know."

Will knew. He watched it tear past the ranch twice a day on its way up or down the valley. There was so much traffic on the new wagon road along the Crystal that he had suggested to Judith that they build a new house a few hundred yards farther west, as far from the road as he could get. Judith had laughed at the idea and Will forgot about it. He and Ardy did, however, build a new bunkhouse for the two new men.

"Never thought I'd get old enough to ree-tire," Ardy said to Will at dinner. The cowboys made do for themselves in the bunkhouse but Ardy continued to eat, and to live, in the main house. "Always thought I'd die whilst tryin' to make some dumb animal do what he didn't want to do. Now I

206

got two men workin' for me and I can just kind of lazy around."

"Don't go getting too lazy, old friend," Will said. "I need you to run this place. You kept me away from the workings so long I don't know much about it."

Ardy grunted. "I kept you away?" His eyes glinted. "You know damned good and well you don't know nothin' about ranchin' 'cause you spent more time on your horse gallivantin' around the mountains than you did workin'."

"And I appreciated the opportunity to do so," Will said.

"What're you gonna do when I die?"

Judith looked up. "Are you thinking about dying?"

"Why not?" Ardy snapped. "I've got six and a half decades on these old bones. Ain't gonna last forever."

"You're too mean to die," Will said. "Besides, we need you around here. Judith's cooking will keep us all alive, anyway."

Ardy cracked a bit of a smile. "I got to admit I'd sure miss them apple pies."

"Then shut up and eat and let's not talk anymore about dying," Judith said.

๛

THE WHITE HOUSE Saloon was a two-story frame building standing at the end of Marble's main street, removed from the rest of the town's structures by forty yards. Inside, the sun cast long shadows from the windows to the opposite wall. Dust and smoke rose slowly to the ceiling and glasses clinked over subdued voices of card players.

Yolanda Peabody-Harrison sat on the piano bench talking to a man who cradled a rifle in his arms. Will made straight for them.

"We need to talk," he said. She turned slowly to look at him and the man beside her stiffened.

"She's busy," he said.

Will refused to look at the man who stood inches taller than himself and who outweighed him by thirty pounds. "Get unbusy," he said.

The room had quieted as the customers watched the unfolding drama. "Maybe the lady don't want . . . "

"Shut up!" Will snapped at the beefy man.

"It's all right, Yates," Yolanda said. She lifted her hand and pushed the gun barrel, which had shifted towards Will's neck, to the side. "I'll talk to you later."

Yolanda motioned to an empty table and Will sat across from her, keeping a wary eye on Yates. "What is it you want?" Her voice was soft with a trace of Taos shadowing the edges. She smiled slightly, but only with her mouth.

"I think you know," Will said. "Your hired guns are building fences around my property."

"Not your property," she said quietly. "Mine."

"You've got me boxed out so I can't get to my horses in the meadow south of Nettle Creek."

She lifted her eyes and locked on Will's. "That's too bad." It was almost a whisper.

"I think there's a law about allowing access," Will said, holding her gaze. "I'll have to cut my way through."

"I wouldn't advise it." She nodded toward Yates and the man grinned, exposing two missing front teeth.

"I'll take my horses out in a few weeks," Will said.

Yolanda crossed her arms, lifted her full breasts and looked disappointed when Will kept his eyes on her face. "Don't take them over my land."

Will fought to control his growing anger. "What do you expect to gain by this?"

"Gain?" Yolanda's smile faded. "Nothing more than the satisfaction of seeing you hurt in some way, big or little. Just an inconvenience here, a bit of difficulty there." She stood. "I'll never let you forget you killed my husband. You need to be wary, Mr. Martin. Now, get out of my saloon. Yates?" She motioned toward the door and Yates was beside Will in three long strides.

"The lady wants you out of here," he said.

Will pushed himself to his feet. "I know the way out." Yates let the gun barrel drop toward Will's stomach.

Will stared at the man, let his eyes drop to the floor and then, before Yates could react, quickly shoved the rifle aside with his left hand. With his right, he grabbed Yates' groin and squeezed.

"Don't make a move," Will said, "or I turn you into a gelding."

Yates froze and Will thought he saw a flicker of amusement in Yolanda's eyes. "Hand me the rifle," Will said. Yates carefully handed it over. "Now, let's kind of amble over toward the door." Will started to walk and, when Yates didn't move quickly enough, gave another squeeze. Yates groaned, then followed. At the door Will stopped and grinned. "I'm surprised," he said. "For such a big fella you sure got a tiny doodah." The room erupted in laughter as Will turned Yates loose, tossed the rifle to the floor and left the building.

Later that evening he packed his pipe as he walked toward the boarding house. He headed for the back, not wanting to go in yet. He leaned against the wall and puffed smoke into the still air. It was quiet in the town except for the sound of the river to the west. The men from the quarries would be coming home anytime now and the noise level would rise considerably. From the back of the boarding house he thought he heard a moan. He listened to the stillness and then heard it again. He nosed around the corner and saw Jacob and Evey locked in an embrace beneath the pine that cast darkness under its branches. He jerked quickly back out of sight. Damn, he thought. *What next?*

Jacob was seventeen, Evey a year younger. She had come to spend most of the summer with Will and Judith and they had done their best to keep the youngsters apart. When Will had announced he was going to Marble, though, Evey had insisted on going with him. It was just one more thing to worry about. *Maybe*, he thought, *it's time to break the news.*

Tom returned from the quarry full of news about a railroad to Marble and wanting to know if what he'd heard about Will's set-to with Yates was true. Everyone was in such high spirits that Will knew he wouldn't say anything that evening.

Evey and Jacob had also heard the story. Evey grabbed Will's arm. "They say you beat off a man with a rifle by grabbing his . . . his thingy!" She blushed.

"Evey!" Tracey laughed and turned a vivid red. "Well." Evey stuck out her lower lip. "Didn't you?"

Will joined the others — all but Jacob — in laughter. "I guess I did, at that."

"That's two pieces of good news today," Tom broke in. "Word came up from Carbondale that Osgood incorporated the Crystal River Railroad last week. Plans to build to Marble."

"That *is* good news," Will said, trying to work up some enthusiasm. He was thinking about the changes in the valley that were sure to come with the railroad. He could almost feel the valley tense as it prepared for yet another influx of people and, this time, steel and steam and gigantic metal monsters that would weigh heavily on the fragile balance between man and nature.

"Know what they're calling you now?" Tom asked. Will shook his head. "The Curse-Killer. The latest story is that you had a day-long fight with that Indian and then threw him off the cliff. And they're saying he wasn't old at all but a young buck."

"My," Tracey exclaimed. "Our own folk hero."

"My father, the Curse-Killer," Evey said. "There are so many stories about you I'm not sure what to believe."

"Maybe you shouldn't believe any of them," Will muttered.

"They say you and that man, Bat Masterson, tamed the wild Dodge City with Doc Holliday. And that you drove the last wagon over the Santa Fe Trail."

"It was one of the last."

"Then, they say you killed Peabody in a gunfight. . . "

"You know the truth of that story."

"Did you get any satisfaction from Yolanda?" Tom asked, changing the subject.

"I'll get to my stock," Will said, sounding more confident than he felt. He walked to the door and looked down the street at the White House Saloon. "Have to head back home tomorrow," he said over his shoulder. He didn't see the looks of intense disappointment on the faces of Evey and Jacob. But he felt their stares on his back and thought he was a damn fool for not telling them long ago.

≈৹৵

THE NEXT MORNING Will shook hands with Tom as he left for the quarry and then went to the livery to get his horses. As he was riding back to the boarding house leading Evey's pony, he saw two men, one of them Yates, riding hard out of town to the north. He wondered only briefly where they might be off to and then stood on the porch saying good-bye to Tracey. He was about to say something about seeing Jacob and Evey kissing, but he stopped short when they came up to the porch. Instead, he bent to kiss Theresa, who also called him "Uncle Will."

"Let's go," he said to Evey and nodded his farewell to Tracey. "See you next time, Jake," he called, but the boy had gone inside without a word.

Within two hours Will and Evey reached the narrowing of the valley just below Chair Mountain and south of the broad meadow where the river meandered past the little coal settlement of Placita. Will was thinking of the appropriateness of the name, which means "little place" in Spanish, when he heard the sharp report of a rifle shot. He had no time to react before Evey's horse went down, throwing her to the rocky bank of the river. The shot echoed off the steep wall of mountain that rose to the east of the river. Before the echo died, Will was off his horse and running toward Evey who lay unmoving on the ground.

A second shot ricocheted off a rock beside him as he stooped to pick up her limp form. Another shot snapped by his head and he ran for the safety of a cottonwood near the river, vowing he would never again leave the ranch unarmed.

More shots splattered the ground around him as Will hugged Evey to the tree, trying to keep her body upright and out of sight. A slug tore off a branch above his head. He decided there were two rifles. For a long moment there was silence. He risked peering around the tree trunk just as a bullet slammed into the tree inches from his face, throwing bark.

210

Will guessed it was Yates and the other man who had left town just before he did.

Evey began to stir. He smoothed her hair and felt a lump on the side of her head. She slowly opened her eyes.

"Be still," he said. "Somebody's shooting at us." Suddenly, another shot echoed off the mountain but no bullet came near this time. Will realized the shot was fired from a third rifle downstream and to his right. The third rifle boomed again, causing the first two to begin a rapid counterattack. At least they're not shooting at us anymore, Will thought, holding Evey closely.

The shooting stopped abruptly and a few seconds later Will heard the sound of hoofbeats as two horses galloped away to the south. He inched the two of them farther to his left and peered around the tree. He could see no one.

"Hello up there!" The voice was deep but sounded young. It came from a clump of bushes near the river about forty yards downstream. "Don't worry," the voice called, "I'm not with those others. I'm coming up."

The bushes shook and a man dressed completely in black showed himself. As he walked toward them Will helped Evey sit on a small rock. He hurried to the river and wet his bandanna in the water, then returned to her and washed her face.

The man blocked the sun as Will looked up at him. He was well over six feet tall, broad in the shoulders and slim-hipped. He carried himself with a careless confidence, letting his rifle dangle at his side.

"Are you two all right?" he asked.

"We are," Will answered. "Thanks to you."

"Not necessary. I was camped down there." He nodded toward the river and long black hair brushed his shoulders.

Will stood and offered his hand. "Will Martin," he said, "and my daughter, Evey."

The man took the hand with a strong grip. "I know," he said. Will studied him for a few seconds but a wide- brimmed hat hid the man's eyes.

Evey was trying to rise. "Sit still," Will ordered. He moved to the man's left and shielded the sun's brightness from his eyes. The man was young, not yet twenty, Will figured. He was not dark-skinned but not quite a white man. "We're obliged to you, Mr. . . .?"

"Matthews. Luke."

"You came along at the right time."

Matthews let his gaze linger on Evey, then turned to Will. "Know what that was all about?"

"Wish I knew," Will said guardedly. He knew, all right. Matthews shouldered his rifle, butt to the sky. "If you two are all right I'll move along.

211

Anything I can do?"

"Thanks, no. We'll double up on my horse. You from around here?"

"No."

Will studied him. The young man had no expression in his long, chiseled face, with high cheekbones beneath deep blue eyes. "I'd like to repay you somehow," he said. "I've got a ranch down toward Carbondale. You heading that way?"

"Maybe." Matthews was not a talkative type.

"Stop by," Will said. "I owe you."

"No, you don't. Maybe I'll see you." Matthews turned and walked with long strides toward the clump of bushes. He walked like he knew where he was going, like he had a reason for going there, like a man who knew himself and what he was about.

TWO MONTHS later, in late October, Luke Matthews walked up the incline toward the Double M's ranch house. The last of the brown aspen leaves mingled with yellow cottonwoods and swirled about his feet. He carried his rifle in his left hand, barrel to the ground, and had a bundle of belongings thrown over his right shoulder. Judith called to Will from the front window.

"Is this the boy you told me about?"

"That's him." There was no mistaking the walk, the black clothes, the broad-brimmed hat, the rare mixture of casualness and confidence that exuded from the man.

Will opened the front door and stepped onto the porch. "Luke. I've been wondering if you'd show up."

Matthews nodded. "Getting cold in the high country." Judith was at the door.

"You've been in the mountains?"

Matthews touched the brim of his hat. "Yes, ma'am."

"My wife, Judith," Will said, and the man nodded again. "Come inside. We're about to have our supper."

Without a word, as though it was expected, Matthews followed them inside. He filled the room and Will caught Judith eyeing him as she put another plate on the table. He was taller than Will by two inches. His body appeared to be solid muscle but he moved quietly and smoothly about the room, like a mountain lion.

Matthews waited politely for Judith to sit and then pulled out his own chair and sat, staring at her face as though trying to memorize it.

When she blushed from the stare he dropped his eyes. "Sorry," he said. His voice had a rich baritone quality and there was no drawl to it. "You remind me of my mother. She was very beautiful. Like you."

"Thank you," Judith said, pleased. She began to pass the bowls of food to Will but paused when Matthews bowed his head and folded his hands in his lap. She nodded at Will who was about to spoon a heap of mashed potatoes. A few seconds later Matthews lifted his head and smiled at them.

"A habit I have," he said. "My mother was a good Christian lady and this was something we always did, even if the meal didn't amount to much."

His smile was a good one that crinkled up the outside of his eyes and showed a dimple in his left cheek.

"I know you have many questions," he said. "I'll be glad to answer them all."

"You do have my curiosity up," Will said. "Glad you're here. My partner is in Glenwood for a few days so it's nice to have some company."

Matthews' blue eyes seemed to sparkle with a hint of amusement. "I knew he was gone. I waited until he left."

After the meal Will built a fire while Judith cleaned up. Finally, seated near the fireplace, Will looked at Matthews, who sat with his feet stretched out in front of him, seeming to occupy half the room.

"I want to thank you again," Will said to him, "for helping us out of a tight spot back in August."

Matthews stared into the fire. "How is Evey?"

"Fine," Will said, surprised Matthews recalled her name. "She went back to Denver early last month."

"Will told me you were camped by the river that day," Judith said. "Does that mean you don't live around here?"

Luke pulled his legs back from the fire and straightened in his chair. Leaning forward and not looking at either of them, he began to talk. He spoke softly, in little more than a whisper. His voice, quiet and low, filled the room with a presence as strong as his physical body.

"I am half Indian. My mother was a Ute who was raped by a white man. She died eight years ago of overwork and, I think, sadness. I was raised on a reservation south of here. My grandfather named me Flies Like an Eagle. He was not actually my grandfather but he helped to raise me. He taught me many of the old ways and my mother saw that I learned the modern ways of the whites. When I was young we picked the name I now go by from the Bible. Luke Matthews seemed to my mother to be acceptable. I preferred David as a name because he was a soldier, a warrior. But my mother hoped to steer me from the path of violence."

Judith stirred, shifted position. "Your mother must have been very

213

wise," she said.

Matthews nodded slowly and turned to Will. "You are the Curse-Killer."

Will moved in his chair, suddenly uncomfortable.

"I know about you," Matthews continued. "I know a great deal about you and this valley. Much of what I know about the valley I knew before I saw it as an adult."

Judith's eyes widened and she started to speak but stopped at the touch of Will's hand on her arm.

"I saw this valley before you," Luke said, looking at Will. "Before most white men. I was born on Owl Point." Judith leaned forward. "Your grandfather . . . ?"

"He was Owl Man. I do not believe you killed him."

"I didn't," Will said, shaking his head.

"I believe you. Tell me, is it true that you are now po'rat, a holy man with powers transferred to you from my grandfather?"

Will tamped his pipe into the fireplace. "I think your grandfather would have liked to believe that."

Luke stared at him. "I, too, would like to believe it."

Judith stood and looked down at Luke. "But aren't you a Christian? How can you reconcile Christianity with these ancient Indian beliefs?"

Luke smiled faintly. "I have come to believe that there are many paths to the one God. My grandfather's God, *Inu'sakats*, might very well be the same God to whom I pray."

"But what about these other . . . things?" Will asked. "The *powa'a*, I think Owl Man called them. This tiny ghost- like thing he says lives in me?"

Luke smiled again, more broadly this time. "Perhaps they are angels," he said. "I think you know what I mean."

Will did know. "Sometimes when I'm in the mountains, especially when I'm near Owl Point . . . "

"You feel them, don't you?" Luke stood, towered over them. "You feel the power in your body, a call to come to the point and to somehow commune with the spirits who live there."

Judith saw Will nod. "There are times . . . times when I think I know what the valley is thinking. Like it's alive, as alive as I am, and that its heart is pumping just below the rocks up there on Owl Point."

Luke sat again and crossed his arms. "My grandfather was a strong judge of men. He told me he would find the one man who could carry on."

"Carry on?" Judith asked. "Carry on, what?"

Matthews smiled again. "Why," he said, "the curse." Will coughed, felt his throat tighten. "You are not a curse *killer*," Matthews said. "You are now the *bearer* of the curse."

214

Will walked to the window. "Do you really believe that?"

Luke shook his head. "I have seen my grandfather work strange miracles," he said. "And I have been told that 'you shall have no other gods before Me.' I believe that all things are possible. And I believe that you were chosen by my grandfather because of your love for this valley. Is it cursed? Who can say? If it is, perhaps you alone have the power to remove it." He laughed slightly again. "Or perhaps Owl Man's power was so great that no man can change this valley's destiny."

"All I know," said Will as he watched the embers of the dying fire, "is that there's something about this whole thing that seems so real it scares me."

Matthews' voice came from the darkness of the corner where he sat, an almost disembodied voice that seemed otherworldly itself. "You must not fear it," he said. "You must give yourself to it. The future of this valley may depend on it."

≈≫≈

THE NEXT MORNING, when Will asked Matthews what his plans were, he got only a shrug for an answer.

"I don't mean just for the winter. Down the line a ways."

"I'll get a job."

Will fired up his pipe. "Osgood may be hiring."

"Not that kind."

"You're not a farmer. What are you good at?"

Luke took a long time getting his eyes from the clouds to Will's face. "Horses."

Will raised his eyebrows. "You know horses?"

"I was raised around them."

"Well," Will said. "Well, hell."

"Your partner is getting old," Luke said.

"You know a lot about us — this place."

"I listen. I watch. It isn't difficult."

"What else do you know?"

Luke squatted on his heels, picked at a weed. "A lot."

Will hunkered down beside him. "Give me a sampling."

"All right. You know more about this valley than any living man. When he was alive my grandfather knew more than you. You've got land from one end of it to the other including a claim at Coal Basin. You've killed a man whose wife will do anything to get even so you're in danger every time you leave your ranch. You've been married before. Pretty soon you'll need someone to run this place." Luke hesitated for a long second, took a breath.

215

"Jacob Collins is your son."

Will felt the blood rush to his face and pushed himself to his feet. "What do you want from me?"

Now Luke stood beside Will. "Mr. Martin, I don't want anything. What I know, I just know. Information isn't hard to come by. Did you know Yolanda Peabody isn't married to this Harrison?"

"I'm not surprised," Will said.

"She brought him in with her mainly on your account, I think. Basically, he's a thief. He goes down to New Mexico now and then, over to Denver, to steal things that he sells to somebody in Taos. They're out to get you in one way or another and I believe they're about to have a go at it."

Will nodded. "I figured as much."

"You need me," Matthews said. "I know horses. I know how to run a place like this. And I can ride with you when it's necessary."

Will studied the man. There was no question Ardy was getting too old and arthritic to keep on running the ranch. Matthews, if he was on the level about his experience with horses, could take over when the time came.

"I reckon I do owe you," Will said.

"Don't hire me for that reason. I'll earn my keep." Will nodded.

"I think you just might," he admitted.

ॐ

WINTER FOLLOWED Ardy back to the ranch, and the weather and the old man were both angry. The wind howled and blew snowflakes through a gray sky. Ardy growled and blew smoke.

"You're always hirin' people without askin'," he complained. "We never hired wranglers in the winter before."

"You need help, old friend," Will replied. "My guess is he's just what we need."

"He's a Injun!" Ardy spit on the ground. "He'll sleep in the bunkhouse. You gonna feed him with the rest of us?"

Will nodded and Ardy rubbed an aching elbow. "Well," he said. "You're the big boss. But you tell him to do what I say. And to keep out of my way."

Luke knew horses. He came and went like a black-clad ghost, saying little, listening, working hard.

"That damn injun is up before me and got the work done time I get to the barn," Ardy said two weeks later. "I think he knows horse-talk. They've got to where they nuzzle him like he's their mother. Sure don't talk much, though."

Luke spoke when spoken to, treated Judith like a regal lady, kept himself

216

and his long hair clean, did his work and let Ardy think he still knew more than Luke.

≪≫

"I HEARD she was killed on a runaway horse," Tracey said of Irene, Osgood's former wife, late one evening after Will had ridden in from Redstone. He had visited with Osgood for an hour that morning. "Whatever happened, I can't say I blame the man for divorcing her, if that's what he did."

"What about the railroad?" Tom paged through a book with eight-year-old Theresa, who sat quietly on his lap.

"Another year, maybe, to Redstone. Longer to Marble."

Jacob stirred from his seat near the window. "Maybe it'll be completed when I get home from college."

"College?" Will turned to him. "What's this?"

"I've been accepted in the pre-law program at the University of Colorado in Boulder," Jacob said with a smile. "I start in the fall."

Will walked to the boy and shook his hand. "How are you fixed for cash? Can I help?"

"No need," Tom said. "Tracey's been putting money aside for years. She had a stash I didn't even know about." Will glanced at Tracey but she wouldn't return his look. "Besides that, Jake earned himself a scholarship."

"I can't wait to tell Evey the news," Jacob said. "In Boulder I'll be close enough to see her often."

"Abby's talking about a finishing school in the East for her," Will put in.

Jacob frowned for an instant but quickly smiled again. "I hope not. I've decided to ask her to marry me."

Will and Tracey froze but Tom jumped to his feet. "By damn, wouldn't that be something, Will? We'd be related."

" It sure would be something, all right," Will said. "It sure would." He made a poor effort to smile.

"I've got to put Theresa to bed," Tracey announced and left the room with her daughter.

Tom seemed not to recognize the lack of enthusiasm with which Will and Tracey had greeted Jacob's announcement. But Jacob noticed and frowned when Will sat down again and stared into the fire without saying any more.

≪≫

EVEY RODE the D&RG to Carbondale and Jake was there with Will

217

and Judith to meet her. When he saw her emerge from a passenger car, Jake went into a stumbling run to greet her. Will winced when he saw the boy's limp and he squeezed Judith's hand. Her soft smile tried to assure him that things would work out.

Evey talked a stream on the ride to the ranch. She was going to school in Denver for another year and then would travel to the East to look at possible finishing schools. She was learning to train horses. Henry had decided to become a minister.

"A preacher?" Will shook his head.

"I think he is well suited for it," Evey said. "Mother has had a great deal to do with his decision, I think."

"I'll bet she has," Will said. "What kind?"

"Oh, Methodist, I suppose." She dismissed the subject and turned to Jake. "I got all your letters and I saved every one. You use awfully big words. Just like a lawyer."

"I can't wait," Jake said excitedly. "Maybe after I do the first few years at Boulder I could finish up at one of the big schools in the East. Maybe Harvard."

"Harvard!" Evey looked at him wide-eyed. "I know you could get into Harvard. You're so smart."

At the ranch Evey kissed her "Uncle Ardy" and then disappeared with Jake.

"We've got to tell them right away," Will told Judith.

"I think so," she said. "He may be proposing right now."

At dinner Luke Matthews ate with his eyes on his food but Evey watched him closely.

"You're awfully tall for an Indian, aren't you?"

"I'm only half Indian."

"You saved our lives last year. I never thanked you."

"Your father thanked me."

There was silence for a moment, then Evey spoke again. "Were you really born on Owl Point? Without a doctor?"

Luke burst into a loud laugh. It was a good, strong laugh that came from his chest. "Yes," he said. "And, no, my mother didn't have a doctor. But my grandfather was something like a doctor."

Evey continued to stare at the man and Jake cleared his throat. "I thought for a while about becoming a doctor," he said. "But I decided the law was more my calling."

Evey turned to Jake and the boy visibly relaxed. "You'd have made a wonderful doctor, too."

Will broke into the conversation. "We'll be going to Marble tomorrow," he said. "Ardy, you and Luke can take care of things, can't you?"

Ardy put down his fork with a hand that shook more than it had all winter. He finished chewing, swallowed, and looked serious. "I been lookin' after things for years," he said. "And, hell, Luke does all the work anyway. You go on."

"But I just got here," Evey said. "I was looking forward to spending some time here with Jacob."

"There's something I've got to take care of," Will said. "We'll all go in the morning."

"All of us?" Judith asked.

He nodded and wouldn't look up. "All of us."

✺

TOM AND TRACEY were surprised to see the four alight from the wagon late in the evening. "I thought you were going to stay down there for a week or more," Tracey said to Will.

"It's time," Will whispered to her while the others carried luggage inside. "Things are moving too fast."

"Oh, my God." Her voice cracked. "So soon?"

"The sooner the better."

"Sooner" turned out to be that very night. After the wagon had been unloaded and the horses stabled, Will asked everyone to gather in the kitchen.

"What's this all about?" Tom wanted to know.

"There's something you've all got to know," Will began. "I've waited far too long to tell you this and I hate having to do it now." He stood behind his chair and gripped the back of it so tightly his knuckles turned white. Judith took Tracey's hand and stroked it. Evey and Jake watched expectantly and Will turned to them.

"I know you two think you're in love . . . "

"Think!" Jake protested, edging closer to Evey.

Tracey looked at her son. "Wait," she said softly.

"What is all this?" Tom asked again, brow furrowed.

Will took a deep breath, exhaled slowly. Do it, he said to himself.

"Jacob and Evaline are half-brother and sister."

"What?" Tom jumped to his feet. Jake and Evey sat in stunned silence. Tom turned to Tracey, then back to Will. Understanding flowed across his face. "You mean . . . ?"

Will nodded. "I'm their father."

Tracey's hand began to shake. Evey and Jake clung to one another. "You

219

and Tracey . . . ?" Again Tom stopped, unable to complete the question.

"It was long before I met Abby and we had no idea that you would ever show up here," Will said.

Jake's face was white and, as he stood, Tom thumped down in a chair, staring at his wife. Jake walked to his mother.

"You and Uncle . . ." He pointed a trembling finger at Will. "You had an affair with him while my father, I mean . . . your husband . . . was still alive?"

Tracey nodded. She looked up and tried to square her shoulders. "Randall was . . . it's all very hard to explain."

Jake turned back to Evey who had remained uncharacteristically silent. "Oh, Evey," he said. Evey stood and the two embraced. Tears streamed down both their cheeks. Will couldn't look at them, turned instead to Tom who had his face in his hands, elbows on the table.

"I should have told you long ago," he said. "We . . . Tracey and I . . . thought maybe nothing would come of the attraction these two had for each other. Obviously, we were wrong."

Tom lifted his head and stared at Will with something like hatred in his eyes. "You were wrong, all right." His voice was hoarse, came out cracking.

"Tom." Tracey touched his arm and he jerked it away.

"You've been in love with him all along." He turned to Will. "You bastard."

Will felt his knees become rubbery. He wanted to sit but stood, facing his old friend. "I'm sorry," was all he could manage.

"Sorry? What the hell good does that do?"

Tracey talked through tears. "We were going to tell you, Tom. Then, all of a sudden you wanted to marry me and . . . and the time never seemed . . . right."

Tom paced the floor, clenching and unclenching his fist. Judith sat silently. Jake held Evey and all looked at Will. "There never would have been a good time," he said.

"But all three of you had to know. Before . . ."

"Before I asked her to marry me!" Jake pulled away from Evey and stood before Will. "I always looked up to you," he said savagely. "I wanted to be like you. Now that I know you're my . . . father . . . I just don't know."

"You mean *she* knew and we didn't?" Tom looked at Judith.

She nodded. "He told me before we were married."

"And you didn't care?"

"I cared," she said softly. "But I knew by his telling me that he loved me and nothing like it would happen again."

Tom looked wildly at the group. Evey was sobbing quietly. "Well, my wife didn't tell me, the one who should have known." He turned on Will.

220

"You son-of-a-bitch. I could kill you."

"I wish I'd told you," Will said, lamely.

"Do you? Do you really?" He stared at Will for a long moment, broke off the gaze, and stormed from the room. The others were quiet as they listened to the front door open and slam shut.

Jake stood behind Evey stroking her hair, then turned to Will with hatred in his own eyes. "If he doesn't kill you," he said, "I just might."

"Sleep on it, boy," Will said. "Maybe tomorrow . . ."

"Tomorrow!" Jake started for the back door. "I think you should be gone by then." He slammed the door behind him.

The three women and Will seemed to hold their breath for a moment. The room was totally silent. Finally, Evey choked back a sob and turned to Will.

"Does my mother know?" she asked. He shook his head. "Oh, my God. I can't believe this is happening. Jacob and I, we had, we had plans." Evey pushed herself to her feet. "There is a curse on this valley," she cried. "It affects anyone who tries to do something good here. Jacob and I . . ." Then she, too, hurried from the room and they heard her footsteps on the stairs as she ran to her room.

Tracey was pulling herself together. "I'm afraid Tom may have gone to the saloon. He hasn't had a drink in years. Once he gets started again . . ."

Will stood, took his hat from the rack. "I'll go check."

Judith took his arm. "Be careful. You don't know what he might do."

Will shook his head. "Tom's my friend. We'll get through this."

❧

LATE AS IT was, noise issued from the White House Saloon and Will pushed open the door to find fifteen or twenty men drinking, playing cards, and talking to the three "doves."

Yolanda Peabody greeted him just inside the door with a broad smile. "He's over there," she said, nodding toward a table off to the side. "He's already gone through one bottle. You two have a fight, did you?"

Will ignored her, walked to Tom's table, and sat. "Get away," Tom said quietly. His eyes were glazed and his hand trembled as he poured from a new bottle. "I don't want to be around you right now."

Will moved the bottle to the far side of the table. "You think this is a good idea?"

"Drinking? I think it's a hell of an idea. A lot better'n you'n Tracey playin' . . . "

"Quiet down!" Will shoved his chair back and pulled Tom to his feet.

221

"I think the man wants to stay." Yolanda pushed herself between Will and Tom. She leaned against Tom, pressing her full breasts against him. "You go ahead and sit," she said, pulling Will's chair closer and sitting beside Tom. She poured a drink and placed the shot glass in Tom's hand. "On the house." She put her arm around Tom's shoulders and whispered to him.

"Come on, Tom," Will pleaded.

"Go away, you bastard."

"My, my," Yolanda purred, a smile decorating her face. "The two old friends have had a falling out. Let's see if I can guess the reason." Will saw Leon Harrison leaning against the bar. He touched the pistol in his belt. Beside him, Yolanda's other henchman, Yates, fingered the trigger of a rifle. "Can it be that Mr. Cordell has found out that you are Jacob's father?" Will started to respond but Tom lifted his head.

"You mean you knew about it, too?" Tom asked.

"Of course. Now everyone will know."

"Everybody knew but me," Tom whined.

"That's not true," Will said. "Peabody found out before he died but . . . "

"Before you killed him!" Yolanda's smile was gone, replaced with a sneer. She turned to the room. "Listen, everyone!" The room quieted slowly. "Mr. Cordell and Mr. Martin have come to a parting of the ways. I fear it is because Mr. Cordell has discovered that his friend here was having his way with Tracey Collins while she was still married to that invalid."

"That's enough," Will said.

"And now he knows that Will Martin is the father of Jacob Collins. He's married to a whore."

Will took her arm and spun her away from the table. She backed against the wall and hissed, "Now everyone knows."

"Come on, Tom," Will urged.

"You're ruined, Martin," she called. "I told you I'd get even."

An older man with a gray beard stained with tobacco juice turned to Yolanda. "Think you could hold it down some?" he asked. "We're tryin' to play poker."

"Don't you care about this?" Yolanda called to the room. "Do you want a man like Will Martin in the same room with you?"

"Oh, hell, Yolanda," the old man said. "Most of us old-timers figured that out a long time ago. 'Sides, we like Tom and Tracey. Now, why don't you leave them two poor fellas alone?" He turned back to his cards and Yolanda stared wildly around the room, finding that no one took much interest in her revelation.

Tom was downing another drink but didn't resist as Will gently took the glass from his hand and helped him to his feet.

"Everybody knows," he mumbled. "Everybody but me."

Yolanda shouted behind Will as he steered Tom toward the door. "Will Martin is an adulterer! Doesn't anyone care? He had your wife, Tom! Lots of times."

"Yolanda," the old man said. "Why don't you shut up?"

"You bastards!" She followed Will and Tom to the door. "You're not through with me yet. You killed my husband. Now I'll get your whore."

At the boarding house Tracey and Judith helped Will get Tom upstairs and into bed. "He'll get over it," Will said.

"I'm not so sure," Tracey said. "He's been terribly hurt."

Will followed Judith down the hall and heard Evey crying as he passed her room. He stopped.

"Leave her alone," Judith said. "It's best now."

WILL WAS THINKING about God as he sat on the rock that rested comfortably along the westernmost rim of Owl Point. He thought about God and the ghosts that Owl Man said inhabited the place. He thought that God had done a fine piece of work on this valley and then seemed to have deserted it. There were those, of course, who he knew would think otherwise — that it was man who had deserted God.

As Will sat on the point and watched man's handiwork being carried out at Redstone far below to the southwest, he began to feel the presence of something that was not human. Perhaps Owl Man had gotten too far inside his imagination, and perhaps his intuition that something otherworldly lived on this point was merely something he wanted to believe.

His view of Coal Basin was blocked by mountains across the river, but he knew the same sort of desecration of nature was taking place there just as it was in Redstone. Dust lifted from the railroad right-of-way and smoke poured from the chimneys of poorly constructed shacks. He was high enough that he could hear no sound of the work that went on day after day below. The settlement was small compared to the immensity of the valley, but to Will it held the danger of the sharp bite of a Kansas rattler. While it poisoned only a small area, the disease spread rapidly throughout the entire body. The result, without some kind of intervention, was death.

He sat and watched and imagined that tiny beings with invisible wings swirled around him, frantically begging him to do something about the activities below. *Stop the cutting of trees*, they seemed to say. *Stop the pouring of smoke and ash into the air. Stop the noise that drowns out the sounds of nature. Stop the digging of holes and the blasting of dynamite and*

223

the laying of track for another fire-spitting, smoke-pouring, noise-making creature that is not of God's — of Inu'sakats' *— making but of man's.*

Suddenly, Will was sure there was another presence on the point. He felt it on the back of his neck the same way he had sensed Owl Man's presence. He turned slowly and saw Luke Matthews sitting against a tree. Luke nodded and Will turned back to the broad flow of valley below him. Luke stood and walked toward him, and Will sighed and said, "You might as well sit down."

Luke sat, scanned the valley and didn't say anything. Will finally turned to him. "You're quiet as a. . . "

"As an Indian?" It wasn't meant to be funny.

"You followed me?"

"Didn't have to. Judith said you'd gone upstream to be alone. I figured you'd be here."

High above, an eagle settled on the wind and floated in one place, waiting for another to join it. "Thought maybe I'd have a vision or something," Will said.

Luke scratched at the red dirt. "Takes more than just sitting. You must believe. And, perhaps you should dance. Maybe some peyote." *Did he smile?* Will wondered.

"No thanks."

"Don't blame you. Want me to leave?"

"Nope," Will said. "Think maybe I'm glad you're here."

Luke lifted his head toward the aspen grove at the back of the ledge. "My birthplace."

"You planning to stay around here?" Will changed the subject abruptly, feeling Luke had followed him for a reason.

"I think I'd like to."

"Think we could put a stop to all this?" Will waved his hand over the valley and they watched the activity below.

Luke stood, stretched, let his long arms play out to the north and south. "Somehow I don't think we'll need to."

"How do you mean?"

"I think the process has already begun and that the fate of this valley was determined long ago. What happens, happens."

"You believe in fate?"

"In a way." He sat beside Will again. "The years we're alive, the time of Redstone or Marble is nothing, really. The God we pray to, even the God my grandfather prayed to — and they may be the same — they have a lot of time. Nothing has to be done today, or even tomorrow."

The boy was right, Will thought. Whatever impact Osgood's venture might have on the valley would be slight in the long run. "What about the curse? You think it's real?"

Will waited a long time for the answer.

"I think there's a force working on this valley, on the country, on the whole of the earth. Whatever types of ghosts, or maybe angels, that my grandfather believed in . . . whatever they can do, they will."

"What if I removed the curse? Owl Man said I had the 'power' or whatever you call it, an ability to prolong it."

"I don't think you could," Luke said. "Anyway, I think the real curse right now, from your standpoint, is Yolanda."

"Good Lord!" Will got to his feet. "You know too damned much."

Luke hunkered on his heels. "Yolanda is the real devil of the valley. I think she must be stopped."

"Stopped? Before what?"

"Before she gets her hooks into you. I think she'll try it through your family."

"My family?"

"I just have a feeling. You must watch her closely."

"I hope you're wrong," Will said. There was a note of resignation in his voice. "But I'm afraid you're not."

STILL, HE didn't make the trip to Marble, and one evening in late August Tracey showed up alone at the ranch. "I put Jacob on the train to Denver today," she said. She was pale and thin and deep lines of worry etched her face. She was not yet fifty but was beginning to look much older. To Will, who had thought she would always look as she did when he first came to the valley, it was a shock. He wondered how he must look to her.

"Tom is still drinking," she told them that night. "I think he's seeing Yolanda."

"What?" A cold shock coursed through Will's body.

"He spends a lot of time at the saloon. I saw her on the street last week and the look on her face told me everything I needed to know."

Tracey's face was drawn. She had pulled her hair back severely and the hard lines of work and worry were clearly evident. "There's more," she said.

"More?" Will slumped in a chair.

"It's Jacob. I've seen him with Yolanda's daughter."

"Hell," Will muttered. "Inez can't be more than twelve."

"She's fifteen and looks twenty," Tracey said. "That's why I encouraged Jacob to leave for school early." A tear welled in her eye. "She's after him, Will — or, at least Yolanda is. She's very beautiful and the boy is simply no

225

match for them."

"Maybe getting him away will help," Judith ventured.

"Maybe. Of course, Tom is no help. He doesn't seem to care. I'm afraid he'll lose his job if he keeps drinking."

Judith took Tracey in her arms and held her tightly. "You've got too much piled on you right now," she said.

Tracey choked back her tears and stood bravely. She let herself be led to the bedroom by Judith and didn't look back at Will who stood helplessly in the middle of the room thinking Luke Matthews' prediction was coming to pass. Yolanda was trying to get at him through his family.

∾∾∾

IN SEPTEMBER of that year — 1899 — Will and Judith received an engraved invitation from J. C. Osgood to attend a reception in Redstone in honor of a guest, Alma Regina Shelgram.

Osgood himself greeted the two at the front door of his home. He wore a dark, three-piece suit with a gold watch chain looped across his increasing girth. He took the cigar out of his mouth long enough to kiss Judith's hand and laughed when she blushed.

Alma Shelgram spoke with a foreign accent that Osgood said was Swedish. "She's a widow," he said. "I met her last summer during my trip abroad. Alma has royal blood. Isn't she beautiful?"

Alma Shelgram was as tall as Judith but much more slender. Large, blue-gray eyes picked up the deep blue of her gown and contrasted sharply with the youthful whiteness of her skin and the honey-colored hair which she wore fashionably piled on top of her head.

Champagne flowed freely and stopped only long enough for Alma to demonstrate her skill as a pianist on an elaborate instrument Osgood said he had brought from Denver. After the applause had died and Osgood had congratulated the beautiful Swede, he motioned for Will to follow him onto the porch.

Osgood held his glass in his left hand while he flipped ashes with his right. He waved the cigar out over the construction of the coke ovens. "By this time next year those ovens will be turning out more than six hundred tons of coke every forty-eight hours," he said. "By then the railroad will be completed all the way to Coal Basin."

"It's hard to believe you've done it," Will said.

Osgood looked at him sharply. "I said I'd do it, and I did. I don't make rash promises. Look over there." Osgood pointed to the southwest at a large meadow that stretched from a grove of aspen at the base of a steep mountainside to the river, a distance of perhaps three hundred yards.

Osgood puffed on his cigar. "No doubt you remember what I said to those numbskulls at the Hotel Colorado the night we dined with you."

"You said a lot that night," Will replied.

Osgood laughed. "I did, indeed. But I also said I would construct an edifice that would put that monstrosity to shame."

Will nodded, sipping his drink. "I remember."

Osgood waved toward the meadow again. "That's where I'll build it. I am to marry Mrs. Shelgram sometime this fall. I'm going to build her a castle."

"A castle?"

"As close to one I saw in Europe as possible. I'm bringing in architects from New York to design it and artists from Italy will hand-stencil every damned wall in the place."

Will let the enormity of the project sink in. The man was made of money.

"We also talked about another matter that night," Osgood said. "That little claim of yours is right in the middle of the area I'm going to mine. I want to buy it from you."

"Sorry," Will said as an idea hit him full in the face. "It's not for sale."

"Not for sale?" Osgood stepped back, straightened up, flicked ashes over the porch rail. "Then it's worthless to you. Why, man, there's no way you can mine that claim."

"I don't plan on it," Will said. "But you can."

"Now, just how the . . . ?" Osgood's eyes brightened and he stepped closer. "You're a canny devil, aren't you? I might have known. What's your offer?"

"You make one," Will said. "You mine it and give me a percentage. I think I just might come out ahead that way."

Osgood laughed again. "I like you, Martin. Wish I had you on my payroll. I'll have the papers drawn up tomorrow. Shall we settle on a percentage?"

"You figure it out," Will said. "Any reason I shouldn't trust you to do it fair?"

As they rode side by side on the wagon later that evening, heading back toward the ranch, Will told Judith about the deal. "That's taking a chance, isn't it?" she asked.

"Not too much of one. If he's putting millions into this project he's pretty sure the payoff will be substantial. We'll have some money coming in regular this way."

"If you say so," she said. "Did you find out much about Alma Shelgram?"

"Me? Nothing."

"Well, I heard plenty." And she told him all of it. Osgood said he had met Alma Shelgram only that summer in Europe but there was some

227

indication that he had known her before that, even prior to his divorce. The story revolved around a man named Arthur Cobb who had committed suicide after a brief association with Alma and a Blanche McKibbon.

"Two women?" Will smiled. "My, my."

Judith chuckled with him. "It gets better," she said.

Cobb was a business failure, the story went, who deserted his family in Boston and went to work at a riding academy in New York teaching beautiful young women, including Alma, to ride. Soon he was employed by her on a rented estate in Mamaroneck, New York. She had his background investigated, however, and fired him when she learned that he was not an English nobleman's son as he had pretended.

"Sounds complicated," Will said.

"Isn't it wonderful?" Judith laughed. "Soon after she got rid of Cobb, Alma went to Europe and supposedly met Mr. Osgood at the Court of King Leopold."

Osgood was in Belgium trying to win the support of King Leopold for his mining ventures. Why Alma was at the Court was a mystery. When the two of them returned to New York together Alma found her former employee, Mr. Cobb, living at the residence of her close friend Blanche McKibbon.

"Now it's getting interesting," Will said.

"Osgood and Alma went to see Mrs. McKibbon when Cobb was away," Judith continued. "They persuaded her to leave with them after Alma told her of the man's deceit."

"Deceit. Living with an unmarried woman. Meeting secretly in Europe at the Court of a king." Will laughed.

When Cobb returned to the house and found that Blanche had left with Osgood and Alma he became despondent. Within hours he had shot himself in the head with a pistol. "He left two notes," Judith said. "He said his death was caused by a woman who called herself Mrs. A. R. Shelgram." Judith poked Will on the arm. "Why do you suppose he would refer to Alma as a woman 'who calls herself' Mrs. Shelgram? Could it be that isn't her real name?"

"You learned a lot in a couple of hours," Will said.

"It's so exciting. Right here in the Crystal Valley. One of the richest men in the nation may have been having an affair with a Swedish Princess while he was still married and it could turn out that she's not of royal blood after all."

Will couldn't help thinking of Alma Shelgram, taller than pot-bellied Osgood, beautiful and talented. "I'm sure glad you had a good time."

A week later Will picked up a two-day-old Denver paper in Carbondale and took it home to Judith. Reporters from New York had followed Osgood to Redstone, pestering him for details on Alma's relationship with Cobb and on Osgood's knowledge of the situation. Finally, Osgood had rid himself of the reporters by issuing a statement:

"I scarcely knew Mr. Cobb. I may have met him on three or four occasions, but really never had an acquaintance with him. It is charitable to assume the man was insane and his letters and accusations were the imaginings of an insane mind. The ladies whose names he has brought into unenviable notoriety were simply kind employers whom he served in his capacity as riding master. His innuendoes against one of them resulted undoubtedly from his discharge for good cause. The two women have confirmed that on several occasions he threatened to kill them. It would be useless to attempt to deny the stories, lies and general misstatements which sensational papers will publish in relation to anyone concerned with this sorry affair."

"I thought Osgood said he met Alma for the first time in Belgium," Judith said, dropping the newspaper.

"That's what *you* said," Will replied.

"Then why does he say he may have met Cobb on three or four occasions? Supposedly, he and Alma took Blanche away while Cobb was gone."

"Judas Priest!" Will stood and headed for the door. "All I know is what Osgood told you. I think it'd be best if we'd all let this thing die and leave the poor girl alone."

He left the house and went outside to smoke his pipe in the cool evening air. Didn't know why he was so suddenly angry. Pretty soon he went back inside and Judith grinned at him as she put a piece of apple pie on the table.

He grinned back and ate it. Later that night he forgot all about Alma Shelgram in the loving embrace of his own beautiful wife.

229

PART VI

1901-1903

The sun was almost to the mountaintops when Will guided the horses out of the shadows of the last narrows and into the sunlight not far from the ranch. He and Judith were returning from their first trip to Marble that spring, and patches of snow lingered along the road while deeper melting snow in the high country gave birth to rushing streams that fed the Crystal.

Tracey had been pleased to see them in Marble but Tom had not been seen during their stay.

"Osgood was in a good mood, at least," Will said.

They had visited with him that morning. The man had been in extremely good humor during their brief stay and had seemed to Will to be busting to spill some secret that Alma didn't want told. Will had thought she might be pregnant but Osgood intimated that he was planning to create "a workers' paradise" that would make Redstone world famous.

Will and Judith were still speculating on what he meant when they drove onto the ranch and saw Ardy waiting for them at the door with a wide grin on his whiskered face and the usual cigarette in his mouth.

"Get down and come inside," he said. "I got a surprise for you." He ushered them into the house and quickly disappeared. Will could only shrug at Judith's question.

Seconds later he was back. "There's someone here wants to see you." He stepped back, still grinning, as Evey walked into the room looking for all the world like a grown-up woman. Will was astounded at the resemblance to Abby in her younger days. He and Judith stood in stunned silence.

"Well," Evey said. "Aren't you glad to see me?" Her long, dark hair spilled to the shoulders of a gray dress trimmed in blue. She walked toward them, seeming to float across the floor, and stood before them. Will stood rigidly, letting his eyes take in the beauty of this nineteen-year-old woman-child who, in the space of only two years, had changed from a teenaged string bean to a young woman of confidence and stunning beauty.

"I have come home," she said, "to apologize. And to tell you that I love you both."

Will took a step toward her on weak legs. "Evey." She was in his arms, then, holding on with all the strength she could muster. Neither noticed when Judith and Ardy left the room.

At dinner, Evey explained to all of them, Luke Matthews included. "I went to a finishing school in Boston. I fully expected to meet a wealthy young man, marry him, and remain there for the rest of my life."

"What happened?" Judith asked.

231

Evey frowned. "Absolutely nothing. I felt nothing for any of them. And they were all handsome and so rich!"

"Rich ain't everything," Ardy put in.

"I agree. And not a one of them measured up."

"Measured up to what?" Will patted a full stomach.

Evey took her father's hand. "To you," she said. "I found myself comparing every man I met to my father. I discovered I was looking for a man just like you. When I finally figured that out, I quit looking altogether."

"He's one of a kind, dear," Judith said with a smile.

"He is!" Evey agreed.

Three of the men had proposed, one a doctor, one the son of a hotel owner, one a banker. All of their hands were white and had no calluses, she complained.

She had dined in elegant restaurants, attended balls with the upper crust of Boston society, gone sailing on yachts and longed for a wagon ride up the Crystal. She had met President McKinley during his re-election campaign and thought his "full dinner pail" slogan was perfect and remembered the miners thrown out of work when the country went to the gold standard. She had visited a country estate and wished she was currying a horse at the Double M.

"I realized my anger with you was stupid," she said to Will. "What happened between you and Tracey was . . ." She turned to Judith. "I'm sorry to bring it up, but it's part of the reason I'm here now."

"Go ahead, dear," Judith said.

"It was a long time ago and it was so . . . so, natural. The circumstances and all . . . I mean . . . it's just that . . ." She stood and threw her arms around Will and talked through tears. "I'm so sorry."

Will stroked her hair. "It's all right."

Evey blew her nose with the handkerchief Judith offered. "Well," she said, hands on her hips now, chin thrust forward. "I'm back. Can I stay?"

"Stay?" Will and Judith said it together.

"At least for the summer."

"Hell, yes, you can stay!" Will hugged her again. "Stay as long as you like." Ardy had turned away and was working at his eye with a fist. "What's the matter with you?"

"Nothin'!" Ardy jerked his hand away. "Got somethin' in my eye. We got any dessert?"

THEY WORKED hard all that summer and Evey seemed perfectly happy to stay on the ranch. She hummed new songs she had learned in Boston: "The Maple Leaf Rag" by Scott Joplin, "Rosie, You are My Posie" from the Broadway musical *Fiddle-dee-dee*. She talked constantly to Judith and Will and to Ardy, too, when he would listen. She was upset to learn that infant mortality in the U.S. was 122 per thousand live births. She had cried when she heard of the death of Queen Victoria that January but was later *thrilled* to learn of Andrew Carnegie's gift of $5.2 million allowing the New York Public Library to open its first branches. She was reading two of the newest books that she said Will and Judith would simply *love*: Booth Tarkington's *Monsieur Beaucaire* and *Lord Jim* by Joseph Conrad. She chattered and worked and hummed and seemed genuinely happy to be where she was.

Her face lost its look of contentment only once that Will saw, and that was when the letter from Jacob came. "He's seeing Inez," she told them all. And she reported that he was surprised to learn she had forgiven Will. She kept the rest of the letter to herself.

It was August before they finally went to Marble, where they learned Tom was on crutches. An explosion at the marble quarry had killed one man and injured several others. Tom's leg had been broken. Many of the miners, Tracey said, were blaming Will.

"It's the Italians and the Swedes," she said. "Since they've come to work in the quarries the stories of the curse have gotten totally out of hand."

"Good Lord," Will muttered.

Tracey's entire body seemed to sag. She huddled in the corner of the sofa like a reprimanded child. Her face was thin. Gray dominated her once dark hair and veins showed in once strong hands.

"They're saying you have the . . . the *power* to remove it but won't because you want all the valley for yourself. They say you own half of it already."

"Surely *Tom* doesn't believe all that," Judith said.

Tracey wouldn't meet her eyes. "He thinks of himself as a failure and almost never talks to me."

"Because of me, again," Will said angrily.

"Partly. But a few months ago Yolanda threw him out."

"Yolanda?" Evey's eyes widened.

"Tom had been sleeping with her, I'm sure. Then around the first of the year he quit spending so much time in her saloon. I heard one of the miners talking at the dinner table about how she told him not to come back."

"I'd be happy about that," Judith said.

"It crushed him. I think it might have been the final blow to his ego. He thought he'd lost me and then she started fawning over him, gave him what he thought he couldn't get from me. Now he's lost that, too."

"Is he still drinking?" Will asked.

Tracey nodded and for a long moment everyone stared at the floor. Then, slowly, Will pulled himself to his feet. "I'm going to have a talk with him."

"He's not here," Tracey said, curling more tightly into herself on the sofa. "I don't know where he is. I never seem to know where he is anymore."

◦◦◦

THE WINTER was a cold one and the snows were heavy. They had rounded up more than 150 horses, sold two-thirds of them and kept the remainder at the ranch. Ardy huddled near the fireplace most days, directing Luke and grumbling about the cold making his bones ache. By midwinter Evey, not Ardy, was riding out with Luke on most mornings.

The mood was not exactly grim, but a sadness enveloped the small family, as it had most of the country in the fall. President McKinley had been shot on September 6. His wounds had not been properly dressed and he died of gangrene eight days later. Theodore Roosevelt, at age forty-two, had become the youngest chief executive in the nation's history. Barely four days before McKinley was shot, Roosevelt had given a speech in Minnesota in which he proposed a rule for U.S. foreign policy. "Speak softly and carry a big stick," he said.

In February, a cold spell settled over the valley, froze the streams, and made trees crack in the middle of cold, windless nights. Horses' hooves broke through a heavy crust of snow and cuts were plentiful. For two days Ardy seldom moved from the fire. He sat bundled in a blanket, coughing, not speaking.

At the end of the second day Judith found Will alone in the kitchen. "We've got to get him to town to see Dr. Castle," she said.

The doctor called it tuberculosis. "We used to refer to it as consumption," he told Will. Ardy lay pale and thin in a bedroom at the back of the house. "He's been suffering from it for some time, I'm sure."

"Doc Holliday died from consumption," Will said. "What can we do?"

The doctor shook his head. "Not much." "Do you want to keep him here?"

"I will, if you want," Castle said. "Ask him. I think he'd prefer to die at home."

"Die? Is it that bad?"

"I don't think he'll last more than a few days."

"Does he know?"

Castle nodded, turned away as Will sank into a chair and let his body sag.

234

He'd somehow thought old Ardy might just live forever. He took a while getting himself together.

At the ranch, they helped Ardy into his bedroom and the tiny man rolled onto his side beneath several blankets and seemed to be immediately asleep.

That night Evey and Judith cried together in the kitchen while Will talked to Luke in the front room. "I'm going to miss that old man," Luke said.

Later, Will sat beside Ardy and tried to get him to eat some of Judith's stew. "Not hungry," Ardy whispered. "No need to waste good food on an old bag of bones like me."

Will put the bowl on the floor. "I wish things were different, old timer."

"No more'n I do," Ardy said around a weak laugh. "But, hell, I done enough in my time. I made it for seventy-odd years. That's pretty good these days."

"It is," Will said. "It sure is."

Ardy tried to turn over and Will helped him. "I been thinkin'," the man said. "Been thinkin' about that injun boy. Want to give him my share of the ranch."

"If you want," Will said. "It's good."

Ardy was silent for a moment. Thinking he had gone to sleep, Will bent to pick up the bowl and Ardy opened his eyes. "Tell you what," he said. "Why don't you ask Judith and Evey to come in here, one at a time. I'll tell 'em my so longs."

"Tell 'em tomorrow," Will said, "after some sleep."

"Plenty of time to sleep. You ask 'em, will you?"

Will sat in the front room staring at the fire until Judith came to ask him to come to bed. "What did he say to you?" he wanted to know.

"He said 'good-bye'," she replied. "He said he was proud that I was your wife and that you were the finest man he'd ever known." Judith buried her face in her pillow and sobbed. She came to Will when he put his arm beneath her, and sometime later they fell asleep.

After midnight Will was awakened by a knock on his bedroom door. It was pitch black in the room. "Who is it?"

"Luke. Ardy's outside."

Will was out of bed in an instant. Dressed and wearing his heaviest coat, he followed Luke toward the barn. Ardy was fully dressed, currying a horse by lamplight. Will and Luke stood just inside and watched. He talked low to the horse and stroked its forehead.

"Might as well come on in," Ardy said, facing the horse. "Or are you gonna stand there all night?"

Luke leaned over the stall while Will went inside to stand with Ardy. "Couldn't that wait until morning?"

"It could." Ardy's voice was rough. He coughed.

They watched him work a while. "Pretty cold," Will said.

Ardy placed the curry comb on a crossbar and faced them. "Tell you what," he said. "Why don't you boys go on back to bed and I'll be along after a while. I'd kinda like to be alone for a tad bit." Will glanced at Luke but the Indian wouldn't meet his eyes. "Whatever you say," Will said, feigning indifference. "Good night, then."

"'Night," Ardy said. Will motioned to Luke who took a long look at Ardy and then followed him out of the barn.

At sunrise, only a few hours later, Will didn't even bother to look in Ardy's room and trudged instead through the crunching snow to the barn. Inside, he found Luke squatting by the stall chewing on a straw. Will stopped and asked the question with his eyes. Luke pointed the straw toward the stall and Will stepped to the opening. Ardy sat propped up against the side, arms folded, head on his chest with his hat down over his eyes. He might have been sleeping, but he wasn't.

"Well," Will said. "Good for him."

"He did it right," Luke said. "Shall I get the shovels?"

"And a pick. Ground's frozen solid."

Later that morning the four of them stood over a mound of dirt behind the barn where the hill started its climb upward. A cold sun sparkled on the snow but gave no warmth. Judith prayed for Ardy — R. D. Metcalf — and Luke repeated the Lord's Prayer, which they all said with him.

As they walked back toward the house, Will said, "You know, I never did find out what R. D. stood for."

"I did," Luke said. "It stood for Reginald Douglas."

Will took Judith's hand and they walked a few more steps. "How'd you find that out?"

"He told me last summer," Luke said as they reached the back door.

Will turned back to stare again at the mound of dirt up the hillside. "Well, I'll be damned," he said.

BEFORE THE SNOW melted in the spring Will received two letters on the same day — one from Abby and one from J. C. Osgood. Abby's was brief. She thought Evey should return to Denver where she could meet some "eligible" men. The ranch was not for the likes of her — their — daughter. She could not understand how Will could agree to let her remain with him through the "dreadful" winter. She presumed that Will had heard that his friend Mr. Osgood had been rejected by the "Sacred Thirty-Six" of Denver.

Will had to laugh. The group was composed of the thirty-six supposedly most prominent families of that city. It was because of the scandal involved in Osgood's marriage to the mysterious Swedish princess, "or whatever she was." He was chuckling over the statement when a paragraph near the end of the letter caught his eye:

> Perhaps you have heard that Jerome B. Wheeler has taken bankruptcy in New York. It happened early in 1901. He has lost everything including the Hotel Jerome and the Wheeler Opera House. My Uncle, Henry Gillespie, while he has not become destitute, is doing little better. He is attempting a mining operation in South America. We have not heard from him for some time.

He put Abby's letter in his shirt pocket and opened Osgood's. It was an invitation to join a party of "notables" for a ride on the Crystal River Railroad from Carbondale to Redstone, where they would spend the night: "Present this invitation as your ticket before 10:30 a.m. on June 18, 1902. All aboard!" They would also take the "high line" to Coal Basin.

"It sounds like fun," Judith said. "Am I invited, too?" "It's addressed to Mr. and Mrs. Martin and Evaline."

"What will I wear? I'll have to make a trip to Glenwood to have my hair done. Where will everyone sleep? That house of theirs is not large enough." She bustled off, probably to begin packing already, Will thought.

"I'm not going back to Denver this summer," Evey announced at dinner that evening. "If you'll allow me to stay, that is."

Judith was pleased. "As far as I'm concerned this is your home for as long as you want it to be."

Will saw his daughter's quick glance at Luke, who might have smiled slightly between mouthfuls of food. Will looked back at Evey but she had turned again to Judith.

"I am so looking forward to the train ride with the Osgoods. Aren't you?"

Later, Will left the table and followed Luke out the back door. "You gonna need some help this summer?" he asked. After Luke nodded, he continued. "Ardy and I used to hire a hand or two every spring. Want to handle it yourself?"

"I can do that."

"I know you can. Do you *want* to?"

"Whatever you want."

Will took Luke's elbow and guided him toward the corral. They climbed on the wooden fence and sat watching the last rays of the setting sun paint the summit of Mount Sopris. Will packed his pipe and looked at the long shadows of two men practically mirroring one another in their postures on the fence. Finally Will decided he might as well get to the point. "Thought you'd take more of a hand in running the place," he said. "Make some decisions. You don't need to wait for me to tell you what to do. The place is half yours, after all."

Luke turned to him. "First you've said of it."

"Ardy told you?" Luke nodded again. "Well?"

Slowly, Luke let himself down from the fence rail and rubbed his backside. "Nobody ever gave me anything," he said. "I'm not sure I like the idea. I always thought I'd earn what I had."

Will tamped out the pipe on the rail, remembering saying something similar to Ardy soon after they met.

Luke stood straight. "How do you feel about me being your partner?"

Will stepped to the ground and squared up with Luke. "Is anything going on between you and Evey?"

Luke shook his head. "I figured. Don't want your daughter sleeping with a half-breed." He waited and when Will didn't reply, said, "How *would* you feel about it?"

"I don't know," Will said honestly. "Is it a possibility?"

"I can't say I haven't thought about it. If it bothers you I'll be gone in the morning."

"Hold on," Will said quickly. He appreciated Luke's forthrightness, and knew the two young people were thrown together often and that, if he were in Luke's situation, he would also be tempted. "Nobody wants you to leave."

"I won't make any promises as far as Evey is concerned," Luke said. "But I won't push her, either. What happens, happens."

Will turned to the house and saw Evey framed in the window, her back to them, washing dishes and engaged in an animated conversation with Judith, who was out of sight. *If ever two women were made for ranching it was those two,* he thought. He turned back to Luke who waited patiently for Will to speak.

"You own half the ranch," he said. "I had some papers drawn up a month ago. Sure am glad you picked Matthews for a last name. Don't have to change the brand. We keep the Double M."

So it was done, and Will knew he would have to let fate play out its hand since both Evey and Luke would be more or less permanent residents. They walked toward the bunkhouse. At the door Will paused. "Anything you need?"

"Not now," Luke answered. "There is one thing."

Will waited.

"We're going to have to face up to Yolanda's bunch one of these days."

"We? It has nothing to do with you."

"It does now," Luke said. "We're partners."

J. C. OSGOOD was on his feet as the train pulled out of the Carbondale depot precisely on time at 10:30 a.m., June 18, 1902. Will, Judith and Evey were the only passengers who were not members of the Colorado Fuel and Iron Company's Board of Directors, officers of the company, or wives of the officials.

"After all, we do have a business deal, don't we, Martin?" Osgood said. "You might as well be considered an officer, being something of a stockholder."

Judith and Will were seated together on the right side of the car and Osgood steered Evey across the aisle to a seat beside Alma Osgood, his wife of barely two years. "But you should sit here, Mr. Osgood," Evey said.

Alma touched Evey's arm as Osgood waved off the suggestion and hurried to greet new arrivals. "I'm so pleased to finally meet you," Evey said to Alma. "I've heard a great deal about you. You are, indeed, beautiful."

"Thank you," Alma said. "Don't worry about my husband. He probably won't sit down the entire trip."

He didn't. Osgood paced the passenger car, talking to individuals or shouting to be heard above the noise. The twenty passengers were seated in a combination caboose-coach which was the final car on a train of eight boxcars. "I had hoped to entertain you aboard my private car, Sunrise," Osgood shouted. "However, I'm having it refurbished in Denver. But we're less than two hours from Redstone."

The train's whistle blasted two longs and a short and everyone in the car started at the sound, the women covering their ears. Osgood laughed delightedly. "You can hear that all the way to Aspen, I'll bet!" he shouted. "The whistle came off a Mississippi River steamboat. One of my engineers told me it sounded like a bull about to break down a gate, so we call Engine No. 1 the *Bull of the Woods*."

Green pastures and fields of potatoes moved swiftly past them as they headed toward Mount Sopris and the narrowing of the valley a few miles to the south. Soon they could see their ranch to the west.

"Do you see it, Evey?" Judith called from across the aisle.

"Is that where you live, Evey?" Alma craned her neck for a better look. "It's very nice."

"It's home," Evey replied and, hearing that, Will and Judith smiled at one another.

Will settled into his seat and felt the mountains shudder with the weight of the train as it snaked its way upstream. Man was leaving his mark in all sorts of ways. Hayfields, potatoes, roads, steel railroad tracks. Before he thought it was possible, Redstone itself was in sight.

Osgood excitedly paced the aisle. "What did I tell you? Barely two hours to travel sixteen miles!"

The train stopped at Redstone's small depot across from the coke ovens. Osgood assembled his guests outside the depot as the *Bull of the Woods* huffed and hissed on the siding. When all had disembarked he signaled the engineer, who waved and gave two more enormous blasts on the whistle and then chugged on ahead toward Placita.

Even with the train gone the noise continued as another train coming down from Coal Basin rode onto the trestle over the river to the south in preparation for dumping its load of coal. Osgood spoke little as he herded his guests onto three wagons for a tour of the town.

The wagons drove onto a single, straight north-south street lined on either side by small houses, each brightly painted a different color. They came to a halt in the center of the street and Osgood stood on the seat of his wagon. "What you see here," he called, holding out his arms to either side, "is the first tangible results of my sociological department's efforts. When we're finished there will be eighty-four cottages for the married miners, each with running water!"

Will couldn't help being astonished at what the man had accomplished in little more than a year. Osgood had told him on the train, in a sudden outpouring of enthusiasm, that the "sociological" department had been the idea of his chief company physician, Dr. Richard Corwin. "It's humanitarian, that's what it is," Osgood had exclaimed. "Humanitarian. My miners will be the best-housed, the cleanest and happiest coal miners in the world."

The man paused and took in the sight with a puffed-out chest and visible pride. "All company-built, company-provided, for only eighteen dollars a month. Each cottage has from two to five rooms, depending on the size of the family. And electricity! Everyone can have electricity for the low sum of thirty-five cents a month per lamp. Look here," he said proudly. "Look at those lawns, gardens. And picket fences. Did you ever see anything like that?"

The caravan moved on, swinging up a curved street to the east that worked its way uphill where a number of larger, more elaborate houses were almost hidden in the trees. These were the homes of superintendents and other officials. Farther up the hillside the three wagons stopped on a street that separated a newly built firehouse from a just-as-new school building. The Redstone Public School was built of red stone and brick. A bell tower topped the building. Next to it stood an even larger structure three stories tall.

"The Redstone Clubhouse," Osgood announced. He waved them all toward the building and ushered them inside. They entered a large lounging room with leather-cushioned armchairs and elaborate settees surrounding refreshment tables. An enormous fireplace occupied one end of the room. To the north was a billiard room and on the south a reading room. Scattered about on the table were magazines and newspapers, some in English and others in foreign languages. On the second floor was a theater that Will guessed would seat three hundred people in chairs with arms. A chandelier with electric lights hung over the room and illuminated a stage perhaps fifteen feet wide.

"I can't believe all this," Judith whispered. "People in *Denver* don't live as well."

Osgood stood on the stage beaming. "We have everything needed for outstanding entertainment," he said. "Scenery, drop curtains, dressing rooms and even an arc illuminant stereopticon." He paced the stage as though he were putting on a performance himself. *And he is*, Will thought.

And still Osgood wasn't through. Back in the wagons, the visitors, awed by what they had already seen, were taken back to the south end of the main street where they stopped in front of an elegant frame and sandstone inn built in the style of a Dutch tavern.

"For my bachelor employees," Osgood said. "It has forty rooms, electric lights, a barbershop, a laundry, reading rooms and steam heat." The onlookers shook their heads in wonderment. "And," he said, "we even have telephones!"

A lady with two moles on her cheek and a large, feathered hat on her head waved her handkerchief. "Why," she said, "it is all so wonderful. But, my goodness, Mr. Osgood. Who would these men want to ring up on the telephone?"

After the laughter had subsided Osgood replied, "Anyone they want to, Mrs. Schellhammer. Anyone at all."

Across the street from the inn stood another large building which Osgood said was the company store. "Everything anyone needs is right here," he said. "My men and their families are cared for as though they were my own children. Now, all of this cost a pretty penny, I'll admit. But the increased productivity will pay off handsomely in profits for all of us."

Several of the new homes had just been completed and were unoccupied. The guests were taken to them to freshen up and prepare for the evening's entertainment at the clubhouse. Will, Judith and Evey were assigned a two-bedroom home. Inside, Judith switched an electric lamp on and off several times. "We should wire our house for electricity," she said. "And get a telephone."

241

Later that night they said good night to Evey and fell exhausted onto the double bed. Will closed his eyes and felt like he could fall immediately asleep but Judith couldn't stop talking about the wonders she had seen. "Mr. Osgood said the instruments used by the Redstone Band were the finest money could buy. They sounded very good, didn't you think? And he said they have a mandolin club and a drama club. It's all too good to be true. Didn't you tell me Osgood once asked you to work for him?" Will nodded sleepily. "We could live in one of those big houses on the hill. Would you like that?"

Will struggled to push himself to his elbows. "I don't think I could work a regular shift one day after another. Not now. Not after the kind of life I've had. Will you let me go to sleep?"

At nine the next morning Osgood stood atop one row of the coke ovens beside a "larry" car which held nearly six tons of finely crushed coal. Will watched Osgood with a group of men who listened to the coal magnate. They stood on railroad tracks that ran alongside the ovens and below a platform where a workman was demonstrating how the ovens worked. It was a warm morning for June and most of the men were already sweating through their suits.

Osgood alone looked comfortable in his suit, vest, tie, gold watch fob, starched collar and round-topped derby. "There are two hundred of them," Osgood said, indicating the long rows of ovens with a sweep of his hand.

Railroad tracks ran on either side of the rows and another track ran along the top of the ovens. "We call them beehive ovens because, even though you can't tell it, they are actually dome-shaped. We flattened out the tops of the rows so we could run the track along the top for the larry cars."

Osgood pointed to the south where the narrow-gauge track from Coal Basin ran across the trestle above the railroad, which continued on to Placita a few miles beyond Redstone. "Those Ingoldsby cars hold about fifty tons of coal each," he said. "The coal we'll use for coking will be processed first at a washery. After we drain off the water the coal is crushed to a fine powder like substance. Then we convey it to stack bins."

Will's eyes strayed to the north where Owl Point jutted out into the blue sky. The morning sun reflected off the tons of snow still covering a shoulder of Mount Sopris beyond the point. Were the ini'pute laying plans to reclaim the valley? he wondered. Could they even expect to accomplish that against the power and money controlled by this man who, as excited as a child, was still explaining the coking process?

"Five or six tons of coal is then dumped from the stack bins to the larry cars which run along the tracks I'm standing on." Osgood explained that the coal was dumped from the doors of the larry cars through the tunnel head on top of each coking oven. With the "charge" in the oven, the coal was leveled and the doors bricked up and sealed. A small hole at the top admitted air. gasses which were then generated ignited and burned slowly downward producing coke.

"The process takes about forty-eight hours," Osgood said, "then the coke is watered down to put out the fire before it is pulled." He waved to the workman who dutifully used a "ravel" to pull the coke from the oven and pile it on the wharf at his feet. "Later the coal cars will be parked on the siding on which you stand and the men will fork the coke aboard. Then it goes back to Carbondale and on to its final destination."

Osgood climbed down from his lofty perch on a wooden ladder and then jumped the three feet from the wharf to the ground beside the men. Will was surprised at the rotund little man's agility. "Now, if you'll all follow me," he said, brushing dust from his suit, "we'll board the wagons again and go back to the club for coffee. Within a hour we'll rejoin the ladies for the trip on the high line to Coal Basin."

Will had turned with the others when Osgood called to him. "Mighty impressive," Will said to the man.

"And profitable," Osgood replied. "I'm glad you came along, Martin. I have something for you."

Will pulled his hat lower on his forehead to block the morning sun and wondered how Luke was getting along with the new hand he'd hired. Osgood was holding out an envelope. "What's this?"

He found the envelope was unsealed. Inside was a check in his name for $1,500. He stared at it, then looked down at Osgood whose smile straightened out his mustache.

"That's only the first installment," Osgood said. "Our little business deal, you know."

Will looked back at the check. "Seems like a lot."

"Bosh! That's only the beginning. You should get one of those every month from now on."

Will's eyes widened. "Every month?"

"Now that the improvements are almost complete, we've got some profits to split up."

"Seems too easy," Will said, placing the check in a pocket.

"Easy for you. Work for me."

The two walked toward the wagons where the others stood in small groups. Will was walking behind one of the wagons when he saw Tom Cordell leaning against the Redstone Depot not twenty feet away. With him were Harrison and Yates and all three were armed. Tom wore the Colt .45 he'd had since their days on the Palo Duro.

"Hello, Will," Tom said.

ːxposed black gaps in his teeth. A Winchester .30-.30 was
ıs. Harrison stood father away, frowning with crossed arms.
ːod stopped and looked a question at Will. "I'll be just a
ı. He walked the ten paces and stopped a few feet away from
... ːou?"

"I'm just dandy," Tom said. Will knew immediately the man was drunk. *Harrison and Yates probably also,* Will thought.

"What are you doing here, Tom?"

Yates took a step forward, keeping his finger on the trigger of the rifle but being careful to not get too close to Will. Tom stood still, not replying, leaning and looking. He, like the other two, was unshaven, his clothes wrinkled and dirty.

"You're not working today?" Will asked, ignoring Yates.

"Not working at all. Got myself fired. All because I didn't show up for a shift a time or two."

"Sorry to hear that."

"Yeah, I'll bet you are." Tom moved toward Will in a shuffling kind of walk, letting his hand stray down toward his holstered pistol. "Looks like you're doin' just fine yourself. Gettin' all cozy with the rich of the world."

Will snapped a look back at the wagons. All were aboard except Osgood who stood by the front seat of the lead wagon and watched. "You coming, Martin?" he called.

Will waved at him. "This won't take long."

There was anger, maybe hatred, in Tom's narrowed eyes. "I heard you were goin' along on this little jaunt and thought I'd mosey down here and have a look at how rich and fat you were gettin'."

Harrison pointed his big belly toward the other three and approached. He twirled a short length of rope in his right hand. It was a newly braided lariat with a bright red tie around the honda. Tom stuck his face toward Will and breathed whiskey on him.

"Kind of early for drinking." *Be careful,* Will thought.

"Early? Maybe late. What the hell do you care? You've got what you want. Money. That big ranch. Land up and down the valley. My wife."

Will's fist came up involuntarily. It came from low at his side and carried all the force he could pack into the uppercut. It caught Tom full on the jaw and the man went back and down hard. Tom lay still a moment, pulled himself to his elbows and shook his head. Yates and Harrison were still, their liquored-up instincts slow to react. Suddenly, Tom's hand went for his gun and Will kicked him in the wrist with the toe of his boot, then stood on the hand.

"Get the hell off," Tom ordered.

244

"I'm sorry, old friend," Will said. "Why don't you go home?"

Tom looked up with bloodshot eyes that told Will the man carried a grudge the likes of which he had never known. "You bastard," he croaked.

Suddenly, Will's hat was knocked away and a stiff rope snaked over his head. Harrison tightened the loop like a noose and yanked Will backwards off his feet. Yates and Harrison dragged him across the graveled area in front of the depot. Will grabbed at the rope around his neck, trying to loosen its grip. He caught the movement of several of the men in the wagons as they jumped to the ground. Another man ran across his line of vision and out of view. Will gagged, unable to loosen the rope.

"Stop that," someone yelled from the wagons.

Tom leveled his gun at the men in business suits. "Stand where you are," he demanded.

Will couldn't breathe. He tried to cough, his face red. He could see Tom standing over him now.

"I think maybe I ought to kill you," Tom said. Will looked into the barrel of the gun and thought of Judith. Tom clicked the hammer back as the pressure of the lariat lessened. He pulled at the rough rope and saw the red tie in his hand.

Tom was grinning as he pointed the weapon at Will's face. "You been diddlin' her even while I was married to her."

"You're wrong," Will gasped. He choked and coughed.

"You ruined my life and I'm gonna make you pay."

"Put down that gun, mister!" It was Osgood's voice. He stood behind Tom with a double-barreled shotgun in his hand. Both hammers were cocked. Tom's face went white. "You're on private property, friend," Osgood said. "I'd suggest you drop that gun or I'll turn you into lunch meat." Tom let the pistol fall to the ground. "All three of you get out of here now!" Osgood waved the shotgun toward Yates and Harrison.

Will shucked the rope from his neck and worked himself to a sitting position, rubbing his neck which was red with rope burns. Harrison slowly coiled the rope as he and Yates backed away.

"I want my gun," Tom said.

Osgood nodded at Will who stood painfully, then walked the two steps to the pistol and bent to it. Rising, he found himself looking into Tom's face once again. He let the shells fall to the ground and handed the empty weapon to Tom.

"You always have to win, don't you?" Tom said, spitting the words out angrily.

"It doesn't have to be this way," Will said.

Tom turned and began to walk slowly toward the other two who,

245

mounted, waited for him. Halfway there, Tom turned. "It isn't over," he said. He pulled himself into the saddle and followed the others out of town to the north, toward Carbondale.

Suddenly, there were men all around Osgood and Will. They talked excitedly, patting Osgood on the back, asking if Will was all right.

"You're a hero, J. C.," one of them exclaimed. "My God, you looked like Wyatt Earp himself with that gun."

Osgood shook his head. "Nothing," he said. "The stationmaster keeps the shotgun in the depot. Any one of you would have done the same."

"Are you all right, Martin? That man night have killed you but for Mr. Osgood here."

Will dusted himself off. "I'm obliged to you, Mr. Osgood. I was darn near out of air."

That brought a laugh of relief from the men and they began to break up, walking toward the wagons. Several of them, though, crowded around Will. "We've heard of you, Martin," one of them said. "You were with Earp and Doc Holliday in Dodge City, weren't you?" Will nodded, tried to push their helping hands away, and felt the rope burns sting his neck. "Don't they call you the Curse-Killer?"

"Didn't you kill that gambler up in Schofield?"

"And that Indian who was terrorizing the valley, too?" "I heard you killed a dozen men in Dodge."

Osgood stepped in and took Will's arm. "Come on," he said. "We'll go up to the club and you can wash up."

"Thanks," Will said, his voice hoarse from the near-hanging. "Listen, I'd appreciate it if you wouldn't say anything to the women. Let me tell my wife in my own good time. No need to get them all upset the rest of the day."

"Of course," Osgood said. "I'll talk to the others."

JUDITH KNEW something was wrong the moment she and Will were seated in another passenger car for the ride to Coal Basin. Evey seemed to take no notice of Will's condition, prattling on about the "exquisite furnishings" and "beautiful appointments" of the inn's dining room where the women had gone that morning for tea. Judith, on the other hand, sat silently beside a quiet Will and studied him carefully. He had pulled the stiff white shirt collar higher on his neck to hide the rope burns and an attendant at the club had done the best he could to clean his clothes.

"Something happened," Judith said. "What was it?"

"Nothing that important," Will lied. "Tell you later."

Osgood again paced the car, delivering his comments about the ride like a tour guide, glancing now and then at Will. "We climbed only twelve hundred feet from Carbondale to Redstone's elevation of 7,200 feet," he said. "Redstone is at a relatively low elevation for a Colorado mining town. Now we're on our way to one of the highest at 9,200 feet."

The train jerked ahead and Will's head was forced backwards with the movement. His raw neck scratched on the starched collar but he thought he did a pretty good job of hiding the pain from Judith. *Where was Tom now?* he wondered. *What kind of confrontation would occur next? What about Tracey and Theresa? Were they all right in Marble or had Tom taken some kind of vengeance on them, too?*

"We'll climb 2,242 feet in the twelve-mile trip," Osgood shouted above the noise of the train. The grade was 4.3 percent, a steep rise, and the track curved constantly, often as much as forty degrees. It doubled back on itself, looping along the edges of canyon walls, making figure eights as it crossed the creek, climbing over a meadow and through deep cuts.

"Only one time on this trip will the train be in a straight line," Osgood shouted. "The rest of the time we'll be constantly turning."

Why did Tom and the other two leave to the north, Will wondered, *instead of heading back toward Marble? Could he be leaving the country?* He looked out the window but instead of the breathtaking beauty the others saw, he looked into Tom's hate-filled face. Instead of the clicking of the wheels on the rails he heard the click of Tom cocking his pistol.

"Look at the wildflowers, Will." Judith nudged him with her elbow and pointed out the window.

Osgood was beside them. "They are beautiful, aren't they? There is so much columbine along the route I've named this stretch of track the Columbine Road."

Will wondered why would Tom take up with Harrison and Yates. Tracey had said Yolanda kicked him out, but he was still involved with two disreputable men who had close ties with her. Will felt the pain in his body again as he thought of being dragged across the gravel, the ropes cutting off his breath. He had been close to death.

"Look everyone!" Osgood shouted. "You'll never see anything more beautiful than this."

At every turn, out one side or the other, the passengers could see far down the valley at the loops they had just negotiated and, beyond them, the imposing vista of the Continental Divide looming to the east, still snowcapped and glaring in the sunlight. The divide's ramparts made a solid wall of mountains that appeared impassable. Below them, Will knew, lay the now-quiet town of Aspen and the remains of Ashcroft and Highlands.

247

To the south, below yet another mighty range, lay Marble and Tracey and Yolanda Peabody. But probably not Tom. Tom had gone north. *North to where*? Will wondered.

They were at Coal Basin. The chilly air and high altitude made the women pull on the coats that Osgood had insisted they bring. "The miners say there are but three seasons up here," Osgood laughed. "Winter, July and August!"

Waterfalls gushed off of sheer mountain walls and brooks fed into Coal Creek from every direction. Will wished he could sit beside one and bathe his raw neck.

"We're taking anywhere from fifteen to twenty-five thousand tons of coal from these mountains every month," Osgood said in the sudden quiet of the car. "We'll use from six to eleven thousand tons of it for coking and ship out the rest for other uses."

Wagons took the group to the Coal Basin clubhouse, which was less elaborate than the one at Redstone. They were ushered into the barroom where lunch would be served. While the others found seats at carefully laid-out tables, Will studied a notice on the wall:

> *The club will sell to its members, or visitors introduced by members in accordance with the rules of the club, wines, beers and liquors, but in order to promote their temperate use and believing that each member or guest has the intelligence and ability to buy what he wants when he wants it without suggestion or aid from anyone, no 'treating' is allowed.*

Osgood stepped to Will's side. "We found that alcohol abuse was the major social problem we faced," he said. "We tried not selling liquor at all but that led to a disgusting amount of bootlegging and we had more of a problem with drunkenness than ever. Now, we sell drinks but this 'no treating' rule seems to have helped the problem."

After the meal of venison a small woman with a round face spoke up. "Are your miners well paid?" she asked.

"Better than most coal miners," Osgood stated. "Our miners make from $103 to $135 per month."

"They must be very happy," the woman continued. "All these foreign people in such adorable little homes and making what to them must be a huge sum of money."

Osgood frowned. "Most are happy," he said. "But a few defectors have moved on west to the fruit country around Paonia. Said they wanted to be their own boss. You simply can't please some people."

He's right, Will thought. There would be no pleasing Tom, at least. No matter what he said or how much he argued the "right" of what happened between him and Tracey.

After lunch the group boarded wagons again and were taken to the mouth of the mine where Osgood explained the details of the operation. Will heard his voice but not his words. He longed to be at home where he could discuss Tom's behavior with Judith. She would have comforting words, perhaps some good advice on how to deal with the man. Finally, they were taken back to the train. Osgood stood in front of his seated passengers and smiled broadly. "Relax and enjoy the scenery," he said. "It will take one hour and forty minutes to get back to Redstone."

It took two minutes less than that and, at the depot, Osgood gathered them once more near the waiting wagons. "You will now return to your lodgings," he said. "We will call for you by six and I have one last surprise for you."

Back in their cottage, while Evey primped in her bedroom, Judith confronted Will. "Now," she said. "Tell me."

He did, trying to include everything. There was no use attempting to hide anything from her, he had discovered. She had a way of finding the truth of everything. She helped him out of his coat and carefully unbuttoned his shirt.

"Will! It's worse than you said."

A look in the mirror convinced him she was right. A lotion that she applied soothed the burns somewhat but the fresh shirt and its even stiffer collar irritated the sores so much that he loosened the tie.

The wagons came on time and proceeded south of the inn, rolling down a narrow road which hugged sheer red cliffs on the left and the Crystal River on the right. Gas lights illuminated the early evening twilight every forty yards. Osgood was unusually quiet although he squirmed on his seat. About a mile south of Redstone, as the cliffs fell away and the river swerved off to the right, the caravan passed through a wrought iron gate. A small chaletlike house stood to the left, just beyond the gate. Ahead, through some pine trees, another building slowly came into view.

"It looks like a castle," Judith whispered. The guests were silent as the wagons creaked past a carriage house that Will thought looked more elaborate than his own home. All eyes were on the building ahead. Even Will had to marvel at the size of the structure. This was Osgood's crowning achievement. It was what he had promised to all who listened that night at the Hotel Colorado in Glenwood.

The building — the castle, for that's what it appeared to be — looked out of place in the rugged western mountains of a still-young American state and, at the same time, it looked as though it belonged there, snug against a rising wall of mountain behind it and commanding a broad sweep of immaculate lawn to the river on the west.

Turrets, chimneys and dormer windows were silhouetted against a sky reddened by a setting sun which seemed to have been instructed, perhaps by Osgood himself, on how to behave on this particular evening. Horses' hooves clattered on cobblestones and echoed across a courtyard which they entered through a European-style gate. As they passed through the gate and gazed at a fountain in the center of the courtyard, Osgood stood in the wagon and tugged on a cord which rang a small bell high overhead, announcing their arrival.

"Welcome," Osgood said. "Welcome to Cleveholm." Women sat with open mouths, staring at the grandeur of the castle. Men cleared their throats and began to stir from their rock-still astonishment. Will had forgotten the pain in his neck and craned his head, trying to absorb the elegance that was beyond anything he had imagined Osgood might create in this wilderness.

"I can't believe this," Judith said as they were led inside. "It must have cost a fortune."

"It did, my dear," Osgood said, overhearing her comment. "It puts that little hotel in Glenwood to shame, doesn't it?"

He moved ahead and Judith leaned toward Will. "He kept his promise and I had almost forgotten it."

"It's not quite finished or we would have welcomed all of you here instead of putting you in those small cottages," Osgood said. Will thought the man had housed them as he did to heighten the contrast with the castle.

Thoughts of his confrontation with Tom disappeared as Osgood himself led a tour of the home. "We have twenty-two bedrooms and the next time I bring you to this valley you shall all stay here." He smiled and looked rather shyly at the floor. "You will also find seventeen bathrooms. All inside."

Men and women alike gasped.

"Inside?" Judith asked in wonderment, and men laughed. She reddened as Osgood motioned them to follow him into the drawing room.

"There are forty-two rooms total," he said. "I modeled it after an English Tudor manor in Great Britain."

The guests spoke in hushed tones as Osgood led them through the large living room. Over a gigantic fireplace the Osgood crest was built into a red sandstone wall. Chandeliers, which Alma quietly said were designed by Tiffany, hung from the ceiling. Ornate furniture filled the room. "The colors we chose, red and green for the most part, are Alma's idea. Royalty, you know," Osgood bragged.

They passed through other rooms where silver goblets, serving trays and centerpieces resided in elegantly hand carved cabinets with curved plate glass. Fireplaces were made of hand-cut green onyx or white marble. Red silk brocade, red velvet, and green taffeta adorned the walls. In the library, green leather wallpaper had been hand-tooled with gold. Artists had been imported from Italy to stencil oak-paneled walls in other rooms. Many of the ceilings were covered with pure gold leaf. A game room was hung with hunting trophies, old rifles and muskets. "Alma is quite a crack shot, don't you know," Osgood bragged, and his wife blushed. A large pool table and round tables for card games took up most of the space. Beneath the pool cues that hung on the wall was a wine closet. The floors of most of the rooms were covered with oriental rugs.

At dinner, served by men and women of various nationalities, Osgood presided like a feudal baron. Alma rang a small bell to signal for another course.

A brave man sitting near Osgood asked the question. "I hesitate to ask," he said, "but I know everyone here is curious about the . . . well, the cost of all this."

"No need to be shy about asking," Osgood replied proudly. "I have personally invested nearly $700,000 in this home alone." Men shook their heads and women's eyes widened. "But you must understand that this is a small part of the complete project, including Redstone. There are more than four thousand acres here. And the road, the outbuildings, including the gatehouse and the carriage house — all of that cost a great deal of money. But, ladies and gentlemen, I will have you know I spared no expense — no expense! — for the good of my miners."

He waited a theatrical moment.

"The entire project has cost the sum of a well-invested, profit-producing total of nearly $5 million!"

Total silence greeted the announcement. A woman whispered, "My God!" Evey's mouth was open. She moved her hand and knocked over a water glass. No one seemed to notice. Then someone began to clap and all the guests broke into prolonged applause. Osgood bowed and beamed.

"This is my home," he said. "Redstone, Coal Basin, Cleveholm — all of this is just the beginning. We will carve a veritable paradise out of this wilderness and our utopian dream will become a beacon to the rest of the world, an example of what humanitarian efforts can do for the working class of the world."

After dessert, wine, cigars for the men, tea for the women, billiards in the game room, more cigars and more wine, a chiming clock suddenly announced it was midnight. Wagons carried weary, slightly intoxicated men and women back to the humble cottages where they would spend their final night before returning to Carbondale.

In the small house which would soon shelter an immigrant worker and his family, Evey could no longer contain herself and began to talk. "Alma went several times to New York to pick out the furnishings and art objects," she

251

said. "She went to Italy to find just the right artists to bring to Redstone. Did you know the castle was built from stone quarried from the hills right behind us? There is a game-keeper's house, too, and a gazebo will be built near the river where they'll have concerts. They even keep the harnesses for their horses in glass-domed cases in the carriage house. Did you ever see such large fireplaces? Mr. Osgood's wealth is so great it is difficult to imagine. Alma is so lucky, isn't she?"

Judith hugged the young woman. "She is, indeed. Now, don't you think you should get to bed? We must get up early for the train."

"But I won't be able to sleep," Evey complained. "I've never seen anything like it. Even in the finest houses in New York and Boston. It's been the most wonderful evening." She kissed Judith and Will and floated into her bedroom, eyes wide and feet clicking on the wooden floors.

Will fell into a chair and gingerly rubbed his neck. Judith sat on the arm of the chair and draped her arms around his shoulders, letting her forehead rest against his. "It's incredible, isn't it? Out here in this remote valley, actually a wilderness. And we have our own castle."

Will turned his head and massaged his stockinged feet which hurt from the tight shoes Judith had insisted he wear. "I'll never be able to give you anything even remotely resembling that," he said. "Makes me feel like a pauper."

Judith tossed her hair and laughed the deep-throated laugh that Will knew was sincere. "Why should you worry about something like that? I couldn't live in a castle, anyway. We have a ranch, land, a home." She pulled him back to her and stroked his hair. "And I love you, Will Martin. More than anything, I love you. You are all the riches I'll ever need."

Will took her hand and smiled. "I love you, too," he said. "Shall we go to bed?" They did, and it was a long time before they fell asleep, wrapped in each other's arms and bone-tired but entirely content with one another.

OSGOOD AND Alma stayed at Cleveholm as the others left on the train the next morning. The ride was a quiet one, with everyone still worn out from the excitement. As the train rounded the shoulder of Mount Sopris and the valley opened up, it stopped to take on a boxcar filled with potatoes and then rumbled on to the north.

"We should see the ranch in a moment," Judith said. Then, as soon as they spotted it they realized something was wrong. "My God! Will! The windows are all broken!"

He jerked upright in his seat and gasped. Curtains blew out of the windows. Debris cluttered the yard. Will reached above his head and pulled the cord that ran along the ceiling from one end of the car to the other. Immediately, the train began to slow. He jumped to his feet and ran to the door at the end of the combination car. Before the train came to a stop he leaped from the platform and ran toward the ranch house. Judith and Evey were close behind. Quickly, other passengers, looking questions at one another, piled from the train and followed. Some of the men ran ahead of their wives, leaving them to fend for themselves. Others pulled on their ladies' hands, urging them on.

At the river, Will found a dying cottonwood and, with the help of two men, toppled it across the river, forming a crude bridge. He helped Judith and Evey across and then ran on ahead. Looking back at the women he saw that several of the men had made their way across the log and others were helping women to cross. He wondered only for an instant why they were following.

He reached his home long before any of the others. The front door was hanging on its hinges. Furniture was strewn throughout the yard; window glass crunched beneath his feet. Inside, broken chairs littered the floor. Lamps and dishes had been smashed. The walls had been scarred with knives and furniture that was bashed against them. Many of the curtains had been torn from the windows and lay on broken glass. The kitchen looked just as bad. He didn't bother going into the bedrooms.

Turning, he saw Judith standing in the doorway with tears streaming down her face. "Why?" she sobbed.

He held her tightly and let her cry out her stunned sorrow. Evey pushed her way past them and stood in the center of the living room gazing at the damage.

Then the others began to arrive. Men panting from the unusual exertion leaned against porch railings, peered through windows and stood in the yard shaking their heads. "What is it, George?" Women were arriving. Beyond them, Will could see the Bull of the Woods puffing smoke on the tracks across the river. "I don't know." Men helped their wives find a place to rest. They sat on ruined chairs and on the edge of the porch. The yard was full of well-dressed men and women who puffed and panted and wanted to know everything at once.

Will pulled free of Judith who seemed to be getting herself under control and found Luke at the corner of the house staring at the ground.

"What happened?" Will asked.

Luke shook his head. "I don't know. We were up on the mesa early this morning. Got back less than an hour ago."

"What do you make of all this, Martin?" Three men from the train walked around the corner of the house. One was carrying a new lariat with a red tie

253

around the loop.

"Where did you get that?" Will asked.

"Found it laying in the yard."

"You recognize it?" Luke fingered the rope.

Will nodded, pulled back his collar to expose the red burns on his neck.

"Who?"

"Tell you later." He turned to the three men, who had been joined by others. "What are all of you people doing here?" The men looked at the ground or at their wives who stood sweating in the sun, dresses filthy where they had trailed across the ground. Sweat streaked the faces of everyone and dark suits were covered with dust. One man who had evidently fallen into the river was soaking wet.

There was a harsh blast from the train whistle and men raised their heads to the sound. Three more short blasts followed. "We'd better get back," a woman said.

Men nodded and began to pair up with their wives and brush off their pants. "Isn't there anything we can do?" one asked.

"I appreciate it," Will replied, shaking his head. "Not now. Why don't all of you get on back to the train? I know your wives want to get on home." Gradually the group began to hurry back toward the tracks.

Inside, Judith and Evey were slowly picking up broken glass and pieces of ruined furniture and carrying the debris to the porch. Will stood in the doorway and watched his wife and daughter move about the room as though in a daze. This act of vandalism seemed to Will to have no clear meaning. It couldn't have been done for vengeance. Nothing short of killing would satisfy Tom. Will speculated that it was an act of pure enjoyment on the part of men who were probably drunk and who felt some sort of power as they destroyed another man's property.

Then, as quickly as it had come on him, the anger passed. Will's head cleared and he suddenly felt almost giddy, happy, free. He smiled and Judith saw it.

"Are you out of your mind?" she demanded. "How can you smile?"

He couldn't help it. He kicked away a broken chair leg, caught Judith in his arms and swung her around, lifting her feet from the floor. Evey stood near the wall, eyes wide. "Father!" she cried, and Will lowered Judith's feet back to the floor. Both women were still red-eyed.

"I think they've done us a favor," he said.

"What?" The women said it almost in unison.

"Sure." He took Evey's hand and brushed Judith's damp cheek with the other. "I told you a long time ago I thought we needed a new house. Now we'll have one."

Judith swallowed. "I liked this one."

"I did, too. But you deserve a better home. It won't be like Cleveholm, but it will be better than this one."

Evey's eyes began to clear as Judith pulled away and looked around the room. "It is a mess, isn't it? But a new house will cost a great deal."

Will fished in the pocket of his coat and found Osgood's check. He smoothed out the wrinkles.

"What's that?" Judith asked, staring at the paper. Will handed it to her and Evey edged closer. "Fifteen hundred dollars? I don't understand."

"It's from Osgood," Will said. "Our profits from the coal claim I filed years ago."

"Profit?"

"That's only part of it." He bent and kissed Evey on the cheek. "We've got one of those coming every month from now 'til doomsday according to Osgood. Of course, part of it belongs to George Sanders and I had a percentage of the claim filed in Jake's name." He turned to Evey. "And part of it is yours."

Evey began to grin and Judith stared at Will. Her laugh began somewhere down deep, like it always did when she was happy, and the three of them hugged each other, laughing and crying and holding on for dear life.

"Where?" Judith asked.

"Where, what?"

"Where will we build the new house? I think I know the spot. Over nearer the creek. But we mustn't disturb those pine trees. I want them to shade the back porch."

"We could make it two stories," Evey said. "And could we have an indoor bathroom like Mr. Osgood's?"

They stood there in the midst of their destroyed furnishings and made plans for a new, larger home, in just the right spot. They crunched across shards of glass and wood and looked through a broken window toward the creek. Judith pointed at the spot she had in mind.

"That's where I've always thought we'd build one day," Will said.

He walked through the kitchen and out the back door as the two women talked excitedly about the details of the new house. He found Luke sitting on his bunk repairing a bridle.

"Tomorrow," Will said. "Early. We're going to Marble."

Slowly, Luke stood and let the grin fill his face. "It's about time," he said. "We've waited long enough."

❧❦

SMALL PATCHES of snow lay along the rough wagon road but as Will and Luke approached Marble the drifts got higher and there were fewer barren spots. At this altitude of more than eight thousand feet, it would take a long time for the sun to burn off the remaining snow. It was late afternoon when they rode past the White House Saloon. Harrison and Yates stepped to the door as they passed and watched warily, evidently warned by someone that Will Martin was on his way into town. There was no sign of Tom.

He wasn't at the boarding house, either. Tracey welcomed Will with an embrace and, in answer to his question, said, "I haven't seen him for days."

Eleven-year-old Theresa bounded down the stairs shouting "Uncle Will!" She gave him a peck on the cheek and asked, "What are you doing here? And who is that?" Luke stood in the background by the door.

"Theresa!" Tracey shot a harsh glance at her daughter.

"It's all right," Will said. *She's just like Evey,* he thought. *Not at all afraid to speak her mind.* "This is Luke Matthews, my partner."

Theresa looked the tall man up and down. "You look just like an Indian."

Tracey blanched but Luke took it in stride. "That's because I am an Indian." He smiled at the girl.

Theresa stepped closer. "I've never seen a real Indian before. Why is your hair so long?"

Theresa followed Luke to a table and sat across from him, staring at the long, black hair. Luke instinctively touched it as Will followed Tracey into the kitchen. "It keeps me mindful of my heritage," Luke was saying.

"I wish I had hair like that." Theresa reached out and Luke leaned forward so she could touch his hair.

"Your hair is very beautiful as it is."

"Oh! Do you think so?"

They were deep in conversation as Will let the door close behind him. While Tracey filled plates he told her of the incident at Redstone and what he had found when he reached the ranch. "There's no proof Tom was at the ranch," he said. "The only thing I've got to go on is the rope."

"Things could have been so different," Tracey whispered. She turned to him and, for a brief moment, let her eyes lock on his. Both looked away at the same time.

As Tracey set the plates on the table, Theresa looked at her with excitement in her eyes. "Oh, Mother. Luke had a horse all his own when he was my age."

"Maybe you'll have one before long, dear," Tracey said.

"But I want one now. I could ride all over the mountains and we could keep it out back. Daddy could build a barn."

At that moment Luke bent his head to pray and Theresa stared at him.

256

When he finished and picked up his fork, she turned to her mother. "Why don't we say grace, too?"

❧❦

WILL AND LUKE were on horseback a mile south of Marble when the sun broke through dark clouds to the east the next morning. Luke shifted in the saddle and looked back down the long valley. "We could do it ourselves," he said softly.

Will shook his head. "Might make a mess of it and end up in jail. We'll let the law handle it."

Four days later they rode back into Marble accompanied by the Gunnison County Sheriff and a deputy. Ollie Schwartz, the Sheriff, had been reluctant to come. "Long way to Marble," he said.

"It's part of your territory," Will replied hotly. "Maybe if you'd had a deputy over there, or showed yourself now and then, I wouldn't have to come for you."

It was twilight when they came down off the mountain and, even that early, the White House Saloon was busy. The rinky-tink piano could be heard as soon as they came out of the trees. The building was alive with light and noise.

"That the place?" Schwartz asked.

"That's where they'll be."

Schwartz spat a wad of tobacco juice. "Mind if we get somethin' to eat first? My stomach's killin' me. I ain't rode this far at once in a long, long time."

Will sighed and glanced at Luke who rolled his eyes. "Over there," Will said, pointing at the boarding house.

Tracey was nervous as she served the men, but Theresa cornered Luke the moment he arrived and begged him to tell her more about his life as an Indian.

"Luke's a fine boy," Tracey said to Will, as they listened to Luke and Theresa laughing together.

"New side of him, all right," Will said.

Sheriff Schwartz finally seemed to have eaten enough. He leaned back in his chair and patted his belly, wiped his flowing mustache with a sleeve, and stood. "Well," he said, "might's well go see what's up across the street." Andy Tomkins, the deputy, jumped to his feet. He was younger than Luke, Will thought, and he didn't know what he was getting into this night.

Outside at the hitching rail, Will fished in his saddlebags and pulled out his Colt. The weapon felt strange on his hip as he buckled his gun belt. He wondered how many years it had been since he'd worn it.

257

Schwartz began a slow walk toward the saloon, Tomkins on one side and Luke on the other, carrying a rifle. Will started to follow and, remembering, returned to his horse and lifted the lariat with a red tie from his saddle horn. He caught up with the others and touched Schwartz on the arm. "Let me go in first and see who's there."

The sheriff shrugged. "Don't make me no never mind." He seemed calm but, as he stepped to the door, Will saw him spinning the chamber of his own revolver.

The harsh light blinded Will for an instant when he entered the room and he stood still, waiting for his eyes to adjust. When they did, he saw Tom sitting alone near the back of the room holding a half-empty bottle. Harrison and Yates were not in sight, nor was Yolanda. Will let the lariat dangle at his side, out of sight as much as possible, and made his way toward Tom.

"Want some company?" He stood over his old friend and Tom let his eyes stray up Will's body to his face.

"Not you," he said, but Will sat beside him anyway.

"I'm going to talk fast and you better listen and hear every word I say because I'm only saying it once," Will whispered. "The sheriff's outside and we've got two other guns with us. I want you to walk real casual-like out the back door. Go home or somewhere but get out of here now."

Tom's eyes widened and his hand shook. "What if I . . ."

"I'm not saying it again," Will cut in. "I'm giving you a chance you probably don't deserve, just for old times' sake. Now git!"

Tom got slowly to his feet, hitched up his pants and strolled toward the back door. He was moving faster when he reached it.

Will walked to the bar. "Harrison around?" he asked the bartender. The man motioned toward the back room. "Tell him Will Martin's here."

"Tell him yourself," the bartender said.

"Never mind, Johnny." Yolanda stood ten feet away, arms crossed. "I'll tell him." She smiled at Will and went into the room at the back. Almost instantly, Harrison appeared at the door. Yates peered around the big man's shoulder from behind. Will didn't think the man knew how to smile, but Yates did as they walked toward the bar. They stopped in the middle of the room. Harrison wore a revolver high on his right side and Yates, the smaller man, carried the rifle that seemed always to be a part of him. Yolanda stood in the background wearing more of a smirk than a smile. The noise in the room let up.

"What you want?" Harrison's voice was low and it cracked as he talked. Tobacco juice stained his scraggly beard. His arms hung at his sides and he clenched and unclenched his fists. Yates grinned beside him, his finger twitching around the rifle's trigger guard.

258

"Got something I think belongs to you," Will said. He tossed the lariat to the floor in front of the two men.

Harrison looked at it a second. "What makes you think it's mine?"

Will let his right hand dangle at his side as he reached to his neck and began to slowly undo the bandanna. "I'm sure it belonged to you a few days ago." He snaked the bandanna from his neck, exposing the still-raw burns.

Harrison grinned, barely, and Yates snickered. He's nervous, Will thought. The little man shuffled his feet. Harrison was the one he had to be careful of and he kept his eyes locked on the big man's.

"Found it at my ranch," Will said, "and thought I'd return it to you."

"I got more," Harrison said, admitting ownership.

Will heard the front door open and saw Harrison look that way. He quickly glanced over and saw Schwartz and Tomkins enter. They flanked the door, young Tomkins looking downright scared.

"Well, shit," Harrison said. With a speed that astonished Will he moved to his right, hand reaching for his holstered pistol. Will saw Yates' rifle level at him and he took a step to his left, reaching for his own gun. A single shot boomed in the room. All three froze.

"Don't nobody reach for no gun," Schwartz said loudly. Will kept Harrison in sight as he let his eyes stray toward the sheriff. He stood, legs apart, gun pointed at Harrison. "You hand over them guns, friends, and we'll do this the easy way."

Again, with an agility that seemed impossible for such a large man, Harrison moved. He sprang to his right and turned over a table with his left hand as his right pulled his weapon, cocking it as it cleared the holster. Schwartz got off a shot that splintered the wall across the room and men dove for the floor. A woman screamed as Will lunged toward Yates. The rifle exploded in Will's ear as he knocked the barrel upwards. A shot was fired from Harrison's direction and Tomkins cried out in pain.

"Well, hell," Schwartz said as he ran for cover behind the bar. Yates was wiry and he wrestled the rifle away from Will, clubbing him on the head with it. Will fell to the floor, saw the rifle barrel come toward him, and heard the back door crash open. Yates hesitated then turned his head. Behind Yates Will saw Luke and Tom standing side by side. Will rolled away from the rifle. Luke lifted his own rifle and Tom leveled a pistol at Yates. Will thought he heard Yates snicker again as he moved the gun away from Will and toward Tom. Two shots sounded as one and Yates fell backward across Will, blood streaming from his neck.

Across the room Harrison stood up and turned slowly toward Luke, who still held his rifle on the man. Harrison looked down at his chest where blood was staining his shirt. "Well, shit," he said, and fell to the floor with a thud.

259

The room was totally quiet for a long second and then Schwartz emerged from behind the bar. He walked to Tomkins, who sat near the door rubbing his leg. "You hurt bad?"

"Don't guess so," Tomkins answered. "Scared the hell out of me, though."

Will shoved Yates' body away and got to his feet. Harrison lay across the edge of the upturned table. He saw Tom holster his pistol as Luke chambered another round into the rifle. The lever action seemed to echo through the quiet of the saloon.

Schwartz stood over Harrison's body. "Killed the hell out of him, didn't you? Never killed a man myself. Hope I never do." He walked toward Will, stopped and stooped over to pick up the lariat. "This is yours," he said, handing it to Will.

"It's his," Will replied. Everybody in the room looked at the large body and pool of blood beneath it.

"*Was* his," Schwartz said, looking around for somewhere to spit. Not finding a spittoon, he spat on the floor. "Satisfied?"

Will coiled the rope and looked at the sheriff. "That's not the question. Are you?"

"I reckon so. Not much question that they was your men, all right. Cut'n dried. Sure hope I don't never have to go through nothin' like that again." He sat on a chair and wiped a sleeve across his nose. "Thought you said there was three of 'em," Schwartz said, with something like a twinkle in his eye. "Wonder what happened to the other one."

"No telling," Will said. "Probably clear to Glenwood by now."

"Probably," Schwartz said. He held Will's eyes for a moment and then turned away. "I got to get me some sleep," he said. "And I b'lieve my deputy needs a bit of doctoring."

A WEEK LATER Will helped Luke and the new man Stone cut and carry timber to the spot near the creek where they would build the new house. He saw a lone rider coming slowly up from the road and recognized him as Tom. He dropped the log and wiped sweat from his neck. The rope burns still hurt when he perspired.

Tom pulled his horse to a halt and kept his eyes downcast as Will stepped to his side. "Howdy," Will said.

Tom had a prepared speech, it sounded to Will, but it came out just fine. "I've been thinking," he said. "I've been doing nothing but think for the past week. I was wrong and I came to apologize. You could have set me up and I'd be as dead as Harrison and Yates. Why'd you let me go?"

Will stroked the neck of Tom's horse and remembered what his old friend had said to him months ago after he'd downed half a bottle of whiskey and Will was trying to get him home to Tracey. "Everything's come easy to you, hasn't it?" Tom had blurted out. "You wandered onto a Texas ranch and landed a job with the best boss in the West. Then you come up here and somebody hands you a silver mine. You have your way with another man's wife and then walk away from her to marry the niece of a silver king in Aspen."

"I didn't walk away," Will had responded.

Tom had waved his arm as though trying to push Will out of his life. "I tried to make my own way. I worked my butt off and for what? Hell, I gave you the first decent clothes you ever had. I taught you cowboying. Tracey still loves you. More'n she loves me."

The fact that Tom felt she no longer loved him had led to the encounter in Redstone and, ultimately, to the destruction of Will's home. Now Tom was here, asking for forgiveness and wondering why Will would have helped him under the circumstances. What could he tell him? It wasn't hard to figure.

"We go way back, Tom. You didn't belong with those two. Figured I owed you."

"Owed me?" Tom finally met Will's eyes. "Way back there in Crystal City you pulled me out of a drunk. You introduced me to a fine woman who I've also got to apologize to. You don't owe me. I owe you."

Will smiled. "I reckon we can call it even. I didn't know you could shoot like that."

Tom managed a smile himself. "Me, neither," he said.

"You going back to Marble?"

"Yep. What kind of welcome you think I'll get?"

"I think there are two ladies up there who'll be mighty glad to see you. Theresa was asking about her daddy."

"She was?" Tom's face brightened.

"Sure, she was. Now get down from that horse. Judith will want you to stay for dinner."

"I came to ask for a job," Tom said softly. He obviously didn't want to say it.

"Nope." Will shook his head.

"No?"

"You got a job in Marble. I talked to the superintendent before we left. Told him you'd been under a strain but I figured you'd got things worked out. Said you'd be back soon."

"But, I . . ."

261

"Oh, shut up. I think things are about to boom up there. Osgood says he might even run his railroad up that way."

Tom broke into a grin. "Well," he said. "Well, hell."

"Well, hell is right. Now get down and let's go eat."

WILL THREW the last of Evey's luggage on the wagon and faced her as she walked from the house.

"A schoolteacher," he said. "You're gonna be a dandy."

"I hope so," she said. "I think it will be fun living in Redstone."

"Evey," Luke Matthews said quietly as he stood by the corner of the house. Evey hurried to him and they talked for perhaps two minutes. Then Luke touched his hat and they turned from one another, Luke disappearing around the building. Judith came from the house at that moment, saw the parting, and caught Will's eye. She shook her head slightly, warning him to say nothing to Evey about Luke.

As the ride to Redstone began, Evey immediately started chattering about the coming winter as a schoolteacher, saying nothing about any sorrow at leaving the ranch — or Luke. Alma Osgood figured prominently in her comments. "It will be so enjoyable to see Alma often this winter. I'm so glad she insisted I take the job."

Later that afternoon, when Will had moved Evey's belongings into the little peach-colored cottage Osgood was providing for her on Redstone Boulevard, the regal Mrs. Osgood showed up in a small black buggy pulled by a small black horse.

"Mr. Osgood and I want all three of you to be our guests for dinner tonight. And, of course, you and Judith will spend the night with us at Cleveholm."

"I thought we'd stay here with Evey," Will said.

"Here?" Alma cast a quick look around the three-room cottage. "No, indeed. I insist you stay with us."

She left with a wave of her gloved hand, climbed into her buggy, and clattered off down the street. Judith frantically began throwing clothes from her luggage.

"What the devil are you doing?" Will asked.

She turned to him wide-eyed. "I don't think I brought anything decent to wear to Cleveholm." She frowned. "Maybe I can patch something together."

"Good Lord," Will muttered as he walked out of the house and stood by the fence making a mess of packing his pipe.

With the help of a light blue shawl of Evey's, Judith turned herself from a rancher's wife to a woman of refinement who looked as though she would be comfortable dining with President Roosevelt himself. The five of them dined at one end of a table that would seat eighteen. A blazing fire took the chill off the evening. The women talked constantly but Will found Osgood more subdued than usual.

After the meal, while the women went into the library, Will followed Osgood into the game room. Osgood made a great fuss offering cigars and going through the sniffing, clipping, and lighting routine as Will admired the hunting trophies on the walls.

"You'll have to take me on a hunt someday," Osgood said. "I hear you're still the best guide in the valley."

"I've been all over it, as you know," Will said.

Osgood disappeared behind a cloud of cigar smoke. As it rose and his face appeared again, his smile was gone. "There's enough coal up there to last a thousand years, Martin."

"Pretty lucky we found it when we did," Will said quietly.

"Luck?" Osgood swiveled in his chair and stared at Will. "Or fate?" He leaned close, pointing his cigar at Will's face. "We also talked about fate, I believe. Fate and destiny." His shoulders sagged. "My destiny may be about played out, I fear."

Will waited. He had thoughts of Osgood dying from a rapidly progressing disease.

Osgood sighed, studied the end of his cigar. "I've made millions in the past years," he said, "and I've also spent millions. I used company money to carry out this sociological experiment. Cleveholm was constructed with my own private funds. I've made it a point never to borrow unless absolutely necessary." He stopped, seemed lost in thought.

"Are you broke?" Will asked.

Osgood laughed loudly. "No, no. Nothing like that." His face clouded over again. "There are men in the East, however, who would like to see me out of the picture."

"Somebody wants to kill you?"

Again Osgood laughed. "No one is trying to kill me, although it is almost as bad. You see, John Gates of Chicago has managed to acquire enough stock in CF&I to exert a certain influence." CF&I, Will knew, resulted from the consolidation of the Colorado Coal and Iron Company and Osgood's Colorado Fuel Company.

"John 'Bet-a-Million' Gates?"

"The same. The man is as dishonest as a Mississippi gambler. Yet the public thinks of the uncouth old bastard as some sort of modern-day Robin Hood." Osgood stood and paced the room. *Talking to himself*, Will thought.

Talking to get it out in the open and just to hear it said.

"I listed the CF&I on the New York Stock Exchange, and immediately Gates bought nearly two hundred shares, making him second only to me as a major stockholder. Not long ago, the United States Steel Corporation offered to buy my company for $105 per share. Gates paid only $68 a share and he has been demanding that I sell out so he can make a quick profit. I have so far refused, telling him I want $125 a share, which I assume no one will pay."

Will stubbed out his cigar and patted his pockets for his pipe as Osgood talked on, still pacing. "Lately, Gates has gotten into cahoots with J. P. Morgan of New York and the two have caused an incredible rise in the price of company stock."

Will found his pipe and chewed on the stem. "That's good, then. You could retire even more wealthy than you are now."

Osgood sat again, leaning toward Will. "I did not spend the millions required to get this company going, to build Redstone and, yes, even Cleveholm, just to sell it and spend the rest of my life lounging about in this castle! My life is work, Martin. Work! The CF&I is like my own child. I will not see it turned over to greedy industrialists from the East who will mangle my grand experiment."

"What can you do?"

"Fight! I will fight to the absolute bitter end. Some of my so-called friends have already sold their shares for big profits and under different circumstances I wouldn't blame them. Now they may force me out of my own firm."

Will got his pipe going. "Isn't there anything you can do?"

Osgood nodded. "I am involved in several complex legal maneuvers which can delay Gates. The worst that can happen now would be for him to throw all of his stock on the market at once, causing a tremendous decline in its value."

"At least you'd have control," Will said. "But I would have no collateral to . . . "

The door opened and Alma Osgood fanned the air. "My goodness," she exclaimed. "How can you two stand all of this nauseating smoke? Come out of that room at once."

As the two men stood, Osgood gripped Will's arm, smiling and nodding at Alma. "There's more," he said. "Despite everything I do for my miners, I fear a strike that would cripple us significantly."

Will looked questioningly at Osgood.

"That agitator John Mitchell has got 147,000 anthracite miners out on strike in the East. They call themselves the United Mine Workers." Osgood shook his head, pointed his cigar at Will. "Do you realize, Martin, that there

264

are nearly one million members of this damnable American Federation of Labor? It's getting miners worked up all over the West, wanting . . . wanting things! And you know the luxuries they have here."

Will nodded, thinking to himself that strikes would never happen this deep in the Rocky Mountains.

"We'll talk again," Osgood muttered and then smiled at the ladies who still stood in the doorway. "You are right, my dear. Let's get out of here, Martin."

Will and Judith were shown to an elaborate bedroom just down the hall from the Osgoods' and were told they would be awakened at seven for breakfast. The long wagon ride and the wine had made Judith tired and she was almost immediately asleep. Will sat in an overstuffed chair, however, thinking about Osgood and what his loss of CF&I might mean to the valley. He wondered if it would mean the end of Redstone and the possibility of a railroad to Marble.

He tried to shake the thoughts of Osgood's problems by concentrating on Evey and her new adventure. She would be an outstanding teacher, he figured. What if she married Luke? Would they stay on the ranch? He would have to build a home for them. The thought pleased him and he ran it around in his mind for a while.

Restless, he went to the door and stepped into the hallway. A small electric light bulb cast a gloomy light as he went to the corner and looked down the hall toward the Osgood bedroom. As he peered around the corner the door opened and Alma walked into the hall. She wore a sheer nightgown and had not put on a robe. Another small light behind her silhouetted her body through the gown. She turned and went to a small balcony which overlooked the large living room below. Alma leaned on the balcony and her breasts fell forward, clearly visible through the filmy material. Will gulped and continued to stare at the beautiful woman. As she turned toward him he started to step back out of sight but found he could not move.

"It's a beautiful night," Alma whispered. She straightened, fluffed her hair with arms raised and let him take in the fullness of her youthful body. "Can't sleep?"

Will shook his head and tried to look elsewhere but failed.

Alma smiled and took a step toward him. "I have the same problem." Although she whispered Will was certain everyone in the house could hear her. He stood, mesmerized by her beauty. She was close to him. He could smell her perfume. "It's chilly," she said, smiling.

Will nodded again, thought of Judith asleep down the hall — and of J. C. Osgood, his friend, asleep a few feet away.

"Did you enjoy the evening?" Alma asked.

265

"Yes, I did," he said. He forced himself to look away and motioned toward his own bedroom. "I better turn in."

He saw her smile, shrug and nod before he turned and started down the hall. Two steps away, he turned back to her. She stood motionless, backlit by the feeble light. "Good night," he said, turned again and hurried to his room.

Judith awoke when he closed the door. "Where have you been?" she asked sleepily.

"Couldn't sleep. Just prowling around in the hall." Judith threw back the covers. "Well, come to bed and warm me up." In an instant he was out of his clothes and huddled up to his wife who surprised him by rolling over on top of him. She put her mouth to his ear and whispered: "Did you see Alma?"

"What?" He swallowed.

"Alma. Did you see her? She told me she has trouble sleeping and often walks around in the middle of the night." Will thought of Alma's body, even as he caressed his wife's.

"I saw her."

Judith moved on his body, kissed him on the mouth, nuzzled his neck. As she straightened he let his hands fall to her hips. "Did she frighten you?"

Will nodded. "Scared the hell out of me."

Judith laughed aloud and Will joined her and rolled her over on her back. They laughed a few seconds more and then the laughter stopped and Will didn't think of Alma any more.

SUMMER QUICKLY turned into fall and the color in the mountains was like light through a prism. Red sumac mingled with the aspen gold and the lighter yellow of the cottonwoods. The pines kept their green as the snow thickened on the peaks and showed white here and there.

"If Osgood would just make good on his promise and build the railroad, even to Prospect, we'd have all the work we could handle," Tom told Will one cool evening in Marble. "I don't understand why the man doesn't start laying track."

Will didn't reply, knowing Osgood's problems were keeping his mind on Redstone and not Marble.

Tom frowned over the need for a railroad but Tracey was grinning from ear to ear. "Shall we tell them?" she asked Tom.

Judith was on her feet. "Are you pregnant?"

They both broke into happy laughter. "No, that's not it," Tom said.

"I'll tell them if you won't," Tracey said, putting her hand on Tom's arm. "Tom has been promoted. To foreman."

266

Will quickly stood. "Congratulations!" he said as the two men gripped each other's hands tightly. "I knew you'd make a go of it."

"Thanks to you," Tom said. He hugged Tracey. "And to this lady, here." Tracey beamed proudly at her husband. "Things are so good it's scary," Tom said. "I've never been so blamed happy. Can you believe it?"

"I believe it," Will said. "I surely do."

᪐᪐

A FEW WEEKS later, just before Thanksgiving, Luke was restless at the dinner table. Though he didn't speak much Will and Judith recognized the man's uneasiness.

"I'd like to go to Redstone," he said, finally. "To see Evey. Would that be all right with you two?"

"Why, Luke!" Judith turned from the sink. "How nice. I know she'll be pleased."

Luke looked at Will. "What about you?"

"Do what you want," Will said, packing his pipe.

Luke stood, took his hat and walked to the door. "I will," he said. "Probably see you Sunday night."

When the door closed behind Luke, Will stood and watched him on the path through the snow toward the bunkhouse. "'Bout time," he muttered and didn't see Judith smiling.

On Sunday night, Luke was back as he promised. Will walked to the barn and helped Luke unsaddle and curry his horse. "How is she?" he asked.

"Fine," Luke said. He ran the stiff brush over the horse's flank then bent to study a hoof.

Will waited a moment and could stand it no longer. "Fine? Is that all? How's she doing? Is she happy? When's she coming home? For Christmas?"

Luke smiled up at him. "She's doing great," he said. "She misses you, said she'd be down here for Christmas."

Will nodded, tossed the curry comb onto a shelf, and started for the door. He stopped, though, and turned back.

"Something else?"

Will hesitated, then turned again. "Nope," he said. "Nothing else." Outside, though, he stopped again and then shoved the door open. It clattered against the wall and Luke looked up. "There is something else."

"Yeah?"

"Yeah. Where did you sleep?"

Luke's normally stoical face broke into a wide smile. He waited a while and let Will stew, knowing it had been difficult for him to ask the question.

Finally, he stood, leaned over the horse's back, still smiling. "Who said we slept?"

Will turned on his heel and began walking quickly toward the door. As he reached it, he heard Luke say softly, "At the inn with the other bachelors." Will tried not to let Luke hear him exhale the deep, relieved breath as he slammed the door behind him.

≈∾

THROUGHOUT the winter, Luke visited Evey at least once a month. She would come back to the ranch for the summer after the school term ended in late May. Will figured they would probably be married by August, maybe even sooner.

He and Luke were at the corral one April morning in 1903 when Judith called from the house. She waved an envelope above her head and Will sloshed through the wet snow to the back door. The letter, from Abby, dealt with only two subjects. The first she addressed quickly, and Will shook his head sadly as he read.

"What is it?" Judith wanted to know.

"Henry Gillespie is dead," Will said. "Abby says he died March 27 of a tropical fever somewhere in South America."

"I recall you said he was mining down there. Was it near Panama, where that big canal is being constructed?"

"Doesn't say. Wherever he was, he evidently hadn't found much of anything. She says he still had a lot of debts."

"It's hard to believe someone like him could be so wealthy and then die penniless."

Will stared at the letter without seeing the words and thought of the Henry Gillespie he had known, the man whose life he thought he was saving when he was actually making a fool of himself. He found it hard to imagine the man dead. He had been a man of movement, of action. And he had such dreams for Aspen. The big tent, the culture, the money that passed through his hands. Gillespie had given Will his own start and had been repaid well for his investment. Now the man, like Aspen itself, was dead. *Well,* Will thought, *that isn't entirely accurate.* Aspen was still alive, though barely. But there would never be another Henry Gillespie. He knew Abby had loved her uncle and he felt for her loss.

He replaced the glasses he was now having to use for reading and studied the rest of the letter.

"I have heard from Evey several times this winter and, in addition to a great deal of information about this Swedish Princess, her letters are full of talk about a half-breed Ute Indian with whom she appears to be in love. Or thinks she is. She tells me this Luke, if that is his name -- more likely 'Big Buffalo' or some such -- is your partner. Why must I learn things like that from someone other than you? You seem to have forgotten how to write, if you ever knew. Surely you can understand how utterly opposed to this relationship I am will forever be. Nothing good can come of it. Must we have half-breed grandchildren? Must she spend her life in that disgusting little valley as a rancher's wife when there is so much in the world that is wonderful? I would like to take her with me this fall to New York to hear a fantastic new tenor named Enrico Caruso sing Rigoletto at the Metropolitan Opera. There she might meet a more appropriate eligible bachelor. But I am certain you are literally delighted with the situation. She is more like the woman you would have liked for me to be, isn't she?

"Evey is talented, Will. She has abilities and training that should create a place for her among the cultured and refined people of the world. Though I was also opposed to her teaching school in Redstone I chose to remain silent about that, hoping a year of it would bring her to her senses. Evidently, it has not.

"I promise you that I will fight this potential marriage to a painted savage with all of my heart and with all the resources I can command. Henry is also opposed to it, as you can imagine, and has vowed to keep her from marrying a 'godless savage' as he so aptly put it."

Will held the letter for a moment and then handed it to Judith. While she read it, he shuffled to the window, and saw Luke repairing a hinge on the corral gate. *If Abby could only meet him*, he thought, *get to know the boy*. He shook his head at the "godless savage" tag his own son Henry had so wrongly placed on Luke. If she could only see him bow his head before every meal. He wouldn't see her marry some white-faced office boy from Denver with soft hands. He would be proud to have Luke as a son-in-law as well as a business partner.

"It's so sad," Judith said, folding the letter. "She simply has no idea of the kind of man her daughter has found."

Will nodded. "It could get ugly. I'd hate to see Evey and her mother at odds for the rest of their lives."

"Let's go to Marble," Judith said out of the blue. "The road will be a mess but we could make it. And we could stop to see Evey on the way."

Will thought about it. "Luke will want to go."

"So?"

He grinned. "We'll go on Friday."

❧

NEARING REDSTONE, Will pulled his horse alongside Judith and pointed to Owl Point. The ridge was snow-covered and cold as it jutted out proudly over the valley. "If there wasn't so much snow I think I'd climb up there," he said. "I always seem to feel better after I've sat on that rock for a few hours and stared up and down the valley." He continued to study the cliff as they rode slowly past it. He thought of his encounter with Owl Man and remembered that Luke had followed him to the point not many years ago. "I wonder why Luke didn't want to come with us today," he said. "It has to be more than making sure the man I hired knows what to do."

Judith smiled. "I think I know."

"Oh, yeah? He wanted to be alone with Evey?"

"That, of course. But there's something else. You'll see." They didn't say anything to Evey about her mother's letter, figuring if she hadn't heard from her by now, she would soon. *Evey seems happier than ever*, Will thought. *These mountains agree with her. Being in love didn't hurt anything, either*, Will decided.

That evening, over a dinner of trout furnished by two of her students, Evey bubbled over with enthusiasm for, it seemed, everything in her life. Her students were "wonderful" children. She reported that Mr. Osgood had provided all the books for her class which ranged from second to eighth grade, and his wife Alma was such a "wonderful" woman.

"They are beginning to call her 'Lady Bountiful' because of all the things she does for the families," Evey said. "She drives her carriage up and down the street, talking to the miners' wives and helping them with their problems. She is such an excellent horsewoman. We've gone on several long rides together. Did you know she plays the piano? She's even composed a song called 'The Redstone Waltz.'"

They watched her trudge happily up the slope to the school the next morning and then rode to Cleveholm. Osgood was in a foul mood but ushered Will into his study.

"I've beaten the damned 'barbed wire king' but I've got another fight on my hands now," he said.

"You beat Gates?"

"Old 'bet-a-million' himself. Can you imagine making a fortune on barbed wire? The idea is revolting."

"How'd you do it?"

"Never mind the details," Osgood said, "but be assured it wasn't easy. It took some intensely complex legal maneuvering on my part. Suffice it to say the man lost a great deal of money."

"He could probably afford it," Will said.

Osgood looked at Will over the top of an unlit cigar. "Let me tell you something, Martin. I like you. Always have. But you don't know much about money. No man, no matter how rich he may be, likes to lose money. It hurt Gates. Hurt him good and I like to think about that." Osgood stood and began the pacing that seemed to be a part of every discussion with Will. "Now, I may have to borrow money --a great deal of it -- and I don't like that idea. But there seems to be no choice if I am to retain control of the company."

"Sorry to hear it," Will said.

"Yes. I could soon be in debt to the fancy tune of up to two million dollars."

"Judas Priest!" Will sat back in his chair. He had thought all along that Osgood had money to burn and that the man would be able to weather any financial storm that blew by.

If the New York Committee has its way things should work out fine, however."

"The what committee?"

Osgood sat again. "It is more commonly known as the Rail Association. It controls the distribution of heavy rails across the country. A price-fixing group, if you will."

"Price fixing? Isn't that illegal?"

"Immoral, perhaps, but not illegal. It's done all the time. Look here. Right now the price of a steel rail is a bit more than twenty dollars. Within a year it should be up to twenty-eight dollars. Now, there's some profit!"

Osgood fanned the air with his cigar. "Meanwhile, those rascals in the east, those anthracite coal miners, actually won a ten percent wage increase – *and* shorter hours! The situation is almost out of hand, Martin."

As they rode on toward Marble Will told Judith about his conversation with Osgood and the man's involvement in price fixing. She didn't seem surprised.

"Alma hinted he has some 'paper' companies that were formed for no purpose other than to funnel money to him," she said. "There are investors who don't seem to be receiving any return on their money. Alma says they're getting restless."

"She told you that?"

"She's worried, Will. I don't think she has anyone to talk to about this sort of thing."

271

Will studied the rocky trail. "Well," he said. "It surprises the hell out of me."

At Marble, though they were pleased to see Will and Judith, Tom and Tracey were also worried.

"We've got a few small contracts," Tom said, "but there's talk that Osgood may pull out completely. If that happens we may not be able to keep the quarries open."

"Maybe it won't come to that," Will said.

"A couple of good things have happened, though," Tom said. "Like a fire back in New Jersey."

Will laughed. "That *is* good news."

"It was good news for us," Tom said quickly, not amused. "Granite walls crumbled to the ground but the marble held up. We think there's going to be a lot more demand for marble for its safety as well as for its beauty."

Luke showed up the next afternoon wearing his usual dark clothing and a huge smile. "Where's Theresa?" he asked, after he had greeted the others.

"Getting out of her school clothes," Tracey said. "Why?" Luke didn't reply. Within moments Theresa ran down the stairs and hugged Luke. "I so hoped you'd come," she said. "Will you take me for another horseback ride?"

"Theresa!" Tracey scowled at her daughter. "He just got here."

Luke couldn't keep the smile from his face. He took Theresa's hand and said, "I think we can go for a ride right now." He lead her out the front door and, when they heard a high-pitched scream from the twelve-year-old, all rushed to the front porch.

Theresa was sitting on a small pinto pony, leaning forward and hugging the horse around the neck. "It's mine!" she shouted. "Uncle Luke gave him to me. It's a late Christmas present."

Will turned to Judith and she looked at the sky. "You knew about this," he said. "Why the big secret?"

She put on a make-believe scowl and shook her finger at Will. "Because that's the way he wanted it."

Tracey and Tom were beside Theresa. "It's too much, Luke," Tracey said. "It's wonderful, but . . . "

"I wanted to do it," he cut in. "She deserves it."

Tom frowned. "I don't have any place to keep a horse." "That's all taken care of," Luke said. "I just stopped off at that big house on the north edge of town with a barn behind it. Part of the present is a year's keep."

Tracey hugged Luke and didn't seem to want to let go. At last he pulled away, took the bridle, and led the horse down the street, Theresa squealing with delight as she patted the horse and squirmed around on its back. "Hang on tight," Luke said. "Tomorrow we'll start some serious riding lessons."

The four adults stood on the porch and watched the small parade move down the street. Tracey looked at Will and said, "Evey better grab onto that man, if she hasn't already."

"I think she has," Judith responded.

And Will muttered, "Well, I'll be damned."

⁂

THE WEDDING would take place at Cleveholm. Alma Osgood had insisted and Evey was ecstatic, as was Judith. The two had been closeted for hours at a time in the past weeks planning every detail while Will and Luke worked to build another house west of the "new" one — the one Will had built after Harrison and Yates, and Tom, had made the "old" one little more than trash. It had taken two trips to Redstone to enlist Alma's help in more plans — plans for the food, plans for the decorations, plans for the reception.

A week before the wedding Will and Luke were ordered to accompany the two women on one last trip so they could walk through the ceremony and take care of last-minute details. In anticipation that the summer would be full of distractions and time away from the ranch, Will had hired two men. Later, Luke said, after things had settled down, he would begin some new horse training and breeding plan that he had devised with Evey.

Will had laughed at that. "You're getting married and expect things to *settle down*? I think you may be in for a rude awakening to the realities of married life."

At Redstone, after Will and Judith had helped with a rather awkward rehearsal during which Evey talked constantly, directing people here and there, changing her mind and then changing it once again, J. C. Osgood motioned for Will to follow him. They walked outside onto a large brick patio which commanded a view across the broad lawn down to the river. Osgood sat in a lawn chair and waved his hand for Will to do the same. Osgood fished a cigar from his pocket. *He always dressed like he was going to dinner with the governor*, Will thought. The man stared across the expanse of lawn.

"It's all over for me, Martin," he said.

Will's hand stopped in the midst of packing his pipe.

"I lost it. It will soon be in all the papers and I wanted you to hear it from me first."

Will sat back in the chair. He couldn't look at Osgood. He looked instead to the north and at the sun shining on Owl Point, the source of the "curse" that now seemed to have had an effect on mighty J. C. Osgood himself. "I'm sorry to hear it," he said. "But I thought you had things under control."

"Things change." Osgood tilted his head back at the deep blue of the sky.

273

"I told you Gates lost a lot of money when he tried to run me out. He sold his shares — at a great loss — to George Gould, Jay Gould's son. In the meantime, John D. Rockefeller also purchased thousands of shares of stock. Between them, they got the majority."

"So they fired you?"

Osgood laughed. "I always said you were good to have around, Martin. No, they didn't fire me. The CF&I was on the brink of insolvency. I had issued bonds to finance improvements at the steelworks but the bonds brought in too little cash." He walked to the edge of the patio, put a foot on the rock wall. Then he turned back to Will and shrugged. "So, I made a magnanimous gesture and offered to resign if Gould and Rockefeller would save the company."

"Is the company that important?" Will asked.

Osgood sat again, leaned forward. "The company is nothing but a piece of paper," he said. "But there are families involved, hundreds of them across the state. If the company goes under, I couldn't stand by and do nothing just to save face."

"Are you broke?" Will was still astonished at the news. This time Osgood laughed loudly. "Not by a long shot.

As a matter of fact, I'm probably still a millionaire. And you'll continue to receive your share of the profits as long as Coal Basin continues to produce."

"I'm not worried about that," Will said.

Osgood studied him. "No," he said. "I was sure you wouldn't be. Money is not important to you, is it?"

"Only when I haven't got any," Will said with a smile. "What about Cleveholm and Redstone?"

Osgood waved away the idea. "They're still mine. I still own this home, the town of Redstone and its eighty-four cottages, and something like forty-two hundred acres of land surrounding us."

"Don't reckon you'll go hungry, then," Will said. "But I am sorry about the other. I know it hurts."

"It does, Martin. It does, indeed. But let's rejoin the women and see if we can soak up some of their happiness over this impending wedding."

WILL WORE a new suit for the wedding and he and Luke laughed at each other as they tugged at tight collars and hobbled on poorly fitting shoes. When Tom joined them in Luke's room they loosened their ties and took off the shoes. "A man goes through hell to get married," Tom said, "and then he goes through more hell 'cause he did it in the first place."

"It's too late to change my mind," Luke said. "Evey's worth whatever it takes."

"She is that," Will agreed.

"I saw Abby downstairs," Tom said to Will. "And your preacher son. Guess her husband didn't come."

"That so?" Will was surprised Abby had shown up.

The Episcopal preacher imported from Glenwood for the ceremony did his job well and Evey, nervous as a cat, managed to get through it without breaking down. Luke, as usual, remained calm. Abby, though not at all resigned to the marriage, had come at Evey's insistence, and had even accepted congratulations in the reception line. She had managed to avoid Will but, at last, had to confront him. "I hope you are satisfied," she said.

"I hope Evey is satisfied," Will replied, looking down at his former wife. She seemed shorter than he remembered, perhaps because Judith was so tall. "Where's Henry?"

"I haven't seen him since before the ceremony," she said, looking Will up and down. "You look fine in that suit. I shouldn't admit it, but I was proud of you, the way you walked Evey down the steps and to the minister. You always were a handsome brute."

"And you were always the prettiest girl at the ball. How are things, Abby? Are you happy?"

"Why shouldn't I be? I have everything I could ever want. I keep busy. I travel."

"But are you *happy*?"

"Why, yes, of course."

Will was unconvinced. "I wish you knew Luke better," he said, changing the subject. "I'm sure you'll like him when you're better acquainted."

Abby frowned. "I doubt that very seriously. Admittedly, he is a good-looking man. But when Evey's attraction to his body wears off and she has to face the reality of living with an Indian on a mountain ranch . . ." Her voice trailed off.

"She's spent enough time on the ranch," Will said, not letting it drop. "She knows what she wants. I'll bet you $100 their marriage lasts fifty years."

Abby cracked a smile. "You're on," she said. "But you realize I'm the only one who is ever likely to collect."

"I appreciate your letters," Will said. "I was sorry to hear about Henry Gillespie."

"Thank you. Will you do me a favor?"

"Sure."

"Write to me now and then and tell me how things are *really* going with

Evey and her godless savage. I know her own letters will be full of milk and honey."

"I expect mine will be, too."

Abby let her eyes fall. "Just be honest with me. And Will, if things go sour, don't let her stay in a bad marriage."

Will lifted her chin with a finger and got her eyes fixed on his. "I'll tell you the truth. But, truthfully, I think this match is a fine one."

"I hope you're right," she said. "Oh, there's Henry." Will saw his son standing in the doorway leaning against the frame. He favored Abby and was nearly a head shorter than Will. He was slight and wore a dark tight-fitting double-breasted suit that made his pasty-looking skin seem almost translucent.

Henry saw his father coming and studied the floor. He barely looked up, and he offered a soft hand with not much of a grip.

"Been a long time," Will said.

"Yes," Henry said without looking at his father. "It has been a long time."

"You're looking fine," Will said, trying hard.

"Thanks."

"Your mother tells me you're at the head of your class at the seminary. Congratulations."

"Thanks."

Despite the boy's evident unwillingness to engage in any kind of meaningful conversation, Will pushed on. "How much longer 'til you're a full-fledged minister?"

"Two years."

"Good Lord, boy, you'll only be, what, twenty-one? Isn't that awful young to be a preacher?"

"I skipped a few grades some time ago. Didn't my mother tell you?"

Will had forgotten. "Sure would have been fine if you could have done the marrying today."

Henry's eyes flashed. "Even if I were ordained and filling a pulpit I would not have officiated at this travesty," he snarled. "The idea of my sister marrying a heathen Indian is more than I can stand. I guess we owe it all to you, don't we?"

"Hold it!" Will snapped. "I didn't make those two fall in love and I have an idea Luke is already more of a man — a good Christian man — than I think you may ever be."

"Why, thank you," Henry said with a sneer. And then he added, "Father."

Will felt his stomach go sour on him and suddenly wished he could take back the words. "Henry," he said, "I'm sorry. I didn't mean . . . "

At that moment a cheer went up in the room as Evey and Luke appeared.

They had changed from their wedding clothes and were preparing to leave. Their first night would be spent less than a mile away across the river in the house Osgood had built before the construction of Cleveholm. In the morning they would take the train to Denver.

Evey searched the room with her eyes and led Luke by the hand to Judith. Both of them hugged her and Will saw Evey talking seriously with her stepmother. They found Abby by a window and she was gracious as Evey hugged her. She appeared relieved when Luke offered his hand instead of embracing her. Finally, they approached Will and Henry.

"I'm so pleased you came," Evey said to her brother. "It has been too long since we've had a chat. I hope you and Luke become good friends."

"Yes, well." Henry gave her a kiss on the cheek. "Perhaps we shall." He shook hands briefly with Luke.

Evey stood in front of her father, holding his hands in hers and giving him such a look of love he thought he might have to look away. "Of all the people here," she said, "you are the finest. You are the kind of man I hope my own sons will be. You remember I told you I was looking for a man like you to marry." She turned to Luke. "I found him."

Evey threw herself against Will and hugged him tightly for what seemed like a long time. When she finally let go her eyes were wet.

"No need for that," Will said. "Be happy."

"I am," she said. "I will be."

Alma Osgood appeared in the doorway. "The carriage is here," she announced. "Do you all have your rice?"

There was confusion and noise as the guests filed through the doorway to the courtyard where Osgood's Oldsmobile, festooned with streamers and tin cans, waited for the newlyweds. Will saw Judith going through the door with Osgood and watched as Henry took Abby's hand and led her out. Will was pushed along with the crowd and looked over the heads of the group as Evey and Luke climbed into the automobile and were driven away by a hired man.

"Good luck," he whispered.

The crowd thinned and he started inside, finding himself beside Henry once again. "What are your plans after you finish your schooling?" he asked.

Henry looked astonished. "I told mother I planned to return to this valley of my birth and convert it," he said. "I was certain she had told you."

"Maybe she did," Will said. "Well, son, you've got your work cut out for you. We're a hard bunch in the Crystal Valley." He smiled, wondering if the boy could be less than serious.

He couldn't. "And are you still communing with ghosts? How is the curse progressing, anyway?"

Will stared at his son, whom he admitted he didn't really know, and perhaps never would. "Just fine, son," he said softly. "Just fine. And thanks for asking." He turned and went looking for Judith.

That night Will and Judith were back in the bedroom they usually occupied when staying at Cleveholm. Judith took a long time coming down from the excitement of the day. She paced the floor, talking excitedly. "Wasn't it just so nice of the Osgoods to allow us to have it here? Didn't Evey look beautiful? Aren't you so proud? And Luke. What a handsome man he is. Did you think the food and the reception were all right? We'll probably have grandchildren before long. I do hope they'll call me 'grandmother.'"

Will sat by the window and looked into the starlit night, thinking about his daughter across the river with her tall Indian husband. He thought of Abby in a bedroom on the other side of the mansion, and of Henry. *Maybe they'll assign him to a church somewhere far away*, he hoped. When he turned back to the room, Judith was stretched out on the bed.

She giggled. "I'm exhausted, and a bit tipsy from too much wine, I think. I'm going to bed. Coming?"

"I'll sit a while," Will said. "I couldn't sleep now."

Judith stood and began to undress for bed. "If you go prowling in the hallway, be wary of Alma Osgood. She likes you, I think."

When Judith was asleep Will did leave the room. He felt cooped up in the small bedroom that seemed to him to have too much furniture for its size. The hallway was quiet and he walked down the stairs to the main room where, in the light from a nearly full moon, he admired again the hunting trophies on the walls. He sat in one of Osgood's leather armchairs. *At least the man still has this, he thought*. He guessed the loss of the CF&I would be, in his world, like the loss of a few horses. But Osgood was hurt by it all. He *had* worked hard, and spent a lot of money to become the coal king of Colorado and, perhaps, the entire West.

He let his head fall onto the backrest of the chair and saw Alma Osgood standing on the balcony that overlooked the room. As on that night long ago, she wore the sheerest of nightgowns. The small light behind her left little to his imagination. For a moment, she looked at him and he stood. Her whisper carried to his ears so loudly he was again sure everyone in the mansion could hear. "It's hot," she said. He nodded and started for the stairs. When he reached the top she stood before him, her long hair falling almost to her waist. "It's been an exciting day," she said softly. She looked him in the eyes and Will's knees felt weak.

"It has been," he whispered, very softly. "And I'm all done in. I'll see you in the morning." He turned back toward his own bedroom and a door opened just down the hall.

Even in the darkness he recognized Henry. His son took a step into the hallway and saw Alma. Quickly, he backed into his room and, as Will walked past, said to his father, "I see you're still up to your old tricks."

Will ignored him and walked quickly past. He was breathing heavily when he closed his bedroom door and stood leaning against it.

"Alma again?" Judith asked sleepily from the bed.

"Henry," Will replied. Under other circumstances he might have gone back for a talk with his son. But he knew it would be fruitless and he lay awake long into the night thinking that the most dangerous "curse" he might have to deal with in the coming years would be his own son.

The next morning the Osgoods and many of the wedding guests rode the train to Carbondale with the newlyweds. Osgood separated the wedding party from the others, though, in his private car, *Sunrise*.

When the train reached Carbondale, Sunrise was unhooked from the Crystal River Railroad and coupled onto the Denver and Rio Grande for the run to Denver. Evey and Luke would ride in a regular coach for the rest of the trip since Osgood had some business associates with him on this leg. During the change-over Osgood pulled Will aside.

"Alma and I are off to Europe," he said. "Perhaps, when we return, we'll get together for that hunting trip we've talked about for so long."

"I'd be proud to," Will said and the two shook hands. Alma politely offered her hand to Will, didn't meet his eyes and then, uncharacteristically, stuck out her tongue at Henry, who watched nearby.

Finally, the long period of saying good-bye and good luck to Luke and Evey was over. As Will was stepping out of the car, Abby was ready to board.

"Give her a chance," Will said to her.

"How could I do otherwise?" Abby smiled. "She's too much like you."

"It was good to see you again, Abby. I hope Henry turns out all right."

"He's going to be a minister," she said with surprise in her voice. "How could he turn out any other way?"

He helped her onto the steps and turned as Henry approached. Out of courtesy, Will shook hands with him again. "Things aren't always as they seem at first glance, boy," he said.

Henry pulled his hand away and boarded the train. Will and Judith stood on the platform and waved goodbye and then they were alone in the quiet.

"It's so wonderful," Judith said.

"We gained a son and lost a man who has been good for this valley," Will said. "I can't believe Osgood is gone."

"They'll be back, won't they?" Judith asked.

"I'm not so sure. I think we may have seen just about the last of Mr. J. C. Osgood in the valley."

They turned and started to walk inside the station when Yolanda

279

Peabody and a beautiful young girl who looked a great deal like her came out onto the platform.

"My, my," Yolanda said. "It's Mr. Martin and his wife." When Will started to brush on past, Yolanda stopped him with a hand on his arm. "I understand there's been a wedding in your family. Congratulations are in order, I'm sure."

"Thank you," Judith said, trying to be gracious.

"What are you doing here, Yolanda?" Will asked.

"My daughter and I have just returned from Denver," she said. "You remember Inez, of course." Will nodded at the young girl. She was not as dark as her mother, but did have the same long, black hair and the perfect complexion on a sculptured face that seemed much older than the nineteen or so she must have been. *About the same age as Henry*, Will noted.

"We had a wonderful visit with your son," Yolanda said with a smile. Will felt Judith's hand tighten on his. "Jacob is such a fine man and he'll make an outstanding lawyer. In only two more years he will take the bar exam."

"That's fine," Will said.

"Do you ever hear from him? Oh, of course not, you poor dear. We do, naturally. I think I should tell you that another member of your family may have a wedding in the not-too-distant future. Then we'll all be together again in the valley. Won't that be wonderful?"

"Together? In the valley?"

"Of course. Your son plans to set up a practice here. With so much mining in the area he is sure to be in demand. He is specializing in mineral law, you know."

Will didn't. "He's planning to come back here, is he?"

"Naturally. He and Inez will probably live in Marble at first but later, who knows? How nice to see you again. And you, too, Mrs. Martin. Good day."

The two women walked away. Inez had not spoken. So, Will thought to himself. Within two years both of his sons would be back in the valley. One a minister and the other a lawyer. And they both hated him.

"It's going to get interesting," he said to Judith. "Real interesting."

"Let's go home, Will," she said. "I want to get back to our home and away from people in general."

She turned and headed for the livery where they had left their horses and wagon before the wedding, knowing they would need transportation back to the ranch. Judith turned back to Will after a few steps and laughed from deep in her throat. "Hurry up," she said. He caught up to her, swatted her on the rump and took her hand as they walked together, heading for home and heading for the future.

Soon, Will's daughter and her husband would be home. And, soon after that, his two sons were to take up residence in the valley. He would have to visit Owl Point before long and think things through. In the meantime, he wanted to be alone with his wife.

PART VII

1905-1914

Will studied Theodore Roosevelt's face while the President carried on a conversation with two aides. At times, especially when he was animated, like now, the face became as round as a Paonia peach. In a thoughtful mood, or when posing for photographs, his face was square.

It was round when the President of the United States finally turned to Will and held out his hand. "Glad you could come, Mr. Martin," he exclaimed loudly. "Sorry to keep you waiting. Everything all set for tomorrow?"

"I'll be ready at sunup, Mr. President," Will replied.

"Bully!" Roosevelt's cheeks glowed a bright red. "Osgood told me I could count on you to get us a bear or two."

"I can almost guarantee it," Will said quickly, and then regretted making such a rash promise.

"Good, good." Roosevelt suddenly frowned. "Where's your wife, man? Didn't she come with you?"

"She's downstairs in our room," Will said. "We didn't know if she should come up now or not."

"Well, go get her! J. C. Osgood said we must meet this remarkable woman. I'll get Edith and we'll have a chat. Half an hour, now."

"She'll be pleased," Will said heading toward the door. "Looking forward to this hunt," the President said. "Looking forward to it with great anticipation. This Hotel Colorado is quite a place, don't you think?"

Roosevelt had won re-election the previous year with 336 electoral votes against 140 for the Democratic candidate, Judge Alton B. Parker of New York, who had been nominated instead of William Jennings Bryan. He was still glorying in his triumph. But he was especially proud of the fact that the Supreme Court had ruled in a five-to-four decision that the Northern Securities Company of 1901 violated the Sherman Act of 1890. The court decision ordered dissolution of the railroad trust and earned the President another nickname: Trust Buster.

Will was puffing from his run down the stairs when he burst in on Judith. "He wants to meet you," he huffed. "Mrs. Roosevelt is going to be there, too."

Judith's eyes widened and she put her hand over her mouth. "What will I wear?"

"Just put on something nice." Will sank into a chair. He was relieved to have his first meeting with the President out of the way. He had been surprised to find that Roosevelt, a former rancher himself, was very much like himself.

While Judith pawed through her clothes, Will recalled his initial surprise

283

at receiving a telegram from the President of the United States. It had come in mid-August saying Roosevelt planned a trip to Glenwood in the fall and that Osgood had recommended Will as the best hunting guide in the state. If he consented to lead the President's party, he was to reply by telegram "soonest." Will went to Carbondale the next day and wired his affirmation.

Now Judith was flustered, dropping a necklace, smearing her makeup, babbling about how she would probably act like a fool. But Roosevelt made them feel immediately at ease. "You are everything Osgood promised," the President said. He stood with hands on hips looking up at her.

"Mr. Osgood told us he had met you but we had no idea you were close friends," Judith said. "We feel so fortunate that he recommended Will as a guide."

"A good man, Osgood," Roosevelt said. His voice seemed to echo around the room. "Known him for years. I even visited Cleveholm once. You didn't know that, did you?"

"Why, no," Judith said.

Roosevelt laughed heartily. "Few people did. I was on my way to Yellowstone on another hunting trip and slipped in there on the railroad one day. Spent the night and sneaked out the next day like a fox. Some fun!"

At that moment Edith Roosevelt entered the room and all three turned to her. "So these are the famous Martins," she said. She sat on a sofa beside Judith. "Mr. Osgood speaks very highly of you, you know."

"Osgood is a fine chap," Roosevelt said. "I've had to have a talk or two with him about this price-fixing thing, but I think we have all that straightened out now."

"How did you meet him?" Judith wanted to know.

The President adjusted his glasses on his nose. "He and J. P. Morgan came to see me right after I was elected in 1901. I had made some, what seemed to them, disparaging remarks about the railroads' policy of giving rebates to customers. Those rebates were putting competitors out of business. The Elkins Act put a stop to that." He chuckled and Will decided that "Teddy" was a happy man. "Osgood has remained a good friend but Morgan thinks I'm a tyrant because I broke up his Northern Securities Company which was formed for no other purpose than to control the key railroads in the West and to reduce competition."

"I know about that," Judith said. "It earned you the title of Trust Buster."

"Enough chitchat about politics," Mrs. Roosevelt said. "What a lovely dress, my dear."

"Thank you," Judith said, beaming. "I think yours is wonderful. Did you get it in Washington?"

"In New York." The two women leaned together as the President motioned to Will, who followed him to the window.

"Bully country you have here, Martin. That Crystal Valley is one of the finest places I've ever been, and I've been just about everywhere."

"We like it," Will said, still awed by the man.

"Now, listen," Roosevelt said, straightening himself and still looking up at Will. "When those namby-pamby staff members of mine start yapping at you to slow down or to take the easy way up a mountain, don't you listen to them. You do what you have to do to put me in a position to make a kill. You hear?"

"Right."

"We never did talk pay. How much are you charging me for this venture?"

"I hadn't thought about it," Will said. "I guess I figured I'd be performing some kind of public service."

Roosevelt guffawed. "Bully, Martin. Bully! But you do a good job and I'll make you a 'square deal.' Get it? A square deal?" He laughed again and Will joined him though he thought it really wasn't that funny.

THEY LEFT by midmorning of the next day even though Will was ready at daybreak. Roosevelt had some papers to sign and telegrams to send, and his entourage of what turned out to be eight staff members and two friends was slow in getting its horses loaded. They rode out of Glenwood to the cheers of crowds of people on the streets and headed north onto the flattops which Will had scouted the previous month. For five days they explored the vastness of the high plateau that Owl Man had crossed on his long trek from the White River Agency after the "Meeker Massacre."

Roosevelt rode beside Will most of the time. "These are fine horses. Breed and raise them yourself?"

Will told him about the ranch and about Ardy and Luke.

"Nothing wrong with an Indian for a son-in-law," Roosevelt said. "The Indians were, *are*, fine and honorable people. I regret deeply what has happened to them."

The hunt was successful. Roosevelt killed ten bears and three lynx and came back to Glenwood in an ebullient mood. "One of the finest hunts I've ever been on, Martin. Thanks to you. And what country! I absolutely loved every minute of it. Have to do it again someday. I'm indebted to Osgood for telling me about you."

"That makes two of us," Will said.

"You'll receive a check from me," Roosevelt said. "And it will be a handsome one, too."

"I'm not worried about getting paid," Will said, "but I have a daughter who is a great admirer of yours. I know she'd think it an honor to have a short note from you."

On the top floor of the hotel, in his suite, Roosevelt kissed his wife and tromped to a small desk where he wrote the note on presidential stationery.

"I appreciate it," Will said, taking the envelope.

"I'm glad we met, Martin. If you ever get to Washington let me know and we'll feed you some of the swill they call food in the East."

Will laughed. "I'll remember that." He shook hands with the President, who was then besieged by aides asking questions, pushing papers at him to sign, and telling him about his upcoming schedule. Will slipped quietly out the door.

Judith leapt on him when he entered their room. "Oh, Will," she cried. "I've had the most marvelous time. Edith, Mrs. Roosevelt, is absolutely wonderful. We spent hours together. Did the hunting go well?"

When he had told her about it she sat on his lap and hugged him. "Will Martin," she said, "you are the most amazing man. If I hadn't married you I'd have never met all those silver barons in Aspen, nor gone to the Wheeler Opera House, nor would I ever have met the President of the United States of America."

"That's all you want me for," Will said with a smile. Judith slowly pushed herself to her feet and laughed low in her throat.

"Oh, no it isn't." She took both of his hands, pulled him out of the chair and toward the bed.

"I'm tired," he said.

"Not that tired," she retorted.

THE NEXT DAY, soon after they returned to the ranch, Evey squealed with delight when Will gave her the note from the President. She read it aloud:

> *Your father and I had a bully hunt. If you are anything at all like him I hope to have the honor of meeting you and your own family someday soon. J. C. Osgood told me you made life in the beautiful Crystal Valley happy, indeed, for his wife Alma. God bless you and yours.*

"How's young Josh?" Will asked. He still found it hard to believe he was a grandfather.

"Fine," Luke replied. "I think he missed his grandparents, though. We've got some news for you." He looked at Evey.

"I might as well tell you," she said. "Henry is here."

"Henry?"

"He's come to settle in the valley. He says he feels 'called' to bring the word of God to this heathen land. He wants to see you."

Will found his pipe and packed it slowly.

Evey turned away and Luke took up the story. "Seems he had a vision — what he called a revelation. He said God himself has been talking to him. Told him you were the cause of all the problems in the valley. He said this curse thing is the work of Satan and that he — Henry — is the man who must rid the valley of the devil-worshippers."

"I don't know any devil-worshippers," Will said.

"According to Henry, anyone who believes in the curse is on the road to damnation."

"There's something else," Evey said.

"Oh?"

"He has a wife."

"Henry is married?"

Luke began to chuckle and Evey turned to him, trying to frown, but had to laugh herself. "You should see her," Luke said. "She's about as big around as a pitchfork tong and she looks like the horse I gave Theresa Cordell two years ago."

Will and Judith joined in the laughter but Evey quickly silenced them. "She's just like Henry," she said. "Every other word out of her mouth was a Biblical quotation. I think she's going to be as much trouble as he is."

"We'll deal with them when we have to," Will said. He was glad to be home again, even if he had been on a bear hunt with the President of the United States.

⋘⋙

"MAY I PRESENT my wife, Reva," Henry said as the two stood in the doorway of Will's house two days later. They had shown up unannounced in a rented surrey, wearing black. Only their hands, necks and faces showed white, and the white on Henry's neck was a stiff ministerial collar. Reva Smythe Tarkington Martin was nearly as tall as Henry. *Lord*, Will thought, *the woman was homely*. Some quirk of fate had dealt her a long, narrow face with eyes set too close between the bridge of a bulbous nose running far down to a narrow cut of mouth that she kept pursed even as she talked.

287

"How do you do?" she said in a metallic voice that seemed to originate just behind her tongue.

"Evey and Luke told us you were here while we were away," Judith said as she poured water for the two of them since they had turned down her offer of coffee or tea, saying they drank nothing but God-provided water.

"Yes," Henry said. "I felt it was my duty to call on you before I began the work which has been assigned to me."

"How fortunate," Judith said, "that the Methodist Church would send you back to your birthplace."

"Yes, well," Henry began. "I am actually here on my own recognizance." He glanced at Reva. "The Church wanted me to take an assistant pastorship at a small church in Limon on the Eastern Plains. But Reva and I decided we had to go where the Lord wanted us to go rather than where the Church would have preferred. Amen."

"Amen," Reva repeated.

Will let his gaze travel across the unusual pair, then looked at Judith, who turned away. "How did you know the difference between what the Church and God wanted?" Will asked.

"He came to me and presented his plan," Henry replied.

"Ah, the vision Evey and Luke told us about."

"Not a vision," Henry said sharply. "A true and wondrous revelation from God himself, amen." The word "God" was pronounced with two syllables, the second being "uh."

Henry looked for a place to put his glass, then kept it in his hand. "I have come," he said, "to rid the valley of its debilitating fear of this evil Indian-induced curse and to bring God-uh back into the lives of those who live here."

"Debilitating," Will muttered, studying his son. The smoothness of Henry's twenty-one-year-old face had given in to lines that creased his forehead and edged his eyes, which had grown hard and less than kind. The beginnings of a mustache looked like sparsely planted grass. He was thin with long and delicate fingers that had done little hard work.

Henry leaned toward his father. "Among the tasks which God-uh has assigned to me, one will be paramount."

"Must be mighty important," Will said. "How'd it come? Special delivery chiseled on a granite tablet?"

"Will!" Judith frowned at him.

"I'm sorry, Henry," Will said. "Go ahead."

Henry and Reva scowled in exactly the same way, as though the expression had been taught in seminary. "I have been told," Henry said, "that you must be brought to God-uh." He put his hands together, as though in prayer. Almost unconsciously, Reva tilted forward, matching her husband's position. "Satan has control of your heart. He has claimed your soul and infused your mind with evil thoughts of spirits and ghosts. When you accept the grace of Jesus Christ and the love of God-uh, the curse, as you call it, will be lifted from the valley and the people therein will rejoice in the happiness of our Lord's bountiful goodness, amen."

"Amen," Reva whispered.

"Amen," Will said. He waited. "Well?"

"What do you mean?" Henry asked.

Will leaned back in his chair, put his hands behind his head, and crossed his legs. "How you gonna do it? What do you do, lay hands on me? Do we sacrifice a lamb?"

Henry's eyes were wide and his hand shook. "The methods by which you will become a member of the fold are not yet clear to me. I know only that I will be the instrument by which you will renounce Satan and beg for forgiveness, amen."

"Amen," Will said quickly. Reva, who had opened her mouth, closed it again.

Henry wasn't through. "I have received His forgiveness and know that I shall dwell in the house of the Lord always."

"Well," Will said, standing. "You're certainly welcome to dwell in my house whenever you're by this way. You just come on in and do whatever God tells you to do. We're usually here." He looked down at Henry. His son, understanding that he was being dismissed, got to his feet. Reva rose with him and turned to Judith.

"Thank you for the water," she said. "We will see much of you, I am sure."

"Anytime," Judith said. She walked to the front door and opened it. Neither she nor Will followed Henry and Reva outside but stood together silently, watching the small surrey disappear down the road.

"I'm so sorry," Judith whispered.

Will shrugged, though he felt terribly sad. "He's taken on a hard life," he said. "I wish he'd been around here more when he was growing up so I could have shown him some of God's handiwork in the valley. I think he'd have developed a different perspective."

"I'm afraid they're going to be a nuisance," Judith said.

Will laughed. "Worse than that. What if they want to move in with us?"

"That's where I draw the line," Judith said. "Even if he is your son."

Will sobered quickly. "I reckon he is that," he said. "But I sure don't like to have to admit it."

⁂

TWO WEEKS LATER when Will and Judith arrived at Marble, Tom had not returned from the quarry but Tracey had news she was eager to tell them. "Your son was here," she said to Will. "He told us about his mission to save your soul. And it seems I am right behind you in terms of wickedness."

"The boy has a lot to learn," Will mumbled.

Tracey put her cup on the table and clasped her hands in her lap. "There's something else. Jacob is here and he's married to Inez Peabody."

All three were silent for a few seconds as Will and Judith let the information soak in. Finally, Will took a deep breath. "We've got the whole family together, don't we?"

Over a late dinner Tom elaborated on Tracey's news. "We've got Jacob in town setting up a law practice and your Henry is up and down the valley preaching the laws of God, as he interprets them. You've got Evey at home and we've got Theresa to bring up here. Hell, we ought to all live together and cut down on the travel time."

"Where are Jake and Inez living?" Will asked.

Tom sighed. "In an apartment over the saloon."

"With Yolanda?"

"Naturally," Tom said. "She's got Jake so messed up he hasn't even been by to say hello to his mother."

"It's his life," Tracey said quickly.

"There is some good news, though," Tom broke in. "You ever hear of Colonel Channing Meek?"

Colonel Meek — the title was honorary — had been president of the Colorado Coal and Iron Company, which had consolidated with J. C. Osgood's Colorado Fuel Company to form CF&I. An Iowa native, Meek had visited Marble in the early 1890s and returned early this year, Tom said, and began buying up lots in and around the town for "one dollar and 'other'."

"Other?" Will got interested.

"Somehow, he'd gotten word that the Colorado-Yule Marble Company was about to incorporate in New York. Even though he had nothing to do with it, the 'other' was promises of stock in this new company. He promised up to $60,000 worth of stock in a company that didn't even exist."

"What happened?" Judith asked.

"About ten days after the company incorporated — for two and a half million dollars, by the way — Meek went to the officers and sold them the title deeds for some of the land he'd bought. And he sold it for one dollar and 'other.' In this case, the 'other' was the presidency of the company."

"Not bad," Will said.

"I think he means business," Tom continued. "He's already bought a

290

lease on the right-of-way between Placita and Marble. And another group of Denver businessmen says they're going to run a railroad from Carbondale to Yule Creek."

"That's wonderful," Judith exclaimed. "Marble may finally start to grow."

As they continued to talk about the renewed promise of Marble, Will paced the floor and thought about Jacob and Inez, just down the street.

"Sit down," Judith said. "Why are you so nervous?"

"I'm not nervous," he snapped, then felt bad for it. "I'm going to see Jake."

A few minutes later Inez answered Will's knock and stepped back silently as he entered. Jacob and Yolanda were seated at a small round table. Jake wore a smoking jacket and brightly polished shoes gleamed beneath the table. Jake, like Henry, wore a mustache, but his was full and black. It swept down over his upper lip and curled slightly at the ends. His hair was slicked back and he looked to Will like a Mississippi gambler. Yolanda hadn't changed much. She wore a low-cut gown and, despite a few new lines on her face, she was still stunning. Inez was a young replica of her mother.

"Well, well." Jake stayed put in his chair. "If it isn't my old man himself. What brings you to town? Come to see my mother?"

Will let it pass. "I hear you're setting up a practice." Jake pulled a cheroot from his pocket and puffed smoke as he lighted.

"I just signed on as legal counsel for Colonel Meek's company." For an instant Will thought his son looked a great deal like Nathan Peabody had when Will first saw the man in Schofield.

"That ought to keep you busy," Will said.

"And wealthy," Jake replied. "Sit down." He kicked a chair out from the table.

"No thanks. Just wanted to say howdy. Something you haven't said to your mother yet."

Jake's face clouded. "You going to play father with me? Kind of late for that, isn't it?"

"I guess it is at that," Will said. He turned to Yolanda. "You happy now?"

She smiled and said softly and slowly, "Why shouldn't I be? How is Tom?"

Will didn't answer, and instead turned back to Jake. "I'd hoped we could be friends."

Jake laughed loudly and reached out to pull Inez to him. He put his arms around her waist, then stared at Will for a long moment. "Why?"

The question startled Will and he involuntarily let his eyes drop for an instant but quickly recovered. "Seemed like a good idea," he said.

Jake's hand strayed to Inez's hip where he let it linger. "Did it?"

Yolanda stood and walked to Will. "Maybe *we* could be friends." Her eyes held his.

"Like you and Tom were friends?"

She tilted her head and smiled. "Why not?"

"No thanks," Will said. "Guess I'll be going."

Inez worked her way free of Jake's embrace and walked smoothly across the room to the door. It was like she was on wheels, Will thought. He stopped at the door and turned. "Hope things work out for you," he said to Jake.

His son smiled. "Why wouldn't they?"

When he turned back to Inez her smile had no warmth, no message of friendliness. It was a smile of the mouth only, a practiced-before-the-mirror type of smile. He decided the girl had no personality, no mannerisms other than those taught to her by her mother and some finishing school in Denver. She closed the door behind him. *I'd sure like to hear her voice*, he thought to himself.

◈◈

MORE THAN eight months later, on November 23, 1906, Will and Judith, Evey, Luke and two-year-old Josh were in Marble when the first Crystal River and San Juan Railroad engine pulled into town. Josh cowered against his mother's breast as the engine blasted its whistle and townspeople fired their guns into the air.

That night, Theresa baby-sat for Josh while the six adults danced to music of the town's string band. Tom asked Judith to dance and Luke and Evey were already on the floor, so Will motioned to Tracey and she moved into his arms, keeping a hand's width from his body. For a few minutes they didn't speak, didn't even look at one another. Finally, as they moved away from Tom and Judith, Will looked down at her just as she looked up.

"It's been a long time," he said. "I've got to be honest. I've still got strong feelings for you."

"And I you," Tracey replied quietly. "What we had was so good."

"Things might have been different," he said.

She shook her head and whispered. "Things are as they should be. What would have happened to Tom and Judith if you hadn't married Abby?"

"Maybe they'd have met each other," Will grinned.

"Will!"

"Well, you're right. We owe it all to Abby."

The celebration went on until almost dawn and, feeling the effects of too much wine, the six walked slowly back to the boarding house.

"That Bates fellow from New York makes things sound mighty good,"

Tom said as they entered the building.

"All you need is a contract," Will replied sleepily.

"That's the goal for 1907," Tom said. "But right now I'm hitting the sack."

In their bedroom Judith wanted to talk. Will climbed into the bed and closed his eyes, hearing her voice as if in a dream. "Charles Austin Bates," she said. "Isn't that a wonderful name? His speech tonight gave me chills."

Bates was with the Bankers Trust Company of New York and was claiming a large part of the credit for Marble's upcoming success. He and his New York friends had invested nearly $1 million in the marble industry, including the construction of the final leg of the railroad. They planned to put another quarter-million dollars into the venture.

"It's been quite a year," Will admitted.

In fact, he had begun paying more attention to the newspapers in recent years, especially since he was personally acquainted with the President of the United States.

Among other things, Roosevelt had been instrumental in getting Congress to create two new national parks — one in Oklahoma and another called Mesa Verde in southwestern Colorado. Roosevelt's hand was seen in many aspects of life. He had called representatives of Harvard, Yale and Princeton to the White House to find ways to stop the growing roughness of football, a game still played with little protective gear. In 1905, eighteen boys had died playing football and 154 had been seriously injured. Will had never seen a football game but decided if it was that rough something ought to be done.

He leaned back on the bed and thought of the evening's celebration. *All because of a train*, he mused. Trains and more and more automobiles were smoking their ways up and down the valley these days, clogging the rough roads and making it difficult for horseback riders or wagons to maneuver. Scared the animals, too. Will could find nothing positive about the automobile. Nothing at all.

He had read not that long ago that more Americans had been killed by motorcars in five months than had died in the Spanish-American War. And he had to agree with Princeton president Thomas Woodrow Wilson. Will carried the newspaper clipping around in his pocket and he could recite the man's words almost verbatim. "Nothing has spread socialistic feeling in this country more than the use of the automobile. To the countryman, they are a picture of the arrogance of wealth, with all its independence and carelessness."

"Man ought to be president someday," Will said aloud.

Judith lay on the bed, eyes wide open. "Between Colonel Meek and Mr. Bates I do believe this is finally the breakthrough for Marble," she said.

But Will was thinking about automobiles and didn't reply.

293

Optimism ran high throughout 1907 and by July of that year Marble's population was at least 250. The Colorado-Yule Marble Company, with Tom as foreman, worked to remove the useless surface rock at the quarry, began construction of a mill along the river on the south edge of town to process the marble and waited for the major contract that would mean prosperity for all. But no contract was made.

Throughout the year, wealthy Eastern businessmen visited Marble to check on their investments. Their optimism was unbounded. Marble had the greatest marble deposits in the world, they were told, and all that was required was the proper equipment for quarrying, dressing and shipping the stone. That, and a major contract.

Charles Austin Bates, who along with Colonel Meek and his business connections now headed a New York investment corporation called the Knickerbocker Syndicate, financed a new $3 million stock promotion. Meek completed his $75,000 mill in August and spent another $70,000 for a massive generator to supply power to the mill and the quarry. Water for the turbines traveled thousands of feet from the Crystal River to the plant through a thick pipe, part of which ran through a lengthy tunnel.

"There is $10 million of marble in these mountains," Meek proclaimed. "And soon we'll be selling it to the greatest cities in the world."

Still there was no contract.

A year earlier no one had wanted town lots, which now began to sell for as much as $250. A lumberyard had more orders than it could fill. Tom and Tracey's boarding house was constantly full, as were the town's hotels. Yolanda Peabody announced an addition to the White House Saloon. Jacob worked eighteen hours a day, Will heard, to handle all the paperwork. The Colorado-Yule Company installed a telephone in the company office and made it available to the public. The city had a park and streets were improved. The school expanded and often had to hold two sessions a day for the increasing number of students. Electric lights brightened local buildings and wires ran from house to house.

Despite these positive additions, there was no contract. Until October.

Again, Will and Judith were in Marble when word came. The Cuyahoga County commissioner had approved the use of Yule marble for the interior of the new courthouse in Cleveland. The contract was worth half a million dollars.

Tom was jubilant. "We've arrived!" he yelled when he heard the news, and then he hugged Tracey and lifted his now sixteen-year-old daughter off her feet.

"I knew it would happen," Theresa said. She had grown into a lovely young woman. *Just like Tracey*, Will thought.

"You've got to see the mill," Tom said to Will. "Colonel Meek says he's going to double it in size. Things are good, Will. Real good."

෴

WILL SAT ON his bed and studied himself in the mirror above the dresser not three feet away. Sometime in the last few years he had gotten old. His hair was turning increasingly white and his mustache, which only a few months ago — or was it a few years ago? — had been a proud black, was now dishwater gray. He covered his upper lip with his hand.

Did it make him look younger? Not with those lines fanning out from his eyes. In only a couple more years he would turn sixty. He stood and flexed his knees. He felt strong. His belly was still relatively flat and he hadn't been sick a day since — when was it? — maybe three years ago in 1905 when he caught a cold.

He walked to the window and looked toward Evey and Luke's house. It was quiet, not surprisingly. Evey and Judith had taken the train to Denver to shop. Luke and the hired men — it took three extra hands to run the place now — were somewhere else, probably up on the mesa.

Will sat back down on the bed and felt useless. And old. Luke had taken over the running of the ranch. Judith took care of the house. Will did whatever struck his fancy, which wasn't much these days. He walked into the kitchen, wadded up a handful of newspaper, then saw a headline about skiing and smoothed out the paper, smearing ink on his hands. *World's First Permanent Ski School Opens at St. Anton in the Austrian Alps*, it said.

Will snorted. *Didn't need a ski school back in the eighties when me and George skied from Crystal to Schofield on nine-foot boards*, he thought. Of course, he reminded himself, he had tried to get Tracey and Jacob down to Crystal too early that year and he and Jake had fallen down the Devil's Punch Bowl.

He didn't want to think about that, though, so he crumpled up the newspaper again, stuck it into the stove beneath a small pile of coal, and set a match to it. He figured he'd boil some water for coffee, and then try to go for a ride up to the mesa. A few minutes later, coffee cup in hand, he stepped out onto the porch and let the midmorning sun warm his face. *June is a good month in the valley*, Will thought. Winter was over and the heat of summer was yet to arrive.

He heard the *clip-clop* of horses' hooves and in a moment saw Henry's secondhand buggy emerge from the cottonwoods near the road and start up the slight grade toward the house. As usual, Reva sat beside her husband. The black horse, black buggy and black-clad couple were an ominous contrast to the background of green trees. *Mighty appropriate*, Will thought, *that those two should wear nothing but black and preach blackness and doom for those in the valley who didn't fear the wrath of God.*

Will's son and daughter-in-law were also in a black mood — blacker than usual. Will made them stay on the porch while he went inside to get water for them and to refill his coffee cup. *Let 'em inside and they'll want to stay all day*, he thought.

Finally, Henry made the reason for his dark mood known. "Colonel Meek has donated land for a church in Marble," he said. "But it will be Episcopalian! We are on our way to Marble to plead with him to create a Methodist church there instead. Or even an interdenominational one. Anything but Episcopalian!"

"What's wrong with the Episco . . . whatevers?" Will watched a trio of clouds meander past Mount Sopris.

"Why, they're almost as bad as the Catholics!"

Will nodded and saw the three clouds become four, then five. They changed shape almost imperceptibly. "That bad, huh?"

Henry's voice was strong, full of pulpit-pounding zeal. "If Meek will not cooperate, I want to build a church somewhere between Redstone and Marble. Perhaps at Bogan Flats just south of Placita. It will serve both communities and those who live between them."

"Takes a heap of money to build a church," Will said. "Got to have land, lumber, windows. All of that."

Will saw Henry glance at Reva and she nodded slightly.

Henry cleared his throat, put his glass on the floor of the porch and leaned toward Will. "You have land," he said. "I believe you have some acreage near Bogan Flats." Will sipped cold coffee.

"We would need only a few thousand square feet of land," Henry said. He lowered his eyes. "Perhaps a spot two hundred feet square near the road."

"Nope," Will said.

Henry sat back in his chair as Reva leaned forward like a seesaw, one end up and the other down. Reva's motion was from the hips. Her back remained straight like a bird whose tail went up as its head went down, pecking at seed. "No?"

"Nope."

Reva looked at Henry. Henry looked at Will. Will looked back and forth between them. "Why not?" Henry asked, at last. "It would cost you nothing and be so small."

Will let his chair fall forward and the two front legs thudded onto the porch. He stood and pitched the cold coffee into the yard.

"Well," he said, "I'll tell you. You two don't think much of me or mine.

296

The first time you came by here you told me I was headed for Hell in a handbasket and that you were sent here by God to convert me." He turned quickly and, as Henry leaned forward, Reva straightened up. *Seesaw, Marjorie-daw*, Will thought. "I'm still waiting to be converted. Waiting for you to give me a good reason why I should become one of your followers instead of going ahead and living by my own religion."

"Your religion?" Henry snorted. "What religion?"

Will bent forward, leaned in close to Henry's face. "I've been thinking about God quite a bit lately," he said softly. "Happens when you get older, I reckon. Now, God and me have known each other for a long time, son." The word came out easily, though he didn't remember referring to Henry as "son" before. "We used to converse now and then as I herded cows down in West Texas. And I'd congratulate Him on the piece of work He did on the plains. When I came up here I was on my way to California . . . " Will straightened at that. *How many years since he'd thought about going to California? Ten? Twenty?* Somehow, the idea had drifted away but now a new thought wandered in and he voiced it.

"I didn't have a vision — a revelation, as you called yours — but God got the message to me that I ought to stay here," he continued. "You understand that? God must have figured there was a good reason for me to be here because every time I turned around there was a new reason for me to stay."

"Like Tracey Cordell?" Henry asked. He masked the look of disappointment with a sneer.

"Her," Will said, "and maybe your mother, too. Where'd you be if I hadn't stayed here?" Henry started to reply but Will put up his hand and the preacher closed his mouth. "I don't much like your style of religion," he said. "Me'n God, now, we've got a pretty good understanding. He puts what you might call 'opportunities' in front of me and, as I see 'em, I take advantage of 'em. Sometimes I foul up but sometimes things work out. I don't see that giving you land for a hellfire church building is one of those opportunities."

Red-faced, Henry stood. He tried with admirable success, Will thought, to control himself. "Did God-uh lead you to kill at least two men? Did God-uh allow you to become the bearer of a curse that could be the tool of destruction for this valley?"

"I don't know," Will said. "Do you believe your God has a purpose for everything that happens?"

Henry nodded, slowly.

"Is it always an obvious purpose?"

"God-uh will reveal Himself and His purpose to us in time."

Will nodded. "Exactly. I reckon there's been a purpose for whatever's happened to me in my purtnear sixty years. And I reckon there's a purpose in

297

me not givin' you land for a church."

Henry could stand it no longer. He slammed his hand against a porch post. "Enough! Your life, at least since you came to this valley, has been full of evil. Adultery, fornication, killing!"

"Amen," Reva said.

"Fornication and killing. Has there been anything else, anything good and fine and . . . and Christian?"

Will didn't reply for a moment. He stared at Henry and felt a wave of deep sadness sweep over him. "I don't think that's for you to decide," he said at last.

"God-uh will decide on Judgment Day!" Henry shouted, waving his arms. "You must accept the Lord Jesus Christ and ask His forgiveness for the black sins that have burdened you. You must bow down to Him and renounce the ways of Satan, throw off this evil curse that hardens your heart to the pleadings of your own son. Only then can you expect to spend eternity out of the hellfire of damnation!"

"You mean," Will said, "if I give you land for a church I'll be saved?"

He saw a light in Henry's eyes, a glimmer of hope. "It would be a grand gesture," Henry said. "A start toward the light of God-uh that will lead you onward and into the arms of Jesus Himself."

"Well," Will said. "Well, well." He turned toward Mount Sopris, now shining in bright sunlight. Reva stood beside her husband and took his hand. Will turned back to them. He shook his head. "Nope," he said. "I think God wants you to get your church another way, if He wants you to have one at all."

Henry's face fell. Reva sat back down. There was total silence for a few seconds until a magpie flew by overhead screeching about something or other.

"You know what you two need?" Will sat back in his chair. "You need some kids. Take your minds off damnation now and then."

"No," Reva said, and kept her mouth puckered up.

"No?"

Henry, still standing, placed his hand on Reva's shoulder. "We have decided not to have children, at least until we have achieved our goals here."

Will nodded. "I see. Well, how do you . . . ? I mean, how do you keep from . . . you know?"

Henry didn't reply but Reva piped up. "Henry and I do not believe that sexual intercourse is necessary to a marriage."

Will looked at the two of them and suddenly felt sorry for these two misguided young people. "That's too bad," he said. "It can be very . . . very nice."

"You should know," Henry said, his face full of anger and what seemed

298

to Will to be outright hatred. "How many women have you befouled with your lust in your lifetime?"

Will was tired of the conversation. "Not a one that I know of," he said. "They all seemed to appreciate it."

Reva gasped and Henry looked into the sky. Will let his eyes drift to the south and thought maybe he'd take a trip to Marble. *Maybe I'll stop over a spell at the hot springs*, he thought. *Maybe climb up to Owl Point.*

"We'll be going," Henry said.

"Well," Will replied, thinking he would start out for Marble now, at least an hour or so after Henry and Reva left so he wouldn't catch up to them on the road. "Don't be strangers, now. You come on by anytime."

Without a word, the two walked to their buggy, climbed aboard and drove off toward the river road. Will thought they really should get a new horse. Maybe he'd give them a horse, at least. He could do that much. But some other time.

IT FELT FINE to sit on his favorite rock on the cliff and survey his valley from Elephant Mountain on the north to Chair Mountain on the south. *It is green*, Will thought. *Lord, is it green.* And red and brown and white, too. And blue above. It was an hour after sunrise and Will was puffing from the climb. A few years ago his legs might not have felt like cornbread but he still congratulated himself on his strength. *Not bad for a fifty-eight-year-old*, he thought.

Down below, Redstone was coming to life. The new owners of the CF&I — he still thought of them as "new" even though it had been five years since Osgood had quit — had continued to mine coal but things weren't the same without Osgood around. People said the man came back now and then, for a few days at a time, but he had never stopped by to visit Will. *Funny how friendships tend to drift apart*, Will mused.

He closed his eyes and remembered that he'd promised to bring Judith up to the point someday but never had. He'd have to do it soon, before they both got too old.

He felt a presence and opened his eyes. As he expected, there was no one there. Or at least he saw no one. But there was something there. The ghosts, or angels, or whatever. The *ini'pute* who inhabited this *ihupi'arat tubut* were there. He felt them surround him. Felt them offer him sanctuary, peace of mind.

Steam belched from a railroad engine on the Coal Basin tracks below and seconds later he heard the *chuff-chuff* of the locomotive. The engines kept getting bigger and more powerful. A few years ago he wouldn't have been able to hear anything this far away. He wondered if Owl Man had actually felt the *powa'a*, the tiny being who he had said lived inside him and directed his power. Or had he simply believed this thing was there and not cared whether or not he felt any sense of being inhabited?

Will felt he was not alone. Someone was with him. Maybe it was Henry's God. Maybe the god to whom Owl Man prayed — *Inu'sakats* — and Henry's God were one and the same. Maybe Henry was right. Maybe he should give the boy some land. What harm would it do? But, somehow, he knew he couldn't and shouldn't. Somehow, God or *Inu'sakats* or some *thing* told him it would be wrong. Wrong for him, wrong for Henry, wrong for the Crystal River Valley.

He stood. He let his gaze sweep the valley, taking in the layers of mountains and rocks, the forests, the river, the snow-covered peaks. "What should I do?" he asked aloud, and the sound of his voice died a few feet from his mouth as it always did. "What should I do?"

And the answer came back quickly and clearly although there was no sound. It came like it always did when he asked the question and it was the same answer. It was the answer he expected and knew would come and yet he was relieved to receive it once again. It was the answer he had received time and time again and that he had always heeded.

Wait, came the answer. *Wait.*

⊷⊶

"IT LOOKS LIKE Yolanda's time is about up," Tom told Will early in December. "The town votes tomorrow on whether or not to go completely dry."

"Dry?"

"There's strong sentiment here for closing down the saloons," Tom said. "Jake's been fighting it, of course. He says prohibition is unconstitutional."

"It figures."

Tom sighed as he lowered himself into an overstuffed chair near the fireplace. "Feels good on these old bones," he said. "You and I are getting on, old man."

As Tom leaned his head back and closed his eyes, Will studied his old friend. Tom had been twenty-two when Will met him on the Texas plains back in 1865. *Twenty-two. Good Lord!* Will thought. Now the man was sixty-five years old. His hair, while not quite as white as Will's, had streaks of gray running through it. His hands, resting on the arms of the chair, were veined and wrinkled.

Will and Judith were both fifty-eight, and Tracey was five years younger. Jake was twenty-seven, Evey twenty-six, and Luke, at twenty-eight, was almost the age Will had been when he first rode into Schofield. Henry was now barely twenty-four, the youngest of the bunch except for seventeen-year-old Theresa and young Joshua, of course. And Abby. He had almost forgotten Abby. *Out of sight, out of mind*, Will thought. She was ten years younger than himself, a mere forty-eight. Thinking about it, he sighed, long and loud.

"What's the matter, old man?" Tom asked, raising his head and smiling. "Can't take it?"

Will frowned. "I climbed up to Owl Point this summer."

The grin filled Tom's face. "Well, ain't that somethin'? What you gonna do next, climb Mount Sopris to show you can?"

A thought flashed into Will's mind and he jumped on it. "Tell you what I am gonna do next summer."

Judith and Tracey came into the room, followed by Evey and Luke, who was carrying Josh. Judith came to Will's side and ruffled his hair. "Just what are you going to do?"

Will stood and put his hands on her shoulders, looked her square in the eyes. "I'm going to do what I started out to do back in 1880," he said. "I'm going to California. And you're all coming with me."

"What?" Judith's eyes narrowed. "California?"

Will liked the idea. "Sure. We'll all go. In the spring. We'll take a train to Sacramento and go see the ocean at San Francisco. Maybe go down to Los Angeles, too."

"Not me," Tom said with a frown. "I'm not interested in California. 'Sides, I'll have work to do."

"Oh, no you won't!" Tracey was at Tom's side and, hands on hips, stared down at him. She turned to Will and Judith. "It's time he quit working. The man thinks he can work until he can't walk anymore." She let herself down onto Tom's lap and kissed his cheek. "Will's right. We're going to take a trip. This is your last winter at the quarry."

"We can't afford it," Tom said.

"Yes, we can. You know," she said, turning to Will again, "we get two dollars and fifty cents a day for room and board and we've been full almost every day for two years. What are we going to do with that money if we don't spend it on something for ourselves?"

"She's got you, Tom," Will said. "It's settled, then. We'll go. The six — or eight — of us."

Evey and Luke shared a quick glance. "Oh, no," Evey said. "Just the four of you. Luke and I'll go some other time. And Theresa is old enough to keep things going here."

301

"I think you're outnumbered, Tom," Will said. He looked at Judith and then at Tracey. "It's settled, then?"

"It's settled," the two women said together and then broke into laughter.

"Hell," Tom said, faking anger. "A man can't even decide for himself when he wants to quit work." Then he, too, broke into a smile and said, "I started out for California once myself. Might as well complete the trip, I reckon."

Later that evening Will saw Evey standing alone on the porch of the boarding house and walked out into the cool night air. "Pretty cold out here," he said.

They studied the stars in the crisp, cloudless sky for a while and pretty soon Will let his eyes fall back to earth and studied his daughter. She was prettier than any girl had a right to be, any girl of his anyway, he thought. "I'm gonna get a jacket," he said. "Want one?"

"Sure. We'll take a walk."

A few minutes later they walked slowly down the center of the street. The town was quiet, except for the sounds of gaiety issuing from the saloons, including the White House which still sat by itself at the end of the street. The buildings were mostly dark, with an occasional night-light illuminating the interior of a store. The two rows of buildings were fronted with utility poles strung with wires, bringing modern electricity up to eight thousand feet in the Rockies. A board sidewalk ran along the south side of the main street and, a little farther down, a small bridge crossed Carbonate Creek.

"Little Josh all right?" Will asked as they passed the millinery shop on the left, the city meat market and the post office on the right.

"Luke is putting him down. He sings to him."

"Luke sings?"

Evey nodded. "He's wonderful with Joshua."

"I figured he'd be a good father when I saw him give Theresa that horse," Will said. As they talked, they strolled through the center of town and passed the shoe store, hardware store, and the Henry Merton store with its jewelry department, prescriptions, and ladies toiletries.

Evey smiled. "I hope he continues to be a good one." She turned to her father. "I'm pregnant again," she said. "You're the first to know. I haven't even told Luke yet."

Right there in the middle of Main Street Will took Evey in his arms and hugged her tightly for all to see. Will Martin hugged his daughter and thought how much he loved her and wished he could love his two sons as much. "That's fine," he said. "That's just fine."

"What are you doing, old man?"

Will turned to the sidewalk and saw a figure standing in the shadows. He saw a flat brimmed hat and the glow from the lighted end of a cheroot and thought, my God, it's Nathan Peabody. Then he recognized Jake and got ready to get a mad on.

"Mighty pretty picture," Jake said. "Hello, sis."

Evey stood back from Will and studied her half-brother. "How are you, Jake? It's been years."

"Fine, just fine. It's been almost ten years, as a matter of fact. Ten years since the old man broke the sad news to us that he'd been diddling my mother and that the two of us were blood relations."

"You're looking prosperous," Evey said, ignoring the remark and speaking before Will could respond.

"I *am* prosperous," Jake said, flipping ashes into the night air. They faded before they hit the dirt street.

"You going to stay around after tomorrow?" Will asked.

"What's tomorrow?" Jake didn't look at Will, kept his eyes on Evey's face.

"I hear they're going to vote the town dry."

"So?"

"So, that'll put your mother-in-law out of business, won't it?"

Jake laughed a hard, sharp bark of a laugh that bit through the cold night air and stung Will's ears. "Hardly," he said. "Actually, things might be even better."

"How can that be?" Evey said, pulling her arms together and pushing up the collar of her coat.

"You'll see," Jake said. "No doubt these temperance-preaching, Bible-thumping do-gooders will get their way and we'll close down the saloon. But even if they *do* vote us dry they wrote a damn poor law."

Evey stepped closer to Will. "What do you mean?"

"I mean it may be illegal to sell liquor, or to give it away, but it will be perfectly legal to purchase it for your own use. There's a lot of people up here who won't have the time to go all the way to Carbondale to stock up."

"So you're going to bootleg it," Will said.

Jake waved his cheroot in the air, dismissing the sardonic tone in Will's voice. "Call it that if you want."

"There's always a way to make a dollar, I guess," Will said. "Right or wrong."

Jake turned to Evey. "Look here, little sis. You and me used to have some downright good times. Why don't you come see me sometime and we'll pick up where we left off?"

Will stepped forward and stood between the two. "Back when you were young I'd never have thought you'd turn out like this," he said to Jake.

Jake shrugged. "Just a thought. She used to be a randy little thing."

Evey started to push around Will but he took her arm and stopped her. "You must have a pretty sad view of womankind."

Jake barked again, something like a laugh. "Why not? They're all alike. My mother, Yolanda, Inez. You too, Evaline. Good for only one thing."

Evey shoved her face up toward Jake's. "I don't know what I ever saw in you," she said. "You've changed. It's that. . . that *whore's* fault."

Again, Jake laughed. He reached out and pushed Evey away and started down the street toward the saloon. He limped a few steps and then turned back. "You're all alike," he said. "You're *all* whores."

Will held Evey's arm as she started toward Jake. Suddenly, she stopped and threw herself back into her father's arms. She sobbed quietly for a moment and then stepped back. "How did it happen?" she asked. "How could he change so much?"

Will shook his head. "You lie down with dogs," he said, "and you get up with fleas."

❧❧

THE STEAM TRACTOR was huge. Its smokestack towered at least twenty feet in the air and had eight-foot steel wheels that turned slowly and noisily beneath the cab. Four wagons, each carrying fifteen to twenty tons of marble, lumbered behind, towed by the machine.

"We used to have nine horse-drawn wagons," Tom told Will that morning. "Now this monster hauls that much alone. It used to carry timber in California."

Will studied the tractor. "Maybe we'll get to see some of those giant trees they've got out there."

"Maybe so," Tom said. "Come on." He had taken the day off so he could show Will around the mill and the quarry. He was like a child showing his toys to a new friend.

Another Ohio town had contracted for Yule marble and Colonel Meek had already doubled the size of the mill to meet the demand for what he expected would be five hundred carloads of marble. He had also built fifty four-room houses which he rented for four dollars a month. Three hundred men worked for the company and Meek promised five hundred men by spring.

"We'll get a ride on the tractor up to the quarry," Tom called. They jumped onto one of the empty wagons and the driver waved at Tom. The ride

304

was much steeper than anything on the Coal Basin railroad. The three-and-a-half-mile trip to the quarry negotiated grades of from six to fourteen percent.

"This time next year we'll have the electric tram built and you can ride up here in comfort," Tom said.

The road slanted suddenly upwards more steeply and, at the same time, a cold wind swept down through the canyon. Snow blew in Will's face. "How high are we?" he asked.

"Right now, I don't know," confessed Tom. "The quarry is at 9,250 feet. There'll be plenty of the white stuff up there. Sometimes we've had to shovel out twenty-foot drifts. Takes a crew of men a week to dig out the road."

The tractor plodded upward, around point after point, through Mud Gulch and across creek beds. Finally, they made a hard left and bounced across one last creek and onto a rocky shoulder of the mountain that was barren of trees. Elk Mountain and Arkansas Mountain, far across the valley above Marble, were suddenly visible.

"This is called Windy Point," Tom yelled.

"I can see why," Will shouted back, pulling his coat collar up higher and holding onto his hat. The road made a 77-degree curve around the point and then dropped down to the base of a waterfall just below the quarry openings. It was snowing heavily and the white marble tailings and chunks of broken blocks on the steep hillside below the quarry blended into the whiteness of the sky, making it difficult for Will to see much of the area.

He and Tom jumped from the wagon, waved their thanks to the driver, and began the climb to the openings. As they got closer Will could see several wooden buildings looking as though they were hung on the side of the mountain.

"I didn't realize the openings would be so far up," he said. Three cavernous holes loomed halfway up the side of the mountain a good fifty or a hundred feet above the canyon floor. Up close, the openings were gigantic. The first, perhaps fifty feet tall, top to bottom, was cut in the shape of an inverted L. The second, almost as big, was square and the smaller, third opening was more rectangular. Will stood in the lofty opening of Number One and looked down into the depths at the working men.

"Isn't that something?" Tom said, almost reverently. "It always makes me think of pictures I've seen of those fancy ballrooms in New York or Paris. Marble floors and marble walls."

Literally millions of cubic feet of marble had already been taken out of the quarry and millions more — maybe billions — were awaiting the quarryman's saw. Tom let Will look for a while and then spoke in hushed tones. "They say it's fifty or sixty million years old. That's something to think about, isn't it?"

"It is," Will said. "It sure is." Here, on this rocky, almost inaccessible mountainside, a solid block of pure white marble extended back indefinitely into the mountain and jutted out just far enough to be found by some greedy prospector. Tom motioned for Will to follow him and they moved back from the opening. To his left Will saw a number of shacks clinging precariously to the side of the steep mountain.

"Quarrytown," Tom said. "Some of the men live there." Will shook his head in awe.

"Up here? In this weather?"

"Last month Colonel Meek hired fifty new men and since the town was full with a lot of people still living in tents, most of the bachelors simply put up shacks for themselves."

Will was studying the steep cliffs that surrounded him when he heard Tom call to a young man who had climbed from the quarry and was heading for Quarrytown.

"Marcello's on my crew," Tom said, introducing the boy as Marcello Barzini. "He's new but he's gonna be a good man. His father is a skilled craftsman down at the mill."

"And that is where I shall be soon. Me, too, skilled," Marcello said. "How do you?" he asked, holding out his hand for Will to shake. Marcello was on his way to his shack in Quarrytown to get new gloves. "This one, how you say, plumb wore out. You come? I show you where I live," Marcello offered.

The shack was tiny, about six feet by ten. It had bunk beds and a wooden trunk. One window faced the northwest and Will thought that was poor planning, considering the winter winds came from that direction. The walls looked as though they wouldn't keep out much wind, in any case.

"You ought to move to town with your dad," Tom said.

"Maybe so, when winter she comes. Too much work getting up and down this hill, though. I am tough. How is Theresa?"

Tom grinned. "She's fine. Just fine." He turned to Will. "Marcello met her at some social deal not long ago."

"I must go back," Marcello said. "You say to Theresa for me, hello."

"I will," Tom said. He and Will watched the boy trudge back toward the quarry.

"How can anyone live in here?" Will asked.

Tom shrugged. "Probably better'n what he had in Italy."

"Lots of Italians up here?"

"And Austrians and Germans and French, and just about anything you can name."

"What about this Marcello and Theresa?"

Tom laughed at Will's frown. "Nothing to worry about. He's a fine fellow

306

and they danced a time or two. She'll be goin' off to school 'fore long and forget all about him."

Will nodded. The snow was heavier. "How do we get back to town?"

"Same way we got up," Tom said. "Follow me."

The ride down was much colder than coming up, and Will was glad to get inside the mill itself. It was the largest building he had ever seen. Outside, cranes carried large blocks of marble from the wagons to a gang truck which took them inside for finishing work. Inside, the noise was deafening. Hundreds of men lined the interior, shaping the marble and finishing it mainly by hand.

"They're the best in the world at what they do," Tom said. "And the best paid, too."

One of the rough-cut blocks was just being lowered onto the nearest of thirty steel-frame gang saws. Each of the sixteen wedges, or "dogs," held one of the saws of the gang. Tom told Will the saws were straight and flat steel pieces, each about one-sixteenth of an inch by four inches deep and up to sixteen feet long. The saws barely touched the marble as they were automatically carried back and forth. Sand and water was poured over the cutting surface. After the piece had been cut to size it would be transported to another area of the mill where it would be shaped properly and then polished to a high shine.

ঞ৻ঙ

"IT TAKES A heap of people, all doing something to the same block of marble and nobody else seeming to know what the other one's doing," Will told Judith that evening. "Somehow, though, every block seems to come out like it's supposed to."

Judith didn't seem much interested in Will's story. "Tracey and I have been talking about our California trip all day. We can't wait to see the ocean."

Theresa bounced into the room at that moment and saw Will and Tom. "How was your day?" she asked and, without waiting for a reply, continued. "I had a perfectly awful day at school. Why do I have to learn geometry, anyway?" Tom started to speak but she cut him off. "Did you go to the quarry? Was Marcello there?" Seeing her father nod, she turned to Will. "I told everyone you're going to California next summer. Do we get to make a trip to Denver so mother and Judith can buy some clothes?"

Tracey's eyes widened. "Why, that sounds like a good idea," she said.

"Oh, good Lord," Tom muttered.

Will was watching Theresa. She reminded him of Evey at that age. He thought of the boy, Marcello. He seemed like a fine enough young man but

307

Theresa was surely smart enough to not let herself get too caught up with him. He was a foreigner, after all, and he might just head back to Italy at any time. Then he felt a flush wash over his face and hoped no one noticed. Evey had married an Indian, after all. But Theresa was heading off to school in another year. She'd meet someone there.

When the vote was counted later that night, Marble had gone dry. The saloons would be closed by midnight at the end of the year. Will thought that maybe Jake would change his mind about turning the White House into a hotel, and maybe Yolanda would leave town. He could only hope and wait.

જીજી

"MAYBE IF Osgood had put up a stronger fight he might still be in control and the mines would be open," Will said to Judith the night they heard the news.

"I doubt it," she said. "Evidently the market simply isn't there any longer."

Will stoked the fire. It was cold, even for January, and the wind had blown hard from the north without letup for three days. "I think he might have found a new market," he said. "I'm sure he wouldn't have simply turned those people out of their homes with no warning."

"No," she said, settling on the sofa and patting the cushion beside her, wanting Will to join her. He did, and rested his head on her shoulder. "Tired?" she asked.

"Yep, I am. Get as old as me you get tired quick."

"Bosh!" It was a new term she had picked up. "I'm as old as you are."

"Don't you get tired?"

"Never."

Will straightened and looked at his wife. *She seemed to get more attractive with age. Something about maturity*, he thought, *that brings out the best.* "I don't believe you."

"I hope those people from Coal Basin are warm," Judith said. "I wonder where they are."

"Scattered all over the country by now," Will said. "I don't suppose we'll ever know why the CF&I shut things down so sudden-like."

Only a few days earlier company officials had announced suddenly there would be only one more trip out on the High Line, Osgood's Columbine Road that ran from Redstone to Coal Basin. The families living at that altitude had abandoned most of their possessions and left with only those goods they could carry.

"It's hard to believe it's over," Will said. "Osgood started Redstone when? Only ten or eleven years ago?"

"He and Alma lived in Cleveholm only a year or so before he was forced out of the company. Do you think they'll ever live there again?"

Will shrugged and decided to turn his attention fully to his wife. He nuzzled in on Judith's neck. He talked, but mainly kissed her neck. "Heard he . . . started two other companies . . . the . . . Victor and the American . . . Fuel. They tell me . . . he's the second leading . . . producer in the state . . ."

"Will! All the lights are on!"

"So what? Osgood has mines in three . . . counties. How do you work these buttons?"

"Will!"

❧❧

NORTHERN NEVADA sped by outside the passenger-car windows and Will wished they were moving even faster. "God-awfullest place I ever *did* see," he said to Tom who sat facing him. Tracey and Judith were across the aisle, talking quietly. They had boarded the train in Glenwood that mid-June and, as usual, Will started for California by heading the wrong way. The D&RG took them east to Denver where they boarded the Union Pacific for the next leg of the trip to Salt Lake City. From there they would ride the Western Pacific to Sacramento, the Southern Pacific to Los Angeles and the Union Pacific again when they headed back east.

Now, though, they were finally pointed west — west to the California Will had struck out for twenty-nine years ago in 1880. Now he was finally going to make it.

By the time they reached the Utah border Will was already wondering about how Luke and Evey were making out at the ranch. He had been astounded at the barrenness of Utah until they started through the Sawatch Range and he felt more at home, since the mountains looked something like his own Elk Range of the Rockies. Luke had hired four hands for the summer and Will knew he wasn't needed, maybe not even missed, but he worried nevertheless.

"Please try and relax," Judith had said to him after he had said something about the Double M for the third time in as many hours. "Things will be just *fine*."

When Will stood on the shores of the Great Salt Lake he said, "The runoff this spring looked pretty good. Don't suppose Luke'll have to be worrying about water."

Tom stood beside Will and shook his head at the salty lake before him. "Can't believe there is such a place as this," he said. "You know, the snow'll be melting up at the quarry by now. The boys in Quarrytown must be feeling

309

good."

"Hush up," Tracey said to him. "Will you two think about something besides work?"

Nevada was a desert. "I saw more grass on one little rise in the Kansas Flint Hills than they got in this whole state," Will said.

Finally, they began to wind upwards into the Sierra Nevada Mountains near Donner Pass and both Will and Tom relaxed once again. In Sacramento they changed trains, and keeping to the timetable Judith and Tracey had carefully worked out over a period of months, went to Yosemite National Park. All four gaped at Bridal Veil Falls and its 620-foot drop. "I'll be damned," Will said. "That makes the Devil's Punch Bowl look like a drop from a teakettle."

"Wonder if we'll ever get a decent road over Schofield Pass," Tom mused.

In San Francisco they listened to stories of the terrible earthquake of barely three years earlier and dined on seafood. "I remember the time fish tasted better'n cow," Will said. "Me'n an old boy named Bronco Jack were lookin' for strays on the Palo Duro when a storm come up like we never saw before. Our horses run off and there wasn't a cow within ten miles. After a day or two we managed to catch us a catfish and it was the only time I ever liked fish."

There was still evidence of the earthquake that had destroyed 28,000 buildings, and all four were glad to get away from the potential danger. They went to Napa Valley and sampled wine until Judith and Tracey got to giggling so much it embarrassed the two men. "Now I know what I looked like when I was a drunk," Tom said. "It sure is quiet in Marble with the saloons closed down. I tell you, I was getting pretty sick of hearing that rinky-tink piano from the White House ever damned night. Wonder how Theresa is doin'? Tracey, you think she's managing all right alone?"

"I'm sure she is," Tracey said with a sigh.

North of San Francisco, in Marin County, they tried to wrap eight arms around a giant redwood tree and needed eight more to make it. Teddy Roosevelt had, by presidential proclamation, created the Muir Woods National Monument only the previous year. He had also created the Grand Canyon National Monument in Arizona.

"If I'd had one of these I could of built Luke's house and three more," Will said, staring up at the mighty tree. "That reminds me, Judith. You know that old cottonwood that's starting to die over by the creek? I'm gonna cut her down and leave the stump for a picnic table."

"That would be nice," she said, shaking her head.

After another long train ride to Los Angeles they walked along a sandy beach, the women touching their toes in the cold water and screaming as the surf spattered them.

Will stood at the edge of the ocean with his pants rolled up and felt the undertow tug at his bare feet, watching the sand disappear around his toes and wondering how deep the ocean really was. He tasted the water and spat it out. "Hell," he said. "You can drink straight from the Crystal River. I been thinkin' about makin' a pond up on the mesa."

They built a sand castle and let a photographer take their picture, all four standing close behind the structure looking foolish and trying to smile naturally. Later, they watched the tide come in and destroy their creation. "Ain't that just like nature?" Tom said. "The elements get you one way or another. Remember those dust storms down on the Llano Estacado? I . . . "

"Will you two please, please stop relating everything to home or someplace else you've been?" Tracey stood before them with hands on hips. "This is beautiful. We're a thousand miles from home. Think about what you're seeing."

"That's what I been doing," Tom said. "This ocean is so flat and wide it reminds me of West Texas." Then he smiled and shut up.

They all had a good laugh that evening, reading about the Los Angeles city engineer's plan to bring water from the Owens River in the Sierras via a $25 million cement and steel aqueduct. The Mulholland Plan would permit irrigation of the San Fernando Valley.

"It'll never happen," Tom said, and Will agreed.

Finally, much to the relief of the men, the trip was over and they were on their way east, back to the Double M and the Cordell Hotel and the Crystal River Valley. Even Tracey and Judith seemed anxious to get home and were willing to talk about the valley and, especially, their children.

"Theresa thinks she might to go to Colorado Women's College," Tracey said.

"When is Evey due?" Tom asked.

Judith beamed. "In late summer. Maybe August."

"What do you want, Will? Another grandson?"

"That would be fine," he said. "But little girls are nice, too."

Tom grinned. "Your kids are making quite an impact on the valley."

"Tom!" Tracey glared at him.

"Well, I didn't mean anything."

"Never mind," Will said. "I guess at least two of them are making names for themselves, at that."

"You've got a lawyer who likes to make up his own rules and a preacher who likes to interpret laws from the Bible his own way."

Will nodded, thinking about Jake and Henry and wondering what the

311

future held for them.

"And, from what I hear," Tom went on, "Evey is making a name as a breeder of some of the finest horses around."

Will brightened, thinking about his daughter. "Her and Luke," he said. "That boy knows horses."

"Indians do, I hear," Tom said, turning away from Tracey's scowl. "All right. All right." He looked at Will and they broke into loud laughter. It was good to be heading home.

✍❧

SOON AFTER THEIR return to the ranch, Will and Judith were visited by Henry and Reva. As they sat on the porch and waited for Judith to bring the usual glasses of water, Will studied his son. The boy was now twenty-five years old. Will found it difficult to think of Henry as a man. Despite the severe dark clothes he continued to wear and the perpetual scowl on his face, he looked young. The scraggly mustache below his nose did little to age him. He was a young man trying to deal with ancient problems of morality and religion.

Henry's "mission" had not changed. "God-uh's will has been revealed again," he said. He looked almost smug as Reva nodded sagely. "You will recall I told you about Colonel Meek's donation of land for an Episcopal church?" Will nodded. "They brought it in not long ago. A small building from Aspen which was no longer being used."

"They brought it on a flatcar," Reva piped up. "They have offered to let Henry use it, and other denominations."

Will raised his glass in a sort of toast. "That's good," he said. "Saves you the trouble of building your own."

But Henry shook his head. "I have refused."

"Well, why in God's name . . . ?" Will leaned forward in his chair. "There was your chance, boy!"

"I knew it was wrong from the first," Henry said. His smile was more of a sneer. "I was proven correct only a few days ago when they consecrated the church building which they have named St. Paul's." He lifted his arms and spread them out wide. "God-uh has seen the evil in this place and has given me my cross which I bear proudly. I know now I must build my own church, a place where the faithful can gather and where the very pores of the wood in the walls will not be polluted with the blasphemous ideas of the unclean."

"Amen," Reva intoned.

"The Episcopalians brought in the Right Reverend Edward Jennings Knight for the ceremony. He was a robust man who seemed in the best of

312

health."

"Was?" Judith asked.

Reva took up the story. "He insisted on walking back to Redstone after the ceremony but became ill on the way. He died two days ago in Glenwood Springs."

"That's terrible!" Judith said. "A heart attack?"

"We don't know and it is not important," Henry said. "That God-uh struck him down in the prime of life is what is important. Don't you see that God-uh has revealed His anger in this way?" He turned to Will. "And can you now see how vital it is that I have land for my own church?"

"I can see you think it's vital," Will answered, sipping water.

"I know it is vital. It may be the single most important event in this valley's history."

"Even more important than when Owl Man cursed it?"

"Of course," Reva replied for her husband. "If . . . *when* we have our church we'll be able to direct the flock in the direction pointed out by our Lord Jesus Christ."

"I have come to ask once again," Henry said, "even to beg if I must, for a small piece of land."

Will shook his head. "I'm not going to do it."

Henry turned quickly away. "I will never understand." He sat on the edge of the porch with his head in his hands. "It would be such a simple act of charity on your part and would mean so much to the Bible Victory Church."

"The what?"

Reva turned to Judith. "It's what Henry has begun to call his church. It represents the triumph of Christ over the devils of Satan who live in this valley."

"It would mean so much," Henry said, his voice muffled by his hands. "Why won't you do it?"

Will moved to the edge of the porch and sat beside his son. He stared off toward the river, scratched in the ground with his boot. "Henry, I just can't. I don't believe in what you're doing in the first place, and if I let you use my land everybody'll think I've thrown in with you."

Reva stood behind them. "What would be wrong with that?"

Will looked over his shoulder at her. "Why, nothing, if it was true. But I don't think it'll ever be true. There's plenty of land. Somebody else will pitch in an acre or two for you."

Henry stood and looked down at his father. His face clouded over and his eyes narrowed. "Then I say this to you. I say may God-uh damn you to eternal hellfire for your refusal to aid His people."

"Amen," muttered Reva.

313

"God-uh has called on you and you have not answered. He has opened wide the door of eternal life and you have chosen not to enter therein. You are damned and I pray that you will see the light of God-uh's love and come to Him on your knees to beg His forgiveness."

"Amen," Reva said again as she followed Henry toward the surrey.

Judith took Will's arm and they watched the two drive away. "I'm so sorry, Will," she said.

"No matter," he replied, but the look in his eyes told her otherwise.

"I feel so sorry for them. They're so young and full of energy. They could do a lot of good."

"But they won't," Will said.

"He cursed his father."

Will shook his head and tried to smile. "Shoot," he said. "I've been goddamned by the best of 'em, and I've goddamned a few myself. Didn't ever amount to much."

"Would a little piece of land be too much?"

He nodded. "It would, to my way of thinking." He took her hand and started back into the house. "You still glad we went to California?"

"Of course. It was wonderful."

"Good. I guess I am, too." He turned to look once more at Henry and Reva and saw the buggy disappear down the road. "Sure is good to be home, even if I am going to Hell," he joked.

A FEW WEEKS later, sometime before dawn, Luke pounded on the door of the house and jarred them out of a sound sleep.

"It's Evey," he said. "The baby's coming."

"But it's almost a month too soon," Judith said. She stood behind Will wearing only her nightgown.

"I'm getting the wagon ready," Luke said over his shoulder as he hurried away. "She wants you, Judith."

The baby — a girl — was born soon after Evey's arrival at Dr. Castle's house. "She weighs less than five pounds," Luke said. "I'm not so sure the wagon ride was a good idea." The baby was little more than a mass of red wrinkles and not much longer than a man's forearm and fist. "We've named her Esther Abigail," Luke told them.

"I'm so worried," Evey said. "She's so small."

Judith took over and shooed Will and Luke out while Evey slept. Pretty soon they were sipping beer in the gloom of the Black Nugget Saloon. "You seem to feel pretty comfortable about Evey and the baby," Will said.

Luke nodded. "If God wants the baby to live, she'll live. If she dies I'll be heartbroken and Evey and I'll have a tough time dealing with it. But I'll figure there's a reason."

"God's will again." Will leaned forward. "Seems like an easy rationalization to me."

"That's a thought, all right," Luke said. "Passing the buck?"

Will nodded.

"Wonder what Henry would think?"

Will smiled. "If he had a child who died, he'd probably think God was punishing him for his sins."

"You're right. And he'd put on sackcloth and ashes and beat himself with a whip."

Will started to reply but overheard part of a conversation from a table behind them and turned his ear toward the speaker, a large man with a full beard who wore the clothes of a miner.

"What's that about Smuggler Mountain?" Will asked him.

"Over to Aspen," the man said. "You know it?"

"I know it."

"Interesting story," the man said in a high-pitched voice that was too small for his body. "Pull up a chair and I'll start over."

"What's going on?" Will asked after he moved his chair.

The man, who said his name was Abe, seemed to enjoy being the center of attention. Three others drifted over to hear. "You know some of the mines have been in operation for the twenty-five years since we went to the gold standard," he said. "Some of 'em, though, just shut down and the owners walked away without so much as a bye-bye. You know the Free Silver Shaft on Smuggler?" Will indicated that he did. "Over the years the mine had filled up with water and the pump had just about rusted away. A couple of men named Brunton and Hyman went to the East Coast and brought back two deep-sea divers."

"Deep-sea divers in Aspen, Colorado?" Two of the men standing around the table began to laugh.

"Sounds strange, I'll admit," Abe said. "But these two fellers put on their diving suits, with those big, round head-pieces, dontcha know, rigged some oxygen lines and went down to fix the pump."

"Those shafts are hundreds of feet deep," Will said.

"So they are. But that didn't bother those fellers. They got the pump goin' and now that mine's drier'n a prairie dog hole in a drought."

"The owners must feel they can still make some money on silver," Will put in.

"Well, I'll tell you," Abe said. "Those that are still minin' are makin' a

315

profit. Not much, but some. Gettin' back to my story, though, these two divers are trainin' a couple of others on how to use them suits in case the shaft starts fillin' up again. I think they're serious about doin' some minin'."

"What are you doing here?" Will asked.

Abe sighed. "Hell, I'm gettin' too old to do that kind of work anymore. Thought about goin' up to Marble and seein' if I could hook on with the quarry but there's talk of a strike up there, so I'm just goin' to Denver."

"A strike at Marble?" Will said. "I hadn't heard."

"Don't know more'n that, friend. Somethin' about the Eye-talians wantin' more money."

"Well, I'll be damned," Will said.

୬୬

TWO DAYS later Will was on his way to Marble. Judith had stayed in Carbondale to be with Evey and Abby was on her way from Denver. Luke was dividing his time between the ranch and Carbondale, and the hired cowboys had things under control while Josh stayed with friends in town. The word from the doctor was that Esther Abigail was going to be fine, but Evey and the baby would have to stay in town for a week or so.

"It's true," Tom said when Will asked about the possibility of a strike. "But it's more than just a possibility. Eighty marble cutters and the quarry men walked off the job today."

"What's it all about? Wages?"

"That's part of it," Tom said. "Why don't you ask one of them yourself. Remember Marcello Barzini, the boy you met up at the quarry?"

"I remember him," Will said. "He lives in Quarrytown."

"Not anymore." Tom motioned upstairs. "He's here now."

"He can afford the $2.50 a day?"

Tom shook his head. "Not exactly. You might say we're kind of subsidizing him. Theresa and Marcello. . . well, you know." Tom's voice trailed off and he looked at the floor.

"You mean that little flirtation of last winter has turned into something else?"

"It looks pretty serious. Theresa is refusing to go off to college this fall. Hell, Will. They're only eighteen."

At that moment Marcello and Theresa walked down the stairs, hand in hand. Marcello was cleaned up and had his hair slicked back. The two made a good-looking couple, Will thought.

"Uncle Will!" Theresa hugged him and Marcello held out his hand. As Will shook it, Theresa beamed.

316

"What can you tell me about this strike?" asked Will.

The boy's face was stern. "It is very simple. A crane runner and his two assistants were, how you say, fired, when they said they would not work extra time with no extra wages. We work all the time, too much, all day and late for too little pay. We have united into Local Number 77 of the International Association of Marble Workers."

"There'll be five hundred men out on strike tomorrow," Tom said. "They say they've joined the American Federation of Labor."

"So you're living here now," Will said to Marcello.

Theresa touched Will's arm. "I couldn't let him stay up there in Quarrytown, now that there might be trouble."

"What about your father?"

"He is living with others in a company house," Marcello said. "They are much too crowded for me to go there, too."

"Jake's acting as company spokesman," Tom said. "Looks like he's winning a lot of support."

"They are afraid," Marcello said. "Most people know that without the company the town will die. But we will die, too, if we are not paid enough for the hard work."

BY THE TIME Theresa and Marcello were married almost a year later, on August 11, 1911, things were peaceful. The Colorado-Yule Company had set production records throughout 1910 as nearly five hundred employees worked feverishly to fill contracts for marble for the Denver Post Office, the Montana State Capitol and other buildings across the country. The mill was enlarged by another two hundred feet. The electric tramway was completed between the mill and the quarries, replacing the old steam tractor Will and Tom had ridden up the steep grade.

The strike had ended when the workers returned to their jobs at a cut in pay. Despite the fact that the town had split into company and labor factions, a sense of normalcy had returned.

Except for Sylvia Smith. Miss Smith had bought the Marble *Silver Lance* and renamed it the *Marble City Times.* From the outset she made it plain that the company was to be a prime target for regular attacks. The weekly paper even managed to get in a dig at the company when it made Marcello's name a household word a few days after the wedding.

COMPANY LEGAL COUNSEL DISRUPTS WEDDING, IS ATTACKED BY ITALIAN BRIDEGROOM

Marcello Barzini Jailed on Wedding
Night for Assault

The newspaper headlines were partly correct. Jake had not actually intruded upon the ceremony itself, but Marcello did spend his wedding night in the Marble city jail.

❧

WILL STOOD in the Sunday afternoon heat sweating through the suit he hadn't worn since his first visit to Cleveholm years ago. He rubbed his neck, thinking of the rope burns.

Judith, standing beside him in a dark wine-colored dress, looked more lovely than ever, he thought. But Theresa, in her long white gown, her face framed with dark brown hair, was stunning. She had become perhaps the loveliest of all the young women of Marble and had been courted by men from as far away as Glenwood. She remained devoted to Marcello, though, and now stood beside him as a Catholic priest, imported from Glenwood, conducted the ceremony.

"I don't care who does it, as long as it's legal," Tom had said. "The boy is Catholic but that doesn't make him bad. I'm not much of anything and Theresa's happy."

Henry, on the other hand, had been furious. "A Papist!" he had literally shouted. "How can you let anyone even remotely acquainted with you marry a Catholic, let alone allow a Papist priest to conduct the ceremony?"

Will raised his hands. "I didn't have anything to say about it."

"It is beyond belief," Henry said, close to tears. "First, my own sister marries a heathen Indian. And now this! Next they'll be bringing in *Negroes* and allowing them to marry white Christians. Soon we'll be a valley of half-breed Episcopalian Indians and Catholic Negroes!" He refused to attend the wedding.

His absence went unnoticed in the throng of townspeople who turned out for the occasion, which took place in a small grove of trees on the south edge of town with Beaver Lake and White House Mountain in the background.

Most of the quarry workers were there, along with *all* of the Italians, Will guessed. Evey and Luke stood near Will. Seven-year-old Josh fidgeted beside his father while Evey held two-year-old Esther. Tracey and Tom stood proudly behind Theresa as the vows were read, and Marcello's father beamed behind his son. The guests wiped sweat from their brows, pulled at too-tight collars, and shifted their weight from foot to foot. Women fanned themselves.

318

Men glanced at each other and sighed, looking forward to the end of the ceremony.

It came, finally, and the entire group of guests began the walk back toward the Cordell Hotel for the reception. Will and Judith were halfway back in the line of marchers.

"It was a beautiful ceremony," Judith said. "And such a lovely setting."

"And hotter'n hell," Will mumbled.

As they reached the edge of town the crowd began to bunch up. Will craned his neck to see over those in front of him. Unable to see the problem, he left Judith with Luke and Evey and pushed his way forward. As he neared the front of the group he heard the voice of Jake Collins.

"This is supposed to be a dry town," Jake was saying. "You've got a hotel full of illegal wine and we can't allow it."

"Who's *we*?" Will put in.

Jake shot a look of hatred at his father. Then the look dissolved into one of superiority. "This is none of your affair," he said. Three other men stood with him.

Tom stepped toward Jake. "The wine is homemade. You haven't got any right to raise the issue, anyway."

"I've got the right of a concerned citizen who wants to see that the laws of this city are upheld," Jake sneered.

Marcello stepped in front of Tom and faced Jake. "The wine is to be given away free of charge. We are not selling it illegally as it is widely known that you do."

"Are you accusing me of something, Dago?" Jake squared up and his three companions moved closer.

"I am saying that you are spoiling a fine day for many people. I would be grateful if you would step aside."

"You would be *grateful*?" Jake swelled up. "You ought to be *grateful* you have a job, Dago. You ought to be *grateful* you're even allowed to stay in this country."

"Leave it alone, Jake." Will stepped to Marcello's side.

"Stay out of this," Jake said. "This is between me and the stinking foreigner."

Marcello's fist came up from his side so fast that few saw it. It went deeply into Jake's midriff and, as the man doubled over, Marcello hit him squarely on the jaw with an uppercut. Jake's head flew up and he went over backwards and lay still on the dusty street. Theresa's gasp was lost in the cheer that went up from the group of Italians who had gathered behind her husband. Jake's three friends stepped forward but Will, Tom, Marcello and Luke, who had joined them, stood squarely in their way. The cheering continued as several of the Italian men formed up beside and behind the four who stood their ground over Jake as he pushed himself to an elbow and rubbed his jaw.

The City Marshal, a small man named Jock Merriweather, arrived from the rear of the crowd and saw Jake lying in the street with four determined men standing over him. "What's going on?"

Jake struggled to his feet. "This man attacked me," he said, pointing at Marcello.

"He was provoked," Will said.

"The hell he was," one of Jake's friends piped up. "We was tellin' these folks they wasn't supposed to have liquor in town when this Dago clobbered him."

Merriweather turned to Marcello. "Did you hit him?"

"I did," Marcello answered, smiling and rubbing his fist. "You bet I did."

"I'm charging him with assault and battery," Jake said, his eyes wild. "I demand that you lock him up."

Merriweather sighed and shook his head. "Oh, hell, Jake. He just got himself married. What you want to go and press charges for?"

"Everyone here saw it," Jake said. His jaw was turning red and swelling. "There's no excuse for this kind of outlaw behavior in a civilized town. Do your duty, Marshal."

The little man with a badge on his coat turned to Marcello. "I'm sorry, son. I ain't got much choice."

"Good Lord, Marshal," Will said. "Jake did everything he could to provoke a fight. We'll all agree to that." Several of those around him nodded. "Can't you just forget it?"

"You forget it and I'll have your badge within a week," Jake snarled. "He beat me up and I'm within my rights to demand he be locked up for my protection."

Merriweather looked at the angry crowd, then turned to Tom. "I'm sorry, Tom."

Marcello smiled at Theresa who stood dumbly, open-mouthed. "It is okay. It was worth it."

The Italians, standing in a group, cheered once again and Marcello waved his hand as he walked off with the Marshal. Theresa broke into loud sobs and Tracey hugged her. Will and Tom stared at each other and a small smile began to play at the corner of Tom's face.

"You know," he said. "I think it *was* worth it."

Jake's sneer disappeared and he turned quickly and walked toward the White House Hotel.

Tom turned to the cheering crowd and held up his arms for quiet. When the noise had stopped he shouted so all could hear. "Everyone follow me! We're going to have a reception in honor of my daughter's marriage to a real *man*!"

Again, cheers erupted and Theresa lifted her tear-stained face to her father. "But he's going to *jail*."

"It's for a good cause," Tom said, still smiling. "Now dry your tears and let's drink some wine and open presents." Within an hour everyone was in fine spirits, thanks to the homemade wine provided by Marcello's Italian friends. Even Theresa was feeling better and had begun to see the humor of the events.

"I want to go see him in jail," she said.

Marcello's father, Guido Barzini, stepped to her side. "We plan a visit later. You are invited too, also."

"Later tonight? Why not now?"

"You'll see." He smiled and drifted away.

"Come open your presents," Tracey called.

Within an hour everyone was in fine spirits, thanks to the homemade wine provided by Marcello's Italian friends.

"Come open your presents," Tracey called.

Included among the many gaily wrapped packages was one from Abby. Theresa called to Will when she found it. He and Judith walked hand in hand across the room.

"How nice," Judith said. "She always was thoughtful." Theresa opened the box and found inside, wrapped in newspaper, a silver pitcher with a tag saying it was from New York City. She dropped the newspaper on the floor as she held up the pitcher for all to see. Will let his eyes drop and noticed the paper. He had just seen the line at the top of the page labeling it the *New York Telegraph* when he saw a small photo of a man who looked vaguely familiar. Then he saw the headline: "Pugilists Set November Date for Big Fight." Below the headline were the words "By Sports Columnist Bat Masterson." The rest of the article had been torn away.

He picked up the paper and stared at Bat's face. It was fuller, rounder, but the big mustache was there and the eyes were definitely Bat's. "Well, I'll be damned," he said.

"What?" Judith turned to him. "Nothing."

"Well," she said. "Don't swear. At least not so loudly."

Will was still thinking about his old friend from Dodge City when the party began to break up at midnight. Will, Tom and Luke walked slowly about, picking up the trash and nodding to the last of the guests as they left.

321

"What a night," Tom said. "I was proud as hell of the boy. He's got guts, all right."

"He does," Will agreed. "And an enemy in Jake, too."

"Hell, Jake's always been an enemy."

Guido Barzini and three other Italian men materialized with Theresa in their wake. "We go visit my son."

"They won't let you in this late," Tom said.

Guido smiled. "Not to worry. Come."

The small group walked quietly up the street, Guido leading the way and carrying two large jugs filled with the last of the wine. Guido put his finger to his lips as they neared the jail, signaling for quiet, and then turned off the street. They followed him up the alley. Theresa giggled and Guido clapped his hand over her mouth. "Quiet now," he cautioned.

Below the high barred window, they gathered in a tight group. Guido stood on a wooden box and tapped lightly on one of the iron bars with a large finger ring. Almost immediately someone was at the window. "Who is it?"

"Tell Marcello his friends are here," Guido whispered. In an instant Marcello was at the window.

"Father?" Guido again put his finger to his lips, motioned for Theresa and lifted her up to the window. Through the bars, the newlyweds managed a brief kiss.

"Are you all right?" Theresa asked.

"I am fine. The Marshal will let me out in the morning."

"Here," Guido said. From somewhere a long tube of macaroni appeared. One end went into a jug and the other was handed through the bars. "Happy wedding night."

"There are three of us in here," Marcello whispered.

"Then share," his father replied.

Within a short time the wine from the two jugs was gone. There was a sharp laugh from inside the jail.

"Sshhh," someone cautioned. Another laugh. A giggle.

"What's goin' on in there?" It was Merriweather.

"Come on," Guido whispered, and he began to run quietly from the window. Theresa forced back a giggle, lifted her white wedding dress from the dust and ran after him, the others following.

Before they rounded the corner of the building, though, they heard the Marshal again. "Why hell!" he said loudly. "You're all drunk!"

The seven ran as fast as they could toward the Cordell Hotel. As they burst inside they could control themselves no longer and broke into loud laughter. Will's side hurt and he had to sit down. Theresa went to her mother and hugged her, still laughing. Tracey and Judith faced them with questions on their faces.

"What a night," Tom said. He kissed Theresa and then hugged Tracey. "This is a night no one will *ever* forget."

❧

THERESA AND MARCELLO celebrated the birth of a son almost a year to the day after their marriage. In a burst of affection for their fathers, they named the child Thomas Guido. He soon became known to the family as T. G., and then Teegee. Theresa and Marcello were both twenty-one years old.

Will was sixty-two but he told himself he felt only fifty. He worried about Tom, though, who had turned sixty-nine that year. To Will, who saw the man failing more and more each time they were together, he looked older. Tom did almost no work. Instead, he sat around the hotel, played with his grandson and put on weight. Now and then he took the train down valley and hopped off near the Double M. He and Will sat on the porch and swapped lies about the old days and talked about whatever came to mind.

"You've got this place lookin' like pure heaven itself," Tom told Will on one of those trips.

"It's Luke and Evey," Will said. "And Judith. I don't do much myself. They won't let me." They sat and smoked and looked over the ranch, down the long expanse of green dotted with yellow dandelions. A whitewashed wooden fence completely surrounded the houses, the corral, and the training track north of Evey and Luke's house. Bright green trim decorated the buildings and a tall gate on the road down below announced in bold green letters that this was the Double M Ranch. "Will Martin and Luke Matthews, Owners," it said.

"You've got the hotel looking pretty good yourself," Will said. "Staying full?"

"Yep. 'Course with Theresa and Marc takin' up three rooms we're not doin' quite the numbers we used to. That new Mexican cook draws 'em in for dinner, though."

They smoked and looked and spat a while. "Things are pretty damned good, aren't they?" Will said.

Tom nodded drowsily. "They are that. Wish we'd of had all this when we were younger?"

Will was quick to answer. "Nope. Been boring as hell." They laughed at that until Tom had one of his stomachaches and had to go inside to lie down. *Pretty strange, those pains*, Will thought. *He ought to see a doctor.*

323

Evey and Luke had earned a statewide reputation for the fine horses they were breeding. Will now had three grandchildren — Josh, Esther, and a six-month-old girl named Iola Ruby. Her first name came from a friend of Evey's named Iola, and Ruby was for the red cliffs in the valley, they explained. *Whatever they want*, Will thought. *But Iola Ruby?*

In Marble, things had never been better. Orders continued to pour in from New Orleans, Chicago, and Denver. More than one hundred men quarried stone and, in the mill — now 1,465 feet by 80 feet — forty thousand cubic feet of stone was processed every month. It was the largest mill in the world and it was fully mechanized. The company issued a monthly payroll of $40,000 to five hundred employees.

Sylvia Smith, however, wasn't happy. The editor of the *Marble City Times* did her best to convince her readers that the company was less interested in producing building stone than it was in selling stock to "suckers" in the East.

"She don't seem to realize that the only reason Marble exists is because of the company," Tom told Will. "If it don't sell stock, it don't operate and people don't work."

When a snowslide struck Quarrytown in March 1912, Miss Smith blamed the company. "The snow looks dangerous above the mill as well," she noted. She was right. A week after the Quarrytown slide the mill was badly damaged by an avalanche off Mill Mountain in the early morning hours. Fortunately, it was between shifts and only the switchboard operator was in the building at the time.

Nevertheless, Sylvia Smith stayed on the attack. *Destiny Keeps Her Appointment and Redresses Many Wrongs*, the headline shouted. In three consecutive issues she hammered at the company and at "Kunnel Meek."

Will and Judith were on hand when three hundred townspeople met in the Masonic Hall to decide what to do about the fiery newspaper editor. Jake was the spokesman for the company and, after a long speech, which Will admitted was an eloquent one, two hundred people signed a petition asking Miss Smith to leave town — for good.

Will and Tom, neither of whom had anything better to do the next day, followed Jake and several others to the newspaper office to present the petition. They hung around and listened to her berate Jake and refuse to leave. They followed at a respectable distance when Jake went to the mayor who then ordered the marshal to escort Miss Smith to jail, "to protect her from the Marble citizens."

"Sure glad this happened," Tom said. "Gives us something to do." The two leaned against porch rails, and smoked. They waited while the business of the day took place and watched people come and go into and out of the stores, up and down the streets.

"Busy place," Will said.

"Sure is," Tom replied. "Here they come."

Jake and three others marched with the marshal to the newspaper office, while Will and Tom followed several yards behind. "Don't you two have anything better to do?" Jake yelled at them.

"Nope," Tom said.

They were at the train station the next morning when Miss Smith was dragged there and told to leave town. When she refused to pay her fare, the conductor paid it for her. Later, they stood outside the newspaper office and watched as Jake directed a number of men who disassembled her printing presses.

"Why are you doing that?" Will asked a man who carried a box of office supplies out of the building.

"Storin' it away," he answered. "Keepin' it safe."

"Right," Will said.

A month later Tom showed up at the ranch and said Sylvia Smith had filed a lawsuit against thirty-seven townspeople, the town of Marble, the Colorado-Yule Company and the Crystal River and San Juan Railroad. The suit was for $22,500 in actual damages and $30,000 in punitive or exemplary damages.

"What's exemplary?" Will asked.

"Beats me, but Jake's named in the suit."

"Serves him right," Will said.

By July, as people continued to talk about the Sylvia Smith lawsuit, the company was working on contracts totaling more than one million dollars. Colorado was third among the states in marble production. In a spirit of generosity, a night school was opened for foreign employees.

"Things are pretty good all over," Will mused to Judith, who smiled and nodded. He said this despite the fact that barely three months earlier a passenger ship named the Titanic had scraped an iceberg and sunk, killing 1,513 people. One of the survivors happened to be Leadville's own Molly Brown.

Henry Ford's assembly line was turning out twenty-six thousand automobiles every month. A Norwegian named Roald Amundsen had reached the South Pole the previous winter. Somebody flew from New York to California in three and a half days. The first direct telephone link between New York and Denver was completed in May. The country's mood was reflected in Irvine Berlin's upbeat "Alexander's Ragtime Band."

And then.

When Colonel Meek donated free marble for the building of a Catholic church, Henry saw his chance and took it. The day the foundation was laid he was standing in the middle of the street three blocks away singing "Onward Christian Soldiers."

Twelve people — nine women and three men who had been badgered into coming along — stood around Henry and Reva while Henry preached to anyone who would listen. A few did, among them Will and Judith.

With spittle running down his chin and sweat pouring off his forehead, Henry railed against the Papists. He spat the words out — the Italians, and the Indians. Pretty soon he was talking about the evils of Negroes and people in general who swore and drank. His flock said "Amen!" and nodded in agreement. When he began to speak of the curse, everyone within hearing distance stopped to listen.

"It's real!" he shouted. "As real as the snow on yon mountain. As real as the . . ." he said, looking around. "As the glass in yon window. As real as a bride's blush."

"Getting a little carried away," Will said to Judith.

"Hush," she said. "He's just getting going good."

Henry was warmed up and he flailed his arms as he preached. "God-uh has sent us a clear message to pray!"

"Amen!" chorused his flock.

"Pray for the Crystal River Valley and all the people therein. Pray for forgiveness for the sins that have been committed here, and for the greed that all have shown, and for the drunkenness and lustfulness that plagues men who seek after pleasures of the flesh!"

"Amen!"

"Yes, the flesh. The lust that is a curse just as the curse of the valley is a curse on all of us who strive to do God-uh's will in this valley of sin and depravity."

"Amen!"

"Satan is at work here. Satan, not some ignorant, illiterate Indian, is behind this curse. We must fight Satan. We must throw off this evil that the devil himself has laid upon this valley. This valley of greed and sin and lustfulness where the carnal pleasures of evil women are sought after, yes, as though a woman's body was as gold and silver itself!"

"Getting good now," Will joked.

"Amen," Judith replied, joining in.

"How will we fight this evil?" Henry yelled. "By joining together as Christian soldiers of the Bible Victory Church which is to be built near Placita on land provided to us by brother Thomason here." He put his hand on the shoulder of a red-faced man in a wrinkled black suit who looked at the ground while his wife puffed up beside him. Henry then turned to those standing

326

along the street. "But we need your help, friends. Yes, we do. We need money to build our church." He smiled and his voice became calmer, even friendly.

Will tugged on Judith's arm. "Come on," he said.

She smiled at him, kind of sadly, he thought. And she said, "Amen."

Halfway to the hotel Jake appeared before them. "You sure do know how to raise kids, don't you, Pop?"

Will hardly looked at Jake. He pulled on Judith's hand and walked past on heavy legs. Behind him, he heard Jake's barklike laugh and he felt old. Old and tired.

ح‌ت‌ه

WHEN COLONEL Channing Meek died a month later, Henry had newfound ammunition for his tirades against the evils he perceived in the valley and stepped up his attacks. It wasn't simply that Meek had died, but the circumstances of his death that interested Henry. Meek was bringing several blocks of marble down from the quarry with four other men when disaster struck. The air brakes on the tram car failed on a steep grade and the car hurtled down the mountain at almost sixty miles an hour. All five of the men leaped from the car and were knocked unconscious. While the four employees were unhurt, Meek suffered internal injuries and died two days later.

Ironically, the marble eventually fell from the car which, with the weight gone, slowed and came to a stop. Had the men stayed on the car, all would have lived.

"But God-uh had other plans," Henry told all who would listen. More people were beginning to listen as events seemed to back up his claims that, until the Crystal River Valley turned to God in great numbers, until the people of the valley prayed as one for salvation, until they drove forever from the valley those whose evil ways perpetuated the reality of the curse, the valley would remain in the hands of Satan himself.

"What will happen with Meek gone?" Will asked Tom.

"That's the question we're all asking," he replied. "And just when things were looking so good, too."

The year 1912 ground slowly toward its close, and news in November that the Wheeler Opera House in Aspen had burned was simply another in a long list of unfortunate incidents that put a cloud over the entire area. The Aspen Times said the fire had been deliberately set by a "fiendish firebug" for the insurance.

"I can't believe it's gone," Judith said. "Remember that wonderful evening we spent there?"

There was other, equally sad news to come. Will received it in a letter from Abby, one of only two he had received from her that year, although she wrote frequently to Evey and, Will assumed, to Henry.

"I doubt that you have heard, and I am sorry to have to tell you," she wrote, "that J. C. Osgood and his mysterious Swedish wife, Alma, have divorced. The news has been in the papers and those who knew them are in a state of shock."

Will handed the letter to Judith and walked to the front window. Pretty soon she was beside him and their eyes drifted toward the south where Cleveholm sat silent and empty. Will remembered Alma standing in the hallway in a thin nightgown. He remembered the joy on Osgood's face when he introduced the lovely young woman to friends.

"Seems like almost nothing happens the way it's supposed to," he said.

"I wouldn't say that." Judith stroked his arm. "Look at Evey and Luke. Even Tom and Tracey."

Will took a deep breath and sighed. "Well," he said. "Anyway, I'm glad this year is about over. Maybe, somehow, things will get better next year."

"WILL MARTIN could do somethin' about it."

"Martin know'd that injun what put the curse on us in the first place, didn't he?"

"Know'd him! Hell, he kilt him."

"Now he's got the injun's power, I hear."

"Will Martin . . ."

"Will Martin . . ."

The townspeople stared at him when he went to Marble, where the curse's imagined effects were felt more strongly than down valley during the cold winter, that January of 1913.

"They need something to take their minds off the real problems," Luke said. "They think about the curse, they remember you and Owl Man. The legend of Will Martin grows."

Henry helped it grow stronger. Upon hearing talk of his father, he increased his exhortations against the curse and against those who helped Satan by drinking and gambling and whoring. He railed against Will Martin for perpetuating the belief in the curse, and for holding fast to his belief that a mystical Indian — or in his eyes, a heathen savage — could have such power.

"Hell," they said. "Martin's been here durn near since the beginning. Owns half the valley hisself, I hear."

"Hell," they said. "Will Martin wants us to keep believin' in the curse so he can gobble up more land."

"Hell, yes," Jake Collins said. "Marble's success doesn't mean anything to him, except that his whore is here."

"Hell," Will Martin said. "What kind of a man calls his own mother a whore?"

And the legend grew: *Will Martin was here when the Indians come through. He himself told the injun to put the curse on the valley. Will Martin and Alma Osgood . . . that's why the divorce. Will Martin and Teddy Roosevelt cooked up a deal to get rid of Osgood.*

"Martin'll own Coal Basin one of these days, you wait and see," they said.

In February, when Mortimer Matthews, now president of the company, went back East to try to raise the $2 million he said was necessary for improvements at the quarry and the mill, people held their breath and waited for news.

"Will Martin's probably worth two million easy, what with that fancy horse ranch and all the land he owns," they said. "And his daughter's married to a injun. What you think of that?"

Two trust companies loaned the company almost two million dollars.

"I hear Martin owned ten thousand head of cows in Texas and sold 'em all 'fore he come up here," they said. "Got the money hid away."

Coupled with a mortgage of nearly half a million dollars the company had incurred in 1905, the new debt seemed almost unbearable.

"Probably have more contracts than we could handle if it wun't for the curse," people complained. "If it wun't for Will Martin."

In March snowslides closed the mill for the first time in its history.

"Damned curse," they said. "Damned Martin."

In April, a jury ruled in favor of Sylvia Smith, the feisty Marble newspaper editor who had been jailed for her outspoken criticism of the company. All parties guilty of damages were ordered to pay a total of $10,344 plus court costs of $592. It was appealed.

"I hear Martin's money was behind Smith's newspaper. Get the company out and he could move in."

"That curse is real and I'm gettin' out!"

Henry was drawing larger crowds at the Bible Victory Church which now met in a log building just north of Bogan Flats. "This hallowed spot may be the only few square feet of land in the valley totally blessed by God-uh!" Henry stated. "You must believe! *Have faith! Pray!* God-uh rewards those who love him. He punishes those who follow Satan. See what is happening? See how God-uh punishes the nonbelievers?"

In August the company signed a contract for $1 million — the largest received by any marble company anywhere up to then — and set to work

329

providing 1.2 million square feet of marble for the Equitable Building in New York.

Economic prosperity began to sway the public's opinion of Will Martin. "Martin ain't so bad. I hear he and Wyatt Earp cleaned up Dodge City by themselves. Hell of a man, Will Martin."

"Martin came out here with nothin' and now look at him. He's what this valley is all about. A man working hard and making something of himself."

In October, J. F. Manning became company president, some said because his contacts in the East would help in the company's bid for the contract to supply marble for the proposed Lincoln Memorial in Washington. Dr. George Merrill, head curator of geology at the U.S. Museum and an expert on marble, came west to look at the Yule Creek deposits. "It is not excelled by any marble in America and I cannot recall foreign deposits which excel it," he reported.

In September the Lincoln Memorial Commission voted in favor of awarding the contract to the company. "The Colorado marble is pure white and therefore it is the most fitting for the memorial," ex-President William Howard Taft said.

"Will Martin killed that injun what put the curse on us. Killed Nathan Peabody, too. Fought for what he believed in and won. Takes a big man to let his daughter marry an injun, even a half-white one. Breeds the finest horses in the state, too. A real credit to the valley."

In January of 1914 the National Fine Arts Commission said it had made a careful examination of all marble submitted as potential for the Lincoln Memorial. "The artistic qualities of Colorado-Yule marble as compared with other submitted, in the opinion of the Commission of Fine Arts, fit it pre-eminently for a structure of the character of the Lincoln Memorial."

"Do not let your heads be turned by one piece of good news," Henry told his congregation. "The devil is still at work, lurking in the shadows of these ancient mountains, leering at the smug men who forget their Lord in good times."

"How you 'spose ol' Will Martin got hisself such a son as that whinin' preacher? Martin drove the Santa Fe Trail and got so sick of mules and wagons he talked the D&RG into comin' to Carbondale, and then helped finance Osgood's Crystal River Railroad up to Redstone. Done a lot for this valley, Will Martin has."

EARLY IN February a winter storm drifted over the lower end of the valley and paused for a long day just above the Double M Ranch. By midmorning Will and Luke agreed that the snow wasn't going to stop for a while and they'd have to round up as many of the nearby horses as they could.

"You don't have to get out in this," Luke said.

"I'm not so old I can't help out," Will said quickly.

"I didn't say that."

"Didn't you?"

"Can't Luke and the hands do it?" Judith asked when Will came into the house to bundle up for the ride.

"Damn it!" Will glared at her. "You, too?"

"I didn't mean anything. Don't be so touchy." She helped him on with his sheepskin coat, found his gloves in the bureau. "Wear your chaps. They keep out the wind."

"I know that," he said, strapping them on. "I'm old but I haven't lost my memory yet."

He started for the door and refused the muffler she tried to hand him. "I'm warm enough."

Will struggled through the deepening snow toward the new corrals closer to Luke and Evey's house. Halfway there he could see neither their house nor his own. Luke and the two cowboys were mounted and waiting for him when he arrived. Luke handed him the reins of a saddled roan. "Sure you want to do this?"

Will hauled himself into the saddle. "Time's wastin'." The four riders lined out toward the mesa to the west, pulling their collars up against a hard north wind that pushed the heavy snow horizontally across their vision. "Been a long time since I've seen a storm like this," Will said, already wishing for the muffler he'd refused. The flurries were so intense that he couldn't see twenty yards ahead, the lead rider a ghost appearing and disappearing in the whiteness.

Right away, they found four horses huddled together, and another half dozen nearby. "We'll spread out!" Luke shouted to be heard over the wind. Will, on the left flank, pulled his bandanna over his nose and immediately felt the ice that had formed in his graying mustache begin to melt from his breath.

He found two horses and left them where they were, moving on ahead to look for others which he would drive back the same route, picking these up on the way. His own horse picked her way down into a draw and out of the wind. They followed the draw for half an hour and found no other horses.

Will was about to turn back when he heard what might have been a whinny. He forced the roan on ahead through snow so deep it scraped his stirrups, and found a mare in a drift struggling to get out. He uncoiled the lariat and dropped a loop over its head. He dallied the rope around his saddle horn and spurred his mount. The mare wouldn't budge. "It figures," he

331

muttered.

He set the roan, keeping the rope taut, and dismounted. He waded through the waist-deep snow, pulling himself along on the rope, and dug down through the snow to the mare's legs. She was buried almost to her neck by now, lying on her side. He helped position her legs beneath her, then struggled back to the roan and gave her a slap on the rump. The roan, trained well by Luke, tried to forge ahead. The downed mare kicked and fought and finally regained her feet. The roan kept going and the mare bucked through the snow toward Will, who sighed with relief. He stepped to the side as the mare kicked past and felt his boot go deeper into the snow. It hit the edge of a rock and slid off. As it did, he felt pain shoot through his leg and he went down.

"Damn!" The word didn't get more than five feet away before it lost itself in the thickening snowstorm. He searched for the horses but they had disappeared into the whiteness. He figured the roan would probably keep going until she fell off a cliff or reached the barn.

He decided his ankle wasn't broken, but it was badly sprained. He tried to put weight on it but the pain went clear to his head this time and he fought off nausea. He let his body sink backwards and settle in the snow. He took off a glove and tried to reach into his boot to rub the ankle but it was already swelling. He leaned back and felt lightheaded.

His rifle was in a case strapped on the roan and the snow covered any driftwood he might use for a cane. The wind whined overhead, and he was thankful that at least he was shielded from its force. As long as he didn't move it, the ankle didn't hurt. He began to shiver and fought off his rising panic. *Somebody will find me sooner or later,* he told himself. *But the storm might last for days.*

He began to scoop out the snow around him. Intermittently working and resting, he soon had himself encased in a barrel of snow. Now he only needed some kind of roof. He thought he'd have to dig a cave and crawl in before long. *Damn, it is cold,* he thought as he pictured Judith sitting by the fire. His ankle began to throb with pain. He jammed his hat down to his ears and pulled up his coat collar, then crossed his arms and beat on his shoulders. *Should have brought that muffler.* He figured that Judith would have some hot coffee and be staring out the window, thinking he'd be along. He thought of their bed and her warm body nestled against his.

"Hey!" He barely heard his own voice. He shifted on his numb rear and scooped out some of the new snow. He wished he could get his boot off. *Probably have to cut it off later and ruin a good pair of boots*, he thought bitterly. He imagined Judith helping him soak his foot in hot water and sitting in front of the fire all warm and cozy.

332

Maybe an hour later — it seemed to Will more like a day — the snow had piled up a foot higher around him as it blew over the edge of the draw and into his resting place. He threw handfuls of it out of the hole for a while and got tired of that and let it pile up.

The wind howled and the fury of the storm increased overhead. Judith would be worried by now, he figured. He got sleepy and closed his eyes, then jerked them open. Have to stay awake. He lifted his good foot and bent his knee, moving the foot back and forth. He tried to do the same with the other but the pain engulfed him again and he fell back.

He imagined Judith's face and stroked it with his hand. "Wish you wouldn't keep your hair tied back like that," he told her. "Let it fall like you used to. Oh, hell. Never mind the gray."

Abby tried to read poetry to him and it made him drowsy. She was too young and too "cultural" to be sapped away up here in this godforsaken valley. If he wasn't careful she'd leave him. She told him to get to bed and go to sleep and he did.

But Tracey woke him up wanting to make love and he heard her husband Randall moving in the hallway and stiffened. "Never mind," Tracey said. "He's dead, you know." She kissed his chest and he stroked her back and Judith laughed that low laugh and crawled on top of him and Abby fought him and scratched and Tracey moaned — no, it was the wind. Judith wasn't in the bed but was in Carbondale having a child who died and he tried to turn over on his side but the covers were binding him and he couldn't move. He called for Abby to close the damn window. Randall Collins came and took Tracey out of the bed and where was Judith anyway? Why didn't she come and warm him with her full body? Abby read poetry to the good side of Randall Collins' face. He smiled at Tracey, who sat on Abby's left laughing at Ardy who was sitting at the kitchen table in his long johns. Judith on top, Abby beneath, Tracey in the crook of his arm, warm bodies sweating, women's voices saying go to sleep. He let his head relax and slept thinking tomorrow he'd . . .

A shock of pain raced from his ankle to his neck and he fought off the hands that were trying to pull him from the warmth of his imagined bed but they wouldn't go away so he opened his eyes and saw Luke bent over him.

"So, you're awake, are you?" Luke brushed snow from Will's legs. "Have a nice nap?"

Will came back to himself and nodded. "'Bout time you got here."

WILL FOUGHT sleep all the way back to the ranch house. When Luke helped him inside and he saw Jake and Henry standing together in his kitchen, he thought he was dreaming.

"What's the matter with you, old man?" Jake asked, and Will wished it was a dream.

Bundled up in a blanket before the fire with his swollen ankle propped up on a stool, Luke explained to Will what had happened. Luke had gone looking for him in the storm, had stumbled across the roan and the mare, followed the draw and found Will buried to his chest in snow.

Henry and Reva had been trying to get to Carbondale. Jake, Inez and their five-year-old son, Nathan Jacob, had been coming from the train at Carbondale. The storm forced all of them to Will's house.

Now they all sat in his living room. Judith was beside him stroking the back of his head. Across the room Henry and Reva sat stiffly, water glasses at their side. Near them Inez rocked Nathan who slept on her lap while Jake stood beside her. Luke peered into the night through the window at the continuing storm and Evey came into the room with a tray of steaming coffee cups. Ten-year-old Josh sat at Luke's feet playing with a toy wagon while Esther, the same age as Nathan, tried to fight off sleep by staring at the black-clad Henry and Reva.

"Ain't this something?" Jake said into the quiet of the room. "All together like it was Christmas or something."

"How does your ankle feel?" Evey asked.

"It's all right," Will lied. His entire body ached.

Jake snorted. "Why don't you admit it hurts like hell." He pulled a cigar from a pocket and lit up.

"Must you smoke?" Reva frowned at him.

Jake looked at her through the fog of smoke. He took the cheroot from his mouth and shrugged, then walked to the fireplace and flipped it into the flames.

Reva sighed. "Thank you."

"You're very welcome," Jake said. He stared at her sitting there straight as a poker, her mouth puckered and her eyebrows pulled down in a tight frown. He looked at Henry and shook his head. He walked back to Inez and touched her hair.

Luke turned from the window. "If this ever lets up we'll have to get some feed to the herd."

Josh tugged Luke's pants leg. "I can help. I can take Grandad's place."

"We'll see," Luke said with a smile at his son.

"Grandad, is it?" Jake nodded toward his own son who continued to sleep in Inez's arms. "I guess it was about time all of your grandchildren got together anyway. I'd been meaning to introduce you to the only one you hadn't met."

"He's a good-looking boy," Judith said, being polite. "He has his mother's eyes." Inez looked at Judith for a long five seconds, then dropped her eyes. Will still had not heard the woman speak. Maybe she's mute, he mused.

"I still don't know how you found me," Will said to Luke.

"I found the horses pointing south so I guessed you were north. Kept riding until my horse almost stepped on you."

Jake barked his short laugh. "Injun blood. All of you are good trackers, I hear."

Luke let his eyes drift toward Jake, where they rested until Jake looked at Henry, who pushed himself to his feet.

"God-uh led you to him. It was a miracle."

"Amen," Reva intoned.

Esther's eyes were as big as spur rowels. "Why do you dress like that?" she asked Reva.

"Esther!" Evey scolded, then picked Esther up, keeping her eyes on Reva.

"We do not believe in gaudiness," Reva replied. "We avoid many things of this world."

Esther turned to her mother. "What does she mean?"

"Never mind," Evey said. "We'll talk about it later."

Jake laughed again. "We'll all have lots to talk about after this night."

Judith held out her arms and Evey passed Esther to her. "Let's find some beds for the children," she said. "Why don't you bring Nathan, Inez, and we'll get them settled."

Josh faced his father. "Do I have to, Dad? Can't I stay up with the grownups a while?"

"It's okay," Luke said. "He'll be all right."

The women left the room, except for Reva, who stared straight ahead. Then she stood. "Suffer the little children to come unto me," she said. "I will help tuck them in and see that they say their prayers." Henry nodded sagely.

When she was gone Jake stepped to Henry's side. "When are you going to get her pregnant?" he asked.

Henry looked away and Jake shifted his attention to Luke. "Did you know Evey used to be in love with me?" Luke sipped his coffee, looking at Jake over the rim of his cup.

"She was young and foolish," he said, finally.

"Young and hot as a boiled potato." Jake smirked.

Henry shook his head. "Lustfulness," he said. "One of the great evils of mankind."

Josh was at Will's side. "What's lustfulness?"

Jake's sharp bark drew all their eyes. "You'll find out soon enough, young fellow."

Will's eyes were heavy. He let his head rest against the back of the chair. Through a haze of drowsiness he sensed the women coming back into the room. He heard someone build up the fire. Later, much later, he woke as Luke carried Josh off to bed. Judith lifted the blanket from his legs and unwrapped the towel from his ankle, replacing it with another. Jake and Inez were asleep on the sofa, his head on her shoulder, mouth open. Henry and Reva were gone from their chairs. Evey and Luke sat in front of the fireplace, his arm around her.

As daylight crept through the window, Will's body ached and his ankle was worse. His leg was asleep and he hit at it with his fist. Judith stirred beside him. "What?" she muttered, wiping sleep from her eyes.

He shook his head. "Where's Luke?"

"Gone to wake the hands. The snow stopped."

Inez was stretched out on the sofa. Henry and Reva sat against the wall wrapped in blankets, still asleep. "Where's Evey?" He craned his neck. "And Jake?" He looked at Judith who pushed herself to her feet as Jake walked into the room from the kitchen with a smile.

"Don't worry," he said. "My half-sister isn't interested in any hanky-panky."

"Like to know how you found that out," Will said.

Jake sneered. "I imagine she'll tell you."

"As soon as you can get on the road I want you out of this house," Will said.

"Can't be too soon for me." Jake walked to the sofa and slapped his sleeping wife on the rump. "Wake up," he ordered. "Time for breakfast."

She rose wordlessly, tried to smooth out the wrinkled dress, and walked toward the kitchen.

"Can she talk?" Will asked.

"When she wants to." Jake smoothed his hair.

"Where's Yolanda?"

"In Taos with her kin. Inez and the kid came up on the train. That's why I was in Carbondale. How soon do you think we can get out of here?"

"Not soon enough."

Jake looked out the window. "Probably be tomorrow before the road's open. You been up to Marble this winter?"

"A couple of times." Will's ankle throbbed.

"How is she?"

"Your mother?"

"Who else?"

"She's fine. All of them are fine." Maybe if he could get the ankle higher

336

yet it would help, he thought.

Jake paced the floor, started to light up a cigar, saw the frown on Henry's face, shrugged and put it back in his coat. "I still can't believe Theresa married that dago," he said. Nobody replied. "Spunky little turkey. I'll say that for him. But a dago, for god's sake."

Henry stirred. "Catholic, too. A Papist!"

"Can you figure it?" Jake said. "Every man in the valley worth anything would have jumped at the chance to get her and she picks out somebody named Marcello." He looked at Will. "And Evey picks out a half-breed injun."

Without looking up, Will said, "And you pick out a half-breed Mexican."

Jake's eyes narrowed and he straightened but then cracked a smile, turning to Henry. "And old Henry here. What'd he pick out? What is she, anyway? Looks more like a goddamn weasel than a woman."

Henry stood up and had to lift his eyes to meet Jake's. "You can't talk about my wife that way."

"I can do whatever the hell I want to do."

"That's enough!" Will pushed himself to a more upright position and felt the pain shoot through his leg. "Let's change the subject."

"Whatever you say, Pa," Jake said. He limped around the room examining the knickknacks, peering out the window. He picked up the framed photograph sitting on the fireplace mantle, the picture of Tracey, Tom, Judith and Will at the ocean's edge in California. He studied it for a long time.

"I've got her eyes, I guess," he said, putting the photo back on the mantle. He put his foot on the hearth and stared into the fire. Turning to Will he smiled. "Must have been a nice trip, just the four of you. You trade off some, did you? You and Tom and the women, I mean?"

Will felt his throat fill, and his breath came fast. "You're pushing it too far, Jake," he said. "I've just about reached the end of my rope with you. I'm afraid we're going to tangle one of these days. So help me, if you *ever* say anything like that about your mother again, I'll . . . "

"You'll what, old man?"

"If it was just you here without your wife and child I'd kick you out right now. Don't push me again, Jake. Men have been killed for calling women more polite names than you call your own mother."

Jake's eyes were wide. "Are you threatening to kill me?"

"Take it however you want."

"You'd kill your own son?"

Will stared at him. "I'm beginning to doubt that you are my son," he said.

"IT WAS THE most uncomfortable two days I've ever spent," Judith said to Tom and Tracey a month later when they were able to get to Marble on the train. "I don't think anyone spoke more than three words at a time that second day. Somebody would say 'pass the gravy' or 'build up the fire' and that was it."

Tom was bent forward in his chair, having one of his stomachaches. "I'd of kicked 'em all out," he said.

"We probably should have," Will agreed. "You ought to see a doctor about those stomachaches."

"Think I might this summer," Tom said.

Theresa and Marcello entered the room, the Italian carrying his two-year-old son Thomas. "Little Teegee wants to say hello to Uncle Will and Aunt Judith," he said. The boy sucked on a thumb and fingered a frayed blanket.

"That contract for the Lincoln Memorial ought to keep you busy for a while," Will said. It had been awarded in March.

Marcello's eyes brightened. "It is good for the future of the town and the company. I am assigned to work in a new shop which is being built at the mill to finish the marble."

He said the contract called for the cutting of thirty-six columns, each forty-six feet tall and seven feet in diameter. "Each column is valued at $15,000," he said. "Can you imagine? I am told it will take nearly two thousand stones, each weighing up to thirty tons."

"Why, that will take forever!" Judith exclaimed.

"We have less than three years to complete the work."

"Can you do it?"

He shrugged. "Of course."

The marble cutters got to work that spring and the Cordell Hotel was almost constantly full. His ankle healed, Will was able to spend a great deal of time on a horse, riding with Luke and exploring the valley on his own. News reached the valley in late June that Archduke Franz Ferdinand, heir to the thrones of Austria and Hungary, had been assassinated, but it was read by most with passing interest. There were a number of Austrian workers at the quarry and the mill, however, and there was talk among them of returning to Europe.

"They say it will mean war," Marcello told Will.

"Crazy Europeans," he said. "Shouldn't affect us."

Marcello looked away. "Austria borders Italy."

Will put his hand on the young man's arm. "Your home is here."

"But I have family still in Italy," Marcello replied, pulling away.

338

᷈᷈

WILL REACHED BACK and took Judith's hand, pulling her up the steep grade past the deadfall. It had been years since he had made the climb to Owl Point and he was astonished at how difficult it had become.

"Can't be because I'm getting old," he said. "Want to rest?"

She did and he was glad. "It's beautiful up here," she said. They were little more than halfway up the mountain. "Why did you wait so long to bring me up here?"

Will felt his breath begin to slow and he looked up at the point. "No reason," he said. "Or maybe there was. Maybe I wanted to keep it all for myself."

It was noon when they stepped out onto the top of the cliff and the valley opened up before them. Judith gasped. "Oh, Will! It's even more wonderful than I had imagined." He didn't reply, and instead led her to the outermost point of the red-floored shelf and helped her sit on the rock which had become his favorite resting place. For a long time neither spoke as they stared out over the expanse of valley.

Down below, Redstone was a tiny toy village and the Crystal River was a gray wire winding through the midst of it all. Across the valley and up the Coal Creek canyon, they could see the area of Coal Basin although there was no evidence that a mine had ever existed there. Will sat on the red dirt beside Judith's rock perch and waited for the familiar presence of something otherworldly to come over him. For a long time nothing happened. He fidgeted.

"What's the matter?" Judith asked.

"Nothing," he lied and pointed to the south. "Elephant Mountain doesn't look so much like an elephant from up here does it?"

"No, but Mount Sopris looks much bigger."

Will watched his wife as she stared out over the mountains. She was a fine-looking woman, he thought, even if she was in her mid-sixties. He wondered where the time had gone. It seemed to him only a couple of years ago that he'd been thirty or so, sitting all alone on the rocky perch, when he was first visited by those tiny beings who exerted a kind of power over the valley. Now, he felt nothing. *Is it age, maturity?* Will asked himself. *But Owl Man had been old and he had felt them.*

Judith turned to him and the early afternoon sun washed her face. It was a fine face, and only somewhat wrinkled. And the hair was graying, braided now and pulled back, not flowing long as in the past. Her body was still full.

"Would you like to make love here?" she asked softly.

He smiled. "How did you know?"

339

Later, the sun was full in their faces as it hovered above the rim of the mountains behind Coal Basin. Clouds were starting to build in the southwest and a breeze had come up. They had sat apart for a time after their lovemaking, each lost in thoughts they didn't share.

Suddenly the breeze turned into a brisk wind that stirred the dust. Judith had let her hair down and it whipped into her face. Will started to say something to her when, like a long-forgotten memory, he felt it. It was another presence, neither man nor animal. He welcomed the feeling but, seconds later he knew he was again among the *ini'pute*. He felt a shock of fear run through his body and involuntarily turned, looking for something he knew he would not, or could not, see. He pushed himself to his feet and had to brace himself against the fierce wind. They were all around him. Like hummingbirds, they darted at his head and quickly flew away, then back. They moved not with the calm, almost angel-like serenity of the past. Now the *ini'pute* were frantic and full of anger. The wind tore at Will's clothes.

Judith was standing. He saw her stagger against the wind and take a step forward toward the precipice. He lunged for her, grabbed her arm and pulled her close. She smiled but frowned quickly when she saw the look on his face. "What is it?"

Will gathered himself. "I think we'd better start down. I don't like the looks of those clouds."

She nodded but he saw the question in her eyes. "I don't like the way it . . . it *feels* up here today. It's not right." She nodded again and followed him toward the back of the outcropping. As soon as he entered the aspen grove he felt better. The feeling of foreboding was gone. He wondered if the reason was because he was out of the wind. No, he decided. It was because he was away from the *ini'pute*, and off the *ihupi'arat tubut*.

He helped Judith across a slide area strewn with rocks, wondering what the change in atmosphere meant for the valley. *It's not good*, he thought to himself. *Not good at all.*

340

PART VIII
1914-1929

Spirits were rising in Marble. Several small but lucrative contracts provided even more work to those already engaged in the company's largest and most prestigious order — the Lincoln Memorial contract. The feeling of optimism spread throughout the valley and few paid much attention to the newspaper reports about the goings on across the Atlantic. But in August, when Germany declared war on Russia and France in quick succession, Judith was more concerned than Will.

"Let 'em settle their own differences," he said. "The United States has no business getting involved."

"I agree," she said, "and so does President Wilson. But this looks bigger than a European fight."

"War is immoral!" Henry cried to his flock and they all said "Amen!"

"The Germans are like the American white men of the 1800s," Luke said. "They'll push and push until they either take it all or they're beaten into the ground."

"I'm glad Joshua is too young to even think about becoming a soldier," Evey said.

And Marcello Barzini scanned every paper he could find, looking for news about Italy and shaking his head.

"I grew up during the Civil War," Will told his grandchildren. Josh, now ten years old, was eager to hear stories about fighting. Esther, a mere five, sat on her grandfather's lap and played with his mustache.

"Were you a Yankee or a Reb, Gramps?" the boy asked.

Will put on a make-believe frown. "My pa was a member of the Army of the Confederate States of America," he said. "And don't call me Gramps. Call me 'Grandpa' or 'Grandfather' or something like that. 'Gramps' makes me feel old."

"Did you fight?" Josh wanted to know.

"Too young, boy."

"But you've killed people, haven't you? My dad says you killed a man in a gunfight at a mine and that you killed a man in Crystal with a chair." Will was silent. "And the kids at school say you killed my dad's grandfather by throwing him off a cliff."

"Don't believe everything you hear," Will said gruffly. Josh left the room disappointed while Will stroked Esther's hair and tickled her tummy.

IN SEPTEMBER, Will looked up from the two-day-old *Rocky Mountain News*. "Where the hell is the Marne? Story in here about the allies stopping the Krauts in the Battle of the Marne."

In October he asked the same question about Ypres. Throughout the winter and into 1915 the war continued to be front page news and President Wilson continued to stand by his statement that the United States would be "neutral in fact as well as in name."

"Thank God for that," Tracey said, looking at her three-year-old grandson. "I pray that no one in this family ever has to fight in a war."

Marcello, hearing these words as he approached the room, turned abruptly and walked away.

In February, Germany began to blockade Great Britain, and in April the Germans used poison gas in the Second Battle of Ypres.

"There's that name again," Will said. "Damned foreigners ought to have names you can pronounce."

"Right," Tom replied with a grin. "Like the Wasatch or the Uncompahgre ranges."

"That's different," Will snorted.

The news that year wasn't *all* bad. The Ford company rolled out car number one million. Rocky Mountain National Park was created on 262,000 acres of Colorado wilderness land that included 107 named peaks above ten thousand feet in elevation. The U.S. wheat crop totaled one billion bushels for the first time. Popular songs included "Pack up Your Troubles in Your Old Kit Bag" and "I Didn't Raise My Boy to Be a Soldier."

Unfortunately, Will thought, *a lot of boys just might be soldiers real soon.*

In early May, a German submarine sank the liner Lusitania and America held her collective breath. Two weeks later Will, Judith, Tracey and Tom sat in the dining room of the Cordell Hotel. It was late and the men were finishing off an apple pie when they heard Theresa slam the door of her room and come sobbing down the stairs.

"He's going," she said, running to Tracey and crying into her shoulder. "Marcello says he's going to Italy."

"What?" All four of them said it at the same time.

"He's so. . . so damned stubborn!"

"But," Tracey said, "to Italy?"

"We have declared war on Austria-Hungary." Marcello stood at the foot of the stairs, a folded newspaper in his hands. "I must join my countrymen."

Judith stepped toward him. "Surely there is no . . . ."

"We are at war," he said. "I would be a traitor to my country if I did not respond when danger threatens."

343

"But you're more American than Italian now," Theresa said.

Marcello straightened and looked lovingly at his wife. "I have relatives there. I shall go back with the others."

"Others?" Tom was on his feet. "What others?"

"All of us. All the Italians who are young enough to fight and some even who are too old."

"All of you?" Tom frowned. "But that'll take most of the skilled labor when we need you the most."

"It cannot be helped," Marcello said. "We talked about returning when Italy signed the Treaty of London last month. Now that we have officially declared war we have no choice."

Theresa sobbed loudly and fell into a chair.

Barely one week later Marcello was ready to board the train with a dozen other young men. Others had already gone and more would follow within days. After Will and Judith had said their goodbyes they stepped back, away from the small, devastated family. Marcello stood in front of his son's grandparents and swallowed hard.

"Please try not to worry too much about me," he said in a soft voice. "I will take care of myself good."

"You do what you have to do," Tom said. "I almost wish I could go with you."

Marcello smiled and nodded, then turned to Tracey. "God bless you," he choked. "You have been the mother I never had. I love you, the both of you."

"You hurry home, now," she said. "Come back to us safely."

Marcello hugged her briefly, turned away, and walked to Theresa who waited by the train. For a long time they looked into each other's eyes and were kissing when the conductor yelled "All aboard!"

"THE NEWS IS all bad," Tom said, throwing the newspaper on the floor. "Trench warfare, poison gas . . ." He stopped and stared out the window.

"Any news from Marcello?" Will asked. He and Judith had not seen the Cordells since their son-in-law left on the train. Now, in late June, they were together on the ranch.

Tom shook his head. "Theresa can hardly stand it."

"What's this I hear about Sylvia Smith?" Will asked, trying to change the subject. He wanted to get Tom's mind on something else besides the European war.

The question brought a chuckle from Tom. Good, Will thought. He studied his old friend. Tom's hair had turned completely gray and, when he thought no one was watching, his face betrayed the pain in his stomach. He was seventy-one years old, and he moved with the slowness of a much older man.

"You heard the Colorado Supreme Court upheld the District Court's verdict?" Tom asked, and Will nodded. "Sylvia came parading into town a week ago with Sheriff Hanlon. They walked door to door demanding that everyone who'd been named in the suit pay up."

Judith and Tracey came into the room from the kitchen. "Tracey just told me about it," Judith said. "Those poor people who couldn't pay on the spot."

"What about them?" Tom asked, and Will saw him clutch his stomach.

"The sheriff actually closed down their businesses," Tracey said. "A lot of them are selling out just to pay her."

"What about Jake?"

Tom frowned. "I heard he pulled a wad out of his coat and paid her cash on the spot."

"Figures," Will said.

"Lot of folks are upset with the company. They think the Colorado-Yule should take the whole debt on itself since it was her comments about the company that caused the ruckus in the first place."

"Lots of good news from up there," Will said sarcastically.

He turned and saw Tracey smiling. "We do have some good news," she said. Will saw Tom's face break into a smile. "Theresa is pregnant."

"That's wonderful!" Judith cried.

"Maybe that'll take her mind off Marcello for a while," Will put in.

As they sat at the evening meal, Luke and Evey and their two children included, Judith and Tracey exchanged glances and Will took a deep breath. "What is it now? Not another California trip, I hope."

"Nothing quite so distant," Judith replied. "We think we'd like to make a trip to Crested Butte, maybe even to Gunnison."

Will and Tom looked less than enthusiastic. "What the hell for?" Will grunted.

"Just for fun." Judith leaned forward. "How long has it been since you've been out of this valley, Tom Cordell? Not since the trip west."

Tom sighed, leaned back, folded his hands on his stomach.

"I think it's a wonderful idea," Evey said.

Luke turned to Will. "Is the road over Schofield Pass still open? I heard it's not in very good shape."

"I've got a feeling we're going to find out," Will said with resignation in his voice.

❧❧

IN MID-JULY the four of them negotiated the rough road — actually more of a trail — around the Devil's Punch Bowl in one of Will's wagons and they made it easily past the small, near-ghost town of Gothic and on to Crested Butte. They pushed on to Gunnison, where Will and Tom lazed around in the lavish LaVeta Hotel while the women shopped. They gorged themselves on food in three restaurants and finally agreed to head home.

They had just started down the incline at the Devil's Punch Bowl when Tom pointed at another wagon that was on the way up. "Mighty narrow," he said. "Can we pass?"

The upward-climbing wagon hugged the inside of the trail, staying away from the loose rock on the outside edge. Throughout the twists and turns of the trail the mountain fell off sharply to Will's right. In places it fell seventy or eighty feet to the foot of the falls. As the approaching wagon got within fifty yards they could tell Jake was the driver. Another man sat beside him.

"Might have known," Tom said. He was sitting on the precipice side of the wagon and anxiously watched for signs of loose rock or a weakening of the roadbed. The two women sat silently on the bench behind the men, holding on tightly and crowding to the left, away from the cliff side.

The two wagons met at a narrow point halfway down. "Howdy," Jake called. "Nice day for a ride."

"Yep," Will said. "Where you goin' with an empty wagon?"

"That's my business, not yours."

Will nodded. "Want to back up a bit so we can get by?"

"Well, now," Jake said with a smirk. "I don't think I do. You can get by here."

Will took a breath. "Doesn't look like it. Shouldn't be much trouble for you to back down a ways."

Jake sat still, toying with the reins. "These horses don't go backwards."

Tom stood and put his foot on the seat, leaning forward toward Jake. "Guess we'll all just have to sit here until you decide to back her down," Tom said.

Jake waited a moment, looking at Tom. "Like hell," he said and flicked the reins. His two horses jerked ahead. There was little space between Will's wagon and the mountainside to his left. His right wheels were close to the edge of the cliff. Jake's wagon crept forward.

"Will!" Judith cried. "It's too narrow."

"Hold 'em up, Jake," Will called. "You can't make it." Jake snapped the reins again. "I'll make it."

He was alongside Will's wagon and it appeared that he might squeeze past. Just when it looked like the wagons would clear each other, Jake's left rear wheel hooked Will's.

The jolt shook Will's wagon and his horses tried to move forward. The wagon tipped slightly to the right, toward the drop-off.

Will turned to see Tom lose his balance, lunged for him and grabbed nothing but air. Tom went over backwards, grabbing at the seat and missing. There was a thud as he hit the side of the roadway and then Tracey's scream drowned out the sound of rocks giving way. As Jake tried to pull his horses back to unlock the wheels, Will's wagon settled back to the left, throwing Will away from Tom. Will saw his friend slip over the edge and disappear.

Tracey screamed and the horses bucked and whinnied. Will leaped from his seat to the ground, ran around the horses, and peered over the cliff. Tom's twisted body lay unmoving sixty beet below.

Tracey was beside him. He felt her grab his arm and lean forward. When she saw her husband, Will felt her knees buckle and he took her arm. "Tom!" she called. "My God! Tom!" She tried to pull away but Will held her and turned to Judith who had joined them. He could see Jake and his companion still sitting in their wagon.

"Hang onto her," he told Judith. "I'll try to get to him." Down the trail forty yards was a switchback where the drop-off was less severe. He trotted downhill, stumbling in loose gravel and feeling his breath come hard. He picked his way down a slide area and traversed a steep incline. Finally, he was beside Tom. He knelt on hurting knees and immediately knew there was no life in the body. A deep gash in Tom's forehead told the story.

Will looked up toward the women and shook his head. They disappeared from view, Judith holding Tracey.

Suddenly, Will realized where he was. Tom had fallen just down river from the spot where Will and Jake had tumbled in the snow years before. He stared at the rocks, then turned back to Tom and forgot about the pain of that winter day. He forgot about Jake altogether as he looked at the broken and lifeless body of his friend, Sagebrush Tom Cordell of the Palo Duro.

EXACTLY ONE week after Tom was buried in the small cemetery north of Marble, Will made his decision. Early that morning he walked to the barn and unlocked the trunk he had stashed there for safekeeping. He lifted the lid and saw his old batwing chaps folded neatly on top. He picked them up and laid them over a rail. He was pawing through clothes and other gear he had saved for no good reason when Luke entered the barn. "What's up?" Luke asked, leaning against a post.

"Looking for something," Will said. He threw an old plaid shirt to the ground and laid his saddlebags beside it. "I carried $15,000 from Aspen to the ranch in these back in '82, I think it was. Money Henry Gillespie loaned me to get all this started."

"I remember the story. It was a long time ago."

Will shot him a look. "Not that long." He continued his search. It *had* been a long time, though. Thirty-three years if he figured right. He found what he sought. He lifted the gun belt from the trunk and weighed it in his hand. Without looking at Luke he buckled it on and was surprised at the heavy weight on his right hip.

Luke stood in his lean, continued watching, and didn't speak. Will pulled the .45 from its holster and spun the chamber. It clicked with the familiar old sound and he saw the chamber contained five bullets. The hammer rested on the empty chamber. The gun felt good in his hand. He had cleaned and oiled the weapon regularly at least once a year.

"You're headed for Marble."

Luke had it right. Will nodded without looking at him and began putting the gear back in the trunk.

"Think that's a good idea?"

"I'm going, ain't I?" Will snapped.

Back in the house, Will headed directly for the bedroom. He threw his hat on the bed, opened the closet door and reached high on the back shelf. He emerged from the room wearing his tall Texas hat with the single star on the side. "Still fits good," he said.

"Will!" Judith was beside Luke.

"Judith," he said. "I don't want to hear a word. I've been thinking about this for a week now and I've made up my mind."

"You're crazy, Will Martin," she said. "If Jake doesn't kill you, one of his gunmen will."

"Maybe. And maybe there won't be any killing at all."

"Why wear a gun, then?" Luke asked. "You're planning on killing him."

"Somebody needs to."

Judith pushed past Luke to front Will. "Not you. You're too damned old, Will." She was ready to cry. She took his arm and tried to pull him away from the door.

Will gently pulled his arm from her grasp. He took her face in his hands and stared at it for a moment. "It's got to be done," he said. "I can't let him get away with the pain he's caused this family."

Judith stepped back, cleared her throat, straightened. She looked him up and down. "You look just like you did when I first met you," she said softly. "Except for the gray hair and the mustache. Where'd you find that hat?"

Will pushed himself to his full height and felt the energy of youth return to his body for a few seconds. He felt like he was ready to ride out onto the Llano Estacado with Sagebrush Tom and round up a few strays. But Sagebrush Tom was dead and Will Martin, an old man now, was the one who would avenge his friend's death. He turned and started for the door, then stopped. He turned back to Judith and took her in his arms. Her body felt good as it pressed into him. He kissed her on the cheek and smiled. "Be back in a few days at most," he said. He turned again and walked out the door heading for the barn and his horse named Malachi, as good a horse as he'd ever had. Almost as good as old Jeremiah, he thought.

He didn't see Luke until he'd been on the road half an hour and the Indian dropped down from the mountainside to his right and rode alongside.

"What are you doing here?" Will muttered.

"Thought I'd come along for the ride," Luke said. He patted the rifle in his case on the side of the saddle.

"No need."

"Maybe not. I'm here, though."

"Well," Will said. "Well, all right."

IN THE TWILIGHT Will saw Jake limping toward the White House Hotel, returning from his office at the mill where he continued as legal counsel. Jake was busy fishing a cigar out of his suit coat and fumbling for matches. He didn't see Will until he was ten paces away. He stopped in the street, scratched a match on his heel and lifted his eyes as he raised the flame. Seeing Will, his eyes widened and the hand holding the match stopped halfway up. His mouth spread in a grin around the cigar.

"Well," he said, "aren't you something?" He laughed his barklike laugh and flipped the match into the street. He fished for another. "What the devil you doing duded up like that? Just what is it you want?"

Will was tired. The long ride had taken most of his strength but he had insisted on confronting Jake that very evening. He was leaning against a porch post now and his legs felt like waterlogged driftwood. His breath came too fast and he wished he was home sitting on the sofa with Judith.

"I owe you for Tom Cordell," he said.

"Oh, good Lord, old man," Jake replied with a shake of his head. "Can't you leave it alone?"

"It can't be left alone."

"You're too damned old for this kind of tomfoolery. What're you gonna do? Kill me?"

Will felt his breath slow. He knew Jake was afraid and felt more confident with the knowledge. "Could be."

Jake took a step forward. He wore a handsome suit of dark wool, a silk tie, and a gold watch fob. A round-topped derby sat on his head. He tried to smile. "You think you're still a cowboy, don't you? How old is that god-awful hat?"

"Older'n you. And you might not get much older."

"Howard!" Jake yelled toward the open front door of the hotel. "McAlester!"

Two men instantly came out the front door and onto the porch to Will's left. He glanced their way. "Always have some help around, don't you?"

"You should have thought of that," Jake said with a smile, putting his hands in his pockets.

Will smiled back. "I did."

"You two boys just hold it right there." The voice came from around the corner of the hotel. As Jake looked that way Luke stepped into the street. "You two men hand me your guns."

The two wore suits similar to Jake's. "We ain't got no guns," one said.

"Now, boys." Luke approached them, reached inside the coat of the first and pulled a small pistol from a shoulder holster. "Now you," he said to the other. The man dropped his gun on the wooden slats of the porch and it made a thud that seemed to echo in the still evening air. Luke motioned them into the street, lined them up near Jake and then stood beside Will with his rifle hanging at his side.

Will still leaned against the post. "You wouldn't be carrying a weapon would you, Jake?"

Jake shook his head. "Mind if I light up? I could stand a smoke right about now." He slowly reached into the pock et of his coat and lifted a match into the air so Will could see it. He struck the match on his heel, as before, but the breeze blew it out. Again he put his hand in his pocket. He pulled it out quickly to show a small derringer with two barrels. He pointed it at Will.

"You always were too trusting," he said.

Will stepped off the porch and let his right hand dangle near his Colt. "Those things aren't very accurate," he said, nodding at the miniature pistol. He took another step.

"The closer you get the more likely I am to get a hit," Jake said, his eyes flashing in the deepening darkness.

"You better be glad I'm coming then," Will replied, taking a third step. He was within a few feet of the three men, with Luke beside him.

"You ought to drop that rifle, injun," Jake said. He took a half step backwards. Howard and McAlester watched him, waiting for orders. Luke held the rifle out to his side at arm's length. They were eight feet away, then six. "Stop right there," Jake demanded. Will took another step. "You're gonna make me kill you, old man."

"Do it," Will said in a whisper.

Jake's eyes were wild. His hand shook slightly. The two men to his right edged away. "Get them," Jake ordered. One of the men took a step forward and Luke swung the rifle at him, catching him on the arm. At that moment, Will lunged forward and hit Jake on the wrist, knocking the derringer from his hand. Luke lifted his rifle to his shoulder and leveled it at the other two.

"You two stand there quiet," he said, "and maybe you won't get hurt."

Will had his Colt in his hand and jabbed the barrel into his son's midsection. "I don't know what happened between us," he said softly. "I know you were hurt when you found out about your mother and me. But that shouldn't have led to the kind of hatred you've shown."

"I never . . ."

"Shut up." Jake did, then found another match, struck it, and lit up with a shaking hand.

"It was Yolanda who turned your head for good," Will continued. "There's no reason for you to hate me so much and I think you know it. You're just too far in to back out without your ego getting bruised."

Jake puffed smoke like a chimney. He took the cigar from his mouth and started to speak but Will cut him off. "Now I've had all I can take from you. That incident up on Schofield Pass was the last . . ."

The cigar came up quickly, and Jake pushed the lighted end into Will's eye. Will grabbed for Jake's hand but hit his elbow instead and the burning tobacco went deeper into his eye socket. He pulled the pistol's hammer back.

"Shoot him!" Luke shouted.

Jake continued to push at the cigar and Will's eye was on fire. Will felt for the trigger, found it and started to squeeze it as Jake ground the burning end in deeper. This was his own son, Will realized suddenly. Will took his finger away from the trigger, felt the pressure of Jake's hand lessen and, out of his good eye, saw Jake raise the other hand. He heard the smash of Luke's rifle butt as it crashed into the side of Jake's head and saw the man slump to the ground.

Jake's two hired guns ran off toward the hotel as Will dropped his Colt and covered his eye with both hands. The pain was intense and he wanted to cry out, but he forced himself to hold it in, groaning slightly. When he opened his good right eye he saw Jake lying on the ground with blood streaming down his face.

"Is he . . . ?" The pain spread to the back of his head. "Is he dead?"

Luke bent to Jake. "Nope. And it's too bad, too." He pulled on Will's elbow. "Come on. Can you get up? We better get you over to Tracey's."

Will tried to stand but couldn't seem to get his legs under him. "My God," he said through clenched teeth. "I ain't never hurt so bad."

A crowd had gathered but they hung back, staring at Jake's body and then swiveling their heads to Will. Jake's men reappeared with several others and they lifted Jake and carried him toward the hotel.

"Help me up," Will said. "I want to walk out of here."

"I'll get some help," Luke said.

"I said I want to walk. Give me a hand." He reached up with his right hand, his left still covering his eye, which was full of ashes. Luke took the hand, pulled Will to his feet and guided him toward the Cordell Hotel.

"Wait a minute!" Somebody shouted from the back of the crowd. "You forgot this." A young boy pushed his way through the men who had gathered around Will and Luke. In his hand he carried Will's tall Texas hat.

"Thanks, pardner," Will said. He felt better with the hat back on his head and tried to walk normally. *A Texas cowboy can take worse than this, he told himself.*

On the porch of the Cordell Hotel he stopped a moment. "Well," he said. "I sure did screw that one up." He took a deep breath, walked inside, sat down on a chair, and passed out.

❦

"YOU KNOW AS well as I do she'll never leave that town," Will said to Judith late in October. The snows had already begun, the color was gone, and the bleakness of another early winter had begun to settle over the valley.

Judith sat beside him at the kitchen table, a steaming cup of coffee in her hand. *She looks tired*, Will thought. *Tired and old like me.* "I hate to think of those two women spending the winter up there all alone," she said. "With Theresa pregnant and Thomas barely three years old . . ."

At Judith's insistence she and Will had pleaded with Tracey and Theresa to shut the hotel down for the winter and move in with them at the ranch, or to at least take rooms in Carbondale where they would be out of the worst of the winter and near a competent doctor. Both had adamantly refused, saying they were used to Marble by now and that the company doctor was available for Theresa when her time came, probably sometime in January.

Will fingered the black patch over his left eye and scratched beneath it, wanting to rub the eye which continued to smart and itch but knowing he shouldn't touch it.

"Does it hurt?" Judith asked.

"No, it doesn't hurt," he assured her for at least the thousandth time. "It just itches like hell."

"And you're still going to let Jake off scot-free?"

"I'll say it one more time." Will sighed and stared at his wife with his one good eye. "If I press charges I'll be the one ends up in jail since I started the fight in the first place. He knows if he raises too much of a stink his bootlegging will come up, along with his part in Tom's death. It's a standoff."

"It isn't fair."

Will nodded his agreement. "Not much is these days."

Two days later Henry and Reva stopped at the ranch.

"Marble is about to receive its just due," Henry said. "If you own land or buildings there you should sell immediately."

Will's good eye narrowed and he tried to smile at Henry as he tamped out his pipe at the fireplace. "Now why would you think that? My information is that the company's getting orders of up to $6,000 a day for mausoleums and monuments and other such. They're grossing nearly $150,000 a month. It'll take another year and a half to finish the Lincoln Memorial contract. And you're telling me to sell out?"

"Mark my words," Henry said. "I have other information."

"Like what?"

"There is a great deal of interest due, for one thing."

Will shrugged. "They'll handle it."

"I also hear that, with the country gearing up for war, the demand for marble is decreasing in favor of other types of building material."

Will studied his son. He was gaunt, pale, and too thin. "How's your church going?"

Henry let his eyes drop momentarily but raised them quickly. "Fine," he said.

"You broke?" Will asked.

Henry allowed both of his eyes to focus on Will's lone good one. "Not quite."

Will waited a while, then said, "You gonna make it?" Henry snapped upright, squared his shoulders. "God-uh will see us through this. But He will wreak havoc upon the evils in Marble as He did, yea even upon Sodom and Gomorrah."

"Amen," Reva piped.

"Oh, good Lord," Will sighed.

"THERESA HAD a girl!" Will shouted the news to Judith as he trudged up the snow-covered driveway to the house in late January of 1916. A rider had brought the letter from Redstone after it had come from Marble with a messenger on snowshoes.

"What did they name her?" Judith asked.

Will scanned the letter. "Martha, I guess. Tracey says 'little Martha and Theresa are doing well.'"

"Thank God."

"The rest of the news isn't so good." Will handed the letter to Judith. "You read it. My eye don't track so good through her kind of writing."

Judith put on her reading glasses and sat on the sofa. "She says the snow has been terrible since late December."

Tracey wrote that by mid-January the snow was six feet deep on the level. The electric trolley to the quarry was stopped and a hundred men used picks and shovels to clear the tracks. Since no marble could get to the mill, it ran short of material and work stopped. As soon as the track was cleared it seemed another storm blew in and covered it once again.

"Any word from Marcello?" Will asked. Judith shook her head.

Throughout the next few months there was little good news. In February the Germans attacked the French at Verdun, beginning the battle that would leave more than 700,000 men dead or wounded.

In late April, ten thousand British troops surrendered to the Turks at Kut-al-Amara rather than face starvation.

Still no word came from Marcello Barzini.

In June, Marble celebrated and, for a while at least, some of its residents were able to take their minds from the Great War and enjoy a special kind of victory of their own. On June 8, months ahead of schedule, the Colorado-Yule Marble Company completed its contract for the Lincoln Memorial. In the two years of work on the contract between five hundred and a thousand men had been employed at the quarries and finishing mill. The company had paid out an average of $95,000 a month in wages. Six hundred freight cars had been required to transport the marble to Washington, each car carrying from fifty to seventy thousand pounds of stone. Forty trains of fifteen cars each had carried the Colorado stone overland.

It had been an amazing feat. This small village, isolated in the central Rockies, had filled the largest single marble contract ever awarded in the United States.

Nationally, there was talk that the U.S. would eventually have to enter the war.

"We'll get into it," Luke stated. "You white people never could stay away from a fight."

Henry and Reva rode throughout the valley preaching the evils of war and predicting the eminent collapse of Marble.

Finally, a letter came from Marcello. Will was in Marble at the time and watched anxiously as Theresa took it to her room. She stayed there for more than three hours. Her eyes were red with weeping when she finally emerged. Marcello was alive, at least. His letter, she said, was full of love for all of them. He did not yet know he had a daughter. Though he glossed over the trials of war, Theresa felt much sorrow in his words.

❧

BARELY A WEEK into July, Judith stayed in bed one morning and was still there at noon. "It's nothing," she told a worried Will, who had brought Evey down from her own house to care for her stepmother. "I've probably got a touch of the flu. Maybe if I sleep a while longer . . ."

Will sat at her bedside, paced the floor, went outside for brief periods of time, and ate little. Judith looked bad to him. Her face was drawn and she had begun to lose weight.

"I'm taking her to Dr. Castle," he told Evey.

Judith refused. "I'm feeling better," she said.

"You ought to have a checkup, anyway."

"I will. Later in the summer."

Three days later, though she looked tired and thin, she insisted she was back to normal and tried to prove it with her outward behavior. She was up early and prepared a big breakfast for Will. Relieved, he went to the barn.

"It's going to be tough this winter," Luke told him. "People aren't spending money on horseflesh like they used to. It's the war scare. You all right?"

"Of course I'm all right! Why?"

"No reason," Luke said, but he looked worried.

"Nothing wrong with me," Will said. To prove it, he offered to take Judith on a trip to Marble.

"You go," she said. "I'm still a bit weak. I need some more rest." She laughed. "Maybe with you gone I can get some."

"I haven't been bothering you any," Will said. "Not that I wouldn't like to."

They laughed together and Will hugged her tightly, feeling slack skin and a frighteningly narrow waist.

Marble should have looked almost deserted in midafternoon. Men should have been laboring in the quarries or at the mill. Instead, small groups stood here and there on the streets, scuffing at the dirt, smoking, talking quietly. "It may be over," Tracey said in reply to his question. "The company went bankrupt yesterday."

355

Will hung his hat on the rack by the door. "But I thought it was making good money."

"Not enough, I hear. They owe nearly three and half million dollars, mostly in bonds."

Will whistled. "And they don't have it."

"Not nearly. How's Judith?"

Quickly, Will told her about his wife's illness. "But she's better. Just a touch of the flu. Where's that baby?"

Tracey took Will upstairs and Theresa willingly let him take the six-month-old Martha from her. "She needs a father figure," she said.

"Any word?" Will asked. She shook her head. "I'm sure he's fine."

Theresa smiled. "I know he is."

In August, Italy declared war on Germany.

WILL PAID LITTLE attention to the war news because Judith was in bed again. This time he wasted no time in getting her to see Dr. Castle. The man kept her in his small hospital overnight and Will found a room at the hotel. Early the next morning he was at her bedside.

"I'd be feeling better except for that awful examination he gave me," she said, forcing a smile.

"Pretty rough on you?"

She leaned toward Will and whispered. "He poked into places no man but you should be allowed."

Will reddened, coughed and recovered. "Want me to get my gun?"

She laughed low, let her head fall back on the pillow. "Just don't let him do it again. And take me home."

Will took her hand and they chatted about meaningless things for a while until the doctor came into the room. Will stood and let the man sit in the chair by the bed. "What's the story?" Will asked.

Dr. Castle took Judith's hand. "I'm glad you're here," he said to Will. He turned back to Judith and looked into her eyes. "I'm afraid I have bad news."

Will saw fear in Judith's face, felt his knees go weak and sat on the edge of her bed, taking her other hand in his own. For a long moment they sat that way, the two men each holding one of her hands.

"Well?" She took a deep breath. "Let's have it."

The doctor swallowed. "You have a cancer," he said. "In the uterus."

Judith gasped and Will felt the shock of fear sweep through him. "A cancer? But . . . ?" Judith turned her head to the side and tears welled in her eyes.

"I'm sorry," Dr. Castle said. He lifted his eyes to Will and shook his head.

"But . . ." Will cleared his throat. "How bad . . . ?"

Dr. Castle shook his head again. "Very bad, I'm afraid."

"You mean . . . she might?"

"Not might." Castle kept his eyes on Will's. Judith's face was buried in the pillow. Will felt her grip tighten on his hand. "I wish there was another way to tell you."

Will bent to Judith and kissed her lightly on her neck. His head was swimming, his stomach churning. He wanted to lie down beside her and take her in his arms. But Judith was tough. She lifted her head and turned to her longtime friend. "How long?"

Castle cleared his own throat. "I'm not sure. Maybe six months. Maybe a year."

Will felt nausea wash over him. Judith's head fell back. "So little time."

"Surely there's something you can do!" Will was on his feet. Now he was angry. "This is 1916, damn it! The wonders of modern medicine ought to be able to cure her!"

Castle stood and faced Will, then took his arm. "I agree," he said. "But cancer is one of the least-understood diseases in the world. We don't know what causes it. We can't cure it."

Will jerked his arm away. "Surgery! You can operate."

"I could," Castle replied, the sadness showing in his face. "But it would do no good."

Will let himself fall back to the bed. He took Judith's hand again and pressed it to his lips.

"I am so terribly sorry," Castle said again. He stood over them looking totally helpless.

"I know," Judith said, her voice hoarse. "Leave us alone now, will you?"

The doctor stood there a few seconds more, then nodded and left. The two of them cried without saying anything to one another. Soon, Will lay down beside her and put his arm beneath her head. She snuggled into him. When he could speak again, Will put his lips to her ear. "I don't know what to say," he whispered. "Except that I love you more than life itself. I wish it was me."

Within half an hour Dr. Castle returned to the room and gave Judith a sedative. Judith reached for Will's hand. "Don't leave," she said with pleading in her eyes.

"I'm not going to ever leave you," he replied, then lay down beside her again and didn't move until her regular breathing told him she had finally fallen asleep.

He slipped from her side and walked to the window. Across the street three children ran screaming after one another in a game of tag. A man and a woman drove past in a wagon laden with store-bought goods. A lady hung washing out to dry. Life went on, oblivious to the painful fact that Judith had just been told that, in all probability, she had less than a year to live.

Will put his hands on the windowsill, leaned forward and pressed his forehead against the coolness of the glass. Judith was going to die. In a very short time she would be gone from his life and he would have to bury her in the rocky ground of the Crystal Valley. But first, for months — perhaps a year — she would suffer. All of them would suffer with her and then, like Tom and Ardy and the others, she would be gone. *Judith is going to die*, he thought, *and there isn't a blessed thing I or anyone else can do about it.*

He rolled his forehead against the window glass, clenched his fists, ground his teeth. "God," he whispered. "God damn it to hell."

He marveled at how many times he had been close to death and survived. And for what? Why couldn't he have the disease instead of her? Why did God allow this to happen to good people? Yolanda Peabody would probably live to be a hundred, he thought scornfully. Jake would survive and continue to be a menace. But Judith was going to die.

❧

EVEY BROKE DOWN when Will told her the news, and Luke took her away into their bedroom. Joshua listened silently and then ran from the house. Will sat with Esther for a while. When Luke came out of the bedroom with red eyes of his own, Will went looking for the twelve-year-old boy.

He found him sitting by the creek, his head in his hands. Will sat down near Josh. He picked up a pebble and tossed it into the water, waiting.

"Grandad?" Good, Will thought. The boy wants to talk.

"Yeah?"

"Dad always said that whatever happens has some good in it if you love God."

"That's what the Book says, I reckon."

Josh studied the ground for a while. When he spoke his voice was barely audible over the gurgle of the creek. "Doesn't Gran love God?"

Will moved closer, rested his weight on his right hand that nested on the ground just behind Josh, allowing him to put his arm around him without seeming to. "Sure she does."

Josh looked away. "She must not. No good can come of her dying."

"Sure doesn't seem like it, does it? Look, Josh. I don't pretend to have many answers. But everyone dies sooner or later. I reckon your Gran's time is just sooner." Will's heart was beating fast. He'd done little more than think about Judith in the days since they had received the news. It was a cruel joke.

358

There was no reasoning it out. How could he talk about it to a young boy who has nothing but long life and the possibility of so many good things ahead of him?

"Will she hurt? I mean, is she going to . . . suffer?"

Will put his hand on the boy's shoulder. "Probably so, Josh. But your Gran's a tough old gal."

Josh was crying. "I don't want her to hurt. I wish she would just die and get it over with."

"Well, now." The same thought had crossed Will's mind. "I kinda think she'd like to stick around a while longer, hurt or no hurt, just to see you and Esther get a little bit older. We've got to put on a good face for her when she comes home. You can do a lot to make her feel better."

"I can?" Josh looked up at his grandfather.

"Sure. Let her know you love her. Take her flowers. Stuff like that."

"I will," Josh said.

"Good boy."

"But Grandad?"

"Yep?"

"I don't understand God."

Will hugged the boy tighter, shook his head. "Neither do I, boy. Neither do I."

HE BROUGHT JUDITH home the last day of August. She walked into the house, made a fuss about the mess and scolded Will. He and Evey had picked a bunch of wildflowers and had them in vases here and there. Judith went from bunch to bunch, smelling and touching them.

Joshua and Esther showed up with more flowers. Josh handed his bouquet to her, couldn't look at her, and ran from the house crying. Esther seemed bewildered by it all. Evey and Luke brought food and everybody tried too hard all evening to smile and laugh and to talk about anything but Judith's illness.

In the middle of the meal she banged her cup down hard on the table. "Listen," she said. "I've tried to go along with this but it's time we put all the cards on the table."

Evey glanced at Josh. "Maybe the children . . ."

"They should stay and hear this." Judith stood straight. "Josh is almost a man now and little Esther can figure things out as much as she can by herself."

Will leaned back, took a breath, wished his heart would stop pounding. "I don't think I can handle this," he said.

Judith snapped a sharp look at him. "Yes, you can, Will Martin. You've been in tighter scrapes than this." She looked at each of them in turn. "I'm going to die," she said. "I've cried and I've fought and I've even swore at God Himself and I've got it all out of my system. I'm going to die."

Esther turned to her mother. "Is Gran going to die?"

"Hush, child," Evey said.

But Judith took Esther in her arms and hugged her. "Yes, I am," she said. "One day soon I will go to heaven and live with Jesus."

"Daddy says heaven is nice," Esther said, playing with the lace on her grandmother's dress.

"It is nice." Judith looked at the others. "I'm not particularly looking forward to the trip but it's one I've got to take and I've come to terms with it. It's time all of you did, too." She handed Esther back to Evey and sat at the table again. "No more pretending. No more skirting the issue. Be sad if you want and get it over with. But don't sit around here laughing at things that aren't that funny just because you think it'll make me feel better. What will make me feel better is to know I'm loved and that I've got somebody to turn to. Understand?"

Everyone, including Josh, nodded.

"Feel better?" Will asked, trying to smile.

"You know," she said. "I think I do."

∞ુ∾

TWO DAYS LATER Tracey, Theresa, Teegee and the baby, Martha, showed up. Tracey cried but, after a few minutes alone with Judith in the kitchen, she came out dry-eyed.

"She give you the speech about treating her normal?" asked Will.

Tracey nodded. "She is some woman, that wife of yours."

"She is that. How're things in Marble?"

"Worse than ever. Half the town burned last week."

"What?"

"It started in the middle of the night. They finally had to dynamite the Swigart Grocery to get it under control. We lost six buildings and the damage may be about $40,000."

"Some people are saying it was set for the insurance money," Theresa said. "But the buildings were insured for only about half of their worth."

"Any damage to the hotel?" Will asked.

"No, luckily. But, with the company practically shut down and half the men out of work, I wonder if anyone will rebuild."

Evey stood and chuckled. "Something funny?" Theresa asked.

"Not exactly funny," Evey said. "I was just thinking about Henry. No doubt he'll blame it on greed and lust."

"Not necessarily in that order," Judith said and joined in the laughter.

It was good to see her laugh, Will thought. She looked thinner, worn, tired. *And no wonder*, reasoned Will. *Lord, she is tough.*

They visited for a while until the younger women left to prepare dinner. Will was left alone with Judith and Tracey. Their conversation soon died and the room fell silent. He stared at the two women, one at a time. In the mirror across the room he could see himself. Three old people, graying and wrinkled, sat around cooling coffee cups in comfortable chairs while the young ones worked and played somewhere else.

Two of the three women he had ever loved in his life now sat close to him. In their old age both were still beautiful to him. Tracey, slender and tall, was the younger of the two at fifty-nine. Will and Judith were both sixty-six. Judith, though not as round and full as only a few years earlier, still carried her body well. Soon, he thought, she would grow gaunt. Will saw himself in the mirror, and realized he was heavier than he had ever been, though he certainly didn't have the large potbelly carried by many men his age. There was more silver hair in the room, he thought, than in a stable full of old gray mares.

JUDITH FOUGHT her disease like a man fighting a wounded grizzly. She refused to let Will see her when she was in pain. "I'm not going to let it get to me," she said. "It's not really that bad." She rested more than she had before and turned in early, but her rapidly thinning face always had a smile for Will or the others. "I'm doing just fine," she insisted.

There was little work in Marble. Fewer than two hundred men had jobs at the company whose president, J. F. Manning, was turned down by the court when he asked for permission to issue receiver's certificates to meet the $20,000-a-month payroll. A district court in Denver ordered the plant shut down as soon as existing contracts were filled.

There was still no letter from Marcello.

In September, the British used tanks for the first time. In December, Judith weighed less than 120 pounds and was in almost constant pain. In February of 1917 the Germans began unrestricted submarine warfare, saying its subs would sink any vessel bound into or out of any Allied port. By that time, Evey was doing the cooking for both families because Judith was barely strong enough to walk to the table. In March, the Germans torpedoed several

American merchant ships without warning. In April they sank nearly a million tons of Allied shipping.

On April 6, 1917, the U.S. declared war on Germany. And on April 15, the Colorado-Yule Marble Company, unable to refinance its debts, ceased operations completely. The town that had produced well over a million cubic feet of rough and finished marble and that had earned nearly five and a half million dollars since 1908 was dying.

Judith Martin was also dying. Her large blue eyes seemed doubly large in her sunken face. Her arms, once full and soft, were thin and scaly. Her voice, once deep and joyful, was little more than a whisper. Her laugh was gone.

Henry and Reva came in November, December, and in January and were each time turned away by Judith. They came in February and March and Will told them to leave her alone.

Then, in June, she began to feel better. She sat up in bed, and ate most of a meal for the first time in weeks. She asked Will to find his Texas hat and put it on for her. When he did, she laughed. "You were the finest man I ever saw," she said.

"I still am," Will replied.

In mid-June Carbonate Creek and the Crystal River went on a rampage, swollen with spring runoff, and washed out the railroad tracks in several places below Marble. The wagon road over Schofield Pass had been torn away by a rock slide the previous year. Nobody had bothered to repair it because they had the railroad to Carbondale. Now it, too, was gone.

In July, not quite a year after Dr. Castle had found the cancer, Judith Martin died. Her family was by her side but they doubted she was aware of their presence. She went quietly in her sleep.

They buried her on the hill near Ardy's grave and Will told Luke he wanted to lie beside her when his own time came. Somehow, Henry knew of her death and showed up at her burial. Against his better judgment, Will allowed Henry to pray over the grave.

"Oh great and glorious God-uh," Henry intoned. "Take this woman into your bosom and comfort her on her journey to eternal life. Care for and comfort this grieving family in their hour of trial. Let all who continue to live in this valley of death come to full realization of your great dominion and power so they may come to you with contrite hearts asking for forgiveness for their manifold sins and . . ."

"Henry," Will said. The man turned to him, his eyes ablaze with the power of God and his arms opened wide. "Henry," Will said. "That's enough."

WILL REACHED the ledge at Owl Point by midmorning on legs so heavy he could barely lift them. Somehow he managed and found his comfortable seat on the big rock, and caught his breath as he scanned the valley. With Redstone barely visible in the trees and the road that paralleled the Crystal River free of traffic, it looked more like it did back in '83 when he climbed to Owl Point for the first time.

"You all right?" Luke asked.

Will snorted at him, wiped sweat from his neck, and lifted the eye patch to dab at pooling perspiration. "It'll take more'n a little climb like this to do me in," he said. "Hell, I'm only sixty-seven, not quite Methuselah yet."

Luke flashed a grin. "Didn't mean to make you mad."

"Not mad."

"Good. I'm going to show Josh where I think I was born. You have a good time."

When the two had disappeared into the aspen grove behind him to his left, he took a deep breath and let it out in a whoosh. It had been a hard climb and his chest was heaving mightily. *Not quite Methuselah but damn near*, Will thought. Finally, his breathing slowed and the sun warmed his back. *If Judith were here she'd massage my shoulders*, he thought. She had been dead only two months and he still couldn't convince himself she wouldn't be there when he got home. *Lord, she was a woman*, he thought. For a while he remembered.

Footsteps crunching in the dirt behind him snapped him out of his reverie. He turned to Luke and Josh. The boy was only thirteen but he was growing fast. *Might be he'll get as tall as Luke*, Will thought.

"I saw where Dad thinks he was born," Josh said. "His mother said it was in an aspen grove. That must be it." Josh sat on the red dirt beside Will's rock and stared out over the valley. After a while he looked up at his grandfather. "Is this the cliff Owl Man fell off?"

"Not fell," Will said. "Jumped."

"Tell me about the ghosts, Grandad."

"I told you before," Will said. He'd been expecting to feel their presence but, so far, had no indication they were still there. *Too many people around*, he thought.

"Tell me again. Please."

Will bent a leg and cupped his hands around a knee. He didn't really mind telling the story. "This place is called Owl Point," he began. "Owl Man named it that after his first vision which was brought to him by *otus asio*, the owl, and by the small birds and the eagle. It is *ihupi'arat tubut*, a haunted place where ghosts dwell." He stopped and closed his eye. He suddenly realized they were there, all around him. Welcome, they said. Welcome.

363

"Grandad? Go on."

"Owl Man was *po'rat*," he told Josh, and heard Luke settle on the ground behind him. Will felt the *ini'pute* in the air like a thousand hummingbirds and smiled to himself. "He was a holy man with powers that allowed him to see the future. Inside Owl Man had lived the *powa'a*, a tiny being who directed the use of his power."

Did a tiny being live in him now? Will wondered, but he could not foresee the future. He had never claimed he could. "Owl Man had healed the *Nunt'z*, the People, and had tried to warn them that the white man's coming would lead to disaster," Will continued. The *ini'pute* were quiet now, and his voice trailed off.

"Grandad?"

Will heard Luke push himself to his feet. "Come on, Josh," he said. "Let's take a walk. Let your Grandad rest."

That's right, Will thought. He was tired. He let himself slide onto the ground and propped himself up against the rock with his hat tipped over his eyes. The sun was warm and he was comfortable. He slept.

In his dream, the valley was quiet. There were no white men to be seen, no human forms at all. Deer walked unafraid to the river's edge to drink. Eagles soared and a bear fished in an eddy. But there was a road beside the river, a white man's road. The coke ovens were there, but they were silent.

Then, suddenly, there was activity. The deer bounded into the trees and disappeared. The bear stood on his hind legs and sniffed the air, fell to all fours, and hurried away. The eagle screeched. A vehicle came down the road puffing smoke. More vehicles arrived, and with them, people. They hurried and shouted and sweated and carried anxious looks in their eyes. A man lay dead. Will tried to make out the face but it was covered by a shroud. Somehow, he knew the body was that of one of his sons. But which one? He strained to see, crept closer to the body, reached for the shroud to pull it from the face.

"Leave him alone."

"But . . ."

"Don't touch him."

The voices weren't part of the dream. It was Josh and Luke. Will opened his eyes and tipped back his hat.

"It's all right," he said. "I'm awake." He sat up too quickly and he was dizzy. The sun blinded him. Which son had it been? What had the dream meant? Will wondered.

"Sorry," Luke said. "Josh wanted to tell you something."

"It's all right," Will said again. He looked at the red ground and the dizziness left. "What is it, boy?"

364

Josh's face gave away his excitement. "I just made a decision. Owl Man was kind of a doctor, wasn't he?"

Will nodded. *"Po'rat."* The *ini'pute* were gone. He wondered if they had given him the dream.

Josh knelt beside him and looked him in the eye. "I'm going to be a doctor, too."

"Well," Will said. "Well, now. That's good. Because of Owl Man?"

"Partly, I guess. But when Gran was sick I wanted to be able to help her and I couldn't. Maybe if I'm a doctor I can help somebody else someday."

Will smiled and pushed himself to a sitting position. "That's mighty fine thinking, Josh. I'm proud."

"Are you ready to go back down? I want to go tell Mom."

"I'm ready," Will said. "And Josh?" He let the boy help him to his feet.

"Yes?"

"You remember that talk we had when you asked me if I believed everything worked out to some good in God's eyes?"

"I remember."

"Well, if your Gran's dying helped you decide to become a doctor, maybe that's the good that'll come of her dying."

Josh's eyes widened. "Maybe so," he said. "I never thought of that."

They worked their way down the mountainside and Will guided them to an area that was heavily overgrown with scrub oak. "I buried Owl Man around here somewhere," he said. "Don't suppose I could find the place anymore."

"Let him be," Luke said. "He'd want it that way."

"I think he would," Will agreed.

"I BOUGHT this Colt back in the late 1870s." Will spun the chamber and Josh, sitting beside him, reached for the gun. Will checked again to see that it was empty and handed it to the boy. He leaned back against the pine tree and watched a leaf float down the stream.

"It's heavy," Josh said.

"You can coldcock a man with that, or shoot him with it."

"Did you ever shoot a man with it, Grandad?"

Will took it back and replaced it in the holster in his lap. "Nope. Never clubbed anyone with it, either. Bat Masterson taught me how to use it, though."

Josh tossed a twig in the creek. "How long does it take to become a doctor?"

"Long time, I reckon."

Another day he and the boy were up in the corrals. "Me'n Sagebrush Tom used to be in the saddle from 'fore sunup 'til after dark, herdin' the damn cows. It's why I'm so bowlegged, don't cha know."

"Does it cost a lot of money to go to medical school?"

"Prob'ly. You don't need to worry about that."

Will sat in the kitchen with Evey and watched her prepare a Sunday dinner. "When we rode the Goodnight-Loving Trail back before 1870 we had a cook named Cookie who didn't know how to cook nothin' but beans and biscuits. Months and months of nothin' but beans and biscuits."

"Dinner is ready," Evey said. "Call the others."

Luke coiled his lariat and watched a hired hand work a horse, teaching it to neck-rein. Luke had filled out in the upper body. His hair was still long, falling to his shoulders, but he had given up the black pants he used to wear in favor of the more comfortable and durable Levis.

"Back on the Palo Duro we'd ride 'em 'til they was broke and then take 'em out to work the damned cows." Will sat on the railing and fired up his pipe. "Smaller ponies, then. Not like these big things you'n Evey raise. Now, Jeremiah, the horse I rode into this valley back in 1880 . . ."

"'Scuse me, Will, but I need to check on something," Luke said, striding toward the barn.

In Marble, Will held Martha Barzini in his lap and balanced Teegee on a knee. Thomas Guido was barely five and Martha was only a year old. "Wyatt Earp and Doc Holliday and me, we was regulars in the Long Branch. And Bat Masterson, too. That was after I met your granddaddy on the Brazos. Me'n Tom, we'd go into Waco and have us one . . ."

"You'd go into Waco and what?" Tracey and Theresa stood in the doorway and grinned at him.

"Well, we'd have a bath and a shave."

Theresa took the children to bed as Tracey lowered the lamps. "Bedtime already?" Will asked.

"For the little ones."

Will looked at her with his one good eye and tried to wink but it looked more like a blink, he figured. "Bedtime for you, too?"

"You're a dirty old man."

"I'm not so old."

"You're right." She stood in the lamplight and, at that moment, it might have been 1880 and Randall Collins might have been upstairs somewhere wearing a black hood and Doc might have been asleep after doing his kitchen chores and Will and Tracey might have been looking forward to a full night together. In the half light she looked young again and Will felt the old, familiar hunger.

"Tracey?"

She walked to him, and gave him a hug. "What?"

"Are we too old? Is it too late?"

She pushed him back and kissed him on the cheek below the patch. "No to both questions. But I'm tired and I'm going to bed. Alone."

She went upstairs and Will walked to the porch. He stood there a while in the silence sucking on a dead pipe. He looked down the street toward the White House Hotel where Yolanda Peabody still lived, practically alone now that Jake had left town. There was a faint glow behind the curtains of a second-story window but that was all. Nobody played the piano anymore.

Here and there a light glowed in one of the buildings where somebody still lived or worked. The hundred or so people who remained in Marble did so out of habit, he supposed. More than thirteen hundred people had abandoned the town in the past months since the quarry shut down.

He yawned, tamped out his pipe, hitched up his pants and went up to bed.

IN JANUARY of 1918, President Woodrow Wilson announced his fourteen points as the basis for peace. But through the spring the Germans launched offensives along the Somme, at Ypres and on the Aisne. In June, after American Marines captured Belleau Wood, Will told Tracey they ought to get married and she turned him down flat.

"Why not? I'll build us a house on the ranch and Theresa and the little ones can come, too."

"That's why, for one reason. We're not leaving here. When Marcello comes home, I want him home, in Marble."

"I'll move up here."

She patted his hand. "Don't look so sad. You'll never move off that ranch."

He put his hands on her still-slim waist and saw her eyes fill up. "Now who's sad?"

She rested her cheek on his shoulder. "It is sad, Will. But I'm too set in my ways now. And I'd be a poor follow-up to Judith."

He thought about it. "And me to Tom." They stood that way and remembered. "Old Sagebrush Tom," Will said. "I'm glad he had you, for a while." He stroked her gray hair. "I remember one time out on the Llano Estacado, me'n Tom and another cowboy, think his name was Bob — yep, it was Bob — me'n Tom and Bob, we was just . . ."

"Will," she said. "I don't want to hear about it now."

367

"Well," he said. "All right. After we're married . . ."

"Will you just shut up?"

THE ASPEN LEAVES were barely tinged with the colors of autumn when Will got sick and tired of sitting around the ranch doing nothing. He saddled a horse named Amos and set off for Aspen with a saddlebag full of Evey's muffins. The trip was uneventful except for waving at folks in wagons, and having to calm Amos after a horseless carriage — a Chevrolet or a Ford, he never could tell the difference — spooked the animal into a jump and Will almost fell off.

Aspen was not quite as silent as Marble but it was just as sad. "Why all the hangdog looks?" he asked a man in a bar.

"Ain't you heard? They pulled the pumps that have been keeping the water out of the Free Silver Shaft on Smuggler Mountain for the past nine years."

Will sipped a beer. "Finally got her dried out, huh?"

The man looked up. "They shut her down. There won't be any mining worth nothin' around here no more."

"Well," Will said. "That about does it, then."

"Yep. That does it."

Will mounted Amos and rode up and down quiet streets of empty homes. Two-story houses lined the thoroughfare. Paint peeled and porches tilted. Windows were broken and weeds littered yards. There were fewer than seven hundred people in Aspen which, not that long ago, had boasted a population of twelve thousand.

Will remembered the night he and Ardy had watched in wonderment as the miners carried their tin "gads" up and down the trails on Aspen Mountain looking like hundreds of fireflies as they changed shifts at midnight. It was a sight no one would ever see again. He thought of Henry Gillespie and the millions he made and lost in a few years' time. He rode past the fire-blackened remains of the Wheeler Opera House and remembered the light in Judith's face after their evening there.

Now it was definitely over. He paused on the bank of the Roaring Fork and looked back at Aspen Mountain. Henry Gillespie had said Aspen would not be another Leadville or Creede or Cripple Creek, a here-today, gone-tomorrow boomtown. There was a glorious future for the town as a cultural oasis in the wilderness, he had said. Now, he looked back and was glad, in a way, that Henry Gillespie hadn't lived to see this day. He looked at Aspen Mountain, at Smuggler Mountain, and thought also about Tourtelotte Park and Lenado and Richmond Hill and Highlands and Ashcroft and all the rest that had produced more than $100 million in silver.

"Too bad," he said aloud, and remembered the similar quiet that pervaded the Crystal River Valley. He thought of the crumbling coke ovens at Redstone, the unused railroad tracks and the tomblike, cold depths of the unworked marble quarries. He also thought of Tracey and Theresa up in Crystal, and he thought sadly that a lot of good people had sure worked their butts off for nothing.

There was a letter from Abby when Will arrived back at the ranch. Jerome B. Wheeler, the man who had built the Hotel Jerome and the Wheeler Opera House, was dead. He had managed to make some money again, she wrote, and had planned to redeem the tax title on the opera house.

"Too bad," Luke said.

Will glanced through the rest of the letter and tossed it on the table. It was mainly about clothes and shopping, since she had written it to Evey.

"Everybody dies," he said sharply. His knees hurt when he got to his feet and he was tired when he got back to his house — his and Judith's. But he couldn't get to sleep and sat up much of the night thinking about death. The death of women and men and towns that had once been so alive.

On November 9, Kaiser Wilhelm II of Germany abdicated and two days later Germany signed the armistice.

"HENRY'S GLOATING that his predictions all came true," Tracey told Will in the spring of 1919. "He said Marble would fall and now that it has he seems almost happy."

"Make *me* happy and marry me," Will said.

She sighed. "Oh, Will."

"For the first time since we've known each other — almost forty years — we're free to do it. Don't make sense not to."

"It does to me." She busied herself with a dust rag. "After Tom and Judith . . . it would be as though we'd just been waiting for them to die."

"Oh, good Lord," Will said, got on old Amos and went back down valley. At least the horse felt good under him. He hated wagons and hated the thought of automobiles even more.

Will had tried to talk Luke out of buying that 1916 Chevrolet but the Indian had been determined. The thing was as black as Henry's surrey and noisy as a steam locomotive. It had room for four people and a cloth top that kept the rain off. Luke treated it like one of his horses: He washed and polished it, and started it up every day or so just to make sure it would still run. It had an electric starter and didn't require the cranking of the old days.

Will went for a ride in it once at Luke's insistence. He admitted it was more comfortable than a wagon but, Lord, he thought, was it noisy! They rode it to Carbondale now and then, and that was about all. Once in a while the family would all pile in without Will and go for a "drive" up and down the road for an hour or so. Then they'd come home and Luke would polish it some more and put it away.

It had big rubber wheels, white on the outside. Two headlights meant they could even drive it at night. Will figured that pretty soon there'd be nothing but automobiles and no need for horses. *Sorry damned world when a man would rather ride in a tin can than on a good horse*, Will thought bitterly.

Just north of Dark Canyon and about at the spot where Will had met Daniel Swensson, Judith's first husband, he saw Henry and Reva coming south in their old black surrey. He found some shade and draped a leg over the saddle horn.

"Nice day for a ride," he said as they pulled alongside.

"It's a nice day for anything," Henry said.

"Glad to see you so happy." Will packed his pipe and studied his son. Henry was in his mid-thirties but looked fifty with dark bags beneath his eyes, lines on his face, and a graying mustache.

Reva peeked around Henry's shoulder. "Henry is building a congregation in Marble," she said, and then disappeared behind her husband.

"Many of those who scoffed at me when I predicted ruin are now joining my flock," Henry said. "Finally, we are seeing the fruits of our labor. The fields of the Lord are indeed fertile."

Will drew on his pipe. He exhaled smoke and waved it away from his face. "Usually are when times are bad," Will said, but when he saw Henry's face cloud over he said, "Forget it. I'm glad for you."

Reva nudged Henry and he nodded. "We must push on. The work of God-uh awaits, you know."

"Yep. Well, you two have a good time now. Hear?" Will sat in the shade while he finished his pipe and thought about Tracey and Yolanda Peabody too. *Two old women tryin' to hang onto the past. Didn't make any sense why any of 'em stayed up there.*

He went on down to the ranch and moped around for a week. Nobody seemed to want to hear about the old days.

One late afternoon he was sitting in a rocking chair on the front porch trying to work up enough gumption to repaint the house when he saw a man standing in the road looking toward the house. He had a duffel bag thrown over his shoulder. Will stood as the man headed for the house. It was hard to make out who it might be with only one good eye so Will squinted and strained to see. The man wore a dirty gray uniform with a peaked cap.

"Is that you there, Mr. Martin?" The man dropped the duffel bag in the yard and took off his cap.

"Marcello!" Will stood and swallowed. He dropped his pipe and lumbered down off the porch. "Marcello Barzini! Well, I'll be damned."

Marcello flashed a smile as big as Italy when Will hugged him tight. "I have come home," he said. "You are fine?"

"Hell, yes, I'm fine! But you? How are you, boy? Why didn't you let somebody know you were coming?"

"I want to surprise them all," Marcello said.

Will held him at arm's length. "You'll do that, all right." He looked the boy up and down. "You look fine, son, just fine. No wounds?"

Marcello shook his head. "Nothing of which I should speak. I mean, nothing to speak of. I am healthy as one of your big horses."

Will laughed. "I think you are, at that. You mean the women don't know you're coming home?"

"They know, but not when. I have been, how you say, hopping the train."

"Riding the rails. Sneakin' rides on freight cars all the way from . . . from where?"

"From New York City."

"Well, I'll be . . . come on in here, boy. We got to get you cleaned up and fed and then up to Marble."

While Evey fawned over the returned soldier, Will went to the barn. Luke found him there. "What are you doing?"

"What do you think? I'm gettin' some horses ready so Marcello and me can head for Marble."

"Tonight?"

"Why, hell yes, tonight. Wouldn't you want to see Evey if you'd been gone that long?"

"You're right. But put that stuff back. We'll take him up in the automobile."

"I ain't ridin' in that thing clear to Marble." Will started out the door with a saddle but Luke caught his arm.

"You stay here, then. I'll take him and we'll be in Marble in less than two hours. How long will it take you on a horse?"

Will couldn't fault the logic. "Hell," he said. "I 'spose you're right." He swung the saddle over a rail. "Never thought I'd see the day . . ."

Luke grinned in the gathering darkness. "Come on, then. Or are you staying here by yourself?"

"Everybody goin'?"

"You bet!"

Luke was out the door and heading for the shed where he kept the Chevrolet. Will followed along, mumbling to himself that he wasn't going to stay there all alone. "I'm gonna see this reunion even if I do have to ride in that damned contraption. It'll wake up everybody between here and there. Damned thing anyway . . ."

It was almost midnight when they puffed into Marble. The car had made the trip easily but Will's legs hurt from holding ten-year-old Esther on his lap and being cramped up beside Evey, who rode between Will and Josh.

Luke screeched to a halt in front of the boarding house and squeezed the horn. The *oogah* echoed down the empty street. A light went on in a second-floor room. Marcello was out of his seat before the car came to a complete stop. He banged on the front door. "Theresa! Thomas! And Martha! Come! I am home!" Luke kept squeezing the horn and the awful oogah brought others to windows and doors.

The door flew open and Theresa was in his arms then and Tracey stood in the background crying. Luke kept *oogahing* until a dozen people had crowded around the car applauding while Marcello and Theresa hugged and kissed and cried, and looked at each other and hugged and kissed and cried some more. Teegee, not yet seven, rubbed his eyes and screamed when the strange man lifted him high in the air, and he ran to his mother when Marcello put him down. Then Marcello held, for the first time, two-and-a-half-year- old Martha, who looked at him with big eyes and smiled a welcome.

Marcello finally got to hug Tracey. He shook hands with some of the townspeople before they began to wander back to their own beds, and then everyone trooped inside.

At dawn, Will went outside and packed his pipe. The children had fallen asleep within an hour of their father's arrival but the adults had stayed up.

Luke came outside and joined Will on the stoop. "Feels good out here," he said. "You ever see anyone so happy?"

"Don't think I ever did," Will replied. "It sure is fine." He rubbed his good eye with a fist. "You think those two will ever get some time to themselves?"

Luke chuckled. "They've got time. All their lives."

Will nodded at the sun that was beaming through a cut in the eastern mountains. He thought of Judith and wished she was there to see it all. He thought of Tracey and wished she'd give in and marry him. *They'd have all the rest of their lives, too, but it sure wasn't as long as Marcello and Theresa had*, Will thought.

"What are you thinking about?" Luke asked.

Will jerked up his head. "Women," he said. "What else?"

❧❧

SOMETIME AROUND his seventieth birthday, Will leaned back in the overstuffed chair that had sat near the living room's fireplace since he and Judith had built the place. He smiled at his preacher son. "Why, things are goin' just fine, boy. And thanks for askin'."

Henry and Reva sat together on the sofa. *They don't look much different than they did the first time they came by*, Will thought, *only older*. "Is your health good?" Reva asked.

"I'm not plannin' on passin' over to the other side right away, if that's what you mean."

Henry's face took on its preacher look. "But one never knows, does one?"

"Guess one never does, at that."

"Have you thought about the consequences of dying without accepting Jesus Christ as your Lord and Savior? What if you died tomorrow? Would you be ready?"

Will lifted the patch and scratched his eyelid. "Ready and willing. Don't do much but take up room anymore."

"I am here to offer eternal life," Henry said.

"Thank you, son." Will straightened. "I'll take it."

"You will?"

"Yeah, I will. I have been feelin' a bit down lately. My shoulder here, where Peabody shot me 'fore I killed him? Been hurtin' some lately, like arthritis or somethin'. And my frostbit toes. They do squeal when I get out in the snow. My ankle's a bit weak, too, where that horse stepped on it. 'Member the night Luke brought me in and all of you — you two and Jake and all — was here? Kind of weak, it is."

"Yes, but you . . ."

"And in the summertime, when I get to sweatin', the rope burns on my neck turn red as hellfire — 'scuse me — as a rose. And do they itch."

"Jesus says . . ."

"I remember one time Sagebrush Tom'n me was pushin' a bunch of cows down that old Indian trail into the Palo Duro Canyon. Tom took off his bandanna and started wavin' it like a flag. Now, me'n Tom . . ."

"We have to be on our way to Marble," Henry interrupted. He and Reva stood as one. At the door Henry turned to his father. "Why don't you and Tracey Cordell get married? I would officiate without charge."

Will scratched his chin. "Why, now, that's a good idea. I'll think on it. Without charge, huh?"

❧❧

373

LATER HE TOLD Tracey about Henry's offer and she laughed. "Do you think it would be legal if he didn't charge us anything?"

"Wouldn't much matter to me if it was legal or not."

She shooed him away when he tried to kiss her on the cheek. "I liked you better when you were married."

"If you'd marry me I'd be married."

When she turned away and didn't answer he thought maybe he had her there. He'd talk her into it one of these days, he thought, if he didn't fall down dead somewhere first. He looked out the window and saw Yolanda Peabody emerge from her hotel.

"What's she do over there?"

"I don't have the foggiest idea. Now and then I see her on the street. She never speaks. And she never seems to have more than one or two roomers."

"Like you?"

Tracey's eyes held on his. "Yes, like me. Business is slow but that doesn't mean it can't change."

Will took her hand. "You wouldn't have to worry about it if you'd marry me and move down to the ranch. Marcello can't be makin' much clerkin' at the general store. I'll teach him to be a cowboy."

"Marcello is perfectly happy. So is Theresa and so am I. Can we change the subject?"

AFTER THANKSGIVING, Abby wrote to Evey and included a newspaper clipping about J. C. Osgood. He had married again, this time to a twenty-five-year-old named Lucille. "Well, I'll be damned," Will said. Esther, now eleven, giggled, and Evey shushed her. "If that old coot can do it . . ." Will got up from the dinner table and threw his napkin on his plate.

"Where are you going?" Evey called.

"Goin' to Marble to ask Tracey to marry me."

"Again?"

HENRY WAS furious. "First the Catholics and now the Mormons!" He paced the floor of Will's living room. Reva sat behind him and nodded her head repeatedly up and down like a duck bobbing for fish in time to Henry's rhythmic rhetoric. He had come to let off steam. Will seldom agreed with him but, with his "flock" dwindling, Henry needed somebody to listen. Will did that well enough.

"Of all the people in God-uh's world to reopen the quarries! Joseph Smith and his golden plates. Blasphemy!" Reva nodded, down and up, down and up. Will found himself nodding along with her. "They will try to convert my people. They will subvert all of my hard-earned success. What next? The Muslims, the Buddhists, the Jews?"

"Lord forbid." Will forced his eye from Reva and had to concentrate to keep from nodding again.

As Henry paced, Will packed his pipe. The eastern division of the Church of Jesus Christ of Latter-Day Saints had formed the Colorado White Marble Company and rumors had it they planned to drive a tunnel into White House Mountain big enough for a standard-gauge locomotive. Henry had heard that marble would be loaded directly into cars in the tunnel and transported to Carbondale on the old Crystal River and San Juan railroad tracks. The Mormons would use the marble for a tabernacle in Independence, Missouri.

"Why you 'spose God let it happen?" Will asked.

Henry whirled around, eyebrows raised. Reva's went up, too. She leaned forward. Will couldn't help himself and leaned forward too.

"It is not God-uh allowing it to happen!" Henry yelled. "It is us! Mankind is responsible for what happens in this valley. But the people are godless. They must throw off this yoke of evil and allow the love of God-uh to flow into every heart."

"God'll get rid of the Catholics and the Mormons?"

"Exactly!"

Will nodded, playing along. "Get rid of the curse!"

"The curse! The devils of Satan must be stopped!"

"Amen!" Reva agreed.

"But those Mormons might provide some work for the poor folks up there," Will said, tiring of the conversation.

"Work!" Henry snorted. "Prayer is what we need. Then work will come. And prosperity. And opportunity. But first, the love of God-uh must be allowed to shine past the dark clouds of Satan's army."

"Better get up there'n get 'em prayin' then," Will said.

Henry's face was set and determined. "It is so." He motioned to Reva and she lifted to her feet without so much as a grunt. She rose like a puff of smoke and glided toward the door behind her husband. "It is up to me," Henry said. "No one else senses the desperate need of this valley for a revival of Christian ethics."

"Get rid of the Papists and Mormons!" Henry shouted as Will waved them out the door.

"Amen," Reva said.

"Amen," Will repeated as they hurried down the lane toward the road, Henry snapping the reins and Reva holding on to the bouncing seat.

❧

UP IN MARBLE, people were bubbling with enthusiasm. "There will be work for me again in the quarries or perhaps the mill," Marcello said. The Yule Marble Company of Colorado had incorporated and other firms were planning on officially starting work in the near future.

"The Yule Company says they'll ship marble out within a year," Tracey said. "And the Carrara Yule Marble Company has already put three men to work repairing its holdings."

"Three men. *That's* encouraging." Will tried to sound sarcastic but it didn't faze Marcello.

"There will be more soon. I am hope to be among them."

"You seen anything of Henry?" Will asked, changing the subject. Theresa covered her mouth to keep from giggling. "What's he done now?"

The day after his arrival in Marble, Theresa recounted, Henry had seen a man carrying a suitcase with a suspicious-looking fluid dripping from it.

"You know we're still supposed to be dry," Theresa said. "Nobody worries about bootleggers too much, but Henry was livid." Henry had run to tell a deputy sheriff who now resided in the area. The deputy and Henry had slipped up behind the man and, catching some of the liquid, had sampled it with their tongues. "Henry insisted the man be arrested and when he and the deputy opened the suitcase, there sat the cutest little puppy you ever saw!"

When he stopped laughing, Will used his bandanna to wipe tears from his eye. "Henry wouldn't recognize the taste of likker but I'm 'sprised at the deputy."

Alone with Tracey later that night, Will pouted. "Don't take it so hard," she said.

He sighed and leaned back. "I'm startin' to get like Henry. Upsets me every time somethin' good happens up here. In his case, it's 'cause his 'flock' deserts him. In mine, it's 'cause it means you got one more reason to turn me down."

Tracey laughed. "You're good for me, Will. But if we were married you'd stop paying so much attention."

"Not for a minute, I wouldn't." She pushed his hand from her knee and laughed again.

Will wasn't laughing. "You're the damnedest, most frustrating female I ever been around."

Will became even more frustrated in late October when he read in the

Denver Post of the death of Bartholomew "Bat" Masterson. He read the obituary twice and then threw the paper into a trash can and went out onto the porch. He was still sitting there when it started to get dark and lights blinked on up at Luke and Evey's house. They had installed electric lights and a telephone. Will still used kerosene lamps and told them he didn't have anybody to call on a telephone.

"What about us?" Evey asked. "You might need us." "Then I'll just holler. You aren't that far away."

Pretty soon Luke came down to the house wondering why Will hadn't shown up for dinner. Without a word Will walked inside, fished the newspaper out of the trash and brought it outside to Luke. After he had read it, Luke put his hand on Will's shoulder. "I'm sorry," he said. "It's rough to lose a friend."

Will tossed the paper to the floor. "Died at a desk of a heart attack. Hell, he was younger'n me." Will leaned against the house and scratched a bug from his wrist. "He was one of the great ones. Him and Doc Holliday and Wyatt Earp."

Luke let it rest. "Dinner's ready. Want to come up?"

Will shook his head. "Not tonight. Think I'll just sit a while." He plopped down in the scarred rocker. "Just sit here and wait to die."

"Fine," Luke said, stepping off the porch. "I'll come back in a couple of days and collect the body. Josh can start digging your grave in the morning."

"Fine. Be sure and throw my spurs in the coffin, too."

Luke smiled. "Who said anything about a coffin?"

"You think I'm not serious? You come back in two days and I'll be sittin' here dead as a rock and twice as hard. You'll never get me unbent to lay me out."

"I'll tell Josh to dig wide, then."

"Good. And deep."

"Right." He sat there a while after Luke left, determined to die. But he got hungry and cold and went inside and fixed himself a sandwich.

Two days later, he took a shovel and hiked up to Judith's grave, which was ten feet from Ardy's. He spaded in and threw a few shovels of dirt to the side. "Might as well get it ready myself," he said to Judith. "Want to make sure I'm as close to you as I can get."

He dug into the rocky ground and hit a boulder big as an anvil and twice as heavy. He was sweating when he got it out. "Wish you were still here, old gal," he said. "We had us some times, didn't we?"

By midafternoon he had a seven-foot-long hole about three feet deep. When he saw Luke walking up the hill toward him, he threw the shovel to the ground, stepped into the hole, lay down, crossed his arms over his chest, and closed his eye. Pretty soon he heard Luke walk to the shallow grave. Will opened his eye a fraction of an inch and saw his son-in-law stare at him a moment, then reach down and pick up the shovel. Without a word, Luke spaded into the pile of dirt Will had made and tossed it into the grave. It spattered on Will's chest and into his face.

He opened his eye and looked at Luke for a moment and then they broke into laughter together.

≈≈≈

THROUGHOUT THE winter of 1921 and 1922, Will couldn't shake the thought of Bat Masterson. They were dying off one by one, all the people who'd ever meant anything to him.

Ardy and Tom and Judith and Doc Holliday and Bat Masterson and Henry Gillespie. Probably Mr. Goodnight by now, too, and God knew who else, he thought. Will was seventy-two and no good to anybody, he told himself. Tracey wouldn't have him. There was little for him to do on the ranch. *Might as well die*, Will decided. *It'd give Henry something to do for a day or so.* He also figured his death would take the preacher's mind off the good news up at Marble, the good news that was bad news to a man like Henry who built his reputation on predicting ruin.

In the spring the Denver and Rio Grande agreed to repair the Crystal River and San Juan line from Carbondale to Marble in exchange for a guarantee of fifteen hundred cars of marble a year from the two mining companies.

As construction picked up across the country, so did the demand for marble. When the first train in five years pulled into Marble in July of 1922, most of the town's four hundred residents were out to meet it. By now, two hundred were employed by the companies and there was actually a shortage of housing. The Cordell Hotel was full every night. Marcello was foreman of a gang charged with repairing the old equipment.

In August, Jacob Collins drove a brand new 1922 Essex down Marble's main street. From the Cordell's porch, Will watched him step from the totally enclosed automobile, limp around to the passenger side and help a tall blond woman from the car. They walked into the White House Hotel and weren't seen for the rest of the day.

"Jake's back," Will told Tracey.

"He is?" He thought he saw her shoulders droop but she was quickly back at work and didn't mention Jake again.

Will was sitting on the porch the next morning when Jake came out of the White House and looked up and down the street. He saw Will and walked slowly toward him. Will waited, watching a much older man than he remembered limp down the dirt street. Jake's muttonchop sideburns were gone but the mustache was still there. He wore a three-button suit and a stiff collar with a black tie. His stomach bulged beneath the suit coat. His face was a pasty white with splotches of red around his nose. He stopped in front of Will and lit a cigar big as a banana. "You still alive, old man?"

Will nodded. "Hello, Jake. You're lookin' prosperous."

Jake smiled around yellow teeth. "I'm doing all right." He stared at his father a long second. "Why don't you get some decent clothes? Think you're still a cowboy?"

"Well," Will said softly. "Where'd you be if I was?"

Jake smirked. "Too bad your silver-mining days didn't pan out, considering they're makin' silver dollars these days. Maybe you'd be as rich as me." His chest puffed up.

"Must be nice," Will said, not really caring.

"That it is." Jake swelled up some more. "We're just back from the East, you know. We were invited to attend the dedication of the Lincoln Memorial. The government's got nearly $3 million invested in it by now, lots of that in Yule Marble. And some of it is in my pocket."

Will smiled and glanced at Jake's belly. "Is that what's bulging? I figured it was something else."

Jake took a puff on his cigar, spat in the street. "You think you're funny but you don't know anything about the world or what's going on in it. Hell, old man. I've got money invested in places you've never even heard of. Did you know there are more than a hundred million people in the United States right now? And that they're smoking forty-three billion cigarettes every year? You wouldn't make in two years anything near my monthly dividend."

"I thought cigarettes were illegal," Will said.

"Only in fourteen states."

"Kind of risky, I'd say."

Jake belched out a laugh. "That's not the only place I've invested. Look, that fellow Lenin over in Russia is begging for food so I'm into agriculture. I've got money in candy bars! You watch how Mounds bars go. And cars, too! Not many people know it, but Henry Ford is making over $264,000 every day. Look, there are over 387,000 miles of paved roads in the country right now and there's more being paved every day. A million trucks and millions of automobiles are using them." He puffed up some more and sneered down his nose at Will. "And you think you're still a cowboy."

Will tried to ignore his contempt but did feel a bit behind the times. "You back to stay or just visitin'?"

Jake put a foot on the porch and rolled the cigar between his fingers.

"Back at my old job. Legal counsel for both the big companies."

Will walked to the edge of the porch. "Saw you drive in yesterday but I didn't see Inez, or the boy. Not with you?"

"Nope. Got a girl, too. Marguerita."

"That's nice. Where's your wife, or are you married to that blond now?"

Jake laughed an unfriendly snicker. "She's just a friend. Inez'll be along."

Will let his eye wander over toward the bright blue Essex which was parked where Jake had left it the night before. Jake spat in the street. "You look awful. That patch and all."

"You ought to see me without it," Will said.

"No thanks."

"You want to say hello to your mother?"

"Nope."

"Figured."

"I'll see you around," Jake said, turning away and limping toward his automobile. The limp seemed worse.

"See you." *I'm afraid I will*, Will thought. All three of his children were again in the valley at the same time.

WILL STAYED on the ranch through the fall, knowing Tracey would be too busy to pay him much mind. *As though she would, even if she wasn't busy*, Will thought. He didn't want to risk seeing Jake, anyway.

At Thanksgiving, though, he rode to Marble in the Chevrolet with Evey, Luke and the kids and, after dinner, met Yolanda Peabody and Inez Collins on the sidewalk. They pushed past without speaking but he got a good look at the two of them. Yolanda was stooped in the shoulders and seemed skinnier. Inez still had a lot of beauty about her but she, too, looked older. A few years ago, before she and Jake left town, her eyes had been large, full of life, and her face had shown with youthful vigor. Now she frowned, her cheeks were sunken, and her eyes, when they met his only briefly, were leaden and dull.

Well, he thought, I've aged, too, and let it pass.

In the spring of 1923 Henry's "flock" was still growing. Every spring mud slide was blamed on the hosts of Satan. Every runaway tram from the quarries to the mill, every broken leg, heart attack, bloody nose and split fingernail was due to a lack of faith in God. Even the holes in the road to Redstone were not the fault of poor maintenance by the county; they were dug by the clawed hands of the Crystal River Valley's own, personal, designated devil. And until God received enough prayerful petitions from His children, the devilish doings would certainly continue.

They continued through May when a fire wiped out three buildings on a Sunday night. In June another mud slide roared down Carbonate Creek. In July a man was mauled by a bear. In August a child choked to death on a piece of meat.

"You could get away from all this and come on down to the ranch and live with me," Will reminded Tracey.

"I could." She winked at him. "But I won't."

"Dammit, Tracey! There's no good reason why you shouldn't."

"I don't want to," she said.

"Well," he replied. "Well, hell."

He saw Jake with the blond woman, Jake with Inez, Jake with Yolanda, Jake with other men. He was never alone, and he was usually with a woman, sometimes one Will had never seen before. Often, they were women he'd bring in for a few days and then send packing on the mail stage. Jake grew larger, obese even, and seemingly richer. Inez began to seem pale, Yolanda bent, the blonde strangely happy.

"How you keepin' all them women happy at the same time?" Will asked him one day when Jake hobbled with the help of a cane between the mill and the White House Hotel.

"Takes a real man to do that."

Will studied the man's girth and estimated his weight in tonnage. He shook his head. "How's your wife?"

"Inez? Fine, I guess." Will let him limp on past without elaboration.

In fact, Inez had begun to attend Henry's Sunday morning services. She sat in the back row, Henry said, and left without speaking. But she was there. "She will be my prize convert," he said. "She will be my shining example of how one gone wrong can feel the forgiving embrace of God- uh."

"There's something wrong with her," Theresa said. "She has a look in her eyes that frightens me."

After the evening meal Marcello motioned Will onto the porch. "Inez is reaching a breaking point. I feel it when I see her. At night sometimes I have seen her walking in the darkness, up and down the street when all are asleep. I also think she follows sometimes Jake."

"She is feeling the power of the Lord God-uh Almighty Himself," Henry beamed. "I can see it in her eyes, which are filled with the great questions of life."

Even when things got better in the spring of 1924 and Henry's flock once again found other things to do on Sunday mornings, Inez was there.

"But she won't talk," Henry complained. "She never says a word. She sits and listens and then leaves quietly. Nevertheless, I know she hears the Word and believes the Word and will respond to my teachings."

381

"Could be," Will said. "I hear things are going pretty well up in Marble."

Henry grumbled and led Reva to the carriage, the same old black carriage he'd driven for years. Maybe the same old horse, too, Will figured.

Things were going well in Marble. Between the Yule Marble Company, the Carrara Company, and the railroad, more than two hundred men were employed and the monthly payroll totaled $25,000. The town's population had reached five hundred. Orders were coming in. In July the two companies merged into the Consolidated Yule Marble Company. Marcello was earning good money. The Cordell Hotel was full. The Consolidated announced late in the year that more than half a million dollars of marble had been sold in the past two years.

"You ain't never gonna marry me, are you?" Will moped in the kitchen as Tracey went about her work.

"Are you finally getting that through your old head? Now, shoo!" She waved him out of the room.

He went out on the porch and watched the activity on the street. He mumbled to himself that he thought when he got to be seventy-four years old he wouldn't be so damned randy.

Will spotted Jake with the blonde, limping away from the White House toward his Essex. Will saw a curtain move in a second-floor window and watched a pale face surrounded by dark hair follow the pair down the street.

Henry and Reva drove into sight and Will worked his way to his feet and went inside. He wasn't up to dealing with Henry just then. The man and his wife had become like ghosts, pale and gaunt, thin and exasperating to most of those with whom they came in contact. They plied the valley from end to end, knocking on doors, stopping people on the road. "God-uh needs your help," Henry said to all. "And you need God-uh's help. Together we can overcome the evil that permeates this place and turn it into a veritable Eden in the wilderness of a desperate world."

In April of 1925, Henry found some renewed hope when a fire started in Shop No. 3 at the mill, spread quickly, and ignited forty barrels of oil. When it was finally extinguished, the fire had destroyed nine hundred feet of the mill and caused more than half a million dollars of damage. Less than $200,000 of insurance was carried.

"The work of Satan!" Henry cried. "Repent! Turn from your lustful, greedy ways and come to God-uh!"

Will had been talking to God quite a bit by then. "Might as well," he told Luke. "My grandkids don't want to listen to my stories, you're too busy and Evey's got other things to do. Tracey won't marry me and everybody else I'd like to talk to is dead."

"What do you talk to Him about?" Luke asked.

382

"Whatever's on my mind. I been tryin' to get Him to change Tracey's mind. And I been makin' quite an argument on Henry's behalf, too. That boy needs some help."

"He does at that. Getting any answers?"

"Yep. Mostly on the negative side."

Luke laughed. "I'm glad you're getting acquainted."

"Acquainted? Hell, we been acquainted for a long time. I just never took much time for a visit. Now I ain't got nothin' else to do."

"Good way to spend your time," Luke said.

Will felt for his tobacco pouch, saw it lying on the table across the room, creaked to his feet and stretched. "Think I'll go on up to Marble and proposition Tracey again. Maybe I can wear her down."

"You really believe that?"

"Nope. But it's about the only fun I got left."

That, he thought, *and riding a horse*. The next morning he saddled a roan named Ephraim and loafed along the river toward Placita. As he passed Redstone he saw activity at Cleveholm. The castle had been literally deserted for years and Will had almost stopped looking at it as he passed. Now, people were bustling about the grounds and he turned Ephraim around and decided to go see what was happening.

"I'VE GOT A CANCER and I've come home to die. It's as simple as that." J. C. Osgood sat in the sun on the brick patio of Cleveholm's northwest corner. Osgood's cheeks were sunken and he had lost considerable weight. His skin had a jaundiced look and his hands shook as he lit a cigar. "I'm not supposed to smoke these but it seems pretty shortsighted, considering that I'm to die soon anyway."

"I'm damned sorry to hear it," Will said. He wondered about Osgood's new wife but Lucille was nowhere to be seen.

Osgood waved the cigar in the air and coughed. "It happens. Always figured I'd live to be ninety or so at least. Now, at seventy-four, I'm counting the days."

"You'll probably see a lot of winters yet," Will said unconvincingly. Osgood was a year younger than him. Will wondered if he looked anywhere near as old as Osgood.

The coal miner tried to laugh. "I appreciate it, Martin. But I had surgery for the damn thing and the doctors told me there was no hope. So I said to Lucille, I said, 'Let's get on back to Cleveholm.' This is the site of the happiest part of my life, you know."

"Well, I'm glad for that, then. Guess you been keeping up on all the news,

Marble and everything."

"Pretty much."

Neither said anything for a while until Will ventured that it was a mighty nice day.

"I've been through some trying times in the past several years," Osgood said softly. He toyed with his cigar, let his head drop as though he wanted to sleep, brought it up slowly. His hand shook. "Labor unions will be the ruination of this wonderful country of ours."

"Another strike?"

"A terrible one, with battles and military involvement."

"Settled?"

"More or less." A wagon passed on the road heading south and Osgood watched it until it disappeared behind the trees. "Tell me about your family. I was sorry to hear about your wife. Judith, wasn't it?"

"Thanks. It was Judith." Will told him the good things, the things about Luke and Evey and the kids, about Tracey, too, and Tom's death, and about Theresa and Marcello. He left out the part about Jake and Henry. Somehow, it didn't seem fitting.

"That's good," Osgood said, almost in a whisper. "You've had a good life."

"So have you."

"Yes, I have." He paused and took a breath. "A far shorter one than you are privileged to enjoy, however."

"Well," Will said, "we don't know that for sure, do we? Hell, I could get myself killed in the next hour."

Osgood cracked a smile. "Don't do that. Stick around and enjoy the grandchildren."

"I think I'd like to do that, all right."

"Where were you heading just now?"

"Goin' to Marble. Got myself a lady friend up there."

"Good. Good. Going to marry her?"

"Kinda doubt it."

"Too bad." Osgood's head fell toward his chest once again and Will turned his eyes away. He would rather remember the paunchy, robust man of 1882 whose short legs carried him up one hillside after another in search of the coal he'd found just west of Cleveholm.

"Martin?"

"Yeah?"

"I appreciate your stopping by. Talking with you brings back some of my fondest memories."

"That's good."

384

Osgood turned slightly toward Will. "I think, however, that this should be our final meeting. I can only get worse, you know."

Will nodded. "I understand." He stood, took Osgood's hand and gripped it for a while. When the coal man loosened his grip Will put his hand in the pocket of his Levi's and, without speaking, went on around the house to his horse.

That night, on the Cordell's porch, Will braced a straight-backed chair against the wall and hooked his feet behind the front legs. Feeling low, he looked for something to take his mind off the day's disappointments — Osgood's impending death and Tracey's continued scoffing at his marriage idea.

Marble was quiet this early in the evening and for a while he couldn't get his mind off his old friend J. C. Osgood. Pretty soon, though, lights started poking holes in the buildings and a few people strolled by with a "howdy!". Will was bent to the front of the porch tamping out his pipe when Jake and the blond woman emerged from the White House Hotel. They angled toward him and he slipped up against the wall in the shadows.

Jake waddled. He put his weight on a cane as he stepped forward with his left leg and leaned far to the right. He lifted the right leg and swung it forward, his body swaying to the left. The woman, speaking softly, cupped his left forearm in her hand guiding the balloon shape up the street. At the end of town they turned west toward the river.

Will stepped out of the shadows but moved quickly back again when he saw Inez slip quietly from the hotel and glance down the street. She lowered her head and followed Jake. *Well*, Will thought, *there isn't anything else to do anyway*. So he pocketed his pipe and set off after Inez. He felt foolish and was glad for the dark as he tried not to crunch too loudly on the rocky ground.

He stopped fifty feet from the riverbank when he saw Inez huddled behind a tree. Jake and the blond woman stood on the built-up bank and stared into the rushing water. Occasionally they spoke to one another. Jake sat on a large boulder and pulled the woman closer, stroking her hip and nuzzling her bosom.

Inez pulled a white handkerchief from somewhere and wiped her eyes. She braced herself against her tree for a moment, then pushed upright and began to walk back toward town. Jake turned his head at that moment and saw her.

"Inez!" he shouted. His voice was small against the rush of the river. Inez turned her head briefly but walked on. Jake struggled to his feet and shouted again: "You get your butt over here!"

Inez stopped, her eyes on the ground, then turned and walked back a few paces toward Jake who was pulling the blond woman as he hobbled, swayed, and lurched toward Inez with a speed that astonished Will. He stayed hidden in the shadow of a pine.

"What the hell are you doing here?" Jake said loudly, grabbing Inez's arm and twisting it. "How many times do I have to tell you not to follow me? Damn it!" The blond woman put her hand over her mouth and giggled.

Will restrained himself when Jake spat on his wife's cheek. He gripped the bark of the tree and clenched his teeth when Jake slapped her and she fell to the ground. What Jake said then was drowned out by the river but the blond woman laughed out loud, then took Jake's arm and led him away. Hating himself for it, Will stayed hidden behind the pine as the two walked past. When they disappeared in the darkness he walked to Inez and stopped a few feet away. As she lifted her face and saw him, her eyes widened and she drew in on herself like a beaten dog. She kept her eyes on him and sniffed, choked and coughed.

"You all right, little one?" Will asked as he knelt beside her. He sat on his heels and let his hands rest on his knees. He made no move toward her, not wanting to frighten her more. Inez nodded.

"I got me a big bandanna here," he said, pulling it from a back pocket. "Do a lot better than that little hanky." He held it out and she took it. She wiped her face with it, blew her nose into it and handed it back.

"Keep it," he said. "Looks like you could use a bushel of 'em."

"Th . . . th . . . thank you."

Glory be! Will thought. *The woman can talk.* In all the years he'd known her, since only a short time after her birth in 1884, Will had never heard her speak. *She was what, forty-one or so?* Will wondered. This was definitely progress. He'd try for more.

"What was that all about? 'Course it ain't none of my business but I'm a good listener if you got somethin' to get off your chest."

Inez stared at him for a moment, then shook her head. But she did hold out her hand and he helped her stand. They each brushed dust from their clothes and Will caught Inez looking at him with a frown. Or was it a question? Will wondered.

"I was takin' an evening stroll when I saw you out here," he lied, then thought better of it. "Naw. I followed you when I saw you trailin' after them two."

Now, Inez's face was expressionless in the moonlight. She let her gaze fall to the ground and took a few steps forward. Then she stopped and turned back to him, nodded something like thanks, and left him standing there in the darkness wondering why he had bothered to help.

He didn't say anything about the incident to Tracey, even when she asked him where he'd gone. "I came out to sit with you," she said.

"My luck. Never around when you're ready."

"Ready! Don't you ever think of anything else?"

"Not much." He patted her hand. "Not when you're around."

"You're good for me. An old woman needs to think she's still got something a man might want besides her cooking."

Will laughed. "Marry me and I'll do the cooking."

"We'd both be dead within a month."

"Maybe so," he said. "But what a month it'd be."

Will hung around town the next day, and the next. He hoped for another opportunity to be alone with Inez and was about to give up on it when, late on his third evening in town, she emerged from the White House and walked up the street. As she passed the Cordell she stopped and stared at Will. He touched his hat brim and thought she motioned with her head for him to follow her. He couldn't be sure in the soft light from the window but he thought she had. Inez walked on and, in a few seconds, Will tagged along. She was waiting near the pine that had hidden him from Jake. He thought maybe he saw her smile as he reached her.

"I wa . . . wanted to say th . . . thank you."

"That's nice," Will said, genuinely pleased. "No need to be nervous about it, though."

"I'm not nervous." The words came out slowly, forced from her mouth like a slow reader struggling with a book.

"Well, that's good," he said. "Guess I shouldn't even have been there. Like to punch that boy sometimes."

She smiled and almost laughed. "Me, t-t-too."

It hit him then: The woman stuttered. Make her talk some more, he thought. "Who is that blond woman?" Inez's smile drooped to a sad frown and her eyes narrowed. Will wondered if he had asked the wrong question.

"C-C-Christine."

Will stared off into the darkness, and listened to the fall of the river. *The poor girl stuttered*, he thought to himself again. But as she talked on, he found he could understand her more clearly.

"I wanted you to know . . . " Inez faltered but surged gamely on. "That . . . . I have always thought you . . . were a g-g-good man. But Jake . . . he . . . ."

"I get the picture," Will said. He stood an arm's length from her and fought the urge to hug her like he might a grandchild who had scraped a knee. But Inez was not a child. She'd simply never been allowed to be a woman.

"I must . . . go back." She brushed past him and then turned. "I always thought . . . I . . . could . . . wike you," she said and was gone.

When Inez said the word "wike," he realized she also had a second speech impediment: She pronounced her l's as w's. No wonder she never spoke in

387

public. Will felt suddenly weak and leaned against the tree. *Some people have problems like we never imagine,* he thought. She probably was in desperate need of a friend and he had made a simple gesture of kindness toward her. *After all these years*, he thought. *Damn Jake. Damn the man, anyway.*

∾

HENRY WAS depressed, and Reva, hard as it was for Will to believe, seemed thinner than ever. Hard lines framed their faces. Narrowed eyes hid below furrowed brows and their mouths drooped at the corners in perpetual frowns.

"I'm sorry, boy," Will said. "Maybe something else was going on."

"It wasn't just last Sunday," Henry sighed. "Attendance began to fall more than a month ago. On the Sabbath last, there were but five in attendance, including Inez."

"She's still coming, then?"

"She is my most faithful parishioner."

They sat on the porch of the Cordell Hotel. It was as close to inside as Tracey would allow them. Even in the August heat Henry and Reva were garbed in black, head to toe with only their white faces, white hands, and Henry's white collar standing out from the darkness. Hands held, they made an H walking to and from their carriage.

"Perhaps," Henry said. "Perhaps I have been too . . . too harsh."

Will waited. He sucked on a dead pipe and fingered a drop of sweat from beside his nose.

"But I wanted salvation for them so strongly . . ."

Down the street, Jake stepped from the White House, leaned against a post, fired the end of a cigar, looked toward Will and let his eyes stay there.

"Tell you what," Will said, watching Jake. "Folks seem to respond better to a nudge than a hammer blow sometimes."

Will watched Jake lower himself from the porch and begin laboriously to work his way across the street toward the Cordell. Henry's voice now sounded forced. "I must admit that I may have chosen an incorrect method to try and reach them."

Will stood and waited for Jake. Henry was beside him, Reva at his side. "I am trying to tell you I'm . . ."

"Wait a bit, boy." Will tamped tobacco ashes into the street. "Somethin' interesting's about to happen, I think."

"More interesting than my apology?"

Will's head snapped toward Henry. "Your what?" Jake was five steps away.

Henry cleared his throat. Reva's face peeped around his shoulder. "Must you make him say it twice?"

Will turned back to Jake, then back to Henry. "Don't go away," he said. "I want to be sure I heard what I think I heard."

"I want to talk to you," Jake growled at Will. "Alone."

Will nodded. "We can take a walk."

"I've done my walking," Jake said. "Maybe my half-brother and her," he said with a sharp glance at Reva, "could go somewhere else."

Will turned to Henry and raised his eyebrows then shrugged his shoulders. Henry and Reva together lifted their noses, joined hands and slowly walked away.

Jake's face was red with the exertion of walking across the street. He leaned heavily on his cane, breathing hard. "I've seen you with my wife," he said.

"Have you?"

"What kind of lies has she been telling you?"

"Lies?" Will had seen Inez only three times since their first brief encounter early that spring. Their visits had been short and she had volunteered no information, certainly nothing that should have stirred Jake up so much.

"Well?" Jake stared at him. The end of his cigar glowed red hot and he puffed smoke like a locomotive.

Will took his time loading his own pipe. "She's a frightened little mouse," he said, matching Jake's stare. "Too frightened to tell any tales."

"Stay away from her," Jake demanded.

"Why?"

The big man leaned forward, took the cigar from his mouth and jabbed it toward Will. "I don't want you around her. Just because she's my wife."

"Is she?"

"What's that supposed to mean?"

"You tell me."

"You're talking in riddles."

Will struck a match, touched it to his tobacco, and drew on it. Make Jake wait, he thought. He threw the match into the street. "Who's Christine?"

Jake tried to smile. "A friend. Nothing to do with Inez."

"I'm sure."

"You're getting me riled, old man."

"Where's your boy, Nathan? I haven't seen him around. Or the girl, either, for that matter."

Jake sighed, put the cigar back in the corner of his mouth. "Good Lord, you old fart. Stay on the subject."

"Thought I was."

"Just stay clear of Inez. Go back to your ranch and sit in a rocking chair." Will stepped toward Jake and the man recoiled, tensed. "What is it you don't want me to know?"

Jake looked at the ground. "Something's wrong with her," he said. "You can't believe anything she says. Stay away."

"Or?"

"Or I may have to send a couple of my men to visit you one of these days. To convince you."

"I don't take threats too well," Will said quietly.

Jake turned and started back toward the White House. Over his shoulder he threw words back at his father. "I mean it. If I see you with her again it'll go rough on you."

He was in the middle of the street when Will called to him. "Jake?"

"What?" The man stopped but didn't turn around.

"Nice visitin' with you."

Jake forged a step ahead, swung his bad leg forward, leaned on his cane, took another step. He grunted into the heat and lumbered away.

"What was that all about?" Henry asked when he and Reva stepped back onto the porch.

"Nothin'," Will said, watching Jake disappear into the White House. He turned to Henry. "You notice anything strange about Inez lately, like she's coming unwound?"

"Coming unwound?"

"Forget it," Will said. "What was it you were saying before we were interrupted?"

Henry took a deep breath. "I came to apologize," he said. "You have been right in many respects, regarding my ministry. I believe now that I should have taken a more, shall we say, gentle approach."

"I'm glad to hear you say it, boy." Will clapped him on the shoulder and dust lifted into the still air. "What you going to do about it?"

Henry looked at Reva and she nodded, gripped his arm. "I thought you might have some . . . some advice," he whispered.

Will felt a wave of sadness sweep over him. Sadness for the years the boy and his wife had wasted. Sadness that he continued to think of a forty-one-year-old man as a boy. Sadness that they had to turn to him, one who had quietly opposed their every effort, for advice.

He took Henry's arm. "Come on over here and sit down," he said. When they were seated, one on either side of him, he refired his pipe, blew some smoke and leaned back. "First thing," he said, "you got to get some different clothes."

❧

LATER THAT NIGHT Will went walking, ignoring Jake's threat and hoping to see Inez. He found her by the river in what had become their meeting place. It was moonless, dark and quiet with the river down to less than half its spring runoff size, so Will could hear her easily when she called to him. She called him "Mr. Martin," and to Will that was all right.

"Over here," he said.

She stood beside him and he could barely make out her shape against the night sky. "I saw . . . Jake . . . t-talking . . . to you."

Will touched her arm and she pulled away. "He told me to stay away from you."

"I am . . . a-fwayed of him."

He waited. Then, "Why? Does he knock you around? What's going on? Tell me, Inez. Maybe I can help."

"There are . . . things." She whispered her words, and kept her face, even in the dark, turned away from him. "Things. I . . . can't . . . tell you."

"Seems to me you need to talk to somebody." His voice was involuntarily a whisper, like hers.

"I mustn't see . . . you again. If he . . . found out."

"What things?"

She sniffed. A white handkerchief fluttered in the blackness. "Things. No one . . . must ever . . . know." She turned and started up the path toward town.

"Wait!" Will called.

"No."

"You're going to Henry's church." She stopped. He couldn't see her but knew she had stopped. "Does it help? Going to church?" He found her in the darkness, put his arms around her, and felt her stiffen. He felt her relax then and nod her head into his shoulder.

"That's good. Henry is proud of you."

She lifted her head. "P-P-Pwoud? Of me?"

"Yes," he lied. Henry was not proud of her, but of himself for "converting" her, or so he thought.

"I want to . . . be . . . with Jesus. But I am . . . unwor- thy?"

"Hush," Will said, patting her shoulder. "Hush that kind of talk. I think Jesus is proud of you, too."

She was silent for a moment, then she raised her head from Will's shoulder and pulled away. When she spoke, her voice was pitched higher, the whisper gone. "There is evil," she said. "Jake and . . . Christine. Satan will . . . they are . . . going to hell." Did she laugh? She seemed taller now to Will.

"God . . . told me."

Inez made a sound that could have been an intake of breath or another laugh.

"Told you?" Will asked. "Told you what?"

"Henry says all things . . . work . . . to good for those . . . who wuv God."

"I've heard that, too."

"Then it will be all wite," she said. She turned and hurried away. She didn't stop when Will called to her and she disappeared into the night.

WILL PUSHED himself from the comfortable chair in front of the fireplace and looked for something to do. He went to the kitchen and put water on to boil. Henry and Reva were beginning to rebuild a following. It had become quickly evident that Henry had been easily led by his wife. He was changing rapidly and Reva was following along. Will looked out the back door and up toward the big house on the rise. Evey and Luke were up there with the two girls. Esther would be seventeen now and Ruby — she hated her first name of Iola — would be, what? Will wondered. He mentally tried to subtract 1912 from 1926 and took a while to come up with fourteen. Josh was away at college in Boulder and in a year or so would be off to medical school. *Lord, they grew up fast*, Will thought.

The fly in the ointment was the death of J. C. Osgood. Will couldn't get away from the news. The coal and steel magnate had died soon after the first of the year. Even after four months, the thought of his passing hurt Will. Osgood's third wife — this Lucille whom Will had never met — inherited everything. Will hadn't even been invited to the funeral, if there had been one. He'd heard later that Osgood's ashes had been scattered over the valley and the Crystal River. *At least that was good*, he thought.

He sat back down in the chair, heard the kettle begin to whistle and sighed as he hauled himself to his feet once more. He set the kettle to the side and, as the whistling faded, thought how quiet it was in his house. He'd just about given up altogether on Tracey. *She was probably right, though*, he mused. *They were too damned old, anyway. But it sure would be nice to have a woman around.*

That led him to thinking about Inez. He hadn't seen her since just before Christmas. He'd been on the porch for a puff on his pipe when she had wandered past. "Wandered" was a good word, thought Will. The woman had stared at him with wide, red-rimmed eyes that may have been seeing something else. There was a look on her face of fear and confusion. Her mouth moved as though she were talking to herself. She walked slowly past the Cordell Hotel, heading off to the south, toward the edge of town. She twisted her hands together and gave no indication that she had recognized Will.

He was still thinking about her when he pulled on his heavy sheepskin coat and trudged up the hill to tell Luke he wanted to go to Marble the first chance they had.

≈∾

THE FIRST CHANCE came in May when the girls had a long weekend away from school. They drove up the rutted, rocky road in Luke's ten-year-old Chevrolet, Will complaining all the way that they should have gone on horseback, knowing it would have been difficult for him but complaining anyway.

As they pulled into Marble past the mill, five teenage boys stood off to the side of the street. One of them saw the two girls and smiled hugely as he doffed his cap at them. The girls giggled and hid their faces.

"Nathan Collins," Luke said, clearly dismayed to see Jake and Inez's son.

Evey turned to the girls. "You two stay away from him."

"Oh, mother," Esther, the oldest, sighed.

Tracey had the usual kiss on the cheek for Will. She pulled away when he tried to hug her and wagged a finger at him with a smile. "You keep your hands to yourself." Will didn't think it was as funny as everyone else.

After lunch, as the adults wandered out back to enjoy one of the first truly warm days of the year, Esther followed Teegee, Marcello and Theresa's now fourteen-year-old son, toward the river. Ruby and Martha, the ten-year-old, played together.

The sun warmed Will and he dozed as he half-listened to the talk around him. The Mormons were 450 feet deep into White House Mountain, still planning to run a railroad track into the tunnel. Marcello was working for the Consolidated company but paychecks were sometimes slow in coming.

He listened to the river, which was beginning to run heavy. An automobile backfired on the street. The hotel was not full but the dining room was busy. Will fell asleep. When he awoke he was alone in the yard. He walked to the back door and called. "Where is everybody?"

Tracey was at the sink. "Marcello took Luke to the mill. I think the others are down at the drugstore."

Her back was to him, her hands in the dishwater. Will leaned against the doorjamb and took a long look. Tracey was still slender, perhaps more than she should be. Her hair was pulled up but strands of it fell to her neck. He quietly slipped up behind her and kissed the nape of her neck. He felt her

393

stiffen a little but she didn't push him away and he put his arms around her. Suddenly it was 1880 again, and they were in another kitchen of a boarding house in Schofield. She was crying as he held her that night and he remembered the strength of his youthful arms. Was she remembering, too? Was that why she settled her body against his and let out a deep breath? It had been the night of their first kiss, the first stirring of passion that had produced a son who now hated them both.

"Tracey."

"Will, I . . ."

Someone knocked on the kitchen door.

Will whispered in her ear. "Don't answer it."

The knocking was persistent. "Mr. M-M-Martin?"

"It's Inez," Will sighed. "What the hell . . . ?"

When he opened the door Inez glanced past him at Tracey and stepped back. He went outside and she stared wildly at him, rubbing her hands together.

"How are you, girl?" Will asked.

"I . . . I . . ." Spittle formed at the side of her mouth.

"Take it easy," he said quietly. "How've you been?"

"Nathan," she croaked. Her voice was harsh. "He and some others . . ."

"Slow down, now." Will smiled at her.

"They're . . . Esther and . . . Teegee . . ."

His smile faded. "What about them?"

"By the river. A fight. You . . . you help."

But Will was already back at the kitchen door, shouting at Tracey. "Something's going on with the kids," he called. "I'll check it out."

He ran. He ran past Inez and over a rock-strewn lot and through a stand of spruce. His breath came quickly and he panted. His legs felt weak and his ankles hurt as the high-heeled boots he still favored caught on rocks and roots. He stumbled up the final rise and looked down at the river. Teegee lay curled on the rocks, the water lapping at his back. Two boys stood over him, one with a broken tree limb in his hand. Off to the right where a cottonwood shaded the bank three boys surrounded Esther. One had her arms pinned behind her while another had one hand on a breast and was trying to lift her skirt with the other.

It was Nathan Collins.

"Hey!" he shouted, but the river drowned out his voice. He shouted again and waved his arms. Esther struggled, kicked out and caught Nathan in the shin. Good for her, Will thought. The bank was steep but he started down anyway, then stumbled and caught himself. He suddenly couldn't breathe. He tried to inhale and felt a weight on his chest, choked and gasped. When his

394

heel caught on another rock his balance was gone and he felt himself falling forward.

"Well, I'll be . . ." he tried to say and then there was blackness and not even the sound of the river.

"ANYBODY TELL Jake?" Will asked later that night.

"He's off somewhere on business," Luke said.

Will pushed himself to a sitting position on the sofa where they had made him lie all afternoon. He felt the aches in his arms and legs, saw the bruises on his forearm. "Somebody doesn't tell him, that kid'll get off scot-free."

"Lie still," Luke ordered. "Jake wouldn't do anything about it anyhow. You know that."

Will stretched out again. "Esther okay?"

"Madder'n I've ever seen her. Wish I could have seen those two women chasing those kids."

"Me, too," Will said with a laugh.

Luke smiled with him. "Tracey said they'd of caught 'em if they'd been on level ground."

"Wish they would have." Will tried to laugh again but had trouble getting air to his lungs and coughed instead.

"What happened to you out there?" Now Luke was frowning.

"Tripped on a rock." *No need to get everybody riled up over probably nothing,* Will decided.

"You've got to be more careful. Pretty stupid of you to go running off like that. You could have a heart attack." He stared into Will's eyes.

"Not me," Will muttered, finding something else to look at. "Strong as a bull." He pounded a fist into his chest a couple of times then thought better of it and quit.

"Right." Luke stood. "I think we'll head back home tomorrow. Take you in to see Dr. Castle on Monday."

"I'm not going to that quack," Will said harshly. He knew Castle wasn't a quack but the times he'd been to see the man the past few years were some of his worst memories. First Ardy and then Judith. "What about Teegee?"

Luke shook his head. "They beat him up pretty good. They were calling him 'dago' and 'wop.' Theresa said it's been going on for quite a while. Happens to all the Italian kids, I guess."

"Teegee's American."

Luke's blue eyes flashed. "So am I. Maybe more American than any of you."

395

"You're right," Will said. "You were here first."

"It's more than that," Luke said. "Thought you read the papers."

"What do you mean?"

"Back in '24. Congress passed a law saying all American Indians were automatically U.S. citizens."

"You never said anything about it."

"Didn't think I needed to."

Will stretched his legs but the aches didn't go away. He kept his hand away from his chest which felt heavy. "Well," he said, thinking about it. "Had to pass a law to make it official, huh? Damn fool politicians."

Finally, he did rub his chest and had trouble taking a deep breath. "Time for a nap," he said.

A WEEK LATER Will was sitting in the comfortable chair on his porch when a strange wagon pulled into the drive and a small woman stepped down. The wagon turned back onto the road and headed north to Carbondale. Will stood and watched as the bent form walked slowly toward the house. When he was sure it was Inez he hurried to her. Despite the warm weather she was cloaked in heavy clothes, a shawl covering her head and shoulders.

As he took her arm the woman turned her face up to him and he fought back the gasp that surged to his throat. Her face was a mass of bruises, one eye swollen completely shut. The corner of her mouth was badly bruised and a scab ran to her chin.

"Good Lord, girl!" Without thinking about it, Will hugged her to him. She whimpered like a whipped pup. He swept her up in his arms and carried her to the house. He was panting heavily as he laid her on the sofa. "Stay there," he ordered. He walked to the kitchen, pumped a glass of water and leaned on the table, letting his heart slow down. Then he went to the back porch and banged three times on the bell Luke had hung there for him. It was the signal that he needed help.

Evey arrived first. She burst in through the kitchen door. He met her at the door to the living room and held out his hands. "Settle down," he said. "It ain't me. But I've got a hurt little woman in here."

"Take her up to the house," Evey told Luke and Esther when they arrived moments later. Luke picked Inez up as though she were a child.

Will followed more slowly and found Evey and Esther locked in the bedroom with Inez. "What do you think?" he asked Luke.

"It's pretty bad. Evey says it isn't just her face. She's got bruises all over her body."

"Jake?"

"Who else?"

"The bastard."

Luke stared at Will, raised his eyebrows.

"Well," Will said, shaking his head. "Well, I almost called him a son-of-a-bitch. The other one's more accurate."

That evening Evey told them the story, or as much of it as she could piece together from the confused and rambling confession she had pried from Inez. Jake had arrived in Marble the day after the incident at the river. Nathan had told him Teegee and several other boys had attacked him and that Will had egged them on. When Inez tried to tell him the true story, Nathan called her a liar. Two of his friends backed up his version and told Jake she had gone to get Will to help Teegee and his friends. Jake had locked her in her bedroom for several days. Frequently, he barged into the room and beat her. Finally, the night before she fled, he had completely lost control and had clubbed her with a board, beating her all over her body. Then he had used his fists on her face. She had found the door to her room unlocked this morning and had simply walked out. A mile north of Marble she had gotten a ride.

"I wanted to take her to town to see Dr. Castle but she's terrified to go anywhere but here," Evey said. "I think I can take care of her but I'd feel better if we'd phone the doctor. Maybe he'll come out here."

When Castle came the next day, he did little more than examine Inez and say Evey had done the right things. After he left, Inez asked to see Will. She lay on the bed beneath a sheet with bandages covering the cuts on her face. One arm was wrapped from elbow to wrist.

"I'm sorry, girl," he said as he sat beside the bed.

She nodded. "I wanted to . . . th-thank you . . ."

"No need. You rest and get better. We'll talk then."

"I need to . . . talk now."

"Well, fine," he said, trying to smile. He pulled his chair closer. "What's so important that you've got to talk even when you don't feel like it?"

Inez swallowed, closed her eyes a moment and then opened them again. A tear trickled down her cheek. "Evey, too. And . . . Luke." She pronounced it "Wuke".

"I'll get them," Will promised.

In a few minutes they were crowded around the bed. Will held her hand as Inez told the story haltingly. It took a long time as she often stopped to cry.

"Nathan," she said, "is not . . . my son." They waited.

She sniffed, swallowed, and tried again. "When Jake . . . and I . . . when everyone th-thought we were . . . in wuv . . ." She stopped again and looked at the ceiling.

397

"It's all right," Will said, patting her hand.

"After my . . . father. . . died . . ." She wouldn't look at Will but he felt her squeeze his hand. "I never knew him. Jake and my mother . . . they . . . from the t-time he . . . found out about you . . ." She nodded toward Evey.

"That we were related?"

Inez nodded. "My mother . . ."

"Yolanda," Will said. "Go on."

"She . . . she and Jake . . ."

Luke stepped back a pace and Evey took a quick breath. Will straightened. "Jake and Yolanda? You mean, they . . . ?"

Inez nodded again. "Nathan is . . . theirs."

"My God." Evey said it softly and slumped to the edge of the bed. Luke leaned against the wall and stared at the floor while Will held the girl's hand and felt the wave of sadness wash over him. He squeezed her hand again and sat there in the silence wondering about the strange ways of people he knew.

There was more to the story and, when Inez had finished and turned on her side to hide the shame, Will still held her hand. He held it for a long time until he thought she was asleep. He found himself alone with her and sat there until he saw the moon through the window. He found Evey and Luke in the kitchen, accepted the offered cup of coffee and sat with them.

"It's horrible," Evey said. "When we were young Jake was so . . . so nice."

"People change," he said lamely.

"It was Yolanda's doing," Luke put in. "I told you years ago she'd try to get to you through your family."

Will toyed with the cup. "Maybe there is a curse." He lifted his eyes to Luke's and saw the man nod.

"You doubted it?"

"I guess I did," Will said.

They sat silently, thinking of the story Inez had taken more than an hour to tell.

Yolanda had decided when Inez and Jake were children that she would use them to exact some sort of revenge on Will for killing her husband. She hadn't been that upset at the loss of Nathan Peabody, Inez had told them, but had played the role early on as a way to gain attention. Later, it became an obsession with her as she and Will had one run-in after another. When Will and Tracey had finally confessed that Jake was their son, and when Sagebrush Tom had taken it so hard, she had even seduced him and then tossed him aside.

"But why Tom?" Evey asked.

"It was simply another way to cause some problems in the lives of Will and Tracey," Luke said. "Then, when the fact that you and Jake were related didn't seem to make any difference to the townspeople, she had to look for some other way to get at them."

"Jake."

"Right. But I never would have thought . . . "

"Inez couldn't have children," Will interrupted. "When they learned that, it didn't take Yolanda long to decide what she would do."

Jake had never loved Inez, the girl had told them. He married her because she was beautiful and because Yolanda promised him a large share of the profits she was making at the saloon and by acting as a go-between for stolen property from all over the state.

Yolanda and Jake agreed that Inez would never speak in public. They terrified her with threats of bodily harm if anyone found out about her speech impediments.

"But why did they do those . . . those things to her?" Evey was close to tears again.

"Yolanda evidently has a sadistic streak," Luke said. "She was angry that she had a daughter who wasn't perfect."

"But to . . . abuse her like that."

Inez had told them of being forced to submit to an assortment of sexual perversions, not only from Jake but from his friends as well. While Yolanda watched. There was no fear of her becoming pregnant.

"I can't believe there are people like that," Evey said, choking back the tears.

"I knew there was something awful wrong when Jake brought in that blonde," Will said. "This Christine."

The blond woman, Inez said, was the mother of four-year-old Marguerita, whom everyone had thought was Inez's daughter.

"I think Inez may be harmed far worse than any of us realize," Evey said "What can we do?"

Her eyes searched from Luke to Will and back again. When both men shook their heads she let her own head fall to her arms on the table and sobbed quietly.

TWO DAYS LATER Henry and Reva drove into the yard in a six-year-old Ford. "A gift of my congregation," Henry told Will, who tried hard not to stare at Henry's gray suit.

"That's fine, boy. I'm proud of you."

Henry turned quickly away. "That's the first time you ever said that to me."

Will took his son's arm and squeezed it tightly. "First time I ever felt like saying it." He glanced at Reva whose pursed lips didn't look quite so lifeless with the little dab of lipstick she was wearing. He was startled at the light gray dress, lighter than Henry's dark gray suit. It made her look — he struggled to find the word — *different*.

"You look downright . . . nice," he said.

He thought for a second that she blushed but quickly decided she'd probably never blushed in her life and wasn't about to start now. There might have been a tight little smile there, though.

"I bring some disturbing news," Henry said. "Jake knows Inez is here. The man who gave her the ride is back in Marble and is spreading the story."

"Well," Will said. "Well, so what?"

"Jake is telling everyone that you've stolen his wife from him. I think he plans on coming to retrieve her."

Will shrugged, feigning indifference.

"With a number of his friends."

"Let 'em come," Will said. Behind the facade of bravado, though, he felt a cold shock of apprehension shoot through his body. There were children here. And Evey.

"Come on in, boy," he said. "And your wife, too. I've got a story to tell you." He took them inside, and for the first time felt good about it.

When he had told them all he knew about Inez he sat back and waited. Neither Henry nor Reva moved for a long moment. Then Henry stood and walked to the window. He stared across the road toward Mount Sopris but Will knew his son was not admiring the scenery. Reva stared at her lap.

Henry turned back to them. "So what I thought was a religious conversion was only the beginnings of madness."

The look of failure that had become familiar to Will began once again to creep across Henry's face.

"I know you helped her," Will said. "She needed something to grab onto and you provided some hope."

"Something!" Henry gripped the back of his chair. "It could have been anything or anybody. God is not part of her life."

"I think He could be," Will replied. "I think she needs your kind of help now more than ever."

Henry's eyes brightened and he straightened. "I must go to her."

"Not yet, boy. Give her some time. And when you do try to bring her the . . . the Word, take it slowly. All right?"

Henry sighed and nodded. "I have learned that lesson well," he said. He turned to Reva. "Haven't we?"

400

Reva looked actually timid as she nodded and Will felt his chest swell a bit. *The boy has some grit after all*, he thought.

঵ঌ৯

THEY CAME after dark. Jake and three others were in the house before Will could snap himself out of the sleep that had overcome him despite his determination to stay awake. He felt someone lift the rifle from his lap and heard a snicker. He forced his good eye open and looked at Jake's sneer close to his face. "Gettin' too old to try and stand guard by yourself, aren't you?" Jake handed the rifle to a tall man in a dark suit and a round-topped hat. "Let's have that Colt, too." Will lifted it from the holster around his waist and Jake snatched it from his hand. "This thing still work?"

"It works."

Jake tossed it into a corner. "Where is she?"

"You're on private property. Get off."

Jake barked his laugh and his yellowed teeth gleamed as somebody touched a match to a lamp. He motioned to the tall man who left the room, then lumbered to the sofa and let himself down slowly, grunting.

"You're too fat." Will started to rise but felt a hand on his shoulder and settled back into the chair. Jake ignored him and looked around the room.

"Why don't you get some electricity in here, old man? You live like a damn hermit."

"She's in there," the tall man said and pointed to the bedroom.

"Well, get her out here, dammit!" Jake pounded his cane on the corner of the table and the picture of the two couples standing in the Pacific Ocean fell on its face.

"What's going on?" Henry stood in the doorway of Will's room in a nightshirt.

Two men took Henry's arms and pulled him into the room. "His wife's probably in there, too," Jake said, and a fat man in a suit barged through the door. Reva peeped something and was shoved into the room. She cowered beside Henry who stood straight and ridiculous in his long white nightshirt.

"She's so damned skinny I can't get ahold of nothin'," the fat man said.

Jake laughed briefly and then sobered as the tall man pushed Inez through the doorway. She stumbled forward, caught herself on a chair back, and groaned. With some difficulty, Jake pushed himself to his feet and limped across the room to her. He stood before her a long moment, then, in a movement so swift Will almost missed it, he brought his cane up from the floor and cracked her on the shoulder. She fell, huddled in a ball and moaned. "You bitch," he muttered.

401

"Everybody drop your guns." Luke's voice was soft but carried the force of surprise. "I mean it," he said. He stood just inside the front door, his rifle leveled at Jake's belly.

"Oh, shit," Jake said. He nodded to the other three men and three pistols thudded to the floor.

"Too bad," Will said, bending to pick up one of the guns.

"Is it?" Jake smiled again. "I don't think so."

"Now *you* drop it, injun," said a new voice that came from a fifth man, this one wearing work clothes, who stood behind Luke and prodded him with a pistol of his own. Luke let his rifle clatter to the floor and the man pushed him inside. Evey, Esther and Ruby came inside, followed by another of Jake's henchmen. "The injun was gone time we got to the house," the man said. "But we got these three pretties."

"Brought yourself an army, did you?" Will asked as he glanced at Inez who still lay on the floor, eyes wide.

Jake braced himself on his cane and turned to his father. "They needed the excitement. Our cars are down the road."

"You walked all the way up here?"

Jake ignored him and turned back to his men. "Get the women over there." He lifted his cane toward the fireplace. "You two" — he indicated Will and Luke — "on the sofa. The preacher, too." He jabbed Inez with the cane. "Get up."

"I . . . c-can't."

"Help her!" Two of the men pulled her to her feet. "Bring her here." The girl's swollen eyes widened as she was dragged to Jake's side. He pressed his face close to hers and smiled. Despite her obvious fear she spit in his face.

"Good for you," Will said.

"Shut up, old man!" Jake raised his arm and Inez tensed but stood her ground. He clubbed her on the jaw and she tumbled to the floor again. "Goddamned retarded slut!" He kicked her in the side. Evey's cry matched Inez's. Jake turned to her.

Evey shook her head. "I never dreamed anyone could be so totally cruel."

Jake left Inez on the floor and lumbered to stand in front of Evey. The four women stood in a row before the fireplace, all wearing nightgowns. Jake looked her up and down and sneered.

"This is my half-sister, boys," he said. "There was a time that she'd of done anything for me. Anything I wanted." A man snickered and Will started to get up from the sofa but was pushed back.

Jake continued to leer at Evey and reached a hand toward her breast. She slapped it away and the man laughed, then turned to the others. "I think we'll take her with us," he said. Then he stopped and his eyes narrowed. "On the other hand . . ." He turned to Esther. "We'll take this one."

"No!" Evey threw her arms around her daughter. Will sensed a sudden jolt of anger and fear, braced his hands and was halfway to his feet when he felt the pain in his head, saw the man standing over him with the gun he had used for a club, heard Evey's cry and thought he heard Esther say, "Grandfather!"

❧

HE CAME TO later, lying with his stomach to the floor and listening to a peal of thunder echo around the mountains.

His back and shoulders hurt. A throw rug was eye-level and a woman's foot twitched near his face. He tried to bring his hands to the floor but they wouldn't move. Hog-tied like a damn cow! he thought. His knees were bent, his hands tied behind his back and held there with a loop around his feet.

"Lie still, Will." Luke was similarly tied off to his right. "Reva's about loose, I think."

"Where?"

"To your left." *Damn.* He realized that was his bad eye. He twisted his head around and could barely see her struggling to free herself from the length of rope which bound her to a chair. A chill wind blew in through an open window and more thunder rumbled off in the southwest.

"A little more," she said. Her thin body was contorted beyond belief, one elbow raised high in the air, the other low to the ground, her torso bent sideways. "If I could just . . ." She lifted a knee slightly, and her elbow was almost in back of her head. "Only a bit . . . oh, Jesus, help me. Now, back this way . . . uh, ahh . . . there!" Her right arm was free. She flashed a broad grin at the others, the first time Will could remember seeing anything near an honest smile on her face. She was quickly free and working on the knots behind Henry's back. "And you've all pitied me because I was so thin," she said.

"Good work, my dear," Henry said.

"Sure glad you didn't fatten her up," Will said.

Evey was squirming desperately in the chair to which she was tied. "Hurry! Esther . . ."

❧

THE CHEVROLET bounced over the rutted road, traveling faster than Will had thought it could. Luke drove silently, his lips a tight line as he concentrated on the dimly lit outline of the road. They had been tied up nearly an hour before Will had come to, Luke had told him. Less than ten minutes

403

after Reva had freed herself, Will and Luke were armed and on their way to Marble. Evey had called the sheriff in Carbondale and she, along with Henry and Reva, were somewhere behind the two men, probably moving much more slowly in Henry's automobile.

"You got a plan?" Will shouted over the roar of the engine. Luke shook his head and Will searched for a handhold as the car went into a muddy rut with the right wheels and hit a hole with the left, splashing water high into the air. "Me neither."

The windshield quickly turned to mud as the rain increased. Luke worked the wipers but they did little more than smear the glass. He leaned out the left side and didn't slow down.

Marble was pitch dark when they arrived, any moon hidden behind low-flying clouds. Luke skidded the car to a halt and shut down the engine. A steady rain peppered the roof of the car and a sliver of lightning off to the right snapped on and off again. Pretty soon a dull drumroll of thunder crept over the western peaks. Luke pointed to the second floor of the White House Hotel. A dim light outlined a window. "They're up there."

"I 'spect," Will replied. He checked the chambers of his revolver for the third or fourth time. "Well?"

Luke glanced at him. "I'm going to get my daughter. You stay here and send the others up when they get here."

"Like hell."

"I figured." Luke checked the load in his double-barreled shotgun. "Let's go, then."

They stepped into the muddy street and were quickly soaked with the heavy rain. They ran to the porch of the hotel and quietly shook water from hats and clothes. Will shivered with the dampness and fingered the trigger of the rifle he carried. There was a sound from upstairs like a woman crying.

The front door was unlocked. "Must of been in a hurry," Will whispered. They walked into the darkened room and the tall man with the round-topped hat stepped from behind the door.

"We left it unlocked on purpose," he said with a smile. The butt of Luke's shotgun came up out of the darkness without a sound and caught the man on the jaw. He lurched backwards, throwing his Colt in the air. Before either hit the floor, Will caught the Colt and Luke caught the man. Will stuck the pistol in his belt and Luke laid his assailant gently on the floor.

Luke was already heading for the stairs at the side of the room. Will hurried after him and was panting heavily when they reached the second floor. "Which room?" Luke whispered. Will nodded toward the second door and Luke walked silently toward it. Luke tried the doorknob and found the door locked. He glanced at Will, shrugged and lifted a booted foot. The doorjamb splintered on the first kick and Luke was inside. Will hurried to catch up, his rifle leveled.

Six people stood stock still. In one swift glance Will took it all in. Inez lay huddled in the far right corner, blood oozing from her nose. Three men in suits stood to the left, one with a wide grin exposing a gap in his teeth. Jake stood over Esther nearly naked and tied to the bed.

"What the . . . ?" Jake turned toward them. His shirt was open and his huge belly hung over unbuttoned pants.

Suddenly, one of the men on the left reached inside his coat and Luke shot him in the chest. Esther screamed as the man slammed backwards against the wall. The room was suddenly a blur of movement. One of the remaining two men made a rush toward them and Will snapped off a shot, hitting him in the knee. He fell with a scream. Jake began a shuffling waddle to his right as the third man reached for a rifle leaning against the wall. Luke blew the side of his head apart with his second barrel.

"Stop where you are, Jake." Luke had thrown his shotgun to the floor and held his Colt waist-high just out of its holster and pointed at Jake's back.

"Don't," Will said. He touched his son-in-law on the arm. "That's enough."

"Is it?"

Will's head began to spin. It was as though he were on Owl Point and the *ini'pute* were swarming round him. There was more to come, he realized. *Let it be over*, he thought. But it wasn't over and somehow he knew it and was afraid. He felt afraid and almost nauseated, but knew he had to stay in charge. Yet he wasn't in charge. Something else had control of events and he was powerless. He could only be aware that something was yet to happen. Be *alert*, he told himself. He swallowed, straightened, fought off the sickness and the increasing pain in his chest.

"Don't move, Jake," Will pleaded. The man stood trembling in the center of the room, facing away from them, his pants drooping below his broad rump. Will nudged Luke.

"Untie Esther, man."

Inez stirred in the corner. She pushed herself to a sitting position, stared at Jake. "If I . . . had a knife. . ."

"Hush, now," Will said.

"I'd . . . cut off . . . your . . ." She looked wildly around the room.

Luke had freed Esther and covered her with a blanket. She knelt on the bed, her arms tightly around her father. "He'll pay, Inez," Luke said. "We'll see to that."

The room was deathly still. No one moved. The man Will had shot in the knee was quiet, perhaps had fainted. Will heard a sob from Esther and, over

405

the roll of distant thunder, the sound of an automobile growing louder. Or was it something else? A humming and a buzzing sound filled Will's ears. A warning of danger nearby? There was no fear, no prickling sensation like you feel when you are alone in the dark and sure someone's following you. Only a sudden knowledge that there was something else. Something evil.

He edged toward Jake. Luke was still bent over Esther, holding her while she sobbed. Inez stared at Jake who trembled as he bent to pull up his pants.

The humming. A car door slammed in the street. Will's head ached. His heart pounded. The room began to spin. He whirled and saw Yolanda in the doorway. She held a gun in front of her with both hands. He saw her smile, saw her breasts swell above the top of the low-cut gown, saw her finger tighten on the trigger. The room seemed upside-down. His chest throbbed and the pain shocked him to action.

He lunged toward the floor, instinctively squeezed the trigger of his rifle, felt something nick at his arm like a bee-sting, heard a roar and a cry, and saw Yolanda fall.

His breath came quickly now. He sucked in great lungfuls of air but couldn't seem to get enough. He hunched there on his knees gasping for all the air he could get and listening to the hummingbirds and wishing the room would turn right-side up again and stop spinning so he could maybe stand up.

Feet thudded on the stairs. "Luke!" Evey's voice called in the hallway. Will saw more people in the room. Evey ran to Luke and Esther. Jake buttoned his pants. Henry was at his father's side.

"Are you . . . ?"

Will shook his head. "Give me a hand, boy. Help me up." Henry took his father's hand, cupped an elbow and gently lifted him to his feet. He put an arm around him, even, and hugged him close.

"My God!" Reva said, leaning into Henry, and Will staggered. "The blood. The death. It is hell itself."

"Quiet, woman," Henry said, and Will thought, *Good for you, boy.*

Now there was a whistling in his ears almost drowning out the humming. *Was it not yet over?* Surely it was over. He forced his way to Yolanda and sat beside her on the floor. His head didn't want to stay upright, and it fell almost to his chest. *Would that infernal buzzing never stop?*

Yolanda was alive, but only barely. Her eyes were half open. Blood soaked her chest just below her neck. She stared at him with glazed eyes.

"Yolanda, I'm . . ."

Her mouth moved. When she was able to speak it was half-whisper, half-croak. "You have killed us both," she said. "First . . . first Nathan. Now me." He heard her plainly even though the humming, buzzing, and spinning continued. There was a sense of panic that filled the air, which smelled of death. Esther clutched her mother, sobbing still. Jake breathed heavily.

Reva tugged at Henry's arm. "Get me out of here," she begged.

"Wait." Henry shoved her aside and she pressed her lean face against the wall, clenched her eyes tightly shut.

Will saw a faint design in the wallpaper. Vertical light blue lines with a small flower print. One flower to the right within its prescribed vertical space, the next to the left. It was a nice print.

Yolanda's eyes closed, opened again. "You will. . ." Her chest swelled. "You will rot. . . in hell."

Will nodded and watched her die. As the breath left her body for the last time he sighed himself. "See you there," he said quietly. He looked at her for a moment longer, then stood on weak and shaking legs and turned.

He caught a movement out of the corner of his eye. Inez had bent and was picking something off the floor. She straightened and leveled the pistol at Jake. Her eyes were wide. Blood had caked on her face and more continued to run from her nose.

"Inez," Will said, and took a step forward. The humming was intense. He wanted to sit, to lie down, to sleep and feel the warmth of Judith beside him.

Inez waved the gun around the room. The back of Jake's neck was bright red and sweat poured onto his shirt. "Oh, shit," he said. "Don't, Inez. Please, don't . . ."

"I have always . . . hated . . . you." she stammered. The gun barrel swung toward Jake again and steadied there. "I have always hated . . . my . . . self."

She shot him in the face. He fell backwards and hit the floor with a dull thud. Reva screamed but no one else moved. They stared at Jake's body, massive there, filling the floor, his face a reddened pulp.

More footsteps sounded on the stairs, the loud thumping of boots. A man with a badge lurched into the room, took in the carnage with a wide sweep and closed his eyes. He swallowed. "Holy . . ."

Will ignored him, and instead turned back to Inez. The humming should have stopped but it was still there, although less intense, expectant, waiting.

Inez tilted her head to the side and smiled at Will.

"Inez, don't!" Will shouted at her but his feet wouldn't move and his chest hurt. The humming became a horrendous roaring in his ears like the Crystal River in full spring runoff gushing through narrows, crashing over boulders. He sucked in air again, as much as he could, but he couldn't move and could only watch with the others.

Inez was still smiling as she placed the barrel of the pistol above her nose, just between the eyes. She hooked a thumb in the trigger guard and pulled.

The humming stopped with the explosion and then there was only the sound of Inez jerking backwards and sliding down the wall. She lay still, the gun on her stomach.

After a few seconds Will sank to his knees and retched in the blood and grime that covered the floor. Reva fainted into Henry's arms and, even through his gagging, Will could hear his son murmur a prayer to the God who so dominated the man's life.

And he thought of Judith, and Tracey. And he hurt. And cried.

∾౬౿

A CLOCK TICKED behind Will, who sat in his favorite chair and thought he should have thrown the thing away long ago. It didn't *tick-tock.* Never had. Instead, it went *tock-tick.* Enough to drive a man to violence. But Judith had bought the clock and she had liked it so Will continued to wind it and listen to it *tock-tick. Seems to be getting louder, too*, he thought.

At least it was fall again and the days were cooler. Will wondered how long it had been. It had been five months but it seemed like only five days. Esther was back in school and had evidently shaken off the trauma of that insane night back in May. There were times when Will thought he saw a hint of sadness and fear in her dark eyes but it never seemed to last long.

Inez, now. She might have turned out just fine if Jake and Yolanda . . . Will stopped the thought. They were all dead now and buried up in Marble where it was probably getting good and cold. He thought he should go up there soon. He hadn't been back since that night. He couldn't seem to make himself go. Thankfully, Tracey had been down to the ranch a time or two with Theresa and the kids.

Tracey had insisted on taking in Jake's four-year-old, Marguerita. The child's mother, Christine, had simply disappeared, either before or after that night, and nobody had heard a word from her since. There was speculation that she must have taken the boy, Nathan, too. *Well, good riddance to them both,* Will mused.

He was a little put out when Henry and Reva came into the house, returning from down valley sooner than they had expected. *There are times, dammit, when you want to be alone*, he thought angrily. Since they'd moved in with him he'd been alone little enough. Had to saddle a horse and ride off somewhere just to get away from people.

Reva sent something like a smile his way and then sidled into the kitchen as Henry plopped down on the sofa.

"What now?" Will asked.

"Reva wants to leave the valley."

"The hell she does."

Henry scowled at him and Will raised his eyebrows. "I told her no."

"No need to leave, now you've got your church goin' so good," Will said.

Henry nodded. "She says we ought to go somewhere else where we can do some real good. I believe I am needed here and here we shall stay."

Will poked at the logs in the fireplace. "When Josh comes back in a few years we'll have us all together again. Gonna make a good doctor, Josh will."

Reva carried a tray into the room bearing one coffee cup and two glasses of water. "Esther will probably be married off by then and perhaps moved to someplace more civilized."

"Hope not," Will said. He nodded his thanks for the coffee and dropped back into the chair. "We'll still have little Ruby for a while, though. She's barely fourteen." He thought about it for a moment. "Theresa's boy, Teegee, he's about the same age as Esther. Maybe they'll. . ."

"Don't count on it," Henry interrupted.

"Then we got Martha. She's ten, I think. And now we got another one. Jake's girl. Little Marguerita. She can't be more'n five or so."

"She's four," Reva said.

"I'll be damned."

"You will, if you keep using that foul language."

"Now look, Reva." Will lifted his cup toward her and then thought better of it. "Never mind. I been talkin' that way too long to quit now. Don't mean nothin'."

Reva turned to Henry. "Have you thought more about . . ?."

"I have," he replied.

"And?"

"And we're staying right here. We are building a good life here. And, besides . . ." He turned to Will. "Besides, I have family here."

Will didn't look at either one of them, and instead frowned into his cup a little, but he felt good inside and he had a feeling Henry knew it.

Henry is coming around, Will thought happily. *He sure enough is coming around.*

THE CHEST PAINS were frequent that winter. Now and then, they were bad. Will didn't say anything about them. He thought about driving the wagon in to see Dr. Castle but never did. He just sat around the house thinking about Tracey and wishing she was living with him instead of Henry and Reva.

He sat around and read the papers and fumed about how the world was going to hell. *Damned little good news in the papers these days*, he decided.

409

Adolph Hitler had published a book called *Mein Kampf* that had everyone nervous about Germany again. *Never happen,* Will thought. *People are smarter nowadays.*

Well, look here. President Coolidge is quoted as saying "the business of America is business." Ain't that something. *Lots of people getting rich back there. Not nearly so many here in the valley.* There was a story about 40,000 Ku Klux Klanners marching around Washington in white sheets. He snickered at the idea. *Too yellow to show their faces.* The Scopes "Monkey Trial." *Now there's a hoot. Bunch of hurrah over that deal.* Will figured he knew a lot of folks who must have had apes for parents. A big mess overseas. *So what else is new?* The Russian Politburo had expelled Leon Trotsky and the newest dictator was a Josef Stalin. Over in China the new leader was Chaing Kai-shek. Will didn't even try to pronounce his name. *Good Lord!* Will thought as he looked at another article. Somebody had put a rocket into space and there was talk about sending a man to the moon. *This Robert Goddard fellow is just the latest wild man the newspapers cotton on to get people riled up and buy their paper. They've got talking motion pictures, a new invention called television and lots of radio to entertain the fat butts who don't have the gumption to get off 'em and go outside and do something.*

Reva nagged at him to get electricity and a telephone but he put her off. "I'll be dead and gone one of these days and you can do whatever you damn well please with the place. But while I'm in charge we're doin' just fine."

Luke and Evey were also doing just fine. They continued to sell their horses across the state. People from Denver and Salt Lake City and Santa Fe and Cheyenne showed up at the ranch to look over the stock. They usually bought something.

Every now and then Will trudged up the hill to visit the graves of Judith and Ardy. The hole he'd started digging for himself was partially filled in and weeds grew in it. He thought about working on it again but decided somebody else could dig his grave. No need to do everything myself, he thought.

He'd sit beside the graves and talk to one or the other of them, sometimes both. He always felt better for it, too.

Tracey found him there one day, late in the summer of 1927 and sat on the grass beside him.

"I'll be joining them before long," Will said to her after he'd received a kiss on the cheek.

"You'll probably live to be a hundred, you old Texas cowboy," she said with a smile. He wondered if he looked as old as she did. She still looked mighty fine. Just old.

"What's the latest up your way?" he asked.

"There is more talk about selling the Consolidated Marble Company.

410

Marcello hopes so. He's back at the general store, you know."

"You got any rooms at the hotel?" Will tugged at a weed and threw it into his grave.

"You know I do. Why?"

He stood, took her hand, and pulled her to her feet. He wouldn't let go of her hands and she didn't struggle. She smiled at him. "I think I might move in," he said. "I got to get away from Reva. I have to do my own cookin' to get anything decent to eat."

Tracey laughed and it was the old, good laugh that was still young.

"I'll pay you," Will said.

She kissed him again, on the cheek, and turned to walk down the hill. "Come on," she said. "I'll cook tonight."

"All right," Will said. "And stay with me. We'll play married."

She laughed again and was several paces ahead when he finally started after her.

THAT WINTER the Consolidated property in Marble was sold to Jacob Smith of Buffalo, New York, for one million dollars and some people thought he might be another Colonel Meek. In June, Marcello and thirty-four others were hired to complete what contracts the company had, mainly a $700,000 project for the Huntington Memorial in Pasadena, California.

"Maybe they ought to forget about marble and concentrate on the other ores," Luke said in the summer of 1928. "I heard the Humboldt Mine's open again and planning to ship a thousand tons of lead, silver and copper a month to Salt Lake City."

"Never do it," Will muttered.

In the presidential election that fall, Al Smith got most of Marble's 130 votes, for all the good it did him.

Lindbergh had flown across the Atlantic by then, there were twenty million cars on American roads, and you could talk on a New York telephone for three minutes with somebody in London for $75. Wouldn't be worth that much for three minutes of talking with anybody, Will thought, except maybe for Tracey.

People were humming "Strike Up the Band" by George Gershwin and "I'm Looking Over a Four Leaf Clover" by Harry Woods. Will didn't know either one of the tunes.

Everybody was having so much fun and drinking so much booze, despite it being illegal, that Will figured he would be dead before the good times got to the valley. It might be fun to be twenty-five these days, though, he figured.

A letter came from Tracey. "Jake Smith sold a half interest in the Consolidated Yule Marble Company to the Vermont Marble Company and Smith himself is buying up more marble land. With Vermont interested in us at last, perhaps prosperity will be ours in 1929."

The year started out well enough. Two miners discovered a vein of gold between Marble and Lizard Lake and a geologist said it assayed as high as four hundred ounces to the ton.

Will put down the newspaper and rubbed his chest. "Are you all right?" Reva asked.

Will nodded. "Don't get excited," he said. "It's not time for electricity in this house yet." But he left the table and went to his bedroom where he stretched out on the bed and waited for the pain to pass. It took a long time and he was afraid.

"I want to go up to Marble," he told Luke the next day. "I can get freed up in a day or two," Luke said. "I'll take you then."

Will shook his head. "I better go now."

Luke looked up sharply from his paperwork. "All right. Go get packed and I'll get the Ford."

"I'm packed," Will said.

In the car, a 1927 model Luke had bought the previous spring, they rode silently until Luke turned to him. "You been having problems, Will?"

"For a while," Will said. He patted his chest.

"We thought so. You better see a doctor."

"You knew?"

Luke kept his eyes on the roadway, a smoother bed these days with fewer ruts. "We all know," he said. "But you're so damned stubborn nobody wanted to say anything."

Will waited a while, then asked, "Tracey know, too?"

Luke nodded. "You can't hide everything from us."

She met them at the door of the mostly empty hotel. "It's about time you showed up," she said. "I was beginning to worry."

Will shot a look at Luke who stared at the ground. "Evey telephoned her," he said.

Will took his bag from the car and pushed past Tracey into the hotel. "Can't even surprise somebody anymore," he muttered. "Damn telephones."

That night, after Luke had left with a promise to return in two days to pick up Will, the two of them sat at a table in the kitchen. Marcello and Theresa were upstairs with their children. Marguerita was asleep and the few boarders had already eaten.

"I been thinkin'," Will said. He warmed his hands around a coffee cup. "I been thinkin' about the old days and some things that might of worked out different."

Tracey kept her eyes from his. "I think of those days often," she said softly.

Will reached across the table and covered her hand with his. "We'd of made a good pair, wouldn't we?"

Finally, she looked at him and the love in her eyes made him want to cry out. "We *are* a good pair."

"You know what I mean."

"I do." She nodded and clutched his hand. "You were the finest. . . you and Tom were the finest men . . ." She wiped away a tear. "And Randall, too."

"Wish I'd of known him in his good days, before the accident," Will said. "At least I got to know you. For a while, there."

For two days they talked and remembered, and laughed and cried now and then. They walked to the river and looked up toward the marble quarry, holding hands. The town looked different from that time when Will had talked Tom into letting him help them build a boarding house. The marble mill, stretching hundreds of feet along the river, had been barely a dream at that time.

"Remember that trip to California?" Will asked and Tracey brightened. "I never wanted to get to California all those years as bad as I wanted to get home after I finally did get there."

"The grass is always greener," she said.

"That was some trip, though. Still got your picture?"

"Of course."

"Me, too."

They went back to the hotel and Luke was there. Will knew it was over and didn't really feel so bad about it. Not as bad as he had thought he might.

After dinner Luke carried his bag to the car and Will stood alone with Tracey once more in the kitchen. They looked at each other for a long moment and then moved together, hugging one another like they never wanted to let go. Will got his face in front of hers and she let him kiss her a long, good one.

When it was over, their cheeks were wet with tears. Will turned his head and quickly wiped a hand across his good eye. "That'll have to do, I reckon," he said.

"It'll do. It will do just fine."

At the door Will stopped again. "You take care of those kids," he said. "They're mighty fine."

She nodded and he knew she wouldn't speak again.

"See you," he said and climbed into the car, knowing it was a lie. He had a feeling she knew it, too.

413

At the edge of town he looked out the rear window and saw her standing there on the porch with a light from the door making a silhouette of her. She raised a hand and Will turned away. He looked down valley and swallowed hard.

❦

ALL SUMMER he waited. He sat in his chair, walked to the corrals to watch Luke and his hands work the horses, climbed the hill to the graves. Nothing happened. He began to feel better, and stronger. *Damn*, he thought. *And I already said my good-byes to Tracey, too.*

He heard that more gold was discovered upriver. There was talk of the government wanting to grant a contract to some company for what would be the largest single block of marble ever quarried. It would be for the Tomb of the Unknown Soldier in Washington, D.C.

"That would make Marble famous," Henry said at dinner.

"Never happen," Will replied.

Suddenly it was fall and just as suddenly, Will was hit with the worst and most painful attack yet. He was sitting on a rail watching Luke trot a horse when he felt the jolt of pain and grabbed for his chest. His head began to spin and he toppled from the rail and hit the ground with a thud. Almost immediately, Luke was bent over him.

"Lie still," he said. "Can you breathe?"

Will tried to nod. "Kind of," he whispered.

Luke picked him up and carried him to the new house. Will motioned the other direction with his head. "My house," he croaked.

"Sorry, old timer," Luke said. "Evey will want you where she can watch over you."

Dr. Castle showed up late in the afternoon and, by then, Will was feeling better. After the doctor had listened to his heartbeat with a cold stethoscope he told Will to stay in bed for a few days. There was some soft talk outside his door that Will couldn't understand, but he didn't much care anyway. He'd known what was coming, after all.

They kept him in bed for two weeks. The telephone seemed to ring day and night and Evey talked into it quietly and never told him what was going on. He didn't give a hoot, but he didn't like being in bed all the time. Henry and Reva came up to see him every day. *At least I don't have to eat her cooking,* he thought.

"Tracey wants to come see you," Evey told him one night.

Will waved it off. "No," he said. "I don't want her to see me this way and we done said our so longs anyhow."

414

"I understand," Evey said.

There were letters and telephone calls that nobody told him about and lots of muttering around the house that he couldn't understand and didn't ask about. *Shoot*, he thought. They didn't even let him read a newspaper. *Just as well, what with one eye and all, and there isn't much I want to read about anyway, thank you,* Will decided. So he slept, or lay there staring out the window as the leaves turned bright red and yellow and then slowly began to go brown and fall to the ground.

One morning there was a commotion in the hallway with lots of scuffling feet and some talking and things thudding on the floor. *Hell*, Will decided. He'd been in bed long enough. So he got up — he didn't have any trouble — and got himself dressed and walked into the living room.

He saw Joshua first. The boy was as tall as Luke and he had filled out in the shoulders. His dark hair was swept back from his face and he broke into a smile at the sight of his grandfather.

Henry and Reva stood in the background. Luke and Evey turned Josh loose long enough for the young man to embrace Will. "I thought you were sick," he said. "You look fine."

"Got tired of that damned bed," Will said lamely.

He turned toward Evey and stared, instead, into the face of Abby. The shock frightened him at first, and his hand went impulsively to his chest. But all he did was breathe faster. She seemed smaller, shorter. There was some plumpness to her that was surprising. Her hair was gray and cut short in the style of the day.

"Hello, Will," she said. She didn't move and the two of them stood there staring at one another while the others looked away, at the floor, or out the window.

"Hello, Abby." She was older but he saw her as the young girl who flirted with him as he held $15,000 in his hands and tried to figure out where he was going to put the money. Henry Gillespie's niece stood before him almost fifty years after that day and Will Martin hunched up his shoulders and took a step toward her. She met him in the center of the room and pretty soon they each held out a hand. He took hers in his and thought, *To hell with it,* and pulled her to him. He was tall and frail, she short and plump. But it was good to hug her and when they broke off everybody was all smiles.

"What are you doing here, Abby? Come to see me off?" The smiles faded and Abby looked away.

"We'll tell you later," she said. "First . . ." She waved a hand over a roomful of suitcases and trunks that Will hadn't noticed. The room was suddenly full of activity, everyone relieved that the meeting was over. Luke and Henry each took the end of a trunk and headed for one of the

415

bedrooms. Joshua hefted two suitcases and followed them. Evey bustled about, taking Abby's coat. Reva disappeared into another room and Will stood there all alone wondering what the devil was going on. At dinner they told him.

Two weeks earlier, on October 24 — "Black Thursday" as it was to be called — the stock market had crashed. Fortunes were lost in minutes. Among those who had been completely wiped out was Winfield Porter, Abby's husband. And among the many who had committed suicide had also been Winfield Porter.

"My God," Will said. "I'm sorry, Abby. I didn't know a thing. Nobody tells me nothin' around here."

Abby nodded, forced back tears and took a sip of water. "I have gotten used to it," she said. "I am a strong person. Winfield was weak. He was strong only as long as he had money."

"You are strong," Will agreed. "Well, I'm sorry. You mean you're . . . broke?"

She nodded again, then smiled. "Completely. When Joshua heard of Winfield's death he immediately came to me. We talked to Evey on the phone and, well, here I am."

Will stared at her. "You're going to live *here*?" He looked at the others. "With *me*?"

That broke the tension and everyone managed a laugh. "With Evey and Luke, at least," Abby said. "I hear you have your own house."

Will snapped a glance at Reva. "I used to," he said. Did Reva blush? "So, what does all this mean? Is the country going to hell or what?"

"Yes," Reva said, but caught herself when Henry frowned.

"We're just not sure yet," Luke answered. "It doesn't look good, though."

"Well," Will said. "We've got the ranch. We'll make out just fine."

There was silence for a moment and then Evey spoke up. "Yes, we will," she said. "And we're all together again." Her gaze took in the entire table. Will realized she was right. Henry and Reva sat near him, Joshua and Esther on his right, Luke at the far end of the table with Evey next to him. Ruby and Abby sat side by side to his left, next to Evey.

"We are that," Will said, looking at his family. "Together again."

⚬ೖ๑

THAT NIGHT the pain returned and he suffered with it alone. *No need to bother everybody at a time like this,* he thought. But it was bad and in the night Evey and Luke came to his room when he groaned too loudly. In another moment Henry was with them and soon Abby followed. Luke stole from the room leaving Will with his two children and their mother.

416

"Just like the old days," he said.

"Hush," Evey said. "Where are those pills Dr. Castle gave you?" Will pointed to the dresser and swallowed one when she brought it with a glass of water from the pitcher.

"Sorry about this," he said. "Go on back to bed. I'll be all right now."

"You go," Abby said to the other two. "I'll sit a while." They were quiet for a long time after the others had left and finally Will reached for her hand. "Wish I knew what to say," he whispered.

"It's just the way things are," she replied. "I have learned to live with the unexpected."

Will tried to laugh. "Me, too."

After another silence, Abby said, "They are wonderful people." Will knew she meant Henry and Evey since they'd both been thinking about their children.

"I was worried about ol' Henry there, for a while," he said.

"I have to admit," she said, then hesitated. "I was worried, too."

"You were?"

"Yes. He is so headstrong. Like you."

"Me!" It was funny for a moment and then he had to cough and the pain got worse for a moment. Finally, it settled back to a dull ache and he breathed deeply and then relaxed. "Don't worry," he said.

She snugged up closer to the bed. "That's funny. I should be comforting you and you're telling me not to worry."

"What have we got to worry about?"

She smiled. "Not a thing."

"You're just as pretty as you ever were, Abby."

"And you're just as big a liar."

"I mean it."

She touched his hand. "I think you do. And thank you. Can you sleep now?"

"Probably so. We'll talk some more tomorrow."

She was at the door when he called her name. She turned. "I can't imagine anyone wanting to be anywhere else," he said. "The valley brought you back, didn't it?"

She opened the door and turned. "Good night," she whispered.

WILL TOOK his pills, saw the doctor again, got up now and then to walk about the house and, once, outside. He felt stronger but knew what was bound to happen. He and Abby talked for long hours each day. She told him about her life in Denver, the life of a rich woman with time on her hands. It was full of parties and music and volunteer work for "good causes." She and Winfield had lived together but, after the first few years of marriage, had realized their seeming love for one another was dwindling rather than maturing. They had developed their own interests, had gone places together because it was expected, had slept in separate bedrooms.

"Then his death . . . ," Will broke in.

"It saddened me," Abby said. "But I was not devastated. Surprised, really, that he was so weak. I could have lived without the money. But not Winfield. Money was his life."

"That's too bad."

"Money never meant anything to you, did it?"

"I wouldn't say that," Will said. "I was glad to have some. Didn't worry too much about it when I didn't."

She laughed. "You were glad to have me, too, when you had me. But you didn't worry too much when I left."

He shook his head. "I should have known this valley wasn't for you. At least, then."

"Well," she said. "I'll have to get used to it again, won't I?"

It was mid-November and the days were shorter, the nights colder, the pain in Will's chest more regular. It was about over, he figured, and one night he asked for Luke and Joshua. When they were in his room and sitting at his side he told them he wanted to go to Owl Point.

"But Grandad . . ."

Will turned to Luke. "You know why."

Luke nodded. "I do."

"But . . ." Josh was close to tears.

"Tomorrow. Early."

"All right." Luke stood, touched Josh on the shoulder. "I'll wake you at daybreak."

"I'll be awake," Will said.

THEY HALF-PUSHED, half-carried him up the steep mountainside. The Ford was parked off the road north of Redstone just upriver from Frog Rock. The climb took most of the morning and they stopped often. The day had started out cloudy with a light mist. By midmorning, however, the sun had broken through and Luke and Josh were sweating with the exertion of getting Will up the incline.

Will had put on his tall Texas hat for the occasion and, at the last moment, had buckled on his spurs. They jangled a little as he made his way upwards. He hadn't seen Evey or the others before he'd left. He figured that was better. He thought he had seen Abby hiding behind a curtained window as they drove out of the yard, but he hadn't waved at her.

Three-quarters of the way up they stopped to rest and Josh sat down beside his grandfather. "I've been at a lower altitude too long," he said, wiping his brow.

"You're coming back here, aren't you?" Will asked.

"I'll be finished in another year. Then I'll come back."

"We need another good doctor. Castle's gettin' too old."

"He'll be a good one, I think," Luke said with a smile.

Will pointed off to his left. "Owl Man is buried over there somewhere."

"I often think about that time I came up here with you and dad," Josh said. "It was the day I decided to go into medicine. You remember?"

"I remember," Will said. "Your grandmother would be proud. It was her death that helped you decide."

They were at the point by early afternoon. Will struggled to the comfortable rock which still sat embedded in the red soil just at the edge of the precipice. He sat down and tried to ignore the pain. He felt dizzy and closed his eyes for a moment. Were the forces still there? It had been years since he had visited this holy spot.

"What did Owl Man call them?" Josh asked.

"They are *ini'pute*," Will answered. "Tiny ghosts who inhabit this *ihupi'arat tubut*. It is a haunted spot and it is very powerful."

Josh looked around him. "And the Indians believed in them and their power."

"They're real," Will said. He turned to Luke. "Do you remember that night . . . in Marble? The night . . . I had to shoot . . .?"

"I remember," Luke said.

"They were there."

"Who?"

"The *ini'pute*."

"In Marble? You?"

"They warned me," Will said. "There may have been only one of them, maybe hundreds. I knew to turn. I knew Yolanda was there and was about to kill me." Josh and Luke stared at him. "It isn't some old man's fantasy," Will said.

Luke looked around him, maybe trying to see some of the ghosts. "I believe you," he said.

"Good," Will said. "It's true. There was something . . . a humming . . . it got louder . . . and I knew to turn. They kept warning me after that. Maybe I

419

could have stopped Inez . . ." Will looked at Josh.

"He knows about it," Luke said. "It's all right."

"Owl Man gave me the power. I never thought . . . "

"Now you know."

"It's real," Will said again, quietly. "Now I must pass it on to someone else." He met Luke's eyes and then, together, they turned to Josh. The boy paled.

"I don't . . . "

"Want it?" Will smiled. "Neither did I."

"But, why me?"

"Because your dad's almost fifty years old," Will said. "And you're coming back here, for good, I hope. You do believe in them, don't you?"

"I . . . "

"It don't matter. I didn't, either. Someday you'll need them, though, and they'll be there. Then you'll believe."

They stared out over the valley for a while. The sun danced on the Crystal River as it had for centuries and the greens and reds and browns blended into a soft bed of forest and mountain. Off to their left Cleveholm glinted through the trees. The little village of Redstone lay quietly below them, the rows of coke ovens silent now, no smoke, no men, no activity. It was good.

"I think I'd like to be alone now," Will said.

Luke stood. "Let's take a walk, son."

Josh rose and was as tall as his father. The two of them might have been brothers.

"We'll see you in a while, Grandad," he said.

Will looked at the boy a long moment. "In a while."

When they were gone he squirmed around on the rock and got comfortable. He fished in his pocket for the pipe, which was now forbidden to him, and fired it up. He inhaled deeply, feeling the pain and welcoming it.

They were all around him then, the *ini'pute* who were his friends, although he hadn't really known it or accepted their powers until that night in Marble. They flitted about like the hummingbirds he remembered. There was no signal this time, no warning. They were simply there, letting him know it.

Owl Man had given them to him that day long ago and he had scoffed at the idea. Now, he felt comfort in their presence. Owl Man had discovered the significance of this point, had accepted the power that was thrust upon him in his youth. Now, Will Martin, the unlikeliest of holy men, was about to pass the responsibility once again. He would pass it to a man who loved the valley and would make it his own. For what was ownership but love and respect? And commitment. Josh would come to accept the gift. He would honor the legacy of Owl Man and respect the beings who inhabited this place of mystery.

Secure in the knowledge, and comforted by it, Will took a long look at Mount Sopris. Its westernmost shoulder was crowned with white from early high-country snows. The Utes had called it the Mount of Sanctuary. Will wondered if it would it be a sanctuary now for Abby, and if it would continue to guard Tracey and her own family.

The pain was worse now and he bent forward, seeking some relief. As he did so, he saw faces in the earth, faces of those who had gone before him. Strong men and women who had shaped his life and made it worth the living. All of them had given him something that provided a direction, a lesson, a way of accomplishing goals that were, often, not so much of his own making but which were thrust upon him. He had often reacted to crises with instinctive decisions that forced his life to veer from one direction to another, like the Crystal River running downhill, bumping into a mountain wall but gouging out a new path just the same and forging ahead to some unseen ending where it would be absorbed into the mighty Colorado.

It was the Grand River when Will rode into the valley in 1880. And the Crystal was Rock Creek. Things change, thanks to men who see a need for change and who aren't afraid to buck the difficulties that change brings.

He'd paid them all back, too. All the men and women who'd done for him when he couldn't do for himself or who saw promise in his ideas, or simply in him as a man. In the red dirt, he saw them and it was a feeling as good as lying next to a good woman and knowing she felt something for you beyond your manhood.

There was Sagebrush Tom, young and lean on a cow pony, then drunk in Nathan Peabody's saloon. Peabody came and went quickly, there in the red dirt, and Sagebrush Tom Cordell reappeared, taking long strides beside Charles Goodnight. And there they were on the Goodnight-Loving Trail with dust in their noses and thinking they'd found heaven itself.

And there was Doc Phillips in his tall black hat, his right eye twitching like mad. And George Sanders, the engineer. Where was he now? Dead, too, probably, like Randall Collins who had worn a black hood and suffered like nobody could ever know.

Sagebrush Tom had his arm around Tracey Collins and she was beautiful and young and strong and had a look in her eye meant for Tom that should have been for Will and was, once. Will had given Tracey and Tom each other, thank God, and it had been good but for Yolanda Peabody.

In the dirt was Henry Gillespie and the other Silver Kings of Aspen who had such high hopes that faded with the gold standard.

Old Ardy himself, the other half of the Double M, was there, then, puffing on a hand-made and swearing at Will 'cause he had to do all the work. Then

Ardy was helping a young Abby down from a wagon and she was all smiles and pert as a yellow daisy wild in a high meadow.

Ardy was snarfing down an enormous piece of Judith Swensson's apple pie and Judith smiled at Will and laughed that low laugh of hers and good Lord it was good.

The creased face of an old Indian was also good and Owl Man danced for him again, for a while.

Pretty soon Bat Masterson showed up in a sombrero that was taller than any Texas hat, and Doc Holliday and Wyatt Earp, too, and was that Teddy Roosevelt?

J. C. Osgood puffed clouds of smoke from a great cigar and waved it over his own kingdom and there stood Alma Osgood in a sheer nightgown with eyes as big as the moon.

Jake and Inez and Yolanda. But he shoved dirt over their faces with a bootheel and they were replaced by Luke Matthews, tall and straight as an arrow, who was the son of an Indian woman and one or the other of two murdering white men. Evey stood with Luke and the wind ruffled her hair and Henry and Joshua were there, too, and the other good folks who had peopled his life.

Back there in the trees somewhere were Luke and Joshua, the two who, more than any others, understood.

The others were gone, or were old and soon to be gone. They had done what had to be done and they had died or would soon die. But Luke and Josh and Evey and Esther and Ruby and Marcello and Theresa and Teegee and Martha and the others would carry on, even after Tracey and Abby were also gone.

There were plenty of good people in the world, Will thought to himself, and damn the stock market anyway. The country would survive.

Things wouldn't be the same, probably, like they weren't the same in the valley with the passing of Schofield and Crystal City, for example. And Aspen, too. Aspen, a town with such a promising future. Maybe it could come back. No, Will thought. Aspen was gone for good. But Marble struggled on. Perhaps this contract for the Tomb of the Unknown Soldier. It could mean a rebirth for Marble. But that was a wild hope, too.

The *ini'pute* were humming about his head again and the images in the dirt faded. He looked out over the valley and it went in and out of focus as the pain in his chest increased again. *Here we go*, he thought. He turned to his left and, like Owl Man years ago, was blinded by the reflection of the sun from the snow in Chair Mountain's bowl.

That day on the point for Owl Man, the day Luke was born. It, too, had been in the fall. Almost fifty years to the day, perhaps. It was fitting.

He sat there on his rock for a long time, the pain coming and going. Maybe he had been wrong. He stood. Maybe he could go see Tracey again. Talk some more with Abby. He turned. An owl sat in the branches of a pine tree and stared with wide, unblinking eyes. The humming increased. Overhead an eagle screeched. Small birds flew across his eyesight.

He felt suddenly strong. He would go back with Luke and Josh. Back to the Double M. He took a step and a shock of pain jolted him to his knees. The owl screeched — *otus asio* — and immediately the humming stopped. The silence startled him, like a youthful nightmare when he tried to call for help and could make no sound. He bent forward, struggled to breathe and was surprised at the pain which was worse than he had expected. Was this it, then? He wasn't as ready as he had thought. There was more to do. He wasn't finished. He wrapped his arms across his chest. Bent to the ground and his hat fell to the red dirt as his forehead touched the ground.

"Well, I'll be. . ."

The eagle described a slow circle above the body. The owl stared with knowing eyes and blinked, once. And the small birds were still. Dark clouds had rolled in over the valley and a quickly moving shadow ran over the Crystal River as it coursed its way through a channel centuries old. The river bounced over boulders and through narrow cuts, past the hot springs and on toward Carbondale.

It began to snow on Will Martin. It snowed all the way up and down the cursed valley of the Crystal River.

THE END

Author's Afterword

This book is a work of the imagination. Although the story is fiction, the "cursed" valley of the title is a very real place.

Much of the story is true and many of those who people its pages are actual figures who had an impact on the valley and its environs. While most of the main characters are fictitious, J. C. Osgood, the coal baron, did develop Redstone and Cleveholm; most of the "silver kings" of Aspen were real people and what is written of them, except for their association with my fictional characters, is based on historic fact.

The Ute Indians did populate the valley although the majority of those who make up the cast of Native Americans are also figments of my imagination. The use and spelling of the Ute language is taken from one source and may be at variance with other resources.

The history of the valley as depicted here and that of nearby Carbondale, Aspen and Glenwood Springs is also based on the way it actually happened. Now and then I have taken liberties with dates and travel times to make the story flow more smoothly.

This novel was begun years ago, long before the first word was set to paper. That it has survived a full decade from its initial publication is testament to the continuing interest in the history of a part of Colorado that I believe mirrors that of the entire West. From its early Native American inhabitants to the adventurous trappers called mountain men to the encroaching miners to the farmers, ranchers and entrepreneurs of today, the tale of this tiny, isolated valley is, in fact, a chronicle of the American West.

There are beguiling stories of the legend of the curse, believed to have been placed on the Crystal River Valley by a Ute holy man in 1879 as he and his band were being driven by the U.S. military to reservations in the southwestern part of the state.

Is the curse real?

That question was the basis for research that resulted in this historical novel which was first published by Pearl Street Publishing of Denver, Colorado, and for which I am grateful.

The original manuscript was much longer than the final, published version. For this 10th Anniversary Edition I've included some material that was excised from the first edition. I am hopeful that the effects of "the curse" do not hamper your enjoyment of this story.

Did the Utes place a curse on the valley? The legend says they did and many old-timers agree. What we do know is that trouble and calamity have plagued many of those who have tried to use this beautiful valley to their own benefit. To that end, perhaps the curse is not such a bad thing after all.

Larry K. Meredith
Gunnison, Colorado
2012

About the Author

An Oklahoma native, Larry K. Meredith was raised in Kansas. He has been a newspaper man, a salesman, an advertising and sales promotion writer for a Fortune 500 company, a college and university public relations director, an instructional technology director, and has owned his own marketing and video production company. Not long ago, he retired from his administrative position with Western State Colorado University in Gunnison, Colorado. Most recently, he served as a library district's executive director.

He and his wife Alley have been part time residents of the Crystal Valley since the 1960s and he has long been interested in its history. Ironically, their son and his family live in "This Cursed Valley" while their daughter and her husband have also resided there.

Log on to www.raspberrycreekbooks.com
to order
This Cursed Valley.
It is also available on Amazon.com, in bookstores and
via Ingram Book Company

Updates about the book and author
Larry K. Meredith
will be posted online regularly.

CPSIA information can be obtained
at www.ICGtesting.com
Printed in the USA
LVHW011815170322
713455LV00006B/27